READER'S DIGEST
CONDENSED BOOKS

READER'S DIGEST
CONDENSED BOOKS

*Selected and edited
by Reader's Digest*

CONDENSED BOOKS DIVISION

THE READER'S DIGEST ASSOCIATION LIMITED, LONDON

www.readersdigest.co.uk

The Reader's Digest Association Limited
11 Westferry Circus
Canary Wharf London E14 4HE

CONTENTS

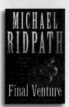

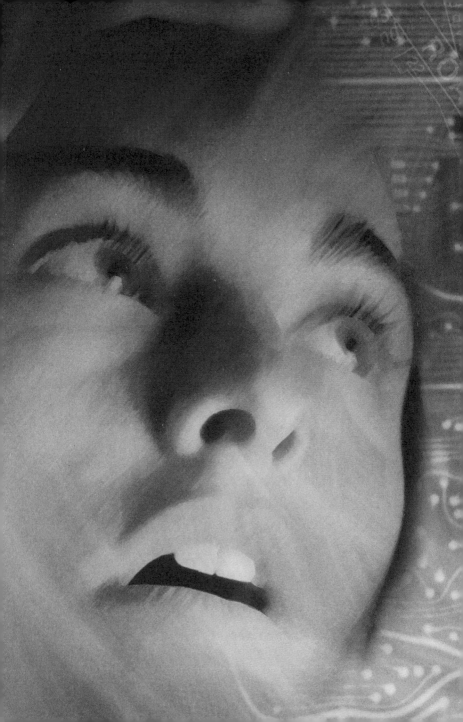

THE
BOMBMAKER

Stephen Leather

Andrea Hayes faces a terrible dilemma: if she refuses to go along with her blackmailers' demands, her daughter will be killed; if she saves her daughter thousands of innocent people will die.
Either way, she isn't coming out of this alive.

t wasn't an especially big bomb. Just a couple of pounds of Semtex, a detonator, a small digital clock and a mercury tilt switch. The man carrying it wasn't overly afraid—he knew that the device had been tested a dozen times, with a torch bulb in place of the detonator. There was no way it could explode prematurely. The timer was set to activate its circuit in thirty minutes' time, and even then the device wouldn't explode until it was moved and the switch was tripped. The Bombmaker had explained everything to him before placing the bomb in the blue holdall that he was now carrying as casually as if it contained nothing more threatening than football kit.

The man looked left and right, then squeezed through a gap in the railings and went down the embankment to the railway tracks. He walked along the sleepers, confident that there wouldn't be a train for an hour, by which time he'd be long gone. He took a quick look at his watch. Plenty of time to place the bomb, then to get to the phone box and make the coded call. This wasn't a bomb designed to kill, it was meant to disrupt. To tie up the police, the army and a bomb-disposal team. That's not to say that it wasn't a serious bomb, but the men who turned up to deal with it would be experts. They'd X-ray it before touching it and they'd see the circuits and then they'd blow it up with a controlled charge. In effect, they'd be blowing up the railway line themselves. Hours of disruption. Great publicity.

He walked up to the entrance to the tunnel and left the holdall a few feet inside. The fact that it was in darkness and close to the tunnel wall would make it harder to deal with. They'd need lights, and they'd also have to close the road that ran above the railway line.

He went back along the tracks and climbed up the embankment, then walked along the road. A blue Fiat pulled up alongside him and he climbed in. 'OK?' said the driver.

The man nodded. He looked at his watch again. Everything was going to plan.

LUCY METCALFE HATED it when her brother played rough. She was a year older than Tim but he was stronger and was worse when his friends were with him. They were kicking a football, but every time Lucy got it, Tim would immediately tackle her, charging in with his shoulder. 'Mine, mine,' he'd shout, before taking the ball off her.

'You're a bully!' she shouted at her ten-year-old brother as he barged into her for the umpteenth time. She stood rubbing her shoulder and glaring at him. 'It's supposed to be a game.'

'Yeah? Well, I'm better than you are.'

'No, you're not better. You're bigger. And uglier. And stupider.'

Tim's friends giggled and his cheeks reddened. He kicked the ball at her, hard, but missed. The ball bounced on the kerb before disappearing through a line of rusting railings. 'Now look what you've done!' Tim shouted. 'Go and get it.'

'Why should I get it?'

'I was kicking it to you.'

Lucy shook her head. 'You were kicking it *at* me, not *to* me,' she said. 'You get it.'

Tim clenched his fists and took a step towards her. Lucy ran, her school bag banging against her hip. 'Chicken!' Tim shouted and started making clucking noises. His friends joined in. Tim waited until his sister was out of sight before ducking through the railings and sliding down the embankment, his friends following him.

The ball was at the mouth of the tunnel. Tim ran over to it and picked it up. As he bent down, he saw something a few feet inside the entrance. A blue holdall. 'Hey, there's something here,' he yelled and waved his friends over.

They ran towards him. Tim grabbed at the holdall, wanting to be the first to open it.

THE MAN REPLACED the receiver and left the call box. He slid into the passenger seat of the blue Fiat, and motioned with his finger for the driver to move off. As the driver's hand reached for the gearstick, they heard a thudding sound in the distance. The two men knew immediately what the noise was. They were both Belfast-born and bred and were no strangers to the sound of exploding bombs.

The man stared out of the window, a sick feeling in his stomach. Something had gone very, very wrong.

Ten Years Later

It had been a long and uncomfortable flight. The men from Beijing had booked Egan a first-class ticket, but he hadn't used it. People were noticed in first class, and Egan had gone through life without being noticed. That was the way he wanted it. He was in his early thirties, a little below average height with receding hair, cropped short. He had pale blue eyes and a squarish face with thin lips. Most people would have difficulty describing Egan an hour after meeting him.

In the arrivals area he saw a liveried chauffeur holding a piece of card with '*Mr Egan*' written on it. Egan shuddered. He considered ignoring the chauffeur, but decided not to in case the man had him paged. He went over to him and nodded.

The chauffeur touched the brim of his cap, reached for Egan's suitcase and led him to a top-of-the-range Mercedes outside the airport terminal. Egan climbed into the plush interior and settled back for the ride to Hong Kong Island.

There was a copy of the *Hong Kong Standard* in the seat pocket and Egan read the business section. The stock market was continuing its downward plunge and inflation was climbing. Egan smiled to himself as he scanned the list of stock prices. The days of the so-called Asian miracle were long gone.

The Mercedes drew up in front of the Mandarin Hotel and a red-liveried bellboy carried Egan's case inside. Egan checked in, showered and then watched CNN until it was time for his meeting.

The men from Beijing were already in the room when Egan arrived, sitting in a line at one end of a long apple-wood table. There was only one other chair, at the opposite end, and Egan sat down and studied the men facing him. Three were in their seventies, with watery eyes and parchment-like faces. The fourth was in his late forties. His name was Deng. The other three had never been introduced to Egan, but he had made enquiries and knew that one was a general in the People's Liberation Army and the other two were bankers. In the United States they'd be retired, enjoying their twilight years on the golf course, but careers were handled differently in China.

'Good to see you again, Mr Egan,' said Deng. He spoke with an

American accent, the result of three years at Harvard University.

Egan nodded but said nothing.

'Everything is proceeding satisfactorily?'

'It is.'

Deng's three companions stared at Egan with unblinking eyes.

Egan leaned forward and interlinked his thick fingers on the table's surface. 'The teams are in place—we're in a position to move to the next stage. But before we proceed, I want to make sure you realise what you're asking.'

'What we're paying for,' said Deng.

Egan nodded, acknowledging the point. These four men had already transferred $500,000 to his account in Zürich, and following today's meeting a further million would be paid. If everything went to plan, Egan stood to receive $7 million.

'Nairobi, 1998. More than two hundred dead, five and a half thousand injured. What you're paying for is much bigger than what I did in Kenya. Timing is the key. It can be done at night and casualties will be minimal. It can be done at lunch time and they'll be digging the bodies out for weeks. I have no qualms either way, but I want to make it clear that if you decide to go ahead with a daytime event, hundreds of office workers could die.'

Deng nodded. He turned to his three companions and spoke in rapid Mandarin. All three men nodded. 'We have no problems with matters as they stand, Mr Egan. If anything, it adds credibility to our scenario, does it not?'

'It could be taken either way,' said Egan. 'I was thinking of the backlash. Africans are one thing, Europeans are something else.'

'Nevertheless,' said Deng, 'we should proceed as planned.'

'No problem,' said Egan. 'As soon as the next tranche is deposited in Zürich, we'll move on to the next stage.'

'The money will be in your account within the hour,' said Deng.

Day One

There were two of them, stocky men wearing matching blue track suits, black Reebok trainers and black ski masks. They vaulted over the back wall and ran to the kitchen door of the house. Then one of the men reached for the door handle. It opened. They weren't surprised. They'd been watching the house for two weeks and they knew the routine. The kitchen door was never locked until the family's golden retriever had been allowed out just after midnight.

The men slipped into the kitchen and gently closed the door behind them. They could just about hear the television in the sitting room. A comedy programme. Loud studio laughter. They reached into their track-suit tops and pulled out guns. Black automatics with bulbous silencers. The men didn't expect to have to use them. But they were prepared to, if necessary.

Their biggest worry was the dog. People could be threatened, but dogs would just growl and bark, maybe even attack to protect their territory. The dog was in the sitting room, so if they moved carefully they wouldn't be heard. One of them eased open the door to the hallway. More studio laughter. They moved on the balls of their feet, hardly breathing as they crept up the stairs.

The men moved along the upper hallway and knelt down at the door to the back bedroom. One of the men was wearing a small rucksack, and he placed it on the carpet. From the rucksack he pulled out a cloth and a bottle containing a colourless liquid. He unscrewed the top and doused the cloth with the liquid, then he nodded at his companion, who opened the door and stepped inside.

They moved quickly to the bed. A small girl was asleep, her blonde hair spread across the pillow, a cuddly Garfield toy clutched to her chest. The man with the cloth held it tightly against the girl's face for a full minute before releasing his grip on her.

The other man put a white envelope on a bedside table and gathered up the little girl. The Garfield toy slipped onto the floor. The man who'd drugged the girl picked up the cuddly toy, hesitated for a second, and then put it into his rucksack.

The two men moved down the stairs as silently as they'd gone up, and two minutes later they were in a Ford Mondeo, driving south with the little girl hidden under a tartan blanket.

'COFFEE?' ASKED Martin Hayes, pushing himself up off the sofa. The golden retriever at his feet wagged its tail hopefully. 'OK, Dermott—I'll let you out.' He looked pointedly at his wife.

'You're all heart,' said Andrea Hayes. Martin planted a kiss on the top of her head, then ruffled her soft, blonde hair. 'Woof,' she said. 'I'll go and check on Katie.'

Martin went to the kitchen and let the dog out before switching on the electric kettle.

'Martin!'

'What?'

'Martin, come here.'

Martin could tell from her voice that something was wrong. He ran down the hall and up the stairs. 'What? What?' he shouted, a tight feeling in the pit of his stomach.

He found Andy standing at the foot of the bed. The bed was empty. Katie had gone. He looked around the room. Nothing. He went to the bathroom. The door was open and he could see immediately that Katie wasn't there, but he pulled back the shower curtain to assure himself that she wasn't hiding there.

'Katie!' he called.

'She's not here. I looked everywhere.'

Martin fought to stay calm. Katie was a seven-year-old girl, and seven-year-old girls didn't just disappear.

'She has to be somewhere,' he said. 'Maybe she's sleepwalking.'

'She doesn't sleepwalk.'

'Maybe she's started.'

They both jumped as they heard a noise downstairs.

They rushed down, shouting their daughter's name. Andy went into the sitting room. Katie wasn't there. She even checked behind the sofas. Nothing.

'Katie, if you're doing this on purpose, you're in big trouble,' she shouted.

The dog came scrabbling along the carpet, pink tongue lolling from the side of his mouth.

'It was Dermott,' said Martin, 'scratching at the door.'

'She's not in the garden?'

Martin shook his head.

Andy put her hands up to her face, her fingers splayed across her cheeks. 'This can't be happening.'

Martin went over to her and shook her gently. 'Come on, love. Pull yourself together. Let's search the house from top to bottom. You check upstairs. I'll check the rooms downstairs. OK?'

Andy nodded uncertainly. Her eyes were brimming with tears and Martin brushed them away. 'We'll check the house and if there's still no sign of her then we'll phone the police, OK?'

'Police?' she repeated.

'We'll find her,' said Martin. 'Go on, check the bedrooms. When I've finished down here, I'll check the loft.' He knew they were clutching at straws but he wanted to do anything other than calling the police. Calling the police meant that their daughter was missing.

He took Andy by the hand and half led, half pulled her into the hallway. He waited until she was climbing the stairs before he went through to the study. Nothing.

He went to the kitchen and began opening all the cupboards,

knowing that it was useless but wanting to check nevertheless.

'Martin!'

Martin's head jerked round. 'What? Have you found her?' Even as he said the words he knew that she hadn't. He dashed upstairs. Andy was walking down the landing, an envelope in one hand, a sheet of paper in the other. 'What is it?' asked Martin. 'What's happened?'

'They've taken her,' gasped Andy. 'They've taken my baby.'

Her legs gave way beneath her and she fell. Her head smacked against the banister, smearing it with blood before she crashed to the floor and rolled onto her back, the letter still clutched in her fist.

THE MAN in the passenger seat of the Ford Mondeo twisted around and lifted the corner of the tartan blanket.

'Is she still out?' asked the driver.

'Yeah. You think I should give her more chloroform?'

'Nah. We're almost there.'

The passenger draped the blanket over the child and settled back in his seat. 'I'm not sure about being so close to their house.'

'Makes no odds. They're not going to know where to look.'

They drove in silence for a while. The passenger spoke first. 'What if they don't do what they're supposed to?'

The driver shrugged but didn't reply.

'Would you . . . you know?' The passenger made a gun with his forefinger and thumb.

'It won't come to that. The threat'll be enough.'

'Are you sure of that?'

The driver threw him a look. 'Are you having second thoughts?'

'No, but . . .'

'There can't be any buts. We've been told what we've got to do and we do it.'

ANDY OPENED her eyes and blinked. For a second or two she thought she'd been asleep, and then the horror of it all came rushing back and broke over her like an icy wave.

Martin was dabbing at her forehead with a damp cloth. 'Easy, love, you had a nasty fall.'

'What happened?' she asked.

'You fainted.'

Andy took several breaths, trying to gather her thoughts. She'd been in Katie's bedroom. The letter. Oh my God, the letter. She forced herself up. 'The letter,' she whispered.

Martin gave her the sheet of paper and she read it quickly.

ANDREA HAYES

WE HAVE YOUR DAUGHTER. SHE WILL NOT BE HARMED IF YOU
DO EXACTLY AS WE SAY. YOU ARE TO TAKE FLIGHT EI 172 TO
LONDON TOMORROW. A ROOM HAS BEEN BOOKED IN YOUR NAME
AT THE STRAND PALACE HOTEL. WAIT THERE FOR FURTHER
INSTRUCTIONS. IF YOU CONTACT THE POLICE YOU WILL NEVER
SEE YOUR DAUGHTER AGAIN. YOUR HUSBAND IS TO CARRY ON
HIS NORMAL ROUTINE. YOU WILL BOTH BE WATCHED. IF WE
BELIEVE YOU HAVE CONTACTED THE POLICE YOUR DAUGHTER
WILL DIE.

Andy blinked away tears. 'Why?' she asked. 'Why us?'

Martin took the letter from her. It was typed, all in capital letters.
'It doesn't say how much they want us to pay.' Martin ran his hand
through his hair, frowning. 'What sort of ransom demand doesn't
mention money?'

'Maybe they'll phone,' said Andy.

'But then why do they want you to go to London? Our money's
here, in Ireland. This doesn't make sense.'

'Sense? Why should it make sense? They've kidnapped Katie, why
should anything they do make sense?'

Martin took her hands in his. 'Don't worry, love. We'll get Katie
back. I promise.'

'You can't promise something like that, Martin.'

Martin shook his head. 'They've obviously planned this, Andy.
They knew where Katie was, they had the note ready. They've got the
hotel room booked in London. Kidnapping is a straightforward
business transaction. We give them money. They give us Katie. OK?'

Andy nodded. What he was saying made sense. It was horrible, but
it was logical. It wasn't a pervert who'd stolen her child, it was a kid-
napper. It wasn't about sexual thrills, it was about money, and she
could just about cope with that. 'What do we do?' she asked.

'We do what they say in the note. You go to London and I guess
they'll contact you there to tell you how much they want.'

'Why us, Martin? We're not rich.'

'We're not short of money, Andy. There are plenty of scumbags
out there who'd class us as wealthy. They don't take mortgages and
overdrafts into account. They see a couple of new cars and a four-
bedroomed house and they think we're rolling in it.'

'We do have the money, don't we?' asked Andy.

Martin stroked her hair and brushed several stray strands away
from her face. 'Whatever it takes, we'll get it. It'll be all right.'

EGAN TOOK OFF his headphones and leaned back in his chair. On the desk in front of him were five digital tape recorders, each linked to radio receivers, one for each of the five listening devices in the Hayes house. He'd planted the devices three weeks earlier while Andrea Hayes had been out walking her dog. They gave him virtually complete coverage of the house.

Egan's studio apartment was in a block just half a mile away from the Hayes house and he'd rented it for twelve months, even though he only expected to be using it for another week. Once the Hayes woman was in place, Egan planned to fly to London to oversee the final phase of the operation. So far everything had gone to plan. Martin and Andrea Hayes were reacting exactly as he'd anticipated.

GEORGE MCEVOY DROVE the Mondeo down the rutted track that led to the cottage. The car swayed and they slowed to a walking pace. The single-storey building was in darkness, and he put the headlights on full beam. 'Home sweet home,' he muttered. 'How is she?'

Mick Canning leaned over and lifted the blanket. Katie was still fast asleep. 'Out like a light,' he said.

McEvoy parked by the side of a wooden garage at the back of the cottage. He climbed out and unlocked the back door of the cottage before waving at Canning to carry the girl in. The nearest house was a hundred yards away and they weren't overlooked at the back.

Canning gathered up Katie, still covered with the blanket, and took her through the kitchen to a white-painted hallway. A wooden door opened onto a flight of concrete steps that went down into the basement. The underground room had been sparsely furnished with a small camp bed, two wooden chairs and a small Formica-covered table. On the floor was a wool rug, and in one corner was a bucket, covered with a towel. Canning placed Katie on the bed, then turned her so that she was lying on her side. Still asleep, Katie murmured and put her thumb in her mouth.

'You all right, Mick?' asked McEvoy. He was standing at the door, looking down into the basement, an expression of barely concealed contempt on his face.

'Yeah, no problem. Do you think we should be with her when she wakes up? She'll be scared, she might start yelling.'

'No one'll hear her,' said McEvoy.

Canning went up the stairs. 'Do you think we should leave the light on?' he asked.

'For God's sake, this isn't a hotel,' snapped McEvoy. He closed the door and slid the bolts across.

Day Two

Martin Hayes awoke with a start. It took him a few seconds to realise where he was. He was in the sitting room, sprawled on the sofa. He rubbed his face. How long had he been asleep? He looked at his watch. It was just after seven. 'Andy?' No answer.

He didn't remember coming down to the sitting room. He'd been upstairs with Andy, lying on their bed, hoping that the phone would ring. Martin went upstairs. Their bedroom was empty.

Andy wasn't in the bathroom, either. The door to Katie's room was closed, and even before Martin pushed it open he knew that he'd find his wife sitting on their daughter's bed. She didn't look up as he went over to her. She was clutching a pillow to her chest, her eyes closed. Martin sat down next to her.

'They've taken Garfield, too,' she said.

'That's a good sign, Andy,' said Martin.

She looked up at him and opened her eyes but they were as devoid of emotion as her voice. 'A good sign?' she repeated.

'They wouldn't have taken her toy if they were going to hurt her.'

She nodded, her eyes still vacant. She was in shock, Martin realised. 'Come on downstairs, you need a cup of tea,' he said.

Andy nodded but she made no move to stand up.

MICK CANNING was frying eggs when Katie started banging on the basement door. 'Help!' she yelled. 'Let me out!'

George McEvoy looked up from his copy of the *Irish Times* and scowled at the door. 'Her ladyship's awake,' he said.

'I'll see to her,' said Canning, handing a spatula to McEvoy. 'You look after the eggs, yeah?'

'Don't forget your . . .'

'Balaclava, yeah, I know,' interrupted Canning. He picked up his rucksack and put on a rolled-up ski mask before unbolting the door.

Katie was standing four steps down, staring wide-eyed up at Canning. The basement was in darkness. Canning unfastened the neck of the rucksack and took out the Garfield toy. 'I brought this for you,' he said, holding it out to her.

'I want to go home,' she said.

'You can't. Not right now.' He held out the soft toy again.

Katie looked as if she was going to argue, then she reached for Garfield. 'Thank you,' she said.

Canning was about to say 'You're welcome' when she hurled the

18

toy at his face and scrambled up the stairs, slipping by his legs before he had the chance to grab her.

Canning ran down the hallway after her, cursing. He caught up with her in three strides, yanked her off her feet, then scooped her up. She began to wriggle and scream as he carried her down the basement steps. 'I want my mummy! I want my mummy.'

'Please, be quiet,' hissed Canning.

'I'll be quiet if you let me go,' she said.

'I can't let you go . . .' Canning began, but he'd barely got the words out of his mouth before she began screaming again. He dropped her down on the camp bed and put his hand over her mouth. It smothered her screams, but Canning had a sudden flash about what he was doing and jerked his hand away as if he'd been burnt. He'd had his hand over a child's mouth. He could have killed her. Smothered her. He took a step back, his hands up as if surrendering. Katie seemed as shocked as he was.

'What?' she said.

'I'm sorry,' he said. 'I didn't mean to put my hand over your mouth. I wasn't trying to . . . I wasn't trying to hurt you.'

Katie swung her legs over the side of the camp bed and sat looking at him curiously. 'Why are you wearing a mask?' she asked.

'So when we send you back to your parents, you won't be able to tell the police what I look like.' Canning crouched down so that his head was on a level with hers. 'Look, I'm sorry if I scared you. But you have to do as my friend and I say, OK? You have to stay down here for a few days, then you can go home.'

'You promise?'

Canning made the sign of the cross on his chest. 'Swear to die.'

ANDY HAYES put down the phone. 'They'll hold the ticket for me at the airport,' she said.

Martin nodded. 'I'll drive you.'

'You can't,' she said. 'You have to carry on as normal, that's what the letter said. You have to go to work, Martin. We mustn't do anything that makes them think we're not cooperating.'

Martin shrugged. 'I guess so.'

Andy's face hardened. 'No, there's no I-guess-so about this. I want you to promise me that you won't call the police or do anything out of the ordinary.'

Martin took her in his arms and kissed her hair. 'I promise.'

She hugged him tightly. 'I'll call you from London. They didn't say that I couldn't do that.'

McEvoy PUT on his ski mask and picked up the tray. On it was a paper plate of spaghetti hoops, a slice of bread, and a plastic fork.

'I'll take it,' said Canning. He was sitting at the table working on the crossword in the *Irish Times*.

'That's all right, Mick. I'll handle it. Where are the scissors?'

Canning gestured with his chin. 'By the sink. You should give her some milk. She'll need something to drink.'

McEvoy put the tray down. He picked up the scissors and slipped them into the back pocket of his jeans, then went over to the fridge, and poured some milk into a plastic cup. 'Anything else I should take her ladyship?' he asked.

Canning ignored him and concentrated on the crossword.

McEvoy went over to the door that led to the basement, slipped the bolts and eased it open with his foot. Katie was sitting on the camp bed, her Garfield in her lap. She looked up and watched him walk down the stairs. He put the tray on the bed next to her and she looked at it disdainfully. 'Spaghetti hoops?'

'Leave it if you don't want it,' said McEvoy curtly.

'What else is there to eat?'

'Nothing. It's spaghetti hoops or nothing.'

Katie sniffed and rested her head on top of Garfield.

McEvoy took the scissors from his back pocket. Katie looked at him fearfully. 'Please don't,' she said, clasping Garfield tightly.

'It won't hurt if you don't move,' said McEvoy.

ANDY OPENED the suitcase and stared at its interior. What was she supposed to pack? She didn't even know how long she was going to be away. She heard Martin climbing the stairs, as if every step was an effort. He walked up behind her and put his hands on her shoulders. 'I don't know what to take with me,' she said.

'Pack for a couple of days,' he said.

'Pack what?'

'Jeans. Shirts. Underwear. Hell, Andy, I don't know.' His fingers moved around her neck and he massaged her slowly.

'Why me, Martin? Why do they want me in London and you here? Why haven't they told us what they want?'

She felt her husband shrug. 'Please let me drive you to the airport.'

Andy shook her head. 'You can't,' she said. 'You have to go to work. You have to do everything as normal, Martin.'

'This is different,' said Martin. 'They know you're going to the airport—they'll expect me to take you.'

Andy sat down on the bed, too tired to argue. She'd barely slept, and it was as if she was thinking in slow motion. 'OK,' she said.

Martin sat next to her and put his arm around her. 'Look, I'll drop you at the airport, then I'll go straight to the office. I'll talk to the bank, see how much we've got on deposit.'

'I hope it's enough,' she said.

'If it isn't, we can raise more,' said Martin. She put her arms around his waist and buried her face in his neck, her body racked by silent sobs. Martin held her, feeling more helpless than he'd ever felt.

CANNING WALKED through the arrivals area, tapping the copy of the *Irish Times* against his leg. He bought a coffee, sat on a stool and cast his eyes over the paper's headlines.

A woman pulled out the stool on the other side of his table. 'Do you mind?' she asked. She was slim in a pale grey business suit, carrying a burgundy briefcase and a mobile telephone. Her shoulder-length hair was blonde, but the dark roots suggested that it had been dyed. There was something unnatural about her eyes, too. They were almost too green, as if she were wearing contact lenses.

Canning waved at the stool. 'Help yourself,' he said. He took a small padded envelope from his jacket and slipped it between the pages of the newspaper, which he folded and placed on the table.

The woman ripped the corner off a pack of sweetener and poured it into her coffee. Canning slid off his stool, nodded and walked away. He didn't see her take the newspaper and put it in her briefcase.

IT HAD BEEN HARD saying goodbye to her husband but Andy had forced a smile and then walked away from the car, through the doors into the departure area.

'Something to drink?' asked the stewardess.

Andy shook her head and closed her eyes. Images of Katie filled her mind. Katie laughing at cartoons on the television, Katie holding her arms out to be hugged. She could almost imagine that she was inhaling the fragrance of her daughter's hair, sweet and clean. She wondered how Katie was feeling. Would she be scared? Andy pictured her in the corner of a dark room, a menacing figure standing over her. She shivered and opened her eyes. What had Katie ever done to deserve this? Andy promised herself that whatever happened she would get her revenge on the men who'd kidnapped Katie.

The captain announced that they'd be landing within twenty minutes. Andy checked her seat belt. At the rear of the plane, the woman with dyed blonde hair and unnaturally green eyes slid her burgundy briefcase under the seat in front of her.

MARTIN'S COMPANY, which he ran with his partner Padraig, was based on an industrial estate twenty miles north of Dublin. The offices were in an H-shaped brick building, with a storage yard for heavy equipment behind and car parking spaces in front.

He parked and walked through reception to his office.

'Coffee?' his secretary Jill Gannon asked.

'No thanks, Jill. And don't put any calls through for the next half an hour or so.' He went inside his office and closed the door. He telephoned his bank and asked for the balance of his accounts. There was a little over £10,000 in his current account, another £30,000 in a deposit account. Martin then called a building society in the Channel Islands and arranged to have a further £90,000 transferred to his current account in Dublin.

His next call was to his stockbroker, Jamie O'Connor. According to Jamie, Martin's stock portfolio was worth just under a quarter of a million pounds.

'Could you sell everything by close of business today?' Martin asked.

'I could, sure. But I wouldn't recommend it. The Irish shares, OK, but your Far Eastern exposure has taken a bit of a tumble recently. I'd suggest you hang on to them.'

'Everything, Jamie.'

'Martin, are you OK? Has something happened?'

'Everything's fine. I just need some cash. Andy's got her heart set on a villa in Portugal and like a fool I agreed to buy it for her.'

'Well, it's your decision, of course. All I can do is offer my professional advice, and I wouldn't recommend liquidating a perfectly decent portfolio of shares to buy a villa in Portugal.'

'Advice noted, Jamie. Close of business today, right? And put the money straight into my current account with Allied Irish, will you?'

There was a slight hesitation from the broker, as if he was about to argue but then decided not to press the point. 'Consider it done.'

'Thanks, Jamie. I'll talk to you again soon.' Martin put down the phone. A quarter of a million pounds, plus the money already in the bank, gave him a total of £380,000. Surely that would be enough? He sat at his desk with his head in his hands. What if it wasn't? What if they wanted more? What would he do then?

ANDY SAT ON THE BED in the Strand Palace Hotel, staring at the telephone. All she had to do was to pick it up and within seconds she could be talking to her husband. Or the police.

She heard a whispering sound at the door and she went over to it. There was a white envelope on the floor. She picked it up, went back to the bed and sat down again. The envelope had been sealed and she used a fingernail to slit it open. Her mind was whirling. Forensic evidence, she thought. Fingerprints. Saliva. DNA. She had to keep the envelope—the police would be able to get information about the kidnappers from it.

There was a single sheet of hotel notepaper inside. Andy read it with shaking hands.

YOUR DAUGHTER IS QUITE SAFE AND SO LONG AS YOU FOLLOW OUR INSTRUCTIONS SHE WILL NOT BE HARMED.

AT NINE O'CLOCK TOMORROW MORNING YOU ARE TO CHECK OUT. TAKE ALL YOUR THINGS WITH YOU.

TURN RIGHT OUT OF THE HOTEL AND WALK DOWN THE STRAND. TURN RIGHT INTO BEDFORD STREET, AND LEFT INTO BEDFORD COURT. YOU WILL SEE A MULTISTOREY CAR PARK ON YOUR LEFT.

GO INSIDE THE CAR PARK. GO UP TO THE THIRD FLOOR. THERE YOU WILL SEE A DARK BLUE TRANSIT VAN. ON THE SIDE OF THE VAN IS THE NAME OF A LANDSCAPING FIRM.

MAKE SURE NO ONE IS WATCHING YOU. OPEN THE REAR DOOR OF THE VAN AND GET IN. CLOSE THE DOOR BEHIND YOU. INSIDE THE VAN YOU WILL FIND A BLACK HOOD. PUT IT OVER YOUR HEAD AND WAIT.

MAKE NO MISTAKE. IF YOU DISOBEY OR IF YOU MAKE ANY ATTEMPT TO CONTACT THE POLICE, YOUR DAUGHTER WILL DIE.

Andy reread the letter several times. A van? A hood? What did these people want from her? She looked at her watch. It was now six o'clock in the evening. Why the delay? Was she allowed to contact Martin? The letter said only that she wasn't to talk to the police. Had they tapped the phone in Dublin? Could she risk it?

She stood at the window and looked out onto the busy street. Who was doing this to her? Who had turned her life upside-down?

MARTIN HAYES LAY staring up at the ceiling. There was no way he'd be able to sleep, but he knew he had to make the effort.

He'd got back home just after seven and had sat next to the telephone for most of the evening, willing it to ring. It had, once, but it was only Padraig. They'd chatted for a while, but Martin had been fairly abrupt with his partner, not wanting to tie up the phone line.

He rolled over and curled up into a ball. His stomach ached, but it wasn't hunger. What he really wanted was a drink, but he doubted that he'd be able to stop at one and he had to keep a clear head.

The telephone rang and Martin grabbed for the receiver. 'Yes?'

'Martin?' It was Andy, her voice little more than a whisper.

'Hiya, love. Are you OK?'

'Can't sleep. I'm just lying here. Martin . . .'

Martin could hear the despair in her voice. 'I'm still here, love.'

'Have they called you?'

'No. Nothing. I've spoken to the bank, and I've sold our shares and stuff. The money's in the bank and all we need now is to know how much they want.'

'Martin . . . I'm not sure if this is about money.'

'What do you mean?'

'They want me to go to a van in a car park around the corner tomorrow. I guess they're going to take me somewhere.' There was a long pause. 'I'm not sure if we should even be talking,' she said. 'Maybe they're listening.'

'If they're listening, love, they know that we haven't gone to the police. OK?'

'I suppose so,' she said, but he could tell that she wasn't convinced.

'Do you know where they want to take you?' Martin asked.

'They didn't say. It was a note, like before. Martin, if it was money they wanted, they'd have called by now, wouldn't they?'

'I don't know what they're playing at, love.'

There was another long silence.

'You haven't been doing business with anybody you shouldn't have? Have you?' she said eventually.

'Andy, what a thing to say.' Martin was stunned. 'The company's never been better.' It was as if she were trying to find some way of blaming him for what had happened. 'What makes you think that?'

'Well, why else would anyone take Katie and then make me do this? It's as if they want you isolated. That's why I thought maybe it wasn't about money.' There was another pause.

'It's late at night and the demons are out, that's all,' said Martin. 'You're thinking too much. If it was to do with the business, there'd have been some lead-up to it, and Andy, love, the sort of people I do business with wouldn't dream of hurting a child.' There was no answer from his wife. 'Andy, did you hear what I said?'

'Yes.' There was a sniff. 'I'm sorry, Martin. I just wish it was over.'

'I know,' said Martin. 'Try to get some sleep, OK?'

'I'll try.' She sniffed again. 'I wonder how they're treating Katie. She'll be so scared.'

'I'm sure they'll be taking good care of her. Everything they're doing depends on us getting her back safely. Try not to worry. I know that's an impossible thing to ask, but try.'

'I'll try. I have to check out at nine. I'll try to call you later.'

Martin said goodbye and replaced the receiver. He had been doing his best to keep his wife's spirits up, but he knew that she was right. This was about more than money. But what?

Day Three

Andy stood in the middle of the hotel room, looking around. She had to let Martin know where she was going, because if anything went wrong it might be the only way he could find out where Katie was. She thought of leaving a message in the room, but the kidnappers might be preparing to search it after she checked out. If they found a letter, there was no saying what they might do to Katie.

Above the writing desk was a framed watercolour of a gondola on a canal, the colours all hazy as if viewed through a mist. Andy stared at the picture. Suddenly she knew exactly what she had to do. She sat down at the desk and opened the leather writing folder that was embossed with the hotel's name. There were several sheets of writing paper, and a ball-point pen. She began to write furiously.

It was just after nine when she walked up to the cashier's desk. A blonde receptionist took her credit card and printed out a copy of the bill. Andy pretended to check the print-out while she had a quick look around to see if anyone was looking at her. An old couple were sitting on a sofa close to the door, and half a dozen Japanese tourists were pulling brochures off a rack. A businessman in a dark blue suit was checking in and a woman in a fur coat was using one of the house phones. No one appeared to be paying Andy any attention. She slid an envelope from inside her jacket, put it on top of the print-out and slid them both across the counter to the receptionist.

'Could you do me a favour?' asked Andy. 'If my husband should pop by in the next few days, could you give this to him?'

The receptionist looked down at the envelope. Andy had written MARTIN HAYES in capital letters.

'No problem,' she replied, and gave Andy a credit-card slip to sign, putting the envelope in a drawer. Andy left the hotel. She followed the instructions she'd been given and carried her suitcase into the multistorey car park. The blue Transit van was on the third floor. There was a sign on the side that said CITY LANDSCAPING, and underneath it an 0181 telephone number.

A man in a blue suit and a red tie drove by in a BMW. Then there was silence. Andy reached out, pulled open the door and threw her suitcase in. She took a last look around the car park and then climbed in and locked the door.

She sat down and scanned the metal floor of the van. There was no sign of a hood. A black hood. There should be a black hood. She crawled over to the suitcase and lifted it up. The hood was underneath it. She felt a sudden surge of relief. So long as everything went as planned, then she'd get her daughter back.

The hood was made of some sort of woollen material with a drawstring around the open end, like a bag that might be used to hold shoes. It didn't feel particularly thick, but even so she was worried about how easy it would be to breathe through. She slowly pulled it on, then put her hands on the drawstring. She couldn't bring herself to tighten the bag around her neck. After taking a few deep breaths to steady her nerves, she sat back against the side of the van and drew her knees up to her chest.

Time seemed to crawl by. Andy tried counting off the seconds, then the minutes, but soon lost interest. It didn't matter whether they made her sit in the van for minutes, hours or days, she had no alternative but to wait. She tried to think of happier times. Birthdays. Christmases. Just lying on the bed, Martin next to her, Katie curled up between them, smiling in her sleep.

Andy stiffened at the sound of a key being inserted into the driver's side door, then a double click as the door locks opened. There was a pause, then the driver's door opened.

'Have you got the hood on?' A man's voice.

'Yes,' said Andy, hesitantly.

'Lie down on the floor, face down.'

Andy did as she was told, folding her arms and resting her chin on her hands. She felt the van lurch as the man climbed in. The passenger side door opened and another man got in.

They drove out of the car park and made a series of turns in quick succession. Andy had no idea in which direction they were heading. More turns. Lots of traffic, the loud hiss of air brakes, a far-off siren. They stopped. A minute later and they were off again. More turns, then a sudden acceleration. They drove in a straight line for a long time, so Andy figured they were on a motorway.

The hood made it difficult to breathe, but she found that, by turning her head to the side and pushing her cheek along the floor, she could create enough space around her chin to suck in fresher air.

Eventually she heard the sound of the indicator, and they turned off the motorway. The driver changed down through the gears.

Third. Second. First. Then a sharp turn to the left and the tyres were crunching over a rough surface. She jumped as the driver sounded the horn, then there was a loud metallic rattling noise from somewhere in front of the van. They edged forward and the rattling noise was repeated, this time from behind them. A gate maybe?

The van doors opened and the two men got out, and a few seconds later they opened the rear doors. 'Out you come,' said one. Andy didn't think it was the driver who'd spoken earlier.

She crawled towards the sound of his voice and then the men frog-marched her away from the van. Their footsteps echoed, making Andy think that they might be inside a large building.

The two men came to a sudden stop, and then forced her down, making her sit on a chair. They let go of her arms and she heard them move a few steps away from her. Andy waited, her hands in her lap, breathing steadily. She had to stay calm.

She tilted her head as she heard one of the men move, then she felt a tug at the hood. She blinked as the bag was ripped off her head. A man sat in front of her, a man wearing a ski mask and baggy blue overalls. In front of him were a notepad and a cheap plastic Biro. Andy already had her speech rehearsed.

'Look, please don't harm Katie. We'll give you whatever you want. You have me now; my husband will give you just as much for me as he will for Katie, so you might as well let her go. He's already told me that he's got the money ready, and he'll pay.'

The man in the ski mask stared at her with unblinking green eyes, saying nothing. Andy suddenly realised that there was mascara on the lashes. It wasn't a man, it was a woman. She heard a chuckling over her shoulder and she looked round. A large man with a wrestler's build was laughing at her. Like the woman, he had on a black ski mask that revealed nothing other than his eyes and part of his mouth, and was wearing similar blue overalls which were strained tight against his barrel-like chest. Next to the burly man was a taller, gangly man, also in a black ski mask and overalls. He was wearing pristine white Nike training shoes.

'Have you finished?' asked Green-eyes.

Andy whirled round to face her. 'What?'

'Have you said all you want to say?' A Scottish accent, but there was a hint of Northern Irish, too. 'Are you ready to listen?'

Andy swallowed and nodded.

'You're free to go, Andrea. We're armed but we're not going to hurt you. If you stay, it's going to be your choice. But if you go, you'll never see your daughter again.'

'Katie's OK?'

'Katie's just fine. And so long as you do as we say, she'll stay that way.' Her voice was soft and persuasive, as if she were selling life insurance and not threatening the life of Andy's only child.

'How much do you want?' asked Andy.

Green-eyes shook her head slowly. 'Hasn't the penny dropped yet, Andrea? Haven't you figured it out?'

Andy looked at her, not understanding. 'What is it you want? If it's not money, what do you want?'

Green-eyes put her gloved hands flat on the table, either side of the notepad and pen. 'Why, Andrea, we want you to do what you do best. We want you to build us a bomb. A very large bomb.'

MARTIN SAT at his desk, staring at his computer screen. All he could think about was his wife and daughter. He'd arrived at the office at eight o'clock, thinking that Andy might telephone him before she checked out of the hotel. She didn't. The kidnappers hadn't called either. His phone rang and he picked it up. It was the headmistress's secretary, calling to see why Katie wasn't at school.

Martin thought quickly. If he said Katie was sick, the woman might ask for a doctor's note. 'It's my wife's mother, Mrs O'Mara. I'm afraid she's had a bit of a fall and my wife has had to go up to Belfast and see her. We didn't have anyone to take care of Katie because I'm up to my eyes in work here. We thought it best if Katie went with my wife. It'll only be for a few days.'

'It's very irregular, Mr Hayes,' said the woman frostily. 'Do you know when we can expect to see Katie again?'

Martin wished that he did know. 'I would think three days. Maybe four. If it's any longer, I'll be sure to let you know, Mrs O'Mara.'

When he put the receiver down, his hand was shaking.

'YOU'RE CRAZY,' said Andy. 'Why would you think—'

Green-eyes silenced her by holding up a gloved hand. 'You're wasting your time, Andrea. We know everything. We know who you are and we know what you are. We're not asking you to do something you haven't done a hundred times before.'

Andy slumped back in her chair and stared at the masked woman. She tried to speak but no words would come.

Green-eyes bent down and pulled a burgundy briefcase out from under the table. She placed it on top, her eyes never leaving Andy's face as she clicked open the two locks and opened the case. She took out a large manila envelope, and tossed it casually in front of Andy.

'What's this?' asked Andy.

Green-eyes nodded at the envelope. Andy opened it and took out a dozen or so photocopies of newspaper cuttings—a mixture of Irish and English newspapers, tabloids and broadsheets. Andy scanned the headlines. BELFAST STORE DESTROYED. BOMB ON MAIN LINE, TRAINS DELAYED. BOMB-DISPOSAL EXPERT KILLED. FIRE IN DEPARTMENT STORE, IRA BLAMED. TWO SOLDIERS DIE IN BOMB BLAST.

Andy stared at the photocopied cuttings. 'If you know everything, then you know why I can't do what you want.'

Green-eyes reached into her briefcase again and took out a piece of newspaper. It was the front page of the *Belfast Telegraph*. There were four black-and-white photographs of small boys in school uniforms, smiling at the camera. The headline was brutal in its simplicity: IRA BOMB KILLS FOUR SCHOOLBOYS. 'Read it, Andrea.'

Andy shook her head. 'I don't have to.' She knew every word by heart and the four young faces were seared into her memory. Four boys killed, another one in intensive care who would later lose a leg and the sight of one eye. Four dead. One maimed. Innocents. And Andy was to blame. She'd carry the guilt to the grave.

Green-eyes pushed the page towards her. 'We're not asking you to do something you haven't already done, Andrea.'

Andy shook her head. 'That was a mistake. A terrible mistake.'

'Casualties of war, the IRA called it. But they never apologised, did they? Even though they were all good Catholic children.'

Andy put her hands over her face and slumped forward so that her elbows were resting on the table. 'Is that what this is, revenge for what happened ten years ago? Who are you?'

'It doesn't matter who we are. All that matters is that we have your daughter. We have the power of life and death over her, Andrea. Do as we say and you'll soon have Katie back home. Refuse, and you'll never see her again. I can promise you something else, Andrea,' Green-eyes said quietly. 'A lot of planning has gone into this. We won't be leaving a holdall in a railway tunnel for children to find.'

Andy shook her head again. 'I can't.'

'Yes, you can,' said Green-eyes firmly. 'You can, and if you want Katie back you will.' She took a small padded envelope from the briefcase and handed it to Andy.

Andy tipped the envelope up and shook out the contents. Blonde curls. A handful. She could tell from the length that they'd been cut close to the scalp. 'Oh no, not her hair,' she said. 'She's so proud of her hair.' She looked at Green-eyes, tears trickling down her cheeks.

Green-eyes leaned forward slowly until her masked face was only inches away from Andy. 'It could have been an ear, Andrea. Or a finger. Think about that.' She motioned at her two companions, and they stepped forward and seized Andy by the arms. The hair and envelope tumbled from her grasp.

Andy pointed at the blonde curls. 'Please,' she said.

Green-eyes walked around the table, scooped up the hair clippings and put them back in the envelope, which she then slotted into the back pocket of Andy's jeans before the two men hustled her away from the table. The men spun Andy round so that her back was to a plasterboard wall. Green-eyes appeared in front of her with a Polaroid camera in her gloved hands.

Andy blinked as the camera flashed and whirred. Then the two men hustled her away down a narrow corridor that ran between the two lines of offices.

EGAN USED a Stanley knife to slit the black garbage bags along the sides, then he pulled them open into single sheets of plastic. It took five to line the boot of the Scorpio, and he used waterproof tape to seal them together. He slit open another three bags and taped them together into a single sheet, then put it and the tape into the boot.

Back in the apartment he checked the action of his Browning, slotted in a clipful of cartridges and gave the silencer a thorough clean.

He had taken a risk planting the listening device in Martin Hayes's office, but without it he'd never have known about Mrs O'Mara's phone call. Egan could tell from the recording that the school secretary wasn't the sort to be deterred by Hayes's clumsy explanation of his daughter's absence. He'd have to do something to silence the meddlesome woman. And quickly.

KATIE WAS SITTING at the Formica-covered table when she heard the bolts slide back. She looked up apprehensively, wondering which of her captors it was. It was the man who'd been nice to her, the one who'd given her Garfield. He was carrying a tray, which he placed on the table in front of her. It was scrambled eggs on a paper plate and a paper cup of milk. She smiled up at him. 'Thank you,' she said.

'I wasn't sure how you liked your eggs,' he said. 'I'm sorry if they're too runny.'

'They're fine,' said Katie. They weren't; they looked horrible, pale yellow and watery, but she wanted to be nice to him. If she was nice to him, maybe he'd be nice to her. She picked up the plastic fork and took a small bite of the eggs. 'Delicious,' she said.

The Nice Man headed for the stairs, but then turned and said, 'Is there anything you like to eat? I'll try to get it for you.'

'Heinz tomato soup. And fish fingers.'

'Same as my kids.'

'You've got children?'

The Nice Man went stiff, as if she'd said the wrong thing. Then he turned round and went up the stairs without saying anything else. Katie looked down at the eggs in disgust. They tasted horrible.

ANDY SAT ON THE FLOOR with her back to the wall in a disused office. The padded envelope was in her lap. In her hands, she held the locks of Katie's hair. She lifted the hair to her face and gently sniffed it, inhaling Katie's fragrance. She closed her eyes and imagined that her face was up against her daughter's neck.

Who were they, these people? Terrorists? Why else would they want a bomb? Could they be Irish? They could be Provisional IRA. Or INLA. Or any of the Republican splinter groups. But then why would they need her? The IRA had their own explosives experts, and if it was them, why the kidnapping? The Army Council could have summoned her before them at any time over the past decade and she would have gone. Maybe not willingly, but she would have gone. So if not the IRA, then who? The Protestants? The Protestant groups didn't have the IRA's technical expertise or access to equipment. Was that what this was all about? Did the Protestants want her to build a bomb for them? Or was someone else behind the kidnapping? Someone else who wanted a bomb built in England. A very large bomb, Green-eyes had said. Andy wondered how big. As big as the bomb the IRA had used at Canary Wharf in 1995? Is that what they wanted from her? And if it was, could Andy do it? Could she give them a bomb in exchange for Katie?

Andy lost all track of time as she sat on the floor, holding Katie's curls next to her cheek. Eventually the door to the office opened and the two men walked across to where she was sitting and grabbed an arm each. The bigger one she thought of as the Wrestler, while the thinner man with the gleaming white Nike trainers was the Runner. Both were still wearing the blue overalls and black ski masks. The Wrestler had put on a black nylon shoulder holster from which protruded the butt of a large automatic.

They pulled her through the doorway and along the corridor to the main factory area. The woman was already sitting at the far side of the table, her arms at rest, her gloved fingers interlinked. She watched with unblinking green eyes as the two men pushed Andy down onto the chair then stood behind her, arms folded.

There was a notepad and pen in front of the woman. The woman picked up the pen and began to tap it on the pad. 'So, Andrea, have you had enough time to think it over?'

'Look, it's not as easy as you seem to think,' said Andy. 'There's specialised equipment . . .'

'What will you need?' the woman asked. Her pen was poised over the notebook.

Andy swallowed. Her mouth was unbearably dry. If she didn't co-operate, if she didn't tell them what they wanted to know, then she knew without a shadow of a doubt that Katie would die. She swallowed again. 'What sort of bomb are you talking about?'

'We want a fertiliser bomb. A big one. Four thousand pounds.'

'Four thousand pounds? That's almost two tons. No one's ever made a two-ton fertiliser bomb before.'

'So we'll get you into the *Guinness Book of Records*,' said Green-eyes.

Andy shook her head. 'You could blow up a small town with a bomb that big. I can't be responsible for something like that.' She leaned forward, resting her arms on the table. 'I can't.'

Green-eyes' lips tightened. 'If you can't, we'll get someone else. But you know what that means.'

Andy put her hands up to her face. 'Jesus, Mary and Joseph,' she whispered.

'Whatever,' said Green-eyes. 'The major component is ammonium nitrate fertiliser,' she said. 'Correct?'

Andy nodded.

'We already have that,' said Green-eyes. 'Just over three thousand pounds. Will that be enough?'

Andy shook her head, trying to clear her thoughts. 'It's complicated. Where are you planning on building it?'

'That's none of your concern.'

'Yes it is. That's what I mean about it being complicated. You need pure ammonium nitrate, but you can't buy it in Northern Ireland, not the pure. The government's not stupid—they know what the pure chemical can be used for, so in Ireland you can only buy it mixed with other stuff. Bone meal, potash, the sort of stuff farmers need.'

'What about in the UK?'

'That's different. Is that what you're planning?'

The woman ignored Andy's question. 'How much would we need? Is three thousand pounds enough?'

Andy tried to concentrate. A 4,000 pound fertiliser bomb. The fertiliser accounted for 80 per cent of the mixture . . . 80 per cent of 4,000 . . . 3,200. She nodded. 'That should be OK, give or take.'

The woman pointed at the far corner of the factory with her pen. Andy turned her head to look. A green tarpaulin covered a mound almost three feet tall. 'You can check it yourself later. What else?'

'Hang on,' said Andy. 'You can't just use it straight from the sack. It's got to be prepared.'

'And how do we do that?'

'Even if it's sold as pure, there'll still be some impurities and you've got to get rid of them first. You have to mix it with alcohol, then strain off the liquid.'

'So how much alcohol will we need?'

Andy did the calculation in her head. 'Assuming you re-use it a few times, a hundred gallons or so. The more the better. It's got to be denatured alcohol. It's used as paint thinner or antifreeze.'

'Where do we get it from?'

'Any biggish paint suppliers should have some.'

'What would happen if we didn't use the alcohol?'

'It might not go off.'

The woman nodded. 'What equipment will you need, to purify the fertiliser?'

'Large containers. Plastic or glass. Stirrers. Wooden or plastic. Then something to heat the mixture. Electric woks are good.'

'How many?'

'The more you have, the faster you can process it. Every pound of fertiliser has to be mixed with alcohol, then heated for three or four minutes. Say you do five pounds at a time, you have to have someone stirring all the time. It's a sort of stir-fry job, you know.'

'So, four. There'll be four of us, so four woks.'

'And electric coffee grinders. I'd get four of them, too.'

'Four it is. What else?'

Andy wanted to lie, to give her wrong information or to withhold something vital, something that would render the explosive inert, but she couldn't risk it. She didn't know how much they already knew. This could be a test, and if she failed the test it could be as dangerous as refusing to cooperate. 'Aluminium powder,' she said. 'You'll need about six hundred pounds.'

'Where would we get that from?' asked the woman.

'Paint suppliers again,' said Andy. 'The best sort to ask for is pyro grade 400 mesh.' She was surprised how easily the technical terms came to her. The information belonged to another life.

The woman scribbled on her pad again.

'Sawdust,' said Andy. 'As fine as possible. Two hundred pounds. Any sawmill will sell it to you. You can say it's for a pet shop. That's what we used to do. And detergent. Thirty pounds or so. Sodium dodecyl benzenesulphonate.' She spelled out the words slowly. 'A chemical supplies company will sell you the pure stuff. But almost any soap-based washing powder will do.'

'And?'

'That's it,' said Andy. 'Ammonium nitrate, aluminium powder, sawdust and detergent. You can add diesel oil if you want. It's not vital, but it helps. You'd need ten gallons or so.'

'And what equipment are you going to need?'

'Desiccators, to dry out the fertiliser. It absorbs moisture, and as soon as it's damp it's useless.'

'Are they easy to get?'

Andy shrugged. 'Depends. You might have to order one.'

'Is there anything else we could use?'

'An electric oven. And baking trays, a couple of inches deep.' Andy did a quick calculation in her head. 'One oven will dry about four hundred pounds a day. So it'll take you about eight days working around the clock to do it all.'

'And if we get four ovens—two days, is that right?'

Andy nodded.

'OK. What else?'

'Respirators. Protective glasses. Overalls. Plastic gloves and oven gloves.' She furrowed her brow as she thought. It had been a long time, and she wasn't sure if she'd remembered everything. She ran through the processes in her mind. 'Thermometers. Metal ones. And a tumble drier,' she said. 'Two would be better.'

'This isn't an ideal home exhibition,' said the woman.

'It's for mixing the fertiliser and aluminium powder,' said Andy. 'It's got to be well mixed. We used to pack it in Tupperware containers then put it in a tumble drier for half an hour or so.'

The woman nodded. 'And once we've made it, it's not unstable?'

'You could smash a train into it and it wouldn't go off. In fact, it's only good for a week or so. Maybe two weeks, but after that the fertiliser will have absorbed water again and no matter what you do to it, it won't go off. So you'll need lots of Tupperware containers, the bigger the better. And lots of black plastic rubbish bags. The more you wrap the stuff, the longer it'll take the water to penetrate.'

The woman made another note. Then she looked up. 'Timer?'

'Depends on when you want it to go off. Minutes, hours, days or weeks.'

'Hours.'

'Any small clock will do. I prefer a battery-operated digital model.'

'What do you pack it in? Oil drums?'

Andy shook her head. 'No. We'll use black bags. You have to pack it around the initiator. If it's in barrels the initial explosion might just knock the rest of the barrels over.'

'OK. Black bags it is. What do you need wiring-wise?'

'Bell wire. Several different colours would help. Soldering iron. Solder. Batteries—1.5 volts. Torch bulbs and bulb holders, for circuit testing. Wire. As many different colours as you can get. Look, what are you going to use this for?'

'That's not your concern.'

'Is it against people, or property? I have a right to know.'

The woman put her pen down and looked at Andy, her eyes narrowing under the ski mask. 'We have your daughter, and unless you do exactly as we say, she'll die. I mean that, Andrea. The men who are looking after her are taking good care of her, but they're just as capable of putting a bullet in her pretty little head or cutting her throat. You have no rights.'

She motioned to the Runner, and he came over and took Andy by the arm, leading her like a naughty child back to the office.

LAURA O'MARA JUMPED as the doorbell rang. It was a quarter past seven, and she wasn't expecting visitors. She put her knitting on the coffee table and turned down the volume of the television set, then peered through the lace curtains. An expensive car, a black saloon, was parked in the road outside her house. She didn't know anyone with a black car. She went over to the door and slid the security chain home. Since her husband had died four years earlier, she'd always taken great care not to let strangers into the house. She eased open the door, keeping a reassuring hand on the lock.

A man in a suit smiled down at her. 'My name's Peter Cordingly,' he said. 'I'm with Dublin City social services.'

He was a pleasant enough chap, with a bland, squarish face, and wire framed spectacles.

'I understand you've expressed concerns about one of the children at your school. Katie Hayes?'

'I only called her father. She was away without permission and . . .'

The man held up a hand to silence her and leaned forward conspiratorially. 'Mrs O'Mara, could I come in and have a word with you about this? What I have to say is a wee bit . . . confidential.'

'Oh my,' said Mrs O'Mara. She unhooked the security chain and pulled the door open, eager to hear what it was that Mr Hayes had done, all thoughts about the dangers of strangers forgotten.

Day Four

Andy woke up as the fluorescent lights flickered into life. She squinted over at the door to the office. The Wrestler stood there with a brown paper bag in one hand and a paper cup in the other. He put them down on the floor in the centre of the room. 'Breakfast,' he said. 'She wants you outside in fifteen minutes.'

'OK.'

The Wrestler went out and closed the door behind him. Andy climbed out of the sleeping-bag that Green-eyes had given her the previous evening. She picked up the brown paper bag and opened it. There was a croissant inside, and a bran muffin. She ate them both, surprised at how hungry she was, but then realised that she hadn't eaten for almost thirty-six hours.

When Green-eyes had given her the sleeping-bag, she'd shown Andy where the bathroom was, at the end of the corridor farthest from the factory area. All it contained was a washbasin and toilet, but it was better than nothing, and Green-eyes had told her she could use it whenever she wanted. There was one stipulation. Andy had to shout that she wanted to leave the office, to give her captors time to put on their ski masks if they weren't already wearing them.

Andy got her washbag out of her suitcase and banged on the office door. 'I want to go to the bathroom!' she shouted.

'OK!' shouted Green-eyes, off in the distance. Andy opened the door and went along to the bathroom, had as good a wash as was possible in a sink, and brushed her teeth.

Green-eyes was waiting for her in the factory area, still wearing the blue overalls and ski mask. The Runner was loading the bags of ammonium nitrate into the back of the blue Transit van.

Green-eyes pointed at the plastic chair on Andy's side of the table. 'Sit down.'

Andy did as she was told.

'I want you to go through the list again,' Green-eyes said to Andy. 'Everything we'll need for a four-thousand-pound fertiliser bomb.'

'Don't you trust me? Or are you testing me, is that it?'

'Maybe I just want to make sure that you didn't forget anything,' said the woman. 'Deliberately or otherwise.'

'When can I see Katie?'

'You can't. She's still in Ireland.'

'I have to know that she's OK. What you're asking me to do is complicated. And I'm going to find it impossible to concentrate if

36

I'm worrying whether or not my daughter is alive. Doesn't that make sense to you?'

Green-eyes tilted her head to one side. 'Maybe you're right at that,' she said. 'I'll see what I can do. Now, let's go through the list.'

The Runner finished loading the Transit van. 'Oy, Don!' he yelled. Green-eyes stiffened. Andy pretended not to notice. 'Pure ammonium nitrate fertiliser,' she said.

The Wrestler came out of one of the offices and headed over to the metal door. He began to pull on the chain to open it and the Runner climbed into the driver's seat of the van.

'Aluminium powder. Pyro grade 400 mesh.' Andy fought to keep her voice steady. She brushed a stray lock of hair from her eyes. 'Sawdust. Soap powder. Diesel oil.'

The van engine kicked into life. Green-eyes began to write on her pad. Andy forced herself to breathe. Had she managed to convince Green-eyes that she hadn't heard the Runner's slip?

O'KEEFE STUFFED his ski mask into the glove compartment. 'I should blow your brains out here and now,' he said.

Quinn looked across at him, his mouth open in surprise. 'What?' He sounded genuinely confused. He braked and brought the van to a halt at the roadside.

'You used my name, you ignorant, stupid piece of shit amateur.'

Quinn gripped the steering wheel. 'What are you talking about?'

O'Keefe jerked his thumb back at the industrial estate behind them. 'Back there. You called me Don.'

'I wouldn't use your name. I'm not stupid.'

O'Keefe seized Quinn by the throat, his big, square hand gripping either side of the younger man's neck like a vice. 'Not stupid!' O'Keefe screamed. 'I'll give you not stupid!' He tightened his grip on Quinn's throat, threatening to crush his windpipe. 'Now, think back, you little shit. Think back to what you said.'

Quinn tried to speak but could barely move his head. O'Keefe let go of Quinn's throat and the younger man gasped for breath.

'I'm sorry. I'm sorry.'

O'Keefe folded his arms and settled back in the passenger seat. 'You've got to be on your toes every second of every minute. This isn't a game. We get caught and they'll throw away the key.'

Quinn put the van into gear and pulled away from the kerb. His hands were shaking on the steering wheel.

They drove to London, and cut across the city towards the financial district. Quinn brought the van to a halt and nodded at the line of half a dozen cars waiting to drive into the City of London. A uniformed policeman waved through the car at the front while his colleague went to speak to the driver of the second.

'Joke, isn't it?' said Quinn. 'What do they expect to find, huh?'

'They're not the ones to worry about,' said O'Keefe. 'It's the eye in the sky that does the damage.' High up on the office building was a wall-mounted camera pointing at the checkpoint.

'That camera picks out the registration number and runs it through the police computer in seven seconds,' continued O'Keefe. 'If it's stolen or used by anyone on the Special Branch watch list, there'd be more armed police around us than fleas on a dog.'

They edged towards the front of the queue of cars. O'Keefe reached under his seat and pulled out a clipboard. The policeman walked up. 'Morning, sir. Can you tell me where you're going? he asked.

O'Keefe showed him the clipboard, with the landscape gardening company's letterhead on the top. 'Cathay Tower,' he said. 'We're doing a rooftop garden.'

The policeman stepped back and waved them on, his eyes already on the next vehicle.

As anticipated there hadn't been any problems. The van was registered and insured in the name of the landscaping company, taxed and MOT'd. Quinn's driving licence was clean, though the name and address weren't his.

The main entrance to Cathay Tower was in Queen Anne Street, close to Bank tube station, but the entrance to the car park was at the rear, down a narrow side street. O'Keefe showed his pass to the elderly security guard. Like the van's paperwork, it was genuine. The office had been rented some three months earlier, and included in the lease were three parking spaces. They were on the second level of the subterranean car park, and Quinn drove down and parked.

They began unloading the sacks of fertiliser onto a trolley they'd brought with them and then went up in the service lift to the ninth floor. The lift doors opened onto a corridor which led to the main reception area where the passenger lifts were. A door led off the reception area to the lavatories; a corridor led to the main open-plan office area which ran the full length of the building. The entire floor was rented in the name of an overseas stockbroking firm, paid for through a Cayman Islands bank account.

O'Keefe walked into the main office area. Quinn followed with the trolley. White vertical blinds covered the ceiling-to-floor windows. The NatWest Tower was almost directly opposite. It would be all too easy for one of the thousands of office workers to look in and see what they were doing. The blinds would have to remain closed all the time they were there.

There were already eighteen sacks of fertiliser piled up in one corner. The two men unloaded the trolley, adding the sacks to the pile. Quinn nodded at them. 'It's weird that gardeners all over the country spread this over their lawns, right? Regular fertiliser. But add other stuff to it and . . . you know . . . bang!'

'Bang? You think a four-thousand-pound bomb's going to go bang? You ever heard a bomb go off? A big one?'

Quinn shook his head.

'Well, I can tell you from the horse's mouth, bang doesn't come into it. Bang's what you get when you burst a balloon. Bombs don't go bang. Not big ones.'

THE MERCEDES SWEPT up the driveway and parked in front of the two-storey house. Two men in dark suits walked up to the car, nodded when they saw who was inside, then walked back to their post by the front door. Deng sat where he was until his bodyguard had climbed out of the car and opened the door for him. He stood for a moment to admire the view of Hong Kong harbour far below him, then walked to the house.

The general was in the study. He indicated that Deng should sit down on a leather winged chair at the side of the window, and looked at him with watery eyes. 'How long?'

'A week. Seven days.'

'And the money?'

'We anticipate receiving payment a month after the . . . incident.'

'Will he wait?' asked the general.

'I assume so,' said Deng. 'It is the only chance he has of getting his money back. It is the only chance any of us has.'

Deng heard footsteps behind him. A man in a dark suit, not one of the guards at the front of the house, walked across the study and emptied a sack in front of the general. Deng grimaced as a dead dog flopped out onto the floor. A spaniel, the fur on its chest matted with blood. 'My daughter's dog,' said the general. 'He is an evil man, that Michael Wong, we should never have done business with him.'

Deng didn't react to the criticism. It had been his idea to bring in Wong as an investor, it was too late for regrets—the only way out of their predicament was to get Wong's money back. And for that they needed Egan, the American. Only he could save their lives and the lives of their families. If they failed, Michael Wong's vengeance would carry far and wide. The dog was just a warning.

McCracken's mobile rang. It was Egan. 'Everything OK?' he asked.

McCracken walked to the far end of the factory area, away from where Andrea was sitting. 'No problems,' she said.

'I'm five minutes away. Make sure she's out of the way, will you?' The line went dead. Like all of Egan's phone calls it was short, to the point, and unidentifiable. He never used names and always spoke in the vaguest terms possible.

McCracken went back over to Andrea. 'Right, you can stay in the office until the boys get back,' she said. 'Take a coffee with you if you want. Keep the door closed until I come and get you.'

Andrea did as she was told. McCracken took off her ski mask and rubbed her face. She made herself a cup of coffee, and as she sipped it she heard Egan's car pull up outside. He let himself in and nodded at her. 'Where is she?'

McCracken jerked a thumb at the office. 'You want a coffee?'

Egan shook his head. He was wearing a black leather jacket over a grey crew-neck pullover and blue jeans and carrying his mobile phone in one hand and his car keys in the other. McCracken studied him as he walked over to the table and picked up her notepad. One word came to mind when she thought of the man who was paying her wages. Bland. Pale blue eyes, receding fair hair, medium height, a squarish face with an average nose, no distinguishing features. Egan studied the list, nodding thoughtfully.

'It's OK?' McCracken asked, going over to join him.

'It's fine. Perfect. How are Quinn and O'Keefe getting on?'

McCracken tilted her head to the side. 'O'Keefe's fine. Very professional. But Quinn . . .'

Egan put down the notepad and narrowed his eyes. 'What?'

McCracken winced under his gaze. 'He's a bit . . . unfocused. Considering what we're expected to do. The next phase and all.'

'It's not too late to replace him, Lydia.' His pale blue eyes watched to see how she'd react.

She knew what he meant by replaced. 'I don't know,' she said.

Egan walked up close to her and looked into her eyes. 'It's got to be your call,' he said. 'Your responsibility. I can't be here all the time.'

'I know. It's just that I haven't worked with guys like him before. He's undisciplined.'

'That's a function of his background, Lydia. He's not a terrorist. You were trained by the best, both mentally and physically. He's a career criminal. But he's good with vehicles and, if anything does go wrong, Quinn's a good man to have in your corner. But as I said, it's your call. Has to be.'

McCracken nodded. 'He'll be OK. Besides, we're going to need everyone to do the mixing.' She gestured at the notepad. 'According to the Hayes woman, there's a hell of a lot of work involved.'

'She's cooperating fully?'

'Carrot and stick,' said McCracken. 'She thinks she's going to see her daughter if she helps us. And that we'll kill her if she doesn't. She keeps asking if she can call her husband. What do you think?'

'Only if it's the only way you can get her to cooperate. He hasn't gone to the cops, so the phones are clean. But if you do allow it, keep it short and watch what she says.' Egan jangled his keys. 'Right. I'll leave you to it. I've got to get back to Ireland.' He reached into his jacket pocket and took out an envelope. 'Be careful with her,' he said, nodding at the office. 'She's not to be trusted, not for a minute.'

GREEN-EYES OPENED the door to the office.

'I'm going to make coffee. Do you want some?'

'What I want is to talk to my husband. And my daughter. I just want to know that she's OK. How could you do this? Don't you have children? How would you feel if someone kidnapped somebody you loved? How would you feel if someone said they'd be killed if you didn't do what they wanted?'

'I'd feel the same as you do,' said the woman. 'I'd feel angry and bitter and fearful. But the difference between us is that I wouldn't do anything to jeopardise the lives of those that depended on me.'

Andy's brow furrowed. 'What do you mean?'

The woman reached into the pocket of her overalls and brought out the envelope Egan had given her. She threw it at Andy and it fell on the floor. It was the letter she'd left at the Strand Palace Hotel. The letter addressed to her husband. Andy closed her eyes.

'That was very, very stupid, Andrea,' said the woman, her voice a low growl. 'What did you think? That we wouldn't be checking on you? Don't whine to me about your daughter being in danger. If anyone's putting Katie's life on the line, it's you.' Green-eyes turned on her heels and slammed the door behind her.

CANNING KNOCKED on the basement door and slipped back the bolts. Katie was lying on her camp bed, curled up around her Garfield toy.

'I feel sick,' she said.

'You're just upset,' he said. 'You're worried, that's all. It's going to be OK. Just a few more days.'

'No, I feel really sick. Hot.'

41

Canning put his hand on her forehead. She was indeed hot and her skin was clammy with sweat.

'Sit up. Let me have a look at you.'

Katie did as he asked and looked at him as he felt her neck.

'Open your mouth.'

She opened her mouth wide. He told her to turn her head so that the light shone into her mouth. The sides of her throat were bright red, but there were no white patches which would have indicated serious infection.

'Are you going to take me to the hospital?' Katie said.

Canning smiled. 'You've just got a bit of flu, that's all. I'll go and get you some medicine. But don't worry, you're going to be all right.'

Katie saw the video camera that Canning had put on the bed.

'I want to take some pictures of you,' he said. 'So that I can send the tape to your mum and dad. So that they know that you're OK.'

'Why don't you let me telephone them? I know my number, it's Dublin six seven nine . . .'

Canning smiled beneath his ski mask. 'I know what your number is, but it's better if we do it with the video camera. Then they can see you as well as hear you.' He picked it up and pointed it at her. 'Now, I want you to say something like, "Hello, this is Katie. I'm fine. They're taking good care of me." You can wave, if you want. But this is really important, Katie. I want you to say that it's Saturday, OK?'

'But it's not Saturday. It's Friday. I'll be telling a lie.'

'But it might be Saturday when they get the message. If you say it's Friday and they get the message on Saturday, they might be worried. You can understand that, can't you?'

Katie nodded. 'I guess.'

'So let's record a message that'll make them happy, then I'll go and get your medicine.'

Canning pressed the RECORD button and nodded.

'Mummy. Dad. This is Katie. Your daughter.' She hesitated.

Canning mouthed the words 'I'm fine' and nodded encouragingly.

'I'm fine,' said Katie. 'But I've got flu, I think. My head hurts and my throat's sore. The nice man is going to give me some medicine to make it better so I should be OK soon.'

Canning mouthed 'Saturday'.

'He said to say it's Saturday and that I'm OK. Mummy, I want to come home . . .'

She started crying and Canning switched off the video camera. He gave her a hug but her little body was racked with sobs.

She curled up on the bed with her back to him and he went

upstairs and into the kitchen. McEvoy was watching the news on a portable television set.

'How's the little princess?' he snarled.

'She's got the flu. I'll go and get her some Night Nurse.'

'Did she do the tape?'

'Yeah. Saturday.'

'Egan wants a week's worth. He won't be happy with one day.'

'The kid's sick,' said Canning.

'She's going to be a hell of a lot sicker if this thing doesn't pan out,' said McEvoy. 'Sick as in dead.'

MARTIN HAYES LEFT the office early. He was in the house by four o'clock, and was making himself a cup of instant coffee when the doorbell rang. The noise startled him and he spilt boiling water over the counter top. He cursed and went to see who was at the front door. There were two uniformed officers of the Garda Siochana, the Irish police, standing on the doorstep, one grey and in his late forties, the other younger and taller. They were both wearing waterproof jackets, flecked with rain.

'Mr Hayes?' asked the older one. 'Mr Martin Hayes?'

'Yes?' said Martin. He had a sick feeling in the pit of his stomach. Two unsmiling policemen could only mean bad news. He held on to the door handle for support, gripping it tightly.

'Is your wife at home?'

Martin narrowed his eyes, confused. The question was totally unexpected. He'd assumed that they were there to tell him that Katie or Andy had been found. And found meant dead, because if they were OK then they'd be on the doorstep with the policemen. 'What?'

'Mrs Hayes. Mrs Andrea Hayes. Is she at home?'

'No,' said Martin, hesitantly.

'What about your daughter? Can we see her, please?'

Martin shook his head. 'She's not here.'

'Where is she?'

'Look, could you tell me what this is about? Is something wrong? Has something happened?'

'That's what we're trying to find out, Mr Hayes.'

Martin could feel his legs start to shake, and he was sure that the two gardai could see the effect their presence was having on him.

'My wife's out. With Katie. They'll be back tomorrow. They've gone up to Belfast to see her aunt. Her aunt's sick and Andy wanted to go and make sure that there was food in the house, stuff like that.'

'And she took your daughter with her?' said the older garda.

Martin nodded. 'I've been really busy at work. I couldn't guarantee that I'd be able to pick Katie up from school. We decided that it'd be better if she went with Andy.'

'And you didn't think of informing the school?'

Martin suddenly realised what the visit was about. The woman in the headmistress's office, Mrs O'Mara, must have called them. He shrugged. 'She's only seven. We didn't think she'd be hurt by a few days off school. It was all short notice. Her aunt called and Andy went the same day.'

The older garda nodded. 'How did she go?'

'What?'

'How did your wife go up to Belfast?'

Martin's mind whirled. Why was he asking that? The reason hit him like a blow to the stomach. There were two cars parked in the driveway. Martin's Range Rover and Andy's Renault Clio. So the gardai knew that Andy hadn't driven up to Belfast.

'She took the train. I mean, they took the train. Andy and Katie.'

'Which train?'

'The Belfast train,' said Martin.

The garda smiled as if there had been a simple misunderstanding. 'The time,' he said. 'What time did the train leave?'

Martin had no idea how often trains went from Dublin to Belfast. 'Morning. Tennish. On Wednesday.'

The two gardai exchanged looks but Martin couldn't tell what they were thinking.

'And your wife's aunt. What was her name?'

'Bessie.'

'Bessie. Where exactly does she live?'

'I'm not sure of the address, exactly. But it's north Belfast.' Martin figured the best thing to do was to keep his answers as vague as possible. Specifics could be checked.

'Has she phoned? Your wife?'

Martin rubbed his nose with the back of his hand. It was unlikely in the extreme that Andy would have gone away and not telephoned him. But if he said yes, could they check? He had no choice, he had to lie. 'Several times,' he said. 'In fact, she called last night.'

The younger garda took out a small green notebook and a pen. 'Could you give us the number, please, sir?'

'The number?'

'Aunt Bessie's telephone number?' said the older garda.

'I don't think she's on the phone.'

'But she phoned to ask your wife to go up and take care of her.'

'She must have used a phone box.'

'But you said she was ill. Needed looking after.'

Martin could feel himself being painted into a corner. 'I'm not sure if it was her that phoned. It could have been someone else, phoning for her.'

The older garda nodded thoughtfully. 'And when are you expecting your wife back?'

'I'm not sure.'

'She didn't say when she called last night?'

'No, she didn't. What's this about? Has something happened?'

The older garda looked at Martin for several seconds before answering. 'We're not sure, Mr Hayes. In fact, it's all a bit of a mystery, really. You know a Mrs O'Mara?'

'She's a secretary at my daughter's school. She phoned yesterday, she wanted to know why Katie wasn't at school.'

'Well, Mrs O'Mara had mentioned to the headmistress that she was concerned about your daughter. Now Mrs O'Mara hasn't turned up for work. We've been around to her house and she's not there.'

Martin put his hand up to his forehead, frowning. 'I don't get what you're saying. Mrs O'Mara isn't at home so you think something's happened to Katie? That makes no sense. No sense at all.'

'That's right,' said the garda. 'It's a mystery. And mysteries annoy the hell out of me. But nothing you've said so far has reassured me that your daughter is safe and sound.'

'What?' Martin didn't have to feign his reaction. 'That's ridiculous! My wife and daughter are out of town, that's all. They'll be back any day now.'

The older garda nodded slowly. He reached into the inside pocket of his waterproof jacket and took out a business card. 'My name's O'Brien,' he said. 'Sergeant O'Brien. Next time your wife phones, would you get her to call me? Just so's we know that she's OK.'

Martin reached for the card. 'Sure. I will,' he said.

The two gardai walked down the path, away from the house.

Martin closed the door and leaned against it, his heart pounding like a jackhammer.

EGAN FROWNED as he listened to the tape. The two gardai turning up was an unexpected development, and it meant he was going to have to revise his plans. Martin Hayes had handled it better than Egan had expected, but doubted that the gardai had been deceived. They'd go away and make further enquiries, but eventually they'd be back.

Egan was surprised that they'd made the connection between the

O'Mara woman and the Hayes girl. Mrs O'Mara was safely buried in a wood some twenty miles south of Dublin—it was sheer bad luck that the secretary had expressed her concerns about Katie's absence to the school's headmistress.

He swivelled his chair around and hit the print button on his computer keyboard. The laser printer whirred and Egan picked up the letter and read it through carefully before signing it. He fed it into the fax machine on the desk and dialled the number of his bank in Zürich. The letter contained instructions to transfer $1 million to another of his accounts, this one in the Cayman Islands.

Egan went over to the window and looked out over the city as the fax machine whirred behind him. He took a swig from a bottle of Budweiser. Behind him, the fax finished transmitting and ejected the letter. One million dollars. The equivalent of twelve years' salary in his last job. Egan had worked for the Defence Intelligence Agency in a black operations department. Blackmail, bribery, assassination—it had been the best possible training for his present career. Egan had left after five years, spent six months travelling the world establishing fake identities and opening a daisy chain of bank accounts, then set up on his own. It had been the best move he'd ever made. A militant Islamic group had paid him a total of $3 million for his work with Muslim terrorists in Kenya and Tanzania. Three months as an adviser with the Palestinian Liberation Organisation had netted him $2 million and his work for the men from Beijing would earn him a further $7 million, minus expenses.

He looked at his Rolex. Everything was going to plan. All he had to do now was to work out the best way of killing Martin Hayes.

Day Five

Canning was stirring a pan of scrambled eggs when McEvoy banged open the kitchen door and stood in the doorway, scratching his stomach. 'What are ya cooking?' he asked.

'Eggs for Katie.'

McEvoy walked across the fake marble linoleum to the cooker and stood behind Canning, so close that Canning could smell the man's stale breath. 'What's this with Katie? It's best to keep your distance, Mick. Don't let it get personal, yeah? Call her anything, but don't call her by her name. If the shit hits the fan, we might have to do her, and it's going to be a hell of a lot harder to do it if you've forged a relationship with her. Get it?'

'Got it.' Canning spooned the scrambled eggs onto a paper plate, then put the plate and a plastic fork on a tray. 'You've done this before, haven't you?'

'Not with a kid, no. But I've held guys before.'

'For ransom, like?'

'No. Not for ransom. I used to work for the Civil Administration Team.'

Canning raised his eyebrows in surprise. He'd known that McEvoy was active in the IRA, but when the IRA needed prisoners or traitors interrogated or tortured, it was the vicious Civil Administration Team that was called in. And most of the men and women they interrogated ended up dead.

McEvoy saw the look of surprise. 'Yeah, the hardest of the hard. That's what I mean about not getting involved. You don't use their names, you don't talk to them and you don't look at them. You treat them like meat because that's all they are. Meat. Dead meat.'

'And are you saying that's what Katie is? Dead meat?'

'She might be. She might not be. Maybe everything's going to go exactly the way Egan's planned, but if worst comes to worst, we've got to be prepared to do what's necessary.' He nodded at the tray. 'Her eggs are getting cold.'

LYDIA MCCRACKEN gave five pounds each to the two shop assistants who had trundled two tumble driers and four electric ovens out of the discount warehouse and loaded them into the back of the blue Peugeot van. Mark Quinn then loaded four large coffee grinders and four electric woks into the van and slammed the door shut.

McCracken got into the passenger seat and told Quinn to drive back to the industrial estate. Most items had now been purchased, and all the chemicals had already been delivered to the office in Cathay Tower. They were ready to go on to the next stage.

It took an hour to get back to the factory unit they were using as their base. It was on a large industrial estate on the outskirts of Milton Keynes, less than half a mile from the M1. McCracken had leased the unit almost a year earlier in the name of a metal tubing manufacturer. There was a parking area at the rear of the unit, with spaces for two dozen vehicles. The blue Transit van in the landscaping company livery was there, along with two courier vans and a grey Volvo. There was also a 250cc Yamaha motorcycle with a black back-box. All the vehicles had genuine paperwork and were taxed, insured and MoT'd.

Quinn parked the Peugeot next to one of the courier vans.

'Don and I'll take the Transit to the airport,' said McCracken. 'Leave the stuff in the van for now.'

They got out of the van and went inside the factory. O'Keefe was sitting at the table, playing patience.

'She OK?' asked McCracken.

'Not a peep,' said O'Keefe, flicking the cards with his thumbnail.

She looked at her wristwatch. 'Right, we're going to drop the Hayes woman at Shepherds Bush at two. Mark, you'd better head off now. Keep your distance. No eye contact, right? Just check she gets there, and that she doesn't talk to anyone or use the phone.'

'No sweat,' said Quinn. He went over to a duffle bag and pulled out a black crash helmet, a leather jacket and a pair of padded leather gloves. 'Catch you later,' he said, heading for the door.

McCracken took her ski mask off the table and put it on, slipped on her leather gloves and went through to the office section, where she called out Andy's name. Andy opened the door. She'd changed into a pair of black jeans and a white shirt.

'Have you got a suit?' asked McCracken. 'Something suitable for an office?'

Andy looked down at her jeans. 'No. I've got these and what I was wearing when you brought me here.'

'You can wear one of mine. We're about the same size.'

McCracken waved at Andy to follow her, and the two women went through to the factory area. McCracken sat down at the table next to O'Keefe. She nodded at the third chair and Andy sat down.

'We're moving out of here,' said McCracken. She passed an A–Z London street directory over to Andy. 'Page forty-two,' she said. 'I've marked the building. It's called Cathay Tower. The address is on a card at the front.'

Andy flicked to the front of the book and found a three-by-four-inch piece of white card. On it was written ORVICE WILLIAMS BROKING INTERNATIONAL LIMITED, and an address.

'We're on the ninth floor,' said McCracken, taking a laminated identification badge from the briefcase and handing it to Andy. 'This'll get you into the building. You go there and wait for us. We'll be there first thing tomorrow morning.'

Andy looked at the badge. It had a small metal clip so that it could be attached to clothing. The name of the broking firm was on the badge. So was another name, Sally Higgs, a scrawled signature and Andy's photograph, the Polaroid picture that had been taken on her arrival at the factory unit.

McCracken stood up. 'On your way to the tower, don't speak to anyone, don't phone anyone. You'll be watched every step of the way. If you try to communicate with anyone at all, we'll simply disappear and you'll never hear from us again. Or your daughter. Understand?'

'Yes,' mumbled Andy. She looked around the factory area as if trying to get her bearings. 'How do I get there?'

'I'll explain that later. But first there's something I want to show you.' She stood up, and Andy followed her across to the computer.

McCracken clicked on the mouse and a view of the Cathay Tower office filled the screen. Andy stared at it, not understanding.

'This is the office we'll be using,' explained McCracken. She clicked on the mouse again. Another view of the office appeared. 'We can see every bit of the office from here,' she said. 'So when you get there, just make yourself comfortable and wait for us. You'll be there on your own tonight, but we'll be watching you.'

Andy nodded, but said nothing.

'You're doing fine, Andrea,' said McCracken. 'Just keep on doing as we ask and you'll soon be back with your family.'

'I want to call my husband. If I don't, Martin'll go to the police.'

'He won't. He'll be too worried about what'll happen to you and Katie.'

'No, you don't know him. He'll want to do something. It's been almost five days since you took Katie. He hasn't heard from me since Wednesday night, so . . .'

Green-eyes stiffened. 'You spoke to him on Wednesday night? You called him from the hotel?'

'You didn't say I wasn't to,' said Andy. 'It was the only call I made. You just said I wasn't to call the police. He needed to know that I was OK. And he needs to know that I'm still OK. Because if he doesn't . . .' She left the sentence hanging.

'I can't trust you, Andrea,' said Green-eyes. 'Look at that business with the letter at the hotel.'

'I'm sorry. That was stupid.' Andy wanted to say more but she didn't want to risk antagonising Green-eyes. Green-eyes hadn't known that Andy had phoned Martin from London. That meant the phone in Dublin wasn't tapped. There had to be a way that she could make use of that knowledge.

Green-eyes went over to a table and picked up her mobile phone. 'What's the number?'

Andy gave her the number and Green-eyes tapped it in. She listened to check that it was ringing, then handed it to Andrea. 'Any tricks, any at all, and it'll be Katie who'll suffer. And I want you to ask him if he's gone to the police.'

'OK. OK.' Andy couldn't believe that Green-eyes was letting her use the phone.

Martin answered and Andy's heart pounded. 'Martin? It's me.'

'Oh, thank God. How are you? Where are you?'

'Martin, listen to me. Did you go to the police?'

'No. No, I didn't.'

Andy put her hand over the receiver. 'It's OK. He hasn't spoken to the police.' Green-eyes nodded and motioned for Andy to continue.

'It's OK,' said Andy. 'I'm here. But you have to listen to me, love. I'm OK, and they say that Katie's OK. Look, Martin, there's something they want me to do for them, then they say they'll let me come home. Katie, too.'

'I've got the money ready,' said Martin. 'Almost four hundred thousand pounds. Tell them I've got the money.'

'They don't want money, Martin. That's all I can tell you. But they've assured me that so long as you don't go to the police, they won't hurt me or Katie. You have to promise me that you won't go to the police.'

'I promise,' said Martin. 'But what do they want?'

Andy ignored the question. 'Just wait there and we'll be back with you soon. We'll all be together again, just like we were before. You can take us to Venice. Like you promised. It'll be so great to go back. You and me, and Katie. It's going to happen, Martin. Just don't do anything to rock the boat, OK?'

Andy was rambling; the words were tumbling out and running into each other as if she were scared that he might interrupt.

'OK, love. I promise. Tell them, I won't go to the police.'

Green-eyes grabbed the phone and pulled it away from Andy. 'That's enough,' she said.

'Thank you,' Andy said. 'Thanks for letting me talk to him.'

Green-eyes switched the phone off. She went over to the table and put the phone in her briefcase and locked it. 'What did you mean about Venice?'

'That's where we went on our honeymoon. He's been promising to take Katie there for ages. She saw the honeymoon pictures and wanted to know why she wasn't there. You know how kids are.'

Green-eyes turned to look at Andy, scowling. 'You weren't trying to be clever, were you, Andrea?'

'What do you mean?'

Green-eyes didn't reply. She sat down, steepled her fingers under her chin and stared at Andy with unblinking eyes.

'He hasn't gone to the police, and now he won't,' said Andy. 'Now he knows that I'm OK.' She dropped down onto one of the chairs. 'Are you really going to use it? The bomb?'

'Does it matter?'

'Of course it matters. Are you building it as a threat, or are you going to set it off?'

'Do you think I'm going to tell you what we're planning to do Andrea? Why would I do that?'

'Have you thought through what'll happen if you explode a four-thousand-pound bomb in London? The backlash will destroy you. Look at what happened in Omagh. It finished the Real IRA. Everyone turned against them.'

Green-eyes stood up again and took hold of her briefcase. 'We've got work to do. Come on.'

MARTIN FELT LIGHT-HEADED, almost drunk with relief. Andy was alive. So was his Katie. Over the past few days his imagination had run riot, and he'd come close to convincing himself that his wife and daughter were dead, that the only option he had left was to go to the police. He thanked God that he hadn't. And if what she'd said was true, she and Katie would be back home soon. His heart had almost stopped when she'd asked him if he'd spoken to the police. He realised that the kidnappers were monitoring the conversation, and if he'd told Andy that the police had turned up on his doorstep they might think that he'd called them. Best not to mention it and hope that Sergeant O'Brien believed his story.

Martin's sense of relief was tempered by the realisation that he still didn't know what the kidnappers wanted. She'd made it clear that they didn't want money. So what was so important that they needed Andy? She was a housewife. She took care of him and raised Katie and she did occasional freelance work for the *Irish Independent* and some Dublin magazines.

So what was it that the kidnappers wanted from her? It couldn't have been her journalistic skills. So what else did she have that they wanted? It was a mystery, and it was driving Martin crazy.

He lay back on the bed, staring up at the ceiling. And what had Andy meant by taking her to Venice? They'd never discussed going there. Hell, they'd never even been to Italy.

MCEVOY LOOKED UP from the portable television set. 'It's almost noon,' he said. 'The flight's at two thirty.'

'Yeah, I know,' said Canning.

'So we'll need the tapes. All seven of them.'

'Look, the wee girl's sick. She can barely talk.'

McEvoy looked at his wristwatch, then pushed himself up out of his armchair. 'Let's see if I can't get the little bird to sing.' He reached for the video camera and a stack of tapes on the table next to where Canning was filling in the crossword in the *Irish Independent*.

'I'll do it,' said Canning.

McEvoy patted him on the shoulder, then gripped it tightly, his fingers biting into Canning's flesh. 'You stay where you are, Mick. I'd hate to tear you away from your crossword.'

McEvoy grinned wolfishly and put on his ski mask. He went down into the basement. The girl was curled up on her bed. She looked over her shoulder as he went up to her.

'Sit up and do as you're told. I don't have time to piss around.'

'I don't feel well,' said Katie.

'Yeah, me neither.' He pulled the wooden chair away from the table and sat on it, facing the bed. 'Right, when I press this button, I want you to tell your mum and dad that you're all right. Tell them that you miss them, tell them anything you want. Then I want you to say that it's Sunday.'

'But it isn't. It's Saturday.'

McEvoy grabbed her by the hair. 'Say it's Sunday, OK?'

Tears sprang into Katie's eyes. 'I don't feel well.'

'You're going to feel a lot worse if you don't do as you're told,' hissed McEvoy. 'Remember how I cut your hair? How would you like it if I cut off one of your ears? And if you don't wipe that sour look off your face, I'll smack you good and proper.'

Katie forced a smile.

'That's better,' said McEvoy. 'Right. Now let's record this message. Then we'll do one for the rest of the days of the week. And if you give me any trouble, I'm going to cut off your ear, OK?'

Katie stared at him with wide eyes. She nodded slowly.

ANDY LAY IN THE BACK of the Transit, the sound of the engine muffled by the hood she'd been made to wear. Next to her was a black briefcase that Green-eyes had given her. That and the dark blue suit and raincoat she'd been supplied with would give credence to her story that she was an office worker having to work a weekend shift.

Outside the van she heard blaring horns and motorcycle engines, and in the distance the siren of an ambulance. They'd turned off the motorway some twenty minutes or so earlier.

The van braked and Andy slid along the metal floor. The van made a series of turns, then came to a halt.

'Now then, Andrea, listen to me carefully. I want you to sit up with your back to us, then take off the hood. Open the doors, close them, then walk away from the van. The tube station is right ahead of you. Don't look back. Just keep walking into the station. And remember, you're going to be watched every step of the way.'

Andy followed the instructions and walked straight to the station, keeping her head down. She knew they'd be watching her in the mirrors and didn't want to give them any reason to suspect that she was trying to sneak a look at them.

She bought a single ticket to Bank station with change that Green-eyes had given her, then went through the ticket barrier and took the escalator down to the eastbound Central Line platform.

She walked along the crowded platform, weaving in and out of the waiting passengers. A businessman in a pinstripe suit was looking at her. He smiled but she ignored him. A tall man in his twenties walked by, nodding his head in time with the music he was playing through a Sony Walkman. He was wearing a denim jacket with a Harley Davidson emblem on the back, and had the volume up so high that other passengers were giving him dirty looks. A woman in a sheep-skin jacket looked up from her *Evening Standard*. Could she be Green-eyes? Andy was too far away to see what colour her eyes were.

A young man in a black leather motorcycle jacket was leaning against the vending machine, picking his teeth with a match. He looked away. Could he be one of them? She'd heard a motorcycle drive away from the factory about half an hour before Green-eyes had told her to get into the back of the Transit.

A breeze on her left cheek signalled the imminent arrival of the eastbound train, and Andy took a step back from the platform. The train pulled into the station and she stepped into a carriage and looked around. The man in the motorcycle jacket was sitting at the far end of the carriage, picking his nose. Was he the one? Andy looked away, not wanting to establish eye contact with him.

Eventually Andy reached Bank station.

After she'd passed through the ticket barrier, she took the A–Z street directory out of her raincoat pocket and used it to find her way to Cathay Tower. There was no sign of the man in the leather jacket.

There was a grey-haired security man with a drinker's nose sitting at a reception desk. He barely glanced at Andy's name badge. She walked past him to the lifts.

From the entrance to a building on the opposite side of the street, Quinn watched Andy go into Cathay Tower. He switched off his Walkman and pulled his headphones down around his neck. From the inside pocket of his denim jacket he took out a mobile phone. 'She's home and dry,' he said.

'OK. Get back to the bike and head up to the factory,' McCracken said. 'Keep an eye on the computer until we get back.'

She cut the connection. Quinn put the phone back into his pocket and put the headphones on, then headed back to Bank station. He'd parked his motorcycle in a multistorey car park in Shepherd's Bush, his helmet and leather jacket locked in the back-box.

CANNING LOOKED UP as McEvoy came out of the basement and bolted the door. 'Easy peasy,' said McEvoy, tossing the video cassettes onto the table. 'I've always had a way with kids and small animals.'

Canning gathered up the cassettes and put them into a plastic carrier bag together with the one he'd recorded.

'Is she OK?'

McEvoy reached for a bottle of Bushmills and poured himself a glassful. 'She's fine and dandy. Don't you worry your pretty little head about her.' He looked at his wristwatch. 'You'd best be going.'

Canning nodded. He didn't like the idea of leaving McEvoy alone with the little girl, but didn't see that he had any choice. McCracken had said that he was to deliver the tapes. He put the carrier bag into his holdall, got his British Midland ticket from a drawer in the sitting room and went outside to the Mondeo.

He drove to the airport, parked the car in a short-term car park, and checked in an hour before his flight to Heathrow.

McCracken was waiting for him in the buffet on the arrivals floor of Terminal One, sitting at a table with a cup of coffee in front of her. Canning bought himself a coffee and a sandwich and sat at a neighbouring table with his back to her.

'Everything OK?' McCracken asked, her voice a whisper.

'Everything's fine,' said Canning, not looking round. He took the carrier bag from his holdall, put it down on the floor and gently pushed it back under his seat.

He heard McCracken pull the carrier bag between her legs, then open and close her briefcase. A few minutes later she stood up and walked away. Canning stayed where he was, finishing his coffee.

MCCRACKEN OPENED the door to the Transit and slid into the passenger seat, placing her briefcase on her lap. O'Keefe started the van and they drove away from the terminal in silence.

O'Keefe broke the silence first. 'What are we going to do with the Hayes woman?' he asked.

'What do you mean?'

'When it's over.'

McCracken tapped her red-painted fingernails on her briefcase but didn't reply.

'She did hear, didn't she?'

McCracken looked at him. 'I'm not sure. If she did, she hid it well.'

'That moron Quinn yelled it across the factory.'

McCracken screwed up her face as if she had a sour taste in her mouth. 'She might have heard, but that's not to say that she realised the significance.'

'Significance!' hissed O'Keefe. 'He used my name. She heard it. If she tells the cops, how long do you think it'd take to track me down? She's got to be dealt with, McCracken. If I go down, we all go down.'

EGAN HAD THOUGHT long and hard about what to do with Martin Hayes. Not that he had any doubts that Hayes had to die—that had been a foregone conclusion once the Garda Siochana had turned up on his doorstep. What concerned Egan was the method; he wanted to cause as few ripples as possible. If Hayes disappeared, the police would start looking for him and they'd start searching for his wife and daughter. They might turn to the media and the last thing Egan wanted was to have Andrea Hayes's face on the evening news.

Egan would have to give them a body, but in such a way that there wouldn't be a murder investigation and that meant that Martin Hayes would have to kill himself.

On the passenger seat of the Scorpio was a length of rope, already knotted, in a white plastic carrier bag. Under his jacket, snug in its leather shoulder holster, was the Browning. There'd be no need to use the gun against Hayes. Egan would give the man a simple choice: Hayes could write a farewell note saying that he couldn't live without his wife and daughter, and then hang himself with the rope. If he refused, Egan would simply tell Hayes that he was going to kill him anyway, and then torture and kill his wife and child. Egan knew without a shadow of a doubt that Hayes would take his own life if he thought it would save the lives of his wife and child.

Egan guided the Scorpio down a tree-lined road, towards Martin's house. He checked his rear-view mirror. There was a police car behind him. No blue light, no siren, just two uniformed officers going about their duties, not suspecting that a few yards in front of them was a man with a gun who would shortly be forcing another human being to take his own life. Egan smiled to himself as he drove. It was going to be so easy, but then the best plans always were.

MARTIN HAYES WAS lying on the sofa watching the late-night news when the doorbell rang. It was the two gardai who'd called the previous day. The older one, O'Brien, tapped the peak of his cap with a gloved hand. 'Evening, Mr Hayes.'

'What's wrong?' asked Martin.

O'Brien smiled without warmth. 'Why should anything be wrong, Mr Hayes?'

'It's ten o'clock at night and there are two officers of the Garda Siochana on my doorstep. I don't suppose you're here to sell me tickets to your Christmas ball.'

O'Brien chuckled, but his younger colleague stared at Hayes with hard, unsmiling eyes. Martin wondered if they'd rehearsed the 'good cop, bad cop' routine before pressing his doorbell.

'Could we come in, Mr Hayes?' asked O'Brien.

Martin held the door open for them and followed them into the sitting room. The gardai didn't sit down and Martin didn't ask them to. All three men stood in the middle of the room. O'Brien took off his cap. 'We were wondering if Mrs Hayes was back?' he said.

'No,' said Martin. 'Not yet.'

'And she hasn't phoned?' he asked.

'Not since you were last here,' said Martin.

'The thing is,' said O'Brien, 'we've spoken to your wife's Aunt Bessie.'

Martin caught his breath. He forced himself to smile. 'Really?'

'Took us a while to track her down, what with the limited information you had. Aunt Bessie. North Belfast. But we had a word with the local police and they were very cooperative.'

Martin felt his hands begin to shake and folded his arms across his chest defensively. 'And?' he said.

'Oh, I think you know what the "and" is, Mr Hayes.'

Martin stared at O'Brien in silence. There was nothing he could say. If O'Brien really had spoken to the woman, then he'd already been caught in a lie.

'Where is your wife, Mr Hayes?' O'Brien asked.

'Belfast.'

O'Brien shook his head, but he was still smiling avuncularly.

The younger garda looked at the door to the hall. 'Do you have a bathroom I can use?'

Martin knew that the garda wanted to look around the house, and while he didn't like the idea of him prowling around, he couldn't refuse without appearing to have something to hide. 'Go ahead,' he said. 'Upstairs. Second on the right.'

O'Brien tapped his cap against his leg. 'Did you and your wife have an argument, maybe?'

Martin swallowed. If he said he'd had a fight with Andy, then maybe they'd be more willing to accept that she'd left without warning. And if she was angry with him, that would explain why she'd taken Katie. He was just about to speak when he realised where the garda was leading him. Andy's car was in the drive. If she'd stormed off after a fight, she'd have taken the car. The garda knew that, and he was hoping to catch Martin out in another lie. A lie that could imply he'd done something to harm his family. He looked O'Brien in the eye. 'No,' he said firmly. 'There was no argument.'

'Sarge!' called the younger garda from upstairs. 'There's something here you should look at.'

O'Brien sighed and smiled at Martin. 'Ah, the enthusiasm of youth,' he said. 'Why don't you come with me, Mr Hayes. Let's see what's got the boy all fired up.'

Martin and O'Brien went through into the hallway. The younger garda was standing at the top of the stairs, staring at the banister.

O'Brien climbed the stairs. He peered at the section of banister that his colleague was pointing at. It was the spot where Andy had fainted and hit her head. 'It looks like blood,' said the younger garda.

O'Brien straightened up. 'I think you'd better come down to Pearse Street with us, Mr Hayes.'

They drove to the Garda station in silence. O'Brien took Martin in and showed him into a small room, barely three paces square. Martin turned to ask O'Brien how long he was going to be kept at the station, but before he could say anything the garda had closed the door.

EGAN SETTLED BACK in the black Ford Scorpio and listened to the engine click as it cooled. He patted his left armpit and felt the reassuring hardness of his Browning Hi-Power pistol. The length of rope was under the front seat. Ahead of him he could see the grey granite frontage of Pearse Street police station. The two gardai had driven round to the back of the building and presumably taken Hayes inside through the rear entrance.

Egan had been about to stop in front of Hayes's house when a sixth sense had told him to keep driving. He had driven on a few hundred yards past the house and waited. He'd seen the two gardai speak to Hayes on his doorstep, go inside, and then the three of them walk to the car several minutes later. Hayes looked pale, and his body language was enough to tell Egan that he wasn't going willingly.

Egan doubted that Hayes would tell the police anything. He'd stick to his story that his wife and daughter were out of town visiting a sick relative. But the police were suspicious, and the more they probed, the more likely they were to discover what had happened.

They'd probably keep him in for a few hours, then release him. They'd have to let him go because they had nothing in the way of evidence against him. And once Hayes was back at home, Egan would pay him a visit. With the rope.

THE DOOR BEHIND MARTIN opened but he didn't turn round. He sat where he was, his hands together on the table, fingers interlinked. Two men came into the room and sat opposite him. Not the gardai who'd brought him to the station—these were men in suits. Detectives. The man who sat directly opposite was in his late thirties, a thickset man with spectacles and a sandy moustache, wearing a grey suit with stains on the lapels and a brightly coloured Bugs Bunny tie. 'How are you doing, Mr Hayes?' he said jovially. 'My name is Detective Inspector James FitzGerald. My colleague here is Detective Sergeant John Power.'

The other man nodded. He was younger, in his late twenties maybe, and considerably better dressed.

'Am I under arrest?' Martin asked.

'No, you're not,' said FitzGerald. He took off his spectacles and wiped them with the end of his tie. He looked up and saw Martin staring at the cartoon rabbit. 'Birthday present from my son, so I figured I had to wear it, you know? The wife bought it, obviously. I think she just enjoys embarrassing me.'

Martin said nothing. FitzGerald put his spectacles back on. 'So,' he said. 'Tell me about your wife, Mr Hayes.'

'What do you mean?'

'Does she embarrass you? Does she sometimes get on your nerves?'

'What the hell are you talking about?'

'Your wife is missing, Mr Hayes. So is your daughter.'

'And you're saying I did something to them, is that it?' He jerked a thumb at the tape recorder. 'Shouldn't this be switched on? Shouldn't you be recording this?'

'All we're doing at the moment is having a wee chat, Mr Hayes. I'd like to keep this low-key just at the moment.'

Martin nodded slowly. 'OK.'

'So, where is Mrs Hayes?'

'She told me that she was going to Belfast. To see Aunt Bessie. But I've just been told by Sergeant O'Brien that she's not with Bessie.'

'So you can see why we're a little concerned, Mr Hayes. What with there being blood in the upstairs hallway and all.'

'Andy tripped. She tripped and banged her head. It was a small knock, that's all.'

'The thing of it is, Mr Hayes, we'd like to reassure ourselves that your wife isn't in any trouble,' said FitzGerald.

'I wish I could help,' said Hayes. 'Look, last time I spoke to my wife, she said she'd be back soon. As soon as she calls again, I'll have her telephone you. How's that?'

FitzGerald leaned forward. 'Are you sure there isn't something you want to tell us, Mr Hayes?'

Martin folded his arms and sat back in his chair. 'This is a complete waste of time. My time and yours. When Andy turns up you're going to look pretty stupid.'

'I'm quite happy to look stupid if it means we find your wife and daughter, Mr Hayes,' said FitzGerald.

'It's not a question of finding them,' said Martin. 'They're not lost.'

FitzGerald and Power exchanged looks.

'Can I go now?' Martin asked.

FitzGerald grimaced. 'We're continuing with our enquiries, and it'd be a big help to us if you stayed here to answer any questions that might arise.'

'Enquiries? What sort of enquiries?'

'We're checking the blood on the banister, obviously. We'd like a Scene of Crime Officer to call round and take a look at the rest of the house. And the garden.'

Martin's jaw dropped. 'What the hell are you suggesting? That I've buried my wife and daughter in the garden?'

FitzGerald put his hands up. 'We're not suggesting anything, Mr Hayes. We're just working our way through a standard set of procedures, that's all.'

Martin glared at the two detectives. He wanted to lash out, verbally and physically, but he knew that the only way he was going to walk out of Pearse Street was if he cooperated. He forced himself to smile. 'OK,' he said. 'Do whatever you have to do.'

Power held out his hand. 'Can we borrow your keys?'

'Sure,' said Martin. He handed then over. 'Be careful of our dog, will you? He might run off.'

'We'll be careful,' said Power.

The two detectives left. Martin put his head in his hands, wondering, whether he should tell them what had really happened to Andy and Katie or continue to lie.

Canning switched on the light and unbolted the door to the basement. Katie was sitting up in bed, rubbing her eyes, when he put the tray on the table. 'Scrambled eggs and beans,' he said.

'What time is it?' she asked.

'Eight o'clock.'

'And it's Sunday today, isn't it?' Her voice sounded stuffy as if her nose was blocked.

'That's right.' He had three comics under one arm. 'I got these for you. Come and eat before it gets cold.'

Katie slid out of bed and padded across to the table. She picked up a glass of orange juice and drank half of it in one gulp.

'How's your throat?'

Katie shrugged. 'It hurts a little bit.'

'Let me have a look,' said Canning and peered down her throat. It was still red, and when he put the back of his hand against her forehead, she still had a temperature.

He took a pack of Day Nurse from his pocket, popped out a tablet and put it on the table. 'Eat your eggs and then swallow this,' he said.

Katie started to eat and Canning put his elbows on the table as he watched her.

'Mummy says that's bad manners,' she said.

Canning raised his eyebrows. 'What is?'

'Putting your elbows on the table while people are eating.'

Canning sat up straight. Katie leaned over her paper plate. 'If you let me go, I won't say anything. I promise.' She waited to see what he'd say, smiling and nodding. Canning smiled behind his ski mask. Even aged seven, children, especially girls, could be so damn manipulative. His own daughter was the same. He could imagine Katie twisting her father round her little finger.

Katie made the sign of the cross on her chest. 'Cross my heart and swear to die,' she said solemnly.

Canning shook his head. 'No, I can't let you go, Katie. Not yet. I'm sorry.'

ANDY LAY ON A SOFA in the reception area, a big, sprawling sofa with huge cushions that seemed to fold round her like clouds. As she drifted in and out of sleep, thinking about the last four days, it felt as if it was all happening to someone else, as if it was a surreal dream.

She half heard the lift doors open and close. It was the Wrestler, pushing a boxed tumble drier on a trolley. He was wearing dark blue overalls with the name of a kitchen-fitting firm emblazoned on the back in fiery red letters. 'Rise and shine,' he said. He wheeled the box by her sofa and into the office. He was followed by the Runner, who was also wearing overalls and pushing another loaded trolley.

Green-eyes came in last, carrying several assorted boxes. Like the men, she was wearing overalls and training shoes.

'In here,' she said to Andy, and Andy followed her through to the main office area. Green-eyes put the boxes she was carrying down on the floor and pointed at the tumble driers. 'Andrea, you start taking them out of their boxes while we bring the rest of the stuff up.'

The Wrestler gave her a small penknife, and she hacked at the tough cardboard with it while her three captors went back outside.

It took them an hour to carry in all the equipment, and another half an hour until all the boxes were opened. The Wrestler had several extension cords, and he plugged in the tumble driers, ovens, electric woks and coffee grinders and checked that they were all functioning.

Green-eyes showed Andy her clipboard. On it was a computer print-out listing all the chemicals and equipment she had purchased. 'Am I missing anything?' she asked.

Andy ran her finger down the list. Everything seemed to be there. Except for one thing. 'You haven't got detonators,' she said.

'That's in hand,' said Green-eyes.

Andy handed back the clipboard. 'In that case, it's all here.'

Green-eyes put the clipboard down on top of one of the tumble driers. 'Come this way,' she said, and she led Andy to a suite of offices, each with a floor-to-ceiling glass panel next to the door so that the interiors were visible from the corridor. One of the offices had been used as a meeting room and contained a long cherry-wood table with a dozen high-backed leather chairs round it. A coffee machine had been put on a sideboard along with several cartons of long-life milk, a bag of sugar and a box of Jaffa Cakes. In one corner of the room was a large-screen Sony television and a video recorder. 'Sit down, Andrea,' said Green-eyes.

Andy did as she was told.

Green-eyes unlocked her burgundy briefcase, took out a tape and fed it into the video recorder. 'You wanted to know that Katie's safe,' she said, and pressed PLAY.

Andy leaned forward with anticipation.

'Mummy. Dad. This is Katie. Your daughter,' said Katie. There was a short pause as if she were gathering her thoughts, then she continued. 'I'm fine. But I've got flu, I think.' She put her hand up to her throat, and Andy copied the gesture. 'My head hurts and my throat's sore. The nice man is going to give me some medicine to make it better so I should be OK soon.'

Katie paused and looked past the lens. Andy had the feeling that someone was prompting her to continue.

'He said to say it's Saturday and that I'm OK. Mummy, I want to come home . . .' The recording ended abruptly and Andy knew it was because her daughter had burst into tears.

'She's sick. I have to go to her,' said Andy. 'She needs me.'

'Don't be ridiculous!' snapped Green-eyes. 'What she needs is for you to do what you have to do. Then you can be with her. We're taking good care of her, Andrea. I promise you.' She stood up. 'First things first. I need you to show the lads what to do. Step by step.'

She took her mobile phone out of her overall pocket and put it in the briefcase, then took out her pistol and flicked the combination locks closed.

Andy followed Green-eyes into the open-plan office area. The Wrestler and the Runner had lined up the four ovens next to each other and were unpacking dozens of Tupperware containers. 'Can we open the windows?' Andy asked. 'It's going to get hot in here.'

Green-eyes looked over at the Wrestler and he shook his head. 'They're sealed,' he said. 'Double-glazed and sealed.'

'Is there a thermostat? If there is, set it to the lowest level.'

The Wrestler pointed to a thermostat on one of the walls and the Runner went to turn it down. Andy looked round the huge office area. 'Right, we need a line of desks here. Close to the ovens.'

The four of them carried half a dozen desks over and lined them up. Then, like an officer mustering her troops, Andy explained what they had to do.

ANDY WIPED her forehead with the back of her arm. She'd changed out of the suit that Green-eyes had given her and was wearing a blue checked shirt and loose-fitting denim jeans, but it was still uncomfortably hot in the office. She went over and looked at the thermostat. It was set to the minimum, but the temperature read-out showed that it was in the mid-nineties.

Green-eyes was at the water cooler, helping herself to a cupful of water. Andy joined her. 'The air-conditioning isn't coping,' she said. 'We're going to need dehumidifiers.'

'It's not too bad,' said Green-eyes. Sweat was dripping down her neck, and the ski mask must have been annoyingly uncomfortable.

Andy poured herself a paper cup of water and sipped it. All four ovens were working, their doors ajar. In each of the ovens were metal baking trays full of the ammonium nitrate fertiliser, four trays per oven. Other trays were lined up on the desks, waiting to be filled. The Wrestler was on his knees in front of one of the ovens, testing the temperature with a metal thermometer.

The Runner was taking trays out of the middle oven and tipping the heated fertiliser into Tupperware containers, which he was then sealing in black rubbish bags.

The doors of the ovens had to be left ajar so that the water could escape, and the temperature had to be constantly monitored because the fertiliser would liquefy at 170 degrees Fahrenheit. It would actually explode at 400 degrees, but it would start to bubble and smoke long before it reached that temperature.

'I want to show you something,' Andy said. She took Green-eyes over to the window. It was blurry from condensation, and water was pooling at the bottom of the pane. 'This is after four hours,' she said. 'It's going to get a lot worse. It's getting too humid.' She nodded at the electric ovens. 'The point of this is to dry out the fertiliser. But if the atmosphere's this moist, the ammonium nitrate is going to soak the water right back up. The windows are sealed, so the only thing you can do is to bring in dehumidifiers.'

'It'll have to be tomorrow,' Green-eyes said.

'Whatever,' said Andy. 'And another thing. We're going to need fans, because when we start to use the alcohol, we're going to have to keep the air moving. If we don't . . . it'll explode. You won't need a detonator. The fumes will be explosive enough.'

JAMES FITZGERALD KNOCKED on the door to Chief Inspector Eamonn Hogan's office and pushed it open as his boss gruffly told him to come in. 'Morning, Jim, how's it going?' Hogan had turned fifty the previous week, though he looked almost a decade older, virtually bald with thick jowls that lay in folds against his shirt collar.

FitzGerald leaned against the door jamb. 'It's about this guy Martin Hayes.'

'The missing wife? Is he still in custody?'

'Helping us with our enquiries,' said FitzGerald.

'What's your take on it, Jim?'

FitzGerald shrugged. 'He's hiding something, there's no doubt about that. But he's not a wife-killer. We've given the house and garden a going-over, and there's nothing to suggest foul play.'

Hogan took off his spectacles and polished them with a large blue handkerchief. 'So what's your feeling, Jim?'

'I don't think he's done anything to her. Or the daughter. Things like that don't happen out of the blue, and there's no history. But I do think he knows where she's gone.'

'Why do you say that?'

'Because if he didn't, he'd have been on to us, right? Wife and kid vanished. He'd have called us, for sure.'

'So why won't he tell you where she is?'

'I don't know. It doesn't make much sense. Maybe he figures she'll come back.' FitzGerald scratched his chin. 'The O'Mara woman is a strange one, too. She's just disappeared into thin air.'

'But the only connection is that she worked at the school, right?'

'Well, it's a bit more than that. She spoke to Hayes that the day she disappeared.'

'You're not suggesting Hayes has had anything to do with her disappearance, are you?'

FitzGerald shrugged. 'I honestly don't know. There's no evidence he ever met her.'

'So it could just be a coincidence.' Hogan sighed. 'God, I hate coincidences,' he said. 'Bane of our lives, coincidences.'

'And another thing,' said FitzGerald. 'He's not asked for a solicitor. If he'd done something, he'd know that his best bet would be to be legally represented.'

'So you're going to treat it as a domestic?'

'I think so, but I'd like us to keep an eye on him.'

'Have a word with uniforms. See if they've got a couple of men spare. Just for a day or two, mind,' agreed Hogan.

ANDY TWISTED the metal tie round the black rubbish bag, then eased it into a second bag and sealed that as well. Even sealed inside two plastic bags, the fertiliser would absorb moisture from the air and would be uselessly damp within two weeks. Green-eyes had said that this wouldn't be a problem. That meant that whatever Green-eyes was planning would be over within a fortnight.

Sweat was beading on Andy's forehead and she wiped it with a towel. Early that morning, Green-eyes had sent the Wrestler and the Runner to buy dehumidifiers and electric fans, and they'd gone some way to lowering the humidity, but it was still in the mid-eighties in the open-plan office.

'I'm going to take a break,' Andy told Green-eyes, who was checking the thermometer in one of the ovens.

Andy went along to the meeting room. There was a Marks and Spencer carrier bag next to the coffee machine, containing a dozen packs of sandwiches. And there was an assortment of canned drinks. Andy popped open a Diet Coke and drank, and then took a smoked salmon sandwich and sat down at the long table.

She looked through the glass panel by the door at the office opposite. Green-eyes had a camp bed there, and it was also where she'd left the briefcase. The mobile phone was in the briefcase, but the case had two combination locks. Each lock had three dials. Zero to 999. If it took two seconds to try each combination, she could do all 1,000 in just over half an hour. An hour to do both locks. Maximum. In all probability it would take a lot less than an hour. But what then? She'd have access to the phone, she knew where the bomb was, and the police would be able to arrest her three captors, but what would happen to Katie? Could she be sure that Green-eyes would confess all and tell the police where Katie was being held?

Andy chewed slowly, barely tasting the sandwich. First things first. She put down her half-eaten sandwich and went to the door, easing it open carefully.

She took a deep breath, then tiptoed across the corridor and opened the door to the second office, her heart in her mouth. The briefcase was on a teak desk. She set the first combination to zero, zero, zero. She tried the lock. It wouldn't move. She flicked the end dial. Zero, zero, one. Still locked. She looked at her watch. She'd try for five minutes, then she'd have to get back to the main office.

THE DOOR to the interview room opened and Martin Hayes looked up. It was the inspector. FitzGerald.

'You can go, Mr Hayes. We've taken up enough of your time.'

Martin ran his hand over the stubble across his chin. He'd been in the Pearse Street station for eighteen hours. 'You're letting me go?'

'It's not a question of letting you go, Mr Hayes. You're not under arrest. You've been free to leave at any time.'

Martin stood up. 'So you believe me?'

'Let's just say we've no evidence that you've had anything to do with the disappearance of your wife and daughter,' said FitzGerald, holding the door open wide. 'But we might want another word with you again soon. So don't leave town, as they say.'

Martin walked away from the grey stone Garda station and caught a taxi near Trinity College. They'd let him go, but it was clear that FitzGerald didn't believe him, and Martin didn't blame him.

He stared out of the taxi with unseeing eyes, wondering what to do next. They'd keep digging, and if they were to speak to his financial advisers, they'd discover that he'd been liquidating his assets and transferring money into his current account. What would they make of that? Martin wondered. They'd assume that he'd killed his wife and daughter and was about to disappear himself.

If nothing else, he'd be hauled into Pearse Street again for more questioning, and the more often that happened the more likely it was that Katie's kidnappers would discover that he was in contact with the police.

The taxi dropped him outside his house and he went inside, where he was practically bowled over by Dermott. He went straight to his answering machine. No messages. He let the dog out into the garden, then made himself a cup of instant coffee and took it upstairs.

Martin went into Katie's bedroom and sat down on the bed. He leaned over to put his cup on Katie's bedside table, and froze. There was a Garda patrol car outside his house. Martin cursed under his breath, backed away from the window and went downstairs.

He paced around the kitchen, clenching and unclenching his fists. They were giving him no choice. He'd have to leave Dublin. If the kidnappers saw the Garda car, they'd think they were there because he'd called them in.

It was late, probably too late to get a flight out of Dublin that night. Besides, there was an outside chance that FitzGerald had men at the airport watching for him. He'd be safer flying through Belfast.

He took a briefcase from his study and emptied it. He put in an unopened flight kit he'd been given on a business trip, together with two clean shirts, underwear and socks. He put his mobile phone in his suit pocket. It was a GSM model and would work in the UK.

He put his briefcase by the back door and then went out into the hallway and looked at the answering machine. What if Andy called again? Or if the kidnappers tried to get in touch? He recorded a fresh message, asking callers to telephone his mobile number.

In a cupboard under the hall were several electrical timers. He went upstairs and fitted one to the plug of a lamp on the dressing table, timed to go off later that night. Then he drew the curtains and went downstairs. He fitted timers to lamps in the sitting room and the kitchen, overlapping the on and off times.

Now what? Both cars were parked in the drive at the front. He'd have to go through the back garden and over the wall, maybe catch a taxi. He shook his head. No, a taxi driver might remember him.

He washed his mug and as he put it on the draining board, he realised what he'd have to do. He called Padraig on his mobile.

'Padraig. It's me, Martin. I need a favour. Big time.'

'Sure.'

'Please can you pick me up on Morehampton Road? Opposite Bloomfield Hospital?'

'No sweat. What's up? Car broken down?'

'Something like that. I'll explain when I see you. Ten minutes, OK?'

Martin thanked his partner and cut the connection. He looked down at Dermott. 'What the hell am I going to do with you?' he said, and the dog woofed softly. If he left the golden retriever in the garden, he might bark and attract the attention of the watching garda, so he decided he'd leave him inside.

Martin picked up his briefcase and let himself out of the back door. The sun was just about to dip below the horizon, smearing the grey sky with an orange glow. He jogged to the end of the garden, clambered over the wall, skirted the golf course and then walked through a car park to the main road. Only then did he start to relax.

EGAN SLID the Browning Hi-Power out of its brown leather shoulder holster and checked that the safety was off. When he had driven past the Hayeses' house, he had seen a Garda patrol car parked in the road outside. He had stopped his Ford Scorpio in a road bordering a golf course, well away from any streetlights.

In his left ear was a small earphone connected to a receiver that allowed him to listen in to the bugs planted in the house. Hayes was going to run, and Egan had only minutes in which to stop him.

He leaned over and took a street map out of the glove compartment and flicked through it. He found the page where Bloomfield Hospital was, and traced a gloved finger from Morehampton Road to the house. Assuming he left through the back garden, Hayes would have to walk close to the golf course. He put the map back in the glove compartment, along with the receiver and earpiece, then got out of the car and walked towards the golf course, putting the collar of his leather jacket up against the wind.

There was a path running round the edge of the course, and beyond it a line of three bunkers. To Egan's left was a clump of trees, to the right an up-market housing estate. Egan kept his face turned away from the golf club's car park, and waited until he was past before taking out his handgun and screwing in a bulbous silencer.

He reached the path and headed towards the trees. In the distance was Hayes, walking towards him, his head down, a coat flapping behind him. Egan picked up the pace. The silencer was efficient, but even so, the farther away he was from the clubhouse the better.

Egan could feel sweat dribbling down his back. He was breathing shallowly, his chest barely moving, the gun tight against his stomach.

Hayes was about fifty feet away. Midway between them was a broad-trunked beech tree, perfect cover for what Egan was about to do.

Thirty feet. Egan began to pull the gun out, his finger already tightening on the trigger.

Hayes stopped. He peered out across the golf course as if looking for someone. Then suddenly he whistled, a piercing shriek that stopped Egan in his tracks. A German Shepherd ran across the grass. It wasn't Hayes, Egan realised. He'd come within seconds of shooting the wrong man. It was just a guy out walking his dog.

Egan started walking again. The man was bending down, patting his dog, as Egan went by. There was no one else on the path, and Egan could see all the way up to the wall at the end of the Hayeses' garden. Somehow Egan had missed him. He turned and went back the way he'd come, walking quickly.

PADRAIG ARRIVED just as Martin was walking by the hospital's gateposts, and flashed the headlights of his BMW. Martin waved. He heard rapid footsteps as the car pulled up and turned to see who it was. A man in a leather jacket and jeans was running towards the car. As he ran he pulled his hand from under his jacket. Something glinted in the BMW's headlights. Something metallic.

Martin pulled open the passenger door and climbed into the car. 'Drive!' he shouted.

Padraig sat stunned, his mouth open in surprise.

'Padraig! For God's sake, drive!'

The passenger window shattered, spraying Martin with cubes of glass. Martin ducked and held his briefcase over his face as Padraig put the car in gear and stamped on the accelerator.

Padraig looked anxiously in his mirror as they drove away. 'Christ, who was that?' he said, his voice shaking.

Martin twisted round in his seat. The man in the leather jacket was walking away from the hospital, his head down and his hands in his jacket pockets.

'I don't know,' said Martin.

'You don't know? What do you mean, you don't know?' Padraig already had the car in fourth gear and they were doing almost eighty.

'Slow down, Padraig. You'll kill us.'

Padraig frowned, and then began to laugh. Despite his pounding heart and shaking hands, Martin laughed too, but it was an ugly, disjointed sound, and both men were soon silent again.

Padraig slowed to just under the speed limit. 'What the hell's going on, Mart?'

'I don't know. I really don't know.'

'Where do you want to go?' asked Padraig.

'North. Belfast. I've got to get out of Ireland, and the police have probably got Dublin airport covered.'

'The police? The police are after you?'

Martin didn't say anything. He picked pieces of glass from his jacket and dropped them onto the floor of the car. Padraig drove, flashing Martin anxious looks as he headed north.

'The guy who shot at you. He wasn't a cop,' said Padraig.

'No,' said Martin.

'So who was he? For God's sake, Martin, I could have been killed back there. You owe me an explanation.'

Martin sighed. His partner was right. He'd put Padraig's life on the line—he had a right to know why.

'Katie's been kidnapped. They took her last week. The kidnappers wanted Andy to go to London. Now the cops have found out that Andy and Katie are missing and they think I've got something to do with it. I figure London's the best place for me. If Andy's left any sort of message for me, it'll be there.'

'And who was the guy with the gun?'

'I don't know. One of the kidnappers, maybe. They must have seen the Garda take me away. Or maybe they saw the patrol car outside the house. If they think I'm cooperating with the cops, they're going to kill Katie.'

'Dear God, Mart.' Padraig pushed down the accelerator and the BMW powered to ninety miles per hour. 'OK. So you go to London. What then?'

'I don't know,' said Martin flatly. 'I really don't know.'

EGAN WALKED BACK to his Ford Scorpio and climbed in. With hindsight, shooting at Martin Hayes had been a mistake. Anyone could have driven by while he had the gun out; anyone could have seen him shooting at the car. He should have let Hayes go and followed at a distance, choosing his moment with more care.

Now Hayes was running scared, but he had nowhere to run to. He clearly wasn't cooperating with the police, and there was no one else he could turn to. Egan had intercepted the letter that his wife had left for him at the hotel, so that was a dead end. And there were only three days left before the bomb would be ready. Even if Hayes told the police everything, there was nothing they could do to prevent the bomb going off. Egan smiled to himself as he drove. Shooting at Hayes had been a mistake, but not a fatal one.

THE GIRL WAS STUNNING, just short of six foot tall in her high heels, with glossy black hair that reached to just above her hips. She wore a yellow evening dress cut low at the front. Her name was Summer. Deng waved at the seat next to him and asked her to sit with him.

She bent forward and swiped a plastic card through a reader in the centre of the table. Customers in the nightclub were billed by the minute for the company of the hostesses. A bottle of champagne arrived. Deng hadn't asked for the champagne, but he knew the score. Girls like Summer didn't come cheap.

An hour later and Deng was in bed with Summer in a Kowloon Tong love hotel. He lay on his back as Summer rode him, her mouth slightly open, showing perfect white teeth, her head thrown back so that her hair brushed against his thighs. She was good, she was very good, and Deng had to fight to stop himself from coming too soon. His hands moved up her soft body and he caressed her breasts.

Deng heard a noise at the door. The sound of a key being turned. 'We've not finished yet,' he shouted in Cantonese. He'd paid for two hours and still had thirty minutes left. There was silence, and muffled voices, then the door burst open. Summer rolled off him and pulled the sheet around her. Deng sat up. It was Michael Wong. And three of his Red Poles. Triad heavies. One of them closed the door and stood with his back against it. The other two had handguns. Big ones.

Wong grinned. 'Good, was she?' he asked in guttural Mandarin.

Deng pushed himself back against the headboard. 'What's this about, Michael?'

Wong walked over to Summer. She looked up at him fearfully, forcing a smile. 'Hello, Summer,' he said. 'Long time no see.'

Summer was shaking, and her smile was little more than a baring of teeth, the smile of a frightened dog. 'Hello, Mr Wong,' she said.

Wong pulled a silenced automatic from inside his jacket and pointed it at her. She froze. He pointed the gun at one of the armchairs and she went over to it and sat down.

'There's no need for this, Michael,' said Deng.

'Where's my money?'

'You'll have it soon.'

'I've heard your promises before, Deng. The Triad entrusted you with twenty million US dollars. Then you come and tell us that we're at risk of losing that investment.'

Deng held his hands up defensively in front of his face. 'We're all in the same boat, Michael,' he said. 'The bank invested more than a hundred million dollars of its own money. We've investors in Singapore and Thailand. We've all . . .'

The gun kicked in Wong's hand. The only noise it made was a slight coughing sound. A bullet buried itself in the pillow by Deng's side and a few small white feathers fluttered into the air. 'I don't care about your bank. I don't care about the other investors. You took the Triad's twenty million dollars and you lied to us.' Wong looked at Deng dispassionately, tapping the barrel of his silenced gun against his lips. 'How can I convince you how serious I am?' he asked. He slowly pointed the weapon at Deng's left foot.

Deng drew his foot back. Wong grinned malevolently and pointed the gun at Deng's groin.

'Or maybe I should blow something else off? Something a little closer to home? Do you have children?'

Deng nodded. 'Two boys.'

'Two sons? You are a lucky man.' Wong tightened his finger on the trigger. Deng's hands went across his groin in a reflex action.

'We want our money. All of it.'

'I told you, you'll have it. Every last penny.'

'That's good. Because if we don't, I'll kill you, your wife, your two precious sons, and every other member of your family I can find. That goes for you and the rest of the members of the board. I want you to tell them that, Deng. Tell them from me.'

Deng nodded furiously. 'I will. Of course I will.'

Wong shook his head. 'But I have to do something to show you how serious I am.'

Deng shook his head even faster, his breath coming in ragged gasps. 'Please don't,' he whimpered.

Wong grinned scornfully. He pointed the gun at Deng's chest, then quickly moved his gun arm in a smooth motion around to his right and shot Summer in the face.

'I'll leave the mess for you to clean up,' said Wong, putting his gun back inside his jacket. 'I'm sure you know the right sort of people.'

Day Seven

Andy woke up to the sound of someone knocking on the office door. It was Green-eyes, with a mug of coffee and a croissant. Andy had spent the night on a leather sofa, with one of her pullovers as a pillow. She sat up and took the coffee and pastry.

'We finished the drying a few hours ago,' said Green-eyes.

'You haven't slept?'

'I'll catch a few hours once we've started on the next stage.'

Andy put her coffee mug down and ran a hand through her hair. 'I could do with a shower.'

'You and me both. But a full washbasin is the best we can do. Sorry.' Green-eyes looked at her wristwatch. 'Ready in ten minutes, right? The troops are waiting.'

Green-eyes went back to the office floor. Andy drank her coffee and ate the croissant, then went to the washroom to clean her teeth.

Green-eyes and the two men were waiting for her in the office area. The four electric woks had been taken out of their cardboard boxes and were lined up on the desks. Andy went over and examined them. They were Teflon-coated, with dials that controlled the heat settings.

'Right,' said Green-eyes. 'What do we do?'

Andy picked up one of the five-gallon cans of alcohol. 'We use this to wash the ammonium nitrate. It gets the impurities out of it.'

She went over to the pile of black rubbish bags and dragged one of them over to the woks. 'You need a container. The Tupperware'll do. Half fill it with the ammonium nitrate, then pour in enough alcohol to cover it. Stir it well for about three minutes, then pour off the alcohol. It should go a dirty brown. You can use it a few times. OK?'

Green-eyes and her colleagues nodded.

'OK, so then we have to evaporate off the alcohol. Pour the wet ammonium nitrate into the wok and sort of stir-fry it, at a low heat —try to keep the temperature around one hundred and fifty degrees.' She looked around the office. 'The fumes can be fierce. I'd suggest we spread out, and use the fans. I warn you, it'll give you a headache.'

'How long do we heat it for?'

'Three or four minutes should do. It's just like when you stir-fry food—keep it hot and keep it moving.'

Green-eyes grinned. 'You might have to give the boys a demonstration. I don't think they're particularly at home in the kitchen.'

She laughed, and Andy started to laugh along with her. She stopped suddenly when she realised what she was doing. She was laughing with the woman responsible for kidnapping her daughter, the woman who was forcing her to build a 4,000-pound bomb in the City of London. What could she be thinking of? She was betraying Katie and she was betraying Martin.

Green-eyes stopped laughing too. 'Go on,' she said. 'What then?'

'You have to grind it up into a fine powder,' said Andy, her voice shaking. 'In the coffee grinders. A couple of minutes should do it. Then seal it back in the Tupperware containers as quickly as possible. Every second it's exposed to the air, it absorbs water.'

The Wrestler held up a hand, pointing a finger at her. 'We've already treated all three thousand and odd pounds of it. Are you saying we have to do it again?'

'That's right. It has to be uniformly pure, uniformly fine or the detonation velocity won't be consistent.'

'It's going to take for ever,' moaned the Runner, looking at the Wrestler, both men clearly unhappy at the prospect of the work that lay ahead.

Green-eyes went over to Andy. 'Why don't you get yourself a coffee, Andrea. I want to have a word with the boys.'

Andrea went off to the meeting room, knowing that Green-eyes was going to give the men a talking-to. A few minutes later the door opened. It was Green-eyes. 'Right. Come on,' she said to Andy. 'Let's get started.'

MARTIN HAYES ARRIVED at Heathrow at nine o'clock in the morning and caught a black cab to the Strand Palace Hotel. He wasn't sure why he was in the hotel—he just knew that it was the only link he had to Andy. She'd have known that too, so if she'd left any sort of trail it had to have been at the hotel. He leaned forward over the reception counter and smiled at the young man in a black suit. 'My wife lost an earring when she was staying here last week. Can you tell me if anything was handed in after she checked out?'

The man tapped away on his computer and shook his head. 'Nope, nothing was handed in,' he said.

Martin sighed. 'Damn. It was hellish expensive. Look, I don't suppose I could have a quick look around, could I? Just to check?'

The man consulted his computer again. 'The room's empty. I don't see why not. I'll get someone to go up with you.'

'That's OK, I don't want to trouble anybody.'

'Security, sir,' said the man. He waved over a teenage bellboy in a beige uniform and handed him a key before explaining the situation.

The bellboy took Martin up to the fifth floor and opened the door. 'An earring, huh?' he said, bending down and looking under the bed.

'Yeah. Gold with a diamond.' Martin went into the bathroom. If he'd been Andy, where would he have hidden a message? The toilet cistern was boxed in and there was no way he could see of removing the base of the bath or shower.

He went back into the bedroom. The bellboy was still on his hands and knees. Martin put down his breifcase, took his wallet out of his jacket and gave the teenager a twenty-pound note. 'There's no point in holding you up. I'll have a look around myself, yeah?'

The note smoothly disappeared into the bellboy's pocket and he left, closing the door behind him. Martin stood in the middle of the bedroom. 'Come on, Andy,' he whispered. 'You must have left me something. You must have.'

He looked at the bed. She couldn't have left anything there—the bedding would be changed after every guest. He went over to the desk and checked the drawers. There was a wallet of hotel stationery and Martin went through it piece by piece. Nothing. There was a banal watercolour above the writing desk. It was a gondola with a young couple cuddling in front, a bored gondolier in a large black hat standing at the rear. It didn't even look like Venice. Martin's breath caught in his throat. Venice? What had Andy said when she phoned? Going back to Venice. He ran his hands around the frame. It wouldn't move. It was screwed to the wall.

With trembling hands, Martin searched through his pockets for a penny. He found one, and used it to take out the screws. He pulled the painting away from the wall and a sheet of paper fluttered to the floor. As he picked up the sheet of paper, he was startled by an angry voice behind him.

'What the hell do you think you're doing?'

The receptionist in the black suit was standing in the doorway. He looked at the picture and at the empty space on the wall.

'I'm sorry,' said Martin. 'I'll pay for any damage.' He folded the paper and thrust it into his jacket pocket, then took out his wallet.

'You'll stay right where you are,' said the man, holding his hands up as if warding off an attack. 'I'm calling Security.'

Martin tossed two twenty-pound notes onto the bed, picked up his briefcase and headed for the door.

'No you don't,' said the receptionist, grabbing for Martin's arm.

Martin hit the man across the head with his briefcase and he fell to the floor. He kicked the door shut, then pulled the bed cover over the man and roughly tied him up with the phone cord before running out of the room. He dashed down the emergency stairs, knowing that the man wouldn't stay tied up for long.

He reached the ground floor and burst through into the reception area. Heads turned as he dashed over to the main doors and out into the Strand. He kept running as hard as he could, the briefcase banging against his leg, his chest heaving with the effort.

Martin looked over his shoulder as he ran. There was no one following him, and he slowed to a jog, then a walk. He took deep breaths, trying to calm himself down.

He walked across the main plaza in Covent Garden, where a clown was walking along a broom handle suspended across a pair of stepladders. A dwarf in a clown suit was walking around a crowd of onlookers, collecting money in a red plastic bucket. Martin threaded his way through the people and went into a large café. He ordered a cappuccino, then took the sheet of paper out and carefully unfolded it. It was a piece of hotel notepaper. The writing was Andy's.

> *Dear Martin*
>
> *My love. If you've found this it can only mean something's gone terribly wrong and that you've called in the police. Dear God, my hands are shaking so much as I write this. Please, just know that I love you, I love you with all my heart. If it has gone wrong, you must never stop looking for Katie.*
>
> *They've told me to go to a car park in Bedford Court and to get into a van. A dark blue Transit van. They say it's got the name of a landscaping company on the side. I don't know where they're going to take me or what they plan to do. I'll do whatever it takes to get Katie back, I promise.*
>
> *Martin, if the worst has happened, if you've had to go to the police or if I'm dead, then there's someone I want you to call. Someone who might be able to find out where Katie is. His name is Detective Chief Inspector Liam Denham. He works for Special Branch in Belfast. Tell him it's about Trevor. Tell him what's happened. He'll help, if anyone can.*
>
> *Please, my love, never, ever forget that I love you.*

At the bottom of the letter was a Belfast telephone number.

Martin reread the letter several times, his mind in a whirl. A Special Branch detective? Trevor? What in God's name was Andy talking about? Special Branch? Why on earth would Andy have been involved with them?

Martin folded the letter up and put it back in his pocket. So far as he knew, Andy was still alive, but the fact that the police were now involved meant that she was in danger. The kidnappers wouldn't know that the police had been called in by Katie's school; they'd assume it was Martin who'd gone to them. And if they assumed that, what was to stop them killing Katie and Andy? Martin had to act quickly. He dropped a couple of pound coins on the table and left the café. He had only one option, the option that Andy had given him.

He walked through Covent Garden and found a call box in King Street. He popped a pound coin into the slot and tapped out the Belfast number that Andy had given him. It was answered on the third ring. 'Yeah?' It was a man's voice. Hard and guttural.

'I'd like to speak to Liam Denham.'

'Who's calling?'

'Look, this is an emergency. I need to speak to Detective Chief Inspector Liam Denham. This is Special Branch, isn't it?'

The line went quiet for a few seconds, then a second man spoke, his voice softer. 'Who am I speaking to?' asked the second man.

'That's not important,' said Martin. 'Just tell Liam Denham that I have to speak with him.'

'That's not possible,' said the man. 'How did you get this number?'

Martin wanted to shout at the man, but he clamped his jaws together and fought to stay calm. Denham could help, Andy had said. 'My wife gave me the number,' said Martin slowly. 'And said that I was to ask for Chief Inspector Liam Denham.'

'And your wife's name would be what?'

'Andy. Andrea. Andrea Hayes.'

Martin heard a clicking sound and realised that the man was typing on a computer keyboard. 'I'm not familiar with that name,' said the man. 'What's your wife's maiden name?'

'Sheridan.'

More typing. 'No. I'm not familiar with that name either.'

'Look, you have to help me,' Martin pleaded. 'My wife said that I was to call this number and to ask for Denham. To tell him that it was about some guy called Trevor.'

Martin heard the clickety-click of the keyboard. Then a sudden intake of breath. 'Mr Hayes, where are you calling from?'

'London. Covent Garden. I'm in a call box.'

'Give me the number.'

Martin gave the man the number of the call box.

'Mr Hayes, please stay by the phone. Someone will call back shortly.'

Martin was midway through thanking the man when the line went dead. He waited in the call box. An elderly man in a blue blazer and yellow cravat rapped on the door with a walking stick. Martin pointed at the phone and shrugged apologetically. 'I'm waiting for a call,' he mouthed. The man glared at him. Martin turned around, he was embarrassed at having to behave so badly.

The phone rang and he grabbed the receiver. 'Denham?' he said.

'I'm afraid Mr Denham isn't available at the moment,' said a woman. She sounded middle-aged, and there was the vague hint of a West Country accent.

'Where the hell is he?'

'Please try to stay calm, Mr Hayes. I'm trying to help you. OK?'

'OK. I'm sorry.'

'Right. Good. Now, my name is Patsy, Mr Hayes. I want you to tell me exactly what's happened to your wife.'

Martin told her about Katie's kidnapping and Andy's disappearance in London. Patsy listened without interrupting. He told her about the gardai coming to his house, and how he'd fled to London. He told them about going to the hotel, and finding the note.

'How did you know to look behind the painting?' Patsy asked.

Martin told her about the brief phone conversation he'd had with Andy on Saturday night.

'Did she tell you anything else? Anything that might suggest where she'd been taken?'

'No. She just said she was OK, and that she was doing what they asked.'

'She didn't say who "they" were?'

'No. No, she didn't.'

'OK, Mr Hayes, you're doing just fine. Now, it's important that you do exactly as I tell you.'

'What about this man Denham? Andy said I should speak to him.'

'Chief Inspector Denham retired some time ago, Mr Hayes. We're trying to contact him now.'

'What's all this about? Why does my wife know him?'

'There'll be time for explanations later, Mr Hayes. First, we want you to go along to a police station in London so that . . .'

'No way am I talking to the police,' interrupted Martin. 'They think I did something to Andy and Katie.'

'You don't have to talk to them, Mr Hayes. But I need you to be somewhere safe until we can meet.'

'We'll meet somewhere else.'

'Where, then?'

'I'll book into a hotel. You can come and see me there.'

'Fine. Which hotel?'

He remembered a hotel he'd stayed at during a business trip to London a few years previously. 'The Tower,' he said. 'It's near the Thames. Near Tower Bridge.'

'OK,' said Patsy. 'Check in and stay in your room. We're trying to track down Chief Inspector Denham now. But someone will contact you later this afternoon. You shouldn't check in under your own name, Mr Hayes, you realise that?'

'Of course. I'll use Sheridan. Martin Sheridan. OK?'

'Fine. Please go to the hotel immediately, Mr Hayes.'

The line went dead.

LIAM DENHAM looked up from the fishing fly he was tying and scowled in annoyance at the rattling window. He pushed up his magnifying visor and put his tweezers down on the mahogany desk top. The window overlooked his sprawling garden, which he and his wife had created from five acres of cow pasture.

Something flashed above the house, clattering and roaring, then just as quickly it had gone. Denham stood up and peered upwards. Seconds later, the helicopter appeared again and the windows shook even more violently than before. The helicopter was a Wessex, dark green. Army colours. Denham took his visor off and turned round to find his wife standing at the door to the study.

'That'll be for you, then,' she said. Like Denham, she was in her early sixties, though she looked a few years younger, with hair that had kept its auburn lustre.

'Aye. I suppose so,' said Denham. He ran a hand over his bald patch and down to the back of his neck. He could feel the tendons tightening already. 'I'd best be seeing what they want.'

He walked out of the study, through the kitchen into the garden.

The door of the helicopter rattled to the side and a figure climbed out in a green flying suit and a black helmet. The figure ducked its head as it walked briskly away from the machine and its still-turning rotors. Denham knew who it was even before the helmet was removed. Even the bulky flight suit couldn't hide her shape. The down-draught from the rotors tugged at her glossy black hair and she shook her head to clear it from her eyes.

'Retirement suits you, Liam,' she shouted above the roar of the helicopter's turbines.

'Hello, Patsy,' he said. He held out his hand and she shook it. She had a soft grip. Deceptively soft, he knew. A lot of men had come to grief underestimating Patsy Ellis. 'Long time no see.'

'We need you, Liam.' Her hazel eyes studied him levelly, gauging his reaction. 'It's Trevor. She's gone missing.'

'Missing?'

Patsy gestured at the helicopter with her thumb. 'We can talk about it on the way to London.'

'Oh, come on, Patsy. I'm retired. And not by choice, either.'

'There's no one else, Liam. No one else knows her.'

'I've got . . .'

'You've got too much time on your hands,' she said.

Denham looked around his garden. At the carefully tended rose bushes. The neat rockeries. 'Aye, Patsy. You might be right at that. Let me get my things.'

He walked back to the house. His wife was waiting for him in the kitchen, a black leather holdall in her arms. She held it out to him. 'I've packed you two shirts. And don't go above twenty a day while you're away.'

He gently cuffed her under the chin. She'd nagged him down to a packet of cigarettes a day and was determined that he'd give up by his sixty-fifth birthday. 'You know me,' said Denham.

She kissed him softly on the cheek. 'Go on with you,' she said. 'That helicopter's ripping the roses to shreds.'

Denham walked briskly to the helicopter, hauled himself inside and sat down next to Patsy.

MARTIN WENT to a cash machine before checking into the Tower Hotel, withdrawing £200 on his Visa card. He booked in for one night, under the name of Martin Sheridan.

He went straight up to the room to wait for the Special Branch detectives. He called up room service and ordered a club sandwich and a pot of coffee and then showered. The doorbell rang as he was getting dressed. When he opened the door, four heavily built uniformed policemen burst in. One of them grappled Martin to the floor, face down, and he felt handcuffs snap around his wrist. 'What the hell's going on?' he shouted.

Martin was ignored. A sheet was thrown over his head and he was half carried, half dragged through a door and down several flights of stairs in a stampede of boots, then through another door. He could hear traffic and realised he was outside. Within seconds he was thrown into the back of a van and it roared off. Someone gripped Martin's arms and helped him onto a hard bench seat. He knew it was pointless to say anything, so he just sat where he was, covered in the blanket. The Special Branch woman had lied to him.

The van drove for half an hour or so, then came to a halt, and the policemen hauled Martin to his feet and into a building he presumed was a police station. He was frog-marched down a corridor and pushed into a room. Hands clutched at his belt and pulled it away from his trousers, then his shoes were torn off his feet. The handcuffs were roughly removed and he was pushed to the side. A metal door slammed shut and there was the double click of a key being turned in a lock. Martin listened, his chest heaving. He slowly slid the sheet off his head and let it drop to the floor. He was alone in a police cell. There was a low bed, nothing more than a concrete podium with a thin plastic mattress on top, a toilet bowl cemented to the floor, and, several feet above his head, a window made of thick glass blocks.

Martin sat down on the bed. He couldn't work out what had happened. They hadn't asked his name, they hadn't charged him, they hadn't taken away his wallet or even searched him. Whatever had happened to him, it wasn't a straightforward arrest. He settled back against the wall. He had no choice other than to wait.

MARK QUINN WAS standing over his electric wok, pushing the ammonium nitrate fertiliser around so that it didn't overheat. On the table next to the wok was a metal thermometer, and he pushed it into the mixture as he continued to stir. His arms ached and his head was throbbing from the fumes. The thermometer rose to 160 degrees Fahrenheit and he turned down the heat.

Sweat was pouring down his face and the ski mask was making him itch furiously. He looked across at the pile of black rubbish sacks containing the treated fertiliser. They'd only done about a fifth. This was going to take for ever. He looked over at O'Keefe, who was clearly as unhappy as he was, then rolled up the sleeves of his overalls and grinned. O'Keefe had a large tattoo on his left forearm, a lion leaping over a flag of St George, and McCracken had told him to keep it covered while the Hayes woman was around.

Quinn looked over to where she was sealing the powdered fertiliser in a Tupperware container. Her shirt was damp with sweat and it clung to her breasts. She'd tied the bottom in a loose knot, exposing her stomach, which glistened with sweat. With her hair tied back in a ponytail she looked more like a teenager than a thirtysomething mother. He stopped stirring and stared at her breasts, the fertiliser hissing in his wok.

She stopped what she was doing and slowly turned to look at him. Quinn stuck out his tongue and licked his lips suggestively. The Hayes woman stared back at him. He could feel the hatred pouring out of her eyes.

'Hey!' O'Keefe yelled, pointing at Quinn's wok with short, stabbing movements. Quinn looked down. The fertiliser was starting to bubble and smoke. Quinn cursed and frantically scraped it out of the wok and onto the table.

McCracken looked up from her wok. 'What's going on over there?'

'Shit-for-brains nearly let his fertiliser overheat.'

'The wok was too hot,' said Quinn. 'That's all.'

'For God's sake be careful,' said McCracken. 'The place is full of fumes. Any sort of flame and the whole place'll go up.'

'I thought that was the big idea,' laughed O'Keefe. His laughter echoed around the office.

MARTIN HAYES was on his feet when the door opened. With the custody sergeant was a couple who looked as if they had just walked out of a church service.

The man was in his sixties, balding and slightly overweight. He was wearing a fawn raincoat over a greenish tweed suit and was carrying a battered tweed hat in one hand.

The woman was younger, in her mid-forties, with skin so white that she must have conscientiously avoided exposing it to the sun. Her hair was cut short with a fringe, its blackness emphasising the paleness of her face. She had bright, inquisitive hazel eyes, and a smile that could have concealed the darkest thoughts. 'Mr Hayes? I'm Patsy. We spoke on the phone.'

Martin glared at her. 'You had me thrown in here?' he said angrily. 'You lied to me.'

'I'm sorry about that, Mr Hayes, but I had to be sure that you wouldn't go running off.' She had a small gold crucifix on a chain round her neck, and she fingered it with her left hand as she spoke. Round her wrist was a gold Cartier watch. She turned to her companion. 'This is Chief Inspector Liam Denham.'

Denham held out his hand. The first and second fingers were stained brownish yellow with nicotine. 'Ex-Chief Inspector,' he said, his harsh accent betraying his Belfast origins. 'Why don't we go and get a cup of tea?'

Martin looked down at his socks. 'They took my shoes.'

'I do apologise for that,' said Patsy. The custody sergeant handed Martin his belongings. The two Special Branch officers waited while Martin sat down on his bunk and slipped on his shoes and belt, then they escorted him from the cell block to a white-tiled canteen.

'Tea?' asked Patsy.

'Coffee. White. One sugar.'

Patsy went over to the counter while Martin and Denham sat at a corner table. Denham dropped his tweed hat onto the table. There was a small red fishing fly close to the brim. 'You don't fish, do you?' he asked as he sat down.

'No. No, I don't. Sorry.' Martin felt suddenly ridiculous apologising for not being an angler. 'Look, what the hell's this all about?'

'Let's wait for Patsy, shall we?' said Denham.

Patsy came over with three mugs on a tray. She put the tray down and passed them over as she sat down.

'How long have you known your wife, Mr Hayes?' asked Denham.

'Ten years.'

'And you met where?'

'Trinity. She was studying English literature.'

'And do you know what she did before that?'

Martin stared at the man for several seconds. Denham returned his stare with no trace of embarrassment, waiting for him to speak. 'No, not really,' said Martin eventually.

'What we're going to tell you is going to be something of a surprise, I'm afraid,' said Denham.

Martin forced himself to stay calm. 'Just tell me what the hell is going on,' he said.

Denham and Patsy looked at each other. There was an almost imperceptible nod from Patsy, as if she were giving Denham permission to go ahead.

'Your wife, Mr Hayes, was once an IRA bombmaker.'

Martin's head swam. The walls of the canteen seemed to bulge in and out, and for a moment he felt as if he was going to faint.

'No,' he said flatly. 'You're not talking about my wife.'

'It was before she was your wife,' said Denham. 'When she was in her early twenties. Before she met you.'

'You're telling me that my wife is a terrorist?'

'Oh no,' said Denham quickly. 'That's not the situation at all.'

'But you said she was an IRA bombmaker?'

'She was recruited by the IRA during her final year of university.'

'At Trinity?'

Denham shook his head. 'Queen's University. Belfast. She got a first in electrical engineering.'

Martin laughed out loud. 'Andy can't change a plug,' he said.

Denham smiled thinly. 'She was recruited by her boyfriend at the time, and was trained by one of their most experienced bombmakers. He was killed a year after she graduated. She took his place. But by that time, she was working for us.'

'Hang on a minute,' interrupted Martin. 'First you tell me she's an IRA terrorist, now you're saying she works for Special Branch?'

'Worked,' said Patsy. 'Past tense. This is all past tense, Mr Hayes.'

'We'd had her under surveillance,' continued Denham, 'almost from the moment she was recruited, but she got wind of it. Smart girl, she was. Took the wind out of our sails by approaching us. We persuaded her to stay with them. Did a hell of a job, for nigh on three years. Until the accident.'

'Accident?'

Denham scratched at a small wine-coloured birthmark on his neck. 'She'd let us know where her bombs were going to be used, and what sort they were. Our bomb-disposal boys always had the edge.

They knew which ones were booby-trapped, and how. Some we'd let explode, providing there was no risk of loss of life. We would release stories to the media that soldiers had been killed, or that a bomb-disposal officer had died. Others we'd pretend to stumble on. There were a million and one ways to make it look as if the IRA had just been unlucky.

'Your wife saved many, many lives, Mr Hayes. She deserved a medal. She played a most dangerous game—not a day went by when her own life wasn't on the line.' He paused. 'What happened was a terrible accident. A small bomb, a few pounds of Semtex. Set to go off with a timer. It had been placed on the Belfast-to-Dublin rail line, under a bridge. Your wife had tipped us off that the bomb was being set, but she didn't know where on the line it was going to be placed. We were waiting for the coded call. It came, but before we could react to it a group of schoolchildren found the bomb.'

'Oh God,' whispered Martin as he realised where the story was heading.

Denham nodded. 'Four boys died. One crippled for life. It wasn't her fault. It wasn't anybody's fault. It was just one of those things.'

'Oh God,' said Martin again. He slumped back in his seat.

'She walked away,' said Denham. 'Told her IRA bosses that she'd built her last bomb. Told us the same. They tried to talk her out of it, and so did we. But she was adamant.'

Martin remembered how Andy had always hated to see reports of bombings on television. How she'd sat with tears streaming down her face on the day that the bomb went off in Omagh. Everyone in Ireland was shocked to the core by the horror of the bombing, but now he knew that there was another reason for Andy's grief. She'd had to live with the deaths of four innocents on her conscience and, knowing what a loving, caring, sensitive person she was, he realised that the strain must have been unbearable.

'She moved to Dublin. Started a new life.'

Martin shook his head, trying to clear his thoughts. 'They let her? They let her walk away from the IRA?'

'They understood why she wanted to leave. She was a woman, and children had died.'

'So they never found out that she was working for you?'

'No. She cut all ties with us.'

'And Trevor? Who was Trevor?'

'Trevor was her code name.'

'This is unbelievable.' Martin stared at the remains of his tea. 'That's what this has all been about? Her bombmaking skills?'

Patsy reached out and gently touched Martin's wrist. 'That's why we're here, Mr Hayes. The fact that your daughter's kidnappers wanted your wife to fly to London suggests that—'

'—they want her to build them a bomb. Here.'

Patsy nodded. 'Exactly. We have to act now. And we need your co-operation.' She had a notebook in front of her and was holding a slim gold pen. 'Now, who else knows what's happened to your family?'

'The Gardai. In Dublin. Inspector James FitzGerald. And a sergeant. Power, his name was, I think.'

Patsy wrote the names down in her notebook.

'Two uniformed gardai called at the house. They're the ones who took me to the Garda station.'

'Do you know their names?'

Martin shook his head. 'The secretary at Katie's school got in touch with them. Mrs O'Mara, her name is. She's disappeared. That's what the police say. That's why they came to see me in the first place. She'd telephoned me to see why Katie wasn't at school, and I guess she'd spoken to the headmistress.'

Patsy looked across at Denham and raised an eyebrow. Then she looked back at Martin. 'Anyone else?'

'I told my partner what had happened. Padraig Martin.'

'What exactly did you tell him?' asked Denham.

Martin massaged his temples as he tried to remember the conversation he'd had with Padraig while he was driving him up to Belfast. 'I told him that Katie had been kidnapped. And that the kidnappers told Andy to go to London.'

'That's just wonderful,' said Denham under his breath.

'I had to tell him something,' said Martin. 'He's my partner. He was nearly killed.'

'Killed? What do you mean, killed?' asked Patsy.

Martin realised he hadn't told them about the man who'd shot at the BMW outside the hospital. He explained what had happened.

'This man, what did he look like?' asked Patsy.

'I didn't see his face, not really,' said Martin. 'He was average height. Medium build. He was wearing a leather jacket. Black or brown. And jeans, maybe.'

'Moustache? Hair colour? Facial hair? A scar? Anything that made him stick out?'

Martin shook his head. 'It was dark. I just wanted to get away.'

'That's OK, Mr Hayes,' said Patsy.

'The note the kidnappers left,' Denham said. 'Do you still have it?'

'No. Andy took it with her.' He reached into his trouser pocket and took out the sheet of paper he'd found behind the hotel paint-ing. 'This is the note she left for me in the Strand Palace.' He gave it to Denham, who read it and passed it over to Patsy.

'The phone conversation you told me about,' said Patsy. 'When your wife told you about this. Where were you?'

'At home. In Dublin.'

'And she called on the land line? Or your mobile?'

'The land line.'

'And she only made one call?'

Martin nodded.

'When she called you, could you hear any traffic? People walking by? Any sounds that might suggest she was using a call box?'

Martin rubbed his face with both hands. 'I don't remember any.'

'Did you get any sense that she was calling from a mobile?'

Martin shook his head. 'I'm sorry.'

Patsy smiled reassuringly. 'Can you run through everything your wife said to you when she called.'

'She said they didn't want money. And that they wouldn't hurt Katie so long as I didn't go to the police. Then she said that after it was all over, we'd go back to Venice. It was only when I saw the pic-ture that I realised what she meant. And that was it.'

Patsy looked across at Denham. He raised an eyebrow

'Did I do something wrong?'

Patsy put down her gold pen. 'No, you didn't, Mr Hayes. But they might have done. It was obviously your wife who initiated the call. It was unstructured, unrehearsed. And the only information imparted was that which your wife wanted to give you. It wasn't a message from the kidnappers. If she managed to get them to allow her one phone call, she might be able to persuade them to let her make another.'

'But if she calls, I won't be there.'

Patsy looked across at Denham. 'I'll get the number transferred to Thames House. We can use that office as a base.'

'And if they call, they'll think I'm still in the house?'

'That's the idea.'

Martin scratched his chin. 'The answering machine's on. I left a message saying that anyone who calls should try me on my mobile.'

'You still have the mobile?'

Martin shook his head. 'It was in my hotel room. In my case.'

Patsy nodded. 'I'll get it for you. But it's best she doesn't call the mobile. I'll get the answering machine turned off.' She stood up. 'I'll make a couple of calls.'

Martin fished his house keys out and slid them across the table.

Patsy smiled and shook her head. 'The people I'll be using won't be needing keys, Mr Hayes.'

EGAN KEPT the Ford Scorpio below seventy as he drove towards London. The ferry crossing from Dun Laoghaire had been uneventful, if a little choppy, and he hadn't even glimpsed a customs officer or policeman as he drove off the ferry. Not that Egan would have been worried if he had been pulled in for a random check—the Semtex explosive and detonators were well hidden within a secret compartment inside the petrol tank.

Egan had taken the explosive from a farmer in Dundalk who had been put in charge of an IRA arms cache back in the early eighties. It was part of a consignment sent from Libya, and had been buried in a plastic dustbin swathed in black polythene. The farmer and his wife had dug up the dustbin as Egan had stood over them with his Browning. He'd taken only as much as he needed—six kilograms. And a pack of Mark 4 detonators. The rest had gone back into the ground, along with the bodies of the farmer and his wife.

LIAM DENHAM LOOKED around the office and nodded appreciatively. 'They certainly look after you, Patsy.'

Patsy sat down in the high-backed leather chair and folded her arms across the blotter on the rosewood desk. She had her back to a large window with an impressive view over the river. There were several oil paintings on the walls, resplendent in massive gilt frames, and the carpet was a rich blue and so thick that it threatened to engulf Denham's battered Hush Puppies. 'Don't be ridiculous, Liam. This isn't mine.'

'Even so . . .' said Denham, settling into one of two wing-backed armchairs that faced the desk. 'It's a damn sight more impressive than my old shoe box.'

'Let's keep to the business at hand, shall we?' said Patsy. 'The phone divert's in place, and if she calls again GCHQ will track it. I reckon it'll turn out to be a mobile, so we're not going to be able to get an accurate fix, but it should narrow it down for us.'

'We're assuming London?'

Patsy sighed and ran her fingers around the blotter. 'I don't think we can, Liam. My gut feeling is yes, it'll be the capital, but we'll both have egg on our faces if they blow up Manchester, won't we?' Patsy picked up a mobile phone and passed it over to Denham. 'It's a digital GSM,' she said. 'But it's not secure, so . . .'

'Mum's the word?'

Patsy smiled. 'Exactly.'

Denham slipped the phone into his jacket pocket.

'Do you think the husband is up to it?' Patsy asked.

'I think so. All he has to do is to keep her talking.' He looked at Patsy. 'What are you going to tell him when he asks what we're doing to find his daughter?'

'That we're doing everything we can.'

'And if he realises that we're not?'

'Liam, our first priority is to prevent them exploding whatever device it is that Andrea Hayes is building for them. If we make any attempt to locate the girl, they'll know we're on to them.'

'So we do nothing to find the girl?'

'We find them here first, then they'll tell us where the girl is,' said Patsy. 'But the converse isn't true. In fact, I'd bet money that the kidnappers don't know the full details of what's going on here.'

Denham nodded. She was right. But he didn't think that Martin Hayes would see it her way. 'And what exactly is it you want from me?' he asked. 'Why've I been brought in from the cold?'

'Hardly the cold, Liam. You've a nice pension, from what I hear.'

'I was sacked, Patsy.'

'You were the only one who dealt with Trevor. You're the only one who knows how she'll react.'

'I've not seen or spoken to her in ten years.'

'You're all we have. You were with her when she was under the most pressure. She knew what they'd do to her if they ever found out she was betraying them. And you were the only one she could confide in.' She paused for a while. 'Liam, I have to know. Given the choice between the life of her daughter and saving hundreds of lives—what would she do?'

Denham shrugged. 'You know why she walked away?'

'Because four children died.'

'It damn near destroyed her. She came close to killing herself. She didn't turn up for a meeting we'd arranged so I broke all the rules and went looking for her. Found her sitting on her bed with the tablets out and a bottle of vodka. It was children, Patsy. That's what pushed her over the edge. So think what her own daughter means to her. She'd die for her.'

Patsy reached for the cross round her neck and stroked it as she studied Denham with unblinking eyes. 'But would she allow others to be killed? If it meant saving her own daughter?'

'She's an intelligent girl is Andrea, you know? Top of her year at

Queen's. You'd never know it to look at her, because she's so damn pretty. The softest blonde hair you ever saw. And her figure. The heads she turned.'

'And you a married man,' said Patsy, shaking her head and smiling. 'What's your point, Liam?'

'The point is, she's going to work out what we both know already. That if they are forcing her to build a bomb, they're not going to want her around after it goes off. And if they're going to kill Andrea, they've nothing to lose by killing the little girl, too. She'll know that if she doesn't do what they want, the girl will die. And she'll know that if she does do what they want, the girl will die. Which leaves her looking for a third way.'

'But she'll be building the bomb?' said Patsy.

'Definitely. Because so long as she's in the process of constructing it, they won't hurt the girl.'

'Which gives us a couple of days? Maybe three?'

Denham nodded.

'There's something else I need you to do, Liam. Somebody's going to have to ask him. And I think it'd be better coming from you.'

Denham lit a cigarette. At the height of the Troubles he'd smoked eighty a day, and he could feel the old cravings returning.

'There's a plane waiting. I'll have transport arranged for you in Belfast.'

'You know where he is?'

Patsy smiled. 'Every minute of every day,' she said. 'I'm going to address the troops.'

She walked down the office to the briefing room. Twenty expectant faces looked up at her as she went over to where two whiteboards were mounted on the wall. The blinds were drawn and the overhead fluorescent lights were on. 'Right, let's get to it, shall we?' she said.

There were four photographs stuck to one of the whiteboards. Three of them were of Andrea Hayes, one was of Katie.

Patsy pointed at one of the photographs of Andrea, a recent head-and-shoulders shot. 'Andrea Hayes. Housewife, thirty-four years old.' She turned to the photograph next to it, this one a blow-up of a passport photograph taken twelve years earlier. 'In a previous life, Andrea Sheridan. Top IRA bombmaker and Special Branch informer.' She tapped the photograph of Katie. 'Her daughter, Katie. Kidnapped from their home in Dublin.'

She tapped the first photograph of Andy. 'Someone wants her to build a bomb. Why, we can work out later. As to when, we think the bomb's likely to be completed within the next few days. Assuming it's a massive fertiliser bomb, which was Andrea Sheridan's speciality, once the ingredients are mixed, their shelf life is limited. We're looking at a time frame of between two days and ten. So, these are our priorities. We need to know who's building the bomb, and we need to know where the bomb is. As regards who, we have video of a vehicle leaving a car park in Covent Garden.'

She moved across to the second whiteboard and tapped a grainy black-and-white print blown up from a still taken from the closed-circuit television video at the car park in Covent Garden. 'Andrea Sheridan is in the back of this van. It is owned by a landscaping company in the Midlands. It's being checked out as we speak, but I don't recommend anyone holding their breath. This has been too well planned for it to be as easy as that.' She pointed to the portion of the photograph showing the van's windscreen. 'Two occupants. Male. They're sitting well back but we can just about make out the bottom of the passenger's face and three-quarters of the driver's. Our technical boys are working on the video now. We've also got all the tickets handed in that day and we're looking for the one that corresponds to their exit time. If we get it, we get the driver's prints.'

She folded her arms and moved away from the whiteboard. 'Whoever they are, the two men in the van aren't working alone. We think it unlikely it's the IRA, or anyone else in the Republican movement. If it was in any way official, there'd be no need for them to use Andrea Sheridan. Her expertise is a decade out of date. We believe that someone wants it to appear that there is an IRA involvement. Now, that leads to two lines of enquiry. First, someone within the IRA must have offered up Andrea Sheridan. Her role as a bomb-maker was known to less than a dozen people. Only one man within RUC Special Branch knew what her position was. Chief Inspector Liam Denham. He is hoping to obtain a list of those members of the IRA who knew of Andrea Sheridan. We have some names already.'

There were four photographs underneath the surveillance shot of the van. 'These are the four known members of her active service unit.' Patsy tapped the photographs one by one.

'James Nolan. The late James Nolan. Scored an own goal in Hammersmith in '93 and blew himself out of a third-floor bedsit in a couple of dozen pieces.'

Several of the agents laughed, but they stopped when she gave them a frosty look.

'Eugene Walsh. Now working for a diving company in the Florida Keys. Our Miami office is looking for him.'

The third face was the youngest of the group, still in his twenties.

Patsy pointed at it. 'Shay Purcell. He's in Mountjoy Prison in Dublin, midway through a life sentence. Killed his girlfriend with a bread knife so he's not regarded as political and won't be getting early release. We'll be speaking to him there.'

She tapped the final picture. 'Brendan Tighe. Still in Belfast. He turned informer about four years back. He's still in the IRA, deep cover, and we know he's sound.'

She turned back to the whiteboard and with a blue marker pen wrote the word 'TREVOR' in capital letters.

'Her code name within Special Branch was Trevor. As of now, that's how she's to be referred to.'

She put the cap back on her marker. 'So, who is behind this if it's not the IRA? You know the possibilities as well as I do.' She named the usual terrorist groups, from animal activists to groups from Libya and Iraq. 'So, we trawl through all the intelligence we have, looking for possibilities. Anyone recently arrived in this country who might be behind something like this. Anyone who's suddenly gone underground. Speak to all your contacts. But tactfully.'

Patsy nodded at the oldest man in the room, David Bingham, her number two. 'David, if and when we locate the men in the van, we're going to want to know where they've been. I'd like you to handle that. I'd also like you to liaise with Chief Inspector Denham when he gets back from Northern Ireland. If he does manage to obtain a list of IRA members who knew about Trevor's role as a bombmaker, other than those names we already have, it has to be our first priority. Any resources you need, you only have to ask. There's to be no contact with the police, at any level, without prior clearance from me. I don't want to see this on the front page of the *Daily Mail*, OK?'

Nodding heads responded.

'Good. This room is our operations centre. If I'm not here I'll be in Jason Hetherington's office down the corridor. Tim, would you come with me? You too, Barbara.'

Tim Fanning opened the door for her and walked with her to Hetherington's office. Fanning was a relatively recent recruit from a City stockbroking firm, where he'd worked as an analyst. Behind them followed Barbara Carter, a twenty-six-year-old psychology graduate who was originally from Dublin. Patsy closed the office door behind them and waved them over to the two armchairs in front of her desk. 'I've got something special for the two of you,' she said, sitting down. 'Martin Hayes is going to need his hand held through this, and I want one of you to be with him at all times.'

The two agents nodded.

Patsy could see from the look on Fanning's face that he wasn't happy about the assignment as he folded his arms across his chest.

'There's something I didn't mention at the briefing, and I want it to remain between us, for the time being at least.'

Patsy had to resist the urge to smile as she saw Fanning's reaction. His whole body language changed. He uncrossed his legs and leaned forward expectantly, eager to hear what she had to say.

'They allowed her to phone her husband. On Saturday.'

Fanning and Carter both raised their eyebrows in surprise.

'Little was said, but our feeling is that, if she managed to convince them to allow her to make one call, she should be able to do it again the closer she gets to completion. Or she'll find a way of getting to a phone without them knowing. Either way, we've arranged with British Telecom and Telecom Eireann to have all calls to the Hayes house routed to an office here. So far as the caller's concerned, they'll be through to the house. We'll be running a trace, but I doubt they'll be on long enough. Still, nothing ventured . . .'

'There is the possibility that she'll ask to speak to her daughter, of course,' said Carter.

Patsy nodded. 'That's where it gets complicated,' she said. 'We'll be monitoring all England–Ireland phone traffic, looking for key words. That's going to be done through GCHQ. But the daughter, is not our prime concern. Though Mr Hayes must absolutely not be aware of that. Are we clear?'

Fanning and Carter nodded.

'Right,' Patsy said, 'let's get to it.'

THEY'D BEEN WAITING for him on the tarmac, the rear door of the Rover already open for Denham as he walked off the RAF Hercules transporter and down the metal stairway.

They drove north towards Antrim, joined the M22 and headed west with the vast expanse of Lough Neagh to their left, until the motorway merged into the A6. The driver was good, Denham had to admit. He drove quickly but safely, and was constantly checking the mirrors, but Denham doubted that anyone would have been able to keep up with them. The speedometer rarely fell below seventy.

The car eventually came to a halt by a stone bridge. The driver turned round to look at Denham and nodded, just once. 'You boys stay with the car,' Denham said. He climbed out of the Rover and walked down towards the fast-flowing stream, holding his arms out for balance as he skidded and slipped along the muddy gravel path.

The man standing in the stream must have heard Denham coming, but he didn't turn his head. He flicked the rod in his hand and a fly whisked through the air and plopped almost silently onto a quiet stretch of water close to the far bank.

'You always did have a hell of a smooth cast, Mr McCormack,' said Denham. Only then did Thomas McCormack turn to acknowledge his presence.

'I'm told you're no mean fisherman yourself, Chief Inspector Denham.' McCormack turned his back on Denham and wound in his line. He was wearing green waders, a quilted waistcoat over a thick green pullover, and on his head a shapeless tweed hat that could have been a close cousin to the one Denham was wearing.

'It's Mr Denham now. Retired almost ten years.'

'Oh, I know that, Chief Inspector, same as I know you're a fisherman. So, would this be a social call?'

'I'm afraid not.'

'You won't mind if I carry on casting, will you? There's a trout, five pounds if it's an ounce, lurking under those leaves over there.'

'You go for it, Mr McCormack.' There was a tree trunk on its side a few steps away from Denham and he went over and sat on it. Denham lit a cigarette. McCormack made three more casts.

'What do you think? Too big?'

'Maybe something brighter?' suggested Denham. 'The light's going.'

'Aye, you could be right,' said McCormack. He wound in the line and replaced his fly with one that had a splash of yellow in its tail.

'Andrea Sheridan,' said Denham. 'Remember her?'

McCormack's eyes narrowed. He looked at Denham for several seconds without speaking. 'That's a name from the past, right enough. Retired, like yourself.'

Denham nodded and took a long pull on his cigarette. Thomas McCormack was an old adversary and, peace process or no peace process, a man to be handled with care. He looked like an elderly schoolmaster, but for many years he'd been a hard-line member of the IRA's Army Executive.

'Maybe. Maybe not. We think she's active again. Perhaps against her will.'

McCormack wound in his line and cast again. Just as the fly plopped onto the water, a big speckled trout seemed to leap from the depths, its mouth agape. It engulfed the fly and disappeared back under the surface. McCormack hauled in the fish and extracted the fly before holding it up to show Denham. 'Six pounds, I'll bet,' he said.

'Hell of a catch,' agreed Denham.

McCormack bent down and lowered the trout into the stream. He let the fish swim free and then straightened up. He waded over to the bank and sat with Denham on the tree trunk. 'What do you mean, against her will?' he asked.

'She has a daughter. Katie. The child's been kidnapped. No ransom, but the kidnappers told Andrea to fly to London. Now she's disappeared.'

'And you're suggesting what, Chief Inspector?'

'I'm not suggesting anything. I'm looking for guidance.'

McCormack wound in his line and began to disassemble his rod.

'I figure that your people wouldn't need to kidnap the little girl to get the mother to do what you wanted. So, I'm ruling out an official operation. An official IRA operation.'

'I'm glad to hear that,' said McCormack, slipping the sections of his rod into a canvas bag.

'I was thinking perhaps a splinter group?'

'Very doubtful,' said McCormack. 'Gerry and Martin wouldn't stand for it.' McCormack propped the bag against the tree trunk and stretched out his legs. 'It's not Republican, Chief Inspector. You should be looking at the other side of the fence.'

'Maybe. But how would they know about her?'

McCormack looked across at Denham, his eyes narrowing. 'I might be asking you the same question.'

Denham stared into the distance.

'My God,' said McCormack, his voice little more than a whisper. 'She was working for you.'

It wasn't a question, and Denham knew there was no point in denying it. He'd known that the moment he asked McCormack about Andrea Sheridan he'd be showing his hand. And that if he expected to get McCormack's help, he'd have to tell him everything.

'For how long?' asked McCormack.

'From day one. Pretty much.'

McCormack shook his head slowly. 'My God. Every bomb, every one she made, you knew about it?'

Denham shrugged but didn't say anything.

'But the people that died? The soldiers? The bomb-disposal . . .' His voice tailed off as realisation dawned. 'You faked them all. You cunning old fox . . .' He took out his hip flask and took a long drink from it, then wiped his mouth with the back of his hand. 'Except for the kids. Something went wrong. The kids died, and she walked away. And you got the push.'

'Somebody had to carry the can. And she was my agent. It's history. Ancient history.'

'Aye. Maybe you're right.'

'But about the matter in hand. You realise what'll happen if it goes off? Her fingerprints will be all over it. Her signature.'

'Which is presumably why they're using her. You don't have to paint a picture for me. We've as much to lose as you do if they succeed.'

'So you'll help?'

'I don't see that I've any choice.' He smiled thinly. 'It's a turn-up for the books, isn't it?'

Denham flicked the end of his cigarette into the stream. 'Aye. It's an ever-changing world, right enough. So, who knew about her? Apart from the two of us.'

MARTIN PACED up and down, staring at the floor.

'Mr Hayes, please. Try to relax.' Martin looked up, his mind a million miles away. He frowned at Carter, his eyes blank.

'Can I get you something? Tea? Coffee?'

'Coffee, maybe. Yes. Coffee. Thanks.' He started pacing again.

Carter and Fanning exchanged worried looks. Carter shrugged, not sure what to say or do to put Martin at ease. She stood up, and went out to get the coffee.

Fanning suggested that Martin sit down. There were two sofas in the office, large enough to sleep on, and there was a small bathroom off to the side, so that there was no need for Martin to leave the room. Patsy Ellis had made it clear that Martin was to remain confined to the office, but that hadn't been a problem—he'd shown no desire to leave. All he'd done for four hours was to pace up and down and from time to time to stare at the two silent phones. The black phone was the line that had been diverted from the Hayes home in Dublin. The white phone was a direct line to Patsy Ellis's mobile.

'I can't sit,' said Martin.

'There's nothing you can do,' said Fanning. 'The ball's in your wife's court. We just have to wait.'

'What if she doesn't ring? What if they don't let her use the phone? The guy that shot at me, he must have been one of them, right? He'll know that I'm not at home. Why would he let Andy call me if he knows I'm not at home?'

'We don't know,' admitted Fanning. 'Patsy said that maybe your wife would be able to get to a phone herself, without them knowing. And just because you were attacked doesn't mean they know you've left the country. For all they know, you could have returned home.'

'So she calls, then what? I know phone traces aren't infallible.'

'You're going by what you see in the movies, Mr Hayes. It's not like that. With a digital exchange, we can get a trace within seconds. Even with a mobile. If she's in the City, we'll know to within a hundred feet where she is.'

Martin wiped his hands over his face as if he were wiping away tears, though his cheeks were dry. 'And Katie? What about my daughter? Are the Gardai looking for her?'

'Patsy thinks it best not to call in the local police,' said Fanning, choosing his words with care. 'We're using our own people. And we're monitoring all calls to Ireland. If they make a call to the kidnappers, we'll know. And we'll have their location. We'll know where your daughter is being held.'

'Oh, come on, Tim. That's not feasible. How can you possibly monitor every single call between England and Ireland?'

Fanning wondered how much he should tell Martin. The man badly needed reassurance, but much of what MI5 did was classified.

He took a deep breath. 'It goes on every hour of every day,' he said. 'The system is called Echelon. It's been around since the seventies, but it's really come into its own in the last few years. It's the brainchild of the Americans, naturally, through their National Security Agency, but it also involves us, through GCHQ, the Australians, the Canadians and New Zealand. Between the five countries, every single satellite, land line and undersea cable transmission is monitored. Every phone call, fax, telex and email in the world. Echelon can search through all transmissions looking for a particular word, or combination of words. It can even search out voiceprints, so we can be on the lookout for a particular individual making a call anywhere in the world.'

'It sounds impossible,' said Martin. 'It's too big.'

'It's big, but computing power is now enormous compared with what it was just twenty years ago. You use the Internet, right?'

'Sure. Who doesn't?'

'And you've used a search engine? Yahoo or AltaVista or one of the others, where you scan the Net looking for specific subjects. Words or combination of words?' Martin nodded. 'Then consider this, Martin. The Internet is old technology. Echelon is several generations ahead. It works at a speed you could never hope to comprehend. We ask it to keep a lookout for the word "Katie" or "Mummy" and it'll flag any phone conversation that takes place in which both words are used. Within seconds we'll know which number is being called, and from where.'

Martin leaned forward. The signs of stress were starting to diminish. He seemed much more relaxed now that he understood what was involved. 'I hope you're right, Tim,' Martin said.

'We are,' said Fanning. Patsy Ellis might not approve of how much of GCHQ's work he had revealed, but Martin was definitely a lot more relaxed having heard it.

THE TWO MEN in Barbour jackets drove Denham back to Belfast in silence. They took him to a nondescript office building on the outskirts of the city, and the one who'd been in the passenger seat escorted him down a white-painted corridor past a series of identical grey doors. The man opened one of the doors and nodded at Denham. 'I'll wait for you here, sir.'

Inside the windowless room was a soundproofed booth, and inside the booth was a metal desk, a plastic chair and a telephone without a dial or keypad. Denham went into the booth and closed the door behind him. He picked up the phone and almost immediately a man's voice asked him who he wished to speak to. He asked for Patsy Ellis. She was on the line within seconds.

'Liam, how did it go?'

'Better than I expected, to be honest. Men like McCormack have changed since the Good Friday agreement.'

'So what did he have to say?'

'He gave me the four who were in Trevor's active service unit, but he obviously knew that we had them anyway. The ASU was under the control of Hugh McGrath, and that we didn't know because he dealt only with Nolan.'

'McGrath?'

'McCormack reckons he's dead too.' Denham lit a cigarette and inhaled deeply. 'He disappeared back in '92.'

'But this McGrath knew about Trevor?'

'Oh, yes. Quite definitely. And another volunteer. Micky Geraghty. He was a sniper, and a bloody good one, but he walked away when his wife died of cancer and went to live near Thurso, up in Scotland.'

'I'll get him checked out. What about the other thing? Is he willing to help?'

'He said he'd make enquiries. But that it wouldn't be easy. It's a hell of a thing to be asking him to do, Patsy. If word got out that he was helping us . . . even under the circumstances, the hard-liners wouldn't think twice about making an example of him.'

'How long before he gets back to us?'

'He couldn't say. He'll put out feelers, ask around, but softly-softly. If he comes across anyone who's gone missing, he'll get back to me.'

'That's great, Liam. Job well done.'

'I was thinking it might be an idea if I return via Scotland. I could pop in on Micky Geraghty. I know it's not exactly on the way, but until McCormack gets back to me, I'm not going to be much use.'

Patsy was silent for a few seconds, thinking it over. 'You're right, it makes sense. I'll speak to our transport people, ascertain where we can get you flown into, and I'll have you met there.'

'I'm a big boy, Patsy. I don't need minders.'

'It'll save time, Liam. Just think of them as drivers.'

'Aye. OK.'

'And Liam? You're not supposed to smoke in the secure communication booths. It screws up the electronics.'

Denham was still chuckling as he left the room.

LYDIA MCCRACKEN SAT on the wooden bench and looked around the garden square. She was wearing a pale blue suit and was holding a small handbag in her lap. Several dozen office workers were strolling around the square, getting a breath of fresh air before heading back to their VDUs and keyboards. Some of them could be among hundreds who'd die when the 4,000-pound fertiliser bomb went off just half a mile away from where she was sitting.

McCracken had helped plant bombs before, though she'd never been involved in the building of one. She'd always believed in what she was doing—that the only way to drive the British out of Ireland was by force—and she'd felt betrayed by the so-called peace process and the cease fire that followed. Her younger brother had been killed in a gun battle with SAS troopers in the early eighties, and two cousins had been shot by British paratroopers when they'd tried to drive through an army roadblock. She wanted revenge against the British for the suffering they'd brought to her country and to her family, and Egan had offered her a way to get that revenge. A bomb in the City would derail the peace process, of that she had no doubt.

'Nice day,' said a man in a dark blue pinstripe suit as he sat down on the bench a few feet from her. He placed a black briefcase on the ground midway between them. It was Egan. He was holding a Marks and Spencer carrier bag and he handed it to her. 'Sandwich?'

McCracken peered inside the bag. It contained two baguettes.

'Thank you.'

'How's everything going?'

'On schedule. Quinn's being a pain though. Keeps pestering Andrea. He makes her nervous, and that's the last thing we need.'

Egan nodded thoughtfully. 'I'll sort it,' he said. He nodded down at the briefcase. 'Take good care of that, huh?'

McCracken smiled tightly. 'I know what I'm doing.'

'I know you do.' Egan stood up and adjusted his tie. 'That's why I hired you for this. Trial run tomorrow, OK?'

'That's the plan.'

'Bring Quinn, will you?'

McCracken picked up the briefcase and put it carefully on her lap. 'I think that's best. I wouldn't want to leave him alone with Andrea.'

Egan walked away. McCracken watched him blend quickly with the other suits and disappear round the corner, then she stood up and walked in the opposite direction. She moved the briefcase as little as possible, all too conscious of the fact that it contained enough Semtex explosive to blow a crater fifty feet wide.

THE HERCULES LANDED at an airport outside Wick, in the far north-west corner of Scotland. There was only one man waiting for Denham this time, standing by a battered old Volvo. He was in his fifties and was wearing a sheepskin jacket with the collar turned up against a bitter wind. 'Welcome to Wick!' he shouted above the noise of the Hercules, and he shook Denham's hand firmly. 'Harry McKechnie. Sorry about the transport. The office car's in for a service so I've got to use my own wheels.'

Denham climbed into the front passenger seat. He took out his cigarettes as McKechnie drove away from the airfield. 'You don't mind if I smoke, do you?' he asked.

'Not if you'll light one for me, too,' said McKechnie. Denham lit two cigarettes and gave one to McKechnie.

'OK,' McKechnie said. 'Michael Geraghty, Micky to his friends, lives about four miles west of Thurso. Place called Garryowen Farm. He runs executive training courses, Outward Bound for the middle-aged. Takes them rock climbing, canoeing, gives them team-building exercises, that sort of thing.'

'Keeping his nose clean?'

'By all accounts, yes.'

The drive to Thurso took the best part of half an hour, then McKechnie turned off the A882 and headed east. After another ten minutes he turned onto a single-track road and slowed the Volvo down to a walking pace. 'That's it, up ahead,' he said.

The headlights illuminated Garryowen Farm, a two-storey grey stone building with a steeply sloping slate roof. There were no lights on. McKechnie stopped the car and tapped his fingers on the steering wheel. 'Shit,' he said.

'Let's have a look around the back,' said Denham.

The two men climbed out of the Volvo and walked towards the rear of the farmhouse. Denham knocked on a black-painted wooden door several times. McKechnie stood back to check if a light went on upstairs, but he shook his head. Next to the door was a large sash window. Denham put his hand against the glass and peered inside. It was the kitchen, and there were no signs of life.

McKechnie bent down and examined the lock on the kitchen door. 'Mortise,' he said. 'Mortise locks are buggers without the right equipment. And I wasn't planning on any breaking and entering.'

He went over to a toolshed and examined the padlock on its door. 'This is more like it,' he said. He had it open within thirty seconds, then went inside and reappeared with a large spade. He grinned at Denham as he went over to the sash window and inserted the end of the blade into the gap between the window and the frame. He pushed down on the handle of the spade with all his weight and the window lock splintered.

'You learned that with Five?' asked Denham wryly.

'Misspent youth,' said McKechnie, pushing the window open and heaving himself into the kitchen, head first. The key was on the inside of the door and a few seconds later the kitchen light flickered on, the door opened and McKechnie waved Denham inside. There was an untidy pile of mail in front of the letterbox.

'You check the bedrooms,' said Denham. He pushed open a door as McKechnie went upstairs and flicked on the light. It was a study—floor-to-ceiling bookshelves lined one wall; the others were wood-panelled with several framed prints of hunting dogs. The furniture was sturdy and worn, comfortable leather chairs with sagging cushions and a large desk with a brass reading lamp. Denham sat down at the desk and pulled open the top drawer. It was filled with papers and Denham took them out. The most recent was three months ago, a letter from a bank to Geraghty, asking him to telephone the manager about his overdraft. He found a diary in the second drawer of the desk, which Geraghty had used to record the courses he ran. The last entry was for five months earlier. From the looks of the diary, business hadn't been good for a long time.

McKechnie came downstairs, and Denham heard him picking up the mail by the front door on his way into the study.

McKechnie dropped the letters on the desk. 'Mail's been piling up for three months,' he said. 'No empty hangers in the wardrobes, toothbrush is in the bathroom. 'What do you think?'

'I think we should give the house a good going over.' Denham pushed himself up out of the chair. At the kitchen end of the hall was a door under the stairs and Denham tried to open it. It was locked. He turned to McKechnie. 'Think your misspent youth can deal with this?'

McKechnie grinned, retrieved the spade, inserted it into the side of the door and pushed against the handle with all his weight. The wood splintered and McKechnie pulled back the door.

Denham wrinkled his nose. A sickly-sweet smell wafted up from the basement below. He took a handkerchief from his pocket and held it to his face as he groped along the wall for a light switch. He found it and flicked it on. The smell hit McKechnie and he took a towel from the kitchen and held it over his mouth and nose before following Denham down into the basement.

It had a concrete floor and white plastered walls. Along the wall opposite the stairs were shelves lined with climbing equipment. In the far corner was a metal trunk. Denham went over to it and opened it. The smell was a hundred times worse, and Denham turned his head away, gagging. McKechnie joined him and looked down into the trunk. The body had been wrapped in black garbage bags and had been bent at the waist so that it would fit

McKechnie went over to the shelving, rummaged through a pile of climbing gear and came back with a piton. He stuck the pointed end into the plastic, ripped a jagged hole in it and tore it away. 'Oh my God,' he said.

Denham took a step back. It had been a long time since he had been confronted by a corpse, but the smell of rotting flesh was something he'd never forget. He moved towards the trunk again, holding his breath. There were two holes in the shirt Geraghty was wearing and the material was stained with dried blood. The little finger and the one next to it had been chopped off. McKechnie grimaced.

'So now we know,' said Denham. He reached over and closed the trunk. 'You tidy up here, Harry. I'll phone Patsy with the bad news.'

ANDY WAS POURING herself a cup of water from the cooler when Green-eyes called her name from the door to the meeting room. Green-eyes was wearing a white sweatshirt with the sleeves pulled up above her elbows, black ski pants and the ever-present ski mask. She was holding a video cassette. 'This arrived,' she said, slotting it into the video recorder and switching on the television.

It was Katie. It was a short message, barely twenty seconds long, just saying that it was Monday, that she was OK and that she wanted to be back home with her mummy and dad. Katie looked much more scared than she'd appeared in the previous video and her voice was shaking. Andy put her hand up to her mouth as she watched.

'She's terrified,' said Andy. 'I want to speak to her.'

'You've just seen that she's OK,' said Green-eyes.

She pulled Egan's black briefcase towards her and clicked the locks open. She turned the open case so that Andy could see the contents. Sixteen oblong slabs of what looked like bright yellow marzipan, covered in thick, clear plastic. Under the plastic on each block was a white paper label with a black border containing the words EXPLOSIVE PLASTIC SEMTEX-H in capital letters.

She then produced and opened a Marks and Spencer carrier bag, took out two bread rolls and broke one in half. Inside were four silver metal tubes, each about three inches long and the thickness of a pencil, with one end crimped around two white wires that had been coiled together. The second roll contained four more tubes.

Andrea picked one of them up. It was a Mark 4 electrical detonator, the type she'd used when she made bombs for the IRA, a lifetime ago. Her hand began to shake, and she put the detonator down on the table. The contents of the briefcase and the bag brought it home to her that she was building a device that was going to be used.

'They're OK?' Green-eyes asked.

Andy nodded.

'You have to build a small bomb for us to use tomorrow. A test.'

Andy's jaw dropped. 'Why?'

'You don't have to worry about why, Andrea. Just do it. And God help you if it doesn't work.'

Day Eight

Patsy Ellis was sitting at the desk looking over a computer print-out when Liam Denham walked in. 'Good morning, Liam. Sleep well?'

Denham grunted. He'd arrived back in London in the early hours and had spent the rest of the night on a couch in an office on the floor above.

One of the three telephones on Patsy's desk rang and she lifted the receiver. She picked up a pen as she listened, making a note on a pad in front of her. She stood up and banged down the phone. 'Briefing room,' she said. 'We've identified the driver.'

Denham followed her down the corridor. On the way she shouted that she wanted everyone in the briefing room. By the time she reached the door there were more than a dozen men and women following in her wake.

Patsy went over to the whiteboard on which were stuck the photographs of Andrea's active service unit. 'Right, thanks to Chief Inspector Denham we now know who gave up Trevor. An IRA sniper, Micky Geraghty. Someone tortured and killed him several weeks ago, presumably for information about Trevor.'

She paused, then tapped the still of the van leaving the Covent Garden car park. 'Now, this is where it gets really interesting. We've identified the driver of the van. One Mark Graham Quinn. A twenty-four-year-old career criminal who has been arrested several times on armed robbery charges. He's always walked, usually because witnesses have a habit of retracting confessions before he's due to appear in court. His prints match those on one of the parking receipts, and our technical boys have a decent match between the video pictures and photographs on file with the Met. We still don't know who the passenger is, but computer enhancement has shown a tattoo on his left forearm. A lion leaping over a flag of St George.

'So what we have is a career criminal working with what we can assume is a Protestant extremist. They've kidnapped a former IRA bombmaker.' She raised an eyebrow. 'Quite a mix, I'd say. Lisa, any news about the landscaping company?'

Lisa Davies shook her head. 'The van isn't theirs. It looks as if the kidnappers just set up an imitation. We're still checking the van itself.'

'OK, keep on top of it. And everyone start putting feelers out on Quinn. But tread carefully.'

ANDY SOLDERED the copper wire to the output from the chip in the digital alarm clock, moving her head to the side to avoid the solder fumes. Green-eyes picked up one of the detonators and began to untangle the two white wires that protruded from one end. 'I thought they'd be different colours,' she said.

Andy looked up from the clock. 'Doesn't make any difference which way it's connected into the circuit. So there's no need to have different colours.'

'So all that stuff in the movies about "shall I cut the black wire or the red wire" is crap?'

Andy smiled thinly. 'No bomb-disposal man would bother cutting the wires to the detonator. There's no point—all he'd have to do is to pull the detonator out.'

Green-eyes continued to unravel the wires. Andy saw what she was doing and gestured with her chin. 'Don't separate the wires. If there's any electrical interference you can get a spark jumping between the two wires and the detonator could go off. You'd lose a hand.'

Green-eyes winced and put the detonator back down on the table. 'It's called the Faraday effect,' said Andy, adjusting the timer and setting the alarm. 'You want this set for five minutes, you said?'

'That's what he said. Five minutes.'

Andy checked the digital read-out: 300 seconds. She showed it to Green-eyes, then showed her which buttons to press to start the timer.

'It's the Faraday effect that's responsible for a lot of bombs going off prematurely. Anything that sends off radio frequencies can do it. Police radios, televisions being turned on and off, even household equipment like fridges and stereos.' Andy realised she was talking too quickly, but she wanted to keep Green-eyes distracted so she wouldn't realise that she'd slipped up. There was someone telling her what to do. Someone who'd told her to set the timer for five minutes.

'There was a volunteer killed a while back, in Aldwych, remember? The bomb he was carrying went off on a bus.'

Green-eyes nodded. 'I remember.'

'The papers said it was because a guy with stereo headphones sat next to him. Turned up the sound, and bang. That's the Faraday effect.'

Green-eyes shook her head thoughtfully. 'Dangerous business.'

'This bomb, the small one. It's just a test, right?' Andy asked.

'We want to make sure that the stuff will explode,' said Green-eyes.

'You think I'd try to trick you? You think I'd risk my daughter?'

'If you've done your job properly, you've nothing to worry about.'

LIAM DENHAM WANDERED into the briefing room and walked over to where Patsy was sitting at a desk, deep in conversation with Lisa Davies. She looked up, her face flushed with excitement.

'Liam. I think we've got a lead on the van they took Andrea away in. The Transit. It's made more than half a dozen trips into the City over the past two months. The last one three days ago.'

Lisa handed Denham a computer print-out. It was a list of dates and times. The first date was about a week before Katie had been kidnapped. At the top of the print-out was a description of the van and its registration number.

'City of London police,' said Patsy in answer to Denham's unspoken question. 'They record all vehicles entering and leaving the centre. I think we can assume that London's the target now.'

Denham handed the print-out back to Lisa. 'What next?' he asked.

'We're going to have to inform the City of London police and the Met. They can start looking for the van. But until we know exactly where the bomb is, there's not much else we can do.'

Lisa's brow furrowed into deep creases. 'Shouldn't we be warning people, giving them the chance to stay out of the City?'

Patsy stood up, shaking her head. 'Absolutely not. There'd be an uncontrollable panic. The City would grind to a halt. Billions of pounds would be lost.'

'Maybe that's what they want,' mused Denham.

'What do you mean?' asked Patsy.

'Maybe it's financial and not political. If it was political, there are easier places to stage a spectacular.'

'That's assuming it is a spectacular, Liam.'

'Six trips? They must be using the van to transport equipment. Six trips is a lot of equipment, so I think it's fair to assume it's going to be a big one. They wouldn't go to all this trouble to build a few letter bombs, would they?'

'That's what you think? They're building the bomb on-site?'

'Why else?'

Patsy considered what Denham had said and then looked at her wristwatch. 'Hetherington's going to be here in a few minutes. I'd better brief him.'

'One thing before you rush off,' said Denham. 'The wee girl? What are we doing to find her?'

Patsy put a hand on Denham's arm and guided him over to a relatively quiet corner of the room. 'It's a question of priorities, Liam. We neutralise the bomb. We take the participants into custody. Then we get the girl back. It has to be done in that order.'

Denham sighed mournfully. 'Aye, you might be right.'

'Have you heard from McCormack?'

'Not yet. I'll give him a call.'

Patsy looked at her watch again. 'I've got to go, Liam. I'll talk to you later, OK?'

Denham watched her walk away. She was right, of course. The bomb took precedence over Katie. But knowing the decision was a logical one didn't make it any easier to accept. Denham had lost a child, a long, long time ago, and the pain was something he wouldn't wish on anyone. He lit a cigarette, then went in search of an empty office from where he could phone McCormack.

'Ah, it's you, Liam,' the IRA man answered. 'I might have guessed. It's names you're ringing for, I suppose.' McCormack laughed softly. 'Right turn of events this, isn't it?'

'The new order, Thomas. Did you come up with anyone?'

'I've one name. George McEvoy. Do you know him?'

'I know of him. Did twelve in Long Kesh, didn't he?'

'That's him. He was with the Civil Administration Team. Lives in Dundalk with his brother, but he hasn't been seen for a month or so.'

'What was he doing with the CAT?'

'What do you think? You know what CAT does.'

'Kidnappings?'

There was a short pause. 'I see what you mean. Yes, he could be the one who's got the little girl.'

'Can you give me his address? I'll run a check on his credit cards, just in case.'

McCormack gave Denham the address and he wrote it down in his notebook. 'Anyone else gone missing?' he asked.

'No one obvious. Did you talk to Micky Geraghty?'

Denham hesitated. McCormack picked up on it immediately.

'What's wrong?'

'He's dead, Thomas. Murdered. Someone tortured him, presumably to get information on Andrea Sheridan.'

'Shit,' said McCormack quietly. 'He was a good 'un.'

Denham said nothing. Geraghty had been an IRA sniper with a good number of kills to his credit. While he took no pleasure in the man's death, he wasn't about to grieve for him.

'Who's handling the arrangements?' McCormack asked.

Denham explained that they'd had to leave the body where they'd found it, in the basement of the farmhouse.

'Do me a favour,' said McCormack. 'Call me when it's over. I'll take care of it.'

Denham promised that he would. The IRA would probably give Geraghty a full military funeral. It would be a celebration of the man's career with the terrorist organisation, but Denham knew it would be churlish not to agree to McCormack's request.

THE DOOR to Jason Hetherington's office was ajar, but Patsy still knocked before entering. He was sitting behind his desk, reading a file, an antique pair of pince-nez glasses perched on the end of his nose. He was wearing a dark blue Savile Row suit with the faintest of pinstripes, a crisp white shirt and a Garrick Club tie. 'Patsy, my dear, thanks for dropping by.' Hetherington was Deputy Director-General (Operational), second only to MI5's Director-General. He was responsible for all the agency's operational activities, and had been Patsy's mentor for the past ten years. 'Any news?'

'It's definitely London,' she said, dropping into one of the chairs opposite Hetherington's desk.

Hetherington took off his spectacles and placed them carefully on top of the file he'd been studying. 'Ah, that's not good.'

Patsy smiled at the understatement. 'A van they've been using has been in and out of the City.'

'And your recommended course of action?'

'We look for the van, obviously. And for Quinn. We'll liaise with the local police, but without saying why. They're just being told not to approach him if he's spotted. We're assuming the device is being constructed somewhere in the City, so we're working through all new leases taken on within the past six months. It's an outside chance considering the possible time frame, but long shots sometimes pay off.'

'And the telephone surveillance is in place?'

'GCHQ are on-line. BT and Telecom Eireann are cooperating.'

'Another long shot?'

Patsy looked pained—she was all too well aware of how little they had to go on. Two long shots and a needle in a haystack.

'She's called her husband once. We believe she'll try again.' She spoke quickly, not giving him the chance to interrupt. 'A stronger possibility is that she'll be able to get to a phone of her own accord. Call her husband without them knowing. Having said that, I feel it's more likely that it's her daughter she'll try to make contact with. The kidnappers have no reason not to allow her to speak to her daughter.'

'Unless she's already dead.' They sat in silence for a while. 'Possible targets?' Hetherington said eventually.

'If it's political, it could be anything from the Stock Exchange to the Bank of England. If it's a high profile they want, they could be targeting the NatWest Tower or Lloyd's of London.'

'So can we at least increase security there?'

'I'm reluctant to inform the local police, Jason. All it takes is one copper warning his wife to stay out of the City for a while and the word would get around. I'd rather keep it in-house for as long as possible. But I think it's time to call Hereford. When we're ready to move we're going to have to move fast. They have a Special Projects team on standby at the Regent's Park barracks, but I was thinking of requesting a sixteen-man troop from Counter-Revolutionary Warfare Wing. We can have them on standby here.'

Hetherington nodded. 'Agreed. What about D11?'

'I'd rather keep Met involvement to a minimum.'

Hetherington put his spectacles on again and peered over the top of them. 'If anything goes wrong and the Met were kept out of it, the Commissioner's going to do everything he can to distance himself,' he warned. 'There could be a lot of mud flying around, and it'll be heading in our direction. It won't be the SAS that gets the blame. It'll be you and me.'

'I appreciate that, Jason. But the more they're involved, the greater the chance that something will go wrong.'

Hetherington pursed his lips. 'Very well,' he said. 'I'll try to get approval for that. Spread the responsibility, as it were.'

He picked up the file he'd been reading. Patsy was dismissed.

ANDY MADE SURE that her industrial respirator was snug against her face, then slid her plastic goggles down over her eyes. Green-eyes had trouble fitting the respirator over her ski mask. 'Why do we need these?' she asked.

'The aluminium,' said Andy. 'You've got to keep it out of your eyes and lungs.' They were standing next to a line of three desks, on which were containers of the dried ammonium nitrate, aluminium powder, soap powder, sawdust and cans of diesel oil.

Andy showed Green-eyes how to measure out the correct amounts of the ingredients into a large Tupperware container.

'What's the point of the aluminium powder and the oil?'

Andy explained as she mixed the ingredients with a wooden stirrer. 'The oil's to help the aluminium to stick to the ammonium nitrate. It's the aluminium that makes it such a good explosive. When it oxidises in the initial explosion, it burns like crazy.'

'And the sawdust and soap?'

'They keep the density down which enhances the detonation. The greater the density, the harder it is to get it to explode.'

They carried their Tupperware containers over to the tumble driers and put one container in each drier.

'Ten minutes on the lowest setting should do it,' said Andy. 'It's just a way of mixing it efficiently.'

'How long will it take to do all four thousand pounds?'

Andy did a quick calculation in her head. 'About twenty-four hours,' she said.

Green-eyes went over to a desk where Andy had been building the wiring circuit. 'This is ready?' she asked.

'I've tested it a dozen times with bulbs,' said Andy. 'I won't put the detonators in until the last minute.'

'Detonators? Plural?'

'It's always safer to use more than one. Sometimes they fail. In Belfast they used three. The last thing they wanted was for an unexploded device to fall into the hands of the army. The IRA's signature would be all over it.'

'What do you mean, signature?'

'The style. The technique. Every bombmaker has his or her own way of putting a device together, as distinctive as a signature.'

Andy looked across at Green-eyes. Did she know about a bombmaker's signature? Did the person she was working for? There was no way of knowing without asking directly, and Andy didn't expect a truthful answer. If they were forcing her to build the bomb so that it looked as if it were the work of the IRA, then they'd hardly be likely to admit it to her. Because the only way the deception would work was if Andy wasn't alive to contradict the evidence.

'Show me again how we set the clock,' Green-eyes said.

Andy went through the procedure, using flashlight bulbs where the detonators would be. The lights winked on as the tumble driers finished their cycle.

Half an hour later they had fifty pounds of the explosive mixture in Tupperware containers on the desk in front of them. Green-eyes reached for a box of medical gloves and put on a pair. 'Did you wear gloves when you prepared the explosive?' she asked.

Andy shook her head. 'No. You have to be able to squeeze the explosive into the form you want it. It'd be like trying to make pastry with gloves on.'

Green-eyes nodded as she lifted a Samsonite hard-shell suitcase onto another desk and opened it.

Andy pulled the lid off one of the containers. The mixture was the consistency of bread dough, and still smelt strongly of fertiliser. She poured two batches of the mixture into the suitcase, then flattened it with her hands.

'You're going to take this away now?' Andy asked. 'Because if you're not, we should hold off making it live until you're ready.'

Green-eyes looked at her watch. 'As soon as it's ready, we're off.'

Andy nodded. 'OK. But remember what I said about the Faraday effect. Stay away from electrical equipment.' She gestured at the line of ovens and the two tumble driers. 'We should unplug those before we make the circuit live. And remember, no mobile phones.'

Andy wasn't sure if mobile phones would have any effect on the circuit. But she wanted to make sure that Green-eyes left the phone in the briefcase when she went out.

'But it's safe, right?' asked Green-eyes.

Andy grimaced. 'It's a bomb.' She patted the suitcase. 'When this goes off, it'll kill anyone within a three-hundred-foot range. So safe isn't really an appropriate description, is it?'

She hollowed out a space in the fertiliser/aluminium mixture about a foot square. She unwrapped one of the blocks of Semtex and placed it in the space, pressing it down with the flat of her hands. Then she lifted up the electric circuit and placed it onto the Semtex, and pushed two Mark 4 detonators into the Semtex at an angle so that they were almost completely buried, just half an inch sticking out. She pressed the batteries slightly, so that they were stuck in the Semtex, then carefully moved the digital clock and the wires leading to it, resting them in the lid of the suitcase. She opened the remaining two Tupperware containers and scraped the rest of the fertiliser/aluminium mixture into the case. Again she used her hands to press the mixture down, kneading it to force out any trapped air. She put two empty rubbish bags on top of the mixture, then laid the clock on top of them. She put another half-dozen empty bags on top of the clock to protect it when she closed the lid.

'That's it,' she said. 'It's live but it won't go off until you set the clock.' Andy closed the lid and snapped the catches shut. 'Keep it flat. If you try to carry it by the handle, everything'll move inside.'

'It's going to look strange, carrying it like that, isn't it?'

Andy shrugged. 'That's not really my problem, is it?'

Green-eyes took off her gloves. 'Right, I'm going to the office to get changed. As soon as we've taken the case out of here, you start preparing all the rest of the stuff. We'll need it for tomorrow.'

'Tomorrow? You're going to do it tomorrow?'

'Just get the mixture ready,' said Green-eyes, and walked away.

Andy shivered. Tomorrow? She had to do something to stop them. But what? What could she do that would prevent them blowing up the building, without endangering Katie?

A few minutes later, Green-eyes came out of the office. She'd changed out of her overalls and into a blue suit with a short skirt and high heels. It made the ski mask she was wearing all the more sinister. The Runner was with her. He'd also taken his overalls off and was wearing a denim jacket and jeans.

Green-eyes nodded at the Wrestler. 'We'll be back this evening. Keep an eye on her.'

JASON HETHERINGTON WALKED into the main briefing room, followed by a man in his twenties with short blond hair. The man had inquisitive eyes that flicked from side to side as he entered the room, taking everything in. He was wearing a brown leather jacket over a pale green sweatshirt, blue Wrangler jeans and Nike training shoes, and looked like a small-time drug dealer on the make.

'Ah, there she is,' murmured Hetherington as he spotted Patsy Ellis crouched over a computer terminal. 'Patsy, I'd like you to meet Captain Payne, Special Projects Team. He and his men have just arrived from Hereford, and they are unpacking their equipment in the gymnasium.'

Payne stuck out his hand. 'Stuart,' he said.

Patsy shook. He had a firm, dry grip, though he didn't try to impress by crushing her fingers. 'Patsy Ellis,' she said. 'Glad to have you on board, Stuart.'

Hetherington motioned with his hand that they should go back to his office, and they walked along the corridor together.

'We're reasonably certain that they're in the City,' said Patsy. 'We've identified one as a career criminal, an armed robber.'

Payne frowned and scratched the back of his head. 'I thought this was an IRA operation.'

'The bombmaker's IRA. But she's working under coercion. Her daughter's been kidnapped,' she said, 'they're threatening to kill the child unless she cooperates. We think the bomb is already in the City but we don't know.'

'OK. So basically we'll have to play it by ear? No rehearsals?'

'I'm afraid not,' said Patsy.

Payne smiled broadly. 'That's what we do best,' he said.

McCracken and Quinn picked up Egan at a service station on the M1 outside Luton. 'Everything OK?' he asked.

'We're on schedule,' McCracken said. 'Tomorrow afternoon.'

'Excellent,' said Egan. He settled back in the seat as Quinn drove back onto the motorway and accelerated towards Milton Keynes.

On Egan's instructions, they kept to just below seventy miles an hour, but it still took them less than half an hour to drive the Volvo to the industrial estate. Egan got out and unlocked the main door, and Quinn drove the Volvo into the factory and parked next to the Transit van. McCracken and Quinn climbed out while Egan opened the boot and looked down at the suitcase. It always amazed him how something so innocuous could do so much damage. Five cubic feet of chemicals at most, a few pence worth of electrical components, and yet it had the capacity to completely destroy the building they were in. Egan put on a pair of medical gloves.

McCracken opened the back of the Transit while Egan carefully lifted the suitcase out of the boot. He carried it over to the van and slid it along the metal floor. Quinn came up behind him. 'Shall I put the Volvo outside,' he asked.

Egan shook his head. 'Get the petrol and douse the offices, yeah?'

Quinn went over to a stack of red petrol cans and picked up two of them. McCracken watched as Egan opened the suitcase. 'Why the gloves?' she asked. 'It's all going to go up in flames anyway.'

Egan looked over his shoulder. 'They can get partial prints off anything these days, Lydia. Even after an explosion. DNA, too. A few skin cells or a piece of hair. The authorities will be all over the place once it goes off. The only prints I want them to find are the woman's.' He checked his Rolex and compared it to the digital read-out on the bomb's timer. Exact to the second. 'Right, show me what to do,' he said.

McCracken talked him through the setting of the alarm, then he pressed the button to activate it.

'OK,' he said. 'Five minutes.' He could feel his heart pounding. By pressing the alarm button he'd irrevocably changed the nature of the beast. Now the bomb was live. Now it had the power of life and death. He shut the suitcase lid and closed the rear door of the van.

'Better get the Volvo out before the fumes get any worse,' he said. McCracken got into the car and reversed out through the doorway.

Over by the offices, Quinn threw down the two petrol cans and went over to the stack for two more.

Egan looked at his watch again. A little over four minutes. Plenty of time, and he calmly closed the rear doors of the Transit.

He walked over to where Quinn was slopping petrol around the corridor between the plasterboard offices, took his automatic out of his jacket pocket and slammed the butt against the back of Quinn's head. The man fell without a sound, and Egan deftly caught the petrol can before it hit the ground. He hefted the unconscious man over his shoulder and carried him and the half-empty can of petrol over to the Transit. He put Quinn in the driver's seat, then poured the rest of the petrol over him before looking at his Rolex again. Two minutes. Time to go.

McCracken was gunning the engine of the Volvo. 'You're cutting it close,' she said.

'Ninety seconds,' he said, pulling open the passenger door and climbing in. 'Anyway, we want to see if it goes up.'

She looked at him expectantly. 'Where's Mark?'

'Mark's not coming with us,' said Egan, taking off his gloves.

'What?'

Egan pointed ahead. 'Lydia, I think if we're going to discuss this, we should be doing it while we're on the move. Don't you?'

McCracken put the Volvo in gear and drove off. Egan looked around casually, checking to see if they were being observed, but the industrial estate's pavements were deserted. McCracken drove quickly out of the estate and onto the main road to Milton Keynes.

'What happened back there?' said McCracken, her eyes flicking between the traffic and the industrial estate on her right.

'You said it yourself, Lydia—we don't need to be carrying a liability. And we certainly don't need Andrea looking over her shoulder at Quinn every other minute.' He looked at his watch. 'Ten seconds. Nine. Eight. Seven. Six.'

There was a flash of light from the skylights at the top of the factory unit, followed almost immediately by a shower of debris erupting from the roof. A second later there was a dull crump that they felt as much as heard.

Egan looked at his watch and frowned. 'Five seconds early.' He looked across at the burning building. It was already well ablaze and little remained of the roof. Thick plumes of smoke were spiralling upwards. By the time the emergency services arrived, there'd be nothing left.

'And that was just fifty pounds?' asked McCracken.

'Pretty impressive, huh? Andrea knows her stuff.' Egan looked across at her and smiled thinly. 'You're thinking of the damage that a four-thousand-pound bomb will do, aren't you?'

McCracken shrugged.

'It's gonna be awesome, Lydia. Absolutely awesome.'

MARTIN REACHED OUT for the black phone, but pulled his hand back when Fanning gave a small shake of his head. 'I keep wanting to check that they're working,' said Martin.

'They're fine.' Fanning ran a hand through his thick blond hair. He tapped the digital tape recorder. 'This monitors the signal constantly. Any problems with the line and it'd show a red light. Relax.'

'Relax?' Martin stood up and paced around the office. Carter and Denham watched him from the sofa. 'What if she doesn't call? What if they don't let her use the phone?'

Carter pushed herself up out of the sofa and went over to Martin. 'Martin, you have to take it easy. When she calls, the kidnappers are going to be listening in. If they suspect you're with someone, they'll cut the connection immediately. You have to stay calm.'

The door opened and they all turned to look at Patsy Ellis. 'There's been an explosion,' she said. 'It was in Milton Keynes.'

Martin bent over as if he'd been punched in the stomach. He struggled to speak but couldn't find any words. Milton Keynes? What the hell did that have to do with Andy?

'Sit down, Martin,' said Patsy. Carter took his arm and eased him down onto a chair.

'We've no idea what happened,' continued Patsy. 'Other than that there was an explosion on an industrial estate just outside Milton Keynes. Early reports are that there was a vehicle inside a factory unit and that it exploded. There was one person killed.'

'Just one?' asked Denham.

'That's the information we have.'

Denham went over to Martin and sat down at the table next to him. 'That's good news, Martin. She wouldn't have been on her own, not with the bomb. If it was an accident, there would have been more killed.' He scratched the birthmark on his neck. 'And there's no reason for her to be in Milton Keynes. No terrorist is going to waste a bomb on Milton Keynes.'

O'KEEFE WHIRLED round as he felt a hand on his shoulder, but instantly relaxed when he saw it was McCracken. She'd put her ski mask on, but he could still see that she was grinning at his reaction. He pulled his respirator down. 'Didn't hear you,' he said. 'The tumble driers.'

'That's OK,' said McCracken. 'Where's Andrea?'

'Getting a drink.' He looked over her shoulder. 'Where's Quinn?'

'Quinn's not with us any more.'

'What? He's buggered off?'

'Not exactly.' She frowned at the line of black bags of the mixed explosive. 'Is that all?'

'Come on, it's hard bloody work, this. There's only the two driers.'

'We've got to get this done by tomorrow or Egan's going to be on the warpath.'

'It'll be done. We could do with Quinn, though.'

'Quinn's dead. He went up with the van.'

O'Keefe put down his wooden spatula. 'What the hell happened?'

McCracken explained what Egan had done. And why. O'Keefe listened in silence, then rubbed his throat. 'He's a hard bastard, is Egan. You trust him?'

'He's come through with everything he promised. A third of our money in advance, this place, the Semtex. He's a pro, and he pays. That's all that matters.'

'Aye, that's as maybe. But we should watch our backs.'

One of the tumble driers reached the end of its cycle and O'Keefe went over to it. 'I'll get Andrea,' said McCracken. 'With Quinn out of the way, she's going to have to pull her finger out.'

ANDY CLICKED the end tumbler of the combination lock and pushed the button. The lock clicked open at 864. She'd done it. She swallowed and looked up at the door. She'd been in the office for almost ten minutes and wasn't sure how long she could stay without the Wrestler wondering what she was doing.

She set the second combination dial to 000 and began working her way through the combinations. After several futile attempts, she had a sudden thought. On her own briefcase she set both locks to the same number. She wondered if Green-eyes had done the same. She set the second dial to 864, said a silent prayer, and pushed the button with her thumb. It clicked open. Her heart pounded. Just as she was about to open the briefcase, she heard footsteps. High heels, crunching softly along the carpet tiles.

Andy snapped the catches shut and slipped the briefcase under the table as the door was flung open. It was Green-eyes. 'What the hell's going on?' she asked angrily. 'I want you out there working, not in here skiving.'

Andy picked up her chicken salad roll. 'I've got to eat, haven't I?'

Green-eyes jerked her thumb at the door. 'You can eat out there.'

Andy stayed where she was. She looked at the video recorder. 'I've had a thought,' she said. 'About the timer.'

'That's another thing. That bomb went off early. Five seconds early. How could that happen?'

Andy pulled at her lower lip. 'The chip, I guess.' She went over to the video recorder and tapped the front where a digital clock was glowing blue. 'I was thinking, the timer in this would be easier to set, I've used one before.'

Green-eyes nodded thoughtfully. 'OK. Whatever.'

Andy unplugged the video recorder and carried it out.

Green-eyes looked round the room, shrugged, and followed her down the corridor.

Day Nine

Martin looked up as Denham walked in. 'Any news?' he asked.

Denham sat down opposite Martin. 'The bomb in Milton Keynes. It was the van we were looking for.'

Martin ran his hands through his hair. 'God. What if it *was* Andy?'

Denham shook his head. 'She was too professional to make a mistake. It couldn't have gone off accidentally.'

'Maybe they wanted to kill her. Maybe they blew her up?'

Denham lit a cigarette and blew smoke at the ceiling. 'If they wanted to kill her, they wouldn't use a bomb, and they wouldn't do it in Milton Keynes. We're pretty sure that it was a deliberate explosion. A test, maybe. Or a way of getting rid of the van.'

'You married, Liam?' asked Martin.

Denham nodded. 'Almost thirty years. Thirty years next year.'

'Children?'

Denham's jaw tightened. 'A daughter. She died a long time ago. Leukaemia.'

'Oh, God. I'm really sorry.'

'Yeah, she was twelve. She'd been sick for two years—in and out of the hospital we were. Chemotherapy. Radiation. Seems like most of the memories I have of her she was wearing a baseball cap.' He blew smoke at the floor.

'Children shouldn't die before their parents,' said Martin quietly. 'If anything happens to Katie . . .'

'We'll find her,' Denham assured him.

Martin's eyes were hard as he stared at Denham. 'You have to find them both, Liam. If they die, I'll die too.'

Denham reached over and gripped Martin's wrist. 'It won't come to that,' he said.

Martin just shook his head and put a hand up to his face, massaging the bridge of his nose and blinking away tears.

Denham stood up and flashed an encouraging smile at Martin, but he was staring at the carpet. He walked to the lift, travelled to the ground floor and walked out of Thames House, putting on his tweed hat and pulling it down hard as he headed towards the river. Out of habit Denham checked over his shoulder several times, but he wasn't being followed. He walked past several call boxes and chose one down a side street, where he dialled the number in Dublin. He smiled as the number rang out. It had been more than a decade since he'd phoned Eamonn Hogan, yet he'd instantly been able to retrieve the number from wherever it was in his brain that it had been filed away.

Hogan didn't answer the phone himself, but an efficient secretary put him through almost immediately. 'Liam, you old rascal, how's retirement?' asked Hogan.

'Not as quiet as I'd hoped,' said Denham. 'Look, Eamonn, I just wanted a word in your ear. Can you talk?'

'Sure.'

'George McEvoy. Remember him?'

'Unfortunately, yes. Did the dirty for the IRA's Civil Administration Team, right?'

'That's him. The thing is, I think McEvoy might be involved in something in your neck of the woods,' said Denham.

There was a pause lasting several seconds. 'This wouldn't be about the Katie Hayes girl, would it? I've been told to lay off that case, that the matter is being pursued at a higher level. Well, am I right?'

Denham cursed silently. 'You know I can't tell you, Eamonn. But I would be grateful if you'd keep an eye out for McEvoy and if he does turn up then I'd appreciate an unofficial call.' He gave Hogan the number of the mobile phone that Patsy had given him. 'That's a mobile and it's not secure,' he warned.

'They never are these days,' said Hogan. 'OK, I'll put him on our watch list. But you be careful, now Liam. You're getting too old for cloak and dagger.'

Denham snorted back a laugh and hung up.

KATIE SAT at the table, flicking through one of the comics that the Nice Man had brought her. She looked round the room. She had to escape. But how? There was only one way out of the basement and that was up the stairs and through the door. The last time she'd tried to run away she'd headed for the kitchen and that had been a mistake because the other man was there. She should have run the other way, to the front door. Then she could run away and shout for help.

She looked up at the single light bulb hanging from the ceiling. She needed to be able to hide in the dark and then run up the stairs before they saw her. She rolled up the comic and swished it through the air. If she could hit the light bulb, it would go out. But she was only little, she couldn't reach. She climbed onto the table and swung the comic at the bulb, but it was still too high.

She knelt down on the table and picked up the wooden chair she'd been sitting on. She hauled it up onto the table, set it down in the middle, and climbed up on it. It wobbled a bit, but not much. She swung the rolled-up comic and hit the bulb. It swung crazily back and forth, then the light winked out, though the glass didn't break.

She stood on the chair in darkness, suddenly afraid. She knelt down, almost lost her balance, then clambered to the floor. She groped around until she found Garfield, then crawled to the bottom of the stairs, where she curled herself up into a tight ball and waited.

ANDY BLEW on the silvery lumps of still-hot solder, then tugged gently at the wire to check that it was firmly fixed to the digital timer's circuit board. She had to force herself to concentrate on what she was doing. Her mind kept wandering to the briefcase and to what would happen if Green-eyes discovered it.

Green-eyes watched her. 'This sort of timer's reliable, is it?'

Andy nodded. 'The big advantage is that it can be set up weeks in advance. The IRA used it to bring down the Grand Hotel in Brighton. Remember, when they almost got Thatcher?'

'I remember. But we won't be needing weeks.'

Green-eyes straightened up and looked at her watch. It was the third occasion she'd looked at her watch in the past ten minutes, and Andy had the feeling that she was waiting for somebody.

Andy soldered one of the wires leading from the digital timer to a nine-volt battery. She'd already soldered another wire to the battery terminal, and she'd connected that temporarily to a bulb holder into which was screwed a small bulb. Three other wires also ran from the timer to three other bulb holders, which were also connected to batteries. Andy was using red wires from the timer to the batteries, blue wires from the batteries to the bulb holders, and brown wires from the bulb holders back to the timer. She fiddled with the timer and all four bulbs lit up.

'Excellent,' said Green-eyes.

'Do you want me to finish it now?'

Green-eyes nodded.

The briefcase full of Semtex slabs was on another table. Andy went over to it and unwrapped the blocks one by one. She began to work the blocks together like a pastry chef, squeezing out the air and forming the high explosive into one malleable roll. It was hard work, and her hands were soon aching. She flattened it out into a rough oblong, then picked it up and put it back in the briefcase, pressing it firmly into all the corners. It filled the case to a depth of almost three inches. The Semtex was, Andy knew, capable of producing a shock wave so devastating that it would virtually vaporise everything within a hundred feet. But its purpose was to act as an initiator to set off the 4,000 pounds of fertiliser explosive. If the Semtex was destructive on it own, combined with the home-made explosive it would be a hundred times more devastating.

Once she was satisfied with the Semtex, she carried the case over to the table where the electrical circuit was. She put it down and turned to Green-eyes. 'If you want me to put the detonators in the circuit, we should unplug all the electrical equipment.'

Green-eyes nodded. She went over and pulled the plugs out of the wall as Andy methodically removed the bulb holders before beginning to wire the detonators into the circuit in the places where the bulb holders had been.

Green-eyes studied the circuit that Andy was assembling. 'And you're going to use four detonators?'

Andy nodded. 'One would do the job.'

'But the more the merrier, you said.'

'They weren't my actual words,' said Andy. 'But you want more than one in case there's a failure. And the more you have, the stronger the original detonation pulse.'

'A bigger bang,' said Green-eyes, with evident satisfaction.

Andy looked up from what she was doing. 'Have you ever seen what a bomb does? The effect it has?'

Green-eyes gave Andy a withering look. 'Of course.'

'So you should know it's not a laughing matter. It's not funny. People get hurt. Legs get blown off. Children die.'

Green-eyes grabbed a handful of Andy's hair and twisted it savagely. 'You're the one who's blown up children, you bitch!' she yelled.

'I'm sorry,' said Andy, trying to push her away.

'Sorry? Sorry for what? For blowing up children?' Green-eyes slapped her across the face. Andy stared back at her, not flinching. Green-eyes drew back her hand to hit Andy again, but there was a loud knock at the reception door. 'Go to the office, now,' Green-eyes hissed. 'Close the door and don't open it until I come and get you.'

LIAM DENHAM was walking towards the office where Martin was being kept when he heard Patsy calling him. He went back along the corridor and found her sitting behind a desk in one of the offices.

'Come in and close the door, will you, Liam,' she said. Her voice was as flat and emotionless as her face, which Denham took as a bad sign. He closed the door and sat down, waiting for her to speak. 'What the hell did you think you were playing at?' she asked looking at him with cold contempt. 'K Division were on the hot line before you'd even hung up. What the hell did you think you were doing?'

'I thought I was helping,' he said.

'You were going behind my back. You were jeopardising an ongoing investigation, and if Hogan makes waves in Dublin you might well be responsible for the death of a seven-year-old girl.'

'In my own defence, I would say that I didn't mention the kidnapping. I just asked him to keep an eye out for McEvoy.'

'Hogan said it. You didn't disagree. If I wanted the Garda Siochana to be looking for the Hayes girl, I'd have made an approach through official channels.'

'And the only official action so far seems to have been to warn them off the investigation.'

Patsy narrowed her eyes. 'What are you getting at?'

Denham sighed. 'I'm starting to feel that in the rush to apprehend the bombers, the little girl is being forgotten. That's all.'

'You're retired, Liam. You're here at my request. You're not here to direct the enquiry and you're not here to criticise my performance.'

'I wasn't being critical, Patsy. That I wasn't. I was trying to help and I'm sorry if you think my attempt was misguided.'

'Misguided isn't the word that springs to mind,' said Patsy. 'I was considering reckless. Irresponsible, maybe.'

Denham sat with his head down, holding his tweed hat with both hands and fingering the fly in the brim. 'Somewhere in Ireland there's a little girl, scared out of her wits, a little girl who doesn't know that she's a pawn in a bigger game. And down the corridor there's a father who doesn't even know if he's ever going to see his daughter again. When all this is over, however it works out, Martin Hayes is going to want to know what we did to try to save his little girl. And just now, from where I'm sitting, it looks as if we're not doing a goddamned thing.' He raised his head and looked her squarely in the eyes. 'I know you have to consider the big picture. But I know what it's like to lose a child, Patsy.'

Patsy stared at Denham for several seconds. 'We're not going to agree on this, Liam,' she said eventually. 'I'm sorry.' She stood up. 'I'd rather you didn't leave the building again, until this is over. I want you here if she does call.' She opened the door for him and together they left the office.

'I suppose there is one good thing to have come out of your little escapade,' she said. 'We know that the GCHQ monitoring works. Your call was flagged immediately Hogan said "Katie".'

ANDY PUT HER EAR to the door and screwed up her face as she tried to hear what was going on outside. She heard a man's voice, but through the door it was little more than a faint rumble.

She looked down at the burgundy briefcase. If she was going to do anything, she had to do it now. The bomb was ready. All that was left to do was set the timer and put it in the middle of the bags of explosive. Andy had reached the stage where she was dispensable.

She knelt down and pulled the briefcase from under the table. The combination locks were as she'd left them, both set to eight-six-four. She flicked the catches and pulled open the lid. The mobile phone was there. But so was something else, something that took her breath away. Five video cassettes, small ones that had been taken from a video camera.

EGAN WALKED OVER to the pile of black rubbish bags. 'All done?'

'All four thousand pounds of it,' said O'Keefe, pulling off his ski mask and rubbing his face. 'We should have asked for more money.'

'You're being well paid,' said Egan.

'What happens to Quinn's share, now that he's . . . retired?'

'Retired?' Egan laughed. 'OK, Don. You and Lydia can split the money I was going to give to Quinn. Happy now?'

O'Keefe grinned and rubbed his gloved hands together. 'Suits me.'

McCracken took off her ski mask and went over to the Semtex-filled briefcase. Egan joined her. 'So everything's ready?' he said.

'All she has to do is push the detonators into the Semtex and set the timer. We don't actually need her for that.'

'No. She has to do it all. It has to look like an IRA bomb, and even the slightest deviation will tip off the investigators. How's she been?'

'She's doing as she's told.'

O'Keefe came over and looked down at the Semtex. 'What happens to her daughter? Afterwards?'

'We'll let her go. This isn't about killing children.'

'And her?' O'Keefe nodded at the offices.

'Ah,' said Egan. 'That's a whole different ball game. She has to go up with the bomb. It's not going to work if she's around to tell her story afterwards.'

'And us?' asked O'Keefe, watching Egan's face for any reaction. 'What about having us around afterwards?'

Egan grinned and put a hand on O'Keefe's shoulder.

'Don, you're as much a part of this as I am. You're hardly likely to go spilling your guts to the cops, are you? I'm paying you to do a job, and providing you behave like a professional I'll treat you like one. Might even have more work for you after this.' He patted O'Keefe gently on the cheek, then pulled a black ski mask from his jacket pocket. 'Right, final stretch. Let's get on with it.'

ANDY ROCKED BACK on her heels, staring at the five small video cassettes in horror. She picked one up. There was a handwritten label stuck to one side. Friday. On the first cassette that Green-eyes had shown her, Katie had said it was Saturday. On the second cassette she'd been shown, Katie had said it was Monday. The five cassettes in the briefcase were for the rest of the days of the week. They weren't being sent over from Ireland. They'd all been done at the same time. Andy felt suddenly sick at the realisation of what that meant. There was no proof that her daughter was still alive. She picked up the mobile phone with trembling hands.

If Katie was really dead, then she had nothing to lose by calling the police. She switched on the phone and its display glowed green. She began to tap out the emergency services number, but stopped on the second 9. What if Katie was all right? What if she was panicking for nothing? What if they'd made the tapes on the same day just to make life easier for themselves?

Andy cancelled the call. They weren't going to let her live after the bomb was ready, she was sure of that. They wanted her fingerprints all over the device so that it looked as if it was the work of the Provisionals. The deception wouldn't work if Andy was around afterwards, so they'd have to kill her. If they were going to kill her, what chance was there that they'd allow Katie to live? She started to tap out 999 again. This time she stopped on the third 9. If she called the police and Katie was alive, what then? Would the police be able to force Green-eyes to tell them where Katie was? She cancelled the call. It wasn't a decision that Andy could make on her own. She tapped out her home number. She had to speak to Martin. She closed her eyes and said a silent prayer as the number rang out.

ALL FOUR PEOPLE in the room froze as the black phone warbled. Carter grabbed for one headset, Denham picked up the other. Fanning sat down and scrutinised the digital tape recorder. Martin took a deep breath and snatched up the receiver. 'Yes?'

'Martin, thank God you're there.'

Martin felt as if he'd been punched in the solar plexus. His whole chest went numb and he couldn't breathe. He tried to speak but no words would come.

'Martin, I don't know what to do. You've got to help me. I can't face this alone. I . . .' Her words ended in sobs.

Denham frowned and scribbled a note on a sheet of paper. He held it in front of Martin's face. *'ASK HER IF ANYONE'S LISTENING.'* Carter took off her headset. 'I'll get Patsy,' she mouthed, and dashed out of the room.

'Andy, love, it's OK. It's OK.'

'It's not OK. They're making me build a bomb, a huge bomb. Hundreds of people are going to die, Martin. But if I do anything to try to stop them, they're going to kill Katie.'

'I know. I know.'

'You know? What do you mean? You can't possibly . . .'

'Andy, is anyone there with you?' Martin interrupted.

'I'm on my own, but I don't know for how much longer.'

Denham took off his headset and reached for the phone. For a second Martin tried to keep hold of the receiver, but Denham flashed him a stern look and Martin relinquished it.

'Andrea. This is Liam.'

'Liam? Liam Denham? What are you doing there?' The confusion was obvious in her voice.

'We don't have time for that, Andrea. I'm in London. So's Martin. Where's the bomb, Andrea? Where've you built the bomb?'

There was a long silence.

'Andrea, are you there?'

'You know what's happened? You know about Katie?'

'Yes. Martin's told us everything. Where are you, Andrea? Where are you calling from?' He scribbled on the paper as he spoke. '*ARE WE TRACING THIS?*' Fanning read the note and gave Denham a thumbs-up and an emphatic nod.

'Please, Liam, don't do anything that'll put Katie at risk. Promise me. Swear to me, Liam, swear to me now.'

The door opened and Patsy rushed in, followed by Carter. She picked up the headset that Denham had been using and put it on.

'We won't do anything that'll put her at risk, I promise.'

Patsy's face hardened and Denham turned away from her.

'I'll hold you to that, Liam. We both know what happened last time . . .'

'It was a mistake, Andrea. A terrible mistake,' said Denham. 'Andrea, where are you?'

There was a slight hesitation, then Andy cleared her throat. 'Cathay Tower. It's in Queen Anne Street, close to Bank tube station. We're on the ninth floor.'

Patsy wrote down the address and nodded at Denham.

'Good girl,' said Denham. 'The bomb, Andrea. How big is it?'

'Four thousand pounds.'

'What type is it?' Denham asked.

'Ammonium nitrate, aluminium powder, sawdust and diesel.'

'Initiator?'

'They've got Semtex, Liam. Semtex and Mark 4 detonators.'

'And what stage are you at?'

'It's ready, Liam. All I have to do is set the timer.'

Patsy ripped off the headset and dashed out of the office, the piece of paper in her hand.

'Liam, promise me you won't do anything until Katie's safe.'

'We'll do what we can,' said Denham, not wanting to lie to her. 'Now listen to me, Andrea. If we're going to locate Katie, you're going to have to get them to let you telephone her. If you can get her on the phone, we can trace it. Just make sure that you say "Katie", do you understand?'

'I'll try,' said Andy. 'But please, you have to promise me, don't let them storm the building, not until Katie's safe.'

Denham closed his eyes and gritted his teeth. He didn't want to lie, but he knew that the bomb was the priority, and that the life of a seven-year-old girl would come a poor second.

PATSY RUSHED into the briefing room. 'Right, everybody, stop whatever you're doing and listen. We have a location.'

Phones were slammed down and all the agents watched her as she wrote the address on the whiteboard. 'Our information is that a four-thousand-pound fertiliser bomb has been constructed on the ninth floor. Lisa, get me a large-scale map of the area, now. Anna, I need architect's floor plans of Cathay Tower. And I need to know the tenants on each floor.' Lisa Davies got up from her computer and dashed out of the room. Anna Wallace picked up the phone.

'Right, everyone else, I want you to split into four groups. We need observation points around the building and we need them fast. Jonathan, find a base that I and the SAS officer in charge can use. I want everyone in the gymnasium in five minutes.'

Jonathan Clare nodded, then half raised his hand. 'Evacuation?'

'No, not at this stage. We don't want them spooked. And we don't know what effect the bomb's going to have. If we fill the streets with people, an evacuation could kill more than it saves, if the worst comes to the worst.'

The agents in the room nodded. 'Right, let's get to it,' Patsy said. She looked at her watch. It was just after eleven o'clock in the morning. The City would be at its busiest.

ANDY CUPPED her hand round the bottom of the mobile phone. 'Liam,' she hissed. 'You mustn't let them do anything until Katie's safe. They'll kill her.'

'I'll do what I can,' said Denham. 'How many of them are there?'

'Three. Two men, one woman. They keep their faces covered all the time they're around me. One of them's called Don. And I think the woman's Irish, but the more I hear her speak the more I think she's Scottish.' She walked over to the television. The remote control for the video recorder was on top of the TV set, and she picked it up with her free hand. She stroked it against her cheek, a faraway look in her eyes, then tucked it into the back pocket of her jeans.

'Have they said why they're doing it?'

Before Andy could answer, she heard a noise behind her. Two figures wearing ski masks were standing at the open door. One was Green-eyes. The other man was a newcomer, wearing a black leather jacket and black jeans. Andy took a step back, her mouth working soundlessly. The man walked quickly towards her.

Andy held the mobile phone in front of her in a futile attempt to keep him away, as he brought the gun crashing down against her temple. She barely felt any pain. Then everything went black.

LIAM DENHAM FROWNED as he looked at the phone. 'She's gone.'

'Gone? Didn't she ask to speak to me?' asked Martin.

Denham continued to stare at the phone, a look of concern on his face. 'Maybe she was interrupted. I don't know. It just went dead.'

'Now what's going to happen?' asked Martin.

'We'll put the building under surveillance, I suppose,' said Denham. 'It's out of my hands, though, Martin. It's Patsy's game from here on in. Patsy and the SAS.'

'But Katie . . .'

'Katie's one little girl. We're going to do what we can, but a four-thousand-pound bomb could destroy the centre of the city. Hundreds could die. Thousands.'

Martin's lip curled back in a snarl and he pointed an accusing finger at Denham. 'If anything happens to Katie, I'm going to hold you responsible. If it wasn't for you using Andy as an informer, none of this would have happened. She wouldn't have built bombs for the IRA, and Katie wouldn't have been kidnapped.'

The office door opened. It was Patsy Ellis. She sensed the tension immediately and motioned with her head for Carter and Fanning to leave. On the way out, Fanning popped the cassette tape out of the recorder and handed it to her.

'What's going on?' she asked.

'He said you're going to send in the SAS,' said Martin. 'If they go in, we might never find Katie.'

'Martin, our best hope is for the SAS to get in there and secure the building so that the explosive officers can disable the bomb. Then we can get them to tell us where they're holding Katie.'

'And what if all the kidnappers are killed? What then?'

'That won't happen. The SAS are experts at this sort of thing.'

'The SAS don't shoot guns out of people's hands, they shoot to kill,' Martin shouted.

'No one's going to shoot to kill,' said Patsy. 'We're going to monitor the situation, see what they're doing. It could be that they'll simply set the bomb and leave, in which case we could move in without a shot being fired.'

Martin put both his hands up to his face and rubbed the palms into his eyes. He sat down at the table and sighed mournfully.

Patsy put a hand on his shoulder. 'We're going to do everything we can to get your daughter back, Martin.' She looked at her Cartier wristwatch. 'We're wasting time arguing about this. We have to go.'

'Go where?'

'We're setting up an observation base close to the target building.' She turned to Denham. 'Liam, you'd better come with us.'

Martin stood up. 'I'm coming too. If you're going to send in the SAS, I want to be there when you do it.'

'Absolutely not,' said Patsy. 'Liam, let's go.'

She made to walk by Martin, but he grabbed her by the upper arm, his fingers digging into the flesh. 'I have the right to be there,' he hissed. 'It's my wife's life on the line here. My wife and my daughter.'

'You're hurting me, Mr Hayes.'

Martin let go of her. 'I'm sorry,' he said. 'But let me come with you. I won't get in the way. I just want to be there.' He gestured around the office. 'I can't sit here, not knowing what's going on.'

Denham looked at Patsy. 'I'll stick with him,' he said. 'And we might need an insight into the way she'll react. It's been ten years since I worked with her. Martin here could be a help to us.'

Patsy looked at the two men, then nodded curtly. Denham and Martin followed her out of the office. Martin patted Denham on the back, unable to find the words to thank him.

They walked quickly along the corridor and down two flights of stairs to the gymnasium. Exercise machines had been moved to the side to give the SAS troopers space to spread out their gear. There were fifteen of them, all dressed in bomber jackets of various colours, jeans and training shoes. Several of the men had opened long, thin metal cases, revealing rifles with telescopic sights attached.

Captain Payne was bent over a map with two of his men. He looked up as Patsy came over and introduced Denham and Martin. Payne tapped the map. 'Cathay Tower,' he said. 'We're going to need the tenth floor evacuated. Minimum.'

Patsy nodded. 'I'll send my people in to clear those offices. Will your men be going in?'

Payne shook his head. 'The troop at Regent's Park under Captain Crosbie is already on its way. I'm to liaise with you and we'll use my men for surveillance and long-range sniping.'

Jonathan Clare walked across the gym towards them. Patsy turned her head and he gave her a thumbs-up. 'We have an observation point,' he said. 'Solicitor's office. Hetherington knows him, apparently and he's gone straight over there.'

More agents were filing into the gym, forming a group in front of a wall lined with climbing bars. 'Is it OK if I address your men along with my people?' Patsy asked the SAS officer, not wanting to cut across his line of command.

'Go ahead,' he said with a grin.

Patsy strode into the middle of the gym.

'OK, we're going to have to move quickly, so this is the only group briefing we're going to have. From here on the one thing we all have to keep at the forefront of our minds is that we're dealing with a four-thousand-pound fertiliser bomb. Bigger than any bomb used by any terrorist group anywhere in the world. Captain Payne and I will be based in an office overlooking the tower. Jonathan has the address and numbers. We'll have radios, but no one uses a radio in the vicinity of the building. Any radio transmission could set off the bomb.

'An SAS troop will be moving into the tenth floor. Gordon, your team and Lisa's are to clear that floor. Subtly. It mustn't look like an evacuation. Lifts two-thirds full, a mixed group in each lift. Everyone out moves well away from the scene. You'll be working with SAS troopers, armed and in plain clothes.' Gordon Harris and Lisa Davies nodded.

'We'll have snipers covering the area, and we're going to want long-distance surveillance mikes and thermal imaging equipment, with all feeds sent to our surveillance HQ. Jonathan, can you take charge of that? Right, let's get to it.'

EGAN GRABBED ANDY by the hair and dragged her out of the office and along the corridor. McCracken followed him, holding the phone which Andy had dropped. 'Find out who she was calling!' Egan shouted. He hauled Andy into the main office area, where O'Keefe was watching open-mouthed, and then let go of her hair.

McCracken checked the numbers dialled and peered at the display. 'Ireland,' she said. 'Dublin. She was calling her husband. That was the only call.'

'What's happening?' asked O'Keefe.

'The bitch was on the phone,' said Egan. He turned to McCracken. 'What the hell was she doing with a phone anyway?'

'I don't know. It was in the briefcase. Locked.'

'Oh, that's all right, then,' said Egan, his voice loaded with sarcasm. 'I told you to watch her. I told you not to trust her.'

He knelt down by Andy's side and began slapping her face, trying to bring her round.

'Why don't we just shoot her now?' said McCracken. 'The bomb's ready. We could set the timers and she'll go up with it.'

Egan shook his head. 'I want to know what she said to her husband. She might have told him to call the cops.'

'All the more reason to kill her now,' said O'Keefe.

Egan studied him with unblinking pale blue eyes. 'Who died and left you in charge, Don? We've still got her daughter—she's not going to endanger the kid.'

Egan went over to the water cooler and carried the reservoir over to where Andy lay. He slowly poured the contents over her until she began to recover consciousness, coughing and spluttering and putting her hands up to try to ward off the torrent of water.

PATSY CLIMBED out of the car and looked up at the office block. 'Tenth floor,' said Bingham. 'Donovan, Scott and Associates.' A black Rover containing Denham and Martin pulled up behind them. The SAS captain and his two troopers carried their kitbags into the office foyer, and they all rode up in the lift together.

Two MI5 agents were in reception, and one of them took them through to a large office where Hetherington was watching a team of half a dozen of the agency's surveillance experts unpack their equipment as he talked into a mobile phone.

The office was huge, wood-panelled, with a massive oak desk at one end, two chesterfield sofas and an oak table with eight chairs around it. The blinds were drawn and the lights were on.

The SAS captain and his two troopers dropped their kitbags on one of the chesterfields and went over to the window. Patsy joined them, and they pushed the slats apart. Hetherington came up behind them, putting his phone away. He pointed to a glass and steel tower directly in front of them.

'The blinds are drawn. White vertical ones. See them?'

'Got it,' said Patsy.

'We've got people to the north and east,' said Hetherington.

'I'd like to put snipers on the roof here,' said Captain Payne. 'Can we have access?'

'It's being arranged,' said Hetherington. 'Our people are installing long-range eavesdroppers as we speak. Patsy, a word.'

Two of the surveillance technicians were unpacking thermal imaging equipment from metal cases. Payne went over to watch as they attached the devices to tripods. They resembled huge pairs of binoculars with soda siphon cartridges attached to the top. They were capable of picking up heat sources through concrete, effectively allowing the viewer to look through walls.

Hetherington took Patsy over to the far corner of the office. 'The PM's been made aware of the situation,' he said. 'And he wants the immediate area evacuated. He's taking the view that if we know there's a bomb in that building, it would be political suicide to allow civilians to remain in the area.'

Patsy nodded. If the PM had made a decision, there was no point in arguing. 'OK. I've requested a team of the Met's explosives officers to be on standby.'

'The Commissioner has been informed and that's in hand. Now, the evacuation. What's the position regarding the building itself?'

'We're clearing the tenth floor and the Counter-Revolutionary team is moving in. Once they're in position, we can use our people to clear the rest of the floors, but it's going to have to be done carefully.'

'Agreed. Carefully, but quickly. If we use the lifts and the stairways how long do you think it'll take to evacuate the building?'

She did a quick calculation in her head. 'An hour, maybe. I'd recommend we take everyone out through the car park.'

'Agreed. Now, regarding the evacuation of the surrounding buildings. The Commissioner wants to set up roadblocks to stop anyone entering the area.'

Patsy pulled a face. 'Jason, if they see what's going on . . .'

'The blinds are closed—they can't see out. We'll tell everyone there's a gas leak. We'll have gas company people all over the place. We'll put a warning on radio and television.'

'That won't fool them,' said Patsy.

'No, but it's better than nothing. We have to evacuate, Patsy. The PM won't stand for anything less.'

ANDY SCUTTLED BACKWARDS, away from the man who'd been pouring water over her. She was soaked, and with every movement of her head she felt as if she was going to pass out again.

'Who did you talk to, Andrea?' said the man. He had an American accent. He pulled a silencer out of his jacket pocket and screwed it into the barrel of his gun, watching her all the time.

Andy looked across at Green-eyes. She was also holding a gun and aiming it at Andy's chest. She looked back at the man. There was no point in lying because they'd have been able to call up the last number dialled on the mobile. 'My husband,' she said. 'I wanted to know if he'd heard from Katie.'

The man's face was hidden by the ski mask, but Andy could see his eyes harden. 'Why would he have heard from Katie?' he asked.

'I don't know. I thought maybe the kidnappers might have called him. I saw the videos. I thought . . .' Her voice tailed off.

The man looked across at Green-eyes. 'The videos were in the briefcase,' Green-eyes explained.

The man nodded and looked at Andy again. 'And you thought your daughter was already dead.' He tilted his head to one side as he looked at her. 'She isn't, Andrea. She's still very much alive. The videos were to put your mind at ease, that's all.'

Andy wrapped her arms around herself, beginning to shiver uncontrollably. 'I don't believe you,' she said.

He gestured with his gun. 'I don't care if you believe me or not. The rules have changed. You're going to set the timer, right now.'

Andy shook her head.

The man levelled the gun at her left foot. 'I'll shoot your foot first. Then your knee. Then your stomach. You'll do it eventually, Andrea, so why not save yourself the pain?'

'You're going to kill me anyway,' Andy said flatly.

'Dead is dead, that's true. But there are degrees of pain.'

Andy turned her head and closed her eyes, waiting for the bullet to tear into her flesh and smash through the bone.

MARTIN TAPPED the technician on the shoulder. The man took his face away from the eyepiece. 'Can I have a look?' asked Martin.

The technician stood to the side so that Martin could look through the binoculars. 'What am I looking at?' he asked.

'Thermal images,' said the man. 'It picks up body heat, any heat sources, you can see right through walls into the building.'

The background was dark and he could make out vague dark green shapes. Desks. Chairs. Pillars. And four light green figures that flickered as they moved. There was no way of telling which was male and which was female, no way of knowing which was his wife.

Anna Wallace came into the room, holding three cardboard tubes. 'I've got the floor plans. This is the ninth,' she said to Patsy, pulling out one of the drawings and laying it on the desk.

Captain Payne walked over and joined Patsy and Anna. He scratched his chin as he scrutinised the plan of the office. 'What do you think?' asked Patsy.

Payne tapped the area of the lift lobby, then ran his finger along the reception area, to the open-plan area. 'This is a problem,' he said. 'It's going to take at least four seconds to take out the door and get into the open-plan area, where the tangos and the bomb are. That's way too long.' He frowned. 'We have to go in through the windows without our guys getting tangled up in the blinds. We're going to have to blow them in. Shaped charges. And with a four-thousand-pound bomb in there, that's going to be a tad . . . interesting.'

'We have visuals!' shouted one of the technicians. There were eight monitors on the table. On two of them were thermal views similar to the one that Martin had seen through the binoculars.

Captain Payne tapped out a number on his mobile phone. 'Yeah, Crosbie? We have visuals. Four tangos. Repeat, four tangos. Call me when you're in position.'

Martin looked at Denham and frowned. 'Tangos?' he mouthed.

'Targets,' whispered Denham. 'Tango means target.'

The picture on one of the monitors began to swing from side to side. Martin could make out more desks, a mound of something in the middle of the office area, but no more green, glowing figures.

'What are we going to do about sound?' Payne asked. 'Do you want us to try through the ceiling? We could push fibre optics through.'

Patsy shook her head. 'Let's see how we get on with our laser mikes on the roof. Shouldn't be long.'

She peered at the monitors on the table, then pointed at a dark green mound in the centre of the office. 'That's it,' she said. 'A four-thousand-pound fertiliser bomb. Enough to blow the whole building to kingdom come.'

THE MAN DRAGGED Andy across the floor. 'Set the timer,' he shouted. 'Finish the bomb or I'll blow your knee-cap off.'

She used the table leg to pull herself up and stared down at the open briefcase. The silver detonators lay on the Semtex, and around them the cluster of different-coloured wires. The timer was glowing, the digits all reading zero.

'Do it,' said the man. He aimed the gun at her left knee.

Andy sat down. She brushed her hair away from her eyes, then picked up an elastic band and used it to tie her hair back into a ponytail. One by one, she pushed the detonators into the Semtex.

She sniffed and rubbed her nose with the back of her hand. 'How long?' she asked. 'What do you want me to set it for?'

'One hour,' said the man. 'Sixty minutes.'

PATSY TOOK her phone away from her mouth. 'Six floors of Cathay Tower clear so far,' she said to Hetherington.

Hetherington nodded his approval. He and Payne were watching the eight screens showing the thermal images. One of the glowing green figures was bent at the waist, obviously sitting, while the three other figures stood around it. Hetherington tapped the image of the seated figure on one of the screens. 'If I was a gambling man, I'd say that was Tango Four.'

Payne nodded. 'She's working on the timer.'

'Tango Four?' said Martin.

'Your wife,' said Hetherington.

'My understanding is that tango means target,' said Martin. 'My wife is not a target. She's a victim. I don't want anyone referring to her as a target.'

'You're quite right, Mr Hayes,' said Hetherington. 'I apologise.'

Before he could say anything else, one of the technicians shouted over at them. 'We have sound.'

There were small loudspeakers on either side of the bank of monitors. There was a hissing sound, then suddenly Martin realised that it was Andy's voice he was listening to.

'. . . going to do? You can't go through with this.'

She sounded close to tears.

'Set it, Andrea.' A man's voice. An American accent. 'Sixty minutes. Do it, Andrea. Do it or I'll put a bullet in your knee.'

'We're going to have to move fast,' said Payne. 'An hour's no time at all.'

'We have to talk to the PM first,' said Patsy.

'What's happening?' asked Martin, looking over his shoulder at Hetherington, who was whispering into his mobile phone, a look of urgency etched into his features. 'What's going on?' He was ignored. He stared at the bank of monitors as he realised for the first time what he was looking at. The man with the American accent was pointing a gun at his wife, and if she didn't do as she was told, he was going to shoot her.

ANDY SAT BACK and closed her eyes. 'It's done,' she said. The digital display showed 01.00.

'Take it over to the bags,' said the man in the ski mask, gesturing with his handgun.

Andy carried the briefcase over to the pile of black rubbish bags. She placed it on top of the pile and turned to face the man.

'And now what? Now you kill me, right?'

The man said nothing, but Green-eyes pointed at Andy. 'That's right, you bitch!' she shouted. 'It goes up and you with it!'

'So I've got nothing to lose, have I?' said Andy quietly. She reached behind her with her right hand and brought out the video recorder's remote control. She slowly raised it in the air so that they could all see it, her thumb moving over the on-off button. 'If I press this, the bomb goes off.'

CAPTAIN CROSBIE ADJUSTED his body armour. 'Right. Orders, group,' he said, and the troopers gathered for the pre-action briefing.

'Two teams of seven,' said Crosbie. 'If we get the green light, we go in on two sides, simultaneously. Three stages. One. Lower the shaped charges. No messing—we only get one chance at it. Stage two. Flash-bangs. Sandy and Coop take care of them. Everyone else goes in immediately afterwards. Four troopers are coming in through the front door, but they're not moving until they hear the flash-bangs.

'We have four targets. Tango One and Tango Two are male. Tango Three and Tango Four are female. Tango Four is the bombmaker, but according to Intelligence she's working under duress. Having said that, all are to be regarded as hostile. Tangos One, Two and Three are armed. Handguns.'

Crosbie then named the two teams, before turning to Coop.

'How are you getting on with the shaped charges?'

'One done. I'll have the other ready in ten minutes.'

Crosbie nodded. The charges were PE4 plastic explosive around light wooden frames that Coop had nailed into rectangles the size of the windows they intended to blow out. If Coop had done his calculations correctly, they would blow in the windows and the blinds, but with minimum damage to the interior of the office, so that the fertiliser bomb would not be accidentally detonated.

ANDY HELD the remote control to the side, aiming it at the briefcase, as Green-eyes and the Wrestler moved to stand behind the man in the ski mask. 'I didn't just wire up the timer,' she said, her voice cracking under the tension. 'I wired up the remote, too.'

'What do you want, Andrea?' asked the man in the ski mask.

'It doesn't matter what she wants,' shouted Green-eyes. 'We've got guns. We'll just shoot her!'

'You can't shoot me,' said Andy. 'Because no matter how good a shot you are, I'm still going to be able to press the button. Even if you kill me stone dead, my hand is going to go into spasm. The bomb'll go off. You'll all die.'

Green-eyes glared at the man. 'Is that possible?'

'If she's wired it that way, yes. The thing of it is, has she?'

Andy swallowed. 'There's only one way to find out,' she said, her voice shaking. 'I'll press the button and we'll all die.'

She raised her hand above her head.

'No!' shouted Green-eyes. 'Don't!' She lowered her gun, but the man in the ski mask kept his levelled at Andy's chest.

CAPTAIN PAYNE LOOKED over at Patsy. 'I recommend we go in now. If she presses that button, everyone dies.'

Patsy exhaled through pursed lips. She looked at Hetherington and raised an eyebrow. He nodded, walked to the far end of the office and began talking urgently into his phone. Neither of them had the ultimate authority to approve the storming of the building. Only one man could do that. Patsy fingered her crucifix.

Martin turned to Denham. 'They can't go in now,' he said. 'What about Katie?'

'Katie's pretty low down their list of priorities right now,' said Denham. 'I'm sorry, Martin.'

Martin looked around the office frantically, as if searching for someone he could appeal to. No one was looking at him. Hetherington was still whispering into his mobile phone; Patsy, Barbara Carter and Tim Fanning were watching the bank of thermal image monitors.

'Patsy, you have to hold off,' urged Martin. 'See what they do. If he lets her talk to Katie, we can find out where she is.'

'It's not my decision any more,' she said, avoiding his gaze.

'What if Andy accidentally presses the button?' asked Martin.

Patsy didn't reply. Martin looked at Denham. 'They're going to shoot her as well, aren't they? That's the only way to stop her pressing the button, isn't it?'

Denham averted his eyes. Martin held his arms out and waved them like a chick trying to fly for the first time. 'For God's sake, will somebody talk to me!' he shouted.

Patsy motioned with her chin at Fanning. 'Tim, take Mr Hayes outside, will you.'

Martin put his hands up in surrender. 'OK, OK,' he said quietly. 'I'll be quiet.' He walked over to the window and stood next to the SAS captain.

Hetherington clicked his mobile phone off and walked over to Patsy. 'The PM says to go in,' he said.

The SAS captain looked over his shoulder. 'That's a green light?' he asked Hetherington.

'Affirmative,' said Hetherington. 'And may God help us all.'

Captain Payne put his phone to his mouth. Martin moved quickly, pushing the phone away with his left hand and grabbing for the man's gun with his right. He gripped the butt of the weapon and pulled it from its nylon holster. It came out smoothly, and before he realised it he was pointing the gun at Payne's head. Martin had never fired a gun in his life, but he knew enough to realise that there was a safety catch and he fumbled it into the off position with his thumb as he took a step backwards.

'Martin, for God's sake, what are you doing?' shouted Denham.

Martin kept the gun pointed at the captain's head. 'Tell your men to keep their hands where they are,' he warned. 'If either of them makes a move towards their weapons, I'll shoot you.'

'Don't be stupid,' said Payne, holding his hands up.

'Martin, I know you're under a lot of strain at the moment,' said Patsy. 'But this isn't helping anyone.'

Martin ignored her. 'Tim, push that desk against the door. Do anything else, anything at all, and I'll shoot him.'

Fanning did as he was told.

'Sit on the desk, Tim. On your hands.' Fanning did so. Martin looked at the SAS officer, and waggled the gun at him. 'Tell your men to take their guns out of their holsters. Tell them to use their thumbs and one finger. Then I want them to eject the thing that holds the bullets. Then they're to kick the guns across the floor to me.'

The captain nodded at his men. They slowly followed Martin's instructions. He kicked the guns under the desk, out of reach.

'Martin, have you thought what's going to happen when this is over?' said Patsy. 'You'll be in court for this. You'll go to prison.'

'Maybe,' said Martin. 'But you haven't given me any choice, have you? If the SAS go in, my wife and daughter are going to be killed. If that happens, I don't care much either way what happens to me.'

He moved to the side so that he could see the thermal image screens. 'Turn up the sound, will you?'

Patsy turned up the volume. Everyone looked at the monitors.

ANDY HELD the remote control above her head, her thumb resting on the on-off button. 'I will do it,' she said. 'You're going to kill me anyway, so I've nothing to lose.'

'Yes, you have,' said the man in the ski mask. 'There's Katie.'

'Katie's dead already.'

The man lowered his gun. 'No. She's not.'

Andy shook her head, blinking away tears. 'I don't believe you.'

The man stretched out a hand as if he were trying to calm a barking dog. 'She is, Andrea. I promise you. She's fine.'

Andy sniffed. Her arm was starting to ache and she wanted to change hands, but she didn't want to give the man in the ski mask an opportunity to shoot her.

The Wrestler cursed and Green-eyes turned to look at him. 'I'm going,' he said. 'You don't need me any more.'

'No,' said the man. 'We all stay until it's finished.'

'No way,' said the Wrestler. 'You've got your bomb. I'm sure as hell not going to be here when it goes off. Just make sure you transfer my money into the bank, Egan.' He turned and walked away.

PATSY LOOKED at Denham. 'You hear that? "Egan", he said.' She turned to Carter. 'Barbara, get onto records. Anything we have on a man called Egan. Aliases, everything. Notify GCHQ, too. Search for any calls mentioning Egan.' Carter nodded and picked up the phone.

'Wait!' said Martin.

'Martin, we have to know who this Egan is.'

Martin hesitated, then nodded. Carter dialled a number and began to whisper urgently into the mouthpiece.

There was a coughing sound from the loudspeaker. On the two screens, one of the green figures slumped to the floor. 'They've shot someone!' said Captain Payne, striding towards the monitors.

'For God's sake, is it Andy?' Martin kept the gun aimed at Payne.

'It's not her,' said Payne. 'He's shot the man.' The SAS captain slammed a fist into the palm of his other hand. 'Now,' he said. 'We have to move now. They're all distracted—we'll be in there before they know it.'

'No,' said Martin. 'We wait until they've made the call. Then we'll know where Katie is.'

'They're not going to let her speak to your daughter,' said Payne. 'They're going to trick her, Martin. It's a distraction—she'll be so focused on the phone. He's killed one of his own people; he's not going to think twice about killing your wife. Think, man. They're not going to let her live, not after this. You've got to let us go in, now. We can do it, Martin,' said the captain, his voice soft and persuasive.

Martin put a hand up to his forehead. 'You're confusing me,' he mumbled.

One of the SAS troopers lunged towards Martin, his hands outstretched, going for the gun. Martin turned, his mouth open in surprise, but too slowly to get his gun round. Denham was quicker—he threw his tweed hat at the trooper's face and stuck out his foot, tripping the man up. Martin jumped back, covering the man with his gun, both hands on the butt, his finger tight on the trigger.

Everyone froze. Martin's eyes were wide and staring and he was breathing heavily.

Captain Payne moved away from Martin, his hands up in surrender. 'It's OK. We're all cool, Martin. No one's going to hurt you.'

'Sorry,' said Denham, picking up his hat. 'I must have slipped.'

The SAS trooper glared up at him, then got to his feet.

'Damn you, Liam,' hissed Patsy.

Denham smiled in a cold imitation of an apology. 'What are you going to do to me, Patsy? Have me sacked?' He nodded at the green screens. 'Let the girl have her chance. She deserves it.'

'Thanks, Liam,' said Martin, covering Payne with the gun.

The office went silent as everyone strained to hear what was being said over in Cathay Tower.

ANDY STARED IN HORROR at the pool of blood that was spreading around the Wrestler's head in a gruesome parody of a halo.

Green-eyes was also stunned. The two women looked at each other, then at the man in the ski mask. 'Why?' asked Green-eyes.

'First rule of this business, always obey orders. Second rule, never use names. He broke both.' He levelled the gun at Andy once more. 'Anyway, we're wasting time.'

In her terror at witnessing the killing, Andy had forgotten the remote control in her hand. Now she waved it in front of her face, her thumb poised over the on-off button. 'If you shoot me, I'll still have time to press this. Then we all die.'

'OK, take it easy,' the man said, his tone conciliatory but firm. 'What is it you want?'

'I want to go home to my family.'

'You can do that. We can all walk out of here, and once the bomb has gone off you can leave.' He looked at his watch. The bomb had been active for almost ten minutes.

'And my daughter?'

'We've no interest in hurting children, Andrea. We just want this building blown up.'

Andy's mouth was so dry that she could barely speak. 'Once the bomb goes off, you're going to kill me anyway. I know you are. You want it to look like an IRA bomb. If I go up with it, that's what everyone will think, that the IRA used me to build it. If I'm alive, your deception isn't going to work.'

Green-eyes and the man looked at each other. Andy knew that she was right. That had been their plan, right from the start.

'So maybe it's better if we all die,' she said. She pointed the remote control at the man as if it were a gun and she was about to fire.

'Wait!' he said. For the first time there was a hint of uncertainty in his voice, as if he finally believed that she might do it.

'I want to know why,' said Andy. 'I want to know why you've done all this. Kidnapped Katie. Forced me to build the bomb for you. Is it because you want to derail the peace process?'

The man in the ski mask snorted dismissively. 'You think we'd go to all this trouble over politics?' He laughed sharply.

'So why, then? If it's not politics, why?'

'It's about money, Andrea. Dollars. Millions of dollars. Hundreds of millions of dollars.'

Andy frowned, not understanding.

The man waved his gun around the office. 'Look around you. What do you see, Andrea? Prime City office space? An appreciating asset?' He shook his head. 'The whole building's worthless. The steel's corroding. It was built on the cheap and now the whole structure's almost ready to come down.'

Andy put a hand to her head. She was confused and finding it hard to breathe, as if something had been tightly wound round her chest.

'The people I work for bought the building last year. They're Chinese—they thought they were getting a good deal and they paid in cash. Four hundred million dollars, a lot of it Triad money. As soon as they handed it over, the vendor disappeared. They were conned. What they thought was a solid-gold investment turned into a millstone round their necks, if you'll excuse the mixed metaphors.'

'So what's that got to do with all this?' said Andy.

The man shook his head impatiently. 'The building has to be rebuilt, which will cost almost as much as they've already spent. But if it should be destroyed in a terrorist bombing, then the government becomes the insurer of last resort. They get paid in full.'

Andy stood transfixed, the remote control in her outstretched hand. 'That's what this is all about? You're going to kill God knows how many people . . . just for money?'

The man laughed harshly. 'For a lot of money, Andrea. A hell of a lot of money.' He paused. 'What if I were to offer you money, Andrea? What if I were to give you half a million dollars to put down that remote control and walk out of here.'

'No.'

'How much, then? How much to buy your cooperation?'

'I want my daughter back. And I want to go home.'

The man stared at her in silence. He clicked his fingers at Green-eyes. 'Give me the phone,' he said. Green-eyes handed over the mobile and he used his thumb to tap out a number. 'I'm calling your daughter,' he said.

Andy narrowed her eyes, suspecting that he was trying to trick her. She held the remote control above her head again.

The phone started to ring and the man put it to his face, keeping the gun pointed at Andy's chest.

PATSY AND HETHERINGTON looked at each other in astonishment. 'Do you believe that?' asked Hetherington. 'That's what this is all about? An insurance job?'

'There's no reason for him to lie,' said Patsy. 'He doesn't know we're listening in.'

Over the loudspeaker, they heard the man call out to Andy. 'They're on the line,' he said.

'I want to talk to her,' said Andy. Her voice sounded strained, as if she was close to tears.

'We should go in now,' said Captain Payne.

'No!' said Martin. 'Wait until she speaks to Katie.' He looked at Patsy. 'They'll be monitoring the call, right?'

Patsy nodded. Martin kept the gun aimed at the captain, but turned to look at the thermal image monitors. As he did, something hit him in the small of the back, pushing him forward. As he fell, Patsy grabbed the gun and twisted it out of his hand. Payne swiftly moved over to her and took the gun from her.

It was Tim Fanning who'd hit Martin, creeping up behind him while his attention was focused on the monitors. Fanning grabbed him round the neck and wrestled him to the ground, and within seconds he was on top, his knees pinning down Martin's arms.

Captain Payne grabbed his phone. 'Stand by, stand by,' he shouted. 'Move in on my word.'

Patsy opened her mouth to give the SAS captain the go-ahead, but before she could speak Denham stepped forward.

'Patsy, they're using the mobile. We can trace the call within a minute. We can find out where Katie is.'

'Please,' begged Martin from the ground.

Patsy looked down at Martin. He looked like a wild animal in fear of its life.

'One minute, Patsy,' said Denham. 'You can give her one minute, can't you?'

Patsy gritted her teeth. 'Damn you,' she said. 'Damn you both.' She held up her hand to Payne, gesturing for him to wait. 'Tim, call the telecom people, right away. Trace that call.'

Fanning climbed off Martin and rushed over to a phone. Martin got slowly to his feet.

Everyone in the room stared at the bank of monitors.

THE MAN in the ski mask kept the gun aimed at Andy's chest as he listened to the phone. 'It's me,' he said. 'Hold the line, yeah?'

'Let me speak to Katie,' said Andy.

'Then what?' asked the man, holding the phone by his side.

'Then you let her go. Then we walk out of here.'

The man shook his head. 'I don't think so.'

Andy waved the remote control. 'You don't have a choice,' she said. 'If I press this, we all die.'

The man smiled thinly, then slowly raised the phone. Andy stepped forward, thinking he was about to hand it to her. He didn't. He put the phone to his mouth, speaking loudly so that his voice echoed around the office. 'Listen carefully. If the line goes dead, kill the girl and get the hell out of there. Understand?' He listened, then held the phone down by his side again. He sneered at Andy. 'Right,' he said flatly. 'Go ahead and press it. If we die, she dies.'

PATSY TAPPED HER FOOT impatiently. It seemed to be taking a lifetime for the telecom experts to trace the call.

The SAS captain walked over to her. 'We have to move in,' he said. 'The clock's still ticking, remember? I make it fifteen minutes so far.'

She looked at him icily. 'I'm hardly likely to forget,' she said.

'Just a few more minutes,' Martin pleaded.

'We don't have a few more minutes,' said the captain. 'We have to get in there so that the explosives officers can get to work on the bomb. If we leave it much longer, even if we go in we won't be able to prevent the bomb going off.'

Martin pointed at the monitors. 'Don't you understand what's going on there?' he thundered. 'If you go in and that phone gets cut off, they'll kill Katie. We have to know where she is.'

'And if that bomb goes off, hundreds of people are going to die!' shouted the captain. 'Including my men.'

The two men stood just feet apart, glaring at each other.

'Easy, gentlemen,' said Hetherington, quietly but firmly. 'We're not fighting each other here. The enemy's over there. Let's not forget that.' He raised an eyebrow at Patsy. She shook her head. 'It's a mobile,' she said. 'Southern Ireland. That's all they know so far.'

Hetherington went over to Martin and put a hand on his shoulder. 'If you're going to hate anyone for this, Mr Hayes, you have to hate me. It's my decision.' He turned to the captain. 'Send in your men.'

Payne took two steps over to the phone he'd been using and picked up the receiver. 'Can you hear me? It's a green light. Go, go, go.'

Patsy slammed down the phone. 'We've got a location!'

'So IT'S YOUR CALL, Andrea,' said the man. 'Press the button and everyone dies. Including your daughter.'

Andy held the remote control in front of her, her hand shaking uncontrollably. He'd beaten her. Whatever she did, she'd lose. She could see from the look of triumph in the man's eyes that he knew it, too.

'It's over, Andrea. Give me the remote control. You know you're not going to press it.'

He stretched out his arm towards her. 'Andrea. It's over.'

CAPTAIN CROSBIE DROPPED the phone and adjusted his respirator. He raised his arm, his fist clenched. 'Go! Go! Go!' he shouted.

His men had split into two teams and on his command, each team dropped a shaped charge down on ropes, while Sandy and Coop stood on the window ledges, abseiling ropes round their waists, and pulled the pins out of their stun grenades. One trooper on each team detonated a shaped charge at the same time. There were two loud explosions from below. Immediately Sandy and Coop disappeared over the edge, and the rest of the troopers took their places, Heckler & Kochs at the ready.

THE WINDOW to Andy's left exploded in a shower of glass. A fraction of a second later, the window behind her also erupted inwards, spraying her back with glass. Two metal cylinders bounced off the floor, the size and shape of cans of beer. Time seemed to stop for Andy. She wondered if the bomb had gone off, if she was already dead and it had happened so fast she didn't know it. She couldn't move. She wasn't conscious of breathing or of her heart beating.

The man in the ski mask started to react, swinging his gun round, bringing it to bear on the window closest to him, his mouth open as if he were about to scream.

The two cylinders exploded at exactly the same time. There was a flash of light, so bright that Andy was instantly blinded, then her world exploded.

THE SAS CAPTAIN moved closer to the monitors at the sound of the explosions. On the eight screens, three green figures were staggering around the office. One of them twitched and then fell. Over the loudspeaker came the muffled rat-tat-tat of rapid fire from a silenced Heckler & Koch. More green figures were flowing into the office, moving quickly and purposefully.

Martin peered over the captain's shoulder. 'Who's been shot?'

'I don't know,' said Payne sharply. Two single muffled shots barked from the loudspeaker. The sound of a silenced handgun.

GREEN-EYES WAS IN SPASM on the floor, though she was obviously dead. The right-hand side of her head was missing, and her gun, unfired, lay close to her twitching right hand. Andy stood transfixed, unable to comprehend what was going on around her. The man in the ski mask had fired twice at three SAS troopers who had come swinging in through one of the broken windows in the wake of the grenades. He'd hit one in the chest, but the bullet had only smashed into the soldier's body armour. The troopers were bringing their sub-machine guns to bear on the man, but he threw himself to the side, rolling behind a desk.

There was a crashing sound from reception and the stamping of boots. Andy held her hands up in surrender, the remote control still clasped in her right hand. 'Don't shoot!' she screamed. Her voice sounded far away, as if it belonged to someone else.

The man in the ski mask rolled again and came up in a half-crouch, taking aim at Andy's chest. With his free hand he ripped off his ski mask. His expression was totally blank as he tightened his finger on the trigger.

Andy sprang to her right and fell against one of the ovens. Two men who'd just piled in through the other window were unclipping themselves from their ropes. One of them swung his submachine gun towards her, but the only sound she could make was a low growl.

The man's silenced gun coughed and a bullet zipped by her head as she fell to the ground and scrambled away on all fours.

She stood up, and one of the SAS troopers fired his submachine-gun. His aim was off and bullets raked the ceiling above her head, shattering the polystyrene tiles. The man with the handgun fired at the troopers and hit one in the respirator. The trooper slumped to the floor, blood pouring from around his face mask.

Andy dropped to the floor and slammed into something soft and yielding and found herself face to face with the Wrestler, his eyes wide and staring, blood congealing between his teeth.

Andy groped for his gun, but when she pulled it wouldn't come free of the holster. As she staggered to her feet, she heard a body crash to the floor and looked up. The man was only feet away from her. His face split into a malevolent grin and he fired at her, point blank. Andy twisted to the side, throwing out her hands for balance, and felt the bullet sear along her outstretched arm and into her shoulder. She screamed in pain and fell backwards.

As Andy hit the ground she saw the man fire at an SAS trooper and hit him in the neck. The trooper twisted around as blood sprayed from the wound.

Andy rolled, pain lancing through her injured shoulder, and crawled under one of the tables. Ahead of her was Green-eyes, blood pooling around her chest, her head twisted grotesquely to one side. Andy saw her gun and grabbed for it, rolling over until she was on her back. The man was bent low. Andy squeezed the trigger, praying that the safety catch wasn't on. Her ears roared as the gun fired again and again as her finger tensed instinctively on the trigger. The upper half of the man's body turned scarlet as bullets raked across his chest.

The last thing Andy saw was three troopers with goggles and respirators staring impassively down at her like giant insects considering their next meal.

THE LOUDSPEAKER was suddenly silent. Then there was a man's voice. A gruff Scottish accent. 'Area secured!'

'Thank God for that,' said Hetherington.

Captain Payne put his phone to his ear and listened, nodding and grunting. He turned to Patsy. 'Tango One and Tango Three are dead, Tango Two is dying. Tango Four is wounded but will survive. You can send in the explosive officers now.'

Martin's mind whirled. Which was Andy?

Patsy came up behind him and squeezed his shoulder. 'It's OK,' she said. 'Andrea's alive. Your wife's OK.'

McEVOY TOOK the mobile phone away from his ear. 'Shit,' he said.

'What happened?' asked Canning.

'Gunfire. Then the line went dead.' McEvoy put the phone down on the coffee table. 'I think it's over.'

Canning paced up and down. 'What the hell are we going to do?'

Egan's instructions had been crystal clear. If the connection was cut, kill the girl. But Egan was probably dead. 'We go,' McEvoy said quietly. 'We pack up and go.' He picked up the holster and fastened it across his chest. 'You check the girl's OK, I'll put the gear in the car.'

Canning pulled on his woollen ski mask, went over to the door leading to the basement and pulled back the bolts. He groped for the light switch and found it, but when he flicked the switch the light didn't come on. He cursed under his breath and moved slowly down the stairs, peering into the gloom. 'Katie. Come here. Stop messing about.' He heard a scuffling sound behind him and turned to see the little girl scampering up the stairs.

Canning rushed after her. 'George, she's coming your way!' he shouted. He took the stairs two at a time and hurtled into the hallway. McEvoy was standing there, his arms outstretched. The girl was frantically trying to pull the front door open. She hadn't noticed that it was bolted. She turned and tried to run to the kitchen, but McEvoy was too quick for her. She skidded to a halt and turned, but her face fell when she saw Canning. He strode over to her and carried her back down to the basement, and dropped her onto the camp bed. She lay there sobbing, her knees drawn up against her chest. 'Calm down, girl, no one's going to hurt you. We're going.'

He heard McEvoy come down the stairs behind him. He turned to look at him. McEvoy's face was set hard and he had his Smith and Wesson .38 in his hand. 'What are you doing?' asked Canning.

McEvoy pulled back the hammer with his thumb. 'She's seen my face, Mick.'

Canning stepped in front of the gun. 'George, listen to me. If you kill her in cold blood, they'll never stop looking for us. We'll be branded as child-killers. If they catch us, they'll throw away the key.'

'I'm not happy about this, but she saw my face. You shouldn't have let her get away from you.' He moved to the side, trying to get a clear shot at the girl.

'No way are you going to do this,' hissed Canning. He grabbed the gun in McEvoy's hand, forcing his thumb between the hammer and the chamber. 'It's over.'

McEvoy tried to pull the gun away from him, but Canning seized McEvoy by the throat and pushed him back against the wall. He put his masked face right up against McEvoy's ear. 'Walk away, George.'

McEvoy glared at him. 'They're going to be coming for us, Mick. I heard what happened. Gunfire. The Sass. Egan's dead. They're all dead—the Sass don't take prisoners. If we don't kill the girl, she'll identify us and the Sass'll be after us.'

'There's a big difference between kidnapping and killing. They'll look for us, sure, but they'll be a hell of a lot more determined if we've killed her. You wanna be a child-killer, George? You want that on your conscience?'

McEvoy nodded slowly. 'OK,' he said.

'We lock her in the basement, then we piss off back to Belfast,' said Canning. 'We can make a call on the way.'

'OK,' said McEvoy.

Canning slowly released his grip on McEvoy's throat. 'Let's get our stuff together,' he said.

McEvoy drove his knee into Canning's groin and hammered the butt of the handgun against the side of his head. Canning staggered back, bent double.

'It's all right for you, you piece of shit,' McEvoy hissed. 'She hasn't seen your face.' He turned and pointed the gun at Katie.

'Please don't,' Katie said, her voice quivering with fear.

McEvoy aimed at her face and his finger tightened on the trigger. Canning lurched to his feet, roared and threw himself at McEvoy's gun arm. He kicked the man's legs from underneath him and McEvoy hit the floor, hard. The gun went off but the bullet buried itself in the ceiling. Canning dropped down on top of McEvoy, fumbling for the gun. He seized McEvoy's wrist with both hands, but he couldn't loosen the man's grip.

McEvoy tore at Canning's woollen ski mask with his left hand and ripped it off Canning's head, grinning. 'Now she's seen us both, what are you going to do?' McEvoy hissed.

Canning said nothing. He grunted, twisting the Smith & Wesson around, towards McEvoy's chest. He managed to get his own finger inside the trigger guard and the gun went off twice. McEvoy stiffened, then blood seeped between his teeth and he rolled onto his back. Canning lay gasping for breath, still holding the .38, and looked around the basement. Katie had gone. He rushed up the stairs and found her in the kitchen, trying to pull open the back door.

'It's locked,' he said.

She stopped fumbling with the handle and slowly turned to look at him. Her lower lip was trembling.

Canning led Katie back down to the basement. She didn't struggle, and when he told her to sit on the bed she did as she was told.

Canning flipped out the cylinder of the .38. Two shots left. More than enough. He clicked the cylinder back into place. He pulled back the hammer. 'Close your eyes, Katie,' he said.

'I won't tell anyone,' she said. 'I promise.'

'The police will find me, Katie. They'll find me and then you'll identify me.'

'I won't. I promise. Please don't kill me.'

Canning pulled one of the wooden chairs closer to the bed and sat down on it, facing the girl. 'Katie, you don't know what the world's like. You're just a kid. Let me tell you what would happen, Katie. The police will catch up with me eventually. They'll send policemen to talk to your mum and dad, and they'll take you all to the police station. They'll be really nice to you and tell you what a brave girl you are. They'll probably give you a Coke or a 7-Up or something, then one of them will sit down and talk to you. Probably a policewoman. Young. She'll talk to you like a big sister. She'll tell you that they've caught me but that you've got to identify me. She'll tell you not to worry, that they'll put me in prison for a long, long time, and that I'll never be able to hurt you or any other little girl again. Then the nice policewoman will take you to a room and she'll show you a window. She'll tell you that there's a line of men on the other side, that you can see them but they can't see you, and she'll tell you to look carefully at all their faces and to tell her which one I am.'

'I won't tell them,' said Katie.

'You're seven years old,' said Canning coldly. 'You won't be able to stand up to them. Close your eyes, Katie.'

Katie did as she was told. 'I won't tell,' she said. 'I promise.' She kept her eyes firmly closed and made the sign of the cross over her heart. 'Cross my heart and swear to die.'

TWO GREEN-OVERALLED paramedics were wheeling a trolley through a police cordon as Patsy, Martin and Denham walked up. Martin ran over to the trolley. It was Andy. She was paler than he'd ever seen her, her hair tied back in a ponytail, dark patches under her eyes. She reached out with her hand and he interlinked his fingers with hers. A large dressing had been taped to her left shoulder and there were two dressings on her arm which had been placed in an inflatable splint. She tried to sit up. 'Katie . . .' she said.

'She's losing blood,' the paramedic said to Martin. 'We have to get her to hospital.'

Andy gripped Martin's hand, her nails digging into his flesh. 'I'm not going anywhere until I know that Katie's safe.'

'You have to go to hospital,' said Martin. 'I'll come with you.'

Denham appeared at Martin's shoulder. 'Our people are on their way to Katie now,' he said.

'Liam?' said Andy. Her eyelids fluttered. She was close to passing out. 'I want to stay here until I know what's happened to Katie.'

Patsy took her mobile phone from her jacket and pressed it into Andy's hand. 'As soon as we know where she is, we'll call you.'

Denham nodded at the paramedics and they wheeled her towards the ambulance. Martin went with them.

'Do you think she's still alive?' asked Patsy as they watched the paramedics lift Andy into the vehicle.

'God, I hope so,' said Denham.

A uniformed policeman examined Patsy's credentials and waved them through the cordon. They rode up to the ninth floor in silence. The doors opened and two more uniformed constables stepped aside to allow them into the office. Half a dozen Scene of Crime Officers in white overalls were moving around like silent ghosts, all their evidence going into labelled plastic bags.

Two Metropolitan Police explosives officers were crouched over the black rubbish bags, gingerly moving them apart.

'Everything OK?' Patsy asked.

One of the EXPOs looked up and grinned at her. 'Safe as houses,' he said. He was barely out of his twenties, with a shock of red hair and acne scars across his cheeks. 'SEXPO's got the detonator. You could drop this lot out of the window and it wouldn't go off.'

'SEXPO?'

'Senior Explosives Officer.' The redhead nodded over at an older man standing by one of the desks. 'Our boss. Dave Hoyle.'

Patsy and Denham went over to Hoyle. He was peering at a digital display through a magnifying glass, examining the wires that protruded from the back of it.

She introduced herself and Denham, but Hoyle just grunted.

'It was live?' asked Patsy.

'Oh, yes. Twenty minutes left on the clock before we got to it.'

'No booby traps?' asked Denham.

'No, it was a simple enough circuit,' said Hoyle. 'No photo-electrics, no tremblers, no collapsing circuits. EXPO-friendly, it was.'

'What about the remote control?' asked Patsy.

'The what?' Deep frowns creased Hoyle's forehead.

'The infrared remote control. She had it rigged so that if she pressed it, it would go off.'

Hoyle's frown deepened. 'No way,' he said. 'Pressing the remote control wouldn't have done a blind thing.'

'Are you sure?'

Hoyle looked offended. Patsy began to laugh. 'She was bluffing,' she said to Denham. 'She was bloody well bluffing.'

Denham's mobile phone warbled and he took it out and put it to his head. Patsy stopped laughing as Denham listened, then frowned. 'Yes, Eamonn.' Patsy watched Denham's face, wondering if it was good news or bad.

Denham put his hand over the bottom of the phone. 'They've found Katie.' A smile spread across his face. 'They locked her in a basement. She's scared but she's OK.'

Patsy grinned. She took a quick step forward and hugged Denham, burying her face in his chest.

Denham hugged her back, then pulled away. 'I have to call Andy,' he said, then he smiled. He held out the phone to Patsy. 'Why don't you do it?'

Three Months Later

The wrought-iron gates swung open and the Mercedes nudged slowly into the compound. Deng didn't recognise the man standing guard by the gate, but that wasn't significant. The firm that supplied him with bodyguards changed the personnel on a regular basis. The only constants were his driver and the man who was sitting in the front passenger seat. Like the rest of the guards assigned to protect Deng, they were armed. Ever since the debacle in London, he'd had three men in the house protecting his wife and sons, and there were always at least two others with him.

He climbed out of the Mercedes and went into his house. The maid wasn't there to take his cashmere coat from him, so he hung it up himself and went through to the sitting room.

His two sons, the elder aged twelve, the other just eighteen months younger, were sitting together on the sofa, an expensive white leather model that Deng had had flown in from Milan. He glared at the boys. 'Didn't we tell you not to sit on the sofa in your school clothes?' he said. 'Why haven't you changed?'

The boys said nothing. The younger one was close to tears.

'What's wrong with you? And where's your mother?'

'She's with me,' said a voice behind him.

Deng froze. He turned slowly. Michael Wong was standing at the door to the kitchen, Deng's wife at his side. Her eyes looked at Deng fearfully, then over at her sons. She gave them an encouraging smile and made a small waving motion with a neatly manicured hand, trying to reassure them that everything was going to be all right now that their father was home. Deng took a deep breath. It wasn't going to be all right. Michael Wong had come for his revenge.

Wong pushed Deng's wife into the room and she ran to Deng and grabbed him round the waist and buried her face in his chest. Two big men in cheap suits and red-and-black-striped ties followed Wong into the sitting room. One of them was holding a silenced automatic. The other had a roll of insulation tape in his hand. As the door swung back, Deng could see three bloodstained bodies on the kitchen floor. His bodyguards. And against the fridge, sitting up but with her head slumped against her chest, the maid. Her throat cut wide open.

Deng looked at them over the head of his sobbing wife, his face impassive. There was no point in showing any emotion. That was what Wong wanted. A reaction. Appeals for mercy. He wanted to see Deng on his hands and knees, begging for his life and the life of his family. Deng knew that any such appeals would be ignored, so he kept his teeth clamped together and waited for the end.

All that lay ahead for all of them over the next few minutes, hours maybe, was acceptance. Then death.

Six Months Later

The doorbell rang and Martin Hayes put down his copy of the *Irish Times* and went to answer it. It was Saturday morning and he wasn't expecting visitors. It was James FitzGerald, the Garda detective inspector. Behind him stood Detective Sergeant John Power.

'Mr Hayes,' said FitzGerald, nodding. 'Sorry to bother you.'

'What's happened?' Martin asked, as Andy appeared at his shoulder.

'We think we've got one of the men who kidnapped Katie,' said FitzGerald.

Andy reached out for her husband's hand. 'You're sure?' she asked.

'Well, he's denying it, but his fingerprints match some prints we found in the cottage. We'd like Katie to come to the station with us, to see if she can identify him.'

'I'll go and get her,' said Martin. He went down the hall and through to the kitchen, where Katie was kneeling on a stool and stirring a bowl of cake mixture with a wooden spoon.

She grinned up at him and held out the spoon, which was dripping with chocolate. 'Do you want some?' she asked.

'I'll wait until it's cooked,' he said. 'Katie, the police think they've found the man. The man who kept you in the basement. They want you to look at him. To check they've got the right person.'

Katie frowned. 'I don't want to, Dad.'

Martin ruffled her hair. 'It'll be OK. I promise.'

He helped her climb down from the stool and held her hand as they walked to the front door, where Andy was already putting on her coat. 'Right,' she said. 'Let's go.'

Power dropped them at the front of Pearse Street Garda station and FitzGerald showed them into a room. Martin was relieved that it wasn't the room where he'd been held before. He put his hand on Katie's shoulder and gave her a small squeeze, as much to reassure himself as to comfort her. FitzGerald asked them to wait, and they sat down while he went back down the corridor, returning a few minutes later with a young uniformed policewoman. She introduced herself by her first name. Teresa. She was in her mid-twenties, blonde with a pretty smile. She knelt down by Katie's side and asked her if she wanted a Coke.

'OK,' said Katie. Teresa asked FitzGerald to get the little girl a Coke, then pulled a chair up close to her and sat down.

'What we want you to do is to look at some men and see if you can recognise the one who took you away from your mummy and daddy. There'll be eight men. We want you to look at them, all eight of them, and then tell us which one is the man who took you. Do you think you can do that for us?'

Katie scowled and looked at the floor. 'I don't want to.'

Teresa leaned forward and put her face close to Katie's.

'There's no need to be scared, Katie. The man can't hurt you. Look at me, Katie.'

Katie slowly raised her eyes and looked at the policewoman.

'Let me tell you how it works,' said Teresa. 'There'll be a line of men, and they'll be on the other side of a window. You look through the window at them, but they can't see you. It's a special glass. You can see through it, but they can't. They just see themselves.'

FitzGerald reappeared with a can of Coke and a plastic beaker. He put them down on the table and Teresa poured some of the soft drink and handed it to Katie. 'So they won't even know you're there. Each of the men will be holding a number. All you have to do is to look at all the men very carefully then tell me which number the man you recognise is holding. You can do that, can't you?'

'I guess so,' said Katie quietly. She took a sip of her Coke.

'If you can tell us which one it is, we can make sure he'll go to prison for a long time. He won't be able to do anything to you again, Katie or hurt any other little girl. You do understand, don't you?'

Katie nodded.

'Good,' said Teresa. 'That's good, Katie. OK, shall we go and have a look at these men?'

Katie nodded solemnly.

Teresa looked at Martin and Andy. 'You can both come,' she said. 'Katie'll probably be more secure if you're with her.'

Andy took Katie's hand and they followed FitzGerald out of the interview room and along the corridor. Martin walked with Teresa.

'How's she been, since the kidnapping?' the policewoman asked.

'Fine,' said Martin. 'She saw a child psychologist for a few weeks afterwards, but there didn't appear to be any problems.'

'Perhaps she didn't realise the danger she was in.'

Martin shook his head. 'No, it wasn't that. She knew exactly what was happening. She just coped with it all, far better than we thought she would.'

FitzGerald held open a door and they all trooped in. It was a long, narrow room with a curtain running virtually the whole length of one side. FitzGerald motioned for Martin and Andy to stand with him. Teresa held out her hand to Katie and Katie took it. 'Right, Katie, my friend over there'—she nodded at FitzGerald—'is going to pull the curtain back, and you'll see the men sitting down on the other side of the window. Look at every one of them at least twice, and then tell me the number of the man you recognise. OK?'

'OK,' said Katie.

'Good girl. You're being very brave, Katie.'

Katie looked over at her parents, and they nodded as if to encourage her. Teresa signalled to FitzGerald to draw the curtain back.

There were eight men, all in their forties, sitting on wooden chairs and staring ahead blankly. They were all holding pieces of cardboard on which was printed a number, from one to eight.

Katie stared at the men. She walked slowly down the length of the room, gazing at their faces. The Nice Man was number five. He was wearing a black pullover and brown corduroy trousers and his hair was all messy. Katie walked back along the window.

'There's no rush, Katie,' said Teresa. 'Take all the time you need.'

Katie shrugged. 'He's not there.'

Teresa knelt down in front of Katie and put her hands on her shoulders. 'There's no need to be scared, Katie. He can't hurt you.'

Katie looked straight at the policewoman. 'He's not there.'

Teresa frowned. 'Are you sure?'

Katie nodded solemnly and made the sign of the cross over her heart. 'Cross my heart and swear to die.'

STEPHEN LEATHER

Manchester-born thriller writer Stephen Leather, who lists among his accomplishments a brown belt in karate, a pilot's licence and knowledge of Thai and Cantonese, is a British thriller writer destined for the top. He started out in journalism as a graduate trainee with the Mirror Group and then did stints at the *Glasgow Herald*, the *Daily Mail*, Hong Kong's *South China Morning Post* and *The Times*. It was in 1992, with the publication of his thriller, *The Chinaman*, that his career as an author took off.

He was working as night news editor for *The Times* and the IRA had launched a bombing campaign on mainland Britain. He decided, in the wake of the violence, to write a novel about a man whose family is killed in a terrorist attack and in it he would describe in some detail the techniques of small-scale bombmaking. In *The Bombmaker* he took this theme further, exploring how a large bomb is put together and how the threat of one might be countered. The information is, he says, 'published if you know where to look' and now even easier to access via the Internet. Contacts in antiterrorist agencies, and the experiences of a friend who is a bomb disposal expert, were also invaluable when it came to research.

In *The Bombmaker*, the puppet masters are Chinese. The Far East, a region of the world that Stephen Leather has been fascinated by since he was a boy, features to a greater or lesser degree in almost all his novels (most recently *The Solitary Man* and *The Tunnel Rats*). He still travels there extensively and is currently based in Bangkok for two months, writing 2,000 words a day of his next novel, *The Stretch*, a London-based gangster story that will star former *Eastenders* stars Leslie Grantham and Anita Dobson when it appears as a two-part drama on Sky One this autumn.

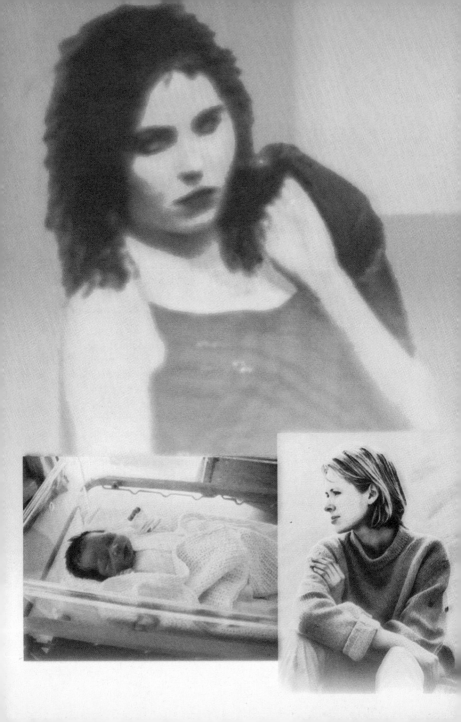

Relative Strangers

VAL HOPKIRK

Andrew Lynton has always been the black sheep of the family, living in the shadow of his successful brother, Calum. But when he finds himself excluded from his father's will, he is beyond placating. Nothing, he vows, will stop him from claiming what is rightfully his.

As he takes his case to the highest court in the land, he turns Calum's world upside-down.

Chapter One

Dan Hargreaves, aspiring partner in one of London's newest research laboratories, was bracing himself for a task he did not usually have to face: telling the anguished father of a terminally ill child that there was nothing either he or his wife could do except wait and hope. Hope for a bone marrow match. Wait for the blood samples to come in. Wait for the tests. Wait for the results.

The father was complaining that the hospital was keeping him in the dark. This was not true but the consultant thought the man needed cooling down, and Dan, the lab's manager, was just the person to do the job. Dan was not pleased. He did not often have to deal with Joe Public and that was the way he liked it.

He and the child's father, Andrew Lynton, had known each other at medical school, but only for two terms. Andrew had decided medicine was not his cup of tea. He was now a car salesman.

Dan barely recognised the bulky figure of his erstwhile colleague when he arrived. Andrew had gained fifty pounds since their university days. 'Andy,' he said, rising from his desk. 'Good to meet up again after such a long time.'

'Thanks for seeing me.' Andrew sat down in the chair opposite and began without preamble. 'I want you to tell me Sebastian's chances. Give it to me straight because the hospital won't.'

Dan ignored this and put on his best pacifying manner. He tapped the file on his desk. 'My people are working round the clock to find a match. Believe me, we're a long way from giving up hope.'

'So there is hope?'

'Of course,' said Dan heartily. 'Every day we're getting in more and more samples, but the most likely match will probably come from within your family.' He rested his hand on the folder. 'It could well be right here.'

'Are you sure you've got samples from all of them?'

'We believe so.'

'May I see?' Andrew stretched out a hand towards the file.

'Sorry,' said Dan. 'We're governed by ethics, confidentiality.'

'Look, the family situation is pretty tense.' Andrew's face was twisted with anxiety. 'I know they all promised my wife they'd arrange to give blood, but what if one of them didn't and it happened to be the match? I only want a quick check.'

Dan hesitated, then chided himself for being ultra-cautious. Andy had flunked out of medical school so soon, the chances of him making sense of the blood reports were zero. But if it gave him peace of mind . . . He handed over the file and waited while Andy looked at it.

'You seem to have them all,' Andrew said, and was about to give the file back when, brow furrowed, he stared intently at one of the pages.

Dan felt a twinge of concern. 'I'll have that back, thank you,' he said. Peremptorily he stretched out a hand.

Andrew pushed the open folder across the desk and sat back. 'You throw up some intriguing data in this business,' he said slowly.

THEY LAY FOR A WHILE without talking, slightly out of breath, damp with perspiration, until Lizzie propped herself up on one elbow. 'It's good to have my lover back,' she said softly.

Calum Lynton, entrepreneur and doting husband, interlaced his fingers with hers. 'I'm sorry I've been such a pig lately. I shouldn't have taken it out on you.'

'That wasn't an apology, was it?' She said in mock amazement.

He managed a smile. 'It's been really tough.'

'You should've told me long ago how worried you were.'

'I know, but I kept on thinking business would perk up. I feel so much better now.' She looked at him, a pleased smile on her face, and he nuzzled the top of her head. 'You can't take all the credit. It might have something to do with the prospect of wiping out our overdraft at long last.'

'Does that mean I won't have to come and work for you?' she asked.

'Not unless you want to.'

Calum had been trying for months to persuade Lizzie to help him in his business organising trade exhibitions. So far she was resisting. Last time it had very nearly been a disaster for their marriage.

The difficulty had been that Calum would not switch off from business, even in the bedroom. The last straw came when Lizzie bought herself an extremely uncomfortable but sexy nightie. Shortly after 11.00pm she had sashayed into their bedroom and posed in front of him. He had looked at her blankly.

'I can't remember whether or not I've sent the invoice to Blakes. Did you take care of it?'

She never went back to his office after that, took herself off to a teachers' training college and now worked as a supply teacher for primary schools in the south London borough of Wandsworth, where they lived. Calum had installed a new right hand, Tess Parker, who seemed to fit the bill exactly.

Lizzie watched as her husband reached for his towelling robe, discarded on the floor. It was way past their normal time for getting up but today was exceptional. In two hours her father-in-law's last will and testament was going to be read in the offices of the family's solicitor and with it, hopefully, their worries would be over.

Calum had been stunned by the suddenness of his father's death a month earlier but, after the post-mortem, doctors had told him the heart attack had been a blessing. His father had had cancer and would have had nothing to look forward to but pain.

All the Lyntons had been asked to attend the solicitor's office, with one notable exception.

'Do you think Andy will turn up?' asked Lizzie.

Calum was examining shirts on his side of the wardrobe. 'He's been told Dad didn't want him there and he ought to obey his wishes. I left a message on his machine telling him I was sorry. What more could I do?'

'What do you think he'll do?'

'Who knows? Apart from being furious, I don't see what he can do. Dad can leave his money to anyone he wants.'

'But you'll look after him, won't you?'

'I'm going to have to do it another way. Dad said often enough he didn't want any of his money to go to Andy and according to Ed Foxton the law says I have to abide by that. But there's nothing to stop me giving some financial security to Edina and Sebastian.'

Since childhood Andrew's complaint was that parents and teachers alike compared him unfavourably with his elder brother. He was unable to accept his father's authority, constantly challenging him over things that did not matter. Calum had often tried to smooth things out between them but it didn't seem to work.

Andrew's jealousy only increased as the years passed. Calum appeared to have everything he did not—supportive parents, a loving wife, a seemingly successful business and a healthy child. Calum and Lizzie had decided, for the sake of harmony, to reduce communication between them to a minimum. Even Sebastian's illness had not led to a reconciliation, although Lizzie maintained contact with Andy's wife. When their solicitor had informed them that Andrew was to be excluded from the reading of the will, they had assumed this meant Calum would be the main beneficiary.

Robert Lynton had never been able to forgive his younger son for what he described as 'a most underhand trick'. Andy was caught stealing from his mother. It emerged that he had been systematically thieving small pieces of jewellery—all of them gifts from Robert Lynton to his wife—for years. Robert had insisted on reporting the matter to the police, and his son had been charged and convicted. He was fined and given 100 hours of community service. Calum could still remember every detail of the terrible scene outside the magistrate's court: Andrew had accused his father of hating him and of always favouring Calum. Their mother had suffered a massive stroke as a result of the shock of the case and had spent the remaining year of her life in a wheelchair. Calum's repeated efforts to get his parents to forgive and forget met with failure and their father never spoke to Andy again.

Lizzie swung her slim legs out of bed, and stretched. The last few months had been difficult for them; worries about the business had naturally spilled over into their private life. Lately, lovemaking had been sporadic, due, Calum reassured her, entirely to his preoccupation with his overdraft. She had readily accepted this explanation, until yesterday. Calum had rung to ask her if she could check a message on their home computer.

The email he mentioned had not been sent, but there was another one sent by Tess, now promoted to office manager. Attractive, curvy, divorced, available. As she scanned the screen, Lizzie experienced a flash of annoyance mingled with unease. She couldn't imagine sending a man a catalogue of items headed 'Good Things About Being a Bloke'. Tess had prefaced the list with one sentence: 'Saw these and thought of you at once!' Some of the items were amusing like 'Flowers fix everything' and 'You never look at the size of a baby's head and cringe'. Others were frankly sexual. Did employer and employee exchange emails about such things? As soon as all this will business was over she would tackle Calum about it.

Lizzie examined herself critically in the mirror. Her gleaming hair was, her husband used to say, the colour of freshly churned butter. Thank God for highlights. Faint lines were beginning to appear at the side of her eyes. Her breasts were, in her opinion, far too large for such a slim frame. Yet whenever she groused about the fit of her clothes Calum told her to stop grumbling, because she was still eminently lust-worthy. Not too bad for thirty-six, he would tease.

Admiration was something Lizzie had grown accustomed to, having been the object of male attention since she was a nubile fifteen-year-old. Her father had died when she was eleven. She and her mother had survived without a male influence in their lives and this affected the way she had dealt with overtures from interested boys. She took refuge in banter to keep all would-be suitors at a distance.

At university Calum was the first man who had not argued, pleaded, cajoled or tried to bully her into bed. Right from the beginning the relationship was serious and it wasn't long before they were making plans to settle down after graduation and earn money for a home. After living with a mother who seemed to have a Gypsy in her soul, Lizzie's dream was to have a domestically tranquil life. They had moved ten times in the years after her father's death. Much as she adored having a mother who was colourful and high-spirited, she vowed that no child of hers would lead such a nomadic life. Even now her mother was travelling round the Far East, seeking enlightenment, she had told her daughter.

Marriage to Calum provided the security Lizzie craved. His mother and father welcomed her into the family with enthusiasm. Lizzie enjoyed their company and the friendship deepened as the older pair began to absorb some of the strain of dealing with their sometimes rebellious granddaughter, Gabriella.

Calum was sitting on the side of the bed, pulling on his socks. He was wearing a dark navy suit; the colour contrasted pleasingly with the reddish glints in his curly hair. He was ageing well and still trim, though a little heavier round the waist these days.

He brushed some imaginary fluff from the shoulders of his jacket. 'It still seems strange not to be able to phone Dad and have a laugh with him,' he sighed. 'I miss him.'

'So do I, but we were lucky he survived that long,' said Lizzie.

Calum straightened his tie and picked up his briefcase to check whether Tess had remembered to put in the papers he needed for an afternoon meeting. Of course she had. Thank God, it looked as though he wouldn't have to make her redundant.

Calum's exhibition design company had flourished in a boom

year, quickly establishing a reputation for attracting influential buyers. Years before, Robert Lynton had given both his sons a gift of £100,000. Calum had used his legacy to start his company, while Andrew had invested much of his in a high-risk property development that had crashed shortly after its inception.

Since then Calum had channelled his energies into making his company one of the most creative exhibition organisers in southern Britain. In those early, heady days there had even been talk of expanding into Europe, but that dream had died when the boom had not lasted. Although Calum's firm was one of the last to feel the pinch, he had been forced to borrow. The bank had been cooperative, accepting the deeds of their terraced house as collateral, but although Calum was managing to repay the interest, he was not on target to reduce the loan.

A couple of times he had been on the brink of asking his father to bail him out. Once, he had almost managed it after a Sunday lunch at the family home, but then his father had said, 'There's a good side to me, son, and there's a bad, and somehow Andy has been unlucky enough to pick up all my faults.'

The old man had stoked the fire and reminisced about the tough days when he had started his own engineering business, a story Calum had heard many times. Then he began complaining that once again Andy was trying to touch him for money.

'Thank God you're not a parasite like your brother,' he had said grimly. 'You're like me. You want to make your own way. Sure, I gave you a helping hand to begin with, like I did with your brother, but you've achieved your success without bothering me again.'

Calum sighed, remembering it all. Well, after today he might be able to wipe out all the debts. That would be the only good thing to come from his father's sudden death.

When Lizzie reappeared from the bathroom, her long neck gleaming with droplets of water above her pink bathrobe, a feeling of warmth came over him. As he laid his arms on her shoulders, he detected a faint tang of peppermint. He loved the smell of her, the feel of her, everything about her. He folded her into his arms and gently planted a kiss on her lips. 'I don't deserve you,' he whispered.

'I agree,' she said, cornflower-blue eyes shining. At that moment the door was pushed open and a teenage voice erupted.

'Yuk! Kissing at this time in the morning. Disgusting.' Gabriella, her thick mane hanging round her shoulders, stood in the doorway, making a face. She was wearing one of the two main colour schemes in her wardrobe: glossy black and matt black.

Her parents broke apart and Calum said, 'I see you've got your Spanish widow's kit on again.'

'Dad, you always say that.' Gabriella smirked at him and did a twirl, revealing bare legs under the folds of the long crepe skirt.

'I think you look just right for what's going on today,' said Lizzie and was rewarded with a smile.

Gabriella paused in the doorway. 'Would Grandpa think I was being horrible if I asked you to guess how much he's left me?'

'No, he'd understand that you're a grasping little minx.'

'I'm not, Dad. I miss him. A lot.'

Lizzie did not doubt this was true. One of the secrets of the friendship between her daughter and Robert Lynton was that Grandpa never criticised, never judged and was somewhat amused by Gabriella's rebellious actions. He was the only one who accepted her right to wear what she wanted, including the nose stud, the Rastafarian plaits, the enveloping widow's weeds and the unwieldy Doc Martens. 'I'm just asking,' said Gabriella. 'I need the dosh.'

'You'll have to be patient,' said Calum. 'Something you're bad at. But you'll know soon enough.'

Lizzie sat at her dressing table, putting the finishing touches to her make-up. Without looking round she said, 'Gaby, don't you think you should tie your hair back?'

'Why? I'm not at school and besides, I like it this way.'

Calum frowned. 'It's a serious occasion, Gabs. Your mother's right.'

'OK,' she called out merrily before disappearing out of the door.

Lizzie turned her palms upwards in a gesture of futility. 'One day that girl is going to do what I ask rather than you and I'll faint clean away.'

Chapter Two

Edward Foxton grimaced. This will was going to cause trouble. Self-made millionaire his client might have been, but his instruction that his younger son was not to be invited to the reading showed he was singularly lacking in common sense when it came to the management of his own family. God knows he had tried hard to change the old man's mind in the cause of justice, fair play and, let's face it, a quiet life for the law firm. But there was just so much anyone could achieve with a client as stubborn as this one had been.

Edward examined the circle of faces round the table. First to arrive had been Robert Lynton's three ageing relatives. Two were cousins, the third was the husband of one of them. His gaze moved to the deceased's elder son. They had become pals at university and had remained close ever since. Calum was sitting with his wife on his right and his teenage daughter to his left. The girl had striking hair, but in Edward's opinion she was a sulky little miss. The only time he had seen her looking anything but petulant was when she was with her grandfather.

He cleared his throat and the hushed talking stopped immediately.

'Robert Lynton's will was drawn up seven years ago,' he began. 'This was before his younger son's, er, transgression and the bulk of the estate was to be divided between Calum and Andrew. However, since his death I have been handed a new will.'

The assembly exchanged meaningful glances.

'This new will,' continued Edward gravely, 'was drawn up three years ago and witnessed by two people known to Robert—his daily, Mrs Brenda Perkins, and her husband, Malcolm.' He caught Calum's eye and removed his spectacles, a habit he had when he was nervous. 'I am satisfied that this document is legal, though I'm bound to say the language is not as precise as I would have wished. Suffice to say, it does reflect his intentions clearly, which is what the law demands.' He replaced his spectacles and began reading.

There were small bequests to the deceased's two cousins and his gardener. Then followed a catalogue of several small bequests to charities Robert and his late wife had favoured, plus a more sizable amount to a Surrey wildlife sanctuary.

Edward took a sip of water and risked a look at Calum, admiring his outward calm, well aware of how much he was counting on his inheritance to rescue his company. Slowly he turned the page.

'"I leave the bulk of my estate, which includes the sale of the house and my shareholdings, estimated after tax at a net total of one and three-quarter million pounds, to my beloved granddaughter, the only grandchild I acknowledge."'

There was delight, disbelief and shock from both the beneficiary and her parents. Edward looked up from the document at Gabriella, who was bouncing in her chair with excitement.

'Sorry,' she said, looking anything but repentant.

Calum's head was bowed. Lizzie sat as if made of stone, and the rest of the room was quiet, staring at the couple.

Edward cleared his throat and went on, '"I believe she displays great intelligence and the sort of bloody-mindedness that has stood me in good stead. But I wish to make it clear that this money is to be put in trust for her until she reaches the age of twenty-five . . ."'

At this Gabriella sighed heavily and her father laid a restraining hand on her arm.

Edward raised his voice. '". . . with ten per cent to be released at the age of eighteen, on condition that she obtains a place at university. A further twenty per cent is to be given to her at the age of twenty-one, or graduation, whichever comes first."'

Edward turned over the page and carried on. '"My elder son will be surprised and disappointed at my decision but he is well set up for life due to his excellent business acumen which, I hope I am allowed to say, he inherited from me. However, as a token of my esteem I would like him to have the entire contents of my library and the portrait of his mother which he has always admired."'

Calum's eyes reflected his disappointment. Edward was not surprised. What Calum needed right now was cash. Lizzie had moved closer to her husband, her expression impenetrable. But for a couple who had seen their life raft snatched away, Edward thought they were putting on a good show. He continued to read. '"As most of you know, I have been sadly disappointed at the activities, both personal and professional, of my younger son, Andrew, who has been given all the opportunities that good education, sound health and an attractive appearance bestow. Despite this he has proved a bitter disappointment to his mother and me. I have written him a letter to be delivered after my death, explaining my reasons for leaving him nothing apart from my Jaguar. No doubt there will be criticism of my actions. As this never bothered me in life, it will not concern me in death."'

Edward ploughed on to the end of the document. '"On the other hand, my elder son has never disappointed me. Calum, you know how much I admire the success you've made of your life and your business. I want you to understand that my primary concern in leaving the bulk of my estate to my granddaughter is to ensure that it will benefit the continuity of what I consider is the good bloodline of the Lynton family."'

Edward looked up and gave Calum a sympathetic glance. He watched as Lizzie gently patted her husband's arm and then the harsh sound of the intercom caused the entire assembly to flinch.

Irritably, Edward flicked the switch on his console, nervousness making him sound aggressive. 'I said I wasn't to be interrupted.'

The voice of his receptionist was hesitant. 'Yes, I'm very sorry. But they're insisting that they see you.'

'I'll come out.'

THE SOUND OF RAISED voices intruded from the outer office. Lizzie tensed, recognising at once the harsh baritone bellowing outside.

'I thought there'd be trouble from Andy,' Calum muttered.

Gabriella leaned forward eagerly. 'Is there going to be a fight?'

'Ssh,' admonished her mother.

The door burst open to reveal the rugged figure of Andrew. He paused in the doorway. To the casual eye the brothers shared few similarities apart from the penetrating green eyes and tawny hair of their Celtic forefathers. In character and ability, they could not be more unalike; Calum was equable and self-possessed, Andrew quick-tempered and mercurial. Silhouetted behind him was a woman with a mass of blonde curls, who lifted a sleeping baby to her shoulder, for all the world like a fox-fur stole.

Edina sometimes gave the outward appearance of being frivolous, but she had earned her spurs in Lizzie's eyes as a formidable tigress protecting her cub. Unfailingly courteous, she had been persistent in rounding up family members, wherever they were living, to request blood samples. Lizzie admired her plucky spirit and had become quite fond of her.

'You didn't think you'd get away with this, did you?' Andrew shouted, glowering at Calum.

Before Calum could reply, Edward said sternly, 'The people here were specifically invited under the terms of your father's will. You were not. The letter your father sent you explains why.'

Andrew snorted contemptuously. 'Dad had no right to do this.'

'He had every right. It was his money,' said the solicitor sharply. 'I must ask you once again to leave peacefully.'

'I refuse.'

There was an explosion of noise as the family reacted to this intransigence. Andrew surveyed the agitated faces. Ignoring the babble around him, he led his wife to a chair and they sat down. His body was relaxed though his arms were firmly folded. Sebastian started to cry and Edina soothed him until he stopped fussing.

'I've no intention of leaving this room until I hear what's in my father's will. There's nothing you can do or say which will make us leave. I'm as much my father's son as he is.'

Lizzie leaned towards her husband and said quietly, 'Ed can't sort this out. You'll have to.'

Calum locked eyes with his brother. 'Andy, Dad wouldn't want us to scrap in public. We have no objection to you staying.'

'You should never have agreed to this in the first place,' Andrew replied ungraciously.

Edward Foxton hesitated then said, 'I would like to place on record that I am agreeing to your presence because your brother has requested it and only because of that.'

'Whatever.' Andrew uncrossed his arms, lolled back in his chair.

'I think it's better all round if we get this over as quickly as possible,' said Edward, shifting his chair nearer the desk and wishing, not for the first time that morning, that he had taken up another career. In a clipped voice he summarised the contents of the will.

Then Andrew spoke. 'Can you beat that, Edina, we get nothing except that bloody old Jag, which I can't afford to run, while Calum's kid cops the lot.' His voice was suspiciously soft. He seemed too calm, too relaxed for a man who had lost his share of a substantial fortune.

Slowly he took Edina by the elbow and urged her to her feet. The baby, awakened by the movement, began to nuzzle her neck. 'Just because you sucked up to your grandfather when he was going gaga, don't think you're going to get away with this. Half that money belongs to me and I'm going to take you to court, young lady. I intend to fight for my rights.'

Edina tugged at his sleeve. 'You've said enough. Let's go.'

'Said enough? I haven't even started. There's things I know, Gaby, things your parents don't want mentioned . . .'

Calum turned to Lizzie. 'Take Gaby out of here.'

'Why?' said Andrew belligerently. 'She's going to have to hear the truth sooner or later.'

Lizzie was already on her feet. She took her daughter's arm and began steering the reluctant girl towards the doorway. Edina caught Lizzie's eye and mouthed, 'I'm sorry.'

Once his wife and daughter had disappeared, Calum turned to his brother. 'Please don't try to blame my daughter. It's not her fault.'

Andrew snorted with derision. 'That's rich coming from you. All the time you've been working behind my back. You're not going to deny you cooked this up with him, are you?'

'Damn right I am. What Dad's done is as much of a shock to me as it is to you.'

'I bet,' Andrew sneered.

'At least let's discuss it. We can work out some compromise.'

'All right. Let's compromise. I want half Dad's estate.'

'He can't do that,' intervened the solicitor. 'It's not his to give.'

'Let's get out of here, Andrew,' said Edina.

'I haven't finished.'

'Well, you don't need me,' she said. 'I'm taking the baby home.'

'Well, big brother, don't think I'm bluffing about going to court. I happen to have an excellent case.'

Edward, who had been watching this exchange with growing unease, interrupted. 'Andrew, I assure you your father's will is watertight. You could spend a lot of money you don't have on legal proceedings. I strongly advise you to accept your father's wishes.'

'Ah, but you see solicitors don't always know everything.' Andrew's voice was teasing. 'Do they, Calum?'

'What are you talking about?'

'I know something you've been trying to keep quiet all these years. And when I tell the world about it, it'll rip this stupid will apart.'

'Whenever your back's against the wall, Andy, you come up with some shock-horror fairy story. What is it this time?'

'This is no fairy story,' Andrew said. 'Gaby isn't entitled to that money.'

Calum felt uneasy. This didn't sound like Andrew's usual bluster. 'Get to the point, Andy,' he snapped.

'Gabriella is not your daughter.'

LIZZIE HAD LEFT a message with Foxton's receptionist to say she and Gabriella would wait at Luigi's, a restaurant nearby.

'Table for such beautiful signorinas? Certainly. Come this way,' said the waiter, waving expansively towards the dimly lit interior.

Gabriella ordered wild smoked salmon and duckling with cherries, the most expensive items on the menu, Lizzie noticed with wry amusement. Lizzie, who had little appetite, opted unenthusiastically for a plate of pasta. The waiter hovered and fussed, continually asking if the beautiful ladies would like wine.

'I wish he'd leave us alone,' Gabriella muttered.

'Take no notice. He flatters all the women who come here, especially the old married ones,' Lizzie said lightly. When Gabriella was in one of her moods, she could be difficult to tease.

'You shouldn't smile at him so much,' replied Gabriella indignantly. 'It encourages him. And besides, you're not old.'

'I feel old, I'm nearly thirty-seven.'

'In eight months,' replied Gabriella. 'How long were you married when you had me?'

Lizzie raised her glass of water to buy a little time. So far she had been able to avoid having to admit that her wedding and Gabriella's birth were only six months apart. She and Calum had been assiduous at keeping the date of their wedding vague. 'Dad and I were keen to start our family straight away,' she said carefully, 'so we could grow up with you. It's just your bad luck we didn't have a brother or sister to take the heat off you.'

The truth was she and Calum had been very keen to have another child, perhaps two, and there was a certain amount of sadness that she had not conceived again.

As she squeezed lemon onto her smoked salmon, Gabriella's good humour returned and she grinned at her mother. 'It's the most wonderful thing that ever happened to me. Isn't Grandpa a star? Oh, the things I'll be able to do now.'

Lizzie was in a quandary. Half of her was miserable for Calum and the other half was nervous for her daughter. She was still trying to come to terms with the shock of the announcement. Never once had Calum's father hinted at what he was planning. Didn't he give a thought as to how it might change Gabriella? Not having to live with her on a day-to-day basis he must not have noticed her truculence, her stubbornness. All their friends assured them that Gabriella was a victim of her hormones. But oh, how difficult it was for her parents to cope with it.

Gabriella had been an angel until a couple of years ago when she was thirteen. Lizzie remembered well the last time Gaby had smiled at her with genuine affection. It was just before her birthday, and with her own hands the child had lovingly created a cake of startling ugliness. Then, almost overnight, it seemed, Gabriella transmuted into the voice of recalcitrance and discord.

Lizzie looked at her watch. Calum would need all the support she could muster. She admired the way he had covered up his despair. But at the moment she was far more worried about Andrew. Why on earth did he think he had grounds to contest the will?

'I could get such a nice flat,' Gabriella was saying. 'What a splash I'll cause at uni with my own Jag outside the front door.'

Lizzie roused herself. 'You did take on board what Grandpa said about waiting for the money, didn't you?'

'No probs.' Gabriella twirled her little finger round and round in the air. 'This is how I'll get money out of Edward Foxton.'

Listen to her, thought Lizzie. She needed to bring Gaby down to earth, but she didn't feel strong enough right then to tackle the job. Better to wait for Calum. So she smiled and nodded, and stirred her coffee so vigorously that it spilled over into the saucer.

'ANDY! WAIT!' Calum ran after his brother's retreating figure.

Andrew ignored him, continuing to hurry along the pavement in the direction of the car park. Their footsteps were the only sound on the concrete stairs as Calum followed him up to the third floor. There he found him unlocking a dark blue BMW.

Andrew climbed into the driver's seat then opened the window. 'Stop following me, I haven't time to discuss anything with you.'

Calum forced his voice into a semblance of calm. 'You can't make allegations like that and then disappear.' He wrenched open the passenger door and flung himself into the seat. 'Look, I know you're disappointed about the money, but a court action only makes lawyers happy. We're still family.'

'Haven't seen much of the family this past year. Been on my uppers too. I'd have liked some support.'

'We're all supporting you, trying to help Sebastian.'

'Leave him out of it.' Andrew adjusted his seat belt.

'I can understand you feeling bitter towards Dad, but why drag Lizzie and Gabriella into it?'

Andrew put the car into gear. 'You'll find out soon enough. Look, get out. I told you I haven't time to talk.'

'No,' said Calum firmly. 'I'm coming with you.'

'Have it your own way,' said Andrew. He drove the car at dizzying speed down the narrow slopes of the car park towards the exit. Outside, with Calum breathing relief that they had made it in one piece, Andrew manoeuvred the vehicle towards the garage opposite and into the 'Eazi Wash 'n' Dry' cavern.

'Got a fiver on you?'

Seething, Calum fished in his pocket and proffered a ten-pound note, which his brother handed to the attendant.

The woman smilingly passed Andrew a ticket, which he keyed into the car-wash machine. He swiftly pocketed the five pounds change and drove forward into the car wash. The huge roller brushes whirred into life, while water and a thick covering of soapsuds rained down on the car.

Calum sat, silent, almost unaware of his surroundings. It was hard luck that Andrew had been cut right out of the old man's estate. On the other hand, Andrew had not turned up at the family home in Hampstead until the day of Robert Lynton's funeral. And afterwards none of them had heard from him until the awful day when Edina visited to beg them to donate a blood sample because her baby needed a bone marrow transplant.

The younger members of the family had been tested first. Apparently, if a match was found among one of them it was more likely to be accepted by the baby's immune system. For once Gabriella had been cooperative, volunteering to go to the hospital as soon as it was suggested. Calum had been proud of how brave she had been. Why the hell should his brother question her paternity? He watched the soap spurt all over the windscreen.

Andrew seemed to read his thoughts. 'You're wondering how I know, aren't you?'

'Know what?' Calum parried.

'Don't be smart. What I can't work out is, did Lizzie tell you before the marriage or after? And did she tell you who Gabriella's father is?'

Calum took a deep breath and told himself to keep calm. 'I'm trying to work out what you hope to gain with this far-fetched story. Of course Gaby's mine. I was there when she was born.'

His brother gave a harsh snort. 'But were you there when she was conceived?'

At this Calum felt an overwhelming urge to strike his brother. Hard. He did not trust himself to speak.

Andrew clicked his fingers. 'Of course. You and Lizzie got married because she was pregnant, didn't you? My God, you were trusting.'

Calum tried to make his voice as noncombative as he could. 'Suppose we stop this fencing and you tell me what you know?'

'Show you the cards in my hand?' Andrew's tone was scornful. 'No, it's for me to know and for you to find out.'

The wash programme ended and Andrew began to ease the BMW forward, past the rows of petrol pumps, to the exit.

'This is where you get out.' He leaned over to open the passenger door. 'I have to meet a prospect who's going to hand over some cash for this little number so I'll see you in court, big brother, and may the best man not win.'

IN THE RESTAURANT Lizzie was saved, by the arrival of a steely-faced Calum, from having to negotiate a trip through a conversational minefield with her daughter. They exchanged the kind of glance that long-married couples do not have to translate: they would discuss the events of the day in private, without their daughter eavesdropping.

Gaby, who was daintily spooning out the last drops of her Belgian chocolate milkshake, jumped right in. 'Uncle Andy's not going to try and take my money away from me, is he?'

'We won't let him. Don't worry.' Calum's breathing was laboured. Lizzie had rarely seen him so out of sorts. She attempted to lighten the atmosphere.

'Your daughter's spent half the money already.'

'Yes, I'm going to buy Mum a whole new wardrobe of designer clothes. And what about a new car, Dad? Yours is past it.'

Calum frowned. 'Your life's going to be exactly the same for the foreseeable future, young lady. No more money, in fact probably less.'

Gaby pouted. 'Whenever anything nice happens you always have to spoil it. I'm sure if I ask Mr Foxton I could get something.'

'Don't you dare try that.' Calum sounded harsher than he had ever been with his daughter.

'I will if I want to,' Gaby flared up. 'It's my money. You always try and run my life. This is one time when you won't be able to.'

Calum beckoned furiously to the waiter for the bill.

'Don't speak to me like that,' he said fiercely to his daughter. 'Ever. Do you understand?'

It was so unlike him that Gabriella was stunned into silence.

Calum softened. 'Sorry, darling. I'm a bit wound up.' He paid the bill and followed them out of the restaurant.

It was a tense trip home, not a word was exchanged with their daughter. She sat, arms tightly folded, staring out of the window.

They managed to find a parking spot not far from the house and, as soon as Calum unlocked the door, Gaby went up the stairs three at a time and slammed her bedroom door so hard the noise reverberated throughout the house. Calum stalked into the kitchen and sat down at the table. He looked at Lizzie miserably.

'What happened?' she asked, picking up a watering can to attend to the plants on the windowsill.

'Andy made a very odd allegation.'

'About what?'

'About Gaby not being my daughter.'

Lizzie set down the watering can. 'That's ridiculous.'

'I told him that, but he insists she's not mine.'

Lizzie pulled a face. 'Darling, what's he on about? You've been my only lover since we met, more's the pity.' She came over to him and pinched his nose.

Calum sighed, but did not return her smile. He trusted Lizzie, but felt depressed by the conversation with his brother.

'Calum. Look at me. You didn't for one moment believe him, did you?'

'Of course I didn't.'

'Who told him such a thing anyway?'

'I have no idea, but he must believe he stands a chance of getting his hands on Dad's money. Why else is he going to contest the will?'

'What? Drag us through court? He's never going to do that. He'd have to produce cast-iron proof that Gaby is not your child and therefore not Robert's bloodline, and he won't be able to do that.'

'He says he can.'

'That's rubbish.'

Calum picked up his jacket from the back of a chair. 'I'll be back as soon as I can.'

She looked at him in surprise. 'You can't just go off and leave like that. We have things to talk about, like the will.'

He pointed out that it was Tuesday and she replied tartly that she was well aware of the day of the week. 'Couldn't you get out of the hockey meeting for just one week?'

He shook his head decisively. 'Can't. I'm chairing it and we're playing at the weekend and several of the players are injured.'

Lizzie was irritated. There was a mutinous child upstairs, she had not recovered from the disappointment of the will and all he could think about was the hockey team.

'It'll take my mind off things,' he said.

'Don't worry about me. I'll get on with my darning.'

He could not help but smile. Domestic skills were not Lizzie's forte. If cajoled she would sew on a button, but that's where it ended.

'Just as well you're good in bed.' He gave her a lopsided grin.

WHEN CALUM RETURNED home later that night, Lizzie was already peacefully asleep. As he lay next to his wife, his mind was churning. She was in her customary foetal position, her back towards him, and he turned his head, watching her for a while.

He had placed his trust in Lizzie from the beginning and had never had cause to doubt her. Nor had he given her cause to doubt him. But here, in the quiet of the night, a disloyal thought persisted: could his darling Lizzie have given herself to someone else after she had started sleeping with him? Immediately he answered his own question: absolutely not.

Calum turned over, trying to compose himself for sleep and hating himself for allowing Andy's poison to affect him.

WHEN SHE HEARD her father come into the house after his hockey meeting, Gabriella forced herself to wait, watching the hand of the clock as it moved with agonising slowness round the dial. He seemed to take an age preparing for bed. She could hear the low hum of the bathroom shower well past midnight.

After another half an hour she judged it safe to move and flung off the duvet. She was already fully dressed, and with boots in hand she tiptoed past her parents' bedroom and down the stairs, cursing at each one that creaked. She had waited until her mother was asleep before risking a call on the hall phone. Cupping her hand over the receiver, she jiggled with impatience, waiting for the phone to be picked up.

As always when she heard his voice, Gabriella lost the indifferent tones she tried so hard to foster and changed into an excited young woman rather than the bored teenager who lolled around the house.

'I've got the money.' There was a pause. 'I'm not kidding. My grandfather's left me all his cash.' Gabriella was sure that somehow she would be able to get her hands on at least a small part of her inheritance. After more whispers she had replaced the phone, her face alight. Then she had gone back to her room to wait.

Now she paused at the front door, every nerve straining. They would be furious with her if they caught her, but they couldn't take the money away. And she hadn't seen him for ages. She wouldn't be long; she'd be back before they missed her.

EDINA NEVER THOUGHT the day would come when she would be pleased Sebastian was in hospital. He had become so lethargic in the solicitor's office, sleeping through most of those heated conversations. Later that afternoon his temperature had risen and the doctor decided to keep him in overnight for observation. Normally she would have stayed with him, but the doctor had taken one look at her exhausted face and insisted that her husband take her home to have a good night's rest.

On the way to their flat in north London, Andy had stopped to buy an Indian takeaway. Instead of sitting in front of the TV to eat it, as happened often these days, she had taken some trouble setting the table and arranging the dishes on a serving platter, between lighted candles. Andy entered into the spirit of the evening, putting on their favourite Frank Sinatra CD.

Halfway through the meal she noticed he had stopped eating. His eyes were brimming with tears. Edina laid down her cutlery quietly. She had rarely seen him emotional, let alone weeping, but experience had taught her that if she asked questions he would clam up.

'He never loved me,' Andy was murmuring, half to himself. 'I know I did wrong. I told him a hundred times I wished I hadn't taken the stuff, but he never believed me. Never understood what drove me to it.' His eyes were guilt-shadowed. 'When I went and saw Mum that last time, she didn't blame me for her illness. She forgave me but he . . .' Andrew wiped away his tears. 'Till his last day he said it was because of me that she'd died before her time. How do you think that made me feel? I loved my mother.'

His expression was so miserable she left her chair and knelt down by his side, squeezing his arm.

'What he wrote in that letter was cruel, but at least we were the only ones reading it,' he said, his voice stronger. 'Then he had to put it all in his will, didn't he, so he could tell all the family exactly what he thought of me.' Andrew clenched his teeth. 'Couldn't he, just this once, have left me to think that maybe, just maybe, he loved me a little? No, he had to bang that on the head.'

'Imagine the vindictiveness of a man who says Gabriella is the only grandchild he acknowledges,' he went on, sounding choked. 'He never saw Sebastian, was never interested enough.'

Andrew pushed away from the table and began to stride round the small flat. 'I meant it, you know. I'm going to fight that will. Gabriella's not his granddaughter and she's not entitled to anything.'

'Oh, Andy, is that wise? It'll cost money and—'

'There are ways, Edina. You leave it to me. I've found a solicitor who'll do it on a no win, no fee basis. I've already talked to him informally.' He clenched his fists. 'I'm not going to let them get away with it. The solicitor reckons if this will isn't allowed because Gabriella has no Lynton blood, then the court will say Dad died intestate. That means they'll divide all his property and money between Calum and me, which is exactly what Dad was going to do in his original will. So that's what I'll accept. And nothing else.'

THE FOLLOWING MORNING Calum lathered his chin vigorously and gave himself a lecture. Get a grip on things. Your wife of nearly six-teen years has never given you a moment to doubt her, she's been supportive and truthful. And opposite her is your brother, a proven liar. Whose word are you going to take?

So why was he feeling miserable when it was all straightforward enough? Calum rinsed the foam off his face and dabbed it dry. He had spent a fitful night and by the time he woke, Lizzie was already up. The aroma of fresh coffee had drifted up the stairwell, and after dressing hurriedly he found her in the kitchen. He kissed the top of her head and picked up a mug of coffee. Automatically she separated the sports section from her newspaper and handed it to him. They sat for a moment or two in companionable silence before he looked up and asked, 'Is the monster up yet?'

'Are you kidding? That girl can sleep for Britain.'

'I used to at her age.'

'Calum, you always stick up for her.'

'I'm trying to be fair.'

'You don't see the way she treats me when you're not around. Sometimes she looks as though she hates me.'

'Come on, you don't usually let her get you down.'

'You know what,' said Lizzie, buttering a piece of toast and handing it to him. 'I can't say I care that your father didn't leave his fortune to you. We've always managed somehow. But I sure as hell worry what effect it's going to have on that young lady upstairs.'

'Do you think we should get her up and have a chat? I'll go with a peace offering, a nice cup of coffee,' he said, rising.

'My God, you're brave.'

'I think it's best to woo her with kindness. One day she'll turn human.' He grinned at Lizzie. 'She's an heiress now and we'll need someone to look after us in our old age.'

As she stirred her coffee, Lizzie reflected that, because of his good-tempered approach, Calum often acted as a buffer between his two warring women. She was scanning the paper for that night's television programmes when there was a shout from the top of the stairs.

'Lizzie, she's not here!'

Lizzie rushed to the hall and peered up the stairwell.

'There's no sign of her.' Calum turned and went back into Gaby's room. Lizzie joined him. It was impossible to tell from the state of her bed whether she had slept in it or not. He met Lizzie's sceptical gaze. 'What are you thinking?' he asked. 'That she crept out last night when we were asleep?'

'It's possible.'

'But she wouldn't stay out all night without letting us know.'

'I'm not so sure. This could be her way of showing us that the money has already given her the freedom to do what she wants.'

Calum said quietly, 'We'll have to put her right about that. We'd better ring round and see if she's with any of her friends.'

Gabriella frequently entertained a legion of friends at home, the chief of these being Natasha Sinclair, the eldest child of Lizzie's best friend, Sarah. She was their first line of enquiry but they met with a negative response. Natasha suggested they try one or two other good friends, but when they did, these teenagers claimed not to have seen Gabriella for weeks. That set off more alarm bells.

Lizzie sat back, her mouth dry, trying to keep a sense of proportion. Recently a teenage girl had been murdered only a few yards from her home after a particularly savage sexual attack.

'Don't let's go off the deep end,' said Calum as she confessed her fears. 'Just because the kid doesn't confide in us where she's off to doesn't mean she's not safe.'

After another hour of not being able to settle to anything, Calum began to search through the bureau in the sitting room.

'What are you looking for?'

'That photograph of Gaby we took at your cousin's wedding.'

'So you do think something's wrong?'

'No, no,' he said at once. 'But I think we ought to phone the police as a precaution, and if we want them to search for her they have to know what she looks like.'

After outlining to the duty police officer what had gone on over the last couple of days and how it had caused a family row, they received a sympathetic response. 'I'm a dad myself. My guess is she's probably trying to teach you a lesson, but you can't be too careful with a fifteen-year-old.' He took down the numbers of the friends they had already contacted, saying that the police were not as easy to fob off as parents. 'We'll get onto it right away. We'll contact you at home as soon as we have any news.'

During the fraught hours that followed, every time the phone rang they both sprang to the receiver, but all the calls were in connection with Calum's business or from friends. By the time it was dark, all pretence of being unconcerned was abandoned. The arrival of two uniformed police constables, one a woman, sent a spurt of panic through them.

'Oh God, has something happened?' asked Lizzie. But the officers quickly reassured her that they had no news and that it was normal procedure for them to search Gaby's bedroom for anything that could help them find her. An entry in a diary, a scrawled note, any clue to her whereabouts.

Lizzie offered them a cup of tea. She was about to pour the first cup when she heard the roar of a powerful engine at the gate.

Calum let out a bellow. 'There she is!'

Lizzie and the officers raced to the window to see Gabriella in the lamplight shaking her hair free from a yellow crash helmet.

Seeing her parents at the window, she gave a defiant shrug and turned her back on them to begin an animated conversation with her helmeted companion. His lanky figure was enveloped in the black leather uniform of a biker, his face masked by his helmet.

Lizzie made for the door fuelled by a mixture of anger and relief.

'We've been worried out of our minds. Where have you been?'

Gabriella looked over her shoulder at the police officers silhouetted in the doorway. 'Why are they here?'

Calum appeared at Lizzie's side. 'Go inside this minute, I want some answers from you.' He gestured towards the biker, who had retreated and looked as though he was about to start up his machine. 'And you too, young man.'

Gabriella shot her father a frightened glance. Then she took the biker by the hand and brushed past her father. Indoors, the young people slumped down on the sofa, apparently unconcerned as the two police officers and Gabriella's parents formed an uneasy semicircle round them.

'I suggest you take your helmet off, sir,' said one of the policemen. 'This could take a while.'

Reluctantly the young man pulled at the visor and took the helmet off. He was certainly a most striking-looking youth, but in Calum's view his appearance was marred by the sullenness of his expression. He was about eighteen or so, too old for Gabriella, Calum thought. The youth slouched on the sofa, arms folded, long legs akimbo.

'Could we be introduced, do you think?' asked Calum.

'This is Luke,' said Gabriella in an offhand manner. The young man gave a barely perceptible nod.

Despite strictures to herself to keep calm and give them a chance to explain, Lizzie could feel her anger growing.

'We can handle this from now on,' Calum said to the officers.

'Thank you,' said Lizzie, 'and we apologise for putting you to all this trouble and wasting your time.'

The policewoman reassured them that it was their job and they were glad that Gabriella had come home.

The policeman turned to Luke. 'Can I trouble you to show me the papers for that motorbike, sir?'

The young man sighed, lazily unzipped his leather jacket and handed over his licence.

The policeman took some notes before handing it back. 'Thank you, sir,' he said.

Calum showed the officers out. On the doorstep the policeman confided that he would check on the name to see if the youth had any form. 'Just so you know who your daughter is hanging around with, sir,' he said blandly. 'After all, she is underage.'

Calum thanked him and returned to the sitting room.

Lizzie's eyes were blazing. 'She's offering no apologies for scaring us out of our wits. No explanation about where she's been.'

'Where were you all night?' he demanded. 'You're only fifteen and still in our charge.'

'You were horrible to me and I wanted to talk to Luke.' She moved closer to the boy. 'You're so old-fashioned. Now I have Grandpa's money I can live the way I want. No stupid curfews.'

'While you're under this roof,' snapped Calum, 'you'll obey our rules. So we'll have no more of this nonsense.'

Lizzie could contain herself no longer. 'Did you sleep with him?'

Luke's arm stretched lazily across the back of the sofa and he lifted up his eyes. 'Nothin' happened,' he drawled.

'Where was she?'

'At my place,' he said.

'Then why didn't you at least phone?'

Gabriella sat, lips clenched, silent, and Luke replied, 'She fell asleep, then she said it was too late and she'd get into terrible trouble.'

Calum walked across to the sofa and looked down at his daughter's rebellious face. 'Fell asleep? That's no excuse. Do you realise what we've been through? The worry you've caused your mother?'

When Gabriella did not answer, Lizzie snapped, 'She's not interested in how we feel, she's only concerned about spending her precious money. She's already promised Luke some.'

'What? But it's not yours yet.' Calum felt a sense of foreboding. The damn will was already causing trouble for this family without a penny of the money being released.

'That's what you say,' retorted Gabriella. 'But the money belongs to me and I'm sure I can get some of it. Luke's got a band and he needs studio time for a demo tape. You don't get anywhere without one. And it only costs two thousand pounds.'

'Haven't you been listening?' Calum raised his voice. 'You can't have any of it for *years*!'

Gabriella was unmoved by her parents' outrage. 'Luke's been trying to raise the money for ages,' she said almost conversationally. 'He's been promised studio time because of a cancellation, but he needs cash up-front. You could lend it to him, couldn't you, Dad? Then I'll pay you back.'

'Why on earth would I bankroll somebody I don't even know?'

'You don't know him, but I do,' Gaby retorted. 'We've been going out for three weeks and two days. Luke's mega-talented and he's very clever too. It's an investment. His group will definitely make it and then he'll be able to pay the money back. In buckets.'

Luke sat motionless, his blank expression unchanged.

'Even if I had the money, and I don't, if you think I'd lend it for something like this you're crazier than I thought,' said Calum sourly.

'The answer's definitely no,' said Lizzie.

This roused the youth to action. 'So I don't get the money?'

Husband and wife spoke in unison. 'Absolutely not.'

Slowly Luke hauled himself to his feet and made for the door, with

Gabriella close behind him. A few moments later Lizzie and Calum heard the sound of the front door closing.

A white-faced Gabriella reappeared. 'I hope you're satisfied. He'll probably bust up with me over this and it'll be all your fault.'

'If he was going around with you because of money, he's not worth it anyway,' said Calum. Then, always the peacemaker, he added, 'Look, if we'd had the chance to get to know him we might've helped. Why didn't you bring him round?'

'Because I knew what you'd say when you saw him. You're both such snobs.'

'That's unfair,' said Calum. 'And you know it.'

'You always say you're not prejudiced, but do you have any black friends? No.'

'Only because it hasn't happened. It's not deliberate,' Lizzie replied.

Gaby began to cry. 'Luke's kind and good and he's always been there for me. And now you've ruined it.'

Calum rolled his eyes at Lizzie.

'I hate you both!' The words were spat out. 'I hope Luke makes me pregnant, then I'd have an excuse to get out of this dump.' With that she wrenched open the door and ran up the stairs before either of her distressed parents could stop her.

'It's our fault,' said Lizzie. 'We've babied her a bit. That's the problem with an only child, and fifteen's quite grown-up these days.'

'How do we deal with this? She must realise she can't roam about London all night without permission. What if we sit her down and talk to her like an adult . . . ?' Calum's voice trailed off.

'Calum, don't you think I've tried? She freezes me out.'

'Maybe I should have a go.'

'I don't think this is the right time. She needs to cool off.'

'So do I.'

THE WEEKEND PASSED with Gabriella spending much of her time in her room. Calum took a phone call from the police officer who gave him the welcome news that Luke had a clean sheet as far as they were concerned. 'And in case you need to contact Luke for any reason in the future,' the officer added, 'this is his address.'

When Gaby finally did emerge, Calum experienced a surge of pity at the sight of her slight body, arms wrapped round herself defensively and lower lip trembling. This was abruptly dispelled when she glared at him.

'Am I grounded?'

Trying not to show surprise, his response was automatic. 'Definitely,' he said, as firmly as he could.

Incredibly, she seemed to accept this and he asked her to go with him to the sitting room for a chat.

'What's the point? We're never going to agree about anything.' She stared at him belligerently and stomped back to her bedroom.

Chapter Three

September was the busiest time of the year for both Calum and Lizzie. A new school term meant hours of extra preparation for her and as a supply teacher she was given tasks that permanent staff were happy to off-load. For his part, Calum had been forced to meet his bank manager again and admit that the expected injection of fresh capital had not materialised. He was given an extension of a month to present proposals for salvaging the situation, and for the first time he began seriously to consider selling his business.

Another exhibition design company called Fair Winds Inc, based in New York, had recently been making noises about a merger. It would mean a lump sum for Calum plus a salary to match his status as head of the British operations. And he would be able to hold on to most of his existing employees. So far Calum had not been desperate enough to consider losing his independence, but he wondered if the time had come. Still, he decided not to worry Lizzie with the problem. She had enough on her plate already.

During the last few days there had been no major upsets with Gabriella, partly because she was rarely to be seen, protesting in the evenings that she had already eaten by the time Calum came home and needed to study for her essays. As a peace move, Lizzie had tentatively suggested that Gaby invite Luke for a meal, but this was rejected. She comforted herself with the thought that although her daughter was uncommunicative, she was not overtly hostile. Hopefully, the storms were abating.

Late one afternoon, her mind whirling with jobs still needing to be done at school, Lizzie took a call from Edward Foxton.

'There's been a development,' he said. 'I've just had couriered from Andrew's solicitor formal notice of his intention to contest the will. They've applied for a preliminary hearing in three weeks' time, so I have to see you and Calum as soon as possible. Tomorrow morning if you can manage it.'

'I can come, but Calum's away at the National Exhibition Centre in Birmingham for the next three days. What's Andy playing at, Ed? He must see he hasn't a hope.' To her consternation Edward did not answer her question but said it was imperative that he talk to them together. Could she see if it was possible for Calum to manage an early-morning appointment?

Puzzled and anxious, Lizzie spent the next half-hour trying to track down Calum.

'You handle it, darling,' he said when she finally contacted him. The success of the exhibition was crucial to the company's perilous cash flow and he did not dare abandon his client.

'I can't. Ed insists we both have to see him. Calum, he gave me the impression he thinks Andy has a case.'

AT EDWARD FOXTON'S OFFICE at seven thirty the next morning, the solicitor did not waste time on the niceties. 'I was sent this yesterday by Blondell's, that's the firm your brother is using. It's a copy of a lab report comparing Calum and Gabriella's blood groups.'

'I thought all that stuff was confidential,' said Calum.

'It is.' He handed over a sheet of paper. 'I can only assume this fell into Andrew's hands because of the testing being done for his baby. Blondell's haven't the best reputation for being too particular, but we won't be able to complain about how they obtained this document; we can only challenge their information if it contains an untruth. Their claim is based on the blood samples being totally incompatible, which means that Calum could not be Gabriella's father.'

'That's utter nonsense,' said Lizzie, angrily.

Calum's eyes were fixed on the report.

When Edward told them he had asked the lab for the test to be done again, Lizzie's jaw tightened. 'Hold on a minute. You don't believe Andy, do you?'

He reached for a jug of water. 'I suppose my first thought was that Gaby must have been adopted. We lost touch for a couple of years and I assumed you hadn't mentioned it. No reason to, of course.'

'She was not adopted,' said Lizzie, startled. 'She's ours. And when the lab checks its work again they'll find they've made a mistake.' The two men made no response. Infuriated by her husband's silence, Lizzie repeated herself. 'You have my word that Gabriella is our baby, Calum's and mine.'

Edward was busying himself riffling through the papers. 'Quite so. This is upsetting for both of you, I see that.' He shifted uncomfortably in his seat. 'I must admit this case is giving me some anxiety because of your father's emphasis on the bloodline.' He picked up a copy of the will and read a sentence which had been highlighted. '"I want you to understand that my primary concern . . . is to ensure . . . the continuity of what I consider is the good bloodline of the Lynton family.'

'That may be so,' Lizzie retorted, 'but I'm not concerned about money here. I'm telling you categorically that Calum and I made a baby together and he was there when I gave birth.'

Calum took her hand and gave it a squeeze.

'Then it's straightforward,' said Edward briskly. 'We have already insisted that the test is to be done again. The lab has asked us to supply another sample of your blood, Calum, and Gaby's, of course.'

'We'd rather not involve Gaby in all this,' said Lizzie quickly.

'I appreciate that.' Edward appeared to be avoiding her eyes. 'But you must see that a fresh test is the only way to settle this.'

Lizzie tried to catch Calum's attention, but he was focusing on the solicitor's desk. 'So the word of a mother who was present at the conception of her own daughter isn't good enough?'

'The law demands hard evidence,' said Edward gently.

'I find that offensive. The reason we married so young was because Gabriella had been conceived,' Lizzie raised her voice, 'by both of us.' She appealed to Calum. 'Tell him.'

Before Calum could answer, Edward interrupted. 'Our best defence is to produce our own tests, one sample from Gabriella and another from Calum. I suggest we send them to the same laboratory so the other side can't make any capital out of a change of testing procedure.'

Lizzie had to give in. They arranged a date for the blood samples to be taken by their local doctor and said their goodbyes to Edward.

They had barely reached the steps outside his office when Lizzie, unable to hide her anger, demanded, 'Why didn't you back me in there? You know that test must be inaccurate.'

'You shouldn't worry,' said Calum, taking her arm. 'I can't see the point of arguing when we'll soon have the proof. And then we can fight back.' As he steered her towards the car park he glanced at his watch. 'I'm sorry to leave you, but I'll have to shoot off or I won't be on site by the time the exhibition opens.' He paused, keys in hand. 'What should we tell Gaby?'

'Nothing,' said Lizzie firmly. 'When they recheck those results it'll kick the case out so there's no need to upset her, is there?'

'Won't she ask why she has to give more blood?'

'Not if I say they need it to help Sebastian.'

She was right. Gaby raised no objection to going to the doctor again to give another blood sample if it meant helping the sick baby.

Lizzie was more unsettled by the potential court action than she would admit. She would have liked their solicitor to have been more dismissive about Andrew's challenge. And why hadn't Calum agreed with her whole-heartedly that the test, if not a fake, was inaccurate?

EVERYONE HAD WARNED them that Japanese rice wine could be lethal. But here she was on her fourth tiny glass and it was having no effect, Lizzie thought.

To celebrate their sixteenth wedding anniversary, Calum had arranged to take her with another couple, Sarah and Hugh Sinclair, to Sushi's, the best local restaurant. Hugh and Calum had met at university and by coincidence had ended up living in the same part of London. Their wives had become close friends when their children began to attend the local kindergarten.

When Sarah's husband Hugh had been made redundant, Lizzie was the first person Sarah turned to, and when Gaby was making life intolerable, Sarah was there with sympathy and gin and tonic. She had been immensely helpful in calming Lizzie after hearing that further blood tests were needed to fight Andy's allegation. 'It's worth the hassle to squash him once and for all,' she had said to her friend.

Calum now started the toasts. 'To my beautiful bride, as lovely now as she was when she walked down the aisle sixteen years ago.'

'To Lizzie.' The other three downed their egg-cup-sized glasses, which were instantly refilled.

Lizzie then raised her glass. 'Here's to the only man I could have married.' Another round of *sake* disappeared.

There was a snort from Hugh, who fancied himself as a comedian. '"Only man"? Come on, who you marry depends on who's around at the time.'

'You mean if Sarah hadn't begged you to marry her you'd have chosen someone else?' Lizzie's eyes danced mischievously.

'Exactly so,' said Hugh, 'and you might've married Peter Rivers.'

'He didn't have a chance.' Lizzie was used to Hugh's teasing.

But he was not to be diverted. 'Peter was pretty keen on you.'

'He was just a big flirt,' she said, noticing that Calum was not joining in the joshing. Surely he wasn't jealous?

'A flirt,' Sarah piped up. 'Like our eldest. If flirting was on the curriculum, he'd get an A grade.'

'That's understandable,' said Hugh. 'He's a carbon copy of me.'

'They all are,' retorted his wife. 'All three of them. I know I must've had something to do with the making of them but who would guess it?' She grinned at Calum. 'As soon as they were born the nurse said, "Here's another little Sinclair. Can't mistake his daddy."' Her hand flew to her mouth when she saw Calum's expression. 'Sorry, that was pretty crass.'

'Sorry for what?' said Hugh, trying to focus.

'It's their case,' said Sarah quickly. 'About the will?'

Light dawned. 'Oh yes. Worrying.'

'Andy must be off his rocker,' said Sarah sympathetically.

'The whole thing's absurd,' said Lizzie lightly. 'Calum and I have decided not to let it upset us. Haven't we, darling?'

He said nothing. If only that were true. These days he woke up long before the alarm, churning Andy's allegation over and over in his mind. How likely was it that the lab could make such a mistake?

'It's spiteful to say Gaby's not your daughter, Calum,' said Sarah indignantly.

Hugh was making a clumsy attempt to get his fingers round the tiny glass. 'Pity she doesn't look like you. It'd make the case go away.'

'Yes, she does,' said Sarah, retrieving the glass from his hand.

But Gabriella did not resemble him, thought Calum, rearranging the chopsticks on his plate. It had not bothered him before, but right now he did not find the subject amusing. He turned and indicated to the waiter that he would like the bill.

'What's the matter with you?' Hugh asked his wife truculently. 'She doesn't look like Calum. Any fool can see that.'

'You've had enough.' Sarah's mouth was set in a thin line.

'We all have,' said Calum.

Lizzie sat tightlipped in the back of the taxi on the way home, while Calum made an effort at desultory conversation by commenting on the standard of the cuisine and the service. Lizzie could not bring herself to respond; she was deflated. The allegations about Gaby's parentage were wicked, but what had Calum said to refute them? Nothing. Thank goodness they were with Sarah and Hugh, who were practically family. But his lack of support rankled.

'I'm tired,' he yawned, and then giving her a gentle nudge, added, 'but not too tired.' She smiled briefly. That was rich, expecting her to feel loving towards him after an evening like this. She could feel irritation building. She stopped herself. If she spurned him, she was fearful of where it could lead. It was the night of their anniversary and she had better get over this antagonism. Of course it was temporary. The second blood test would prove Calum was Gaby's father and all would be well again.

As HE WAITED for Edward Foxton to finish his phone conversation, Calum gazed round the familiar oak-panelled reception area.

When Edward had requested another meeting at short notice, the timing was impossible for Lizzie so Calum had come alone.

For the umpteenth time he chastised himself for being nervous about the result of the new test. How could he doubt he was Gaby's father? It was preposterous. Not Lizzie. Never his Lizzie. Since their romance had begun at university they'd been steadfastly faithful to each other. There'd been several times when he could have been unfaithful. Hotels shared by exhibition personnel provided fertile ground for adultery and he'd be lying if he said he hadn't been tempted once or twice by stunning models on the promotion staff. And Tess Parker.

Calum had been assiduous about never being alone with Tess since an encounter a couple of years ago. It had been after a particularly hectic week in which they had been thrown together from daybreak until late evening. After packing up he had invited Tess to share a brandy in the deserted exhibition suite. He had found himself kissing her and reacting to her ardent response. It had taken every ounce of self-restraint to break away and apologise for losing control. 'I wanted it as much as you,' she had said to him.

He and Tess had not referred to it the next day or afterwards and he vowed he would be careful not to put himself in that situation again. But recently she had made it clear she would not be averse to taking their relationship further, sending him the occasional email to amuse and distract him from his worries.

Calum watched as Edward unlocked his desk and extracted a slim buff folder. 'There's no easy way to tell you this, Calum. I'm afraid the original tests have been proved correct. You could not possibly be Gabriella's father.'

'I can't believe that. How can you be so sure?'

Edward shook his head. 'I'm sorry, Calum. Our experts tell me there's a ninety-nine per cent probability you are not her father.'

Calum gazed at his friend, his heart beginning to pound. 'There must be another explanation. May I see?'

As he looked at the meaningless codes produced by the laboratory, Calum's eyes began to blur and dimly he became aware of Edward sliding a glass of brandy across the desk.

'It's a mistake, it must be. And this test isn't a hundred per cent certain, Ed.' His eyes pleaded for reassurance.

'I don't think there's been any mistake.' Edward pointed to a paragraph of the accompanying letter from the lab and quoted, ' "These results conform to the previous ones in every particular".'

'But there's a one per cent chance that I am her father.'

'Calum, I would very much like to offer you hope, but I can't. I'm sorry, but you're going to have to accept . . .' his voice trailed off.

Calum stared at the pens on Edward's desk. Eventually he asked, 'What am I going to do, Ed?'

The solicitor's face exuded concern. 'I don't think you should do anything, not at the moment. You need to think about it rationally.'

'Rationally! All these years Lizzie made me believe Gaby was mine. Can you imagine what it means to know your whole life is based on a lie? Why didn't she trust me enough to tell me the truth?'

Edward said nothing.

'I was sure there was no other man in her life,' Calum said forlornly. 'Just last week she laughed at me for suggesting there was. That's hard to take. Even after sixteen years she didn't have the guts to tell me the truth. I'd respect her more if she had.'

'Calum, I want you to think about your next step very carefully.' Edward stood up and began to pace the room. 'How you handle this could make or break your relationship. Whatever happened is history,' he went on. 'You can't change it. But,' he took off his spectacles and rested them on the desk, 'what you do now will determine the present and the future.'

Calum bowed his head to try to regain some control. His throat was closing up and he felt perilously close to tears.

'As a father myself,' said Edward, 'I can't imagine what this is like for you, but as your lawyer I have to remind you that we're fighting a court case. I'd rather not raise it now, but we need to take soundings for a new strategy. I've already consulted a barrister and—'

'Damn the will. This is my life you're talking about.'

'I'm sorry, Calum, but I also act for Gabriella and I have to put up the best case I can on her behalf.'

'Does Andy need to be told about the second test?'

'I'm afraid so, but we'll vigorously contest any case he puts up and our strength is the bond between Gabriella and her grandfather. I'm reasonably sure the judge will go with Robert's clearly stated intentions in his will.'

Calum stood up abruptly. 'Do what you have to do.' Before going through the door, he paused. 'Who could he be?' he asked agitatedly. 'The man who fathered Gaby?'

Edward raised his shoulders in a gesture of bafflement and Calum went on, 'How can things ever be the same between Lizzie and me?'

As he walked towards the car, Calum's first thought was to go straight to Lizzie's school, yank her out of the classroom and force her to admit the truth. All these years he had admired her honesty and her courage. He had misread her completely. She was devious, scheming and, what was worse, gutless. Why hadn't she been brave enough to confess that she had made a mistake?

He got into the car and tried to steady his shaking hands. Edward's advice had always proved to be wise in the past and he could see the sense of it. Do nothing impulsive. Think of your marriage. Think of Gaby. She was another victim of this deceit. At least he could try to protect her as much as possible.

He phoned Tess to cancel his afternoon appointments. Her voice was full of concern and for a moment he was tempted to confide the whole hideous story to her but thought better of it.

As he sat staring miserably through the windscreen, the germ of an idea began to form. He went onto autopilot on the drive home. He would have a couple of hours to himself before Lizzie's school day ended. Gaby had swimming lessons and would not return till late afternoon.

At home Calum made straight for the bedroom, where he sank to his knees to rummage under the bed. He pulled out two large shoe-boxes covered in a film of dust. He upturned one of them onto the bed and there, in a pile, lay mementos of his youth—letters, school reports, diaries and souvenirs.

Rapidly he emptied the other box. This one contained hundreds of snapshots. Memories flooded back as he began to place the pictures into two separate piles, those taken in the last sixteen years and, the smaller pile, from his university days. He sifted through the larger batch and picked out a photo showing a group of friends at a barbecue. The picture triggered sudden, dark memories. He sat motionless, remembering.

That was the night he'd gone to look for Lizzie in the garden, with her drink, only to find her half in shadow talking to Peter Rivers. Peter had been part of the crowd, about ten of them from college days, but he always seemed to drift, ostensibly casually, towards Lizzie, as several photos showing his tall figure standing next to hers testified. Calum and Lizzie had had a terrible fight, Lizzie accusing him of mistrusting her. But he had seen the sensuous look on Peter's face. The row was a catalyst for straight talking between them and they vowed to be honest with each other and brave enough to discuss problems before they became insurmountable.

What a fool he'd been. All this time his friends had probably been laughing at him; they would know all about her and Peter carrying on behind his back. But why the hell hadn't she gone off with him when she'd found she was pregnant? Maybe, he thought bitterly, Peter had made himself scarce. Although he did not think of himself as a violent man, at that moment Calum felt a desire to destroy everything he and Lizzie had built up together. Everything had been based on deceit.

LIZZIE CLOSED DOWN her laptop, pushed it to the back of the desk and gave her arms a good stretch. She was feeling more positive about everything. Today would surely mark the end of a nightmarish few weeks and then, thank God, they would get back to normal.

It was only four o'clock and there were dozens of tasks still to be tackled, but she could concentrate no longer. She wanted to hear about Calum's meeting with Edward Foxton.

As she walked swiftly from the bus-stop she saw with surprise that Calum's car was parked outside the house. What had brought him home this early? She opened the front door and called his name. He answered from the bedroom so she made her way up the stairs. He was sitting on the bed surrounded by photographs and postcards.

'Are you feeling OK?'

He ignored her and continued to sort through the souvenirs.

'I've been waiting for you to phone all afternoon,' she said in a tone of mild reproof, moving towards him with every intention of giving him her customary kiss. He drew back.

'What did Ed say?' she asked.

At last he looked at her. 'Is this him?' He held up a photograph. 'Don't try and pretend.'

She took the photograph and stared at him dumbly.

'Peter Rivers,' he said. 'He's Gabriella's father, isn't he?'

She sank down on the edge of the bed, the photo still clasped in her hand, and stared at her husband's pale, stricken face. Calum's voice was quiet. 'The second test is exactly the same as the first. I can't be Gabriella's father.'

She stared at his wild eyes. 'Calum, can't you see? The lab's made a mistake again.'

'You never give up, do you? Can you imagine how humiliating it was, sitting in Ed's office, realising how you've made a fool of me all this time?' He snatched the photo back from her. 'Take a look at this. His jaw, his nose, his colouring. It's Gabriella. The evidence was staring me in the face.'

Peter Rivers. Tall, dark-haired, a jester. Lizzie remembered his ironic sense of humour and how it matched her own. There was a spark between them, she had to admit, and she enjoyed his admiration. He paid her extravagant compliments which she could never take seriously because compared with Calum he was lightweight.

Calum broke into her thoughts. 'Peter was always hanging around you like a dog on heat. I suppose he wouldn't marry you, so you came to the poor sucker who did.'

All the frustrations of the past weeks engulfed her. She wanted to scream and rant about the unfairness of being accused of such a deception by a husband who was supposed to trust her word above all others, but some inner voice urged caution.

'I've lived with you all these years,' she said steadily. 'Is this what you think of me?'

'How can both sets of tests be wrong, Lizzie? Answer me that.'

'I don't know, but I do know that you're Gaby's father.'

Calum ignored that. 'Why didn't you have the guts to tell me before I was forced to find out?'

Her restraint evaporated. Anger propelled her towards him and she began to pummel his chest with her clenched fists. 'You're the only man I've been with since we met,' she shouted.

He took hold of both of her wrists. 'You were so concerned to find a name for your illegitimate baby you didn't care about me.'

My God, he actually believes that, thought Lizzie, dismayed. Unsteadily she pulled away from him and went to the dressing table. If he would not accept her word, what could she do? Right now she was too distraught to think straight. And their daughter—and despite what Calum was saying, she was their daughter—would be home at any moment.

Lizzie tried to compose herself. She had to keep Gaby in ignorance of the calamity that had befallen them. She and Calum could pretend to be disagreeing about something else for a time, but if the court case went ahead Gaby would have to be told about Andy's allegation. For now, it was essential that they carry on as normal.

Somehow she had to prove that the lab had made a mistake. Again. They were testing the same blood and using the same procedure; obviously they had reproduced their error.

THE BABY WRIGGLED as the cold hands of the doctor touched his stomach. He squealed and rolled over, his large hazel eyes alive with mischief.

'He's doing well, isn't he?' said Edina. 'Since you changed the drugs he's been really lively.'

The doctor's face registered none of her hope. In the seven months since Sebastian had been diagnosed as suffering from leukaemia Edina had wanted the doctor to express some optimism, but he was the pragmatic type. Polite, professional and kind he might be, but Edina occasionally wished he would hold her hand and squeeze some reassurance into her system. Sebastian had been in remission for nineteen weeks and she and Andy had just emerged from the 'holding-the-breath' stage and were about to enter the 'maybe-it's-gone-for-good' level, when he had suffered a relapse. The memory of the day it happened would never leave her. That was when, for the first time, the doctor mentioned a bone marrow transplant. He had been glancing at the database and thought there might be a couple of potential donors; but it was a hit and miss affair and she could help in the search. Family members were the best sources, they often produced a match.

His voice had gone on sonorously while Edina, not taking in the words, watched her baby singing to himself as he played with his fingers. Why did this have to happen to her little angel? Why? Anger gave way to uncontrollable grief. Andrew came rushing back from work and for the rest of the day and night she did little but weep helplessly on his shoulder.

During the first months of their marriage Andrew had been inconsiderate and bad-tempered, especially when his business ventures failed. She had often thought that their marriage would surely not have lasted had it not been for Sebastian's illness. Having a sick child bound you in ways she could not have anticipated.

Andy had changed. He often made supper when she'd had a tiring day and, though he worked long hours, insisted on taking over at night when Sebastian was fretful. She was sure that if only Andy's family could see this compassionate and caring side of him, it might change some of their perceptions.

Now she was woken from her reverie by the doctor, who had finished his examination and was packing away his instruments.

'I think we'd better admit him to hospital immediately, Mrs Lynton.' Her blood froze because he actually took her hand in his.

'Why?'

'Before we can do the bone marrow transplant we have to get his body ready for it. We need to do transfusions with blood and platelets and these can't be done with Sebastian as an outpatient.'

'Now?' she had managed to croak. 'Right now?'

'He can't wait much longer, Edina.'

He had called her by her first name. The message could hardly be clearer. He thought Sebastian was going to die.

LIZZIE'S FAITH in Calum had been damaged. In her mind she could understand his confusion when confronted with the results of the blood tests, but in her heart she believed he had let her down.

It was fortunate that Gaby did not seem to notice the extent of her parents' alienation and as her eating times rarely coincided with theirs they were saved having to make polite conversation. They were physically estranged but living in the same house, both suffering yet unable to comfort each other. Calum walked out of the room each time Lizzie attempted to convince him that he was Gaby's father.

She decided to talk to Edward. Calum had a high regard for him; maybe she could persuade him to intervene on her behalf.

His voice on the phone was crisp. 'I'm sorry, Lizzie, I'm trained to accept evidence, not someone's word, however fond I am of them.' He sounded distant, not like the friend she had known for years.

'I see,' she said. 'Well, I'm not happy about that.' She slammed down the phone. If Edward wouldn't help her, she would have to confront the lab herself.

THE WHITE-COATED laboratory technicians were hard at work on blood samples. It was laborious and time-consuming. For bone marrow work they had to establish the human leucocyte/antigen typing through testing white cells against numerous antibodies.

Today their specific task was to recheck a test in the batch on the Lynton child. They had already handed over the results of a second test to a firm of solicitors for some kind of paternity case. Then the boss had insisted on this third check.

Dan Hargreaves picked up the Lynton file. 'Finished?'

His assistant nodded.

'Come up with anything different?'

'Nope, exactly the same. Why wouldn't it be?'

'People always hope it's an error.'

'They wouldn't be so keen to give their blood if they had any idea of how much one tiny drop can tell us.'

'Too true.'

'And it didn't help that the client read that smart-arsed comment, "Not his kid. Bet he doesn't know."'

Dan did not reply, but gazed out at the darkening sky. That note could spell curtains to the promise of a future partnership, not to mention a subpoena from the ethics committee of the General Medical Council. But today all he was concerned about was Mrs Elizabeth Lynton. She was accusing the lab of making a mistake with the tests. She was wrong but he had to mollify her, then steer her away from any idea that Andrew Lynton had decided to contest the will as a direct result of the lab's indiscretion. If the news leaked out that the laboratory was insecure, then it would be the end for the business and certainly for him. As it was he had been verbally flayed by his boss for allowing a client access to a confidential report. He hadn't been able to deny it. Andrew Lynton's solicitor had assured the lab that if it cooperated, the information would be treated with every discretion. He had also made it perfectly clear why his client required a copy of the lab report on the blood samples given by Calum and Gabriella Lynton. Dan's protestation that it wasn't he who had written the damaging comment was dismissed contemptuously. If the report hadn't been shown in the first place there would be no repercussions, serious or otherwise.

Dan did not anticipate problems with Elizabeth Lynton and hoped it would not take long to get rid of her. Carefully he straightened the pen and ink set on his desk. He had to give the impression of a top professional at work, someone whose laboratory simply could not make a mistake.

As Lizzie walked through the doorway, Dan's business smile was firmly in place, but it gave way instantly to genuine pleasure at the sight of this attractive woman. 'Do sit down, Mrs Lynton,' he said, indicating the chair opposite him. Nice legs, he thought. 'Would you like some tea? Coffee?'

When she refused he said, 'I believe you're unhappy about a test we did here.'

'I certainly am. It is inaccurate and it's caused me and my family a great deal of trouble.'

He was sorry to hear that, he said, but it was highly unlikely the lab had made a mistake.

'Are you saying you never make mistakes?'

'No one's infallible, but we've done a third test and the results are exactly the same as the first two.' He spent the next few minutes explaining exactly how the tests were done.

When he had finished, she shook her head. 'Gaby is my husband's child. I wasn't a virgin when I met my husband, but I assure you that I haven't made love to anyone else since we started going out.'

Dan stopped himself saying what a great waste that was. 'If you tell me you're the mother, that's good enough for me,' he said with a confidence he did not feel. 'But we have established that your husband could not be the father.'

Her face crumpled. 'I don't understand. You say you believe me . . .'

'I do, but I'm a scientist and I deal in logic.' He went through the possibilities in his mind and felt sudden inspiration. He rose and crossed over to a filing cabinet to take out a buff folder. 'There has to be another explanation,' he said. 'You've told me you're telling the truth so it means we need to test for other comparable components.' She looked perplexed. 'Wider tests might give us more clues.' There was something about her sincerity that made him want to help.

'The sensible thing would be for me to take a sample of your blood for testing,' he said. 'I'm surprised no one has asked for one before.'

'There was no reason. I'm not related to Sebastian and they tested only the Lynton family, not those who married into it.'

She took off her jacket and Dan applied a tourniquet, pressing her wrist gently to try and raise a vein. Her skin was pale and delicate and smelt of freshly picked lavender. 'You'll have to be patient for the results,' he said, extracting the syringe carefully from her arm. Finding out what blood group she belonged to was a mere ten minutes' work, he told her, but DNA comparison, to settle matters of paternity, could take as long as three or four weeks.

'Will I have to wait that long?' Lizzie asked in alarm.

Dan shook his head. 'The lab's pretty busy, but I'll ask them to rush through a preliminary test on your blood. It should be ready in about two or three days' time.'

Whatever the result of the test, what this desirable, vulnerable woman needed at this moment was to be rescued from a slough of despond. He was just the man to do it.

CALUM PUSHED HIS CHAIR back and grinned at Tess. She always made him feel better. Lately they had been spending more time together after the others in the office had gone home. She had been offering him practical advice and together they were working on the redrafting of clients' contracts.

'I'm fed up with all this,' he gestured to the pile of invoices. 'Let's go to the pub.' Calum had no desire to rush home.

As Tess and he settled into a small booth, she launched into the ramifications of a conversation Calum had had that afternoon with Fair Winds Inc in New York.

The restrained lighting in the pub highlighted the glisten of her lipstick and her generous mouth moved rapidly as her story gained momentum. For a moment he speculated what it would be like to silence her with his own lips. Until now he had stifled all memories of that solitary occasion when he had almost lost control. Last time he had had a reason to fight temptation. He was enjoying a damn good marriage. Not any more.

He was conscious of Tess looking at him quizzically over the rim of her glass. 'What are you thinking about? You've been miles away.'

'Better you can't read my mind.'

She raised her eyebrows. 'Would I enjoy it?'

Already regretting his provocative comment, he did not respond.

Tess rotated the stem of her wineglass slowly through her fingers. 'You're having a tough time at the moment, aren't you? And I'm not talking about the business.'

Warmed by the alcohol and needing a sympathetic ear, he found himself telling her of the terrible discovery about Gaby's paternity. Tess listened, her eyes full of compassion. He talked about the tension at home because Lizzie kept on insisting there was some mistake with the test. Then he blurted out, 'I can't understand,' he said. 'Why, when she's been found out, won't she admit the truth?'

Tess gave a deep sigh. 'Haven't you heard the saying "deny, deny, deny"? If the test proves you're not Gaby's father, what else is there for her to say? And she'll probably keep on denying it. She has to.'

'Even after two tests say the same? That's ridiculous.'

'I'd do exactly the same.' She took a sip of wine and stared at him over the rim of the glass. 'If it meant I'd keep you.'

LIZZIE WAS DREADING the sound of the key in the lock. She prayed that Calum would be late and she would be in bed and could pretend to be asleep. Anything to put off the terrible moment when she had to tell him that the laboratory had been right about his test. No ifs or buts. She had tussled with the idea of not telling him about her visit to the lab. But she wanted to let him know that the doctor had believed her when her husband of sixteen years had not.

The phone rang and made her jump. It showed how tense she was, she thought, picking up the receiver. But it wasn't Calum. Tess Parker asked her to tell Calum she would bring the file he'd left in the pub to their morning meeting.

Lizzie smacked the phone down, irritated that she was in a state of stress waiting for him to come home, while he was apparently having a relaxed drink with the attentive Tess. When at last she heard the sound of the front door opening and Calum came in, it was apparent from the loosened tie and his glazed eyes that he'd had more than his customary pint of beer.

She gave him Tess's message. but his face gave nothing away.

'I've something important to discuss before you go off to bed,' she then said carefully.

He looked at her warily before easing himself into a chair. Lizzie described her visit to the laboratory and her interview with Dr Hargreaves and he straightened quickly, asking if they had found out anything new. When she said the test had given the same result, the light went out of his eyes.

'So there's got to be another explanation,' she went on quickly.

'There is,' he said icily. 'You were pregnant by another man.' Abruptly he got up, turned on his heel and stalked out of the room.

THE YELLOW-SPOT BALL ricocheted off the scarred wall and Edward Foxton charged towards it, walloping it at a vicious angle. He was a wily player but Calum was the better strategist.

Edward made an unsuccessful lunge.

'Game, third set and champ.' Calum held his racket above his head in a victory salute and he and Edward made their way towards the showers. As the hot water cascaded down his body, Calum reflected how he conformed to Lizzie's criticism that men compartmentalised their emotions. She would have insisted on hearing the latest development on the court case rather than bide her time until the game was over and they were sitting in the clubhouse bar.

They ordered a ploughman's and a pint of bitter, then Calum could restrain himself no longer.

'So tell me.'

Edward shrugged. 'Bit of a problem. It's not straightforward, I'm afraid. I felt sure our barrister, Tim Goodman, would quibble about the way your father expressed himself in the second will and he did.'

'The bloodline?'

'Precisely. Tim thinks it could make for complications because judges' interpretations can vary.'

'Why didn't Dad mention Gabriella's name in the will?'

The solicitor shifted uneasily in his seat. 'Because it wouldn't have occurred to him there were any other granddaughters.'

The waiter appeared with their order and they supped their pints meditatively.

'With all the evidence we're going to present about the bond between Gaby and my father, we must win, surely?'

'Nothing's certain, but I think we have a good chance. Tim Goodman mentioned that the judge might want to talk to Gabriella.'

Calum put his glass down with a thump. 'I hope not. I don't want her to be put under that kind of pressure. She doesn't yet know about the blood test. Lizzie and I are hoping that Andy will settle so there won't be a case and she won't have to know.' Observing his friend's questioning gaze, he added, 'Yes, we will tell her, but at a time when we think she can handle it better.' He told Edward that he had tried speaking to his brother but Andrew would not come to the phone or return his calls.

'I don't think there's any chance of his settling out of court,' said Edward. 'He wants the will declared null and void. In which case your father would be deemed to have died intestate and then the whole estate would be shared between you and Andy.'

Privately, Calum thought he would not quibble with this outcome. Then he felt guilty. It had been his father's expressed desire for his money to go to Gabriella and, whatever he thought about the decision, he had to fight for it. He thought for a moment. 'OK, you don't think he'll settle. But I'd like you to have one more try. We haven't any cash, but when he knows I'm prepared to sell the business perhaps he'll change his mind.'

Edward agreed to put another offer to Andrew, but warned Calum not to assume his brother would be satisfied with what he could raise. They drank in silence for a minute before Edward gave an embarrassed cough. 'How are things with you and Lizzie?' Calum's expression was so melancholy that he added quickly, 'If you'd rather not talk about it . . .'

'No, you're one of the few people I dare confide in. Ed, every time I look at her I'm reminded I've been living with a liar all these years. The problem is I'm stuck. I can't do anything because I have to think of Gaby. She needs me.'

Edward nodded sympathetically.

'I love her as my own, nothing will change that, and you know the strange thing about all this? The fact that she's not mine doesn't worry me nearly as much as I'd expected it would.' Calum raked his fingers through his hair. 'It's Lizzie's duplicity that really hurts. I feel cheated.' He appealed to his friend. 'Is that any basis for the future?'

EDINA STIRRED HER COFFEE, aware that Andy was still speaking about the court case, but too tired to concentrate any more. The doctors had told her that Sebastian was responding reasonably well to the preoperation tests and if a match could be found they would go ahead immediately. Please God, let it be soon. None of the relatives had matched up, but the hospital was still testing the hundreds of volunteers who had come forward.

The baby's illness had brought her and Andy closer. She had been surprised at how gentle and loving he was with Sebastian. It was a side of himself he rarely showed to outsiders.

Edina did not want any court case. She hated the idea of fighting with the family when they had been so good about Sebastian. She had no legal knowledge, but it seemed to her perfectly clear that Robert Lynton wanted his money to go to Gabriella, so whatever the solicitors were putting into Andy's head, she did not think they had much chance of winning.

She had never set eyes on the old man. By the time she met Andrew he was not speaking to any of his family, but when Sebastian was born Andy's mother came to see him and gave Edina a cheque for £500. She never came back again. Andy said that was because she was completely under his father's thumb. Edina thought it a shame Robert Lynton had not seen his only grandson. But if he didn't want to acknowledge Sebastian, she didn't want any of his money. She had not got the courage to say any of this to Andy.

There was a sharp cry from the next room and at once Edina sprang up from the table and ran to attend to her son.

Chapter Four

In the early dawn the scene outside Gaby's school was chaotic. Parents, trying to be helpful, were hampering the driver in his efforts to load the coach. Baggage was piled everywhere and it was raining. Invariably the pupils began their annual half-term trip to Lyon with damp anoraks and hair dripping down their backs. The unearthly hour of 4.00am had been chosen so that the coach would pick up the Dover ferry in time to make a reasonable start on the French autoroute. They should leave in five minutes.

Gaby was sitting in the front seat, headphones already clamped in place, when Lizzie spotted a familiar navy-blue Rover screeching to a halt alongside the bus. Calum had said his goodbyes to Gaby the night before so what was he doing turning up here to see her off?

He tooted the horn twice before climbing out, then came to stand alongside Gaby, waving at her until he caught her attention. A broad smile crossed her face and she got up and clambered off the coach.

'Dad. What are you doing here?'

He clasped her in his arms and held her tight.

'What's the matter?'

Lizzie thought she could see the beginning of tears.

'Nothing, Gabs. Nothing at all. I just wanted to see you.' He let her go. 'You know you're my favourite daughter.'

'Dad,' she laughed, as she always did, 'you've only got one.'

Never had this familiar litany sounded more poignant to Lizzie, and she assumed his unexpected appearance was as much a message to her as to his daughter.

The last pupil turned up and the driver was finally able to depart. Hands waved frantically until the vehicle was out of sight. There was an awkward moment when Calum, standing by Lizzie, muttered, 'Come on, then.' She had to explain to Sarah that she did not need a lift home.

On the journey back, Lizzie attempted to discuss Gaby's packed schedule, but Calum rebuffed her efforts with a curt, 'I saw Edward yesterday. It seems Andy is determined to go to court.'

'We can't let him do that. We've got to settle.'

'Do you think I haven't tried? I've asked Ed to have another go but he's pessimistic about the chances.'

Lizzie twisted her wedding ring as she always did when she was stressed. The pounds were dropping off her and the ring was now so loose it was in danger of falling off.

'Then Gaby's going to find out everything,' she said dully.

'Not if I can help it. I think we should sell out so that we can make Andy a decent offer. I intend to leave for America tomorrow to see if Erik Schroeder at Fair Winds still wants to take me over.'

'Sell the business?'

'There's no other option. It's still doing well enough to interest Erik and I hope you agree that we should.' Lizzie owned 12 per cent of the shares and, when she hesitated, he reminded her that he would still head the British arm.

Lizzie was taken aback, but she could offer no alternative and so reluctantly agreed. Once or twice over the last few days she had ditched her pride and made an attempt to discuss their problems. But, if anything, his hostility seemed to be increasing and each time she made a peace move he would walk out or change the subject.

This unravelling of their marriage had happened at such speed, that she began to question how solid its foundations had been. Surely, if Calum had truly valued her all this while, he would have tried to find some solution for them, instead of pushing her away. If their relationship had disintegrated to such an extent, would they ever be able to put it together again?

CALUM KEPT an obedient eye on the semaphoring air stewardess as she indicated the emergency exits. He had an appointment the following day with Erik Schroeder, the egocentric chief executive of

Fair Winds Inc, and he was preparing himself for tough negotiations. He had a rough figure in mind although he doubted it would be enough to satisfy his brother, whose motive in all this Calum assumed was to safeguard the future of his son. No other reason could excuse his actions.

Calum eased open the seat belt as the overhead sign was switched off. His mind turned back to the business. He had been forced to tell the staff that it needed an injection of cash, and this was unsettling for all of them. There were eight people on the payroll and Calum was conscious that a number of them had left good jobs to come to him. They were rightly nervous that their jobs were not as secure as they'd once thought.

He accepted a glass of orange juice from the stewardess, leaned back and tried to blot out the question that had been troubling him. Just supposing Lizzie had confessed the truth about her pregnancy at the time; what would he have done? The answer came at once. However much he loved her, he could not have married her.

LIZZIE HAD LEFT HOME far too early for her appointment with Dan Hargreaves and she arrived forty-five minutes ahead of time. Fortuitously, his last meeting had been cancelled and the instant she saw his welcoming smile, some of her tension evaporated. Surely his relaxed manner must indicate he had good news for her. But her optimism was short-lived.

'I'm really sorry,' he said, 'there's a slight delay and the last few pieces of information are being collated now. It won't be long. Under an hour, I'm told.'

She could not hide her disappointment.

'While they're doing the last of it why don't I take you to the wine bar round the corner?' Dan suggested.

She nodded gratefully. 'A drink is exactly what I could use.'

Dan Hargreaves was an amusing companion, and as they drank she found to her surprise that her worries receded. Perhaps it was the combination of a couple of glasses of chilled chardonnay and the candlelight in the darkened cellar, but for the first time in weeks Lizzie began to relax and she found herself confiding in Dan about Gabriella's inheritance and the fight for the money between the two brothers. He appeared riveted. He was such a sympathetic listener that Lizzie wished she could tell him how serious the rift was between her and Calum. But she was saved from any possible indiscretion when he straightened suddenly and took off the pager attached to his waistband.

'It's the lab,' he said. 'I'll find out what's happening. Excuse me.'

She watched his athletic figure hurry towards the phones, certain the call was to do with her test. She had no clear idea how it could prove that Calum was Gaby's father; she simply trusted that it could. Why else would Dr Hargreaves have suggested taking a blood sample from her?

He returned to their table and sat down. Lizzie stared at him, her heart pounding in her rib cage. His expression was solemn. Iron fingers gripped her insides.

'This is going to be hard to understand,' he said, his expression grim. 'It's a scientific fact that a mother's blood always matches that of her child in some respect. Yours doesn't. Which means,' he swallowed, 'there's no possibility that you gave birth to Gabriella.'

Lizzie's face was white. Her body started to shake. 'I saw her being born. They put a mirror at the bottom of the bed. I saw her come into the world and then Calum cut the cord. She's our baby.'

'You saw a baby being born. But it wasn't Gabriella. It couldn't have been.' He leaned over and took her ice-cold hands in his. 'I think there must have been a mix-up somewhere along the line at the hospital and you were given the wrong baby.'

This was not happening. Not to her. She could not speak, could not feel the contact with him. Dan poured some bottled water into a glass and handed it to her. Gratefully she gulped it down.

After a few moments she managed to stammer, 'I don't understand . . . how could it happen?'

'That's what we have to find out. What happened right after the birth? Tell me exactly.'

Searing pain, she remembered. Labour had lasted for more than eighteen hours. By the time the midwife told her it was time to push, Lizzie had been debilitated, full of drugs, and weepy. The midwife had handed the newborn baby to Lizzie, but she was too weak to hold her for more than a few minutes before Calum took over. He cradled his daughter and began crooning to her as Lizzie sank into exhausted oblivion. When she awoke, the staff nurse told her the baby had been taken away to the special care unit for jaundice treatment.

'How long was she there?' Dan asked.

'For about two days. I struggled up there, with Calum, and held her hand, talked to her . . .' She bit her lip. She must not break down.

'You didn't notice anything different? Her size, her colouring?'

'No, but I'd had only a short glimpse of her when she was born and I was exhausted, full of drugs, and in the first few hours they let me sleep.' She added, more defensively than she intended, 'Calum held the baby and he didn't notice anything was wrong either.'

'Did you breastfeed?'

'Yes, the following day.'

'And as far as you were concerned it was the same baby that you visited in the special care unit?'

She nodded. Dan was quiet for a time then asked a question which surprised her. 'What day of the week did you give birth?'

'Sunday,' said Lizzie immediately. She remembered Calum reciting that rhyme to her about Sunday's child being the most favoured.

'Sunday's the day when a mistake like that could happen,' he said. 'Hospitals are often short-handed at weekends. Two babies could have arrived in the special care unit at the same time,' he said, 'and the identity tags could have been accidentally switched. Security systems weren't as rigorous then as they are now.'

Surely she ought to have known at once? Wouldn't some instinct have told her that the baby who returned from the special care unit wasn't hers? But when she voiced this thought to Dan he reassured her. 'Don't blame yourself. You bonded with the baby at your breast. Why should it occur to you that she wasn't yours?'

She would never forget Gabriella's eyes fixed on her face during those close moments of breastfeeding. Lizzie masked her face with both hands as a flood of emotion threatened to swamp her. There were so many memories . . . watching Gabriella's expression as she lay sleeping in her cot, or toddling round the garden, or grimacing at her first taste of carrots . . . And all the time, all fifteen years of it, she had been loving the wrong child.

Lizzie let her hands drop into her lap, took a deep breath and asked Dan the question she had been avoiding.

'What,' she asked quietly, 'could have happened to my child?'

He frowned. 'It won't be easy to find out. But you've had a great shock and I'm not sure you should make any decisions about that, not right now. Once you start to search, other people are sure to find out why you're asking questions and you have to think through the consequences before disrupting so many lives.' He paused for a second. 'Why not talk it over with your husband?'

'He's in America.'

'Is there anyone else you can talk to? I don't think it's a good idea for you to be on your own.'

Lizzie nodded, thinking of Sarah, but Sarah was in Norfolk with the rest of her brood for the half-term holiday. She did not say so to Dan Hargreaves. She was already feeling she had unburdened herself too much to someone who was a comparative stranger. Before making a quick exit, Lizzie thanked him profusely for his help and promised to keep in touch.

Of course she had to tell Calum, but first she needed time to marshal her thoughts, to work out the full implications of the bombshell that threatened to fragment their lives. Poor little Gaby. She dreaded the moment she would have to tell her she belonged to neither of them. The girl's future rested on the way she handled this.

Back home, Lizzie lay on the bed completely worn out. It was incredible that the hospital might have accidentally switched the babies and yet nothing else made sense of the blood tests. Dr Hargreaves had told her there could be no other explanation.

She levered herself off the bed and began to forage around the top of her wardrobe until she found the small holdall she had taken with her to hospital. Lodged in the corner of the bag was a piece of tissue paper containing the doll-sized pink wristband bearing their surname and Gabriella's date and time of birth. She examined it carefully. How could the hospital have made such a cataclysmic mistake?

The one comfort to spring from all this mess was that her attitude to Gaby was unchanged. She hoped she was being honest with herself, but at the moment it did not matter, one way or the other, that she was not her biological mother. And whatever criticisms she could make of Calum's behaviour towards her, she could discern no change in his attitude to Gaby since he had been told about the blood tests. Knowing her husband as well as she did, she was certain that whatever his true feelings, Gaby would never be the loser.

Lizzie glanced at her watch and made a rapid calculation about New York time. She dialled the number of his hotel.

CALUM, TOO, was looking at his watch. He had just left Schroeder's office on the East Side and had an hour to get across the city for his meeting with his accountant and lawyer. He had left an important document in his room and having hailed a cab he asked the driver if he could wait outside the hotel. Talks had gone well with Schroeder and he was feeling more relaxed than at the start of the trip.

Calum raced into the hotel and up to the ninth floor. It did not take him long to find the paper he needed. But when he glanced through it he saw that one of the figures was wrong. It could skewer everything. He'd have to phone the office and get them to fax a new copy. As he reached out for the receiver, it rang. Please God, let it be the office and he could get Tess onto it right away. But it was Lizzie.

'Is this a good time?'

'Afraid not, I'm rushing off to a meeting. Gaby OK?' If he phoned

Tess she could probably fax the new figures to his accountant's office before he arrived.

'Yes, she's fine. Look, I've had the results of my blood test.'

'Lizzie, I'm sorry, I can't talk now. I'm only interested if this changes the picture. Am I Gaby's father?'

'No, but—'

'Then I'll have to phone you back later.'

'Calum, I kept on telling you there had been a mistake and I've found out that—'

'Sorry, Lizzie, I'm going to be late, I really have to go. Bye.'

Lizzie replaced the receiver, fuming. How dare he not listen? Where the hell were his priorities? She sighed, but Calum was bound to phone back. She cracked open a couple of free-range eggs into a bowl to make an omelette for her supper. The automatic whisking motion was quite soothing and she began to daydream about her child, the baby who had spent nine months in her womb.

The family might have left Britain, emigrated. She could be anywhere in the world. She would be the same age as Gaby, of course. Would she look more like her or Calum? And then she had another thought. If she tracked the girl down, she might be the one to save Sebastian. Lizzie would have loved to pick up the phone and tell Edina what she had discovered, but it was too early.

It was a perfect omelette, but after two small bites Lizzie's appetite vanished. She poured herself a glass of white wine, took it up to the bathroom and turned on the taps. Relaxing in the hot water did much to soothe her anger at Calum's peremptory manner. Involvement in the negotiations for the sale of the business was all-consuming, she told herself. She was foolish to assume that he would be ready and able to talk just because she was. But as time passed and still Calum did not ring, her mood changed to one of self-pity. If only her mother were around. At least she could be relied on to listen. But her mother's itinerary was vague. She had promised a contact number when she reached a hotel where she might stay for a while, but so far Lizzie had heard nothing.

She allowed herself to wallow in her misery and, alone in the house, she wept for the life she had lost.

It was late when Lizzie climbed into bed. Calum hadn't phoned. Miserably she wondered why she'd ever thought he would. Nothing about his attitude towards her lately suggested he was remotely interested. Well, she would track down their daughter without his help. He would have to be told, but in her own time. Lizzie switched off the light. After a few minutes, her brain whirling, she switched it on again.

Calum's sudden trip to America and Gaby's half-term visit to France meant that for the first time in years she was alone. She would not have to explain her movements or account for her absence to either of them. It was as if God was saying to her, 'Here is the perfect opportunity. Make the most of it.'

Where would she start? She could imagine the reaction if she marched into St Martyn's Hospital and asked if she could examine their records of fifteen years before. Whatever story she managed to cook up she was certain she would be shown the door. She needed the help of an insider. Would Dan Hargreaves help? All she wanted was to be steered in the right direction.

'Don't ask, don't get,' parroted Lizzie as she psyched herself to phone his laboratory at the start of the business day.

When Dan heard she had made up her mind to try to find her natural daughter he did not try to dissuade her. On the contrary, he immediately offered to help. She was delighted but also surprised and slightly puzzled. A telephone contact or an introductory letter to the hospital authorities was all she had hoped for. Why would he be willing to give up his time to join in the search? Then she chastised herself for being suspicious. Surely it was Sebastian's welfare that was motivating him. She accepted his help gladly.

'We'll have to be careful about our reason for requesting to see records from fifteen years ago,' he said. 'If there's the smallest sniff of the hospital being to blame for a mess-up, those files will be buried under concrete.'

'I'm not interested in blaming anyone,' she told him. 'I just want to find the child.'

'I know that and you know that, but St Martyn's Hospital will never accept that somebody won't want to make money out of this. Trust me.'

The least suspicious way to gain admission to the records department would be to ask the authorities at the hospital, for whom he had done work in the past, if he could examine their files for a research project on teenagers born fifteen years ago. He'd say he planned to interview them, naturally with parental permission.

'There's no time like the present,' he said. 'Let's try our luck tomorrow afternoon. Your cover can be as my assistant,' he added, smiling, 'although if you were, I think I'd find you too distracting.'

What did he expect as a reward? Lizzie wondered uneasily, and immediately dismissed the thought. He was only trying to keep her spirits up. He had not made her feel the least bit uncomfortable and she was feeling more positive and hopeful than she had for days.

THE ARCHIVE SECTION of St Martyn's was attached to the hospital, only a few hundred yards away from Dan's laboratory. It was little visited these days; current data was accessed by computer.

They were shown into a basement room by a harassed young clerk, who brushed off their explanations and gestured towards a row of daunting-looking cabinets. 'There you go. The files you want are in the second cabinet on the right. Mind if I leave you to it?' He quickly vanished.

The first drawer Lizzie looked in contained files dated six months before Gabriella's birthday. Two more drawers brought her no nearer to the correct date.

'I can't find anything here, can you?' she asked Dan.

He shook his head, clearly annoyed. 'What was the guy talking about? He doesn't have a clue about which files are where.' He continued to rummage through the folders. 'Here we are. This is more like it,' he announced triumphantly. 'The week beginning November the 11th.' He isolated several of the folders before placing them on a nearby desk. 'Your call, I think.'

Now that the moment had arrived, Lizzie had ambivalent feelings about opening this Pandora's box. Would it be better for her, for Gaby, for Calum to leave the folders undisturbed?

Dan saw her hesitation. 'You don't necessarily need to act on what you find, do you?' He divided the files into two piles. They sat down and agreed to consult each other before discarding any possible candidate. Taking a deep breath, Lizzie began examining her folders. Rapidly she began to extract the ones bearing the date November 11. The 11th had been a busy day, with fifteen babies delivered. Only five were girls. Dan replaced the files containing data on male babies, while Lizzie went through the others until she came to the one marked 'Lynton'.

Below the columns in which the time, weight and length of the baby was recorded was a comment column. In it was a note that an Apgar score taken immediately after birth, then again five minutes later, gave Gabriella seven out of ten for colour, breathing and response. Except for a slight touch of jaundice, Gaby's physical condition was apparently perfect.

After scrutinising the other files Lizzie told Dan, 'We can discard two of these right away. I remember this woman. She was a jazz singer and was in a private ward so we didn't see her much. But she and her husband were both from Jamaica, and this baby,' she tapped a file with her fingernail, 'has Chinese parents.'

'Here's one that's a possible,' Dan said, scanning the folder. 'No, forget it. This child died three days after birth.' Lizzie felt a shiver pass over her body. His eyes darted over the details. 'She wasn't your child, the blood groups aren't compatible.'

Only one folder remained unopened on the table. Dan picked it up and Lizzie's breathing stopped as she waited for him to check the medical compatibilities.

'Now this looks more promising,' he said, handing her the sheet. The child was the third pregnancy of Nancy Ewing, married to Derek Walter Ewing. His occupation was given as long-distance lorry driver. The baby girl had the same birth weight as Gabriella and measured about the same in length. She also had the same Apgar score. But what clinched it was the added detail: 'Respiratory problem. Fluid in lungs. Transferred to special care unit 22.15.'

There was no other file left, no other baby of the right sex and blood group. This had to be her daughter. The immensity of what was happening suddenly overwhelmed Lizzie and it was some time before she could compose herself. Dan came round to the back of her chair and put his hands on her shoulders. There they stayed until Lizzie became aware that her wet cheek was resting on one of his hands. She lifted her head abruptly and began to apologise.

'It's completely understandable,' he said quietly, taking out a handkerchief and wiping her face gently. She was embarrassed at showing such raw emotion to a comparative stranger. It should have been Calum by her side, comforting her, assuring her that everything would turn out right. Dan picked up the folder, appearing not to notice her discomfiture. 'Does the name ring any bells?'

Lizzie shook her head, frantically trying to remember the small room with its six beds. 'I don't think she was in my ward.'

'According to this file the Ewings lived in Fulham,' he said. 'Here's the address.' He walked towards the filing cabinet holding the Ewing folder. 'What do you want me to do? Put it away? Or give it to you?'

If it wasn't for the possibility that the Ewing child could be a match for Sebastian, there were good reasons to forget she existed. When Lizzie told Calum, he would inform Edward. Would he have to tell the court if Andrew went ahead with this case? Wouldn't the girl have a claim? Then Andrew might gain nothing for himself, or for Sebastian. Either way, the cat would be out of the bag. It would certainly turn Gaby's world upside-down. Lizzie baulked at the thought.

But where was her baby? What was her name? Did she look like her or Calum? Was she happy?

If she did manage to track down her child, Lizzie told herself, she wouldn't have to say anything at first, would she? To anyone. But wouldn't it be wonderful just to set eyes on her?

Slowly Lizzie reached out a hand and took the folder.

SARAH HEARD the desperation in Lizzie's voice on the phone early the following morning and without hesitation agreed to meet her in the park, away from telephones and domestic interruptions. She had just come back from Norfolk and said this was the perfect excuse to get away from the chaos.

Late October was Lizzie's favourite time of year, warm enough to enjoy being outdoors but with a hint of autumnal crispness that invigorated the spirits. But this morning nature did not work its usual magic and by the time she spotted Sarah her mood had not improved.

The two friends walked towards a park bench.

'Lizzie, tell me what's happened,' said Sarah. 'Is it the court case?'

Lizzie shook her head, her eyes downcast. She turned to look at Sarah. 'Calum is definitely not Gabriella's father.'

'But I thought you said—'

Lizzie put up a restraining hand. 'There's an explanation. I had my blood tested and I'm not Gaby's mother either.' The words came tumbling out. 'There must have been a switch in the hospital when she was born. I was given the wrong baby, Sarah. She's not related to either of us.' Her tears, so long held back, spilled over and a stunned-looking Sarah reached over to comfort her.

'Lizzie, Lizzie, how awful for you.'

'I don't think I've taken it in yet. I can't.' Lizzie put her hand over her eyes. 'I feel so stupid. For God's sake, I talked to the baby in the womb. I used to play her Beethoven. I've always believed that a mother has certain instincts about her offspring, so why didn't I sense that she wasn't mine?'

'Don't torment yourself, Lizzie.'

'I used to overhear the other parents in the hospital ward say their baby looked like this aunt or that grandmother, but Calum and I could never see any of our relatives in Gaby.'

Sarah replied mildly that many kids did not resemble their parents. 'What does Calum say about this?' she asked. 'I bet he feels terrible about accusing you of two-timing him. This is proof that you weren't lying.'

Lizzie's mouth tightened and she told Sarah about the rushed phone call. 'I know how business gets him stressed, but he still hasn't phoned back and I'm damned if I'm going to ring him again.'

'I know how you must feel but—'

'Don't try to defend him. You don't know the half of it. He said I trapped him into marriage and that I did it only because I wanted to give "my illegitimate baby" a name. You can't believe how close I was to walking out on him. The only thing that stopped me was Gaby.'

Sarah's voice was grave. 'He'll have to find out some time.'

Lizzie looked sombre. 'I suppose you're right.'

'No suppose about it,' said Sarah briskly. 'What do you intend to do about Gaby?'

Lizzie groaned. 'The last thing I want to do is tell her when she's already so difficult to handle. I'm going to wait till she's older.' She added, with the trace of a smile, 'Like forty.'

Sarah gave her hand a squeeze. 'God, what a mess. It's like a Grimms fairy tale. You know, the princess snatched from her cradle and replaced by the foundling?'

'Yes . . .' Lizzie's expression was anguished. 'Except I know who took my baby home.' Lizzie recounted what she and Dan Hargreaves had discovered in the hospital archives.

Sarah stared at her. 'What a traumatic time you've had,' she sympathised. 'Why didn't you tell me? At least you wouldn't have had to go through this alone.' She paused for breath then added, 'But you must tell Calum.'

'Not yet. Not until I find out where the child is.' Lizzie was adamant.

'Oh, Lizzie, you're on dangerous ground. Please be careful.'

'I will. The idea petrifies me, but I want to know whether she's happy, what she looks like, what her first name is. Wouldn't you?'

'Of course.' Sarah looked troubled.

'And then there's Sebastian. This girl is his cousin. That's another very good reason to track her down.'

'You're going to need the wisdom of Solomon to sort this out.'

'I know.'

Sarah looked at her. 'Would you like some help?'

Lizzie kept her eyes wide open so that the tears wouldn't spill over. 'Yes, please.'

THE NEXT MORNING Sarah drove Lizzie to Fulham, having left Hugh to entertain the children.

As she manoeuvred her car into a rare parking spot off the Fulham Broadway, she asked, 'So what's the plan?'

'We can't assume they still live around here,' said Lizzie, trying to quell her nervousness, 'but I thought we could make enquiries at the local shops, talk to the neighbours, find out something about the family if we can.'

They started at the local newsagent's, then at the bakery and finally at the corner shop. Their approach was studiously casual. Did anyone know of a family called Ewing? They drew a blank. Frustrated, they decided there was no other course but to go to the actual street.

Few of the houses showed any sign of life. They were standing across the road from number 53, Lizzie nerving herself to go over and knock at the door, when a heavily built woman pulling a shopping trolley turned into the gate.

'Could that be her?' Sarah asked quietly.

'Doesn't she look too old?'

Sarah agreed she did, but they crossed the street to talk to her. 'I wonder if you can help me.' Lizzie tried not to sound breathless. 'I'm looking for an old friend by the name of Nancy Ewing, and when I knew her she lived in this house.'

The woman shook her head. 'We've been here seven years and that wasn't the person who sold the house to us.' She opened the door, giving every impression of wanting to cut short the conversation.

'What happened to the people who sold you the house?'

'Mr and Mrs Hudd? Don't know,' the woman replied.

'Did they leave a forwarding address?'

'If they did it was seven years ago,' said the woman impatiently. 'I haven't a clue where it could be.' She looked at their crestfallen faces and relented slightly. 'You could try the estate agents. They're just round the corner.' And with that she banged the door firmly shut.

'That was easy, Dr Watson,' said Lizzie.

'I don't think,' replied Sarah, looking at her watch. 'Let's go. I promised Hugh I'd be back in an hour to feed the kids.'

They soon discovered the estate agents had changed hands twice in the intervening years, but fortunately one of the employees had managed to survive all the buy-outs. When it became clear that Lizzie was not there to enquire about property, her welcoming smile faded.

'Sixteen years ago? All those records are somewhere in the basement.' She made it sound as far off as the moon.

Lizzie allowed her desperation to show. 'Believe me, I wouldn't ask you if it wasn't vital to get the address of Mr and Mrs Hudd.'

'Well, I'll see what I can do. Come back in about two weeks.'

Sarah had inspiration. 'What if we gave you fifty pounds for your time?' The estate agent looked over her shoulder at her bustling colleagues, none of whom showed any interest in what was going on. Lizzie slipped the cash to the estate agent who took the notes and put them into her pocket. 'We close at five. Come back then.'

THE HUDDS WOULD have to live in Dorset, a good four hours' drive on the motorway.

'Can't you put it off till the weekend?' Sarah asked, before adding with a groan, 'No, dammit. I'm sorry. I can't get away then either. I promised the kids an outing and Hugh can't stand in for me.'

'That's a pity,' said Lizzie, 'I don't want to go alone. Maybe I could . . . hang on, there's a call waiting. It's probably Calum.'

'Are you going to tell him?'

'I'll have to.'

But the call waiting was not from Calum. Lizzie recognised the husky voice at once. Dan Hargreaves wanted to know how the search was progressing. 'Quite well,' she said, and explained her tussle with the estate agent.

'So are you going down to Dorset?'

'I suppose I'll have to, but it might be a wild-goose chase.'

'You could phone.'

'No, I'll get far more out of them face to face.'

'You're right.' A thought struck him. 'If you haven't anyone to drive you, why don't I come with you?'

Lizzie was wary. 'Why would you do that?'

'Are you serious? How often do you think I come across a situation as unique as this?'

Lizzie was uncertain how to react. It was a generous offer but she wasn't sure how keen she was to have a stranger involved in something as personal as this search.

'Besides,' he carried on cheerfully, 'it's not something you'd want to do on your own, is it?'

'No, it isn't,' she said emphatically, thinking that undoubtedly his status as a doctor, planning medical research, was a far better cover when asking personal questions of strangers.

As they made arrangements to meet the following morning, Lizzie felt a surge of excitement. Nor could she put it down solely to the fact that her search had started in earnest. Dan Hargreaves wasn't the kind of man she met at hockey club dances or at school and that gave him added appeal. But only up to a point, she told herself sternly, I'm not on the lookout for an affair.

When Dan Hargreaves's vintage racing-green Morgan drew up

outside her door, Lizzie was impressed. She slipped onto the calf leather-covered seat, sniffed that distinctive, expensive aroma and almost purred. 'I feel like a princess,' she said.

Dan gave her a dazzling smile. 'Anyone who appreciates this car is definitely on my wavelength.'

The next few miles were spent with an amused Lizzie listening to Dan proclaim his love for a car he confessed he had lusted after for years and worked hard to afford. 'I know I go over the top about my Morgan but really, when I meet a woman I love more than this thing, then I'll know it's real.'

His exhilaration amused her and she liked him the better for it.

'What does your husband make of this?' he asked.

'I haven't told him yet. He's still in America, in the middle of important business negotiations.'

'Then I'm glad I'm around to give you some company,' Dan said.

'I'm very grateful,' she said, and for the first time was full of anticipation about what the next hours would bring.

Dan noted that she seemed more relaxed and smiled to himself. He had been ordered by his boss to keep close to her in case she made trouble for them. So far she had not mentioned the lab in connection with the court case and he was there to ensure as far as he could that they were kept out of the frame and away from the medical ethics committee. At least this way he might find out what she planned to do.

He gave Lizzie a disarming smile and suggested it might be easier if he approached the Hudds, assuming they were still the occupants of the house.

It was dusk when they located the terraced house in a quiet cul-de-sac in Thurlston. There were lights shining from a downstairs window.

Lizzie watched from the car as Dan's six-foot frame approached the front door. His knock was answered by a short female figure, but in the gloom Lizzie could not make out any features. By now her palms were moist and she let out a sigh of relief as Dan was ushered through the doorway. They must be accepting his story.

Her thoughts turned to Calum. When he returned from America she must tell him. But could they repair the damage that all this business had caused? She wasn't at all sure. What an unreal situation she was in. How on earth could this be happening and her husband not knowing a thing about it?

LIZZIE WAS STIFF with suspense. For the past ten minutes her gaze had not wavered from the entrance to the pebbledash house. She straightened as the door opened and Dan appeared. He waved his hand in farewell to someone standing inside the house and turned towards the car. Sliding into the seat next to her he seemed distracted. 'Good news and bad. The Hudds do live there but I'm afraid we have to come back in the morning.'

'Why?' Despite her efforts, Lizzie's frustration was evident.

'Mr Hudd works nights so he wasn't at home and he's the only one who knows where the papers are.'

'What time does he get home?'

'Around half past seven, and he goes straight to sleep so you'd better not be late. It might be best if you stayed somewhere here overnight. There must be a decent pub in the nearby village.'

'Yes, I suppose you're right.' She felt a mixture of disappointment and relief that he had not included himself in the plan. But however awkward she felt, Lizzie was dreading an evening alone with her thoughts and Dan would be a welcome diversion. With what she hoped was a relaxed and casual tone she asked if she could treat him to dinner as a thankyou for driving her down. After a slight hesitation he accepted.

The nearby village of Thurlston-on-the-Green was full of carefully maintained thatched cottages and a stuccoed building with a wrought-iron pub sign proclaiming the Prince of Wales.

The pub landlady suggested they had a meal in front of the fire while she prepared their room.

'My room,' said Lizzie firmly. 'Only one of us is staying.'

The landlady examined the register. 'Double or single? We're not busy and you can have your pick for the same price.'

'That's very generous,' said Lizzie. 'Then let it be a double.'

The cloth on their table was starched white cotton and in the centre was a posy of seasonal flowers and a candle in a silver holder. Lizzie drank her wine more swiftly than she meant to. In her heightened state it had more effect than usual. She began to feel uncomfortably warm. She dearly longed to take off her jacket, but she worried it might send the wrong signal. Nervously she began to toy with the top button, then stopped abruptly when she noticed Dan's eyes fixed on her moving fingers.

From that moment the atmosphere changed. Lizzie sensed an undercurrent between them. She found it difficult to meet Dan's gaze. Even the most prosaic questions seemed to have hidden meaning. When he asked if she'd like to have another glass of wine she found herself colouring. Was she being naive or was he trying to lower her guard?

Lulled by the pleasant ambiance and fuelled by several glasses of a fine Bordeaux, Lizzie relaxed. At the end of the meal two glasses of dessert wine appeared with the landlady's compliments, but Dan refused, saying with a charming smile that he had to drive back to London. Lizzie squinted at her watch and looked brightly at him. 'It'll be quite late when you get back. I feel really guilty, I shouldn't have persuaded you to stay for dinner.' He merely gazed at her, saying nothing, and she hurried on. 'I suppose you have a full day at the lab tomorrow, otherwise I'd suggest you stay over as well.'

He spoke so quietly she had to lean towards him to hear.

'This all started out with me wanting to play the great detective,' he said quietly. 'It was a welcome break from my routine in the lab. But now something's changed. I don't only want to help you. I find I'm thinking about you. Often, at the most inappropriate times.'

Lizzie was taken aback. With all that was going on in her life how could she cope with extra complications? For a moment or two they avoided eye contact, then Dan said, 'I didn't mean to embarrass you. I think I'd better get on my way. I'll just have a black coffee.'

Lizzie found herself in a quandary. She did not want him to believe she planned to jump into bed with him, but it was late and he had been drinking. She surprised herself by saying, 'Now don't be silly, you've had too much wine to drive. You might scratch your car.' His expression registered such shock that she had to laugh. It took little more to persuade him and when the coffees turned out to be laced with brandy and cream, he took it as a sign that he should indeed spend the night at the Prince of Wales.

As he sipped the coffee the conversation became more personal. He stared at her quizzically. 'Let me get this straight. You've been married for sixteen years and you've been faithful all that time?'

'Don't make me feel like a freak. There are more of us around than you think.'

'Let's think about this in a scientific way.' His eyes were twinkling. 'You married at what? Nineteen, twenty? And you don't seem to me to be the wild-child type, so I wonder how much experience would you have had?'

Too dangerous to answer, thought Lizzie, smiling enigmatically.

'What a challenge,' he said mischievously and held her gaze so long she was forced to look away.

Eventually he went to book himself into a room and the moment came when she had to get up. She walked up the narrow staircase towards the bedrooms, acutely aware of Dan's eyes following her. In the corridor he opened his palm and showed her two large gold keys.

'You choose.'

As Lizzie reached out to pick up one of the keys, his hand closed over hers, trapping it in his grasp. In a sudden movement he pulled her towards him. His lips were soft and the kiss was gentle, but her body responded fiercely. Not since her first days with Calum had she experienced such an electrical charge. The kiss ended and he let her go, which was just as well because she could not have pushed him away. They stared at each other, short of breath. 'I'll see you in the morning,' she said, trying to sound like a strong-minded married woman. She turned and quickly opened her bedroom door, locking it behind her with a certain amount of regret.

AFTER A FITFUL few hours' sleep, she went into the shower. Hoping to shock herself awake, she set the thermostat to cool. They planned to leave in half an hour to see Mr Hudd and she needed to have all her wits about her.

Dan was already at reception when she came downstairs. He was about to take a credit card from his wallet when she laid a restraining hand on his arm.

'I insist on paying. If it wasn't for me you wouldn't be here.'

'That's true, but I'm still not letting you pay for me.'

The landlady observed this interchange with some interest before accepting a credit card from both of them.

While she was dealing with the bills, Dan turned to Lizzie and gave her a smile that reassured her he wasn't bearing a grudge. 'If you'd been braver we could've saved the price of a room,' he teased.

There was a definite nip in the air as they made their way to the car park. 'We ought to be in time to catch Mr Hudd before he goes to bed,' said Lizzie, wrapping her coat more tightly round herself.

'Don't worry about that,' said Dan. He produced a slip of paper from his back pocket. 'We don't have to go back. His wife already gave me the name and address last night.'

'Are you telling me you had this all the time?'

'Yup.'

She raised an eyebrow. 'You planned for us to stay overnight.'

' "Planned" is such a harsh word,' he grinned. 'Let's say I hoped.'

Dan opened the passenger door for her. She watched as he strode round to the driver's side. Part of her was flattered, but she was also angry. He was well aware how anxiously she had been waiting for the Ewings' address. She was searching for her lost child, for God's sake, not some sexual adventure. She would have respected him more if he'd been straight with her. Then again, she thought, she would never have spent the night in the same hotel with him if he had been honest. From now on she would not be so trusting of him.

Lizzie studied the slip of paper and saw with dismay that the address was in Glasgow. As the car sped along the motorway back towards London, she began to think about how she could find out if the family still lived there without alerting them to her search. It was a long way to go without checking they were still at this address.

'The Glasgow address might be out-of-date,' Dan said. 'The Ewings could be living anywhere. Wasn't he a long-distance lorry driver?'

'Yes, but at least we have his full name from the hospital records. Perhaps we can get a phone number for this address,' she said.

Dan pointed to the car phone. 'No time like the present.'

Lizzie drew a blank. The female operator could find no trace of a D. W. Ewing in Glasgow. Lizzie switched off, her face disconsolate.

'Cheer up,' said Dan. 'We'll just have to carry on with this detective business.'

'OK, Sherlock, what ideas do you have?'

'It looks as though we're going to be forced to spend more time together.' He gave her a roguish look. 'Fancy some haggis?'

She couldn't help smiling, but her answer was swift. 'You've been a great help and I'm grateful, but I don't expect you to come to Glasgow with me.'

Dan slid his gaze to Lizzie's profile. Was he losing his touch? She appeared to be relaxed, not uptight at all. Why then had she turned down his offer to go to Glasgow? Perhaps he had come on too strong last night. He did not want her to feel uneasy with him. His boss would still want to be briefed about her plans. He would have to find an excuse to see her again.

Chapter Five

Back home, away from the magnetic influence of Dan's personality, Lizzie was delighted to find Sarah had managed to persuade her mother to stay with the children so she was free to go to Scotland.

On the plane journey they had rehearsed their cover story, that they were tracking down babies born on a certain day in a certain hospital as part of research for a magazine article. If the Ewing girl turned out to be alive and well, the next step would be somehow to persuade her to give a blood sample, needed as part of the research. Lizzie wasn't sure how they should approach this. Still, one step at a time. They had to find the Ewings first.

The address proved to be a three-storeyed Victorian house badly in need of a coat of paint. It was distinguished from the others in the run-down terrace only by the name in faded lettering on the window above the door.

'Gallagher's Guesthouse,' read Lizzie as they sat in the car outside the house. 'Oh, Sarah. We've come all this way for nothing.'

'Not for nothing,' she said. 'We could always pretend we wanted a room, and these people might know where the Ewings have gone to.' Sarah became businesslike. 'Look, it's possible they gave this address because they were staying here temporarily.'

'You're probably right and it's all I've got,' Lizzie said, opening the car door and climbing out.

Until that moment she had been able to control the flutters in the stomach. But the idea of being so close to finding her daughter made her shiver with apprehension.

After what seemed an age, the door opened abruptly and a whippet of a woman stood in the hallway apologising for the delay. She was probably in her early forties and looked as though she could do with a decent meal and a good haircut. Lizzie took in the greying hair, the deeply etched lines around the faded features.

'We're looking for someone who gave this as their address.'

'A lot of people do that, lady.' The woman grimaced. 'Running away from wives, debts, you name it. Are you bailiffs?'

Sarah immediately reassured her and said they were looking for a family called Ewing. The woman stiffened so she added hastily, 'They've done nothing wrong.'

'Then why are you looking for them?'

'Nancy and I had babies on the same day in the same hospital.'

'So?'

'We are looking for the Ewing child because we need her help with a magazine feature we're doing.'

The door opened a fraction. 'I'm her mother. I'm Nancy Ewing.' She peered across at Lizzie. 'Come in and tell me what this is about.'

Nancy Ewing led the way to a sitting room, cheaply and shabbily furnished. She motioned them to sit down and Lizzie perched nervously on the edge of an armchair.

Apparently Nancy Ewing had taken over the boarding house after the death of her mother, Mrs Gallagher. Her two older boys had left home not long after her husband had been killed in an accident while driving a defective lorry. Life had been a struggle for her and her daughter Anna-Maria since then.

Anna-Maria. A pretty name in such an unattractive setting, thought Lizzie, and ventured the question she had been itching to pose since the monologue started. 'Is she about? Your daughter.'

The woman's face clouded. 'No. I never know where she is these days.'

'Isn't she at school?'

Nancy Ewing's expression was bitter. 'She's been bunking off since she was twelve and finally the school got fed up with her. They asked me to take her away and now she works in a pub.'

'She's working in a pub?' Lizzie tried to sound neutral.

'She lied about her age, said she was eighteen. I threatened to report the landlord because he didn't check, but she said she'd leave home if I did. Mind, she looks eighteen.'

'Do you have any pictures of her?' asked Lizzie eagerly.

Nancy Ewing sighed and stood up. 'Maybe I have some from a year or two back.'

She returned with a much-creased envelope containing one of those sterile school pictures. The girl might have been described as pretty had she not been staring at the camera with undisguised hostility. A wave of anticlimax engulfed Lizzie as she examined the picture for some sort of family likeness. Apart from the girl's colouring, she could see little of her own parents or grandparents or Calum's. At a stretch, maybe that mane was a little like Calum's.

'Fifteen's a difficult age, isn't it?' said Lizzie, hoping to draw out Mrs Ewing. 'They know everything.'

The woman gave a groan of agreement. 'She won't listen to anything I say. I don't know what she gets up to and she comes in at all hours of the day and night. I really worry about her.'

Lizzie stared at Nancy Ewing with growing despair. How could this depressed, defeated woman cope with a turbulent teenager? And she could be Gabriella's natural mother! As Lizzie looked at the faded, lined features, there was little hint of what Nancy might have looked like at Gabriella's age. Fleetingly she had an image of her own daughter's life. The pony rides, the swimming sessions, the ballet lessons, the trips abroad. Nothing was barred to her. How different were the limits set on Anna-Maria's life.

'Doesn't she have something she wants to do?' asked Lizzie. 'She can't want to work in the pub all her life, or does she?'

Nancy gave a sardonic laugh. 'Oh, she's got ideas all right. To be a film star, if you please. She's been talking about drama school, but how can a girl like her get into one of those? She'll be lucky if she isn't pregnant with three kids underfoot already by the time she's twenty-one. And I know who the mug'll be looking after them.'

Oh God, thought Lizzie. If she's mine I'll have to get her away. I'd never be able to rest knowing that my daughter is in this dead-end place, in a dead-end job and facing a dead-end future. But she pulled herself up sharply. How could she presume to judge the relationship between mother and daughter? They could have a real bond. Anyone hearing her moans lately about Gaby would certainly get the wrong impression about their feelings towards each other. And in any case, the deal she'd made with herself was to do nothing impulsive.

Her conscience began to trouble her. If this was the Lynton grand-child, did she have the right to deprive her of a share of the inheri-tance? On the other hand, Robert Lynton had definitely intended his money to go to Gabriella. Shouldn't she just leave matters as they were? But Sebastian's needs were more important than any of this. It was vital they persuade the mother to cooperate in getting a blood sample. Mrs Ewing was looking at her expectantly.

'About this research we're involved in,' said Lizzie, 'would you mind if I talked to your daughter? Where would she be now?'

'At the pub, I suppose—if she's turned up.'

The wind was whipping up the debris on the streets as Lizzie and Sarah made their way, following Nancy Ewing's directions, to the Pack Horse. They had expected Anna-Maria's place of employment to be as run-down as her mother's boarding house and were sur-prised to discover a well-tended turn-of-the-century pub out of kilter with the area it served.

Lizzie hung back, smoothing her hair and brushing the shoulders of her jacket.

'Are you OK?' asked Sarah, taking her arm.

She nodded, biting her lower lip.

'Look, you don't have to go through with this,' Sarah said. 'We could turn right round and go home.'

'No.' Lizzie pushed open the door. 'It's not only for me. She might be a match for Sebastian.' The pub had been newly refurbished and had stalls complete with gleaming brass rails and leather-type ban-quettes. Behind the bar was a young woman laughing uproariously. A shaven-headed youth was perching on a stool in front of her. Although she bore little resemblance to the photograph, Lizzie recognised the springy curls. She saw that hair, that subtle reddish colour, every day of her married life.

The girl turned towards them enquiringly and Lizzie ordered two glasses of white wine. As Anna-Maria hunted for a half-opened bottle of Frascati, Lizzie took the opportunity to scrutinise her. She was slim, and above average in height, but then Calum was over six foot. Her narrow-fitting jeans clung to a pair of extraordinarily long limbs. It was one of the best assets of the Lynton family physique. Lizzie was nerving herself to talk when the young woman pre-empted her and asked, 'I haven't seen you in here before. Are you just passing through?'

Lizzie explained that they were visiting the area and had just come from her mother's house.

The girl's face showed immediate alarm. 'What do you want with me? Are you from the police?'

'No, we're not,' said Lizzie.

'Then what do you want?'

'It's private. Let's have a talk at a table.'

Anna-Maria darted a look at the youth on the bar stool, who was studiously uninterested, then followed them to a banquette, where she sat down in the corner and glared at them.

So this aggressive young woman could be her daughter. Try as she might, Lizzie could conjure up no maternal feelings, no instinct that she had given birth to this young woman.

'Who are you, then? What d'ya want?' Suddenly Lizzie glimpsed the girl Nancy Ewing had been describing, pugnacious and hostile.

Trying to appear unruffled by the girl's antagonism, Lizzie explained how she and Nancy Ewing had met in hospital. 'You were born on exactly the same day as my daughter.'

'So?'

Sarah cut in and said she was working on a nationwide research project. This appeared to evince a spark of interest and she explained that the reason they wanted to track Anna-Maria down was because they were focusing on children born on her birthday, recording all physical and medical details. Anna-Maria seemed intrigued and asked pertinent questions. The girl might have bunked off school, but she seemed to have natural intelligence. Lizzie wondered what might have happened if she had been brought up in different circumstances. It was time to broach the vital question. Would Anna-Maria be willing to cooperate with the research?

At once she was suspicious. 'What would I have to do?'

'Nothing much. We'd need to take some pictures.'

'That's fine, so long as you pay me something.'

'No problem.' Lizzie took a deep breath. 'And you'd have to give a small sample of your blood.'

'Give blood? No way.'

'It won't hurt, I promise you. Your doctor will clear it with the laboratory in London and arrange everything.'

'I'm telling you no. I'm not doing it.'

'This is very important,' Lizzie said. 'It's linked to a research project which might help thousands of people.'

'Look, I don't ask for help. Nobody helps me and that's the way I want it.'

'All the samples are anonymous.'

'How many times do I have to tell you people? Stop bugging me. Leave me alone.' She stood up. 'I have customers. I have to go,' she said, stalking across the near-deserted pub to her position at the bar.

IN THE CAR outside, Sarah tried to comfort Lizzie, but she would not be consoled.

'I handled it all wrong,' she said despondently.

'No, you didn't. Did you see her pupils? That girl's on something, so she's going to overreact whatever we do.'

'I should've spent more time winning her confidence before jumping in like that.'

'It wouldn't have made any difference. My guess is she's afraid of what a blood test might show about whatever drugs she's on.'

'She's only fifteen.'

Sarah shrugged. 'You heard her first reaction when you said you'd been to her home. She's obviously been in trouble with the police.'

Lizzie took out a handkerchief. 'But I can't just abandon her. Not now I've met her. There must be something I can do for her.'

'You have to be cautious about this. You can't just break the news.'

'I know that, but perhaps Calum and I . . .' She trailed off. 'We could see she gets some money.' The mention of Calum's name brought Lizzie back to reality. Whether or not her marriage was over, it was imperative to bring Calum into the picture. Anna-Maria was his responsibility too. Anything that needed to be done, any decision that needed to be taken must be decided by both of them. She had invested so much hope in this trip, for her own sake as well as Sebastian's, yet here she was, on her way back to London, little nearer to knowing the truth.

GABRIELLA ARRIVED back home from Lyon in the early afternoon. She flung a bulging rucksack heavily onto the hall floor and burst through the kitchen door demanding, 'Anything to eat? I'm starving.' Then she darted back out and dragged her rucksack into the kitchen. She delved into it, throwing out clothes and toilet bag, and

Lizzie glowed with pleasure at the sight of her lively face and felt an overwhelming urge to protect Gabriella from unhappiness. She might not be of her flesh, but Lizzie could not imagine a situation where she would regard Gaby as anything other than her daughter.

When Gabriella had nearly emptied the rucksack, she glanced up and spotted the tender smile on Lizzie's face. 'Don't tell me you missed me,' she grinned.

'I did.'

'Good, because I've brought you something.' And she unwrapped a bottle of Bordeaux wine, proudly displaying the label. It was wonderful to know that Gabriella was trying to please her and Lizzie took the bottle, saying it would be saved for a special occasion.

Lizzie had prepared a plate of sandwiches and sat down at the table watching Gabriella munch away. It was like old times, sitting down together, laughing at things that had happened. Lizzie revelled in the feeling of intimacy, something she had not experienced with Gabriella for months.

Then the telephone interrupted their laughter and, as ever, Gabriella raced to pick up the receiver.

'It's Dad,' she called excitedly over her shoulder and spent the next couple of minutes telling him about her trip. After a moment or two she asked, 'When are you coming home?' As she listened, a puzzled frown flickered across her forehead. 'Surely you have some idea? OK . . . see you then. Want to talk to Mum now?'

Lizzie rose but her daughter shook her head. Gaby's frown deepened and after a few seconds she said quietly, 'OK, I'll tell her,' and replaced the receiver. 'He didn't want to talk to you, said he was in a hurry.' She looked puzzled. 'I've never known you two not to speak, especially when he's out of the country. Have you had a fight?'

'We had a bit of a tiff before he went.'

'It's not serious, is it?'

'I don't think so.'

'You don't think so?' Gabriella's voice rose. When her mother did not reply, her alarm was obvious. 'Are you going to split up?'

Lizzie rose from her chair, opened a cupboard and began rearranging the packets and tins, desperately trying to think of how she could change the subject.

'This'll blow over,' said Gabriella. Her voice sounded firm, but she was eyeing her mother apprehensively. 'You and Dad have the best marriage of all the parents I know. You're just going through one of the "downs" they talk about, aren't you?'

'Probably, we'll see,' said Lizzie.

'I hate it when you say "we'll see".'

To Lizzie's great relief the doorbell chimed and Gabriella took off at great speed to see who it was. When she returned she was carrying an expensive-looking arrangement of lilies and ferns.

'Aren't they beautiful? You see, this is his way of saying sorry or whatever. Dad loves you. Forgive him. Go on, Mum.'

Lizzie smiled. It was an exceptionally lovely bouquet.

'Let me open the card,' said Gabriella eagerly. She ripped open the tiny white envelope and with a flourish extracted a gold-edged card. Her mouth formed the words, but as she read them silently her animated expression faded. Lizzie was faintly alarmed.

Gabriella's voice was dead as she parroted the message on the card. 'I must see you again. D.'

Lizzie's eyes widened.

'Who is D?' Gaby's eyes stared with hostility.

Lizzie said quickly, 'He's a friend. Just a friend. There's nothing romantic between us, certainly not on my side.'

'He doesn't seem to think so. And isn't it funny that he's come on the scene when you and Dad aren't talking?'

'This has absolutely nothing to do with the problems between your father and me.' Lizzie was frantically searching for something she could say. 'All this man's been doing is helping me.'

'Helping you with what?'

'I can't go into it. When you understand what's going on . . .'

'I understand all too well. Dad's the one I feel sorry for. I bet he doesn't know that behind his back you've been having an affair.'

'Gaby, I haven't been having an affair. I wish I could explain.'

'Then why don't you?'

'Because . . .' Lizzie hesitated. It was tempting to tell Gabriella the truth and get herself off the hook, but this was something she needed to do with Calum first. 'I will tell you, but not yet,' she said weakly.

'You're so horrible. You know you're in the wrong.' Her eyes brimmed with tears. 'And Dad doesn't know . . .' She paused then burst out, 'He doesn't know that his wife is . . . a lying whore.'

Gabriella flung the bouquet on the floor and with a furious look at her horrified mother stomped upstairs.

SHAKEN, LIZZIE SAT on the chair in the hall and tapped number three on the speed dial for Sarah's number.

'I've just had the worst-ever fight with Gaby.'

'You must be getting used to that by now.'

Lizzie gave a wry laugh. 'This was different.'

When Sarah heard all the details, she was appalled. 'She actually used those words?'

'I'm quoting verbatim.'

'What are you going to do about it?'

'I intend to give Dan Hargreaves a piece of my mind. After I'm finished with him he won't send me so much as a daisy again.'

Sarah stifled a laugh. 'It's a bit rich to tick someone off for sending flowers. He couldn't know your daughter would read the note.'

'But why's he done it, Sarah? The more I think about it, the more I reckon it's not because of my charms but a self-preservation thing. I can't help wondering how Andy got wind of the fact that Gaby wasn't Calum's daughter. Something must have persuaded the lab to send his solicitor the full report of Gaby's blood test.'

'What are you saying, that Dan somehow cocked up and has taken time off work to trail after you because he's worried about his job?'

'Precisely. If he let Andy see the report, it's a breach of confidentiality, at the very least.'

'He's been very helpful, why are you now so suspicious?'

'Because of the flowers, Sarah. And he didn't need to write such a provocative message.'

'Are you going to be all right?' Lizzie could hear the concern in Sarah's voice.

'Let's see. My marriage is coming apart because my husband thinks another man has fathered my baby. My daughter's just called me a whore. I'm going to have to tell Calum that yes, he isn't her father but nor am I her mother.' She took a hurried breath. 'And my real daughter's probably a junkie. Apart from that everything's hunky-dory.'

'I'm glad you still have a sense of humour.'

'Sarah, only on the outside, believe me, only on the outside.'

As DAN SAT WAITING for Lizzie in the cellar wine bar he reflected that this invitation couldn't have come at a better time. His boss had been pestering him to find out how far she had got in her search and what she was going to do about it. Flowers fix everything, he mused. Women were suckers for that kind of thing.

He spotted Lizzie's shapely figure in the doorway, glancing uncertainly at the tables. He half rose and caught her eye. When she arrived at the table, Dan took both her hands in his, giving them a firm squeeze. 'I'm glad you phoned. You look stunning.'

There was no reaction to his greeting and for a moment he was disconcerted. But hell, she had asked to see him, not the other way round. She sat down, extricating her hands and drawing her chair slightly away from his. He began to pour out the wine he had already ordered, then raised his glass. 'To many more occasions like this.'

Her expression was stony. 'Why the hell did you send me those flowers? And what did that message mean?'

'It meant what it said—that I wanted to see you again,' he said mildly, and when she still did not soften added, 'Lizzie, you affect me in a way I've not experienced before. I've never wanted to help a woman as much as I do you. That must mean something.'

Lizzie leaned back in her chair and considered him. 'Please, Dan. Stop. Don't go down that road. I know you don't mean it.'

'You're wrong about that, and don't tell me that after what your husband's put you through your marriage is fine and dandy, because I won't believe it.'

She flushed. 'Whether or not it's over doesn't affect you.'

'So the signals I picked up in Dorset meant nothing? Your body responded to me. You can't deny that. But I respected your wishes not to take it any further and I sent the flowers because I wanted to get to know you better.'

'I'm sorry you did. My daughter read your note.'

Dan forced himself to look contrite. 'That wasn't my intention. But how else could I get through to you that I didn't want our relationship to end?'

She lifted her chin in a gesture of dismissal and for one of the rare occasions in his life Dan Hargreaves felt he was not going to be able to manipulate a woman.

'I don't suppose your protestations would have anything to do with worries about your lab's breach of security?'

'I don't know what you're talking about.'

'I'm sure you do. How else could Andrew have found out about Gabriella's parentage except from you?'

'I swear it had nothing to do with me or my lab,' he said with as much sincerity as he could muster. 'You're forgetting how many people had access to that report, like the hospital and the bone marrow organisation, to name two.' He was rewarded by the flicker of doubt that crossed her face, and pressed home his advantage. 'But that's all past and I don't think we should waste time talking about it. Tell me about Glasgow. Did you find your daughter?'

She nodded.

'What are you going to do about her?'

'I'm sorry, but I think it best if I don't tell you.'

Dan tried to mask his irritation. 'But if it wasn't for me you wouldn't have found her.'

'Dan, forgive me. This is intensely private and I don't want anyone outside the family to know our business.'

It was clear he wasn't going to be given any details. The boss would be furious. Could he appeal to her better nature? 'You led me on,' he said. 'You made me believe your marriage was over.'

'Come on, Dan. Don't tell me I'm the first married woman who's turned you down.' Her face had resumed its glacial mien. Lizzie pushed back her chair and stood up. 'I don't want to see you again and I don't want you to contact me either.'

His chair scraped against the floorboards as he stood up hurriedly to have one last throw of the dice. 'I care about you.'

'No, you care about the lab.'

'You're wrong. This is personal. Between you and me, and nothing to do with the lab.'

'I'm not sure my solicitor will see it like that,' she said tersely before making her way swiftly to the door.

Dan sank back into his chair. If she planned to exploit that moment of weakness, the one time when, against his better instincts, he had bent the rules, she would be sorry. He couldn't risk waiting around to see if he was fingered in the case. He had to strike first.

ANDREW CLICKED the flashing 'You have new mail' message on his computer to open his mailbox. The In-box heralded five new items. Four were from fellow car dealers hoping to close deals. Good. The fifth message made his eyebrows shoot up in surprise.

'I have new information about Gabriella's parentage. She was the product of a baby switch at St Martyn's Hospital. I can give you the name and location of where I believe the real Lynton granddaughter is living now. It's worth fifty thousand. I am prepared to divulge this if you guarantee my anonymity. Your call. D. Hargreaves.'

Andrew stared at the words on the screen, hardly able to believe what he was reading. My God, a baby switch? Could it be true? That sulky Gabriella not only wasn't Calum's child, she wasn't even Lizzie's. If he could provide proof, this was a bonus his legal team could use to muddy the waters still further. Andrew could smell the inheritance getting closer. How he wished his father was still alive and could be told about his precious Gaby. Then he had a sobering thought, guilty that it had not occurred to him immediately. The real Lynton granddaughter could be a match for his baby. This thought was closely followed by another: if the court accepted that bloodline, not Gaby, was what mattered to Robert Lynton, this girl's family might try and snatch the whole estate and he could be left with nothing. He would have to be very sure of his facts before he had a conflab with his lawyers.

He stared at the screen for a moment or two, thoughts jumbling around his head. Calum couldn't have a clue about this, judging by their last conversation. But what about Lizzie? If she had been aware of the swap she'd have told Calum.

Everything was suddenly clear. He had to get to the girl first, and he would size up the situation before deciding how much of the story to tell her. He was sure he could persuade her to help Seb. Andrew leaned back, considering his options. Dan had said fifty thousand. What a hope. He didn't have five hundred.

Then a slight smile played on his lips. Maybe it was time to call in the reptiles. Newspapers, as he had once discovered, had deep pockets for stories like this. He would have a better chance of getting to the girl first if he could squeeze money out of a newspaper to pay his informant. Andrew began to type. 'Am unable to raise fifty grand though I could, at a pinch, raise twenty. Acceptable?' He pressed the 'SEND' button.

The answer arrived within thirty minutes. 'Unacceptable. Fifty or nothing. Up-front, no messing around. This is my bank and account number. Please confirm soonest. When the funds are cleared I'll be in touch with the information.'

'How do I know your information is reliable?' Andrew typed.

A few minutes later he got his reply. 'Common sense. I wouldn't risk my career like this on a scam.'

Arrogant sod, thought Andrew. He wasn't above risking his precious career for some straightforward extortion.

Andy picked up the phone, punched in the *Chronicle*'s number and asked the switchboard for Craig Garrett.

'Craig? Remember me? Andy Lynton. I helped you with that car scam story.'

'Yeah, it was a good one. Got any more like that?'

'Much better than that.'

They arranged to meet at a pub a couple of miles away from the Canary Wharf office.

Craig Garrett was regarded as a bovver boy in the *Chronicle* offices, with a reputation for stamping on ideas and colleagues in his efforts to remain the editor's current favourite. As a result, his colleagues were always on the alert to try to find ways to get their own back. But Craig's reputation in the office did not matter to Andrew. His sole aim was to come away with the promise of the money he needed to pay Hargreaves.

In the pub Craig allowed him only one sip of beer before he got down to business. 'OK, what you got for me?' Succinctly Andrew sketched in the main planks of his impending court case, and that the young heiress was a fraud, not his brother's child at all.

Craig drank his pint and set the glass down on the table with a clunk. 'Sorry, mate,' he said, rising from the bar stool, 'it's not sexy enough for my editor. If there was a celeb involved or there was some sleaze maybe we'd be interested.'

Trying to hide the desperation in his voice, Andrew said, 'Have another pint. I'm not finished yet.'

'I haven't got much time. Get on with it.'

'That little bitch doesn't deserve the family money,' said Andrew. 'My baby's dying of leukaemia. He needs it more than she does.'

The reporter sat down again. 'Dying baby? That's more like it.' He narrowed his eyes. 'What's the kid look like?'

Andrew bought him another pint and then took a family snapshot out of his wallet and was pleased to see the journalist nodding at the sight of Sebastian's smiling face.

'I have to be straight with you. We only take on cases we can win. The *Chronicle* never loses its campaigns.'

Andrew winced. How the hell could he guarantee that? For a fleeting second he had a vision of Edina's wrath if she suspected he was using Sebastian's illness as a lever to prise money out of a newspaper. Andrew adopted the tone of voice he reserved for clinching a deal. 'The hospital is very hopeful they'll find a donor match for Sebastian any time now.'

Craig leaned back, his eyes glazing. 'I have it. A great headline: "SOS: Save Our Sebastian". Yeah, that's quite good. The editor might well go for it.'

Andrew shifted in his seat. 'Let's put all the cards on the table, shall we? How much would I get for this story?'

'Money for this? You're joking? We're doing you a favour. We're going to try to save your kid. You ought to pay us.'

No money? Andrew decided to call Craig's bluff. 'If you don't think it's worth anything I'll take it someplace else.'

'Fine,' said Craig curtly. 'You'll soon find that all papers operate the same these days. They don't lash out like they used to.'

Andrew was stuck. If he let Craig walk away he'd have to try to interest another newspaper. But he didn't have contacts with other newspapers. What would induce the man to pay good money? Only a story that was rare. Like a baby switch at a hospital. He thought hard about whether he dare risk it. That could scupper everything.

But he needed the funds to find the girl's address. Without that information he couldn't help Sebastian.

'Would your editor pay money for another twist to this story?'

'Can't say till I know what it is,' Craig said.

'I told you that the girl, Gabriella, isn't my brother's child, right? I've just found out that there was a baby switch at the hospital—my brother and his wife have been bringing up the wrong child.'

To Andrew's disappointment Craig's expression seemed not to alter. 'That could be interesting,' he said.

'How much?' pressed Andrew.

'Maybe I could screw the editor for a few grand.'

When Andrew said he needed fifty to get the address, Craig choked on his beer. He wiped the beer froth off his lips and said slowly that it might be possible if the story made the front page and the centre spread. With the proviso that not a word about the baby switch would be printed until after the court case, the two men shook hands. Satisfied he was sitting on an exclusive, Craig ordered a couple more pints and took out his reporter's notebook. Much research had to be done before a word could be printed in the paper.

BACK IN HIS OFFICE Craig congratulated himself. Andrew Lynton thought he was a smart operator. Fifty grand? Dream on. It was his practice never to let a punter know when he was being ridiculous. It had been simple to fillet Andrew. The information from his contact was now unnecessary. It had taken him only a few minutes to find out the name of the hospital where the swap had taken place. Craig had every intention of getting his butt down there and obtaining the details himself. It wouldn't half get him in good with the editor. And, boy, did he need that at the moment.

His boss was trying to suck up to the Establishment and had got himself appointed to the Press Complaints Commission. This meant that Craig had to identify himself to the hospital as a newspaperman or risk the sack if he was found out. With his mortgage, no story was worth that.

Unfortunately the administrator at St Martyn's had suffered badly at the hands of the press when a dying celebrity had been under siege by journalists. Craig was given short shrift. Reluctantly he decided he would have to nail the missing heiress by being obvious and hang the consequences. When it came to his livelihood or Andrew's problems, there was no contest.

Would his editor go with it? Craig had not yet proved to his own satisfaction that the baby switch story was on the level, nor had he tracked down the girl, but he needed time and expenses to do both. He typed out a memo to the editor, taking more care with the words than he'd done for most of the stories he had written lately. ·

Four hours later, back came his memo with the editor's note scrawled at the bottom: *OK, but watch budget. £5,000 top whack.*

GABRIELLA'S MOOD was not improved when early the next morning her mother rapped on the bedroom door. After the third knock she snarled, 'Go away.'

'Phone call for you. It's Natasha. She says it's urgent.'

Blearily Gabriella looked at the alarm clock and reached to the floor where her dressing gown lay, wondering why Tasha was phoning at this hour.

Her friend sounded agitated. 'Look at the *Chronicle*. Page five.' She lowered her voice. 'It's not good news. Ring me straight back when you've read it.'

The paper was sticking through the letterbox. Sitting cross-legged in the hallway, Gabriella leafed through till she found page five.

The story was all about Sebastian's search for a bone marrow donor. And there was a picture of her, not a very good one, she thought, annoyed. Where had it come from? What was the bad news? Tasha already knew that she was not able to help her small cousin. Then she began reading the boxed-off story underneath her picture. She drew a breath. This was nothing to do with helping Sebastian. It was about some fight her Uncle Andy was having over Grandpa's will. HEIRESS CHALLENGED IN COURT, ran the headline.

An heiress. Gabriella was pleased. She would show this to her school friends. Why hadn't her mother told her she would have to go to court? She walked slowly up the stairs, reading on.

'The will is to be fought in the High Court on the grounds that Gabriella Lynton, aged fifteen, is not the descendant of wealthy businessman Robert McDowall Lynton.' What were they on about? 'Blood tests have allegedly established that the deceased's elder son, Calum Lynton, is not her biological father.'

Gabriella's mouth dropped open. Not her father? How dare they print such rubbish. It was a lie. A stinking, horrible lie. Newspaper clutched in her hand, Gabriella went up the remaining stairs two at a time and burst into her parents' bedroom. Her mother, bending over the washbasin, her mouth foaming with toothpaste, looked round in surprise.

'It's all a lie. Isn't it?' shouted Gabriella flourishing the *Chronicle*.

Lizzie dabbed at her lips with a towel and reached for the paper.

It seemed to Gabriella that her mother was never going to answer. 'Tell me.'

Lizzie dropped the paper onto the floor and sat down heavily on the bed. Gabriella waited for the denial. It never came.

Finally she shouted, 'But he *is* my father, he is, he is.' By this time her mother was in tears and Gabriella watched her in silence.

'I'm sorry, Gaby,' said Lizzie, trying to compose herself. 'What they say is true.'

Gabriella stared at her wide-eyed. 'Why haven't you told me before? How dare you keep something like that from me?'

Lizzie took a deep breath. 'I didn't know myself until a short while ago and I hoped you wouldn't find out, especially like this.' The two women continued to stare at each other. 'Sit down, darling, and let me tell you what happened at the hospital when you were born.'

White-faced, Gabriella slumped onto a chair.

'Your father was there and he's been with you ever since, so he is your father.'

'That's what you say,' retorted Gabriella angrily, leaping up. 'Why don't you just answer me straight. How many men did you sleep with when you were seeing Dad?'

'Gabriella! Don't talk to me like that.'

'I'll talk to you however I want. Who is my father?' she asked witheringly, before delivering her parting shot in the doorway. 'I bet you don't even know.'

Gabriella had no clear idea what to do next. She was only fifteen, but as soon as she got the first lot of money she would be off. Then a painful thought struck her. If Dad wasn't her dad, then she wasn't entitled to Granddad's money. She was trapped in a house with a woman she hated. Worse, she didn't even know who her real father was.

DAN HARGREAVES CHECKED the date in the *Chronicle* story again. November 11. That double-dealing bastard Andrew Lynton had gone behind his back to the paper. He'd given him seventy-two hours to come up with the money and since then the man had been stalling him. Yesterday's email was the most blatant yet. He had been so busy coping with his sick baby, he wrote, he hadn't had time to round up the cash. It was obvious what his game was. He was hoping the newspaper would find the girl and he wouldn't have to shell out. If this story brought the right girl forward then his information would be worth zilch. It was time to cut out the middleman.

Dan rang Craig Garrett, whose by-line was printed above the story.

TOUGH BASTARD, thought Craig as he put the phone down. There was no way he could get his hands on the £50,000 Dan had asked for unless he worked a scam. He had done it before, but not on this scale. He reckoned it was worth the risk. He was one of the few on the paper for whom the editor would sign an authority to draw up to £5,000 to pay an informant. The editor's handwriting was so bad, few could read it properly, and the way he had scrawled the figures, it was a simple matter for Craig to match the colour of the editorial pen and squeeze in an extra nought to the £5,000 mentioned above the signature on the memo.

A few hours later Craig met his informant. Dan gave him all he knew about Anna-Maria Ewing in Glasgow and readily agreed to accompany Craig to verify the birth details at the Family Records Centre. Other checks confirmed everything Andrew had told him, so Craig handed over a large bundle of crisp fifty-pound notes fresh from the paper's cashiers. Then he booked seats for himself and a photographer on the following day's flight to Glasgow.

THE PHONE WAS RINGING as Calum walked into his hotel bedroom in downtown Manhattan. He hardly recognised the voice of his wife, she sounded so distraught.

'Gaby has found out you're not her father.'

Calum felt a sense of outrage. 'Why did you tell her? We agreed to do it together.'

'Don't jump to conclusions,' she retorted. 'Of course I didn't tell her. The *Chronicle* did.'

'How the hell did they find out?'

'Andrew, I suppose.'

Calum was silent for a moment, then said sadly, 'That's ruined everything. I wanted to tell her myself. How's she taking it?'

'Badly. She was hysterical.'

Poor kid. Gabriella was volatile at the best of times. They would have to handle this really carefully. He was midway through the takeover negotiations but this took precedence over business. He would take the first plane out of New York. Lizzie immediately offered to meet him and he said he would let her know the time of his arrival. Calum's next call was to Tess to tell her he was on his way back and did not need a lift from the airport. Then he flung his clothes into his suitcase and went downstairs to settle the bill.

When he'd heard Lizzie's distressed voice on the phone his gut reaction had been to respond at once. He was still angry about her deceit, but lately he had begun to feel some guilt that he had not given her a chance to give her side of the story. Could their marriage be rescued? Only if they could forgive each other. Maybe that was possible, but forget? Never. Did he want to try to make it work? That was something only time could answer.

AS THE DOORS from the customs hall parted to make way for his luggage trolley, Calum spotted Lizzie's white, strained face at once. She was leaning over the rail, scanning the crowd.

They greeted each other hesitantly and did not embrace. Calum suggested they have a coffee before starting the journey home, and they found a table in a large snack bar. Lizzie sat down and Calum went to stand in line to pay for a four-cup cafetiere.

When eventually he brought the tray over to their table he noticed the dark smudges under Lizzie's eyes. They started drinking the coffee in silence, Lizzie twisting her wedding ring round and round her finger. At last she said, 'I know you want to talk about Gabriella, and she is very upset as you can imagine, but right now there's something else I have to tell you.'

He waited apprehensively. Her voice was so low he had to lean across the table to hear.

'Look, there's no easy way to say this.' She stopped. 'We've already found out that Gabriella isn't your daughter. Well, she isn't my daughter either.'

His first thought was that she had lost her mind.

'I had my blood tested and it showed the same incompatibility between our blood types as they found in yours. It proves without a shadow of a doubt that Gabriella is not related to either of us.'

Calum could hardly grasp what she was saying. He gripped the edge of the table until his knuckles whitened. 'That's not possible. I was there, I watched . . .'

'I know, I was there too.' She gave a mirthless smile. 'There's only one logical explanation. They made a mistake in the labour ward at St Martyn's. Somehow two babies were switched. One of them was ours.' Her voice was gentle as she reminded him of the over-busy labour ward, the short-staffing, the special care unit where two babies could be swapped without the mistake being detected.

Calum rested his forehead on his hand. 'And we didn't notice?'

'I've asked myself why we didn't a hundred times.' Her face was a study in misery. 'But we had only a brief glimpse of our baby before she was taken off for the jaundice treatment.'

Calum remembered his blind panic at the time, but he had been assured Gaby would be fine. And when he had visited her in the special care unit all he'd been concerned about was seeing if there was the correct number of fingers and toes. Had that been their baby or had she already been swapped?

'When you started to breastfeed . . .' Calum was hesitant. 'I just wondered whether you might have noticed anything was wrong.'

Lizzie shook her head. 'I had no doubt she was ours. I'll never forget the way she looked up at me in those early days and the way her fingers curled round my hand.'

Calum could see she was making a supreme effort to hold back tears. She took a deep breath. 'I've found the baby who was switched. In fact, I've already been to see her.'

'*You've what?*'

'She lives in Glasgow. Her name is Anna-Maria Ewing.' Lizzie explained how she had gone through the records at the hospital with some lab doctor who had been helpful, finally tracking the family down, via Dorset, to Glasgow with Sarah.

Calum stared at the table. He was conscious that Lizzie was watching him carefully. 'How sure are you that this girl is really ours?'

'Anna-Maria Ewing was the only girl baby in the unit who was about the same weight and length as Gaby.' Lizzie paused. 'And she has your colouring, your hair. And your long legs.'

Calum was silent. 'What is she like? As a person, I mean.'

'Bright, lively. A bit suspicious of strangers asking questions. Her mother says she's quite a handful and rarely goes to school. I think Anna-Maria has had a few run-ins with social services—and the police. Sarah reckons she takes drugs.'

'God. And she's only fifteen.'

Lizzie nodded. 'She might be a match for Sebastian, but she absolutely refused to give blood.'

'She could be terrified of needles, like Gaby,' said Calum with a weak smile.

'Maybe,' said Lizzie. 'I imagine you want to see her for yourself.'

'I'm curious about her, certainly, but I don't plan to dash off to Glasgow, not yet at any rate. My only priority at the moment is Gaby. She's a good kid and she's part of us—even if we didn't give life to her. I love her, probably more now because she needs me more. She needs both of us.' Calum glanced at his watch. 'I suppose we'd better get back and break the news to her.'

Lizzie began to gather up her things. 'Gaby's not at home. She's staying at Sarah's house at the moment because we had a terrible fight after she read the article. She says she never wants to see me again. She thinks I probably don't even know who her father is.'

Calum's eyes widened with shock. 'I'm so sorry, Lizzie.'

She turned wordlessly and he followed her to the parking bay.

As he stowed his luggage in the boot of the car, he caught a glimpse of the back of Lizzie's head through the rear window. A surge of sympathy overwhelmed him. He had been in the wrong, catastrophically in the wrong. He could barely imagine the agonies she must have suffered since that first awful session in Ed Foxton's office, and he winced at the memory of the night he had thrown that photograph of Peter Rivers at her. Calum settled into his seat, making no effort to start the engine. He tried to take her hand, but she pulled away. That nearly made him lose courage.

'Lizzie, I should have believed you when you said you'd never had an affair. I was wrong not to trust you from the start.'

She gazed steadfastly ahead and showed no reaction.

A note of desperation crept into his voice. 'The only thing I can say in my defence is that the tests were done twice and they were conclusive. Lizzie, I'm very, very sorry.'

She sat bolt upright, her chin jutting out. 'Sorry,' she said fiercely. 'You think by saying it that's enough? Can you imagine what I've been going through these past few weeks?'

Calum stared at her anxiously. 'I wish . . . I wish I could put back the clock, but I can't. Will you try to forgive me?'

Her eyes seemed to darken. 'I'm not sure I can. You were prepared to chuck away sixteen years of marriage, just like that.' She snapped her fingers. 'After those tests came in you wouldn't even consider any other explanation. Well, there was one. And we need to tell Gabriella, so I suggest we just think about that now.'

Miserably Calum switched on the engine, shifted into first gear and soon joined the slow-moving line of vehicles snaking its way along the M25 motorway.

Chapter Six

However many stories he was sent on, Craig never failed to get a buzz. It was what kept him on the road rather than behind a desk issuing orders. This assignment was turning out to be a breeze.

In fact, waiting around in front of Gallagher's Guesthouse was the hardest part. The electoral register had given him the Ewings' address and he and the photographer had arrived at lunchtime. By five o'clock, when even Craig was beginning to fret, he saw a figure in a black leather skirt riding high on her thigh, swaying down the street. 'That can't be her,' he whispered to the photographer. 'She looks well over fifteen.' But it had been, and he thought moodily that they would have to scrape off some of that pancake stuff to make her look more appealing to readers and less of a tart. He could already see the editor nodding approvingly at the headline splashed across five columns: WE FIND THE GIRL THE WHOLE OF BRITAIN HAS BEEN SEEKING.

TOP OF THE POPS resonated through the untidy bedroom. There was a firm knock at the door. 'Tasha, I need to come in.'

Gabriella shook her head violently. Raising her voice, Natasha called out, 'Gaby wants to be left alone, Mum, and so do I.'

'Sorry, that's not an option.' Sarah was firm. 'Open up. Now.'

Natasha sighed. 'Best to get it over with.' She unlocked the door.

Sarah came into the room and sat on the bed. 'Tasha, could you turn that TV off, please?' Her daughter muted the sound but left the set on. 'Gaby, your parents are downstairs.'

The girl's lips compressed and Natasha put her arm round her friend's shoulders.

'I think you ought to see them,' said Sarah. 'They're very upset.'

'Good.'

'I know how you must feel—'

'You don't. No one does,' said Gabriella vehemently.

'You're very hurt, I know, Gaby,' said Sarah. 'It must have been horrible to find out the way you did, but you'll have to go home some time. You all need to talk about this. It's the only way.'

'No. They've both been lying to me.'

'No, they haven't. There is an explanation and they want to tell you what it is. You owe it to them to at least hear them out.'

Gabriella stared unblinking at the television.

'Please,' urged Sarah. 'Go and see them. If you don't want to say anything you needn't. Just listen.'

Gabriella aimed the remote control at the television. Again the strident mixture of bass guitar and violins filled the room.

Sarah strode briskly out to join Lizzie and Calum, who were sitting at opposite ends of the sitting room.

'She won't come down.'

'I'll go up and talk to her,' said Calum. With that he sprang to his feet and went up the stairs..

'Would you like a drink?' Sarah asked, but Lizzie declined.

Calum reappeared, a sullen-faced Gaby behind him. 'I told her we had something really important to talk over,' he said to Lizzie, 'and I suggested we had a bite to eat on neutral ground. She's opted for McDonald's.' He turned to Sarah. 'Thanks for all your help.'

NEVER WERE PEOPLE so at odds with the relentlessly cheerful atmosphere of the restaurant than Calum, Lizzie and Gabriella.

'I remember Mum and I bringing you here for one of your birthdays,' Calum said. 'I think you must've been about six.'

Lizzie nodded but Gaby continued to stare down at her tray, toying with her hamburger.

Calum took his child's hands across the table and readied himself for the most difficult task he had ever undertaken.

'I'm sorry that you had to find out in the most hurtful way possible that I'm not your biological father. But that doesn't matter a hoot to me,' he said softly. 'You are my daughter and you always will be. It's important you believe it.'

Gabriella's eyes were stretched wide. 'I want to,' she said, 'but why didn't you tell me? It wouldn't have been such a shock.'

'I didn't tell you because until very recently I didn't know.' Calum explained how the facts had come to light as a result of the blood test Gaby had given to help Sebastian. Somehow Andrew had found out and was using it to fight the will.

'Don't you mind? That Mum must've . . .' Her courage failed her.

'I thought the same as you, darling,' Calum came in quickly, 'that your mother must have been with another man. I'm not proud of myself. I should've realised . . .' He paused and his voice became stronger. 'We owe your mother a very big apology because she didn't lie. There was a mistake at the hospital.'

Gaby stared from one to the other.

'What happened, Gaby, was that you were switched with someone else's baby. As far as we can work out, a few hours after you were born, the wrist tags must have been muddled up and then they were put on the wrong babies.' He cleared his throat.

Gaby's breath quickened. 'So I'm not yours?' she said to Calum. Then she turned her pale, almost translucent face to Lizzie. 'And I don't belong to you either?' Her face crumpled and she started to sob, her head bent, her body shaking. A few curious glances were thrown in their direction.

The three sat motionless in the booth, Lizzie aware that Gabriella would need time to absorb the enormity of what she'd been told. Calum held on tightly to Gaby's hands and squeezed them three times. This was their secret code for 'I love you'. She made no motion to repel him but did not squeeze back as she normally did, though slowly the harsh weeping began to ease.

'Gaby, nothing's really changed,' said Lizzie at last. 'We're still the same people and we love you.'

At this her face crumpled again. 'But I don't know who I am now.'

Lizzie was trying to control her emotions as she took Gabriella in her arms and gave her a hug. She noticed Calum swallowing hard as he stroked Gabriella's hands.

'Darling Gabs, I'm still your father, still your dad, and Mum's still your mum.' He waited for a moment to see if his words were having any effect. 'We've been with you since the minute you were born, haven't we? In every sense of the word we are your parents.'

Lizzie smiled encouragingly at Gaby's pale face.

'You have to say that, don't you?' Gabriella managed weakly.

'But we mean it,' said Lizzie. 'From the moment you were put into my arms, you were mine. My daughter.' She enunciated each word carefully, hoping that Gabriella could take it in. 'And that's how I still feel.' Her heart was thumping uncomfortably. 'Darling, it's not who your parents are that's important. It's who *you* are.'

Gaby nodded, but then her tears started again. 'Mum, why didn't you tell me before?' She stood up, making off in the direction of the toilets. Lizzie half rose as if to follow, but Calum shook his head.

'She needs a bit of breathing space.'

For a few moments husband and wife looked at each other. Lizzie sighed. 'I'm worried about how she'll cope with the court case, all the awful publicity. We won't be able to shield her for ever, but maybe she ought to stay at Sarah's place while it's on.'

'Good idea,' said Calum, his eye on the toilet doors.

A few minutes later Gabriella returned to the table, calmer, her eyes red but with questions on her mind.

'How did you find out about the hospital's mistake?' she asked, and listened quietly as Lizzie told her the entire sequence of events.

'Have you met the other people?'

'I have,' said Lizzie. 'I met your natural mother, briefly.'

'What's her name?'

'Nancy. Nancy Ewing.'

'And my . . . father?'

'I'm afraid he was killed in a road accident a few years ago. His name was Derek.' Lizzie told her about Nancy Ewing, her appearance, her home and what she did for a living. Her heart twisted as she waited for Gaby to ask about Anna-Maria.

'And what about . . . ?' Gaby couldn't finish the sentence.

'I met her too,' said Lizzie gently.

'Do you think Grandpa would've left me the money if he'd known this about me?' Gaby asked quickly, as if she couldn't face hearing about her mother's natural daughter.

'Absolutely,' said Calum with all the force he could muster. 'He loved you, Gaby; you made him laugh. And he liked spending time with you. Of course he would've acted in exactly the same way. I'm convinced of it.'

'When can I see her, my mother, I mean?'

Calum chose his words carefully. 'I can understand your need to find out everything about your natural mother and her family. I promise to help you meet them, but right now we have to concentrate on the court case. And maybe that's for the best.' He patted her hand. 'We all need time to come to terms with what's happened.'

'We're going to ask Uncle Andy to settle,' added Lizzie. 'He's been against it so far, but we'll go on asking until the last minute because we don't want our private business in the papers again.'

They were able to persuade her of the wisdom of being away from home when the story broke in the newspapers. The suggestion from Calum that she could stay with Natasha had the necessary effect and Gabriella seemed pleased with the chance of being cosseted by Sarah and the rest of the Sinclair family.

They were preparing to leave when Gabriella asked, 'Do I have any brothers or sisters?'

'Mrs Ewing has two other children, much older than you, who live away from home,' she replied. 'Two boys. And Anna-Maria.'

'The one who was switched with me?'

'Yes.'

'I'm really Anna-Maria Ewing, aren't I?' Once more her eyes filled with tears. 'And she's Gabriella Lynton. Your real daughter.'

RESTLESSLY CALUM RUMMAGED through the fridge, but nothing tempted his appetite. He poured out a generous measure of whisky. A wave of sadness engulfed him. Upstairs, the woman with whom he had shared everything, had shrunk away from him when he'd tried to embrace her. Was he such a bad person? He had made one mistake. A major one. But did she intend to push him away for ever?

Frustrated, he took a large gulp of the whisky. He drained his glass and began to crush the box that had housed the whisky purchased on the plane. He pressed the pedal of the waste bin with his foot to drop in the cardboard, but the bin was full. Of flowers.

Lizzie was sitting at the dressing table taking off her eye make-up.

'I found the remains of a bouquet of flowers in the bin. Why did you chuck them away?'

She looked round for a second, then resumed what she was doing. 'Gaby and I had a fight. She got hold of the wrong end of the stick, as usual, and ruined the flowers.'

Calum was uneasy. He did not want to press her. Having been proved wrong about practically everything lately, he didn't want to upset Lizzie further, yet he couldn't help asking the next question. 'Who sent them to you?'

'Dan Hargreaves, the doctor at the lab who was so helpful. I told you about him.'

'That was good of him,' he said vaguely, before retracing his steps back down to the kitchen. A puzzled frown creased his forehead. Why was this man sending his wife flowers?

GABRIELLA'S MIND was spinning as she lay in the bath. Calum wasn't her dad. Lizzie wasn't her mum. They'd said nothing had changed, but her feelings were hard to sort out.

Who *were* her parents? Pictures from her childhood kept popping up in her mind. Lizzie taking her to ballet classes, Calum bringing her home a little teddy bear when she had a cold. She had brought Angus Bear with her to Natasha's and that night, as every night, she would sleep with him under her pillow.

Was it possible for them to meet the daughter they had created together and not prefer her? How could they help but compare this daughter with herself, who was sometimes irritable and often, let's face it, horrible, especially to Lizzie. Anna-Maria was a mixture of their genes. She probably took after Calum, even-tempered, and like Lizzie, loved classical music. She could imagine the three of them, cosily listening to some concerto or other, and shuddered at the thought.

She'd bet a million pounds that Anna-Maria would prefer Calum and Lizzie to her own parents. Anyone would. But her real mother would probably be heartbroken at the loss of Anna-Maria and wouldn't want a strange daughter to replace her. Anyway, how could she live in Glasgow, away from everything that was familiar to her?

Gabriella pulled herself out of the bath and reached for a towel. It would be too painful for her to welcome this real daughter into the house, to share her with Calum and Lizzie. From now on she had to become more independent and she had better start right away.

She would have a talk with Luke. He was clever. He would help her decide what to do.

IN THE KITCHEN Calum was taking out the bin liner. He emptied it over the kitchen floor. It did not take him long to find what he was searching for, the florist's card. It was ripped into four fragments but it was easy to piece them together: 'I must see you again. D.'

Calum stared at the message. Gaby must have seen the card. No wonder she had got the wrong end of the stick, as Lizzie had put it. He massaged his aching forehead but realised that despite his jet lag he would never be able to sleep.

Impetuously he dialled Tess Parker's number. He would discuss the last-minute demands from Schroeder, anything to divert his mind from what had happened in the last twenty-four hours. But when her answering machine clicked in, he sighed and left a brief message. Maybe a drive might clear his thoughts and make his body accept the switch from New York to London time.

As he steered the car aimlessly through the streets, his mind returned to the image of the crushed flowers in the bin. What did Dan Hargreaves mean to Lizzie? Was he the reason she kept pulling away from him? Calum's head ached as the questions went round and round in his mind. Would he have been so suspicious about a bunch of flowers if his relationship with Lizzie hadn't already been strained by his lack of trust in her? He didn't think so, but that didn't help. He needed Lizzie to meet him halfway. Suddenly feeling dog-tired, he turned the car and headed for home.

LIZZIE LAY in the darkness, tossing and turning, waiting for Calum to return. She had heard the sound of his car pulling away from the house and wondered where he could be going at this ungodly hour. Unbidden, the image of Tess rose up in her mind. Lizzie thumped her pillow and resolutely turned her back on that line of thought.

Two hours later she heard the click of the front door and Calum's footsteps as he made his way to the bedroom. She pulled the duvet over her head and pretended to be asleep.

Breakfast was an ordeal. They pussyfooted around each other until Lizzie felt like yelling with frustration.

Eventually Calum retreated to his newspaper as she started clearing up. Making her voice deliberately casual she said, 'You went out very late last night. Where did you get to?'

He put the paper down and stretched. 'Nowhere, I just got into the car and drove round and round. I needed to think.' He stood up. 'If you don't mind I'm going to try to have a little more sleep before I go to the office. I'm no good to anyone like this.'

Part of her was grateful he was going off, because she was in no mood for a confrontation. Had he gone to Tess? Lizzie was surprised at the dull ache inside when she imagined him and Tess making love. She needed to stop thinking about it. To occupy her mind she would mark some tests she had set her class.

When the phone rang she jumped.

It was Tess; she needed to speak to Calum. When told he was asleep she asked Lizzie to tell him that the figures he had asked for last night were on his desk. Lizzie stopped breathing for a second. 'Was he with you last night?'

There was a pause before Tess said, 'I'd better not say anything more. I don't want to be involved.'

Calum had lied. Driving around aimlessly, indeed, when all the time he'd been with Tess. Bastard. If this was the way he was going to play it she would apply for the full-time job she had seen advertised in the staffroom at her current school. The post had accommodation offered with it. That would be a neat solution to their problems. Despite their occasional bust-ups, she suspected Gaby would choose to live with her if it came to the crunch.

Calum reappeared downstairs a short time later, dressed for the office. Lizzie was sitting at the kitchen table and greeted his smile with a frosty stare. He appeared not to notice and walked over to the sink to fill the kettle. 'Couldn't sleep.'

'Calum, Tess phoned and as good as told me you were with her last night.'

'I can't think why she would've done that. It's not true.'

'You expect me to believe you rather than her?'

'Yes, I do. Just like I'm expected to believe you.'

'What's that supposed to mean?'

'I read the note with the flowers. I think you slept with that man.'

Lizzie turned her back on him. 'You're wrong.'

Infuriated, he strode over to her. 'Tell me what's going on!'

'I don't have the energy for this at the moment. Please, I want us to call a truce. We have too much on our plate. Let's leave to one side what we're going to decide about us.'

Calum's face was strained. 'Us?'

'You know what I mean.' When he said nothing she sighed. 'All right, I'll spell it out. I still feel bitter that you didn't believe me. I hope I'll get over it but I don't know . . . and now you accuse me of sleeping with Dan Hargreaves after you've spent half the night with Tess.'

'That's not—'

'Just hear me out. I don't want an explanation. I don't want to hear excuses or reasons. I simply want to concentrate on Gabriella.'

'I agree with that,' said Calum grimly.

'As far as she's concerned, things have to appear as normal as possible. However difficult it might be I think we ought to put on a civilised front for the next few weeks.'

'What about sleeping arrangements?' Calum asked.

'We'll call a truce on that as well,' Lizzie replied. 'I suggest we share the same bedroom for Gaby's sake. In a day or two, if we find it impossible, one of us could move to the spare room.'

Calum's face was impassive. The phone rang and Lizzie seized it gratefully. It was Edward Foxton. Andrew's court case would take place in five days' time. Edward wanted them to come to his office as soon as possible. He had already briefed their barrister, Tim Goodman, and needed to discuss Tim's comments with them.

In the car on the way to Edward's office Lizzie wondered how he would react to the news of the baby switch.

'Do we have to tell Edward about Gaby?' she said to Calum. 'I'd much rather we kept it to ourselves.'

'I think we should,' Calum replied. 'We can trust Edward to keep it quiet, but if it leaks out we don't want our team to have surprises.'

'I'M AFRAID your brother's after blood,' said Edward as soon as they had sat down. He fingered the corner of his file, tied with pink cord, and gave a shame-faced grin. 'No pun intended.'

When there was no reaction from either of them, he went on, 'Andrew wants his day in court. I stressed that you were willing to sell the business, but he said if you gave him every penny you owned he wouldn't make what he stood to gain through the court, and it's my impression he won't compromise.'

'I'm not surprised,' said Calum. 'And he's right, I can't come close to matching what he hopes to get out of my father's estate, that much became clear when I was in America.' He glanced at Lizzie before continuing, 'There's been another development which we feel you should know about.'

Lizzie recounted how she had organised her own blood test, and how it showed she could not possibly be Gaby's mother.

'We could sue the hospital, you know,' was Edward's first reaction after Lizzie explained the theory that there could have been a switch in the special care unit. Typical legal mind, she thought.

'I think we have enough on our plates right now without another money-grabbing court case,' she said coldly.

'As you wish,' said Edward smoothly. 'Tim Goodman is quite clear in his mind about the line to take. In his opinion Robert's intention is what matters and I can't think the fact that there might be another Lynton baby out there changes that.'

Lizzie caught Calum's gaze and gave him a hard stare. She could see no reason to tell Edward that she knew exactly where the other Lynton child lived.

'I'll brief Tim Goodman about the baby switch,' Edward went on. 'But, as I say, in my opinion that won't change our tactics. You've given us terrific evidence of how close Gabriella was to her grandfather. Those home videos will be invaluable should we need to show them, and there's plenty of back-up in the way of letters and photographs.' He extracted a large birthday card from the folder. 'This is particularly helpful because the inscription, "My dearest granddaughter", is in Robert's own hand and reflects the language of the will.' He took off his glasses and polished them absent-mindedly. 'With all the ammunition we have, I'll stick my neck out and predict we won't need to call Gabriella into the witness box.'

'Thank God,' said Lizzie. 'I couldn't bear her to be questioned by a hostile barrister.'

'Judges don't usually like dragging young people into court unless it's strictly necessary,' said Edward. 'But there are no guarantees.'

CRAIG GARRETT flung his pen across the desk in a fit of irritation and barked into the receiver, 'For God's sake, I'm not asking for a cure for cancer. It's a blood test I'm after. You do them day in, day out. We need to find out if this girl is a match for Sebastian.'

He listened for a moment and then said slowly, 'No, I've told you people before, it's only the preliminary test results we need. The DNA test is for the paternity suit in court. Yes, I'm well aware that takes three or four weeks. If you don't pull your finger out the Save Our Sebastian campaign and possibly the kid as well are going to die on us, so I expect you to get results *fast*.' He crashed the receiver down, picked up his contacts book and mobile phone and prepared to return to the Ewings hotel and the dreary attempts at friendliness. To have this wonderful holiday in London, all Anna-Maria had to do, he had told her mother, was to give a sample of her blood to determine whether she was a match for the sick baby. He had to keep them sweet; the court case was due to start tomorrow. If only the lab would pull their finger out.

The news, when Craig finally got the call, made him more determined than ever to keep the Ewings the exclusive property of the *Chronicle*. Anna-Maria's bone marrow was not a match for the baby. One knock did not kill the story, though. Maybe a donor would still come forward as a result of the publicity. In the meantime he would have to fall back on the court case. This had all the ingredients of high drama now that a baby swap was involved, and Anna-Maria would be at the centre of it. He was keeping the Ewings under wraps until the afternoon of the first day's court hearing. Naturally he would write the story from the angle of saving the poor baby. But he would wrap it round every twist and turn of the family feud and the switched babies, emphasising how the *Chronicle* had tracked down this unassuming Scottish lass, unaware of her good fortune. It was a classic. Better than a Lottery winner story. But he'd better keep the negative result of Anna-Maria's blood test to himself. Best for the editor, Andrew and the court not to know about it for the present.

God, he was fed up with the Ewing mother and daughter. All they wanted to do was look at Buckingham Palace or go shopping. He was damned if he was going to use up his precious expense account trailing round the shops with them. Thank goodness it was only for a couple more days.

As SHE HAD to get up early to get to court, Lizzie decided to try to get a good night's sleep before the ordeal. At their last meeting Edward had not exuded his usual confidence and she and Calum were both uneasy. Despite the shared burden of the court case, the atmosphere between them remained frosty.

As he sat in the kitchen, toying with a cup of coffee, Calum had a sense of foreboding. For the first time he faced the possibility that Lizzie might walk away from all that they had built up together. He loved Gabriella and, however drawn he might be to his biological child, he could not imagine life without her. She was staying the night at the Sinclairs' and impulsively he picked up the phone and dialled their number. Gaby was a night bird. She was sure to be awake.

'Sarah? It's Calum. Sorry to ring so late but could I have a word with Gaby if she's still up?'

A moment later she came on the line.

'Hi, Gabs. You OK?'

'Fine, thanks.' There was a pause. 'Are we going to win tomorrow?'

'I hope so. Edward Foxton certainly rates our chances.'

Her next question surprised him. 'If we're successful and I get awarded the money and everything, do you think I could ask the court for an advance?'

'What for?'

She hesitated for such a long time he thought she wasn't going to answer. 'It's for Luke,' she finally admitted.

'You're not still on about that demo tape of his, are you?'

'He's very talented.' Her tone was wheedling. 'It's only two grand.'

'Gaby, the court won't agree and if they did, we wouldn't.' Desperate to change the subject, he went on, 'We've had several people phoning for you saying they were friends of yours. They wouldn't leave names so I'm sure they were reporters.'

'I'm sorry to miss the excitement.'

He laughed. 'Now you be good, young lady, and we'll see you at home tomorrow. Sleep tight.'

'Bye. I love you.'

His heart missed a beat. 'I love you too. Bye, pussycat.'

Calum replaced the receiver and his eyes began to prickle. Not once had she called him Dad.

Across London, in a Canary Wharf hostelry, Andrew Lynton was having a few pints with Craig. On the table lay the page proofs for the feature in the next day's *Chronicle*, with a prominent Craig Garrett by-line above the story about the baby switch and how a fortune lay at stake.

'I thought the girl was quite a hard little piece. How did you track her down?' asked Andrew, examining the large picture of Anna-Maria with his child.

Craig tapped his nose. 'Contacts, my boy.' Much against Craig's better judgment he had allowed the Ewing mother and daughter to have a pub supper with Andrew the previous evening. It was a pain, but Mrs Ewing had insisted on meeting the girl's uncle since she could not see her real daughter right away.

'When will we know about Anna-Maria's test?' Andrew asked.

'Another week or so.' Craig wondered briefly if he ought to tell him that her test had proved she was not a match. Aw, what was the point? The doctor at the hospital should be the one to do that.

'Craig, I put you onto this story. Don't you usually pay your sources?'

'Ah,' said Craig heartily. 'You gave me half a story. I had to find the address for myself. I'm afraid that cost plenty, the records people and so on. The expense of keeping the Ewings in the style to which they are unaccustomed is very high. There's virtually nothing left over.'

Andrew frowned and Craig went on, 'I told you, I'm paying you in kind. Look at the help I'm giving you with Sebastian as well as with fighting your case.'

'Craig, I'm grateful for the help you're giving Sebastian but this isn't fair. If I'm awarded money from the court it'll take ages to come through. I was counting on the *Chronicle* money to pay legal bills.'

'Didn't you tell me you had negotiated a no win, no fee deal with your lawyers?'

Andrew was silent.

'There you are then. Sebastian's getting his treatment on the NHS. And you'll win your case. We all score.' Craig fished a twenty-pound note from his wallet. 'But I don't want you to be out of pocket. Buy us another round.'

Andrew, still smarting, had to hold his tongue because this man had so much power over his life. Reluctantly he went to stand at the bar and tried in vain to catch the eye of the harassed barman.

Craig spotted the figure of a neighbour he had roped in to share the burden of minding the Ewings. She was the wife of a retired printer and knew the ropes and he could trust her not to gossip. Right now she was hovering hesitantly in the doorway and he waved his hand in the direction of his table, and shouted to Andrew to add a bitter lemon to his order.

By the time Andrew returned bearing a tray of drinks, Craig was listening to an account of a shopping trip the neighbour had organised for the Ewing duo.

'They'd never been to Harrods before,' she was prattling on. 'I hope you don't mind, Craig, but I bought them each an outfit.'

Craig struggled to keep his composure. The woman was saving him from having to spend time with the pair but he didn't want to draw his editor's attention to the spiralling costs. He immediately banned any more shopping trips.

'But what am I supposed to do with them?' she asked, puzzled.

'Tomorrow they'll be going with me to court,' said Andrew, 'so you won't be needed.'

Craig banged his glass on the table. 'I've not paid out all this cash to hand them over to other papers. You can have them in the afternoon only. And they're under strict orders from me not to stir out of their hotel until I come and fetch them. After lunch.'

'But my people want her there in the morning, in case—'

'Tough,' said Craig, tapping the advance copy of the paper. 'Once the others see this story they'll be on the hunt. We've got our follow-up for the next day's paper. I want our rivals to have as little time as possible to get in on the act.'

Andrew could see no point in arguing and bade Craig a frosty farewell. He was in a fury. He had every intention of using the Ewings in any way he saw fit, and if his lawyers wanted them in court from day one, minute one, they would be there.

He made straight for the hotel where the Ewings were holed up and told them that the plan had changed.

'All we ask is that you sit in a nearby room during the proceedings so if the judge wants to see the real Lynton granddaughter, he'll be able to.'

Mrs Ewing insisted that Craig had drummed into them that they should not leave the hotel without his express say-so, and that they should go to court only when he decreed, but Andrew smothered all doubts with the clincher, 'Didn't he tell you? He's changed his mind about you going to the court.'

Chapter Seven

The morning of the case was unseasonably bright, judging from the intensity of light coming through her windows. A butterfly flapping its wings would usually be enough to wake Lizzie, but she had slept for more than seven hours, a record these days. Drawing back the curtain she looked into the street—and into the lens of a cameraman standing inside the gate. With an angry exclamation she grabbed at the fabric and drew it closed rapidly. She had better warn Calum.

He was already in the kitchen making coffee, his face drawn. Determined not to provide more tabloid fodder they agreed to leave the house separately and meet down the road. They had put on their coats and were about to leave when the phone went.

Calum gave a tut of annoyance. 'Leave it. We haven't time now,' he said. But he was too late. Lizzie had already lifted the receiver.

'It's Sarah,' she mouthed at him. Then her expression changed to alarm. 'No, she isn't here.' More murmurings from the other end. 'I'm sure he didn't say that.' Lizzie looked at Calum. 'Apparently you spoke to Gaby last night and told her she could come home.'

Vehemently he shook his head and took the phone. 'Sarah,' he said, 'I thought we all agreed she should stay with you until the court case was over?'

There was a torrent of words and Calum interrupted. 'I didn't say anything to her about coming back here to sleep. What time was that?' The answer did not please him. 'She hasn't turned up?' He listened again. 'No, no, don't apologise. We'll sort it out. Goodbye.'

'Oh God, not again. What's she up to?' asked Lizzie.

'It might've been my fault,' said Calum slowly. 'Last night when I phoned, Gaby brought up the subject of Luke and money for that bloody demo tape. And I told her off.'

'I bet she's with him. Let's go to his house,' suggested Lizzie. 'Where did you put his address?'

'Second drawer in the dresser.' Calum looked at his watch. 'Ed will go ballistic if we're not on time.'

'We can't just leave her like that. I won't be able to concentrate on anything unless I know she's all right,' said Lizzie agitatedly. 'It shouldn't take too long, he only lives about half a mile away.'

Diversionary tactics forgotten, they went out of the front door together to face the flashlight of one persistent photographer.

Luke's home was in the middle of a small terrace in a poorer part of the borough. The house had been freshly painted and Persil-white net curtains were at every window.

A wary-sounding voice answered their knock. 'Who is it?'

Calum called out, 'Gabriella Lynton's parents.'

A woman peered from behind the curtain attached to the door. Apparently satisfied, she turned the lock and asked them to come in. She was a slim woman in her early forties and introduced herself as Luke's mother, Margaret Abbott. When Calum asked politely if their daughter happened to be in her home, Margaret nodded.

'She's upstairs. I can wake her if you like, but are you sure you want me to?'

Lizzie bridled slightly. 'We'd like to talk to her. We'd arranged for her to stay with a friend and we can't understand why she left and came here without saying anything to us.'

Margaret smiled reassuringly. 'When she arrived, quite late last night, I asked if you knew she was here. Come to think of it she didn't exactly answer the question. It was late so I said she could have a bed for the night. I thought I was doing the right thing.'

'You did,' said Calum swiftly, 'and we're grateful.'

There was an uncomfortable silence before Lizzie said she thought it best to wake Gabriella. Margaret agreed at once and Lizzie promptly followed her lithe figure up the narrow staircase.

Gently Margaret turned the knob of a room at the side of the corridor and stood back to allow Lizzie to enter.

In the gloom Lizzie saw the familiar sprawl of Gabriella's long hair across the pillow. One leg was protruding from under a blanket on what appeared to be a truckle bed. Lizzie stifled a sigh of relief to see she was alone in the bed and wearing the pink candy-striped pyjamas they had given her for Christmas. She tiptoed out of the room, followed by Margaret.

'That's Luke's room,' said Margaret, indicating another door on the side of the corridor. 'He's still asleep too.'

As the women entered the kitchen, Calum looked up expectantly. 'She's dead to the world,' Lizzie told him. 'I think you'd better go to court on your own and I'll wait until she wakes up.'

'I have a suggestion,' Margaret said. 'I could keep an eye on Gaby. If you'd like to go with your husband, Mrs Lynton, I promise your daughter will be quite safe here.'

'I wouldn't like to miss the hearing,' Lizzie admitted, giving Calum an enquiring look.

'I don't like to leave without talking to her,' said Calum, 'but we certainly don't want her anywhere near the court today.'

Sensing their need for reassurance Margaret said, 'There'll be no funny business in my house. Your girl is far too young and I'm strict about that sort of thing.'

Lizzie was by no means convinced that her daughter and Luke were not already lovers, but she did recognise that for a few hours at least her daughter would be under supervision. She and Calum agreed to leave Gaby there until they could collect her after the court had adjourned.

OUTSIDE THE Courts of Justice a clutch of photographers and television cameramen were pushing and shoving to get the best position beyond the wrought-iron gates. The fine Gothic building was alive with a cross-section of Britain's defendants, litigants, barristers and sundry court personnel, all talking earnestly.

Since the first edition of the *Chronicle* had dropped onto their desks, rival newspapers had been on the trail of anyone connected to the Lynton case. So far their attempts to get first-hand information had been thwarted. Lynton family members would not talk, the daughter had seemingly vanished and the *Chronicle* had the Ewings well sewn up.

That morning Craig had strutted into the Ewings' hotel feeling pleased at the reaction to his story. But his mood swiftly turned to fury. Anna-Maria was all ready to go to court for the start of the hearing, overriding his command. The bitch had apparently done a deal with Andrew, who had managed to assure them that it was in their own interest to attend court. Craig had no option but to climb down.

He looked with distaste at Anna-Maria. Her nails were painted a violent shade of purple and her make-up looked more like a mask.

'Wipe that stuff off your face,' he demanded.

'I won't.' She looked away. 'I've got spots.'

'Good,' he said with a grin. 'The judge will think you're a sweet little teenager instead of what you really are.'

'I think you're wonderful as well,' she simpered at him. But she disappeared into the bathroom and emerged a few minutes later, her naked face shiny from the lashings of cleanser she must have used. Craig scrutinised the final effect. Plain clothes. No accessories to distract the eye. Simple hairstyle. And she had acne. Perfect.

CALUM AND LIZZIE ditched their car at an underground car park near London Bridge and hailed a taxi to take them to the Strand entrance of the courts. Almost blinded by a continuous flash of halogen bulbs, they swerved round the pack and, ignoring questions flung at them by reporters, dashed up the stairs and into the safety of the lobby.

Hovering inside were Edward with Tim Goodman. Edward ushered them quickly up the stairs. He showed them into a small, dark room.

'We have something pressing to discuss before we go into court,' he said, taking off his gloves.

'Andrew's offered to settle?' asked Calum.

'Afraid not,' said Tim.

'What did you think of the stuff in today's paper?' asked Tim Goodman.

'We haven't had a minute to read anything,' replied Lizzie.

Tim opened his briefcase and took out a bundle of newspapers. 'All this is an unfortunate complication but I'm glad we knew about it in advance,' he said, spreading newspapers on the table and picking out the *Chronicle*. He handed it to Calum and Lizzie.

The first thing they noticed was a page one headline proclaiming: BABY SWITCH DRAMA. They stared at the paper in dismay.

'How the hell did they find out?' asked Lizzie.

The story gave every detail of the switch, with quotes from a worried hospital registrar and information about the two families involved. The last paragraph was particularly obnoxious, the great, crusading *Chronicle* claiming credit for tracking down the natural daughter of the Lyntons who could 'Save Our Sebastian'. A further story on the centre pages carried a large picture of a smiling Anna-Maria with Sebastian on her lap and the heading: I HOPE TO SAVE THIS BABY. The biggest photographs were on the opposite page, side by side. One was of Gabriella taken at a school concert, above which ran the headline: THE 'FAKE' HEIRESS? The other was of Anna-Maria Ewing with the headline: IS THIS THE REAL HEIRESS?

Tim Goodman gestured at the newspapers. 'Can anyone tell me how the *Chronicle* tracked down the Ewing girl and, more importantly, how they knew the two girls were switched at birth?'

'I'm positive the Ewings couldn't have told them,' said Lizzie. 'When I met them they did not know anything about this and it certainly didn't come from Calum or me.'

Calum broke the short silence. 'I bet you anything you like that Andy's involved.'

Lizzie tried to control the flush that was threatening to engulf her cheeks. It might not have been Andrew. Dan Hargreaves was with her when the Hudds handed over the address. It could have come from him. Apparently her discomfiture had gone unnoticed, for Calum was asking whether the publicity would affect the case.

'Can't see that it will,' replied Tim. 'Not the main issue anyway.'

Edward began polishing his glasses. 'Should the judgment go against us . . .' The sight of their startled expressions made him add hastily, 'not that it will, but hypothetically speaking this so-called "true heiress" could get her own lawyer and sue the family for your father's money.'

He and Tim began collecting their papers, preparing to leave for the courtroom.

'Any idea what the judge is like?' Calum asked Tim.

'Lord Nash? Decent old soul. Quite sound. We could have got much worse.' Tim adjusted his wig. 'He doesn't like long speeches, tends to doze off in the afternoon if you're not careful.' He looked from one to the other. 'I'm a betting man and I like our odds.'

ACROSS THE HALL in a room identical to the one being used by Edward Foxton, opposing counsel was having a briefing session with their client. Andrew Lynton could hardly contain his glee. The publicity could not have been better if he had written it himself.

'How do you think this will affect our chances?' he asked.

'There are never any guarantees in this business,' said Zak Blondell.

'I have no intention of giving my brother or his wife something else to gloat about,' said Andrew. 'I have to win. They've been working against me a long time and it's my turn to come out on top.'

Jocasta Hutcheson, his barrister, was firm. 'I told you from the beginning, we have to fight this on points of law. You can't allow emotion to cloud the issue, however hard done by you feel.'

'When do we play our trump card?'

'If and when we have to. Once the judge is aware that another granddaughter exists, one that carries on the Lynton bloodline, the case could take a direction we can't control. You don't want to lose the money to her, do you? But if I see that things are not going our way I might need to introduce her into the proceedings as evidence.'

She was interrupted by a tap on the door. It was Zak's clerk shepherding Anna-Maria and her tense-looking mother into the room.

'Here you are,' said Andrew heartily. 'Don't you two look smart.'

'Any trouble with the press?' asked Zak.

Anna-Maria brightened. 'Craig was trying to stop the photographers taking pictures of us. I kept my head down like he said, but they got one or two.' She gave her mother a conspiratorial smile.

'We can't worry about that now,' said Andrew before introducing them to his barrister, who reassured the two women it was very unlikely that they would be called in front of the judge.

'Then why are we here?' asked the girl.

'We didn't want to take any chances,' said Jocasta.

'Blood tests are all very well,' Zak explained, 'but we haven't yet got the full results of your DNA test, which is a weakness in our case. So if the judge requests proof of your existence, then here you are.'

Mrs Ewing was looking uncomfortable. 'I don't know about any of this. I only agreed to come because I want to meet Gabriella Lynton.'

'You will,' said Andrew quickly, 'when the case is over.'

THE JUDGE settled himself onto his throne-like dais and the slender figure of Jocasta Hutcheson rose to address the court.

After a brief outline of her client's claim, she used reports from the laboratory to prove that Gabriella Lynton was not of the Lynton bloodline. 'My Lord,' she said, 'we maintain that Gabriella Lynton has no claim whatsoever on this money because she is proved not to be Calum Lynton's daughter. It is our view that if Robert Lynton had known this, he would have structured his will differently. Our case is that he would have reverted to his original will and split the estate between his two sons Calum McDowall Lynton and his brother, my client, Andrew McDowall Lynton. We maintain that these two are the rightful heirs. I hope Your Lordship will agree and rule in my client's favour.'

She sat down only a few minutes after she had risen and the judge looked over his spectacles at her, his eyes warm.

'Thank you for that masterly and succinct summary, Miss Hutcheson, for which I, and I'm sure others in this court, are properly grateful.' He beamed expectantly towards Calum's defence team.

Tim Goodman duly took his cue. 'My Lord, we are here to defend the provisions of the will of Robert McDowall Lynton. In our opinion it is quite clear that the deceased intended to leave the bulk of his fortune to, and I quote directly from the will, "my beloved granddaughter". Gabriella Lynton is the young woman he helped to raise as his granddaughter from the time she was born, until virtually the day he died. He intended his money to go to Gabriella Lynton and no one else and I hope Your Lordship will grant him his wish.' Tim Goodman sat down and the judge nodded approvingly.

Jocasta stood up immediately. 'With great respect, My Lord, my learned friend conveniently omits to mention another sentence in the will.' She flourished a copy of it. 'May I be permitted to introduce this to the court as document A?'

The judge nodded and his clerk handed it up to the bench.

'In the will, Mr Lynton clearly states that his primary concern is to ensure that his money will allow the continuity of what he calls "the good bloodline of the Lynton family".' She paused. '"Good bloodline of the Lynton family",' she repeated. 'My Lord, can there be any mistake as to what Mr Lynton intended? He wanted to leave his hard-earned fortune to the person he had every reason to believe had his blood in her veins. But the sad fact of this case is that there exists a blood test which shows he was mistaken. I have a copy of this test result which I would like to introduce to the court as exhibit A.'

The judge's clerk handed up the document.

Jocasta raised her voice slightly. 'This test proves beyond a shadow of a doubt that there is a ninety-nine point nine per cent probability that Calum Lynton did not father Gabriella Lynton. In other words, My Lord, she is not his child and therefore not of Robert McDowall Lynton's bloodline, one of the main tenets of the disputed will.'

There followed various other legal submissions. Then Tim Goodman presented his evidence supporting his argument with regard to the close relationship that had existed between Gabriella and her grandfather. The judge was passed a bundle of letters which he studied closely. Next a television monitor was wheeled into the courtroom and he was asked to scrutinise a series of short video extracts showing Gabriella and her grandfather.

Jocasta scribbled a note to her assistant: *This is strong stuff. We'll have to bring in the evidence about Anna-Maria. I'm pretty sure he won't want to see her, but have her stand by just in case.* Jocasta stood up and asked politely if she could address the court. She wanted to introduce some new evidence. She asserted that this new evidence, though not directly affecting the case, would have repercussions on any judgment His Lordship was minded to make.

Tim Goodman attempted to speak but he was silenced with a small movement of the judicial index finger. The judge's bewigged head moved in the direction of Jocasta. 'Continue, Miss Hutcheson.'

'I'm obliged, My Lord.' She paused for maximum effect. 'We believe the case hinges on one simple premise. If the deceased wanted his bloodline to continue, then the beneficiary should be someone who is of his blood, not Gabriella Lynton who is not related to him in any way. It is on this point that we wish to introduce new evidence.'

Lizzie, sitting on a bench behind their barrister, watched anxiously as Tim Goodman began to talk urgently in Edward Foxton's ear.

'I have decided to accept this last-minute submission from the plaintiff,' boomed the judge, pausing to take a sip of water. 'I'm sure you won't prolong the case beyond its allotted time,' he turned a page over in front of him, 'will you, Miss Hutcheson?'

Jocasta stood up. 'My Lord, as you have heard, Calum Lynton is proved not to be the biological father of Gabriella Lynton.' The judge nodded. 'We have now been given to understand she is not the offspring of the mother either.'

Jocasta went on to paint a picture of a hospital, short-staffed on a Sunday, when human error resulted in the identity bands of two babies being switched and the babies then given to the wrong mothers.

'We have managed to track down the child born on the same day in the same hospital as Gabriella Lynton,' Jocasta pressed on, 'and by comparing hospital records, we are given to understand there is the strongest probability she is Robert Lynton's biological grand-daughter. Her name is Anna-Maria Ewing. She is at present in the court building should Your Lordship request her presence.'

Calum and Lizzie exchanged despairing glances.

Lord Nash tapped his pen rapidly on the blotter.

'There is no need to include that information. Please strike that name from the record,' said the judge sternly. 'Miss Hutcheson, since relationship to the mother is not relevant to this case, please confine yourself to what is pertinent.'

Defeated, Jocasta sat down. She'd given it her best shot. What more could she do?

Tim rose to his feet. 'My Lord, Miss Hutcheson would have us believe that Robert Lynton wanted his money to go to some unspec-ified granddaughter. He did not. He had one particular person in mind, not some young girl of whose existence he was unaware. My Lord, Robert Lynton forged a bond with Gabriella Lynton and she and no one else is the rightful heir to his estate.'

The judge had completed his notes. He removed his spectacles and put them in their case. 'I will need time to consider this evidence and I may propose a deferred judgment. I suggest we break for lunch, which will give me time to give the matter some thought.' The judge used the arms of his imposing chair to ease himself up and fifty or so bodies rose automatically as he shuffled out of the courtroom.

LUKE'S MOTHER would have been hard-pressed to recognise her son. He actually looked animated, jabbing a forefinger in the direction of the television. The lunchtime BBC news was on.

'Bloody hell, it's your mum and dad!'

Gaby moved towards the set and watched intently as the camera focused on her parents walking through a throng of people milling around the courts. The screen switched to a reporter who was interviewing a black-robed barrister. 'I can't say any more than I said in court, that we have evidence that Gabriella Lynton was switched at birth with another baby girl in the hospital.'

The screen was filled with a picture of a smiling young girl cuddling a baby, taken from the pages of that morning's *Chronicle*.

'That's her,' Gabriella's voice was choking. 'That's their real daughter. Look at her hair, it's just like Dad's.' She began to sob. Clumsily Luke took her into his arms, but she shoved him away.

'Why does it have to be all over the stinking television?'

On screen the reporter had turned to camera and was explaining that the case would continue after lunch but that the judge had indicated he might defer judgment.

'Why wouldn't they let me go to the court? They always treat me like a baby.' She stared sightlessly at the floor.

Luke said nothing.

'I know why they wanted me out of the way,' continued Gabriella moodily, 'because she was going to be in court. They wanted to see her, probably talk to her. They're not worried what happens to me.'

'I don't think that's right,' Luke said. 'Remember how worried they were when you didn't come home that time?'

For a moment Gaby looked uncertain as memories of Lizzie's troubled face, flanked by that of a police officer, came into her mind. She hadn't meant to frighten them then, but, when she wanted to say she was sorry, somehow the words came out all bolshily and as usual it ended in a row. And whatever she wanted to do, give money to Luke for his demo tape, go to court, it was always 'No'.

'You should be there now,' he said. 'It's your money that they're talking about.'

'But it's not my money any more, is it?' Gaby said miserably. 'He isn't my grandpa.'

Luke made no reply.

'But Grandpa always said I was his favourite. He used to love it when I beat him at chess. He said I was the brains of the family.'

'See, that's the sort of thing you should tell the judge,' said Luke. 'I'll take you there on the bike.'

'If I go,' Gaby said softly, 'will you promise to stay with me the whole time?'

THE WOMAN TUGGED at her bra strap, which was cutting into her shoulder. As she eased it, there was a sharp ping as the safety pin gave up its unequal struggle. She was watching the television set with unusual concentration, giving up a silent prayer that she was mistaken about what she had seen on the BBC 1 lunchtime news. She had switched channels to catch the later BBC 2 news as well, in case the story was repeated. Urgently she called out to her husband, who had promised to be there at the start.

'Ron,' she shouted, 'it's starting. Hurry or you'll miss it.'

The door burst open with a whoosh that caused a heap of newspapers on the kitchen table to scatter onto the floor.

'It's right at the beginning.' Her voice was sharp and he sat down on the arm of the chair and squeezed her arm affectionately.

'I'm here now, hon.'

After several other news items, when the waiting seemed interminable, the woman clutched her husband's sleeve. 'There.'

He craned forward, gazing unblinkingly.

'Am I right? What do you think?'

Slowly the man turned to look at his wife. 'No doubt about it.'

She sagged back into the chair. 'What are we going to do?'

He gave a deep sigh. 'Nothing. Much better to leave matters be.'

AFTER LUNCH the judge decided he would defer judgment. The instant he was out of the chamber a buzz erupted from all sides. Lizzie was visibly trembling and Calum slid along the bench to put an arm round her shoulder. Edward was looking sombre as he conferred with Tim Goodman. Calum decided to approach them.

'Do you think we've lost?' he asked.

'Certainly not,' said Tim, but to Calum's ears he could have sounded more forceful. 'This judge isn't known for fast judgments and this is an unusual case. We've done everything possible. I'm sure we'll get the right verdict,' he added when Lizzie joined them.

Lizzie listened with half an ear. It was too late to worry about the case. She was more concerned for her daughter.

'Calum, we must get to Gaby before she hears about the verdict from the papers or the TV.'

THE BLACK-HELMETED DUO on the motorcycle came to an abrupt halt in the central reservation of the Strand not far from the Courts of Justice. As they clambered off the machine Luke muttered hurriedly, 'Keep your helmet on.' He gestured to the crowd of pressmen. 'You don't want to be recognised by that lot.'

Cautiously they skirted round the jostling bodies, trying to see what was causing all the commotion. Facing the cameras was Andrew, with his arm round a young girl. To one side stood a thin woman with greying hair and with a pang Gabriella realised she must be her real mother. She stared at Nancy Ewing.

Gabriella's gaze then shifted to the girl at Uncle Andy's side. She recognised her at once, from the television news and the newspaper. This was her parents' real daughter. And then she saw Calum and Lizzie. Neither of them noticed the two figures in black leather on the far side of the jostling reporters.

Suddenly Calum saw his brother extricating himself from a small group of media people. Andrew and another man were shepherding the young girl and the older woman towards a waiting car and for a second Calum met his brother's eyes. Then the car drew away into the dense traffic to the accompaniment of flashing cameras.

Until that moment Calum had persuaded himself that he did not want to meet the girl or have anything to do with her or her family. But after seeing her in the flesh, he was overcome by sadness at the thought of her being hijacked by his brother for his own ends. She must regard him, her father, as the enemy. How could they build up a relationship after such a bad start?

GABRIELLA STARED after Calum and Lizzie. She had seen the way Calum looked at Anna-Maria, had seen his expression. Luke had seen it too. 'Maybe this wasn't such a good idea,' he mumbled. Gaby's distress was palpable, every line of her body was taut, as if she dared not move in case she fragmented. Clumsily he tried to console her. 'It'll be all right.'

That brought a flash of the old-style Gaby. 'No, it won't. You saw the way he looked at her. He wanted to go to her, here, in front of all these reporters and photographers. It's like he wanted to claim her, to say she belongs to them and I don't.'

Gabriella was overcome with misery. She'd willingly give up every penny of the damn inheritance if she could only put back the clock.

'Come on,' said Luke. 'I'll take you home.'

LUKE'S MOTORBIKE turned the corner and Gabriella saw with trepidation that the family car was parked outside the house. They pulled up behind it and Gaby got off. Luke stayed where he was.

'Come in with me, Luke?' Gaby pleaded. 'I can't face them on my own.'

'Yes, you can,' he said. 'They won't want me there, and I'm supposed to be practising with the band anyway.'

Slowly, Gaby turned and walked to the house. She was halfway up the path when the front door opened and Lizzie, followed closely by Calum, walked towards her. Lizzie opened up her arms and Gabriella found herself sinking into the embrace, something she had not permitted herself to do for the last couple of years. Calum's arms encircled the two of them and for a minute the trio rocked back and forth, not uttering a word. Eventually Calum broke away and Gaby was surprised to see his eyes were wet with tears. Lizzie continued to hold her arm tightly as they walked through the front door.

'Why don't we have a cup of tea?' suggested Calum.

'Come on, Gabs,' Lizzie said gently. She led her into the kitchen where Gabriella took a deep breath and nerved herself to ask the question that had been tormenting her.

'I saw your real daughter outside the court,' she said. 'What happens to me? Do you still want me here?'

Calum swallowed hard. 'Of course we do.'

Lizzie stood in the doorway, her eyes moist with tears. 'You're ours,' she said, her voice breaking, 'you always will be.'

Gabriella hesitated for a second. 'When I saw Mrs Ewing . . . my mother . . . standing there on the pavement, I didn't feel a thing.'

'It was the same when I met Anna-Maria in Glasgow,' said Lizzie, 'I didn't feel anything either.'

'I think I'd like to meet her—Mrs Ewing, I mean,' said Gaby. 'She did give birth to me, after all. Do you think that would be possible?'

'We can try,' said Lizzie. 'But they may not feel the same way about making contact and we can't force it.'

'If it happens, I hope you won't be disappointed,' Calum said.

'Why should I be?'

'Mrs Ewing and Anna-Maria were working with the newspaper against us. And people only do that for money.'

For a minute there was a glimpse of the rebellious teenager. 'How can you say that?' said Gabriella hotly. 'They're probably not very well off and anyway Anna-Maria was with Sebastian in the newspaper photograph. She could be trying to help him as well.'

'Yes, she could,' said Calum quickly.

'And you might be disappointed by your daughter,' Gaby said.

Calum smiled and shook his head. 'You're my daughter.'

EDINA WAS SITTING at the side of the cot, her fingers clutching the rungs. On the other side Andrew took hold of Sebastian's hand. The boy was so weak it seemed an effort for him to open his eyes.

Through the glass partition Edina saw the doctor. He exchanged a few words with a nurse and hesitated before entering the room. For a few minutes he busied himself with the charts at the end of the cot but she realised he was trying to tell her something. Something bad.

'I'm afraid we've had the test on the Ewing girl and she isn't a match.' Edina did not move. Andrew came swiftly round the cot and sat beside her, his arm round her shoulders. The doctor put on a cheerful-looking smile. 'We had many people volunteer after that newspaper publicity and the lab's working at full stretch so don't think there's no hope. There is. There always is.'

This wasn't the cool, detached medical professional. He was involved, concerned, and seemed to be trying to convince himself. He was scaring Edina far more than he would ever know. There were no tears left as she watched her child slowly dying.

ONLY A FEW DAYS AGO, Lizzie reflected, she had been in the High Court and the focus of a great deal of attention. Now she was trundling a supermarket trolley past the bakery section, ignored by her fellow shoppers. She caught a glimpse of her drawn face reflected in a glass cabinet. She looked haggard. Hardly surprising as the three of them had marked the ending of the case by talking until the early hours, thrashing over everything that had happened.

One thing they had all agreed on. The horrendous problems thrown up by the case had been put into context. The money and who ended up with it was far less important than whether they were still a family unit. Calum was more relaxed about the business; Erik Schroeder had made a reasonable offer and Calum had decided to go ahead with it to pay off his debts. And he had come to terms with the idea that someone else would be running the business.

As she tore off a number at the delicatessen counter, Lizzie experienced a pang of guilt remembering how she had turned her back on Calum's tentative overtures in bed last night. She couldn't deny she still had feelings for him, but however much he tried she wasn't able to overcome her hurt. She couldn't banish the vision of him making love to Tess from her mind. His denials and explanation did not ring true. Nor could she bring herself to talk about her future plans, but she knew she couldn't postpone it much longer. She had applied for the full-time teaching job with flat attached, and the governors had promised a decision within the week. If she were offered the post, that would definitely bring things to a head because she would have alternative accommodation for herself and Gaby. Did she want that?

She was startled out of her reverie by a shopper who accidentally bumped into her trolley. She wheeled it hurriedly to the check-out and began to unload the groceries, glancing at her watch. She had promised to go and sit with Edina at Sebastian's bedside.

CALUM TOOK STOCK. After her initial bewilderment Gabriella seemed to be handling all that was thrown at her with remarkable maturity. He was reasonably confident that the bond between them would not be broken by the events of the last few weeks. Naturally she wanted to meet up with her new family. So did he. That would happen in time. But how much longer could he and Lizzie postpone a decision about their marriage? What did he want? Could any marriage be the same after what had happened?

He longed for an evening with someone who understood him and could pamper his bruised ego. He thought of Tess, as he did too often these days. Lizzie was convinced he'd been having an affair with her. Every time he tried to convince her she'd misunderstood Tess, she cut him off. He came up against a brick wall whenever he tried to bring up a discussion about their marriage. He was attracted to Tess, he couldn't deny it, and the fact was that lately the temptation to do something about the attraction had been growing. And if Lizzie continued to turn away from him, what was the point of resisting?

MRS EWING KEPT UP a constant bleating about how Craig Garrett had double-crossed her. 'He promised I could meet my daughter as soon as the case was over.'

'And so you will, I'll make sure of that,' said Andrew absently, keeping an eye on the central information board. Only another half an hour to go before the departure of the Glasgow train.

'We can't do a thing until the judgment is announced,' he said firmly. 'When I win I'll organise your trip back, all expenses paid.'

Nancy Ewing still looked doubtful. Andrew gave a sideways glance at Anna-Maria.

'We should stay down here until it's all over,' she muttered.

'There's nothing I'd like better,' he replied, forcing a smile, 'but I can't afford it and Craig's newspaper won't pay anything more.' The truth was the *Chronicle*'s editor had washed his hands of the story and was off to fresh pastures.

Andrew helped them into the carriage with their suitcases. When the train disappeared round the corner he heaved a sigh of relief.

ON THE DAY of the judgment the Lynton family made their way to the court in a state of high tension. During the night Gabriella had been at her most irritating, leaping in and out of bed to get water, toast—any excuse she could think of to postpone sleep. Calum and Lizzie, after a night of fragmented dreams, had woken up heavy-eyed and fuzzy-headed.

They were late starting off and the morning rush hour was made more unbearable by a tailback all along the Embankment. But nothing seemed to faze Gabriella, who didn't show any of the ravages of lack of sleep. She kept up a steady stream of conversation about what she would do with the inheritance, seemingly impervious to Lizzie's attempt to douse her expectations.

They arrived in court number five with only minutes to spare. They were barely seated when the clerk called for silence to announce the arrival of the judge.

The seats behind Andrew's legal team remained empty. The only reason for Andrew's absence must be that he was needed at the hospital. Lizzie sent up a silent prayer for the sick baby.

To her surprise the judge caught her eye as he made his way to the dais. He looked like a medieval king seated on his throne dispensing justice and wisdom to his loyal subjects below.

'From the beginning,' he said in his summing up, 'this case seemed to be fairly straightforward. Paramount, surely, must be that Robert Lynton's wishes be carried out. What were those wishes? That his beloved granddaughter, his "bloodline" as he put it, should be his heir. But what was the importance of that term, "the bloodline"?'

Lord Nash paused, gazing around the courtroom over his half-moon spectacles. 'I had to ask myself, did this man show affection towards Gabriella Lynton simply because she was the product of his bloodline? That, of course, is the nub of the case. I was reassured by the evidence presented to me that the deceased was impressed by Gabriella Lynton's intelligence and robust attitude to life.' Gabriella, who had seemed subdued by the authoritarian atmosphere in the court, perked up at these words. 'But did the fact that she had considerably brightened his later years give me to understand that he intended to reward her with his entire fortune? That is what I had to decide.' Gaby's shoulders drooped.

'My conclusion is that the bond between the deceased and Gabriella Lynton was such that the continuation of the bloodline was of secondary importance.' The judge paused. 'I therefore find against the plaintiff and in favour of the defendant.'

'Dad,' she whispered urgently. 'Which one are we?'

At this Lizzie let out a laugh, which she quickly stifled when she found the judge staring at her.

Tim Goodman leapt to his feet, as did the others, as the judge majestically left the stage. The courtroom door was barely closed behind him when Tim turned round and clapped Calum on the back. 'We won. Well done, young lady,' said Edward to a bemused Gabriella.

Lizzie squeezed her daughter's arm. 'I suppose I'll have to start being nice to you from now on.'

Gabriella returned her mother's smile. 'Oh, Mum, don't be daft. Let's go to eat so that we can talk about going up to Glasgow.'

ANDREW WAS GIVEN the bad news by his solicitor and his instinctive reaction was to instruct them to start appeal proceedings. Gently the solicitor informed him that in the opinion of their barrister that would be a waste of funds. They could not accept a further brief on a no win, no fee basis.

Andrew waited at Craig's usual pub, nursing a brandy until the reporter appeared. But instead of commiserating with Andrew, Craig began cursing him for destroying his career. 'I'll be lucky to be in charge of paperclips,' Craig snarled, 'and it's all your fault.'

'I did all this to save my kid,' Andrew stuttered.

'Give it a break, Andy,' said Craig. 'OK, you might've used some of the money for Sebastian but, face it, your greed got the better of you.'

Andrew was seething. 'At this moment my child is lying in hospital, clinging to life. How do you think I felt finding out that Anna-Maria wasn't a match? Something you didn't bother to mention.'

Craig was momentarily repentant. 'Yeah, sorry about that. It didn't pan out for any of us. And I'll probably be out on my ear.'

Andrew stood up and stared down at Craig with a look of such distaste on his face that the newspaperman was temporarily silenced.

'You can always get another job. I can never get another Sebastian.'

A MEMO LANDED on Craig Garrett's desk an hour after the Press Association's report on the judgment was sent down the lines. It requested his presence in the editor's office. An unauthorised payment of £50,000 had come to light and an explanation was required. Craig decided there was no point in keeping the appointment and started to assemble the belongings he had accumulated over the past eight years.

AS THEY SAT ROUND the kitchen table that night, Calum opened a bottle of newly chilled Veuve Clicquot and raised his glass in a toast.

'Here's to you, Gabs.'

She took a sip and lifted her glass. 'To all the great things I'm going to do for everyone, you two and Sebastian and, oh, lots of others.'

The three of them clinked glasses and Lizzie grinned. 'Are you including Luke in that? I wonder if you'll still know him when you get the first instalment.'

'Probably. He's been a good friend to me. But he doesn't need money for that demo tape any more. He's given up the idea.'

'Why's he done that?' asked Calum.

'He's got a scholarship to Oxford. Isn't that wonderful?'

Calum spluttered, 'Good for him!' Lizzie remembered Gaby mentioning that he was clever. It had obviously been more than just a partisan view.

Gabriella spent a happy half-hour discussing what she wanted to do with the money. First of all she wanted to help her mum and dad. Then, she would certainly like to help the Ewings. 'We could ask the court if Grandpa's money could be split between the two of us, me and Anna-Maria. That would be fair,' said Gabriella.

'I don't think it's as easy as that,' Calum said. 'Ed wouldn't agree, and as he's the executor of the will he has some influence. But certainly there's a way you could help, perhaps with the interest on the capital.'

As for Sebastian they were still desperately anxious about him, but he was getting the best possible medical treatment and did not need money at this point in his life. Andrew had told them that the events of the past few weeks had shown him that family was more important than money. Now that the case had ended, he was determined to heal the breach with his brother.

'Maybe later,' said Calum, 'you could set up a trust that would protect Sebastian's future. It would give Andrew less to worry about.'

Gabriella agreed enthusiastically.

Chapter Eight

Lizzie had promised Edina that she would visit Sebastian in hospital as often as she could; she had already been there once this week. She made her way down the corridor to Sebastian's ward, but when she opened the door there was no sign of the child. Heart racing, Lizzie went to look for a nurse, fearing the worst.

'Where's Sebastian?' she asked breathlessly. 'He isn't . . . ?'

The nurse broke into a beaming smile. 'Oh no. He was operated on an hour ago. They found a donor. Isn't it great?'

'That's wonderful news,' said Lizzie, overjoyed.

'They had to operate immediately,' said the nurse. 'Poor little mite was sinking fast and they couldn't wait. Thank God they found a match at last. His mother's been with him all the while, but she's just gone for a coffee.'

'How is Sebastian doing?' Lizzie asked.

The nurse smiled. 'The early signs are promising. He's stable but we won't know for a few days yet whether or not the match will work.'

'Could I see him?'

'I don't see why not. He's in an isolation unit. But I'm sure the ward sister will allow you to peep through the window. Go to the third floor, second door on the left, then the first room on the right.'

Lizzie peered through the small window of the isolation room. A couple of nurses obscured the view of the bed. She hovered outside until they came out.

One of them noticed her and said pleasantly, 'Are you the mother? You can only stay for a minute.'

Lizzie was surprised that she was apparently being allowed into the room only hours after the operation and without a sterile gown or mask, but they must know what they were doing. Lizzie walked over to the bed towards the slight figure beneath the covers. Why wasn't he in a cot?

She stared at the sleeping face on the pillow, transfixed. She was looking down at a mirror image of herself.

Hardly able to believe the evidence of her own eyes, Lizzie's legs gave way and she sank onto the chair by the side of the bed, her gaze still on the face of the young girl lying comatose. The same wayward tuft of hair at the forehead, the same texture, the same skin colouring and the same features. Nose, shape of face. Hers.

Every now and then the girl would murmur incoherently and Lizzie experienced a wave of compassion that she could not explain. Who was this young person? What was she doing here? A nurse arrived and glanced at her before taking an electronic thermometer from her pocket. She inserted it briefly into the girl's ear.

'She's doing well. She's been so brave, we're very proud of her.'

Lizzie did not trust herself to speak and the nurse said brightly, 'I've just come on duty. Are you her mother?'

Mutely Lizzie shook her head and the nurse looked puzzled. 'You must be a relative, you look so alike. Wasn't it a miracle she was a match for Sebastian?'

Lizzie was trying to frame a reply when the door opened again and a plump, anxious-looking woman put her head round the door. 'Is it all right to come in now?' she asked, and the nurse beckoned her in before leaving to continue her rounds.

The woman leaned over and landed a soft kiss on the forehead of the sleeping girl. 'Alison, darling, I'm here and Dad's on his way.' She straightened and shot Lizzie a penetrating glance. 'You're Elizabeth Lynton. I read about you in the papers and saw you on the telly.'

Lizzie swallowed. 'Who is this? Your daughter?'

The woman hesitated. 'No, she's yours. Haven't you realised that?'

Lizzie stared dumbly at her and the woman began to explain.

'It was on the news. They were talking about this court case and they mentioned a mix-up with babies at the hospital. Then I saw you with your husband, in front of the courts. You were only on the screen for seconds, but when I saw your face I thought I was looking at our Alison. I only had to see you to know the truth. The resemblance is uncanny. I made Ron, that's my husband, look at the next news bulletin and he saw it immediately, too.' She put out her hand. 'Let me introduce myself. I'm Angela Simmons.'

Lizzie's eyes began to mist over and, seeing this, Angela Simmons took hold of Lizzie's hand.

After a while Lizzie said, 'I'm very pleased to meet you.' She took a deep breath. 'By the "truth" you mean you've been bringing up my daughter and I've been bringing up yours?'

'It seems like it, doesn't it?' said Angela Simmons quietly.

Lizzie looked again at the still figure lying in the bed and was overwhelmed by a strong, sure instinct that this girl, who was her double, was the daughter who had been taken from her all those years ago. The child she and Calum had conceived.

Angela said sympathetically, 'I'm sorry to break the news to you like this. It took me days to come to terms with it. Actually, I haven't really, but I've had a little longer to take it in than you.'

Lizzie gulped. 'I'd got used to the idea of another girl being our child. We were making plans to go and see her. But I don't understand this. Why didn't I discover her right at the beginning?' She described the start of her search to Angela and added, 'I checked those hospital records myself, meticulously. There were fifteen babies born on November the 11th and I'm positive there was no Simmons among them. How could I have missed you?'

'Easily.' Angela's face lightened. 'You see, she wasn't actually born in the hospital. Alison,' Angela paused for half a second, 'my baby, I mean, was born in the taxi on the way there. She wouldn't wait, the little minx. I won't forget that night in a hurry.'

'I didn't see any Simmons baby in the records,' said Lizzie.

'Presumably you were only looking for babies born on November the 11th?'

'Of course, that's the only day I was interested in.'

'My baby was born on November the 11th, but just before midnight. By the time we arrived at the hospital it was half past twelve and it was chaos. They'd had a terribly busy time. So my baby's birth was registered as the 12th, the following day.'

'Was she sent to the special care unit?' Lizzie asked, and Angela nodded.

'Bingo,' said Lizzie. 'I'm sure that's where our babies were switched.'

Angela patted her hand. There was a moment of quiet between them before she asked, 'Do you have a picture of Gabriella?'

Lizzie opened her handbag and took out a small photograph. 'It's not very good, she always turns her head away.'

Angela studied the features for some time, and her square, rather stern face became much softer.

'Very striking,' she said after a while. 'Reminds me a bit of Ron's mother. She was a beauty. Tell me, what sort of girl is she?'

Lizzie's face puckered. 'We've had our ups and downs. I suppose I'd call her spirited. Speaks her mind. Typical teenager.'

'Stubborn. Just like Ron's mother.'

'And Alison,' Lizzie asked, almost shyly. 'What's she like?'

Judging by Angela's description, Alison had much the same interests as Gabriella. She was popular at school, interested in art and music—like my father, thought Lizzie—and very impetuous. 'She just scampers off without thinking sometimes and it gets her into trouble.' Like me, thought Lizzie. A worry was beginning to penetrate her thoughts. She had been so positive Anna-Maria was the one. Though she was certain this time, Lizzie suggested to Angela that it would be sensible to do a DNA test on both families. Angela nodded, continuing to watch Alison in silence, but the girl's eyes did not open.

Angela smiled. 'Seeing you sitting there is like looking at an older version of Alison. My husband and I have always been puzzled at the differences between her and the boys. After all those years of wondering who she took after, everything now makes sense. But I don't think we'd have done anything about finding you for fear it would upset her.'

'So why did you?'

'It was that poor Sebastian. When we heard about him and how he might die, we felt we had to help in case Alison was a match. We contacted the donor unit and they found out she was.'

'Does Alison know anything about the circumstances of her birth?' Lizzie asked.

'No, she doesn't. Ron and I didn't have a wink of sleep thinking about what was the right thing to do. Eventually we persuaded the whole family to volunteer to be tested so Alison wouldn't think it was unusual to be picked out.'

There was movement from the bed and Angela bent over the supine figure. 'Darling? Alison, can you hear me? It's Mum.'

At the words, Lizzie's eyes filled with tears. For Angela was Alison's mother, as she was Gabriella's, and whatever happened in the future, Angela needed to be alone with her child right now. As silently as she could, Lizzie crept out of the room into the corridor and watched with a thudding heart as a nurse hurried in to attend to her patient.

Before she set off for home, Lizzie wanted to talk to Edina.

The canteen was almost deserted; there was no sign of anyone. Lizzie ordered a double espresso and sat down at one of the corner tables. She had been there for only a minute or so when Angela appeared at her shoulder.

'I hoped you might be here,' she smiled. 'I didn't want you to dash off before we'd at least exchanged telephone numbers.' She sat down and Lizzie began to write down her telephone number and address while Angela gave details of her home in Bromley in Kent.

Nervously Lizzie gazed round the canteen and asked, 'Have you met the baby's parents?'

'I saw the mother briefly,' said Angela. 'She was the only one allowed to see Alison as she was being prepped.'

Lizzie began to fret. 'Do you think she noticed the similarity between Alison and me?' she asked.

'I don't think so. She was in such a daze and thrilled about finding a match, I don't think she was concentrating on anything else.'

'That's good,' said Lizzie, relieved. She explained about the court case. 'The father was involved with the *Chronicle* and he might reveal to the journalists who you are.'

Angela looked alarmed. 'My family doesn't want to see itself splashed all over the newspapers. We made anonymity the main condition of helping.'

'Then you shouldn't have anything to worry about.'

Angela straightened, two tiny spots of colour in her cheeks. 'We're not doing this for the money they talked about on the television. It was only to save the baby's life,' she said. 'We're fine as we are.'

'I'm sure,' said Lizzie, and Angela's hunched shoulders relaxed. She had a strong conviction that whatever decision she and Angela made about the future they would make together, and the secret would remain within their two families.

'We four parents have to think carefully what to do,' said Angela. 'First of all we'll have to decide whether or not to tell the girls.'

'Gabriella's already been told she was switched at birth, but she thinks it was with the Ewing baby. She wants to go and see them. It wouldn't be right to do that now.'

Angela looked downcast. 'Alison will be so upset, I don't know how we're going to break the news. I wonder if we ever should.'

'Only you and your husband can make that decision. We thought it best not to keep secrets, but then we had a court case to face.'

Angela gave Lizzie a steely look. 'I would like to meet Gabriella, but it's not as if we're going to switch them back, are we?'

'Certainly not. That's the last thing I'd want to do,' said Lizzie. 'But having said that, there's nothing to stop our families from becoming friends, is there?'

At this Angela leaned over and clutched Lizzie's hand. The two mothers smiled at each other and, overwhelmed by events, their eyes filled with tears. When they had regained control, Lizzie smiled. 'I think I need another coffee. Can I get you one?'

'Yes, please.'

As she queued at the coffee urn, Lizzie looked round idly and saw to her dismay that Edina was making straight for her. Lizzie smiled at her, hoping she would not betray her anxiety.

'Thanks for coming.' Edina's face was transformed and she appeared to be in a state of euphoria. 'Isn't it wonderful news? I know he's going to be all right. Other babies have been cured and I'm sure Sebastian will be too.'

Lizzie prayed that Edina would not notice Angela sitting in the corner. The last thing she wanted was for the three of them to have a cosy chat and for Edina to find out who the donor was.

'Here's your two coffees, love,' said the canteen assistant to Lizzie.

'Sorry,' said Lizzie, flustered. 'I only wanted one. Unless you'd like it, Edina?'

She shook her head, apparently unaware of Lizzie's confusion. 'Just water, please. I daren't have any more caffeine. I've been drinking coffee all day.' Lizzie risked a glance towards Angela. The corner table was empty. Smart woman.

'The people here have been incredibly supportive,' said Edina, 'especially that nice doctor, the one who gave us the good news. He was as pleased as if it had been his own child.'

'That's understandable,' said Lizzie. It would be natural to ask who the donor was and she was anxious to learn how much Edina had been told. 'Who was the donor?' she asked, heart pounding.

'It's a young girl. I saw her briefly before the operation but I don't know anything about the family. I'll never be able to repay them, never.' She sipped her glass of water. 'Of course, Dr Hargreaves said they were prepared to carry on trying to find a match for as long as it took.' Edina was unstoppable. She painted Dan Hargreaves as a cross between St Francis of Assisi and Albert Schweitzer. 'He's been a great help all along. I shouldn't tell you this, but when he saw Andy at his lab he couldn't have been more sympathetic. But then they were at med school together, you know.'

Alarm bells clanged in Lizzie's head as Edina prattled on, walking ahead to find an empty table.

'Dr Hargreaves was the one who first put us onto that girl in Glasgow.'

Lizzie tried to quieten her pounding heart. 'Dr Hargreaves told you about Anna-Maria?'

'Yes, he saw the article in the *Chronicle* and went straight to them with his information. Andrew says he needed money for his lab. Apparently they paid him fifty thousand pounds. I don't mind, it's in a good cause.'

Lizzie's eyes narrowed. She wondered how much of that money had gone into Dan's own pocket.

'You can imagine how I felt when the girl turned out to be no use for Sebastian.' She clapped her hand to her mouth. 'I'm sorry. I shouldn't have said that. Not about your real daughter. But then, without him you wouldn't have found her. You should thank him as well, Lizzie.'

'Yes,' murmured Lizzie. 'I should.'

'What are you going to do about her?' asked Edina. 'And what about Gaby?'

'There's a lot we have to think about,' said Lizzie. 'We haven't made any decisions yet.' That bloody Dan Hargreaves, she thought. All this agony, this publicity, because of his greed.

Edina was talking about the court case. 'I've been so upset about it. I did try to persuade Andy to settle, Lizzie.'

'I know. It's all sorted out now. Where is he, by the way?'

'I wish I knew. Things happened so fast I've not been able to tell him about the operation.' Her face began to crumple. 'He's never around when he's needed.'

Lizzie consoled her as best she could until, unexpectedly, Edina's face brightened. She was staring into the middle distance and pointed to a tall figure making for the counter. 'Look, there he is.'

'Andy?' asked Lizzie who had her back to the counter.

'No. The doctor,' smiled Edina, waving vigorously to catch his attention. 'Dr Hargreaves, over here.'

For a moment Dan hesitated, then, tray in hand, made his way towards them and sat down at their table. As he and Edina began to discuss Sebastian's progress, Dan unloaded his cup of coffee, sandwich and an apple and aimed a dazzling smile at Lizzie.

'Dr Hargreaves, this is my sister-in-law, Lizzie,' Edina said.

'What a pleasure to meet you,' he said, stretching out his hand. She wanted to wipe that self-satisfied smile off his face.

'Edina's been telling me how wonderful you were. Fancy being able to find out Anna-Maria's address. So clever of you.' She paused as if to think. 'And that national newspaper who did the story about them, how on earth do you think they got to Glasgow so quickly?'

Abruptly Dan put down his sandwich, his eyes wary.

Bull's-eye, thought Lizzie.

'It was so brave of you,' she said, 'risking your professional reputation like that.'

Edina was looking puzzled. Lizzie leaned forward and dropped her voice. 'By releasing information about Anna-Maria this man has jeopardised his entire career for Sebastian,' Lizzie told her.

'I didn't realise.' Edina's eyes were shining with adoration.

'I think you're exaggerating my part in all this, Mrs Lynton,' said Dan, his smile long disappeared.

'Oh, don't be so modest. You know very well doctors have to keep their records confidential. If anyone reported you to the BMA, you'd be struck off.' She paused. 'Instantly.'

Dan flinched.

'Don't worry, Dr Hargreaves,' Edina's voice was practically a whisper. 'Nobody will find out anything from us.'

'Let's hope none of us features in any newspaper article from now on,' said Lizzie briskly.

By now Dan Hargreaves's skin had taken on a satisfying greenish hue. She rose from her chair. 'I must be off.' As she reached under the table to pick up her handbag, her elbow jutted against the edge of Dan Hargreaves's coffee cup. Piping hot liquid flooded across the table and down onto his expensive trousers. He leapt up, holding his groin, shouting in pain.

'Oh, how stupid of me,' she gushed, handing him a paper napkin. 'I'm very, very sorry.'

LIZZIE COULD HARDLY CONTAIN her jubilation when she returned from the hospital and burst into the living room to find Calum and Gabriella watching television.

'I've got some great news,' she said.

'Wait, wait.' Gabriella picked up the remote control and activated the video. Calum switched off the set.

'They've found a donor, and fingers crossed, it looks as if Sebastian's going to be OK.'

She could not tell which of them was the more delighted.

Calum asked the crucial question. 'Who was the donor?'

'Someone who heard about the story on the television and volunteered a blood sample.'

Calum nodded. 'So that publicity was helpful after all.'

Tentatively Lizzie confessed the entire story. She began by describing her feelings on catching sight of a girl in the hospital who was a mirror image of herself when she was a teenager and ended, without interruption from either of them, with the decision that they should await a DNA test before doing anything.

There was a silence and Lizzie and Calum exchanged nervous glances before Gabriella asked eagerly, 'Is she still at the hospital? Can we go there now?'

'Her mum wants Alison fully recovered before she breaks the news. You can understand that, Gaby.'

'Yes, yes. You're right. In a way this makes everything simpler somehow,' she went on. 'I mean with the Ewings.'

'And it explains why I didn't feel anything when I met Anna-Maria,' said Lizzie. 'Thank God we didn't jump in and get involved with the Ewings' lives.'

WHEN THE ENVELOPE arrived from the laboratory, confirming what the two mothers already believed, Lizzie was at home alone, having a free morning from school. While Anna-Maria had no genetic characteristics in common with the Lyntons, Alison's matched theirs in every important particular.

Lizzie's immediate reaction was to ring Angela, and the two women spent an hour on the telephone, eventually deciding two things. Alison must be told as soon as possible. And the parents did not have the right to make decisions about the future without the girls being fully consulted. They both admitted they were afraid of the situation running out of control. Once the girls had set eyes on their natural parents, would one or both want to share their lives with them? And if they did, what then? It was a question neither mother wanted to confront.

In the event it was Alison who resolved the dilemma. She refused point-blank to meet the Lyntons, and no amount of persuasion from Angela would make her change her mind. Ron backed Alison's stand, saying he, too, thought it unwise to 'muck around' with people's lives.

Angela desperately wanted to meet Gabriella, but told Lizzie it was best to leave matters for a while. In time, when the girls were a little older, perhaps then they could organise something.

Lizzie was struck by the sudden realisation, when she heard the Simmonses' decision, that the emotion uppermost in her mind was not disappointment but immense relief. She could sympathise with Alison. Perhaps it was not wise to open up this can of worms.

Gabriella was very disappointed, but decided not to worry her parents by telling them. However, the next day, when she came home to an empty house, she decided this was an opportunity to give fate a little push. She fished in her satchel to find a number then punched it in. When the receiver was picked up at the other end and the speaker identified herself, Gabriella took a deep breath. Now or never.

'Hi. It's Gabriella.'

'How did you get my number?'

'I dialled 1471 after your mother's last call. I love using it.'

A giggle. 'So do I.'

A long pause followed, before Gaby said she was sorry that they weren't going to meet. There was no response and Gaby summoned up her courage. 'Isn't the whole thing scary?' she asked. 'It's like something on the telly, not real life.'

'You feel like that? So do I. It was horrible finding out. I cried my eyes out.'

'So did I.'

There was another pause. 'Aren't you dying to see if you look like one of them?' Gaby asked.

'In a way. But Mum's told me the kind of person Mrs Lynton is and . . .' she stopped.

'And what?'

'My family's very different to yours. Dad isn't a company director.'

Gabriella laughed. 'Actually, neither is mine now.'

There was an answering laugh down the line that broke more ice. Alison began to confess that she had been unwilling to meet her natural parents because they were bound to be disappointed by her. Exactly what she'd felt, Gabriella told her. Sensing that the opposition was softening, Gabriella set about drawing out from Alison what she called the teenage junk: boys, school and clothes.

They agreed to keep their conversation secret and made arrangements to talk again later in the week. 'You're the only one who really knows how I feel,' said Alison.

'Ditto.'

SEBASTIAN WAS SITTING up in the hospital cot babbling his entire repertoire of eight words, smiling and rosy-cheeked.

Edina beamed at the nurse. 'I realise we'll have to wait at least four weeks before we know whether the transplant has worked, but look at him . . . He hasn't been this perky for months.'

Andrew had been mortified that his mobile phone had been switched off at the crucial time. He explained to Edina that he had been in such turmoil that he had taken a walk along the Embankment to try to clear his head. The phone had been buzzing with business calls and he had needed a rest from it.

I'm sorry you weren't here,' said Edina. 'It was amazing to see the life-saving liquid being injected into him. It was all over in under an hour.'

The nurse, who had spent the morning briefing the hospital's press office on the baby's progress, picked up one of the dozens of toys that had flooded in when news of his operation had been leaked to the press. She dangled the toy in front of the baby. So far the hospital had managed to protect the identity of the donor and the Press Complaints Committee had issued a statement saying they would take a dim view of any media outlet that infringed the right to privacy.

Andrew turned to the nurse. 'I can't tell you how grateful we are. I'd like to thank the donor.'

'She's already gone home,' said the nurse, smiling at Sebastian, 'but she and her family were insistent that they didn't need thanks.'

After the nurse left, Andrew told Edina he'd been wondering about whether or not to phone Calum. 'The excuse could be Sebastian, but even then I wonder if he'll take the call. He must be so angry with me.'

'I wish you'd make the effort because I want Sebastian to grow up as part of a family. It's been difficult for me and Lizzie. I haven't really told you how lovely she's been, even during the court case.'

Andrew looked chastened. 'I wish I'd behaved as well as that.'

His wife stood up and stroked his hair. 'Never mind, that's in the past.' They held hands, watching lovingly as their son tried to chew the ear off a hand-knitted panda.

Chapter Nine

The date of the meeting was preordained—November 11, the sixteenth birthday of Gabriella Lynton and Alison Simmons. It came about as a result of countless telephone conversations between the two girls. Once she had established a friendly relationship with Gabriella, it was Alison who persuaded Ron that she would be happy to meet the Lyntons. Finally he succumbed.

It was the season for fireworks and Gabriella suggested they have a bonfire and serve sausages and baked potatoes. Calum and Lizzie agreed, thinking a less formal event would be a useful ice-breaker.

The Simmons were due at six. An hour before, Gaby decided she must change her outfit. For the third time. Lizzie, as nervous as her daughter, did not try to persuade her that the cropped leather skirt was perfect, but just urged her to hurry up.

The cake had been iced and took pride of place in the centre of the table. Gabriella had squeezed out the slogan in pink icing: Happy Birthday To Us! and Lizzie allowed herself to hope that the event might be less of an ordeal than she feared. As she watched Calum joshing with Gabriella, pouring out white wine and soda for her, Lizzie reflected on how this turmoil had affected Gaby. She seemed to have undergone some kind of metamorphosis. She hadn't exactly become the perfect daughter, but the truculence and hostility towards her mother had been diluted. Indeed, she and Gaby had been able to plan this party together without a single cross word. Almost.

It was a cold night and the first thing Lizzie noticed about Alison was how pink her cheeks were. As she stepped shyly into the hallway,

Lizzie heard a faint intake of breath from Calum. She could understand his amazement at seeing a younger version of herself. Alison stood hesitantly and, unable to speak, Lizzie folded her into her arms. The girl's body tensed and Lizzie broke away quickly. She mustn't overwhelm her.

Angela was not having quite the same reaction from Gaby, who was hugging her natural mother joyously. When Gabriella finally prised herself away from Angela's embrace, Ron came and patted her awkwardly on the shoulder. Gabriella had been steeling herself for the traumatic moment when she faced her natural parents, but she felt it was turning out OK, less embarrassing and upsetting than she had feared.

Calum made no move towards Alison, busying himself hanging up coats and shepherding his guests into the sitting room. Finally, he nerved himself to approach her and politely asked what she would like to drink. Alison looked up at him shyly and smiled. He stepped back. 'You look so much like my wife.'

At this the room grew silent and Ron, noticing Gabriella's disquiet, said in a booming voice, 'No need for that, my girl. You're the spitting image of my mother. God rest her soul.'

The tension was broken then and the chattering started in earnest and never faltered for the rest of the evening. Photograph albums were spread across the floor, and everyone exclaimed over the likeness of the girls to relatives, many long dead.

Angela Simmons took hold of Gabriella's hand and examined her little finger. 'There it is,' she said, and went on to explain how many female members of her family shared the same physical trait, a slight curve in the finger. 'It's meant to be very lucky, you know.'

The two fathers went outside to set up the fireworks display. All smiles, the rest spilled out to watch the catherine wheels and rockets cascading into the night air. Lizzie had an immense feeling of well-being. Crucially, what had to emerge from this was that both the girls would remain secure within their existing family units. The circle in which they had grown and developed would not change; it would only grow larger.

The display over, they trooped back inside and Ron began making moves to take his wife and Alison home.

'Before you go, we have a little present for the girls.' Lizzie beamed conspiratorially at Angela, who went over to the table to pick up two small boxes. They were identical in size and wrapped not in traditional birthday paper but the kind used to welcome babies.

Alison was the first to rip open the lid. For a moment she stared at the contents, before squealing with delight. Lizzie held her breath as Gabriella tussled to open her box. A second or two later she held aloft a tiny plastic wristband, the sort used to identify newborn babies. Alison waved hers in front of her.

'Isn't it tiny?' she cried.

'I can't believe we were ever as small as this.' Gabriella's face was full of wonder. 'Mine says Simmons.'

'And mine says Lynton,' Alison laughed.

There was silence in the room for a moment, broken by Calum. 'But you are who you are. You'll always be Gabriella Lynton,' he said, glancing at her.

Ron put his arm round his daughter. 'And you'll always be Alison Simmons.'

Lizzie raised her glass at the giggling girls and clinked a spoon against it. 'A toast—no, two.' Obediently they all fell silent. 'First to Sebastian who brought us together and who's making wonderful progress, thank God.'

They cheerfully drank to that, and then she said, 'And to Gabriella and Alison. Both families have gained a daughter.' Lizzie looked fondly from one young face to the other. She longed to have a proper conversation with her newly found daughter, but this noisy gathering was not the right time. Observing her over the past few hours had convinced her that Alison did not have Gabriella's confidence or brio. But little by little, she hoped to establish a good relationship with her. She would not allow it to affect her closeness to Gabriella. In any case she was certain that the growing bond between herself and Gaby was strong enough to withstand the introduction of this new girl into their lives.

Across the room Calum raised his glass towards Alison and she gave him a shy smile of acknowledgment. He looked forward to talking to her about her new family. He would set out to make her proud of her ancestry and some day she might be persuaded that for the sake of Robert McDowall Lynton she would add his surname to hers. And if she did, the last wish of his father would have been honoured. The bloodline of the family *and* the Lynton name would continue.

THE SIMMONS FAMILY was long gone and Gabriella had trundled up to bed exhausted. Without the conversational shield provided by their guests, Lizzie and Calum were skirting round each other in edgy silence as they cleared the debris of the evening's meal.

'We should get Alison over on her own,' said Calum, putting the glasses into the cupboard. 'That's if you're still around.'

Lizzie went quite still. She searched for inspiration to answer him without spoiling what had been their first pleasant evening for months. 'It's too late for this kind of conversation.'

He stared at her for a second then asked quietly, 'Too late in the evening or too late in the marriage?' When she did not respond he went on, 'How long do you want me to wait, Lizzie? There's a limit to the number of times I can say how sorry I am.'

She turned her head away.

'So you can never get over it? Is that what you're telling me?'

Why couldn't he leave it alone for now? Her voice sounded snappier than she intended as she said, 'If you push me you'll get an answer you won't like.'

'I'm tired of being the supplicant,' he replied.

That did it. She flung a tea towel onto the draining board and told him she fully intended taking the job she had applied for and that she and Gabriella would be living in the flat provided. Seeing the fright in his eyes she added hurriedly that he would be welcome to visit Gabriella any time he wanted.

'Why are you doing this?' he shouted.

'Calum, we married very young, with little experience of places, people,' she hesitated, 'or other lovers. This gives us the opportunity to live on our own and see whether we can function as separate entities, as individuals. Perhaps marriages have a shelf life . . .'

Calum's eyes took on a glitter that Lizzie had never seen in all the years of their marriage. He stared at her with such anger that a thrill of apprehension ran through her.

'How dare you chuck this marriage on the scrapheap! You're going to give up all we've built up without making the smallest effort?'

She bridled at this, but in the face of his fury thought it best not to retaliate.

'Is it that bloody man who sent you flowers? Are you going to him?'

'Definitely not. There's no one else involved in my decision. But what about you? You and Tess?'

'We've never had an affair. She's been very supportive—no more than that.'

'You lied to me. You said you were driving around the night you came back from New York, but Tess told me you were with her.'

'You misunderstood her. She—'

'She's in love with you, isn't she?' Lizzie interrupted.

'Yes, I think she may be.'

Lizzie took a deep breath. 'Then I'm happy for you. This is your chance to make a fresh start. Let's face it, things have been said and done between us that I'm not sure can be undone.'

This seemed to push him over the edge and he moved swiftly towards her, grabbing her by the shoulders and swivelling her round. Panting with fury, he pressed his face close to hers.

'You're a fool, Lizzie, if you don't see how much you mean to me. I don't want you to leave me.'

She tried to speak but couldn't because he began to shake her angrily and, despite herself, Lizzie was moved by his passion. Here was a man who was prepared to show deeply felt, raw ardour.

'I've always had to be the peacemaker, the comforter and I'm fed up with it!' he continued. 'I'm not going to let you walk away without a fight.'

For several seconds they faced each other, then, with a low groan, he pulled her towards him and kissed her with such force that she reeled back.

Calum's kisses had always been gentle, soft, sensuous. This one was full of desperation, but the feeling behind it excited her. He began to pull at the lapels of her blouse and eased her gently onto the kitchen floor where he continued to undress her, muttering how much he loved her.

Lizzie's body responded as he entered her.

Afterwards, as she lay back, she was overcome by shyness. It was almost like being with someone new. She felt a little awkward.

Calum propped himself up on his elbow. 'It's good to have my lover back.'

'Ditto.' She smiled at him, moved at the intensity of love shining from his eyes.

Calum surveyed the crumpled clothes scattered around them. 'I don't know how that happened.'

'Don't apologise. I liked it.'

'It was the thought of another man making love to you. It sent me demented.'

'You should talk. I've had a few bad moments over Tess.'

He leaned over her. 'I don't think I encouraged her.' Lizzie's eyebrows shot up. 'Well, not much.'

'I don't blame her for trying,' said Lizzie. 'I suppose it looked to her as though we were finished. I shouldn't have left a tasty morsel like you just lying around.'

He traced his forefinger round her cheeks. 'You're not bad yourself, Mrs Lynton, and if you thought I'd step back and let that Dan feller whisk you away then you were very much mistaken.' He became reflective. 'The good thing that's come out of this is that it's taught us about priorities. For me it's you and Gaby.'

'And our other daughter.'

'Of course. In time. We'll have to get to know her.'

They went up to bed and lay in companionable silence. 'I think you ought to try to get to know your brother too. I think Sebastian has made him examine his priorities as well.'

Calum frowned. 'That's going to take time. I'm not sure I can forgive him for what he's put us through.'

'I'm not excusing what he did, but Sebastian was dying. We all concentrated on him and Edina, but Andy must've been nearly mad with worry as well. I wonder how we would have reacted in those circumstances.' Calum looked away, but Lizzie gently turned his face towards hers. 'We should make the first move, for Edina's sake. She wants Sebastian to grow up as part of a family. I think we owe her that, don't you?' Calum said nothing and she went on, 'What's the solution? To let this feud fester on?'

'I suppose I could make an effort,' he paused, 'because you want me to.'

'You have to want to yourself, but I suppose that's better than nothing.' She smiled at him. 'I'll ask them over for a meal.'

Lizzie snuggled into the crook of his arm and as neither of them felt sleepy they spent the rest of the night talking about the future. They admitted that over the past few years they had been neglecting each other's needs. They came to the conclusion that one of the things that had gone wrong was that they had few shared interests. Calum's absences on business and for hockey coaching had driven Lizzie to spend her leisure time separately from him and this inevitably had led to a breakdown in communication.

Calum volunteered to dispense with most of his hockey duties and Lizzie suggested they choose a hobby in which they could both participate. As one of his mad ideas for the future was to sail in a catamaran to the West Indies, she wondered if they might take up sailing when Gabriella had gone to university, an idea he seized upon enthusiastically. As for Lizzie, she wouldn't take the job that would have meant leaving home, but would look for another full-time post.

It was as if their marriage had been reborn, as if they had found the roots of their relationship. Lizzie reminded Calum of the saying, 'Good timber does not grow in ease. The stronger the wind, the tougher the trees.'

'This *will* make us stronger,' he said. 'We've been given a second chance.'

Lizzie lay back smiling and lifted her face for her husband's kiss.

VAL HOPKIRK

Val Hopkirk is the pseudonym used by co-authors Val Corbett (right) and Joyce Hopkirk (left), who first started writing fiction six years ago as a trio with friend and journalist Eve Pollard. Together, the three women wrote four novels, the first, *Splash*, becoming a best seller. When Eve Pollard left the group, Val and Joyce were keen to carry on together. *Relative Strangers* was the result, and they are already busy writing their next novel.

'It works well,' says Joyce. 'Hard work but excellent fun. We have known each other for so many years and have been through such a lot together—childbirth, divorce, buying and selling houses—that we are very tolerant of one another. Of course we have our little temper tantrums now and again, but we both enjoy working together. We literally take it in turns to sit at the typewriter, and, when we've finished a book, it's so much a joint effort that it's difficult to remember who thought of what.'

Prior to writing fiction full-time, both women had impressive media careers. Joyce Hopkirk worked on newspapers and magazines as a journalist and editor, launched the ground-breaking magazine *Cosmopolitan* in Britain in the seventies and subsequently the British edition of *Elle*. Val Corbett started her working life as a newspaper journalist before moving into television, where she directed several documentaries for the BBC and co-wrote the successful comedy, *Life Without George*. She was a director of Goldhawk Television, an independent production company, until her recent decision to become a professional writer.

Joyce concludes that with their different backgrounds she and Val contribute different strengths to their writing partnership. 'Because of her experience in television, Val is much better at dialogue than I am, but I think I'm more of a wordsmith because I've played around with words all my life.'

Final Venture

MICHAEL RIDPATH

Simon Ayot, newly married to a beautiful young biotech researcher and about to pull off a major deal at the venture-capital firm where he works, seems to have everything going his way.

But all that is about to change, for beneath the veneer of prestige and professionalism that the partners and associates present to the world, ambitions and rivalries simmer. And when millions are at stake, the rewards, it seems, are worth killing for . . .

I should have told her the night before, when I came home very late smelling of wine. Or that Friday morning, early, as I fought a thick head to crawl out of bed and into work for eight o'clock.

But I hadn't. If I had, she might, she just might, have stayed.

I was cooking supper when she came home from the lab. Shepherd's pie and baked beans. You can't get shepherd's pie in America unless you make it yourself. I needed the English comfort food to absorb the remains of the previous night's alcohol.

'Simon?' she shouted as the door slammed.

'Yeah!'

I heard her steps make their way through the living room of our small apartment, and felt her arms slide round my waist. I turned and kissed her, then broke away and turned back to the beans, which were beginning to bubble.

'Shepherd's pie?' she asked.

'Yep.'

'Was it a rough night last night?'

'You could say that.' I stirred the beans.

She poured a glass of wine and brought it over to me. She was wearing a black V-necked sweater and leggings. There was nothing under the sweater, I knew; no shirt, no bra. I knew her small, pert, lithe body so well, yet I couldn't get enough of it. In the six months we had been married, we had been all over each other all the time.

'I spoke to Dad today,' she said, a wicked smile on her face.

'Oh yes?' Dad was Lisa's father, Frank Cook, a partner at Revere, the venture-capital firm I worked for. I had him to thank for my job there, and for introducing me to his daughter.

'Yes. He says he bumped into you last night. You seemed to be having an enjoyable evening. And there was I thinking you were slaving away at cash-flow statements.'

I felt a rush of panic. Lisa saw it, but the amused smile remained on her face. 'He saw me?' I gulped. 'I mean, I didn't see him.'

'You must have been too wrapped up in your date.'

'It wasn't a date. It was Diane Zarrilli. We were both working late on one of her deals, and then she suggested we go out for a drink. We passed a restaurant, so we got something to eat as well.'

'You told me you went for a drink with some people from work.'

It was true. I had mumbled that as I had crawled into bed after midnight. 'You got me,' I said.

'Dad seems to think I should be careful of this Diane woman.'

'She's nice. You haven't met her properly yet. You'd like her.'

'She's very attractive.'

'I suppose so,' I murmured. It was undeniable.

'You lied to me, Simon Ayot,' Lisa said.

'It wasn't exactly a lie.'

'Yes it was.' She moved closer to me, pushing me back towards the cooker. Her hand shot out and gently squeezed my balls.

'Ow!' I squawked.

She giggled, her brown eyes flashing up at me. She walked backwards, pulling me towards the bedroom.

Ten minutes later, the smell of burning beans drifted in.

'No.' Gil Appleby, Revere's Managing Partner, and my boss, folded his arms across his chest, daring me to protest.

No? It couldn't be no. I couldn't let it be no.

I had promised Craig the money only a few days before. When we had initially invested in his company, Net Cop, six months previously, we had committed to provide more funds when the company needed them. Craig needed them now. Without our cash, his company would go bust. It shouldn't have been a problem.

The Monday morning meeting of the partnership, where new investment opportunities were discussed and any problems in Revere's investment portfolio dealt with, had started in the usual way, with Art Altschule talking about BioOne. Art liked to talk about BioOne whenever he could. It was Revere's most successful investment, and Art's deal, and he didn't want any of us to forget it.

Eventually, Gil glanced down at the papers in front of him. 'OK. Net Cop. A three-million-dollar follow-on. Tell us about it, Simon.'

I cleared my throat. 'As you no doubt remember, Net Cop plans to make the switches that direct the billions of information packets that fly around the Internet every day,' I began. 'They've completed the design of the switch, and they need a further three million dollars from us to go on to build something that they can show to potential customers. We agreed to put in further funds provided Net Cop met various milestones. As you can see from my memo, they've met these milestones. Internet traffic is growing exponentially, and Net Cop has tremendous potential. In my opinion, we should continue to support Craig Docherty.'

At thirty-two Craig was three years older than me, a wise old man in his business. He had vision, drive, energy, and an absolute determination to see Net Cop succeed.

There was a brief pause as I finished. Everyone was watching me. The five partners: Gil, Frank, Art, Diane and Ravi Gupta, the firm's biotech expert. And the other two associates, Daniel and John, who I knew would support me, but who didn't have a vote.

No matter how many presentations I made, the board room didn't get any less intimidating. One set of windows overlooked Boston Harbor, the other the great canyon that was Franklin Street, with the Bank of Boston building guarding one wall. Looking thoughtfully over Gil's shoulder, as if weighing the pros and cons of the discussion round the table, was a bust of Paul Revere himself. Silversmith, patriot, energetic horseman and wealthy entrepreneur, he mocked the computer geeks and disgruntled middle managers who came before him. He didn't seem too impressed by my arguments, either.

Gil sat stiffly in his usual place at the middle of the table, leafing through the briefing papers I had prepared. 'The original plan called for a follow-on investment to be made after one year. We are only six months into the deal. Why so soon?' He peered at me through his thick glasses. The lenses made his eyes look unnaturally small and hard. I had seen him use this effect many times to unsettle hopeful entrepreneurs. It was working with me.

'There are more competitors springing up all over the place. Craig wants to make sure Net Cop is the first to ship product.'

Gil's face, wrinkled and weather-beaten from countless days spent under sail in Massachusetts Bay, watched me, thinking.

'Frank. You helped Simon with the deal. What do you think?'

I glanced over to my father-in-law. Despite his fifty-seven years his hair was still light brown, his body athletic, and his face handsome.

But his eyes, which usually twinkled kindly, were agitated, worried.

'I don't know, Gil. I've got some problems with this one.'

What? Frank was supposed to be on my side.

'Yes?' said Gil.

'I think Simon has drawn the wrong conclusions,' Frank said. 'There's much more competition out there now. Maybe we should think about that.'

'But Craig has thought about it,' I said. 'That's why he's speeded up the development process!'

'I'm not sure about Craig Docherty, either.'

Out of the corner of my eye I saw Gil flinch. Venture capitalists are proud of backing people, not businesses. Once you begin to doubt the person, then it is very hard not to doubt the business.

'You liked him six months ago, Frank. What's changed?' Art was always quick to spot an opportunity to criticise Frank's judgment. He and Frank jostled for the position of Gil's right-hand man.

'That's true. We all did. But from what I've seen of him since then, I think he's unreliable. He believes so much in the success of his company that he loses track of what's going on around him. The original plan was for twelve months to the development of a prototype. You can't do it in six without screwing up the product.'

'But he's been working eighteen-hour days, seven days a week!' I protested. 'And his staff are all working just as hard.'

'So he's driving them too hard,' said Frank. 'He'll screw up.'

'Are you saying we should drop Net Cop?' asked Gil.

Frank rubbed his chin. 'We took a risk with the first two million. That's what we're supposed to do as venture capitalists. But the deal looks different now. It would be a big mistake to drop another three million.'

The bastard! Net Cop would be dead.

'I disagree,' I said. 'I'm sorry, Frank, but the market thinks that Craig's switches are better than everyone else's. He has easily the most advanced security and encryption features, and that's exactly what the big telcos and ISPs want these days. He's got a winner here.'

Frank was silent. Then, for the first time that morning, he smiled. 'I admire Simon's enthusiasm. I've got to admit this looked like a good deal when we invested. But not any more. Sorry, Simon.'

Gil took a deep breath. 'OK, do we go ahead with the extra three million? Frank, I take it you say no?'

Frank nodded.

'Art?'

'No.'

'Ravi?'

With curly grey hair, a bow tie, and half-moon reading spectacles on his brown face, Ravi looked more like a professor than a venture capitalist. He thought for a moment, but he shook his head.

'Diane?'

Diane sat there with perfect poise, her thick dark hair framing her high cheekbones, her small delicate lips puckered in thought.

'I think we should go with it,' she said at length. 'I take Frank's points, but we knew when we did this deal we were in for five million. It's an exciting market, and maybe we have got a winner here.'

I gave her a quick smile. I appreciated the support.

Gil listened to her with respect and nodded. 'Thank you, Diane.'

The room was silent as Gil studied the papers in front of him. Then he sat back and delivered his verdict. 'No.'

It felt like a physical slap in the face. I had lost a deal.

Gil took some pity on me. 'I'm sorry, Simon. I go with Frank on this one. When a deal turns sour, you should take your losses. I'd like you to get hold of the lawyers and work out how best to present this to Net Cop. But I don't want to lose our two million if we can avoid it. Salvage what you can.'

My first bad deal, after two years with the firm. I could live with the blow to my ego. I couldn't live with going back on my word.

'Without the extra three, Net Cop's finished. I can't do it.'

Gil looked at me sharply. 'Simon, we've decided to pull out. Now it's your job to do just that.'

'We made a moral commitment, to give Net Cop the funds. *I* made a moral commitment. I can't go back on that.'

Art, who had been quiet throughout this, suddenly burst in. 'Hey, quit playing the English gentleman with us. This is business. We back winners, and when they stop being winners, we drop them—'

Gil held up his hand. 'OK, Art, OK,' he said calmly. He turned to me. 'We had a moral commitment to invest more money, provided we were happy with the way the business was being run. But we're not. It's not your decision, it's ours. All we ask is that you carry it out.'

They were all staring at me. 'I can't,' I said, and picked up my pen and pad and left the room.

I SAT AT MY DESK in the empty office I shared with the other two associates, my brain tumbling over what had just happened.

I had joined Revere straight from Harvard Business School, and from the beginning I had been determined to succeed, to make the serious money that American venture capitalists can earn, to break out of the traditional constraints of my past: my father's title that had now become mine, public school, university, the army.

America was a land of opportunity for anyone who believed they had ability and who wanted to make a success of themselves. And I had been doing well. I had worked on many deals, and the second that had my name on it, PC Homelease, had made $8 million for Revere in six months. It had won me recognition in the firm as someone who was either smart or lucky. Gil thought highly of me and, until today, so had Frank. I badly wanted to make partner; at a lunch a few months before, Gil had hinted at the possibility. Was I now going to throw it all away?

The other two associates returned from the meeting.

'Have you got a death wish, or something?' asked Daniel, as he threw his legal pad onto his desk by the window. Short, thin, with dark hair and pale skin, he was the most aggressive and probably the brightest of us. 'Once they say no, they mean no, you know that.'

I shrugged.

'Man, that was rough,' said John. 'They mauled you in there.'

'It certainly felt like it.'

'I think you were right, though. If you say you're gonna do something, you've gotta do it.' He gave me a friendly smile.

'Bullshit!' Daniel said. 'Art's right. You've always got to do what makes financial sense.'

There was no point in arguing with Daniel on the question of ethics. To him, the concept of 'market forces' was a religious system. If something's price goes up it's good, if the price goes down it's bad. We had both been recruited from Harvard, and had been given plenty of academic justification for the supremacy of the pricing mechanism as a moral tool. Daniel was a natural believer.

John was very different. Tall and athletic, with mousy brown hair and big blue eyes, he looked younger than his thirty years. His father, John Chalfont Senior, had built up Chalfont Controls into a multi-billion-dollar corporation and was one of America's richest men. But John Junior had little interest in hard work or money. His ambition seemed to be to lead an ordinary life, which, given who his father was, was not easy to achieve. Joining Revere had kept his father happy. Daniel said John would never make it at the firm. He was probably right. But John did what he was asked to do competently enough. He did a lot of work for Frank, who seemed to be happy with him.

'What are you going to do now?' John asked.

I sighed. 'I don't know. I'm thinking of resigning.'

'Don't do it, Simon,' said Daniel. 'Seriously. Shit like this happens. What's with Frank anyway? I've never seen him so mean.'

'Neither have I.'

Frank would normally have backed me up on something like this. And if he had disagreed with my conclusions, he would have gently guided me to what he believed was the right answer, not waited for maximum humiliation. It had to be me and Diane. That was the only logical explanation. Frank was very protective of his daughter.

I picked up the Net Cop papers and tried to focus on them.

My phone rang; it was an external call. 'Can you take that, John?'

He punched a button and picked up the phone. He listened, mouthing the word 'Craig' at me. I shook my head. 'I'm sorry, Craig, he's in a meeting . . . I'm sure he'll be back to you when he has some news . . . OK, goodbye.'

'Thanks,' I said, as he put down the receiver.

Gil's decision had been taken. I had to face up to the fact. I couldn't leave it to someone else at Revere, or even worse, some hard-nosed lawyer, to tell Craig. I had to do it myself, face to face. I owed him at least that much.

NET COP WAS LOCATED in an industrial park in the romantically named Hemlock Gorge, a small wooded valley just off Route 128 in Wellesley. The whole company was basically a room of engineers at computers on the first floor of a low, brown, all-purpose building.

I received a wave from Gina, the company's only secretary, and looked for Craig. On one side of the room sat the hardware engineers; the software engineers were on the other. To get these two groups working together, a small team of 'bilingual' engineers sat in the middle. Many of the staff were surprisingly old; Craig liked to hire experienced people—the enthusiastic nerds of the eighties who now had wives, children and a little common sense. A great team, Craig said. They had already achieved more in six months than much bigger firms had achieved in two years.

I spotted the man himself drawing, at breakneck speed, over a double whiteboard in the corner. Boxes and arrows spread across the large white surface in bewildering confusion. Two engineers were listening to him.

I crossed the room and coughed gently.

Craig turned round. 'Hey, Simon! Howya doin'?' He was grinning broadly. 'So, when do we get the dough?'

'That's what I wanted to talk to you about. There's a problem.'

'A problem? What kind of problem?'

I could feel eyes all around the room resting on us. 'Can we talk about it in private?'

'OK,' Craig growled, and led me over to his small corner office.

I took a deep breath. 'Revere has decided to make no further investment in Net Cop,' I said. 'Sorry, Craig.'

'You're not going to give us the money?' Craig's face reddened, and his thick neck bulged, the veins clearly visible. 'Why the hell not?'

He took a couple of steps forwards and stared up at me. He was only five feet six inches tall, but he worked out regularly. He was a tight bundle of muscle in jeans, trainers and a black T-shirt, strong, tough and very, very angry.

I groped for words. 'The market has changed. Too many companies are out there and it's hard to tell who the winner will be.'

'We've been through this a million times. You wanna know who's gonna be the winner? We are!' Spittle darted from his lips as he pounded his chest with a meaty thumb.

'I'm sorry,' I said. 'But there it is.'

'You can't do this, Simon. You're committed in the investment agreement. We've met the milestones. Where's the money?'

Reluctantly I tossed across a copy of the investment agreement, with the words 'will be determined at the sole discretion of Revere Partners' highlighted in yellow.

Craig glanced at it and then scowled. 'What about this, then? "Such approval not to be unreasonably withheld." I'd say you assholes are being unreasonable.'

I sighed. 'Your lawyers can spend money with our lawyers discussing that if you like. It doesn't really matter. We'll win, and even if we don't, there are two more clauses we can use. Face it, Craig, if we don't want to put in more money, we don't have to.'

Craig threw the agreement onto the table and moved over to the window. 'You gave me your word that we would get the money, Simon,' he said quietly, his back towards me.

'I know,' I replied. 'I haven't been able to deliver. I should never have made you a promise it wasn't in my power to keep.'

Craig spun round. 'I've put everything into this business. Not just all my money. I gave up a good, well-paid job with stock options. I hardly see Mary and the kids, now. And what about those guys out there?' He waved his arm towards the room. 'If I have to let them down . . .'

He stood silently for several moments.

'Who was it, Simon? Who turned us down?'

'It was a partnership decision. A consensus.'

'Don't give me that bullshit! You at least owe me the truth on this one. Now, who was it?'

'Frank Cook,' I said.

'The bastard!' Craig shook his head.

'Craig, you'll get the money. It's a great opportunity for someone.'

'Oh, please. Like, some other venture capitalist is gonna leap in with a ton of money once you guys have pulled out. Come on! We're screwed, and you screwed us.' Craig's face was filled with contempt.

'You can try. I'll give you the best reference I can.'

'Like they're gonna call you! They're gonna talk to Frank Cook, and you know what that bastard's gonna say.'

Craig was right. Frank would make clear his reasons why Revere had pulled out. Craig glared at me. 'Just get outta here.'

'Craig, I can help—'

'Just get out!'

I nodded slowly and left, vowing never to get myself into that situation again.

BACK AT THE OFFICE, Daniel was scanning stock prices on his computer. He made no secret of the fact that his ambition was to make many millions very quickly, and he saw the stock market as the quickest way to that end. For the most part his investments seemed remarkably successful. He had an uncanny knack for spotting takeovers before they happened, and for anticipating the rapidly changing fads of technology investors.

He looked up. 'Craig wasn't too happy, huh? Did he try to kill you?'

'Nearly,' I said.

'So, what are you going to do?'

I slumped into my chair. 'I don't know.'

'Tea?' John asked.

I nodded. 'Thanks.'

He was back a couple of minutes later with a cup of tea for me and some complicated latte-type coffee for himself. He looked over Daniel's shoulder at his machine. 'Forty-three and a quarter, eh?'

We all knew what he was looking at. It was the same little number everyone at Revere looked at every day. The BioOne stock price.

'Edging up,' said Daniel as he turned his attention to a pile of letters and business plans.

I tried to concentrate on work, but it was impossible. I couldn't forgive Frank. We had immediately liked each other when he had interviewed me for a job at Revere, and he had watched my developing relationship with his daughter with approval. It was only in the last six months, since the wedding, that his attitude to me had cooled. I no longer felt welcome at his house by the shore and I was sure that he engineered times for him and Lisa to meet up when he knew I couldn't be there. In a way, I understood. Belatedly, he had realised that once Lisa married me, he would cease to be the most important man in her life. To his fear of losing his daughter was now added concern that she might be mistreated by a philandering husband. I needed to talk to him.

He was in his office, which was expensively kitted out with the mixture of high-technology and old furniture that Gil believed gave the impression of a leading venture-capital firm with money. Frank was on the phone, and he waved me to a chair in front of his desk.

I waited. He continued talking, avoiding my eye. The shrugs, the hand movements, the expressions were the only signs of his Jewish ancestry, and the only resemblance to Lisa. He looked the archetypal White Anglo-Saxon Protestant, while she took after her mother, with her dark hair and eyes and her sharp features.

He eventually finished his phone call, and turned to me.

'I'd like to talk about this morning,' I began.

'There's nothing to say. We said it all at the meeting.'

'I don't think so. There's more to it than that. I know you saw me having dinner with Diane.'

He leaned forward. 'Simon, understand this. Your marriage to my daughter has no bearing on how I treat you at work, and I resent the implication that it does.'

'What else am I supposed to think? We did that deal together. Nothing's changed. All the milestones we set have been met.'

'I disagree, Simon. I think plenty has changed. It was a judgment call. Now, I don't want to have any more of this conversation.'

'Oh, come on,' I said. 'You might have disagreed with me, but there was no need to humiliate me—'

'I said, I don't want to have this conversation.' He looked down to the papers on his desk.

I knew there was more I should say, but Frank didn't want to hear it. I made my way back to my desk, passing Diane in the corridor.

'Cheer up,' she said.

'Why? I've just screwed everything up.'

'No, you haven't. Here, come into my office.'

I followed her. Her office was smaller than Frank's, and tidier. Cool, crisp and modern. I slumped into an armchair. She sat on the sofa opposite me, relaxed, an encouraging half-smile on her lips, her long legs resting against the side of the sofa.

'Everyone has a really bad day sometime in the firm. It's like a rite of passage. You've had your good deal with PC Homelease. Now you've got your bad one. They'll all be watching how you handle it, you know. If you bounce back, they'll think the better of you.'

'We'll see,' I said. 'Thank you for your support, by the way.'

'I thought you made the right call.' She smiled quickly. 'Now,' she got up and took a sheaf of papers from her desk. 'Take a look at this for me. It's a company called Tetracom. They have a new idea for microwave filters for cellphone networks. The technology looks very interesting and I've scheduled a trip to see them in Cincinnati next Thursday and Friday. Can you make it?'

I hesitated. An overnight trip with Diane, however innocuous, would be bad timing. 'Um, I don't think I'll be able to,' I said. 'This Net Cop business is going to take some sorting out.'

'Oh, come on. It's only a day and a half. And I'd like you to work on it. I think we make a good team.'

When a partner specifically wanted you to work on something it was stupid to refuse.

'Do you have a problem with travelling with me?' Diane asked sharply. She was standing there, soberly dressed, next to her large desk, a partner of the firm I worked for. Telecoms was her area of expertise, and it was a field I was trying to specialise in myself. How could I have a problem?

'No, of course not. I'll do my best,' I told her.

'Good. This is an important deal, you know.'

I smiled and left.

'I saw you slinking into Diane's office,' Daniel said as I returned to my desk. 'You two sure are spending some quality time together.'

I LEFT THE OFFICE at six, early for me, and walked home from the Financial District over the Common to Beacon Hill. It was a warm evening for early October, but the first of the leaves were beginning to turn. I walked slowly, trying to relax, letting the low sunlight caress my face. There was no doubt that fall was the best time of year in Boston.

Halfway up Beacon Hill was Louisburg Square, where Gil lived, supposedly the most expensive piece of residential real estate in New England. Our apartment was at the bottom of the hill, down a pretty little street of dappled sunlight, green leaves and black railings.

I had just taken a bottle of Sam Adams from the refrigerator when Lisa came in.

'You're early,' I said.

'So are you,' she replied, and gave me a kiss. 'It's kinda nice, isn't it?' She hugged me. 'What's wrong? Bad day?'

'Horrible day.'

'Oh no. What happened?'

I got her a beer and we sat down together on the sofa. She tucked herself under my arm and listened as I told her about the meeting.

She exploded. 'I can't believe Dad did that! He shouldn't jerk you around at work. Let me call him right now.' She untangled herself from me and moved towards the telephone.

'No, don't do that, Lisa!' I said. 'That'll only make it worse.' I pulled her to me and kissed her. 'It's sweet of you to be so concerned. So far, I've managed to keep my relationship with Frank at work purely professional. I'd like to try to stick to that.'

'OK,' she said. 'But no way should he have done that to you.'

'No, he shouldn't have.' I took a swig of my beer. 'I promised Craig the money. And now Gil expects me to pull the plug. I'm not sure I can live with that. Maybe I should resign. What do you think?'

She was silent. I waited.

'Do you really want to give up?' she said eventually.

'No, of course I don't want to give up. But sometimes the only right thing to do is resign.'

'It sounds like you've got a real problem. You can either run away from it, or you can try to solve it. Sure, you've let Craig down and got him in a horrible mess. So you've got to get him out again.'

'Net Cop is history. No other venture firm would touch him.'

'Not yet, it isn't,' Lisa replied. 'I've never seen such a determined guy as Craig. He's smart. So are you. You'll figure something out.'

Her confidence in me was touching. 'I'll think about it.'

The phone rang. I picked it up. I heard the clear English tones of my sister.

'Helen! It's the middle of the night in London, isn't it?'

'I couldn't sleep. And I thought this would be a good time to get you at home.' She sounded tired. Tired and worried.

'What's up?' I said.

'I spoke to the lawyers today. They think we can appeal. I don't know what to do about it.'

'What makes them think we'll win an appeal?'

'They've found two more expert witnesses who will say that the doctor was definitely negligent. They're good. Well respected.'

'They'll need to be paid, of course.'

'So will the lawyers. Especially the barrister. That's the killer.'

It was. Helen had already spent all her meagre savings on the lawsuit. And I had spent all mine. And Lisa's. And after all that, Matthew still had cerebral palsy, and Helen had still been forced to give up her career so that she could look after him.

'Have you spoken to Piers?'

Piers was Matthew's father, an unsuccessful TV scriptwriter who had disappeared from Helen's life just before the boy had been born.

'There's no point. He has no interest, and he has no money.'

'What about Mother?'

'Come on! I haven't spoken to her for six months!'

Our mother, Lady Ayot, hadn't approved of her daughter having a baby out of wedlock. Besides which, she had no money either.

'What do you want to do?' I asked.

Helen sighed. 'If we win, we could get a large settlement. And we'd get costs, so I could pay you back.'

'That doesn't matter,' I said. What mattered was how my younger sister was going to look after her son without a job, a husband, or any money. I was very fond of her. She deserved better. 'And if we lose?'

'I've lost everything anyway,' Helen said. 'It's you I'm worried about. I was going to leave you out of it. Tell them that we couldn't afford to go to appeal. But . . . It's our only hope. And . . . well, I thought you wouldn't want me to make up your mind for you.'

'You're right,' I said. 'I'm glad you called.' I sighed. 'How much?'

'Fifty thousand pounds.'

We had to try. Somehow, we had to try.

'Leave it with me,' I said. 'I'll think of something.'

'Thank you,' she said, a glimmer of hope in her voice.

I put down the phone.

'She wants to appeal and it's going to cost fifty thousand quid.'

Lisa winced. 'Where are we going to get that from?'

I shrugged. I had no idea. I slumped back in the sofa.

There had been complications at Matthew's birth that had led to him being deprived of oxygen for a few minutes. The doctor had made some mistakes. When it became clear that Matthew had cerebral palsy, Helen had decided to sue, with my support. It had been an easy decision at the time: Matthew, now two, needed constant care, and Helen was finding it very hard to cope. But the case had quickly become more complicated than any of us had expected. Although Lisa and I agonised over the money, it became harder and harder to pull out. In the end, I always came to the same decision: I wasn't going to abandon my sister.

'I'm sorry about all this,' I said to Lisa, taking her hand.

She squeezed it. 'Don't worry. I'd do the same for my brother.'

WE WERE LYING naked in bed together, reading. Lisa was engrossed in a novel. I was skimming the Tetracom material Diane had given me.

'We had some good results today,' Lisa said.

I put down my papers. 'Really?'

'Yes, we'll be able to try BP 56 on humans soon. We won't know it works until it has gone through the whole clinical trials process, but so far the animal work is looking very good.'

'That's great. Well done, my love.' I leaned over and kissed her. It was Lisa who had first suggested that BP 56, a small molecule called a neuropeptide that she had isolated, would have a beneficial effect on Parkinson's disease. And it now looked as if she was right.

She smiled. 'Poor Henry is so excited he can hardly control himself.' Henry Chan was her boss and the founder of Boston Peptides. 'But we're going to need cash from somewhere to fund the clinical trials. Venture First doesn't want to put up any more.'

I told her that the rumours in the market were that Venture First, the small venture-capital firm that had provided initial funding for Boston Peptides, had itself run out of money.

'So what kind of people do you get to take these drugs during the clinical trials?' I asked.

'Volunteers. Medical students, mostly. They get paid for it.'

'They must be mad.'

'It's perfectly safe. We do very thorough tests on animals. If there's a major problem it will show up.'

'So why do the tests on people at all, then?'

'There are often side effects,' Lisa said. 'Headaches, nausea, diarrhoea.'

'You'd never catch me doing it.'

Lisa glanced at the papers I was reading. 'What are all these?'

'Oh, a deal that Diane is working on for a company called Tetracom. It looks quite promising.'

'Diane, huh?'

'Yes.' I tried to come out with the next bit casually. 'We're going to Cincinnati next week to visit them. I'll be out Thursday night.'

She pulled back. 'OK,' she said, picking up her book again and studying the page intently.

'Do you have a problem with that?' I said.

'No.' She didn't look up from her book.

'I mean, I have to go. It's my job to work with Diane.'

Then she looked up, a spark of anger in her face. 'To tell you the truth, I do mind, Simon.'

'There's nothing to worry about. You should know that.'

'I think perhaps there is,' Lisa snapped. 'The two of you alone in some hotel. If she has got her eye on you, that's when she'll make her move, Simon.'

'Lisa! She's a partner in my firm. A colleague. A boss.'

'She's done it before! Dad told me.'

'Huh,' I snorted. 'He put all this into your mind, didn't he?'

'I just don't trust that woman.'

'You don't even know her.'

'OK,' said Lisa. 'You go then.' She turned out the light.

We lay in bed, backs to each other. I was angry. I really had no choice but to go. And Lisa really ought to be able to trust me.

I was still fuming, when I felt a finger brush gently up my spine.

'Simon?' she whispered. 'I have an idea.'

'What is it?' I turned to face her.

She pulled herself close to me. 'I'm going to wear you out so completely that Diane will dump you.'

'Sounds like a good plan to me,' I said.

The scull cut through the river and the slight head wind towards the Boston University Bridge, where the Charles River narrowed. A mile behind me was the Union Boathouse from where I set off three mornings a week. I was into a good rowing rhythm now. The air was crisp, the water blue, and the sky clear. Out here, I could think.

My conversation with Helen had depressed me. I knew she was near the end of her rope, and I wanted so badly to help her. I was the lucky one, with a wife I loved and a job I enjoyed. It wasn't fair. I wanted to share some of that luck with her.

Although the job wasn't going brilliantly at the moment. My anger at Frank and the other partners was hardening. But there was nothing I could do to change their minds. I could disappear in a huff, my honour intact, my résumé a shambles, and try to find another job. But I'd be throwing away a promising career at a place I liked. Or I could do as Lisa suggested. Try to sort the mess out myself.

As usual, Lisa was right. I would stay and help Craig. I wouldn't let Net Cop die.

I reached the Harvard boathouses and turned round.

Lisa's reaction to my going to Cincinnati with Diane bothered me.

She didn't have anything to be jealous about. Diane was attractive. I liked her. We got on well together. But I loved Lisa. I loved her so much, and I didn't want to do anything to jeopardise that.

I didn't want to end up like my father. He had inherited a small estate in Devon, a baronetcy and a desire to join the family regiment, the Life Guards. He did everything that a dashing cavalry officer was supposed to do. He gambled, entertained lavishly, womanised, found a beautiful wife and drove armoured cars round godforsaken parts of the world. Women loved him, and he loved women. My parents did their best to keep the state of their marriage from Helen and me, sending us first of all to bed, and then to boarding school, but of course they didn't succeed. When I was ten, they divorced. I hated my father for hurting my mother. But I also admired him. Throughout my teenage years he used to take me off on a series of unplanned trips: scuba-diving in Belize, rock-climbing in Canada, and later, when I was at university, to nightclubs in London and Paris. Then one day he died of a heart attack. He was forty-five.

Against my mother's wishes, I joined the Life Guards after Cambridge. I did it partly out of a sense of loyalty to my father, but also because I thought soldiering would be fun. It was, and I was good at it, but in my middle twenties I realised that my life of tradition and privilege was for me a cold prison cell, and I left.

I bitterly regretted my parents' divorce. At ten I had solemnly resolved never ever to do the same thing myself. And now my father-in-law was suggesting I was going the same way.

Lisa's parents were also divorced. Frank had walked out on his wife when Lisa was fourteen. Lisa had never been given a satisfactory explanation and, like me, had never quite forgiven her father. Her mother quickly remarried and moved to San Francisco, taking Lisa and her brother with her. Frank had stayed single.

I wanted to make quite sure that neither one of us followed in our parents' footsteps.

I looked over my shoulder and saw the Union Boathouse speeding nearer. My arms and shoulders ached. It had been a good outing.

'So what are you going to do with Net Cop?' Daniel said next morning, glancing up from his computer.

'Find it some money.'

He raised his eyebrows. 'How?'

'God knows. Any ideas?'

It was always worth asking Daniel for ideas. Despite his cynicism, he could be very creative.

He paused for a moment. 'What about Jeff Lieberman? He invested in BioOne, didn't he? He might have a go at Net Cop.'

Jeff had been at business school with us. He was an able student, and he and I had had a lot of time for each other. He had headed off for Bloomfield Weiss, a big investment bank in New York. I had told him about BioOne, and he had made a significant investment in the Initial Public Offering.

'It's worth a try,' I said.

I looked up his number and dialled it.

'Jeff Lieberman.'

'Jeff, it's Simon Ayot.'

'Simon! How're you doing?'

'I'm fine.'

'And how's my little BioOne?'

'Forty-four this morning. Way above where you bought it. Jeff, I was actually calling about another company we're involved in.'

'Tell me more.'

So I told him all about Net Cop. The deal caught his interest. It had that magic word 'Internet' attached to it. I told him that Revere had backed out, but that just seemed to whet his appetite.

'OK, thanks, Simon. Send me the information. I'll let you know.'

'I put the phone down.

'Was he interested?' asked Daniel.

'He might be.'

'I'm going to New York this weekend. I can see him if you like.'

'Thanks. Do that.'

Just then, John strolled in, whistling and clutching a large latte. He glanced at the screen full of stock prices in front of Daniel. 'Doesn't matter how long you stare at it. It's not going up.'

'You never know,' Daniel muttered.

'You've got to own half of BioOne by now,' said John. 'You must be sitting on a big profit, surely.'

Daniel sighed. 'I bought a load at fifty-eight.'

'Warren Buffet would be proud of you,' said John, smiling.

'It'll come back,' said Daniel irritably.

After the Initial Public Offering BioOne's stock price had shot up, increasing fourfold. For the last year it had marked time, hovering around sixty dollars, until the recent slump with the rest of the biotech sector.

'Still, our glorious partners are doing OK,' John said. 'I wonder how much their stake is worth?'

'About fifty-five million dollars between them,' answered Daniel.

'Fifty-five million!'

'Absolutely. Revere invested five million in '94. That five million is now worth about two hundred and seventy-five million. The partners get twenty per cent of the profits and there you are.'

Trust Daniel to have the numbers at his fingertips. Of course Gil would get the most. Art would get a big chunk, because he had done the BioOne deal originally, but Frank would get a lot too. The newer partners, Ravi and Diane, would have much smaller shares.

'So, what's it feel like to have a father-in-law worth millions of dollars, Simon?' Daniel asked.

'It's all paper profits,' I said. 'And anyway I get the impression I'm not the favourite son-in-law at the moment.'

Daniel smiled grimly. 'I kinda got that impression too.'

'What does Lisa think of BioOne?' John asked.

'Not much,' I answered. 'She had a friend who worked there who hated it. Apparently the Technical Director is a scumbag. You know, Thomas Enever, the Aussie. He runs a regime of total secrecy there. He's the only one who knows what's going on.'

'I think she's wrong,' said Daniel. 'Enever's brilliant. Touchy, but brilliant.'

'He must be,' I said. 'I don't know the first thing about biotech.'

'Neither does Art,' said Daniel, laughing. 'And it's the only investment he's ever made here that's worked.'

I smiled. Daniel occasionally helped Art out on BioOne, and was the only person apart from Art who had had contact with the company. When Art had decided to invest in BioOne, four years ago, he'd been backing an old friend from his computing days, Jerry Peterson, now BioOne's chairman. Art knew nothing about biotech, but he got lucky. It had turned out that BioOne had the world's most promising treatment for Alzheimer's disease. Once the drug was approved by the Food and Drug Administration, it would turn into billions of dollars of sales. That was why BioOne was valued at $1.5 billion on NASDAQ, the high-tech stock exchange. It was difficult though, to begrudge Art his luck, especially since the whole firm was benefiting.

I WAS LYING on the sofa in our small living room, an open book resting face down on my chest, my eyes closed, when I heard the door bang. I looked at the clock on the wall. Ten o'clock.

'Hi.' Lisa plopped down next to me. 'It's dark in here.'

I had been reading by one weak lamp. I liked the room like that in the evening.

'Shall I turn some lights on?' I asked.

'No. It's nice. But you could get me a glass of wine.'

'Sure.' I opened a bottle of Californian red, and poured us a glass each. Lisa drank hers gratefully, and kicked off her shoes.

'My brain hurts,' she groaned.

I kissed her temple. 'I wish you didn't have to work quite so hard.'

'No choice. We have to get BP 56 to a point where we can attract more money before we run out of cash. We've got to get the animal data written up for the FDA so we can go on to the human trials. It's a nightmare.'

'I bet.'

'You didn't resign, I take it?'

'No. You were right. I'm going to try to save Net Cop. I don't know how. A guy from business school might put some money up. But we'll need a lot more than he's got.'

'You'll find it,' Lisa said. 'Any more ideas about Helen's appeal?'

'I'd like to go for it,' I said. 'I called the solicitor this morning. Apparently these new expert witnesses are very convincing. But we just don't have the money.'

Lisa seemed to hesitate. 'I saw Dad today,' she said. 'For lunch.'

I felt a mild burst of irritation at my wife and my father-in-law conspiring to see each other behind my back. 'You didn't tell me.'

'No. I wanted to ask him whether he could lend us some money for Helen.'

I was shocked. 'What did he say?'

Lisa bit her lip. 'No.'

I winced. 'You shouldn't have asked him, Lisa. It was nice of you to try, but this is my family's problem. It has nothing to do with him. As he seems to realise,' I added bitterly.

'It wasn't that,' said Lisa. 'He doesn't approve of medical litigation. He thinks it's screwing up this country's medical system. I said I'd go up and see him on Sunday at Marsh House,' she went on hesitantly. 'By myself.'

'Lisa! Look, I can't stop you seeing him every now and then,' I said. 'But it's as though he's trying to edge me out somehow.'

'Oh, Simon, don't be ridiculous. We always used to see a lot of each other. I love him. He's my father. Why shouldn't I see him?'

'I think it's unhealthy.'

'Unhealthy? After I went begging to him for money!'

'I didn't ask you to,' I muttered.

Lisa glared at me, put down her wine, and stood up. 'Good night, Simon,' she said, and marched from the room.

I let ten minutes pass before I went into the bedroom. Lisa was already in bed with the light off, her back to the middle of the bed. I took off my clothes and crawled in behind her.

'Lisa? I'm sorry.' I kissed her softly under her left ear. 'It was really good of you to try to get the money for Helen. Of course you should go to see your father on Sunday.' I kissed her again. Suddenly, her body relaxed, and she rolled over to take me in her arms.

IT TOOK THREE DAYS before Craig would see me again. He seemed in a better mood. We called some of the newer, smaller venture firms, who were more desperate for deals, to try to elicit some interest. We also drew up a list of his potential customers, and began to work on a presentation for them.

It was seven o'clock on Friday evening, and I was preparing to leave. 'We'll get there,' I said.

Craig allowed himself a smile. 'Yeah, I guess we will.'

I looked at him closely. 'Have you got an idea you haven't been telling me?'

'Have a good one, Simon,' said Craig, grinning widely. Wondering what on earth he could be up to, I left for home.

I HAD HARDLY seen Frank at all since our awkward discussion earlier in the week. I was worried about the steady deterioration of our relationship, and I wanted to do something about it. So, with Lisa's encouragement, I decided to have another try. I left Lisa in her lab where she usually spent her Saturdays, liberated my Morgan from its garage, and headed north, to Marsh House.

Woodbridge was a small town about twenty miles outside Boston, a frozen relic of early colonial prosperity. Marsh House was four miles to the south of the town, nestled in the expanse of salt marshes that filled many of the bays along this coastline. It was quiet there, isolated, and very beautiful. Frank came almost every weekend to escape the bustle of Boston.

I pulled up onto a patch of grass next to the small, white wooden house. Frank's Mercedes was there. I rapped on the door.

Frank appeared, dressed in a checked shirt and jeans. He wasn't pleased to see me. 'What are you doing here? You should always call before you come.'

This took me aback. True, Lisa always called before she visited her father, but I hadn't wanted to give him the chance to refuse to see me.

'Sorry,' I said. 'I wondered if you could spare me a few minutes?'

Frank grunted, and led me in to the living room. The furnishings were old, basic but comfortable. It was warm; wood was burning in the iron stove. Frank sat in an old rocker, and I sat in a wicker sofa with faded cushions. He looked tired, as though he hadn't slept the night before. His eyes were dark and strained, and he fidgeted.

'I was bothered by the Monday morning meeting last week. I wanted to talk to you about it.'

'I thought we'd been through all that at the office.'

'I know, but I wanted to see you outside Revere.'

He watched me impatiently.

'I just wanted to say that I think you're reading too much into my dinner with Diane. You have nothing to fear about Lisa. I love her very much, and I would never do anything to hurt her.'

'Sure you do,' he said. 'Who you have dinner with is your own affair.'

'Precisely.'

'As long as you don't hide it from my daughter.'

'I didn't hide it.'

Frank raised his eyebrows.

'I mean, I didn't tell her. But I would have. If it was important. Which it wasn't.'

'I've seen the way Diane looks at you. That woman is bad news, Simon. A friend at Barnes McLintock told me she wrecked a marriage there. I don't want her doing that at our firm, and especially not when the marriage in question is my daughter's!'

I bit my tongue. There were things I wanted to say, but I didn't say them. I had come here to look for a reconciliation, not to pick a fight. 'OK, Frank, I understand. I give you my word I won't do anything to jeopardise our marriage. And I don't want all this to interfere with our professional relationship.'

'It won't,' said Frank. 'I told you that on Monday. And like I told you, that's not the problem. If I were you, I would concentrate on not making any dumb decisions like promising a company more money when you haven't got the backing of the partnership.'

I felt anger rise in me, but controlled it. I was getting nowhere.

'And if you've come here to ask for money, the answer's no. I'm sorry about your nephew, but I told Lisa no, and I meant no.'

I stood up straight. 'I didn't ask you for money.'

'That's OK, then.'

'All right, Frank, I understand. Thank you for seeing me.'

I held out my hand.

Frank turned away as though he hadn't seen it.

'OK. Goodbye, Simon.'

I let myself out, then drove a couple of miles to Shanks Beach. A stiff breeze blew off the sea, and waves crashed against the shoreline, scattering wading birds. I walked along the water's edge, head down, dodging the occasional wave that reached further up the sand than the others. I kicked a chunk of driftwood as hard as I could.

Something was wrong with Frank; I had no idea what it was. But if I concentrated on saving Net Cop, and limited my contact with Diane, then everything would blow over. Give it time.

I spent an hour on the beach, and then drove to Net Cop. I was told Craig wasn't in. So I headed home.

'WHY DON'T you come with me to see Dad tomorrow? I don't like you two not getting along. You're both important to me. I'd like to straighten things out between you.'

We were eating dinner, some kind of pasta dish Lisa had put together. I put down my fork. I really didn't want to see Frank again that weekend. 'I tried it and it didn't work,' I said. 'I think it would be better to leave things alone.'

'That's typical of you, Simon,' Lisa protested. 'You never want to talk about your feelings. I'm positive it will help to talk it over.'

This was a common complaint of Lisa's, although actually I had talked more about how I felt with her than I had done with anyone else. But perhaps she had a point. Where I had failed, there was a chance she would succeed. It was worth a try.

'OK, we'll go,' I said.

LISA RAPPED on the cottage door. No reply. She rapped harder. Still nothing. She turned the doorknob. The door was locked.

'His car's still here,' she said. Her father's dark blue Mercedes was still parked where I had seen it the day before.

'He must have gone for a walk,' I said.

We looked around. In front of us stretched the marsh, a soft carpet of brown and gold grass. No sign of Frank. Behind was the wooded knoll down which we had approached the house. There was no sign of him there, either. In fact there was no sign of anyone.

'Come on! Let's go down to the dock,' said Lisa.

I followed her along the rickety wooden walkway down to the creek. The tide was out, so the dock itself had floated down below the level of the surrounding marsh. We sat on the end of the walkway. It was a surprisingly warm day for October. The smells of the marsh, salt and vegetation rose up to meet us. You couldn't see the sea from here; the marsh was surrounded by thickly wooded islands. Just beyond Hog Island, a mile and a half in front of us, was the ocean.

'I love this place,' said Lisa. 'You can imagine what it was like to be a kid here in the summer. Swimming, fishing, sailing. I really missed it when I went to California.'

In fact it was here we had first met. Frank was having a barbecue for a dozen or so people and I was listening to Art talk about what he described as Massachusetts' draconian gun laws. I disagreed with him. Art launched into a tirade about the constitutional right of Americans to bear arms, when a slight, dark-haired woman leapt to my defence. Barbed comments flew back and forth for about five minutes, to the embarrassment of most of the onlookers, before Frank diplomatically suggested that the woman show me his old dinghies, kept in a dilapidated boathouse a few yards away.

She did as she was told, and we spent much of the rest of the evening together. I was drawn to Lisa straight away. I liked the way she said what she thought, I found I wanted to talk to her, and I found her physically attractive. She mentioned the only French film I had happened to have seen, and on the strength of my enthusiasm, suggested we see something else by the same director. I suddenly became very interested in French films.

Now she turned and kissed me.

I smiled. 'What was that for?'

'Oh, nothing.' She smiled and took my hand, and we made our way back to Marsh House.

Lisa rapped on the door. No reply. She looked around anxiously. 'It's strange he locked the door. He usually leaves it open when he's here. Let's see if we can see inside the house.'

So we walked round the building, looking in through the windows. The living room was empty, as was the kitchen. There was a small dining area between the two, with a high window.

'Here, get on my shoulders,' I said to Lisa, crouching down.

'OK.' She giggled, and climbed onto my back. I slowly straightened my legs, bringing her up to the level of the window.

The giggling stopped abruptly. She stiffened, and her fingers clawed at my hair. 'Simon,' she whispered. 'SIMON!'

I swung her down to the ground. Her eyes were wide, and she was gasping for breath. I grabbed the window ledge and hauled myself up.

'Jesus!' I dropped to the ground and sprinted round the house. I threw myself at the front door, the wood cracked and it burst open. I rushed over to Frank's body.

He was dead. Two bullet holes gaped through the back of his checked shirt. Lisa pushed past me and threw herself onto him, grabbing his face, sobbing 'Dad, Dad, Dad,' over and over again.

3

'**Just a few** more questions, Mr Ayot.'

Sergeant Mahoney sat on the sofa in our small living room. His card said he was from the State Police Crime Prevention and Control Unit assigned to the Essex County District Attorney's Office. He was a big man, running to fat, with thinning red hair and bright blue eyes. One corner of his mouth seemed permanently raised in a half-smile of mild amusement, or mild disbelief, I couldn't tell which. He was probably pushing fifty, and had the air of someone who had seen a lot. A female colleague had taken Lisa out for a cup of coffee.

'I'd like to go back over some of the things you told me yesterday. It looks like you were the last person to see Frank Cook alive.' The blue eyes watched my every reaction. 'The coroner thinks he died some time before ten on Saturday evening. Now you say you came to see him at about two thirty that afternoon?'

'I think that's right, yes.'

'Why did you go to meet him?'

I hesitated. 'Frank and I had had an argument at work about an investment. I wanted to try to straighten things between us.'

'I see.' He remained silent, holding my eyes.

I had no desire to tell Mahoney about Frank's suspicions over me and Diane. But I had even less desire to be caught hiding them. I decided it was best to be as straightforward as possible.

I sighed. 'I thought the real cause of the disagreement was that Frank suspected me of having an affair with one of my colleagues. I wanted to persuade him that there was no danger of that.'

'Did Mr Cook believe you?'

'I don't know. I don't think so.'

'Did you have another argument?'

'Not exactly,' I said, truthfully.

'But you didn't leave best of friends?'

'No.'

'What time did you leave the house?'

'I don't know. Three o'clock, perhaps.'

'Where did you go then?'

'I went for a walk on the beach. Shanks Beach. And then I drove to the office of one of our companies, Net Cop.'

'Did you meet anyone on this walk? See anyone?'

'There were a few cars in the car park.' I thought hard. 'I think there were one or two people on the beach.'

'How long were you there?'

'About an hour.'

I then gave Mahoney the details of Net Cop and the people I had seen. He promised to check with them. I was sure he would.

'Do you know how much Frank Cook's estate will be?'

The change of tack surprised me. 'I've no idea.'

'Close to four million dollars, we think. And Mr Appleby says that in another year or two Mr Cook would have had another ten from one of Revere's investments. That will still go to his heirs. Which brings me to another question. Who are Frank Cook's heirs?'

'Lisa, I suppose. And her brother, Eddie. Maybe her mother.'

Mahoney grunted. 'And, as Lisa's husband, you might expect to get some money as a result of Mr Cook's death.'

'I suppose so. But I've never thought about it until now.'

'Do you own a gun, Mr Ayot?' Another change of tack.

'No.'

'Do you know how to use a gun?'

I paused. 'Yes. I used to be in the British army. They teach you how to use a weapon.'

'I see.' The blue eyes hardened. 'Have you ever killed anyone?'

'Yes,' I said quietly.

'Was it while you were in the army? In Ireland, maybe?'

'Yes.' I had killed two members of the Provisional IRA, but I wasn't proud of it. 'I don't have to answer this sort of question,' I said sharply. 'Am I under suspicion, or what?'

Mahoney relaxed. 'Look, we've got a job to do here. We're just gathering information, that's all. Thank you for your help, Mr Ayot.'

With that, he was gone, leaving me feeling distinctly uneasy.

I DIDN'T HAVE much time to worry, though. Lisa needed me. She seemed dazed, sometimes crying, sometimes just staring into space. Her pain scared me. So far in our lives together, we hadn't faced anything more serious than a broken dishwasher. I had no idea how Lisa would cope with what had happened. I wanted to wrap my arms round her and defend her from it; I did the best I could. But I couldn't protect her from the fact that Frank was gone.

He was to be buried the next day. Lisa's mother and brother were flying over from California, and would be staying at a bed and breakfast round the corner from our apartment. We picked them up from the airport that evening.

They were easy to spot. Eddie was tall and thin with dark hair cut so short it was little more than stubble. Their mother, Ann, was a bustling dark-haired woman who, with the help of careful attention to clothes, make-up and hair, was still striking. The three of them embraced, tears running down the cheeks of Lisa and her mother, Eddie's face a foot above them, his eyes blinking.

Then Ann gave me a hug. I extended a hand to Eddie, who shot me a cool glance before shaking it.

I cooked them supper in our apartment. Lasagne. A bottle of red wine before the meal, a second to accompany it.

'What I don't understand,' said Ann, returning to the subject that was on all our minds, 'is why anyone would want to kill Frank. He never had any enemies. He was such a *nice* man. Always.'

Then why did you divorce him? I thought. Ann's attitude towards Frank and my mother's attitude towards my father were poles apart. My mother had been a reluctant attendant at her husband's funeral, her face betraying no emotion whatsoever. But there could be no doubting the genuine sadness Lisa's mother felt.

'Have the cops any ideas who did it?' Eddie asked.

'Simon seems to be their best guess,' said Lisa. 'He was the last one to see Frank alive.'

I glanced across at her sharply.

Eddie looked at me. 'Really?' Lisa's senior by two years, he was in some kind of postgraduate school at the University of California in San Francisco. He was both polite and suspicious towards me, his little sister's husband. Since his father had left, he had taken on the role of head of the family; his mother and sister hung on his every word. And, of course, I had been introduced to Lisa by his father. This put me on the wrong side of the family divide that figured so prominently in Eddie's mind.

'It's true,' I said. 'He and I had had an argument at work, and I went up to Marsh House to sort it out. I didn't get anywhere, so I left. Apparently he was killed some time between then and ten o'clock that evening.'

'Don't look like that, Eddie,' said Lisa, finally aware of the difficulty she had raised. 'Of course Simon had nothing to do with it.'

'Of course not,' said Eddie, with an indulgent smile.

She smiled back, glad to clear up the misunderstanding. But from Eddie's glance towards me I wasn't at all sure she had done any such thing. 'The police will catch whoever did this,' she said.

'I hope they do,' said Eddie. 'I'd never thought I'd say this, but he deserves the chair.'

There was a brief silence, then Ann spoke. 'I thought you got on so well with Frank. I'm sorry you parted on such bad terms.'

'So am I,' I said, pouring Eddie some more wine. 'I do feel bad about it. There's a lot I'd have liked to say to him before he died.'

'Me too,' said Lisa flatly.

THAT NIGHT, as I lay in bed, trying to get to sleep, I felt the bed shudder gently. I touched Lisa's shoulder. It was shaking.

'Come here,' I said.

She rolled over into my arms and I felt warm tears trickle down my chest.

'You know that plaid shirt Dad was wearing?' she said. 'I gave that to him for his birthday last year. He really liked it. And now it's covered with his blood.'

I squeezed her tighter into my chest. She cried some more. Eventually, she broke away, sniffed and reached for some tissues.

'It must be awful for Eddie,' she said. 'He hasn't seen Dad for six years. He's barely spoken to him since he and Mom broke up.'

'Why do you think it got to him so badly?'

'I don't know. It would have been better if they'd told us the real reason they split up. They just said they didn't want to live together any more. But Eddie thought Dad was running away from us. He never forgave him.'

'I suppose that's why Eddie's so angry,' I said.

'Because he feels guilty about not seeing Dad? Probably. I'm angry too. It's just so wrong for someone to die like that.'

We lay in silence for a while. Then Lisa spoke: her voice was so quiet I could hardly hear it. 'When I was little and felt bad or scared, Dad used to sing to me. I wish he could do it now.'

I couldn't sing to her, but I could hold her. I didn't let her go until, a long time later, I heard the regular breathing of sleep.

FRANK WAS BURIED in a Jewish cemetery in Brookline where his family used to live. The ceremony was simple. After the Kaddish, the rabbi spoke of Frank in his younger days, and Gil made a short eulogy, honest and very moving. Only about twenty or so people were there: family and close friends. I was annoyed to see Sergeant Mahoney standing at the back, his sharp eyes scanning the gathering.

The shiva, or visitation, was held at Frank's sister's house a mile or so away. Technically it should have lasted seven days, but Eddie had to get back to his studies, and Frank was at best a lapsed progressive Jew, so the family had decided on the one evening. The mourners were joined by others who came to pass on their condolences.

Frank's sister, Zoë, a tall, black-haired woman with kindly eyes, did her best as a hostess, smiling and nodding, patting hands. I extricated her from an earnest man wearing dark glasses, who had been talking to her for several minutes, and brought her a piece of cake.

'Oh, Eddie, thank you so much,' she said. 'I know these people, but half the names don't come. And I don't want to offend them.'

'You're doing very well,' I said, not bothering to correct her mistake over my name.

'Aunt Zoë!' Lisa rushed up and gave her aunt a huge hug. 'Has Simon been looking after you?'

Aunt Zoë looked momentarily confused and then glanced towards me apologetically. 'Yes. Yes, he has, dear. How are you?'

'Oh, fine, I suppose. Can you believe all these people?'

'I wish he could be here to see them all,' Zoë said.

She was accosted by a friend of Frank's and moved away.

'She looks OK,' Lisa said.

'Yes,' I said. 'But she called me Eddie.'

'No, really? It's so sad. She's only fifty-two.'

Aunt Zoë, Lisa had told me earlier, was suffering from the early symptoms of Alzheimer's.

Her husband, Carl, a heavy man with a grey beard, several years older than his wife, now came and joined us.

'How is Zoë, Carl?' Lisa asked.

Carl sighed. 'You know she lost her job at the library?'

'Oh, no,' Lisa said.

'She forgets names of people, names of books, and she has some trouble telling the time. But she still remembers me, she always knows where she is and what day it is. There's a lot further to go. Unless the drug Frank recommended really works.'

'Drug? I didn't know Dad recommended any drug?'

'Yes,' said Carl. 'It's a new drug for Alzheimer's they're testing.'

'Is it neuroxil-5?' Lisa asked. 'Made by a company called BioOne?'

'That's right. She's been taking it for seven months now, and it looks like things have stabilised.'

'That's good news,' I said. I, too, hoped that neuroxil-5 worked.

THE NEXT MORNING, Lisa, her mother, her brother and I all set off downtown for Frank's lawyer's office to discuss his will. As we waited in the law firm's smart reception area, an uneasy silence settled on us. Up to this moment, none of us had talked about Frank's legacy. It had seemed in bad taste to discuss it. Eddie, in particular, seemed nervous, his long fingers playing with the teaspoon by his cup.

After five minutes, the lawyer bustled in, a balding portly man with a mild face but intelligent eyes. He introduced himself as Bergey and led us through to his office.

'Thank you all for coming in to see me today,' he said, having seated everyone round a table. 'I'm Mr Cook's executor. Now, ordinarily I would simply mail a letter to the beneficiaries of a will, but in this case, I thought it made sense to take advantage of you all being in the same place at once, to explain the will in person.'

Bergey had our attention.

'First, Mr Cook held an insurance policy of three hundred thousand dollars, which is to be divided equally between his former wife and two children.' He smiled quickly at us, and cleared his throat. I had the impression we were coming to the tricky bit.

'Second, Mr Cook's estate goes in its entirety to Elizabeth Rebecca Cook, his daughter. Excluding interest in funds managed by Revere Partners, it is valued at a minimum of four million dollars.'

We were all watching Eddie. You could see the anger boiling up inside him. He glanced at all of us, and then addressed Bergey. 'He can't do that, can he? I have a right to half his estate.'

'I drew up your father's will myself, Mr Cook. He made it after careful consideration. He was quite clear in his intention.'

We all looked away. We knew why Frank had ignored his son in death. It was because his son had ignored him in life.

'Simon, you're behind this, aren't you? You stole my inheritance from under my nose,' protested Eddie.

'What? How do you get that idea?'

'I've seen how you worked your way into Dad's favours. Getting the job at Revere, getting Lisa, being the perfect son-in-law.'

'Eddie, Frank didn't consult me about his will, I can assure you.'

'Yeah, but you and Lisa spent so much time with him.' He turned on his sister. 'The only reason he cut me out is because I stood by Mom.'

Lisa looked shocked. 'Eddie, I loved him,' she said. 'I don't want his stupid money.' She turned to the lawyer. 'Mr Bergey. Isn't there any way I can renounce half of it? Give it to Eddie?'

'Hm,' the lawyer frowned. 'You do have the right to renounce all or part of your inheritance, up to nine months after the date of death. Since your brother is not a named default in the will, the funds would be disposed under the laws of intestacy, which means Edward Cook would be the next in line.'

'Great,' said Lisa. 'Let's do it.'

Bergey cleared his throat. 'I strongly suggest that you think carefully before you decide on that course. Mr Cook was very clear that he wanted everything to go to you.'

Lisa glanced at Eddie. 'I'm sure it's what I want. But I'll think it over if you like. Perhaps I can see you next week?'

'Very well,' said Bergey.

Eddie smiled at Lisa. 'Thank you,' he said.

IT WAS WITH RELIEF that I immersed myself in the problems of Net Cop and Tetracom back at the office. But I was soon disturbed by a summons from Gil. He sat me down on the sofa in his oak-panelled office, the largest in the firm, and poured me a cup of coffee.

'Thank you for coming in today, Simon. I know you must have a lot on your plate at home.'

'It's no problem. It's good to have the distraction, to be honest.'

'I'm sure,' said Gil sympathetically. He cleared his throat. 'This is a difficult question, but I think it's important to clear the air. The police have been asking all of us here all kinds of questions, from which I'd guess they view you as a likely suspect. Are they correct?'

'You mean, did I kill Frank?'

Gil nodded.

I met his eyes, held them. 'No, Gil. No, I didn't.'

He paused and sat back. 'Good. I believe you. I want you to know that you have my total support, and that of the firm. If there's anything I can do for you, please ask.'

'Thank you,' I said. 'Um, there is one thing. I wonder if you could give me the name of a good criminal lawyer. I doubt I'll need one, but you never know.'

'Certainly.' He went over to his desk and rifled through his Rolodex. 'Gardner Phillips. He's an old friend of mine and a fine trial lawyer. Here's his number.'

I jotted down the details. 'Thanks.' I made as if to get up.

'One moment, Simon.' He looked at me closely through his thick glasses. 'Net Cop. What are you planning to do about it?'

'I don't intend giving up quite yet. Craig Docherty and I are trying to find some other sources of funds.'

'Any luck?'

'None yet. But we've only just started.'

'I see. I'm worried about Craig Docherty. I think Frank might have been right about him. He came to see me last week, and threatened me, said he would go to the press with the story of how Revere allegedly hadn't met its commitment to him.'

I groaned. How could Craig have been so stupid? 'What did you tell him?'

'I told him to leave. I won't be blackmailed by my entrepreneurs.'

'He was probably just upset,' I said

'But it clouded his judgment. If he did something that stupid once, he's going to do something just as stupid again.'

I saw Gil's point. 'What do you want me to do about it?'

'Carry on with Net Cop. Get every last dollar you can out of it. But tell Craig Docherty that if he breathes a word to the press that might harm Revere's reputation, he'll be fired from Net Cop, and he'll never get venture backing from anyone in this town again.'

'WHAT WAS THAT all about?' asked Daniel back in our office.

'Gil wanted to know whether I killed Frank. It seems I'm everyone's favourite suspect.'

'You're certainly mine,' said Daniel.

'Thanks for the support.'

'Poor Frank,' said Daniel. 'Revere will be screwed without him.'

'I know what you mean.' Frank was easily Revere's most able investor. Gil's record was patchy and Art's was downright appalling— BioOne excepted. Ravi and Diane had made some promising investments between them, but it was too early to tell how they would do.

'Where's John?' I asked.

'Sick.'

'Huh. It must be serious. He's such a healthy sod, you don't expect him to actually take a day off work.'

'He's taken Frank's death pretty badly. You know how much they worked together,' Daniel said. 'Oh, by the way, I saw Jeff Lieberman in New York at the weekend. He might be interested in Net Cop. Give him a call.'

'I will. After I've straightened out my favourite lunatic CEO.'

IN THE NET COP offices later that day, I found Craig had recovered his optimism and energy as he came bounding over to me.

'Hey, Simon, howya doin'? I heard about Frank Cook. I'm sorry.' We went through to the glass-enclosed office. 'So, is there any chance Revere might change its mind about the money now?'

I recoiled. 'No, Craig, no chance at all.'

'Too bad.' Only then did Craig seem to read my expression. 'Guess that was in bad taste, huh?'

'You could say that,' I replied. 'It also wasn't such a great idea to try to threaten Gil Appleby. What were you thinking of?'

'Hey. I was angry. I was desperate. I was willing to try anything.'

'Well, he told me to tell you that if you squeak a word to the press, we'll fire you and make sure you never get backing from a venture-capital firm again.'

Craig sighed. 'OK, I get the message. I'm sorry.'

A thought struck me. 'When I left Net Cop the day before Frank was killed, you seemed awfully cheerful. That had nothing to do with his death, did it?'

'No, of course not,' said Craig.

I looked at him suspiciously, but his face was all injured innocence.

He stood up and moved over to a whiteboard in his office. On it there was a string of names, venture capitalists in one column, industry players in the other. Many of the names were crossed out.

'We're getting no luck with the VCs,' Craig said, 'but some of the equipment suppliers are nibbling. I've fixed up a meeting with Luxtel in New Jersey tomorrow . . .' Craig rattled on, once again totally absorbed with the success of his company.

Inspired by his enthusiasm, I called Jeff Lieberman. He liked the Net Cop deal. His colleagues had agreed to put in $150,000 for an appropriate share of the company yet to be haggled over. It was much more than I had expected and Craig was impressed. Net Cop would need more funds to develop the prototype, but Jeff and his friends had bought us a couple more weeks to find them. It was something.

I WENT STRAIGHT HOME, walking rapidly across the Common.

It was a grey evening and a few spots of rain spattered my face. There weren't many people about. I looked behind me, back towards the elegant Georgian spire of Park Street Church and the giant buildings of the Financial District towering above it. An old lady stumbled by, muttering to herself. Behind her was a young Hispanic man in jeans and a dark jacket. His eyes darted up at me as I sat down, and he seemed to hesitate for a moment, then walked past, eyes on the pathway beneath his feet. Was I being followed?

LISA LOOKED PLEASED to see me. I hugged her. 'Did your mother and Eddie leave all right?'

She nodded. 'The plane was right on time.'

'That was a pretty unpleasant meeting this morning, wasn't it? It was very generous of you to cut Eddie back in.'

'I didn't want Dad's death to cause any more strain on our family. It's only fair to let Eddie have his share.'

'Eddie is very lucky to be your brother.'

Lisa looked at me. 'You don't like him, do you?'

'It's more a case of him not liking me. But after a while, I have to admit I begin to feel the same way about him.'

'He's a wonderful person, really. After the divorce, whenever I had a problem, he was there. Eddie encouraged me to study biochemistry, to go to Stanford. He made me believe in myself. Thanks to him, I did a pretty good job of getting over the divorce. I guess *he* never did, though. That's why he's so touchy about Dad.'

'It must have been rough on him,' I said, to mollify Lisa. What I really thought was that Eddie was a spoilt brat, who had thrown a temper tantrum and been rewarded with a couple of million bucks.

'At least now we can help Helen out on her lawsuit,' Lisa said. 'You should call and tell her. But remember, we'll have to wait till probate comes through.'

I smiled at her. 'I'll ring her tomorrow,' I said. 'She'll be very happy. Thank you.' I kissed her. 'How do you feel?'

'Lousy.'

'You're coping well.'

'Thanks to you.' She held me. 'I'm so glad I married you. I couldn't deal with this alone.' We held each other in silence, then she stirred in my arms. 'I think I'll go to work tomorrow. I can't stand hanging around here.' She broke away. 'Oh, the police came.'

'Again?'

'They searched the place. They seemed awfully interested in some of your clothes. They had tweezers and little plastic bags.'

'Did they find anything?'

'I don't think so. You look worried.'

'I am. I feel they're blocking all the exit routes before they attack.'

'They can't do anything to you. You're innocent.'

I looked down at Lisa's trusting face. She trusted the US justice system and she trusted me.

I met Craig at the airport the next morning, very early, and we made our way by aeroplane and rental car to suburban New Jersey. We were making a presentation to Luxtel, a massive telecommunications equipment company that was a possible reseller of Net Cop's switches, and therefore a possible provider of finance. I was there to field the difficult questions about why Revere had pulled out, putting it all down to market conditions.

Luxtel really liked Net Cop's switch. Craig promised 99.99 per cent reliability and this impressed them. But they felt it was too early to make a firm commitment to buy, let alone to invest.

As Craig drove our rental car back towards Newark airport in silence, his jaw set, I tried to sound optimistic. 'There's one definite customer, if we can get the money.'

'I have to make this work, you know,' Craig said.

'I know.'

'No, you don't. This is just another deal for you,' he muttered. 'I've put everything into Net Cop. I'll have to make it succeed. The alternative . . . there is no alternative.'

I worried about it all the way back to Boston. I was not prepared to let Net Cop die, but to build the prototype the company needed serious dollars from serious players.

I DIDN'T GET BACK to the office until midafternoon. Daniel was out at BioOne. I wasn't sure where John was. I surveyed the pile of papers screaming at me from my in-box. Tetracom. Diane was in Cincinnati, without me, visiting the company. I'd told her I ought to stay with Lisa, and she had understood.

I had been working for about a quarter of an hour when John burst in. 'Man, these quilt guys are something else!'

'What happened?'

The National Quilt Company was a quilt manufacturer that had been bought by a marketing man named Andy McArdle with the backing of Revere. His idea had been to turn the company round by realising the potential of 'comforters', American-style duvets, for merchandising. Art had done the deal with John, and put John on the board.

'It was wild. You know I told you about those merchandising deals they'd signed for the fall season? Some goon ordered a few hundred thousand Mutant Turtle comforters no one wants to buy. Warehouse full. Big problem. I suggest maybe they ought to go back to making comforters with cute patterns on them. Flowers and suchlike.'

'Radical.'

'Not as radical as McArdle. He's done a ton of research on the number of single-person homes and the under-thirties, and his conclusion is . . .' John looked at me. 'Go naked.'

'Go naked?'

'Yup. We spread naked women all over these quilts. They get

bought by the millions of men out there who are sick of flowers or turtles on their comforters. National Quilt makes out like bandits.'

'Did you let him do it?'

'Yeah. On a small scale. The company's screwed anyway, and I'm curious to see what happens. I figure if this company goes down the toilet, then it's McArdle's fault, not mine.'

I wasn't convinced, but I let it pass.

SERGEANT MAHONEY came to see me that afternoon. I took him into a small meeting room.

'How are you getting on?' I asked him. 'Do you have any suspects yet? Apart from me?'

'We're making progress. We have been able to narrow down the time of Mr Cook's murder. The phone records show he called John Chalfont at three twenty-four that Saturday afternoon. Mr Chalfont recalls they were talking about a deal they were both working on. So we know Mr Cook was alive at that time. Mr Chalfont says he called Mr Cook back later on that afternoon. Mr Cook didn't answer, but his answering machine did. The call was timed at four thirty-eight. So where were you between three twenty-four, and four thirty-eight?'

'Walking on the beach. I told you.'

'Yes, you did,' said Mahoney. 'Trouble is we haven't found anyone who remembers seeing anyone who fits your description.'

'Oh,' I said. Damn!

'Can you think of someone who might have seen you? Did you stop for gas? Go into a store somewhere?'

'No,' I said. 'Are you sure no one saw my car? You'd have thought someone would have noticed the Morgan.'

'You'd have thought so,' said Mahoney. His blue eyes twinkled, and he smiled his irritating half-smile. He thought he'd got me.

'I definitely was there, Sergeant,' I said.

'All we're trying to do is confirm your story, Mr Ayot. Now, according to Daniel Hall, you and he discussed your father-in-law's wealth as recently as last week. Is that true?'

I remembered the conversation. 'Oh, yes. That's right. We did. Or rather he did. Daniel is obsessed with how much money everyone makes, especially the partners. I wasn't very interested.'

'Not interested, huh? That money will be useful for you to fight your sister's lawsuit with, won't it?'

'Yes,' I said carefully.

'How much have you already spent on your sister's lawsuit?'

'About forty-five thousand pounds. She's spent twenty.'

'And unless you can find the money to continue with this lawsuit, then you can kiss goodbye to that forty-five thousand pounds?'

'That's right,' I admitted.

'OK. I understand that your wife asked Mr Cook for some money to help pay for this, but Mr Cook said no. So when you went to see him yourself did you talk about money?'

'No. But I suppose Frank did. He thought I'd come to see him to ask for money. I hadn't. I told him that.'

'I see,' said Mahoney. 'Thank you for your cooperation, Mr Ayot.'

The interview was over and I showed Sergeant Mahoney to the elevators. The irritating little smile never left his lips.

It was very hard to get back to work. I was worried. Although Mahoney hadn't come right out and accused me of murdering Frank, he was steadily building a case against me. Lisa must have told him about Helen's legal case. She probably didn't see the harm in it. But I wished she hadn't.

All this reminded me that I had intended to call Helen that afternoon to tell her about Lisa's willingness to fund her legal bills. But something stopped me. I didn't want to get her hopes up until I was cleared of blame and the true culprit found.

LISA DIDN'T ARRIVE home that evening until nine. She looked tired and depressed as she flopped on the sofa.

I passed her a glass of wine. 'You did a long day's work.'

'Well, what do you expect?' she snapped. 'I've been out half the week. There's a ton of work to be done.'

I was taken aback by the outburst. 'I'm sure there is,' I said neutrally. I sat down beside her and put my arm round her.

'Sorry, Simon. It's just that Boston Peptides is in real trouble. We're out of cash. I didn't realise how bad it was. I've agreed to no pay cheque this month, but that's hardly going to help.'

I sighed. 'Have they no leads on any more funds?'

'No. If only we could get all the animal work finished on BP 56. It would make us a much better proposition for any investor.'

Lisa had put everything into BP 56. If Boston Peptides went bust it would be a huge disappointment for her. I squeezed her, and she pressed herself close into me. Then she began to cry.

AT WORK the next morning I arrived to find John looking over the *Wall Street Journal*. 'Forty-four and a half,' he said, quoting BioOne's stock price without looking up.

'It's creeping back,' I said.

I checked Chelsea's web page. The Internet was a godsend for English football supporters trapped in America.

John interrupted me. 'Hey, did you hear about Boston Peptides? BioOne's going to take it over. Art and Daniel were working on it all yesterday.'

I put my head in my hands. 'Oh, hell.'

John was surprised by my reaction. 'It'll be good for Lisa, won't it? BioOne will give Peptides the backing to expand its R and D.'

'I don't think Lisa likes BioOne very much, John.'

Daniel strode into the office, bags under his eyes, briefcase pulling down one arm.

'I heard about Boston Peptides,' I said. 'John told me.'

'It's a good deal,' said Daniel, arranging the papers on his desk. 'Boston Peptides has a promising drug for Parkinson's, and BioOne has the muscle to see it through.'

I sighed. I could see the commercial logic.

'They're making a presentation this afternoon at two,' said John. 'You coming?'

'You bet,' I replied.

'Oh, Simon,' Daniel said. 'Art asked me to tell you to go see him first thing this morning.'

'About BioOne?'

'I guess so.'

Art was in his habitual position, leaning back in his leather executive chair, one hand pressing the telephone to his ear, the other clasping a can of Diet Dr Pepper. It was the kind of work he liked. It involved talking, not thinking.

He beckoned for me to sit down. I perched on the small chair on the other side of his desk. He cut an imposing figure. He was a big broad man in his fifties with grey hair cropped close to his head. He exercised regularly, and most of his size was muscle, rather than fat. He had served in the Marines, as he had reminded me on many occasions, and he still affected a tough-guy attitude.

Ten minutes later, he finally put the receiver down. 'I guess you heard. We're buying Boston Peptides.' By 'we' Art meant BioOne. He identified himself so closely with that company that in his eyes he was indistinguishable from it.

'Congratulations,' I said neutrally.

'Now, we're not quite ready to make an announcement yet. Also, we've been negotiating with Boston Peptides' backers, Venture First, directly. Henry Chan and his management team know nothing about the deal. So, it's very important that you don't tell any of this to Lisa.'

I swallowed. 'OK,' I said. 'I understand.'

Art leaned back in his big chair. 'We're going to try to keep you out of this deal as much as possible, Simon, but in such a small office it's impossible to keep anyone entirely in the dark. Besides, that's not the way we work here.' He smiled briefly. 'But anything you do hear, you keep to yourself, OK?'

BioOne's gleaming, high-tech building was in Kendall Square, a prestigious location within shouting distance of the Massachusetts Institute of Technology. Daniel, who had crunched the numbers, said the rent played havoc with BioOne's bottom line. But no one cared. Once BioOne had a treatment for Alzheimer's on the market, the dollars would flow in.

John and I were a couple of minutes late and Gil, Art, Ravi and Daniel were waiting with a small prim woman of about forty with short dark hair and very large glasses. Lynette Mauer.

Like many other venture capitalists, Revere Partners didn't invest its own money, but managed a series of funds holding money raised from institutional investors such as insurance companies, pension funds, or family foundations. Lynette Mauer was Chief Investment Officer for the Bieber Foundation, a substantial family trust that was the biggest investor in our funds. Gil had no doubt brought her along to see our star investment at first hand.

When Art saw me he frowned and whispered something to Gil. It was clear he hadn't wanted me there. Tough.

A smartly dressed woman approached and led us through a series of corridors, flashing her identity card at winking green lights. Eventually we reached a door marked DR THOMAS E. ENEVER, TECH-NICAL DIRECTOR. The woman knocked, and showed us in.

Two men greeted us. One I recognised. He had silver hair and a young fresh face, and wore an open-necked shirt and slacks, every inch the successful entrepreneur. He was Jerry Peterson, BioOne's chairman and Art's old buddy. The other man was tall and thin. What was left of his hair was oiled back over a shining brown fore-head. He had a long narrow face, etched with deep downward-sloping lines. Dr Enever, I presumed.

Gil made the introductions. Jerry Peterson sat everyone down.

I looked round Enever's large office. There were shelves with thick books and serious science periodicals neatly filed. But there was also a big executive desk, and a suite of executive armchairs.

Jerry Peterson cleared his throat. 'Before I hand over to Thomas here, I'd just like to say that I know you'll be real excited by this opportunity. In neuroxil-5, this company has a blockbuster drug, a world-beater. But the acquisition of Boston Peptides and its anti-Parkinson's drug, BP 56, will give us an exciting new prospect to talk about for the future. Thomas.'

Enever smiled thinly, as he sat stiffly in one of his armchairs.

Art caught his attention. 'Thomas, before you start, I wonder if you could just explain to Lynette here what neuroxil-5 does.'

'Why certainly,' said Enever. 'Alzheimer's disease is a complicated illness that no one really understands.' His accent was a hybrid of American and his native Australian. 'Over a period of many years, it kills millions of brain cells. At first the effect is too small to be noticed. Then the patient begins to forget small things, then larger things until eventually the body forgets how to function, and the patient dies. In the brain of an Alzheimer's patient, the pathways of the brain's neurotransmitters become blocked. A twisted plaque builds up in certain parts of the brain releasing molecules known as free radicals that attack the brain cells. Then the brain cells themselves become flooded with calcium and die. Most treatments focus on one or other of these processes.'

Enever's face was animated, as he talked. 'But these are the symptoms, not the cause. We have identified the gene that, at a certain stage in a patient's life, sets in train these effects. These messages are carried by molecules of ribonucleic acid or RNA. We have developed a molecule that neutralises the RNA emitted by this gene, thus preventing the Alzheimer's from developing further. This is neuroxil-5.'

'So the patient is cured?'

'Not exactly. Once the brain cells are dead, we can't resurrect them. But we can prevent the death of more brain cells, and hence slow down or even stop the progression of the disease.'

'And how many Alzheimer's patients are there?' Mauer asked.

'It's difficult to say. The government estimates there are four million in the US alone. And of course those numbers will grow as other medical advances allow people to live longer.'

'That's a huge market.'

Enever smiled. 'Billions of dollars.'

Lynette Mauer paused, blinking through her glasses. 'And how is the drug progressing?'

'The clinical trials are going excellently at the moment. Provided they don't throw up any problems, neuroxil-5 will be on the market by the end of next year.'

'Thank you, Dr Enever,' Art said. 'Now, perhaps you can tell us something about Boston Peptides.'

Enever launched into an enthusiastic description of BP 56 and its prospects for treating Parkinson's disease. Then Jerry talked about the deal itself, and Daniel handed round his figures.

'How are you going to integrate Boston Peptides into your business?' Ravi asked.

'That won't be a problem,' said Enever. 'We're really just buying the drug. Many drugs are discovered like this, more or less by accident, but they need professional guidance to get them to market.'

I stiffened. I didn't like this.

'Boston Peptides doesn't have the capital or, quite frankly, the management expertise to develop this treatment for Parkinson's disease to its full potential. At BioOne we are fortunate that we have people who can do that.'

Art threw me a worried glance. I knew I should keep my mouth shut, but I couldn't. 'So you will have to make changes at Boston Peptides?' Out of the corner of my eye I could see Art's glance turn into a glare.

'Oh, undoubtedly. We'll have to let some scientists go. They've done their part, now it's time for others to take over.'

Done their part! Lisa and her colleagues had devoted many years to BP 56, and Enever was planning to shuffle them off. I fumed.

ALTHOUGH IT WAS FRIDAY, Lisa didn't return home until after nine again. She looked shattered. She turned on the television, and said she didn't want any supper. So I cooked myself an omelette and ate it at the kitchen table.

Just as I was finishing, she came in and put a muffin in the toaster. She didn't look good at all. Her face was pinched into an expression of fatigue and cold despair.

'How are you feeling?'

'I feel really bad, Simon,' she snapped. 'My father's dead, I'm tired, my head hurts, and I wish I was someone else someplace else.'

I shut up, finished my omelette, and fled to the living room.

I heard a cry from the kitchen. 'Damn!' A pause. 'Damned toaster!' and then a crash.

I rushed through to see the toaster on its side, smoke pouring out of it. Lisa was shaking with anger. 'It's burned the damned muffin!'

I pulled the plug out of the wall socket, and looked in the toaster. The muffin was indeed stuck. I grabbed a knife and forced it out. I turned to see Lisa trying to hold back tears, her face red.

I put my arms round her, and she buried her head in my shoulder and began to sob.

'Shhh. It's only a stupid toaster. Don't worry about it.'

She broke away. 'I need a tissue.' She fetched one, and blew her nose. 'I'm OK now,' she mumbled, with a half-smile.

We sat on the sofa in the sitting room, my arm round her. I wanted so desperately to comfort her, but I could tell she didn't want to talk. We just sat there. I realised I had to tell Lisa about the takeover, no matter what Art said. Once it was made public, she would know that I had kept the information from her. That would really make her angry. It wasn't a good time, but no time seemed like a good time these days. So I summoned up my courage.

'I heard some news today. You mustn't mention it to anyone at work. They told me to keep it quiet. Even from you.'

Lisa turned to me. 'What is it?'

'BioOne is going to buy Boston Peptides.'

'No! Are you serious? Does Henry know?'

'I don't think so. They've been negotiating with Venture First.'

'I can't believe it,' she said. 'We need the money, but BioOne!' She glanced at me sharply. 'I suppose Revere is behind this?' Her eyes narrowed with suspicion. 'You didn't tell them what I'd said about our cash problems, did you? Because if you did . . .'

'Of course not!' I fought to control my own rising anger. 'Look. At least you'll have the resources to finish working on BP 56.'

'Yeah, but Thomas Enever will take all the credit, and I'll be lucky if I'm doing anything more than washing out test tubes. That man's awful, Simon. I've heard all about him.'

'He can't be that bad,' I said, although from what I'd seen of him I feared perhaps he might be.

Lisa pulled away from me. 'You don't understand, do you? Everything I have worked for for the last four years has been sold out to a total asshole. By my husband's firm, for God's sake!'

'Lisa . . .'

'I'm going to bed.'

I AWOKE at a quarter to nine the next morning and found Lisa gone. To the lab presumably. I pulled on my rowing gear and jogged down to the boathouse where Kieran was waiting for me. He was a tall, rangy Irishman from Trinity College, Dublin, whom I had met at business school and who had found himself a job at one of the many management consultancies in Boston. Most Saturday mornings we rowed pairs together.

'I read about your father-in-law. I'm sorry.'

'Thanks.'

Kieran could tell I didn't want to talk, and knew to let it drop. 'Let's get this thing in the water.'

We threw the boat into the river, and I stepped in first. I was rowing stroke, Kieran bow. We soon set up a good rhythm. My heart pumped blood, oxygen and endorphins round my system, cool air flowed over my exposed skin and I began to relax.

After ten minutes of rowing, my mind began to turn to Lisa. I had known Frank's death would fall very hard on her. But work was getting at her as well. The timing was terrible. She seemed to be almost physically ill—tired, with headaches, and that dreadful look of despair. She had completely overreacted to the toaster burning her muffin. And it had been unlike Lisa to fly off the handle when I had told her about the takeover . . .

'Hey, slow down, Simon!' Kieran called behind me. 'I had a heavy night last night.'

'Sorry,' I shouted back. I had speeded up without realising it, so I reduced my pace to a more sedate thirty strokes per minute or so.

'That's better. We'll win the Olympics *next* weekend, if that's OK.'

We rowed along steadily, sliding underneath the graceful bridges spanning the Charles.

'Simon?' Kieran called. 'A bunch of the boys are getting together on Tuesday at the Red Hat. Do you want to come along?'

'I don't know. There's a lot going on at home.'

'Oh, come on. It'll be good for you.'

He was probably right. 'OK,' I said. 'I'll be there.'

LISA ARRIVED HOME at about five, looking exhausted. 'Hi, Simon.' She smiled and kissed me.

'Hi. How are you?'

'Tired. Very tired.'

'I brought you some flowers.' I went into the kitchen and came back with some irises. She liked irises.

'Thank you,' she said, giving me a quick kiss. She disappeared into the kitchen, and returned with the flowers arranged in a tall vase.

'Simon, I'm sorry I was so horrible to you yesterday. I don't want us to become one of those snappy couples. I don't know why I did it, but I'm sorry.'

'That's OK. You're under a lot of pressure,' I said. 'I understand.'

'I guess that must be it.' She sighed. 'I just feel hollow inside, like I'm empty. And then suddenly something seems to boil up in here,' she put her hand on her chest, 'and I feel like I want to shout and scream, or else just cry. I've never felt like this before.'

'Something like this has never happened to you before,' I said.

She looked at her watch. 'If we go now, do you think we might get into Olive's?'

I smiled. 'We could try.'

Olive's was an Italian restaurant in Charlestown. We made it before the rush, and were seated at one of the large wooden tables. As always, it was crowded, with lots of noise, warmth and excellent food.

'Remember the first time we came here?' said Lisa.

'Of course I do.'

'Do you remember how much we talked? They kept on trying to throw us out, and we wouldn't go.'

'I do. And we missed the first half of that Truffaut film.'

'Which was crap anyway.'

I laughed. 'I'm glad you admit that now!'

I suddenly realised Lisa was staring at me. 'I'm so glad I met you,' she said.

I smiled at her. 'And I'm really glad I met you.'

'I'm really sorry I've been such a pain. It's funny. It sort of comes in waves. Thinking about Dad. One moment I'm fine and the next I feel awful. Like right now I . . .' She paused, and a tear ran down her cheek. She tried to smile. 'I was going to say I feel fine now, but look at me.' She sniffed. 'I'm sorry, Simon. I'm just a mess.'

I reached over and touched her hand.

She blew her nose. 'I wonder who killed him,' she said. 'Some burglar probably. The house is pretty isolated. I guess the police haven't got anywhere yet, or we'd have heard.'

'Oh, I didn't get a chance to tell you. Sergeant Mahoney came to see me a couple of days ago at the office.'

'What did he say?'

'He just asked me some questions about where I went after I left your father. Apparently Frank spoke to John on the phone when I was walking on the beach. Mahoney still hasn't found anyone who saw me. I didn't get the impression he'd made much progress in any direction but I think I'm still his number-one suspect.'

'Oh, Simon.' She squeezed my hand.

'Did you tell him about Helen's legal case?'

'Yes, I did. Why? Did he ask you about it?'

'Yes. He implied that it was convenient Frank had died. That now we can afford to fight the appeal. It makes me sick thinking about it.'

'I'm sorry, Simon. He asked whether we'd had any financial disagreements with Dad. I thought I should tell the truth.'

I smiled at her. 'That's OK. I suspect it is best to tell the truth.

Otherwise he'll catch us out and it'll be even worse.'

'Don't worry, Simon. They haven't got any evidence.'

'Not hard evidence, no. But I have to admit, I am a bit worried.'

The waiter brought a bottle of Chianti, and I poured us both a glass. The conversation moved on. We didn't talk about Frank or Boston Peptides or BioOne for the rest of the evening. For a couple of hours we were as we had been before Frank's death.

Eventually they threw us out, and we decided to walk up the hill behind the restaurant to the Bunker Hill monument. It was a warm evening and we sat down under the tall obelisk neatly hemmed in by black railings and crisply mown grass. We looked out over the Charles River to the lights of Boston. 'I like it here,' I said.

'That's strange, considering it's where so many of the evil British redcoats met their final destiny.'

'At the hands of a bunch of violent tax-dodgers.'

'Not paying taxes is a fine American tradition,' Lisa said. 'And one that our wealthiest citizens are proud to follow.'

'Anyway, wasn't the battle fought a few hundred yards from here?'

Lisa kissed me. 'Smart-ass.'

At the Monday morning meeting, Lynette Mauer sat next to Gil, watching him with an expression close to awe, lapping up everything he was saying. To be fair to Gil he never told us to behave differently when an investor was present but, inevitably, troubled investments were skated over rather than dissected, and we talked a lot about BioOne. This was good news for me, because I didn't have to talk about Net Cop. It was good news for Art because he was allowed to expound upon his favourite subject.

'The Street can't get enough of BioOne stock,' he was saying. 'The price is up to forty-five.'

'OK, and what's the value of Revere's holdings?' asked Gil, for Mauer's benefit.

Art paused as though he hadn't really thought about the question before. 'I'd say just shy of three hundred million.'

'Good. Now I think you'll all agree that we had a very interesting meeting with Jerry and Dr Enever last week. Can I take it we support the Boston Peptides deal?'

There were nods around the table. It was pointless me protesting. This was just a formality, and anyway I wasn't a partner.

'Excellent,' said Gil. 'Do you have any questions for Art, Lynette?'

Lynette Mauer smiled sweetly at Gil. 'It does seem to be a very successful investment, Art. Well done. I see you have been looking after our money well.'

Art beamed.

'I do have one question. It's something I saw in the paper at the weekend about Alzheimer's.' She shuffled through her papers, and pulled out a piece of newspaper. She scanned it quickly. 'It's something about galantamine. It's supposed to be a more effective treatment for Alzheimer's than what's on the market at the moment. Might this be a threat to neuroxil-5?'

'Ah, no, not at all,' replied Art quickly. 'Neuroxil-5 prevents the build-up of beta-amyloid, the substance that eventually kills the brain cells. No other treatment has succeeded in attacking this beta-amyloid in the way neuroxil-5 does.'

'I understand that,' said Mauer. 'But it says here that this drug galantamine inhibits cholinesterase, which is what kills brain cells. So which is it? The beta-amyloid stuff or the cholinesterase stuff?' Mauer looked at Art ever so sweetly, as though she was completely confident he would be able to answer.

Art was stumped. He didn't have a clue.

Ravi jumped in. 'I happened to catch that article about galantamine too.' He had all our attention. As he addressed Mauer over his half-moon glasses, he spoke quietly and with authority. 'I think the truth is that Alzheimer's involves a complex tangle of different biochemical reactions in the brain. It seems likely that drugs like galantamine delay the onset of Alzheimer's, but BioOne believes that neuroxil-5 neutralises the gene that is behind all these processes, including the production of beta-amyloid *and* cholinesterase.'

Mauer smiled at Ravi. 'OK, I understand, thank you very much.'

Art was trying to smile. But he was furious. His neck was reddening as though any minute his head would begin to boil.

We moved on to new deals, of which the most interesting was Tetracom. Diane was an excellent presenter. Listening to her, it seemed that we should sign up on the spot. We were all impressed.

Gil finished up by turning to Mauer.

'Lynette, perhaps you could tell us something about the Bieber Foundation's plans. As you know, we're raising a new fund next year. We look forward to welcoming you into it.'

Lynette smiled. 'Yes, there is something I'd like to say.' Our interest quickened. This wasn't in the script. 'I'd like to thank all of you for the work you've done for us over the last few years. Your returns have been good, thanks in large part to BioOne.' A nice smile for Art. 'And of course to Frank Cook, who was responsible for so many successful investments.' She paused, out of deference to his memory. There was a but. We were all waiting for the but. 'But we have had a recent change of policy. In future the Foundation will consolidate its investment in venture capital into two or maybe three firms. We will be reviewing all our venture-capital investments.'

Gil looked confused. 'I'm sure we can count on your continued investment in our funds, Lynette,' he said smoothly.

'Perhaps. But I wouldn't rely on it, Gil. I have analysed Revere's returns, and if you take out BioOne and Frank Cook's investments you are left with a performance that isn't quite as good as some of your competitors'. You seem to have missed the Internet bus almost entirely.'

'Art looked into that market, and concluded it was all hype. We firmly believe those companies are overvalued.'

'They've made a lot of people a lot of money,' said Lynette.

In truth, many of the Internet stocks had been hyped to the stratosphere. But most of our competitors had made money putting them there, and Mauer knew this.

'Perhaps we should discuss this in my office,' said Gil hurriedly.

The meeting broke up.

Daniel strolled over to the small woman. 'Ms Mauer?'

'Yes?'

'Daniel Hall. I noticed you are a major investor in Beaufort Technologies. I just wanted to suggest that you should perhaps take your profits. The stock is due for a big correction.'

'Why? What's wrong with Beaufort?'

'Nothing,' Daniel said. 'It's just that the market's love affair with three-D animation is wearing thin. It's going out of fashion.'

Gil was glaring at Daniel but he had Mauer's attention. 'Thank you,' she said and followed Gil out of the room.

'You just about kissed goodbye to your career back there,' I said to Daniel as we made our way back to our office.

Daniel smiled. 'Beaufort's going down. And when it falls, Lynette Mauer'll be glad I warned her, and so will Gil.'

'Maybe. If we still have a firm by then. If Bieber pulls out, so might some of the other investors.'

'Oh, Revere will survive,' said Daniel.

Maybe. Or maybe Revere was falling apart about our ears.

'AYOT, COME with me! Gil's office. Now!'

It was Monday afternoon. Art was standing at the door to the associates' office, his face red.

I slowly followed him. Gil was standing stiffly behind his desk as I came in, his weather-beaten face grim.

'Sit down, Simon,' he said coldly.

I took one of Gil's armchairs. The two older men seated themselves opposite me. Art could barely contain himself. His big forearms were wrapped across his chest in an effort to suppress his anger.

Gil leaned towards me. 'Apparently someone has told the Boston Peptides management about BioOne's bid for the company. This has raised major difficulties with the negotiations, which were at a delicate stage. Art tells me that you are responsible. Is he correct?'

Oh Lisa, Lisa!

I nodded. 'I'm sorry. I did ask her to—'

'Sorry!' screamed Art. 'I tell you not to do something, and you go right ahead and do it! Sorry isn't good enough. If you can't trust your own wife, you shouldn't have spoken to her! Stupid bitch.'

'Hey!' I rose from my chair, the anger boiling up inside me.

'That's enough!' Gil put his hand on my arm. 'I know you're angry, Art, but let's keep the personal comments out of it.'

I glared at Art and sat down.

Gil turned to me. 'What you did was a serious breach of trust.'

'I know. I'm sorry, Gil. It's just it was the kind of secret I didn't want to keep from my wife.'

'That's not good enough, Simon, and you know it,' Gil said. 'We're a small firm, and we have to be able to trust each other. And it's not a question of us making you lie to your wife. We were just expecting you to behave professionally. That's not unreasonable, is it?'

I sighed. 'No, it's not.'

'OK. Let this be a warning to you. I don't expect to see any breach of your colleagues' trust again.'

'OK, Gil. And I am sorry.'

I marched straight back to my desk and picked up the phone, ignoring the stares of John and Daniel. I punched in a number.

'Lisa Cook.'

'You told Henry about the takeover, didn't you?'

There was a moment's silence. Then Lisa's voice, curt and crisp. 'It was important to Boston Peptides. Henry told me he would treat the information carefully.'

'Well, he didn't, did he? Lisa, I can't believe you'd do that! I only told you about the takeover because I felt I could trust you. But I couldn't could I? The deal's blown wide open, and I just got a massive bollocking from Gil. It's lucky I wasn't fired.'

'Simon, I . . .' Lisa was clearly taken aback by my anger. I had never been that angry with her before. 'I'm sorry, Simon.' Lisa's voice was cold now. 'I did what I had to do.'

'It's almost as though you place your loyalty to Boston Peptides above your loyalty to me.'

'And why shouldn't I, just for once? I just don't think you understand that my job is as important to me as your job is to you. Goodbye, Simon.'

And there was a click as the line went dead.

There was complete silence in the room.

'Don't tell me she forgot to fold your socks again,' said Daniel at last.

I smiled, deflated, and tried to go back to work.

That afternoon, Diane dropped by my desk. I hadn't spoken to her since her Cincinnati trip.

'How was Tetracom?' I asked.

'Fascinating. I've got a good feeling about this one. I'm going out there again next Monday. I'd really like you to come with me. I need some help, and . . . well, I'd like a second opinion.'

It was always flattering as an associate to be asked for an opinion, and it looked as if Tetracom might go all the way to investment. It was obviously smart for an associate to attach himself to a deal that eventually got done. But was it sensible to go on a trip with Diane?

She noticed my hesitation. 'It would be great if you could make it, but I'd understand if you have to be with Lisa.'

Be with Lisa? She could look after herself for one night. That bit about me thinking my work was more important than hers rankled. It simply wasn't true. She had betrayed my trust in her for the benefit of her career: I could go on a business trip for the benefit of mine.

'No, I'm sure she'll be fine,' I said. 'I'll be glad to come.'

BY THE TIME Lisa arrived home my anger at what she had done had subsided a little. She looked terrible, lines of fatigue and misery ravaging her face.

'Lisa, I'd like to talk to you about the takeover.'

'There really isn't any point, Simon.'

'But, Lisa . . .'

'There's no point. Have you had dinner?'

'Not yet.'

Lisa ordered some Chinese to be delivered, and picked up her book. I turned on the TV. When the food came we ate in silence.

I had developed a headache myself. I rummaged around in the bathroom cabinet for Lisa's Tylenol. Inside a paper bag were two bottles of pills, unlabelled. I forgot the Tylenol, and took the bottles into the living room.

'Lisa. What are these?'

She looked up. 'BP 56,' she said. She looked me in the eye, defying me to say anything.

'BP 56! But that hasn't been tested on humans yet.'

'It's been thoroughly tested on animals. And if there are any problems with the drug, I need to know. We can't afford to wait until we've gone through all the paperwork with the FDA.'

'I don't think it's a good idea, Lisa. Why didn't you tell me?'

She sighed. 'Because I knew you wouldn't like it.'

It seemed to me foolhardy for Lisa to take this untried drug, but I knew there was no chance of me persuading her not to.

The phone rang. I picked it up.

'Can I speak to Lisa?'

I recognised Eddie's voice. No 'hello', no 'how are you?'

'Hold on.' I looked up. 'It's Eddie.'

'I'll take it in the bedroom,' Lisa said.

She emerged twenty minutes later.

'How is he?' I asked.

'I'd say he's quite upset,' Lisa replied icily, picking up her book again.

'By the way,' I said. 'I'm going to Cincinnati with Diane next Monday. I'll be out one night.'

Lisa looked at me sharply. 'Next Monday?'

'Yes. We've been through this before. I have to go.'

'OK,' she said. 'You do what you have to do.'

BioOne made a public announcement the following morning about its intentions for Boston Peptides. I looked at the press release on my computer. The text was pretty bland, apart from one killer sentence.

'Daniel! What's this about "substantial cost savings at Boston Peptides"?'

'BioOne thinks it can cut some duplicated costs. It can move Boston Peptides into Kendall Square. And other things.'

'Like firing people?'

Daniel shrugged. 'That's what happens in takeovers. You heard Enever. Hey! The stock's up four to forty-nine.'

'Well, that's wonderful, then.' I put my head in my hands. Lisa was going to love this.

SURE ENOUGH, the announcement had caused uproar at Boston Peptides. But at least Lisa was willing to talk that evening.

'People are upset. They're talking about resigning.'

'Is Enever really that bad?'

'Oh, yes. You know what they call him at BioOne? Enema.'

'Sounds attractive.'

'It turns out he didn't even discover neuroxil-5. Most of the work was done at the institute he worked at in Australia. He was just one of a team. He brought the idea to America and patented it here.'

'How did he get away with that?'

'One of the team tried to kick up a fuss. I don't think he got anywhere. Enema's lawyers argued that neuroxil-5 was slightly different from the drug the Australians had developed.'

'Sounds like a great guy.'

'Yeah. Also, there are rumours that some of BioOne's early research results were manipulated.'

'Why the hell did we back him?'

Lisa sighed. 'He sounds convincing. The stock market loves him. I'm worried he'll muscle his way into running things at Boston Peptides, and hog all the credit for anything we produce.' She switched on the TV. 'Weren't you going out with Kieran tonight?'

'No, that's OK. He won't miss me. I'll stay here with you.'

'Don't worry about me,' said Lisa neutrally. 'You go, Simon.'

So I went.

THE RED HAT was a dark basement bar only a few minutes' walk from our apartment. Kieran was already there, with half a dozen others from our business school days. Pitchers of beer were bought and drunk. After some tedious talk of business school, 'I-banks', 'VCs' and pay cheques, the conversation regressed to women, drink and sport. I forgot Frank's death, Sergeant Mahoney and Lisa's problems, and my brain went pleasantly fuzzy.

I arrived home at about half past ten, ready to tumble into bed. Lisa was sitting on the sofa, crying.

'Lisa!' I moved over to sit by her on the sofa.

'Get away from me!' she cried.

I stopped in mid-stride. 'What's wrong?'

Lisa sniffed, and took a deep breath. 'I found it, Simon.'

'Found what?'

'The gun. The gun that shot Dad.'

'What! Where?'

Lisa glared at me. 'Right there!' She pointed at a large closet. 'I was looking for an old photo album. I found it OK, but underneath was a revolver in a plastic bag. A Smith and Wesson model six forty, three fifty-seven Magnum. The police said that was the type of gun that killed Dad. And two bullets were missing. It's the gun all right. I want to know how it got there.'

I had no idea. 'Someone must have planted it.'

'Yeah, right. Like who?'

'I don't know. Hold on. Didn't the police search the closet last week? They didn't find anything then.'

'No. But it was definitely there this evening.'

'Let me see it,' I said.

'I threw it in the river. I didn't want it in the apartment.'

'Oh, Jesus. You shouldn't have done that, Lisa. I could have given it to the police.'

'Give them the evidence they need to arrest you?'

'But don't you see? It might have helped clear my name. If I gave it to them voluntarily, they would hardly suspect me, would they?'

'It's easy for you to say that now.' She shook her head, and more tears came. 'It was horrible to see it. The thing that killed Dad. I couldn't stand having it here in the apartment. I had to get rid of it right away. And I thought I was doing you a favour!'

This was ridiculous. I rushed over to her, and put my hands on her shoulders. 'Lisa. Lisa! Look at me.'

Reluctantly, she did.

'How can you believe I murdered your father? You know me. How can you think I'd do something like that?'

Lisa held my eyes, and then looked away. 'I can't bear to think about it. I don't know what to believe.' Her hands reached my chest and pushed me away. 'Let go of me!'

I stood back. Frustration boiled up inside me. 'Lisa. It wasn't me. I didn't kill your father. I've never even seen the bloody gun. I didn't kill your father!' I shouted. 'You must believe that.'

The echo of my denial reverberated though the small room.

A LONG, CRUEL DAY at work followed. I couldn't focus on anything properly. I couldn't even focus on what the gun was doing in our apartment. All I could think about was Lisa, and that evening I waited for her with apprehension. When I heard the front door of the apartment slam, I walked out to meet her.

'Hi,' I said. 'Good day?'

Stupid question. 'Simon. BioOne is going to take the place apart. No, it wasn't a good day.'

'Sorry. I made a salad.'

'Great,' Lisa said with little enthusiasm, and picked up her mail. 'I won't be a minute. I just want to call Eddie.'

She disappeared into the bedroom. She was half an hour. I reread the newspaper and tried not to get angry, but failed. Eventually she came out, her eyes red.

As we sat down, I felt a turmoil of opposing emotions. One was a powerful desire to comfort her, to try to heal the terrible hurt she was feeling. The other was anger that she wouldn't trust me.

We sat in silence munching the salad. A tear ran down her cheek. At first she tried to ignore it, and then she sniffed and wiped it away.

'Oh, Lisa,' I said, moving my hand across to her. 'Talk to me.'

She put down her fork, then sniffed again. 'What about?'

'I need to know whether you think I killed your father.'

She took a deep breath. 'The truth is, Simon, I just don't know. I've been thinking about it all day, and I'm totally confused. The police think you killed Dad, Eddie thinks you killed Dad, and I'm left wondering whether I'm just the stupid little wife, living with a murderer. But you're right, how can I even think you'd do something like that?'

'You have to trust me, Lisa—'

'Simon, I'd love to trust you. But I can't.' She paused, taking in deep breaths, trying to hold back the tears. 'Today I decided I'd just try to ignore all my doubts, but I'm not sure I can.'

'You can, Lisa. You can.'

She shook her head. 'No. It won't work. I'm confused, I'm tired, I've never felt so miserable. Everything is just . . . falling apart. I don't have the strength to stay here when . . .' She couldn't finish the sentence.

I was losing her. I knew I was losing her. 'Lisa . . .'

She seemed to be making a superhuman effort to contain the turmoil within her. Suddenly, she threw down her fork, pushed her plate away, and rushed for the bedroom, slamming the door behind her.

I opened it. She was pulling a case down from the closet.

'Lisa! What are you doing? You can't leave!'

'Why not? I can't stay.' She stuffed clothes into the bag.

'Lisa. Don't go. Please stay here. We can work through this.'

I walked over to the case, and tried to pick it up.

'Leave that alone!' she screamed, and pulled it back. 'I'm going to stay with Kelly.' Kelly was a friend of hers from work.

'Lisa . . .'

She strode towards the door, carrying the bulging bag.

I hardly slept at all that night. I needed to get out of the apartment, so I went in to work at Revere as soon as was decently possible, and stared at Tetracom papers without really taking in their contents. I waited for a quarter past nine, by which time Lisa would be sure to have arrived at the lab.

'I'm just nipping out,' I called over to John. 'I'll be back in a quarter of an hour.'

Out on Federal Street, I flipped open my cellphone and dialled Boston Peptides' switchboard.

'Can I speak to Lisa Cook?'

'I'll see if she's available. Who's speaking?'

'Simon.'

I wasn't surprised when the voice told me Lisa was unavailable.

I waited five minutes. Then I tried again. I put on an American accent. 'Oh, hi, can I speak with Lisa, please? It's her brother, Eddie.'

There was a pause, and then Lisa's voice came on the line. 'Eddie!'

'It's not Eddie,' I said. 'It's me.'

'Listen, Simon, don't you ever try to pretend—'

'No, Lisa, listen to *me*. We were both upset last night. We need to talk it through again when we're both calmer.'

'There's no need, Simon. I've made up my mind. I can't stay with you. Not when I think you might have killed my father.'

'You said "might". You're not sure, then, are you?'

There was a pause at the other end. 'Look, I'm confused, OK? I feel lousy. Really bad. I just want to be away from you for a while.'

'I understand that's how you feel. But I don't understand why. I have a right to know. Why don't we meet for a cup of coffee, and you can try to explain it? I deserve at least that.'

There was silence on the phone. 'OK. I guess you're right. Can you get here now?'

'Yes,' I said. 'I'll be there right away.'

I took a cab. Despite its name, Boston Peptides was housed in a scruffy-looking building in Cambridge, in the wasteland between MIT and Harvard. On one side was a small engineering company, and on the other was an open patch of land that was temporarily being used as a soccer pitch. Lisa was waiting on the steps.

'Let's walk,' she said, and we made our way towards the soccer pitch, where two teams of kids were playing.

We sat on a wall and watched them for a few moments, both of us nervous of starting a conversation that could end in disaster.

I waited for Lisa to say something. She didn't.

'You shouldn't listen to Eddie. Eddie's wrong. He hates me. He hates himself,' I said.

'Maybe Eddie can see things more clearly than I can.'

I lost the calm I had been trying so hard to maintain. 'Lisa. You know me. I'm your husband. I love you. You know I'm not capable of killing your father.'

Lisa turned to me. 'Then what was the gun doing there?'

'I don't know,' I said in exasperation.

'Let's look at the evidence here, Simon.' She was talking fast now. 'One, you were the last person to see Dad alive. Two, you and he had a fight. Three, you know how to use a gun. And four,' she looked at me defiantly, 'I found that gun hidden in our apartment.'

'That doesn't mean anything. Why would I kill him, anyway?'

'I don't know. You need fifty thousand pounds to fight your sister's lawsuit. We'll have that now.'

'Oh, come on.'

'All right. Maybe you *are* having an affair with Diane. Maybe Dad found out. Maybe you wanted to keep him quiet *and* get your hands on his money.'

'That's absurd. I'm not having an affair with anybody. Someone must have planted the gun.'

'Like who? The police? It was in a *Boots* plastic bag. Do you think Sergeant Mahoney goes to England to pick up his deodorant?'

'None of that proves anything.'

'It's a hypothesis. And a plausible one,' said Lisa. 'And I will go with it, until you can disprove it.'

'This isn't some scientific experiment, Lisa. It's me you're talking about. Us!'

Lisa looked at me, her eyes filling with tears. 'But I've only known you, what, two years? I don't know anything about who you are, really. I know you're clever, I know you can hold a lot inside without talking about it, but perhaps I don't know what is really inside you. Of course the Simon I fell in love with wouldn't have an affair or kill anyone. But did that Simon ever really exist?'

I wanted to argue, but there seemed little point.

'Come back,' I said simply. 'Please.'

Lisa took a deep breath, and shook her head. 'No, Simon.' She stood up. 'I've got to get back to work.'

'You said you'd only be a quarter of an hour,' John said.

'Sorry.' I gave him a quick smile.

'Your voice mail has been working overtime.'

I ignored the winking light on my phone, and played over my conversation with Lisa again and again. I still couldn't quite believe that she had just walked away from me. I had obviously become part of the black world that seemed to surround and threaten her. I couldn't bear the thought of her believing that I had killed her father. Her love was the most precious thing in the world to me. The idea of it turning to hatred hurt. It hurt a lot. Well, I would prove to her that I was innocent.

I asked myself the vital question. If I hadn't killed Frank, who had? I realised it was unlikely that it could have been a burglar. The police hadn't mentioned any signs of a break-in, nor had I seen any. Frank had been shot some way inside the house. It seemed most likely that he had known whoever had shot him, or at least that he had voluntarily let his murderer into the house. I realised I didn't know much about Frank's life. Presumably he had other friends, but I knew nothing about them. Lisa said there hadn't been any girlfriends since he and her mother had got divorced.

I thought about the gun. I had checked the apartment for signs of a break-in, but there were none. And no one had been in the apartment since the police had searched it apart from Lisa and me. In theory the police could have planted it. But why? Anyway, if he had planted the gun, wouldn't Mahoney have 'discovered' it in his search?

The Boots bag didn't mean anything. It was undoubtedly mine. Whoever had been in the closet would have spotted it.

I didn't think Ann could have killed her ex-husband. She seemed to have recovered from their separation quite successfully and was now happily remarried. At the funeral, she spoke of Frank with fondness. But Eddie was much more likely. He had never forgiven his father for leaving, had barely spoken to him for years, and the prospect of Frank's legacy seemed very important to him. And he was very eager to blame me for the crime. The other 'family suspect' was Lisa. Lisa I just couldn't believe. Which left the possibility that it might be one of Frank's colleagues. There were rivalries at Revere. Frank and Art didn't much like each other, vying for position as Gil's right-hand man. But it was generally a civilised, pleasant place to work. It wasn't the kind of place where people shot each other.

Or was it? I needed to find out more. I walked down the corridor towards Frank's office. The door was locked.

I sauntered further along the corridor to Gil's assistant's desk.

'Connie, I'd like to get into Frank's office. I need to see if he has some papers on Net Cop. Do you know who has the key?'

Connie seemed to like me, which was at times very useful.

'I think Gil has it, Simon. Go right in, there's no one with him.'

I went in.

'What can I do for you, Simon?' Gil smiled at me.

'I need the key for Frank's office. There are some files on Net Cop in there that I want.'

Gil reached into his desk for a key. 'Here you are. Please return it as soon as you're done with it.'

Frank's office looked much the same as it had the last time I was there. It was reasonably tidy, but there were papers in his in-box, and on top of the wooden filing cabinets. Yellow Post-Its reminded him of things he would never now do.

I had worked with him closely enough to know my way round his filing system, so the first thing I did was to look for his Net Cop file and pull it out. I ignored the bulging files on his other deals and concentrated on his more personal stuff. He didn't have any secrets. No locked drawers. No coded files. A very full diary, but none of the appointments seemed out of the ordinary. And then I came across a file labelled 'Fund IV'. In it was a letter from Gil to Lynette Mauer, dated September 9. The second paragraph grabbed my attention:

> As you know, I am planning to reduce my involvement with the day-to-day management of Revere Partners. While I will continue to provide advice related to our first three funds, I will take no role in the new fund. I am confident the strong team of partners that I have been fortunate enough to assemble over the last few years will ensure that the performance of our fourth fund will be as strong as those preceding it.

So Gil was going to retire! Very interesting. And now that Frank was out of the way, his successor was obvious. Art Altschule. I shuddered. No wonder Lynette Mauer was worried. She didn't trust Art. She saw BioOne for what it was, a fluke.

I stuffed the letter back in the file and had just turned on Frank's computer when his office door opened. It was Gil.

'What are you doing, Simon?' he asked, his forehead wrinkled. 'You've been in here a long time.'

'I'm looking for a memo Frank wrote when we originally invested in Net Cop,' I said.

The small brown eyes bored into me through those thick lenses. I sat still, trying to keep a keen-associate look on my face.

'I don't think you should be rooting around in Frank's computer. You've been in here long enough. If you haven't found it yet, you're not going to find it.'

I switched off Frank's machine, grabbed the Net Cop file and left, feeling very small. I should be much more careful in future.

I MADE MY WAY slowly home that evening, delaying my return to the empty apartment. On an impulse I stopped at the 7-Eleven and bought bacon, sausage, eggs, the works. Within minutes, the sounds and smells of a gigantic fry-up filled the kitchen.

The bell rang. I swore and answered the door. It was Sergeant Mahoney, accompanied by his detective sidekick. I let them in.

'Hang on a minute. Sit down, while I sort out the stove.'

When I returned to the living room, Mahoney was looking at a picture of me in my Life Guards uniform, complete with red tunic and breastplate, that stood on Lisa's desk. She had appropriated it because she said I looked dashing.

'What can I do for you?' I said.

'We'd like to ask you some more questions about Frank Cook's murder,' Mahoney said, sitting on the sofa. His sidekick perched next to him, notebook ready.

I thought about refusing to talk, or about insisting that I call the lawyer Gil had told me about, Gardner Phillips. But I wanted to find out certain things from him. 'OK. Go ahead.'

'Where's your wife, Mr Ayot?'

It was obvious Mahoney knew the answer already. 'She left me. She's gone to stay with a friend.'

'Is this a permanent separation?' he asked, raising an eyebrow.

'Oh, no,' I said. 'She's upset by her father's death. She says she needs some time alone. Or at least without me.'

'Your wife says that she's working on a big project with Kelly Williams, and it makes sense to stay with her for a while.'

I sighed. 'She's just trying to keep up appearances, I suppose. It'll blow over. She'll be back here soon.' I tried to sound confident.

Mahoney smiled. 'OK. I didn't believe her explanation, anyway. But then, I don't believe yours either.' He left the words hanging there for a while. 'Do you know anything about a gun?'

'No.'

Mahoney leaned forward. 'You and your wife had an argument last night. You raised your voice. You said,' here he examined his notebook, '"I've never even seen the bloody gun. I didn't kill your father." Did you say those words, Mr Ayot?'

I closed my eyes. A neighbour must have heard me. This was a question I didn't want to answer. 'I think I'd like to talk to a lawyer.'

'OK. Have him give me a call in the morning. In the meantime I have a warrant to search your apartment again and your car.'

It didn't take them long. It was a small apartment and they knew what they were looking for. I then led them the couple of blocks to the Brimmer Street Garage where my Morgan was stowed.

'Look, Sergeant Mahoney,' I said as we stood outside. 'I didn't kill Frank. I want to find out who did. If you give me some information, perhaps I can help.'

Mahoney turned his bulky frame towards me. 'I am very confident we will find Frank Cook's murderer. And we won't need any help from you.'

With that, he and his colleague walked down the street, climbed into a car and drove off.

As soon as I was back in the apartment, I telephoned Gardner Phillips's office. Fortunately he was still there, even though it was after eight o'clock. He suggested a meeting in his office the next morning.

Then I dialled Kelly Williams's number.

'Oh, hi, Simon,' she said breezily, as though this was just a normal social call. 'I'll just see if Lisa's around.'

There was a long wait. Finally Kelly was back on the line. 'She's just stepped out, Simon. I'm not sure when she'll be back.'

'No, she hasn't. She's there and she doesn't want to talk to me. Just put her on the line for a moment. It's important.'

'Sorry, Simon. I'm not going to spend all night running back and forth between the two of you.' Kelly's reply was friendly but firm.

'OK, OK. But can you at least give her a message from me? Can you just tell her "Thank you for standing by me."'

'OK. I'll tell her.'

I hoped Lisa would understand my message. I wanted her to know that there was still a lot between us. That I wanted her back.

GARDNER PHILLIPS's office was in a modern building close to the Court House. It was only a small detour for me on my way to work.

Phillips himself was a decade or so younger than Gil, with a neatly trimmed beard and an air of confidence that I found very comforting. He listened carefully to my story, taking notes. I told him everything, including how Lisa had discovered and disposed of the gun.

'There's no doubt they're trying to build a case against you. But they have a way to go yet. They need to find the weapon, or a witness, or something else to tie you in. The important thing, from now on, is not to talk to them unless I'm present.'

'Even if I can straighten them out on something?'

'I'll straighten them out if they need straightening out. I'll talk to Sergeant Mahoney this morning.'

After a difficult weekend, during which I missed Lisa badly, Diane and I headed off to the airport.

Tetracom was located in a suburb a few miles south of Cincinnati, in northern Kentucky. The company had bought and refurbished some old red-brick industrial buildings, looking nothing like the gleaming high-tech ventures I was used to. Diane introduced me to the management team, and we were ushered into a shabby office.

The purpose of this session was to nail down the answers to some questions about Tetracom's competitors. The management coped well. The CEO, Bob Hecht, seemed to know his product and his market inside out. He had assembled a good team and they seemed determined to make the product work. As cellular telephony spread around the globe, so did demand for filters, and Tetracom's appeared to be better and cheaper than what was out there at the moment.

We had dinner with Hecht and his colleagues back at the Cincinnatian Hotel where we were staying. It was a credo of venture capital that you should get to know the management team thoroughly before making an investment.

The Tetracom team left just before eleven. I was about to go to bed when Diane suggested a drink. We headed for the bar, and I ordered a single malt, Diane a brandy.

'So what do you think of them?' she asked.

I gave Diane my analysis, which was that I was impressed, but worried that existing companies in the sector might come out with their own new technologies to match Tetracom's. We talked about that for a while, and then Diane asked me the $4.7 million question.

'Do you think we should invest?'

No deal was ever perfect, but this was closer than most. I nodded. 'Provided we can get comfortable about the competition, yes.'

'Good. So do I. We'll do some more research when we get back.'

I smiled and raised my glass. 'To Tetracom.'

'To Tetracom.' Diane sipped her brandy. Even though she had been up since six that morning and hadn't had a chance to change, she looked cool and poised in a simple, well-cut black suit.

'What do you think about Revere, Simon?' she asked.

I decided to trust her. And I hoped I might find something out. 'I'm worried by what Lynette Mauer said last week. Not just worried about us losing an investor in our funds. I'm more concerned she might be right. Now Frank's gone we've lost the partner with the most consistent track record.'

'What about Gil?'

Diane was watching me closely over her brandy. I decided to be open. 'I suspect Gil won't be around Revere much longer either.'

She raised her eyebrows. 'How do you know about that?'

I shrugged. 'Lynette Mauer is obviously worried, and I don't blame her. Without both Frank and Gil, Art would run the show. I just don't trust his judgment.'

Diane frowned. 'It's exactly what I've been thinking about a lot recently.' She had implicitly criticised one of her partners in front of an associate. I felt in a strange way honoured by her confidence.

'What were relations like between Frank and Art?' I asked her.

She thought for a moment before answering. 'They were always polite to each other. Or at least Frank was always polite to Art. And I never heard him say anything bad about Art behind his back. Art was always polite about Frank, as well, but what he did try to do was ease Frank out of the loop. He would schedule important meetings when Frank couldn't make them, he'd spend a lot of time with the investors, and so on. Frank let himself be outmanoeuvred. He knew that ultimately he could rely on Gil's support.'

I paused before asking my next question. 'And if Frank was still alive, do you think he would have taken over from Gil?'

'Oh, undoubtedly. But I think some way would have been found for Art to save face. I don't know, some new title or position or something.' She drained her glass. 'Do you want another?' I nodded and she beckoned to the waiter. 'Why are you asking me all this?'

'I wonder who killed Frank,' I answered simply. 'The police seem to have decided it was me.'

'That's ridiculous.'

'I'd love to be able to point them in another direction.'

Diane leaned forward. 'I can understand your concern. But be careful. If we start pointing fingers at each other over Frank's death, we'll tear the firm apart.'

'Do you think I killed Frank, Diane?'

'Of course not,' she replied unhesitatingly.

'Thank you.'

We sipped our drinks in silence. It had been a long day.

'How's Lisa?' Diane asked.

'She's left me,' I said.

'No!' Diane looked genuinely concerned. 'I'm sorry.'

I didn't want to talk about Lisa. And just for the moment I didn't want to think about her. It was good to be away from Boston and Lisa and the mess of Frank's death.

We talked of other things, of England, of New Jersey where Diane had grown up. I hadn't realised her father was an electrician, yet she had managed to get herself into NYU and then Columbia Business School where she had graduated top of her class. She was a classic example of poor girl made good.

It was nearly one o'clock when we finally called it a night. As we rode up in the lift together, Diane stood close to me. She kissed me on the lips. I was too tired, too confused to respond, but I didn't pull away either. Then, as the lift stopped, she flashed me a quick smile. 'Good night,' she said, and was gone.

I had another terrible night's sleep brooding about Frank, Lisa and Diane. I woke up still tired, with a headache.

At breakfast Diane looked great, and acted as though nothing had happened the previous night. Perhaps it hadn't.

BACK IN THE OFFICE, John was looking seriously worried.

'What's up?' I asked.

'National Quilt is screwed,' he said. 'The bank's getting antsy. They don't like all this inventory build-up. They want the working capital line of credit cleaned up by the end of the month.'

'And you're not going to make that?'

'No way.'

'What about the "Go Naked" strategy?'

'I think it makes them even more worried,' said John gloomily.

'Oh.' That sounded like a problem. 'What's Art's advice?'

'I started talking to him about it, and then he suddenly had an urgent phone call. He said if things were looking tough I should raise it at next week's Monday morning meeting.'

'Sounds like he doesn't want to know.'

'That's exactly what it sounds like.' John sighed. 'I guess this is all part of becoming a grown-up venture capitalist.'

John headed off to visit the ill-fated quilt company, leaving me to spend the day at my desk. I gathered together some pretty good information on Tetracom's competitors that seemed to suggest their product really was special. But it was difficult. I spent long periods of time staring into space, worrying.

Daniel was involved in some heavy-duty number-crunching. Eventually he stopped and stretched.

'So you think we might do Tetracom, huh?'

'I think so. Or else I'm wasting my time with all this.'

'And how was the lovely Diane?'

'Missing you badly, Daniel.' I kept my composure.

'Naturally.' He smiled. 'Hey, how about a drink after work?'

WE WENT TO PETE'S, a bar on Franklin Street, in the middle of the Financial District, and had a cold Sam Adams each.

'So how come you were staring into space all afternoon?' Daniel asked.

I took a long draught of the cool beer. 'Lisa's left me.'

'Oh, no! I'm sorry. Why did she do that? Did she find a one-eyed leper who was better looking?'

'Thanks, Daniel.'

'If she's free, so am I. Have you got her new number?'

I ignored his comment. However offensive it was, Daniel's kidding eased the gloom a bit. 'She thinks I killed Frank.'

Daniel winced. 'Oooh. That could take some forgiving. I do hope she's wrong.'

'Yes, she's all wrong. But the police seem to agree with her.'

'What, that nice Sergeant Malone who asked all those questions?'

'Mahoney. That's right.' There was one question I needed to ask Daniel. 'Did you tell Mahoney we were talking about how wealthy Frank was just before he died?'

Daniel winced. 'Yeah, I did. Sorry. But he did ask, and I had to tell him the truth.'

'Don't worry.' I sipped my beer. 'But what interests me is, if I didn't kill Frank, who did?'

'Good question,' said Daniel. 'It wasn't me. I was in New York.'

'No need to be so smug about it. What's the office gossip? I don't seem to hear any of it any more.'

'People usually steer clear of the subject. When they don't, there's one name that comes up quite consistently.'

'Mine?'

Daniel nodded.

'But people can't really think I murdered Frank?'

'I don't think they do. Which leaves us kind of stuck.'

'What about Art?'

Daniel thought for a moment. 'Not a bad choice. He hated Frank. But where was he when Frank was killed?'

'I don't know,' I said. 'And I can scarcely ask. You've worked with Art more than I have. Do you know much about his background?'

'He's known Gil a long time. I think they were at Harvard together. After that they both went to Vietnam. Gil was in a regular unit; Art was in the Marines. I think Art saw some pretty hairy action, but he never talks about what happened.'

'I can understand that,' I said. There were one or two things in my own short military career I would rather not discuss.

'But you know how Art likes to brag,' said Daniel. 'Anyway, after Vietnam he got an MBA, and then started some company selling minicomputers. He sold it for something like twelve million bucks to ICX Computers. But once ICX got in there they found they had bought a can of worms. The accounts were rotten. ICX hit Art and his partner for ten million. Art's partner killed himself.'

'Jesus.'

'The story is that Art didn't know anything about it. And I can kind of believe that. There's quite a lot Art doesn't know. Then Art's old buddy Gil started up a VC firm, and asked Art to join him. Art arrived a few months before Frank, I think. Then he had several years' mediocre investing until he lucked out on BioOne.'

We drank our beer. I thought through other possibilities.

'Gil?' I suggested.

'I don't think so,' said Daniel. 'He's so straight. And they were friends. Besides, why would he do it?'

'No reason I can think of.'

Daniel sipped his beer thoughtfully. 'But what about Diane?'

'Diane?' I said. 'Why would she want to kill Frank?'

'I don't know. But she's devious. A skilful political animal. She was one of the youngest partners at Barnes McLintock, the management consultants, but she left some collateral damage in her wake.'

'What happened?'

'It seems her boss advised Pan United Airlines to change their image to appear less American. They lost a quarter of their passengers within six months. They tried to sue. Diane somehow persuaded Pan United that she had always thought it was a bad idea and she came up with some smart ways to fix the problem. Barnes McLintock didn't get sued, her boss got fired, and she got promoted. I heard the guy didn't stand a chance once Diane had him in her sights.'

'I see.' I remembered Frank had said something about Diane

breaking up a marriage. 'She didn't have an affair with him, did she?'

Daniel laughed. 'No, but there was something with an associate. A young guy. Married. He walked out on his wife and left the firm. Then she dropped him a few months later.' He looked at me curiously. 'You'd better watch yourself with Diane, Simon.'

'Oh, come on, Daniel. There's nothing between us.'

'She's after you.'

The trouble with Daniel was you could never tell whether he was joking or being serious. But either way I knew he was right.

'I still don't think Diane would kill anyone,' I said. 'That goes way beyond political scheming. No, I think Art is our best bet.'

'There is one interesting thing about Art,' Daniel said. 'I think he used to be an alcoholic.'

'I've never seen him drink.'

'Precisely. And he doesn't act like the temperance type.'

'You mean he must have given up?'

'Absolutely. Except I think he might be back on the booze. He's called in sick unexpectedly three times in the last three weeks. And on Tuesday morning I could swear he smelt of whisky.'

'That's not good. Do you think some recent event might have started him off again?'

'It's a theory,' said Daniel. 'But it's nowhere near as convincing as the theory that you did it.'

'Great,' I said, and drained my beer.

An hour or so later we left Pete's, mellow but not drunk. The nights were beginning to get cold. I hunched my shoulders and pushed my hands deep into my suit pockets. It was late, and it was quiet in the heart of the Financial District.

Two big men approached us along the narrow sidewalk. We paused to let them pass by. But they didn't. Their eyes locked on Daniel and me. I heard rapid footsteps behind us.

I pulled my hands out of my pockets, too late to prevent a heavy blow to my stomach. I doubled up, gasping. Two more punches followed, and I slumped backwards against the wall.

They bundled Daniel into an alleyway. I heard the blows coming thick and fast. Daniel cried out. My head slowly cleared. In front of me stood a big hard man, his fists clenched, ready to strike again. I thrust my fist upwards with all my strength. The blow caught him on the side of the head, and sent him stumbling into the street. Out of the corner of my eye I could see the other two move towards me. I turned to face them. Then one of them muttered something in a foreign language that sounded like Russian, and they backed off.

'Daniel, are you OK?' I crouched over him. He was conscious but groaning. 'I'll call an ambulance.'

Daniel sat up. 'No, don't do that. I think I am OK. It just hurts. Get me a taxi, Simon. I'll go home.'

His nose was bleeding, and so was his lip, and he had a huge red mark on one cheek. I picked him up and half carried him to a busier street. We waited a couple of minutes for a taxi. I gently placed Daniel in the back seat and climbed in with him.

'You're a great guy to be out with in Boston at night,' said Daniel, trying to stem the flow of blood from his nose with his hand.

'They didn't know who we were, did they?'

'Didn't they?' said Daniel. 'Did they steal anything? I've still got my wallet, I think.' He patted his pocket to make sure.

I checked mine. It was still there. The thought that people I didn't know might want to beat me up bothered me. But Daniel was right. They hadn't taken anything.

'Did you hear them at the end?' I said. 'One of them was speaking Russian I think. What would a bunch of Russians want with me?'

'Face it,' said Daniel. 'Nobody likes you.'

DAYLIGHT and a clearer head didn't help answer the question, as I walked into work the next day. On the Common the leaves were at the peak of their colour: oranges, yellows and browns.

I was walking past the Meridien Hotel, when I saw Diane coming the other way. She crossed the road at the junction, and disappeared into the entrance. I wasn't surprised; it was a favourite breakfast haunt for downtown venture capitalists. Then, as I reached the junction, I saw the diminutive figure of Lynette Mauer also headed for the Meridien. Interesting.

I arrived at work before Daniel. When he made his entrance, I saw that a black eye had materialised, his cheek shone purple and red, and his bottom lip had a nasty black-red scab.

'What happened to you?' exclaimed John.

'Some guys tried to beat up Simon. I got in the way,' said Daniel.

'Why did they want to beat you up?' John asked me.

'I wish I knew,' I muttered.

Work had to be dealt with. I went to see Diane with the analysis of Tetracom's competition. It clearly impressed her. Just as I was about to leave her office, I paused. 'Oh, I think I saw Lynette Mauer this morning going into the Meridien. She didn't see me.'

'Oh, yes?' said Diane neutrally.

'You didn't see me, either, I don't think.'

Diane smiled. 'OK, you caught me.'

'So what were you and Mauer talking about?'

'Oh, you'll find out soon, I hope.' Diane's smile broadened. 'Let's just say someone had to take the initiative around here.'

Back at my desk, I checked my computer for BioOne's stock price. John saw what I was doing. 'Forty-eight and five-eighths. Down three-eighths, going nowhere,' he said.

I looked up. Now seemed like a good time to ask. 'John, who do you think killed Frank?'

He looked at me sharply, surprised by the question. 'I don't know. I haven't thought about it much, I guess.'

'You must have some opinion.'

He looked uncomfortable. 'To tell you the truth, Simon, the whole subject is something I'd rather not think about.' He swallowed. 'I liked Frank. I just can't believe . . .' He paused. 'He was a good guy, you know. He wasn't just a good venture capitalist. He was a great person. I'm going to miss him.'

I was a little surprised by his emotional reaction and decided not to push him any further on the subject of possible suspects.

'The police said that Frank phoned you the day he died?'

'That's right.'

'What about?'

For a moment John looked confused. 'Oh . . . a deal we were working on. Um . . . Smart Toys, I think it was. He called me asking for some information. I had the papers at home.'

John turned back to his work. I turned to mine. But something wasn't quite right with what John had said. I dug through the agendas for recent Monday morning meetings, and found the one for October 12. There was a section labelled DEAD DEALS that listed all the deals that had been turned down in the previous week. Sure enough, there it was: 'Smart Toys, October 8'. Frank had killed the deal on the Thursday before he died. John had lied to me. Why?

I decided not to confront him yet. I had work to do. I attacked my emails. One was from Jeff Lieberman. It said some of his firm's managing directors were interested in investing in Net Cop, and could Craig and I meet them that afternoon?

I was just mulling the message over when the phone rang.

It was Craig. 'Hey, Simon. Good news or what?'

I hesitated. I hated to dampen Craig's spirits, but it was important we keep a sense of perspective. 'It's nice, Craig. But don't get your hopes up. We're still a long way off the three million we need.'

'Yeah, but Bloomfield Weiss is one of the biggest investment banks in the world. They got to have dough. There's no one else to try. If these guys don't put up, then there's no Net Cop to save.'

He was right. I looked at my watch. 'I'll see you at the airport for the one o'clock shuttle.'

BOSTON HAD SOME big buildings downtown, but New York's were huge. We were dropped off outside a fifty-storey black monstrosity just off Wall Street, with the words BLOOMFIELD WEISS in small gold lettering just above the entrance.

A high-speed lift propelled us up to the forty-sixth floor, where we waited in a plush reception area for Jeff Lieberman. We had decided that Craig should wear his usual uniform of T-shirt and jeans. At least then he'd look like the brilliant computer geek he was, rather than a muscle-bound construction worker in his Sunday best.

Jeff met us and took us through to a conference room. More suits came in. Or more strictly they were shirts: half of them wore identical heavy white oxford shirts with bright ties, while the other half wore expensive polo shirts and slacks in honour of dress-down Friday. Craig was nervous. So was I. These were well-groomed, powerful men of money. Whereas Revere doled out the odd million here and there, Bloomfield Weiss sent billions spinning round the globe twenty-four hours a day.

Jeff deferred to a tiny man named Sidney Stahl.

'So, Craig. Jeff's given me the bullshit. Tell me what you really do. You got ten minutes.'

'Sure,' Craig said, and he began talking. The Bloomfield Weiss hotshots were entranced.

Forty-five minutes later there was a knock at the door, and a worried-looking young man in a nice suit caught Stahl's eye.

'OK, OK,' Stahl said. 'Sorry, Craig. I gotta stop you there.' He turned to look at the group. 'I'm in. What about you guys?'

Heads nodded all round the table, with a mixture of deference and bravado. If Sidney thought it was a good risk, then so did the others.

Stahl stood up. 'I like you, Craig. You've got our money, but only if you and Jeff can agree on a deal. I don't think you'll find him a pushover.' He left the room, followed by everyone but Jeff.

Jeff grinned at me. 'I bet you didn't think it would be that easy.'

I smiled broadly back at him. 'What was all that about? That's not the kind of investment committee you get in venture capital.'

'That's the point,' said Jeff. 'It's a kind of informal investment club made up of some of the big-hitters in the firm, who choose to invest personally in deals that are too small for Bloomfield Weiss. It's a kind of macho thing. Putting up their own money for a big risk. But don't knock it. These guys have had some spectacular home runs.'

'Um, there is one thing we didn't cover,' I said. 'How much are we talking about?'

'How much do you need?'

My eyes flashed up at Jeff. 'Three million dollars.'

'Then I guess we're talking about three million dollars.'

CRAIG WAS ECSTATIC on the flight back. He gave himself and me a blow-by-blow commentary of what had happened, as though he still couldn't quite believe it. The Bloomfield Weiss syndicate would end up with a large chunk of the company, Craig would keep a chunk, and Revere's holding would be diluted. The deal still needed Revere's approval, but it looked very much as though Craig would get to build his prototype. Net Cop was going to work.

'Thank you, Simon,' Craig said, finally.

I was pleased. But it still left all my other problems out there.

Craig noticed my silence. 'Hey, Simon, what's up? You've been fighting for this as much as I have.'

I smiled at him. 'Yes. And I am truly very pleased.'

'So?'

So I told him about how I was everyone's favourite suspect for Frank's murder, and that I needed to find out more.

'Perhaps I can help,' he said. 'My dad retired from the force a few years ago, but he knows a lot of people there.'

'Perhaps you can,' I said. 'The man leading the investigation is Sergeant Mahoney. He doesn't like me. It would be interesting to find out a bit more about him.'

'I'll ask around.'

'And can you see if you can find out whether the following people have a criminal record. Do you have a pen?'

Craig raised his eyebrows. 'What do I need a pen for? I know *pi* to twenty-nine decimal places.'

'OK, sorry. The names are Arthur Altschule, Gilbert Appleby, Edward Cook—that's Lisa's brother, and Diane Zarrilli.'

'OK, I'll see what I can do.'

'Ow!' A STAB of pain ran down my shoulder as I carried the boat to the river with Kieran.

'Are you OK, Simon?' he asked.

'I got into a spot of bother a couple of nights ago. My shoulder still hurts.'

'A spot of bother? Do you mean a fight?'

'You could call it that. I was mugged on the street outside Pete's. With Daniel Hall.'

'How much did they take?'

'It was odd. They didn't take anything.'

'Oh, I see. So they just didn't like your face?'

'I don't know what they didn't like.'

'It was probably Daniel. Did he make some smart-arse comment?'

'I don't think so. He thinks it was me they were after. I've been in some trouble recently.'

'Must be some pretty bad trouble.'

'I suppose it is,' I said. 'But even so, I don't know why anyone would want to beat me up. One of them spoke Russian.'

'Really?'

We threw the boat in the water, and set off at a slow pace.

'I read somewhere that the Russians are the new boys in town when it comes to organised crime,' said Kieran. 'Drugs, money-laundering, loan-sharking. Remember that guy Sergei Delesov?'

'Yes.' He was a very able Russian in our class at business school.

'There was a rumour he was mixed up with some of them.'

'Delesov? A Harvard graduate?'

'That was the rumour. I think he's running some bank back in Russia now.'

We rowed on at a steady pace and the aching in my muscles eased a little as I warmed up. Kieran told me not to worry, he could use a gentle start to his Saturday.

WEEKENDS ARE TOUGH when you love someone and they hate you. Especially if you're alone. The full reality of Lisa leaving me was sinking in, bringing with it the awful thought that she might not come back. The loneliness of that thought crushed in on me.

Craig burst in on my moping on Saturday evening.

'That was quick,' I said, getting him a beer.

'The Boston Police Department never sleeps,' said Craig. 'Or at least the computers still work at weekends.'

'So, what have you got?'

'My dad knew Mahoney. He worked in Boston for twenty years as a street patrolman and then a detective. He got transferred to the State Police. He'd get a hunch and he'd play it. Often he'd be right.'

Oh, great. I was his hunch on this case. 'What about the others?'

'There are a coupla Edward Cooks with records in California, but none of them looks like your guy. Nothing on Gil. Nor on Diane.'

'And Art?'

'Now, this guy has an interesting file. He was involved with a company that sold UNIX boxes. His partner, a guy named Dennis Slater, liked to invent customers who he'd sell the same box to several times over. When they sold the company, Slater was found out, and he blew his brains out.'

'The police investigated Art?'

'That's right. But there's really no hard evidence that he did it.'

'Can you get anything on the investigation into Frank Cook's murder?'

Craig shook his head. 'Sorry, Simon. An ongoing murder investigation is a much bigger deal. It would be hard for my contacts to nose around that sort of thing without being noticed.'

I nodded. 'That's a shame. I'd love to know if Mahoney has found out anything else about Art.'

'You could always ask Art.'

I looked sceptically at Craig. 'He's hardly likely to go on his knees and confess to me.'

'No, but he might tell you if there's proof that he didn't do it. If you ask him in the right way.'

'Maybe I will. Thanks, Craig, that's helpful.'

I decided the best place to talk to Art was at his home. So late on Sunday afternoon I drove out to Acton. The Boston area is stuffed with the most prosaic place names from the southeast of England. Acton, Chelmsford, Woburn, Braintree and Norwood, to name but a few. I hadn't found Chipping Ongar yet, but I was sure it was lurking there somewhere.

Acton was nothing like its west London namesake. Winding rivers, stony fields of pumpkins lined up as if on parade, brightly painted wooden houses, tiny blue lakes and trees everywhere. The clear autumn light reflected off the oranges and reds of the maples, and despite the reason for my visit, my spirits rose as I drove up to Art's large yellow-painted house.

His wife, Shirley, answered the door. Although she must have been about fifty, she was trying to look twenty years younger. Counterfeit blonde hair, tight blue jeans and careful make-up did their best, but didn't quite succeed. We had got on very well at the previous year's Christmas party, but it took her a second to recognise me. Then she gave me a broad smile. 'Simon, how nice to see you again!'

'I'm sorry to disturb you over the weekend, Shirley,' I said.

'No trouble at all. Do come in. Art's around.'

I stood in the hallway as she fetched her husband.

'What's the problem, Simon?' Art was dressed in neatly pressed khaki trousers and a denim shirt. He looked bleary-eyed.

'Um, I wanted to ask your advice about something.'

Art decided he was happy to play the role of wise uncle. He showed me through to the living room, flicked a remote to turn off the TV and picked up a can of Diet Dr Pepper.

'Want one?'

'No, thanks,' I said.

'Cup of tea?'

'Actually, yes, please. That would be nice.'

'Hold on a moment, I'll get Shirley to fix it.'

I sat down in an armchair.

'What's the problem?' said Art, returning from the kitchen.

'Well,' I began. 'It's about Frank's murder, actually. The problem is, the police seem to think I'm responsible.'

Art didn't say anything at all at first, just looked at me carefully, as though he agreed with the police's assessment. But then he decided to be polite. 'Gil has made it clear to all of us that he supports you, and so we should. How can I help?'

Shirley Altschule appeared with a dainty Wedgwood cup of tea.

'Thank you, but can I just have a drop of milk?'

'Oh, why certainly,' she said quickly, and retreated to the kitchen.

When she had gone I said, 'I need to find out who *did* kill Frank. And to do that, I need to ask some questions. I wonder if you could tell me where you were on the Saturday he was killed?'

'What?' Art swigged his Dr Pepper. 'I didn't kill him. I had to answer these questions from the police. Why the hell should I answer them from you?'

'I'm sorry, Art. The police won't tell me the results of their investigation, so I have to re-create their investigation for myself. I know it's a bore for you, but I just need to eliminate everyone in the firm.'

'Well, I was at home with Shirley all that day when Frank Cook was killed, wasn't I, honey?'

His wife, who had just returned with a delicate jug of milk, threw me a sharp look. 'That's right. You worked in the yard most of the afternoon, and then we rented a video in the evening. But we've told the police all this. Surely you don't think—'

'Of course I don't, Mrs Altschule. Anyway, with what you've told me, I can cross Art off the list, even though he wasn't really on it to start with.'

She gave me a worried look. 'I'm just going down to the store, Art,' she said. 'I'll be back.'

I waited until she had left, and then I continued my questioning. 'Have you any idea who else might have killed Frank?'

'No. I can't believe it can have been anyone at Revere, though. It was probably some wandering psycho. The cops will get him in the end. I just hope they find him before he kills any more people.'

'I tell you though, it's horrible when you feel the police are after you,' I said. 'It shakes your faith in the justice system.'

'I bet.'

'I hear the same kind of thing happened to you once. After your partner committed suicide?'

'Who told you that?' asked Art, sharply.

'Oh, I forget who. It's just rumour. It's probably all wrong.'

Art looked at me. 'No, it's true.' He glanced at his watch. 'What do you say to a real drink? Jack on the rocks OK with you?'

I nodded. Art reached behind a bookcase and pulled out a bottle. He found two glasses on a shelf, and took some ice from a small refrigerator. Within a moment a large drink was in my hand. Art took a big gulp. 'Aah. That tastes good. Yeah, I've had my turn as a number-one suspect,' he said. 'It was a bad time. My partner had been ripping off our company for years. We were both being hit for a giant warranty payment. And then the stupid son-of-a-bitch went and killed himself. The cops blamed me. They didn't have any evidence, but I had a motive, and my only alibi was Shirley, and they didn't believe her. They also held the fact that I had been in 'Nam against me. That really pissed me off. It was as though just because I had been out there fighting for my country, I was some kind of murderer. But in the end they couldn't pin anything on me.'

'I know what you mean. That's what Mahoney holds against me.'

Art looked at me curiously. 'But you didn't fight in any war, did you? I thought you guys just pranced around on horses at the Queen's tea parties.'

'No, I never fought in any war,' I said. 'But I did spend a year in Northern Ireland. I think that's what Mahoney didn't like.'

'That figures,' said Art.

'What was it like in Vietnam?' I asked.

Art looked at me suspiciously. 'It wasn't what I expected. It wasn't how a war should be fought.' He took a large gulp of his whisky. 'I try to forget it. I don't always succeed, but I try.'

This reply was so unlike Art, so lacking in bravado and bluster, that it caught me by surprise.

He emptied his glass and refilled it. 'Hey, do you want to take a look at my gun collection? You were a soldier, you'd appreciate it.'

'I'd love to,' I said.

We left our glasses, and Art took me down to the basement. One wall was lined with sturdy-looking metal cabinets. Art took out a key, and unlocked one of them. It held half a dozen antique muskets, rifles and carbines, most from the American Civil War. The other cabinets held modern weapons, including some from the Second World War. There were assault rifles, semiautomatics, and a variety of handguns. No three fifty-seven Magnums though.

We returned to the living room. Art was mellow and relaxed.

'What did you think of Frank?' I asked.

He took a deep breath. 'We had very different philosophies on how the firm should be run. Frank was very analytical. I'm more seat-of-the-pants. Sure, Frank was a bright guy. But for a real big winner like BioOne, you need something more. It's a kind of imagination, a willingness to take risks. Courage, leadership. Call it what you will.'

'Do you think he would have taken over when Gil eventually retires?'

'Possibly,' said Art. 'Gil liked Frank a lot. But what Revere needs now more than ever is leadership, and that's something I can provide.' He poured himself another drink. 'I have the best investment track record at the firm. I think I'm the obvious choice.'

Just then, Shirley came in, carrying some grocery bags. 'Art, can you help me with these?' she called. Then she saw the whisky glass. 'Art!' she snapped.

'What?' His tone was angry. Belligerent.

'Art. We agreed.' Her voice was exasperated.

'Shirley, I'm just having a drink with my colleague here.'

She dropped the shopping, and grabbed the glass in his hand. She threw the whisky into a plant pot.

Art's face reddened. 'Don't do that,' he growled. His voice was low, sinister. His wife froze. There was something close to fear in her face.

She seemed to take a second to summon up her courage. 'Art. No more drink, OK?' She threw a quick glance at me.

'Don't worry. He's just going,' said Art, glaring at his wife.

'Can I help you with the shopping, Mrs Altschule?' I said.

'OK. That would be very kind.' She headed for the door. I followed her. Her car was parked in the driveway, the boot open.

'I'm sorry,' I said. 'He offered me a drink and I accepted.'

She sighed. 'It's not your fault. If he wants to drink he will.'

'When did the drinking start?'

'About a month ago. A bit before Frank died.'

'Do you know why?'

She looked at me hesitantly.

'I know Gil is planning to retire,' I said. 'Did he tell Art that Frank was going to take over the firm?'

She took a deep breath. 'Art's very ambitious. He's always assumed Gil's job would be his eventually. When Gil told him Frank would get the job, he felt badly let down. I've never seen Art so angry. He ranted on for an hour or so, and then left the house. He came back in a taxi at midnight, drunk.' She bit her lip. 'It was the first drop he'd touched for nearly ten years, since his partner killed himself. Once he started, he couldn't stop. It's not going to do anything for his chances.'

'But now Frank's dead, doesn't he think the job's his?'

'He says he does. But his confidence is shaken. He doesn't trust Gil any more.' She glanced at me sharply, as though she regretted what she had just said. 'My husband didn't kill Frank Cook,' she said icily. 'I know that. He was here with me all the time. And he might be violent sometimes, but he's not a murderer.' She looked me straight in the eyes. 'Now, help me carry these in.'

THE MONDAY MORNING meeting started on a positive note. Diane wanted to bring the Tetracom management in to present to the partnership that Wednesday. She warmed Gil up nicely. Art stayed suspiciously silent, ignoring me completely. Then we came to Net Cop.

I outlined the deal I had struck with Jeff Lieberman. Revere's holding would be diluted, but if Net Cop really did work as well as I hoped, we could still make a healthy profit on our original investment. Gil was pleased, and gave his blessing.

Then came the National Quilt Company. John explained that it was likely that the company would have to file for bankruptcy the following week.

'What?' said Gil, frowning. 'I didn't know we had a problem here. You're on the board, aren't you? Couldn't you see this coming?'

John shrugged. 'I guess I missed it.'

Gil turned to Art. 'This was your deal originally, Art. What went wrong?'

'It's difficult to tell,' said Art. 'Three months ago the company seemed stable. So I handed it to John. Since then the management seem to have gone off on some crazy strategy to put naked women on their bed covers. I guess that's what the trouble is.'

'What?' said Gil, turning to John. 'Is that true?'

'Uh. Yes,' said John. 'Or, at least, I mean . . .'

Gil's patience was wearing very thin. 'And you let them do it? Why, for God's sake?'

John panicked. He could have said that the build-up of inventory had been caused by purchasing decisions that were taken when Art was on the board. He could have said that he had tried to talk to Art but Art hadn't wanted to know. But he didn't. 'Sorry.'

Gil glowered at him. 'This is just the sort of company we cannot afford to lose. Especially now when we know that the Bieber Foundation is looking at what we do so closely.'

John cowered. These were strong words from Gil.

Gil turned to Art. 'I'd like you to see what you can salvage from this one.'

'Sure,' said Art. 'I'll see what I can do.'

'Well, I think that just about wraps it up,' said Gil, picking up his agenda. 'I think the meeting's over.'

AS SOON AS WE were back in our office I said to John, 'Why didn't you stand up for yourself in there? Art dropped you in it completely.'

John shrugged. 'Picking a fight with Art would only make it worse. There was nothing I could do.'

'You've got to stand up for yourself,' I said.

John shook his head and slumped back in his chair. 'I swear, I've got to get out of this job.'

'Hey, you can't give up just because one deal goes bad.'

'It's not just that,' said John. 'I've lost my taste for this place. I'm just not turned on by money like the rest of them.'

'What do you mean, not turned on by money? You've been to business school. You know it's the only thing that matters.'

John ignored my irony. 'That's what someone like Daniel might think. But not me. You know, my father has his grand plan for me. Business school, venture-capital experience, then I make my own millions. But since Frank . . .' John paused, suddenly finding it difficult to control his emotion. 'Since Frank was killed, I just wonder what's the point. I guess there comes a time when I'm just going to have to tell my father who I really am. Maybe that time is soon.'

I smiled with sympathy. A death can mean different things to different people. It was natural, I supposed, that Frank's sudden departure from this world should make John wonder what it was all for.

I called Craig to give him the good news about Net Cop and worked through till lunch. I was just finishing a bagel at my desk when in marched Mahoney, accompanied by two other detectives, and Gil, looking stern.

'Afternoon,' I said, as I chewed my last mouthful of bagel.

Mahoney didn't return my greeting. 'I'd like you to come with me to the DA's office and answer a few questions.'

'HAVE YOU EVER seen this before?' Mahoney was holding a silver-grey revolver.

With a heavy feeling in the pit of my stomach I said nothing.

We were in the DA's office in Salem, and this time I had exercised my right to have Gardner Phillips present. Mahoney had brought in reinforcements as well in the shape of Assistant District Attorney Pamela Leyser. She was a well-groomed blonde-haired woman in her late thirties, very crisp and businesslike. I shook her hand and smiled at her. She didn't smile back. Gardner Phillips had absolutely insisted that I say nothing. He was watching Mahoney like a hawk, looking for a slip-up in his questioning.

'It's a Smith and Wesson three fifty-seven Magnum. It was used to murder Frank Cook.'

No response.

'Do you know where we found it?'

Of course I did. But I made no response.

'It was in this plastic bag.' Mahoney held up a bedraggled Boots bag. 'Do you recognise it? I believe it comes from a British store.'

No answer.

'We found the bag with the gun in it in the Basin. Your wife threw it there, didn't she?'

Nothing.

'We have a witness who saw her running out of your street carrying something heavy in a plastic bag. We have another who saw her running back towards your house from the direction of the river, carrying nothing.'

Mahoney carried on, piling up the evidence against me. I wanted to tell him that he had got it all wrong. But I put my faith in Gardner Phillips and kept quiet. The Assistant District Attorney watched it all, unblinking. Although she said nothing, both Mahoney and Phillips seemed intensely aware of her presence.

Eventually the questioning ceased and I was led along a corridor. I still hadn't been arrested, and I was technically free to go, but Gardner Phillips wanted to have a few words with Pamela Leyser. I passed a small waiting area, and saw Lisa sitting there, a middle-aged man in a suit next to her.

'Lisa!'

She turned. She looked surprised to see me, but she didn't smile.

I moved towards her. 'Lisa—'

Gardner Phillips pulled me away. 'It's much the best thing if you say nothing to her. She's got a lawyer. I'll talk to him.'

I was put in an interview room while Phillips went off to talk to the Assistant DA. It took a while. I was scared. Shut in this room I could feel my liberty slipping away from me. Arrest could not be far away. And with it jail, a trial. And what if they found me guilty? I'd spend what was left of my youth, and presumably the better part of my middle age, in prison. Everything I'd aspired to, everything I'd lived for, would be gone.

Lisa was the one person I really needed to talk to about this, the one person on whom I had learned to rely. If I felt she was truly on my side, it would all be much more bearable.

Eventually Gardner Phillips returned.

'I've spoken with the Assistant DA,' he said. 'They don't have enough evidence to arrest you. But they are close. Very close. I've agreed that you'll voluntarily give them your passport.'

'Did you talk to Lisa's lawyer?'

'Yes. She's taken the Fifth Amendment, which means she has chosen to say nothing to avoid incriminating herself. Fortunately, she will also avoid incriminating you.'

'So what happens now?' I asked.

'The police will try to find more evidence against you. And believe me, they'll try hard.' He gave me a half-smile. 'I guess we'll be seeing a lot more of each other.'

I suddenly felt cold. 'I wish I could prove I didn't do it.'

'You don't need to. All we need to do is make sure there's a reasonable doubt that you're guilty.'

I stared out of the window. That's all, I thought. But a reasonable doubt wasn't good enough for me. I was innocent, and I needed everyone to know it. Lisa in particular.

AFTER LUNCH the next day, I told John I would be out at a meeting for the rest of the afternoon, and drove the Morgan out to Woodbridge.

Marsh House stood alone under a large sky of gathering rain clouds. A strong breeze from the sea was flattening the marsh grass, and rocking the trees behind the house. Everything was as it had been the day Lisa and I discovered Frank's body, except that the Mercedes had disappeared, presumably taken by the police.

I let myself in with Lisa's key. The house was cold and dead quiet. The air had a musty smell to it, and a thin layer of grey film covered some of the surfaces. Most of Frank's stuff was still there: books, magazines, photographs of Lisa and Eddie. His desk had been emptied. There were no papers left, no notebook or diary that might have given some clue of his thoughts before he died. Just a flower-patterned pencil box that Lisa had made for him when she was a girl.

I climbed the stairs. Out of Frank's bedroom window I could see the clouds thickening and darkening over the marsh. I tried to imagine what the house must have been like twenty years before, with the noise and bustle of a family on holiday. A small Lisa and a larger Eddie playing on the porch or returning from an afternoon's swimming along the walkway across the marsh. For the last fifteen years this had been Frank's sanctuary, the place where he liked to come alone as often as he could. Why had he given up his family? He loved his children. He seemed to at least like his wife. It was a mystery.

As I descended the narrow staircase, one of the pens that lay in the patterned pencil box caught my eye. I recognised it from somewhere. It was a maroon ball-point pen, with an acorn logo and the words OAKWOOD ANALYTICS embossed in gold lettering along its side. I turned it round in my fingers, trying to remember where I had seen the name before. But it wouldn't come.

I took one last look around, and left, driving up the dirt track back to the road. The clouds were upon me now, and it started to rain. Houses were scattered along the track, nestling among the trees. The majority were only occupied in summer. I wondered whether any of the occupants had seen anything the day Frank died.

The first two houses were empty, but the third showed signs of occupation. I braved the rain, and knocked.

The door was opened by a pleasant middle-aged woman, her grey-streaked hair pulled firmly back from her forehead. She reminded me of the doughty ladies you see in English rose gardens.

'Yes?' she said doubtfully.

'Hello. I'm Simon Ayot, Frank Cook's son-in-law. Did you know Frank Cook? He used to live in Marsh House.'

'Oh yes. Of course I knew him. Not well, mind you. That was an awful thing to happen to him. How terrible for you.'

I smiled. 'I wonder if I could ask you a couple of questions?'

'Of course. Get yourself out of the wet.'

She led me through to a living space with a view of the marsh.

'Coffee? I have some brewed.'

I accepted gratefully, and soon cupped my hands round a steaming mug. I sat down on an old sofa.

'My name's Nancy Bowman, by the way. How can I help you?'

'I wanted to ask you about the day of the murder. Whether you saw anyone strange hanging around.'

'The police asked me this,' she replied. 'As I told them, there was one strange man I saw a couple of times that weekend. He seemed to be some kind of photographer, or perhaps a birdwatcher. I saw him on the road out there, and down behind Marsh House. He seemed to be waiting for something. He had an expensive-looking camera.'

'What did he look like?'

'Young. In his thirties I should think. Short, but quite big, if you see what I mean. Not fat, just broad.'

'And what was he wearing?'

'A T-shirt and jeans. I remember thinking he must have been cold but he looked like a tough fellow.'

'Have you seen him before or since?'

'No, just that weekend.'

'I see. Did you see anyone else? Me, for instance?'

'No. Not that I can remember.'

I stood up. 'Thank you very much, Mrs Bowman. That's very helpful. And thanks for the coffee.'

I drove back to Boston. Nancy Bowman's description was unmistakable. Craig. He had been in Woodbridge the day Frank died. Craig knew Frank was opposed to further investment in Net Cop. I remembered that when I saw him just before Frank was killed, he had been smiling, as though he had found a solution to his problems. Could he have been dumb enough to have murdered Frank in the hope that Revere would change its mind about Net Cop? With a shudder I realised that it was conceivable. I knew how absolutely determined Craig was to make Net Cop succeed.

THAT EVENING I was sitting at home at the computer, idly scanning Chelsea Football Club's web pages, when I heard the key scrape in the door.

It was Lisa, and she looked angry.

I leapt to my feet, my rush of joy at seeing her again immediately tempered by her expression. 'Lisa!'

'Can you help me with some cartons?' she muttered.

'OK.' I followed her outside, where a man and a small truck waited. A dozen or so collapsable cardboard cartons lay on the sidewalk. I took half of them and Lisa took the other half.

'I take it you're not moving back in, then?' I said, tentatively.

'No I am not, Simon. I'm going back to California. Roger has offered me a job.' Roger was Roger Mettler, her old professor. He had been trying to entice her back to Stanford for years.

'California!' I felt a rush of panic. 'What about Boston Peptides?'

'Oh, don't pretend you don't know,' she spat.

'What do you mean? What's happened?'

'I've been fired, that's what's happened,' she said as she wrestled with the first of the cartons.

'No! I don't believe it! They need you, don't they? I mean you're responsible for BP 56.'

'Well that's not what Enema thinks. He says I don't fit into the BioOne way of doing things. Damn this thing!'

She was folding the flaps of the box together in the wrong order.

'Here, let me,' I said.

'Leave me alone!' she snapped.

I left her alone. 'What happened?'

'I asked too many questions about neuroxil-5.'

'What's wrong with it?'

She threw the half-constructed box to the floor. 'Simon, the drug stinks and BioOne stinks. Now let me pack and get out of here.'

'Lisa, sit down. Let's talk for a moment.'

She hesitated, then sat in a chair. Her face bore the stony expression of misery it had worn since just after Frank died. A tear ran down one cheek. She sniffed. I took hold of her hand and crouched beside her. 'Listen, Lisa. I love you. I want to help you. You must let me.'

Lisa didn't answer. She sat still and straight, the tears now streaming down her face. She wiped her nose with the back of her hand.

'I need the old you,' Lisa said, her voice trembling.

'But you've got me.'

Lisa shook her head. 'I don't know who I've got, Simon. I don't know whether you killed Dad. I don't know whether you used me to sell out my company and get me fired. I don't know whether you've been unfaithful to me. I don't know you at all. And it scares me.'

'Of course you know me, Lisa. I haven't changed. I love you, and you love me. Please stay.'

Lisa took a deep breath, fighting to regain control. 'If I stay here, I'll go crazy. I need to rebuild my own life, Simon. Now let me go. I'll come back and do all this tomorrow morning. Please make sure you're not here.'

Then she stood up, and she walked out.

THE NEXT MORNING I drove straight to Net Cop's offices in Wellesley.

Craig was pleased to see me. 'Hey, Simon! So they let you out?'

'Their evidence didn't stack up. But I'm not off the hook yet.'

'That's too bad. Hey, did you know we signed the deal with the Bloomfield Weiss guys yesterday?'

I shook my head. Craig's attention span for anything other than Net Cop was about ten seconds. I wasn't surprised. That was, after all, why I had backed him.

'That's good, Craig.'

'Yeah. We're starting on the prototype right away and—'

'Craig?' I interrupted. 'Do you mind if I ask you about something else for a moment?'

Craig looked a little annoyed, but he nodded. 'OK.'

'Were you on the marshes at Woodbridge the Saturday Frank Cook was murdered?'

'Oh,' said Craig.

I raised my eyebrows.

'Yeah. You could say I was. Did someone see me?'

I nodded. This next question was a difficult one to ask, but I had to ask it. 'Craig. Did you kill Frank?'

He paused. Breathed in through his nose. 'No,' he said at last.

'Well, what were you doing in Woodbridge?' I asked.

'That's a little difficult to explain.'

'So try. Look, Craig. I'm the one who's facing the murder charge here. I need to know.'

'OK.' He moved over to a locked filing cabinet in the corner of his office. He took out a brown manila envelope and handed it to me. Inside were a dozen or so black-and-white photographs. They were pictures of Frank with someone. A man. They weren't sexually explicit, but the nature of the relationship was obvious. In one they were holding hands. In another Frank's arm was round the other man's waist. The other man was John.

I now knew what the word 'gobsmacked' meant. But as I thought about it, the pictures made some kind of sense. They explained why Frank had left Lisa's mother, for a start. They explained why we hadn't heard of any other relationship since then. I now remembered where I had seen the Oakwood Analytics pen. On John's desk at Revere. I had used it to write his phone messages for him.

It had never occurred to me that Frank was gay. He didn't fit any of the gay stereotypes, except perhaps for a certain neatness in the way he dressed. John had kept his private life very private. He had a mythical 'girlfriend' back in Chicago. In fact, I remembered Lisa speculating a year or so ago that he might be gay. Only two days before, John had told me that maybe it was time to tell his father who he really was. Now I understood what he meant.

A host of questions leapt to my mind. How long had this relationship gone on? Was it serious? And then of course the most important question of all: Did this mean John had killed Frank?

'When did you take these?' I asked.

'The evening before Frank was killed. I followed him from Boston out to Woodbridge, and got them on the porch with a zoom lens.'

'And on the Saturday? Did you see him on the Saturday?'

'No. I came over about lunchtime. John's car wasn't there. Frank spent most of the time outside working on a boat. He had just gone inside when you came along.'

'So you saw me?'

Craig nodded. 'I saw you arrive, and then I left. I figured his boyfriend was unlikely to show up and do anything photogenic while you were there.'

'How did you know about Frank and John?'

'I intercepted Frank's email at home.'

'I didn't know you could do that.'

'I can,' replied Craig. 'He was getting these messages from some guy called John that showed they were very good friends. They were supposed to be spending the weekend in Woodbridge. So I thought I'd go up there and see if I could take any interesting photos.'

'To blackmail Frank with?'

'I just wanted him to give the go-ahead for Revere to put in the investment Revere owed us,' protested Craig.

'That's blackmail, Craig.'

'Look!' said Craig, his old anger returning. 'I had to do what I had to do.'

'No, you didn't. Oh, Jesus.' I ran my hand through my hair. 'Did you tell the police any of this?'

'No. I was sure it wouldn't look good to the cops.'

'But you knew I was in trouble. You could have helped me!'

Craig looked uncomfortable.

'I'm going,' I said. 'I'll keep these?' I held up the photos. 'You've got the negatives.' I put the photos back in their envelope, and moved towards the door.

'But, Simon. We need to talk about the prototype.'

'No, we don't, Craig. You can worry about Net Cop if you like. Personally, I need to prove I'm innocent.'

IT WAS NEARLY midday by the time I got back home. Lisa had already been and gone, taking her stuff with her. The apartment felt even emptier and lonelier than it had before. I pulled out the photos Craig had given me and looked at them again. What would Lisa make of this? Frank had deceived her for all these years, living a double life. His secret would be much harder to confront now that he was dead than it would have been when he was alive. Lisa's memory of him would be altered. I resolved to keep the photographs from her for as long as I could.

TETRACOM WERE MAKING their presentation that afternoon. I arrived at the office at three o'clock. Apart from John, who was at National Quilt, everyone was there: Gil, Art, Diane, Ravi, Daniel and me. Art had arrived late back from lunch, a glassy look in his eyes.

Bob Hecht and the Tetracom management were slick. The presentation was tailor-made for a venture capitalist's investment committee.

Afterwards, Diane thanked Bob and asked for questions. Gil asked an obscure question about purchasing power and lower margins, Ravi asked about threats from Far Eastern manufacturers. Good questions, answered well. Diane looked pleased. Daniel was just beginning to ask a question when he was interrupted by a low growl. We all looked towards Art, who was drawing lines along the bottom of his pad as if he was crossing something out.

Diane raised her eyebrows to encourage Daniel to continue speaking. Bob Hecht smiled towards Art. 'Yes, sir?'

'Huh?' said Art, looking up. His eyes, which had been dull before, now glinted dangerously in his red face.

'Do you have a question, sir?'

Art cleared his throat. 'Yes, I have a question. Why does a chickenshit company like yours have the gall to ask us for money?'

'Art!' snapped Gil. 'I'd appreciate it if you'd ask a more specific question.'

Art looked at Gil. Looked at Hecht again. Smiled. 'OK,' he said. 'How many venture-capital investors have you been to see?'

'You're the first,' replied Hecht immediately. 'We wanted to go to the best first.'

'The first since when?' asked Art. 'Isn't it true you went to a bunch of venture capitalists last year and they all turned you down?'

For less than a moment there was a brief flutter of panic on Hecht's handsome, sincere features. But we all saw it. 'It's true that last year we did have a couple of informal discussions with some VCs. Just to help with our planning.'

'And who were they?' Art demanded.

Hecht rattled off eight of the biggest names in venture capital. Diane's face reddened. She should have asked these questions.

'I see,' Art said. 'And why didn't you go back to these firms, Mr Hecht? Was it because you knew they wouldn't give you money in a thousand years?'

'No!' protested Hecht. He knew he was in danger of losing us. He sighed. 'There was another member of the team, then. I subsequently found out that he was the one the VCs didn't like.'

'Oh really? And what was his name?'

'Murray Redfearn.'

Art and Gil exchanged glances. So did Diane and I. It was clear that they had heard of him and we hadn't.

'Murray Redfearn was involved in a couple of spectacular disasters in the late eighties,' explained Gil. 'A lot of venture capitalists lost money on him.'

Hecht nodded. 'We only found all this out later. So we bought him out, developed the product further, and here we are.'

'You lied to Ms Zarrilli,' Art said.

'No, I didn't,' protested Hecht. He glanced towards Diane for help.

Diane paused. She had a fine line to tread. 'I didn't ask the question, Art,' she said, 'and I should have. But I must admit, Bob, it would have been nice if you had been more open with me on this.'

'Damn right,' said Art. 'Now why don't we tell these jerks to piss off and let us get back to work.'

Hecht reddened. One of his colleagues, the Chief Financial Officer, looked as though he was about to explode.

'Art!' snapped Gil. 'That's enough. Thank you, Mr Hecht,' he said. 'That was a most interesting presentation. Diane will be in touch with you very shortly.'

There was an awkward silence as Diane led the Tetracom team out to a conference room, where we had agreed they would wait for the committee's decision. Gil was red-faced, glowering at Art. He no doubt suspected Art was drunk. Diane returned in a moment.

'What do you want to do, Diane?' said Gil.

'First I should apologise,' she began. 'I should have asked the questions Art did. Thank you.' She smiled charmingly at him. He grunted. 'I still believe in the deal, though. I think it is a truly great opportunity that any other firm would be quick to snap up if they had the chance. So I'd like to ask for investment approval subject to checking out Bob Hecht's story. I think he's probably telling the truth. But it'll be easy to check with the other venture capitalists.'

'OK, let's take a vote. Ravi?'

Ravi took off his glasses, and began to polish them. 'Provided Hecht isn't hiding anything else, I think we should go ahead.'

'Art?' Gil turned to him warily.

'No way.' Art stared at his Managing Partner belligerently.

That was probably his biggest mistake. Gil was in a nervous frame of mind, and if Art had subtly played on that he might have succeeded in killing Diane's deal. But Gil would not tolerate open war among his people. 'We do the deal,' he said.

DIANE GAVE the Tetracom people the good news, and then gave Hecht a firm but polite roasting. Hecht seemed confident that Diane's checks wouldn't bring up any nasty surprises, and on that basis we started work on the term sheet.

We broke at nine for dinner. We went to Sonsie's, a chic restaurant on Newbury Street. Diane, with her mixture of charm and firmness, had Tetracom eating out of her hand.

We left at eleven. I was walking into the street to hail a cab when she caught me. 'Simon, I know it's late, but I'd like to go through those financial covenants again. Could you spare a half-hour to go over the numbers now? I'm sure it'll help us tomorrow.'

She was right. It would. I was tired and I wanted to go to bed, but Diane was the boss, this was a deal, and venture capitalists didn't go to bed early if there was work to be done on a live deal.

'OK,' I nodded, 'I'll get a cab.'

'No need to go all the way to the office,' said Diane. 'My apartment is just around the corner.'

I was too tired to argue. 'All right,' I said. 'Lead the way.'

It was, literally, around the corner. The electrician's daughter from New Jersey had done well. The furniture was either expensive and comfortable or expensive, antique and European. The art was expensive, modern and American. The whole thing was all very tastefully done, and very relaxing.

'Coffee?' she asked.

'Sure.'

While she fiddled about in the kitchen area, I pulled out my laptop and crunched some numbers. She returned with the coffee, kicked off her shoes and sat down next to me at the mahogany dining table. The legal documentation contained a set of financial ratios. If Tetracom's management broke them, they would be forced to hand over most of the company to us. Before morning, Diane and I had to sort out the level at which these ratios needed to be set.

In less than half an hour we'd cracked it. I leaned back on the chair, and rubbed my eyes. 'I'm knackered,' I sighed. 'Don't you ever get tired?' Diane looked as cool as she had several hours before.

'Sometimes. But the excitement of the deal keeps me going. Don't you find that?'

'No. Late-night deals send me to sleep. I think the Commonwealth of Massachusetts should pass a law that agreements negotiated after eight o'clock at night are invalid.'

She smiled, and sipped her coffee. She suddenly seemed to be sitting uncomfortably close to me. Or too comfortably close.

'Simon? Remember in Cincinnati when we talked about the firm?'

'Yes.'

'Well, things are developing. Can I get you a drink?'

'OK.' I was curious to hear what she had to say.

We moved through to the sitting-room area, and Diane produced a glass of Scotch for me, and a bourbon for her. We sat opposite each other. Safe. She tucked her long legs discreetly under her and leaned back in her armchair.

'Art was blasted today,' she said. 'And it wasn't the first time. The guy has suddenly dredged up a drink problem from somewhere. He's sliding downhill fast. Gil's worried.'

'Is he still planning to retire?'

'He'd like to. He's considering sending Art to a clinic.'

'But that won't solve anything. Art would be a disastrous Managing Partner of Revere. He was pretty awful before this. But with an alcohol problem? Gil might as well shut down Revere now.'

Diane gave a small smile. 'That's an interesting point of view.'

'Oh, come off it, Diane, it's obvious. You think that. I'll bet our investors think that.'

'As a matter of fact, they do,' she said, the smile playing on her lips.

I remembered Diane's breakfast at the Meridien. 'I get it. You've spoken to Gil and Lynette Mauer about this, haven't you? And other investors too, I'll bet?'

Diane did not respond.

'Get rid of Art, and make you Managing Partner? Will it work?'

Diane allowed herself a grin. 'Lynette is on board. Gil is wavering, but I'm working on him. But I'll need to build a team. I'll need to recruit an experienced venture capitalist at partner level. And then there's Ravi, and you. I need your help.'

'As a partner?'

'Yes. I'm sure you can handle it. I like the way you work. I believe you'll be very good at this game.'

My mind raced. I badly wanted to be a partner of Revere. But I was wary of corporate politics. Diane was trying to get me to support her against Art. That was OK. Against Gil wouldn't be.

'You're hesitating,' said Diane.

'Oh, sorry. It sounds a great opportunity. I was just thinking it through. I don't want to become involved in some coup against Gil. I owe that man a lot.'

'And he likes you too,' said Diane. 'Art is putting pressure on him to fire you. But Gil wants to keep you on.'

So Art wanted to get rid of me? Somehow I wasn't surprised.

'What about the police investigation?' I asked.

'I know you didn't kill Frank,' said Diane smiling. 'Eventually, so will everyone else. It will blow away.'

I was grateful. I had no right to expect such trust from her. 'Thank you. In that case, thanks for the offer. What do I have to do?'

'Not much for now. The main thing is, I need to know I can count on your support when I need it.'

'You've got it.'

She gave me a smile that warmed my tired body. 'I know this is none of my business, but how could your wife leave you when you are in so much trouble?'

I stuttered an excuse. 'She was under a lot of pressure. She thought I'd killed her father. I can understand what she did.'

It was all true, but as I was saying it I felt a surge of anger. Diane was right. Lisa should have stayed with me!

'You look miserable. Let me get you another drink.'

Lisa had pissed off to California; why shouldn't I have another?

Diane disappeared, and returned with another glass. Somehow she had put some music on, Mozart or something. She sat down next to me on the sofa.

'Cheers,' she said.

I swallowed my whisky.

'Relax, Simon. You need to relax.'

Slowly she leaned over and pulled at my tie, taking it off. She let her hand rest against my leg. Her scent flowed over me. I turned to look at her. Small delicate face, flawless skin, full lips slightly apart. She leaned over and kissed me. It was a soft gentle kiss, safe, yet promising much more. I responded. I wanted much more.

She stood up. 'Come on,' she said, slowly moving towards a closed door off the hallway.

I stood up, and began to follow her. Then the muzzy feeling of warm relaxation suddenly snapped.

'Look, I'm sorry, Diane. This isn't right. I've got to go. Now.'

I turned, grabbed my tie and searched for my jacket and briefcase.

Diane leaned against the wall, the smile still on her lips. 'Stay, Simon,' she said quietly. 'You know you want to. Stay.'

'I'm sorry. I just can't.' I found my stuff, and rushed for the door.

I was ten minutes late for the next morning's meeting. Everyone was as fresh as a daisy, except me. Diane treated me as though we hadn't been entwined on her sofa only a few hours before. I couldn't concentrate.

I hadn't been back at my desk for more than five minutes when my phone rang. It was Diane. She wanted to see me.

I entered her office with trepidation. But she gave me a friendly smile, and immediately launched into a discussion about Tetracom. Gil had made two calls that morning to venture capitalists who backed up Hecht's story. The remaining calls were to the West Coast, and they would have to wait a couple of hours, but Diane was now confident that Tetracom's cupboard was bare of skeletons. A deal was probably less than a week away.

Our conversation finished, I stood up to go. I was almost out of there, when Diane stopped me. 'Simon? About last night.'

'Um . . .'

She held up her hand. 'No, it's OK, I don't want to talk about it now. But why don't you buy me a drink some time?'

'I'm not sure that's a good idea,' I said.

'Oh, come on,' she said. 'You owe me at least that.'

She was right. I smiled quickly. 'Yes, of course.'

'Good. Friday?'

'Fine.'

I returned to my desk wondering what Diane was up to, what she wanted. How would she take me pulling back? Perhaps it would harm my chances of making partner in the new regime? Well, if it did, that was just tough. I had been wrong to go as far as I had with her, and I would never, ever let anything like that happen again.

'What's up, Simon?'

It was Daniel, looking at me with extreme curiosity. 'Don't ask,' I replied. I glanced over to John's empty desk. There was a lot I needed to talk to him about. 'Where's John?'

'Out at National Quilt all day,' Daniel answered.

I checked my emails. There was one from Connie saying I was invited to Gil's club for a drink at seven that evening.

THE DEVONSHIRE CLUB bar was small and cosy, with red leather upholstery. I was tucking into a beer and a huge array of crisps and nuts on the small table in front of me when Gil arrived exactly ten minutes late. He shook my hand, sat down and caught the waiter's eye for a martini.

'Thanks for coming, Simon,' he said. 'How are you holding up?'

'OK, I suppose.'

'Simon, I wanted to talk to you about the future of the partnership. You may have heard, I'm planning to pull back from my involvement in Revere.'

'I had guessed that.'

'It's a small place. Word gets around. Now, obviously I want to leave the firm in as good shape as I can. But with my departure there arises the question of succession.'

This was getting interesting. 'I see.'

'My intentions would have been for Art to take over from me. Now Frank has passed away, he is the most senior partner, but he hasn't been well recently. I'm not sure whether he will be up to the job. Which leaves two choices.' He paused to sip his martini.

Two? I thought there was only one.

'Diane,' Gil went on, 'or a senior venture capitalist from outside.'

That was an eventuality Diane hadn't considered, I thought, or at least not one she had discussed with me.

'I don't want Revere to blow apart once I leave, so I'd like you to give me your word that you will continue to work under whomever succeeds me. You're a good man, Simon. The firm needs you.'

I had as good as promised Diane I would pledge my support to her. Now what could I say?

'Can't you stay on a bit until all this becomes clearer?' I asked.

'In theory I could. But my kidneys are in a bad way. I'll be on dialysis soon, my doctors tell me.'

'Oh, no! How soon?'

'It could be six months or it could be six years. Whatever it is, I want to enjoy my last few years of mobility. So I need to sort out Revere now. So, will you promise to stay no matter who becomes Managing Partner? At least until he, or she, settles in?'

I owed Gil. I didn't really owe Diane. 'Yes, Gil, I will,' I said.

I WENT STRAIGHT from the Devonshire to John's apartment. He lived in the South End, in an apartment in a three-storey terraced house next door to a gallery and a real estate agency.

He was surprised to see me, but let me in. He had changed out of his work clothes into jeans and a loose cotton shirt, which hung outside his trousers. His apartment was nicely if minimally decorated. A wooden floor, a glass table, some attractive modern lamps and bowls.

We sat down. He offered me a beer, which I accepted, and then opened one himself.

'What a shit day,' he said. 'Why can't we let companies die quickly?' He took a swig of his beer. 'So. What are you doing here?'

'I wanted to ask you about something a little . . . awkward.'

John stiffened. 'What?'

'A photographer gave me these.' I passed him the envelope. He opened it, and took out the prints. His face froze.

'So?' he said, blinking.

'I'm trying to find out who killed him.'

John let his face fall into his hands. I watched in silence. Eventually, he looked up. 'I don't know,' he said. 'I loved him. We had a fight the night before he died. The last time I saw him was when I stormed out that Saturday at one o'clock in the morning. I just wish I could have left him on better terms.'

'I'm sorry.'

'It's been awful,' said John. 'The worst part about it is I haven't been able to talk about it with anyone. Or at least anyone who knew Frank.' He was desperately trying to hold back the tears.

'What was the argument about?' I asked gently.

'Oh, I'd been seeing other men. Frank didn't like it. None of them meant anything. It was just casual. But he didn't understand. I was Frank's only lover. I don't think he really admitted to himself that he was gay until he met me. He was very uptight about it.'

'Wasn't that why his marriage broke up?' I asked.

'Eventually Frank admitted that that was the reason, but he didn't realise it at the time. He just thought he had no sexual interest in his wife any more. I was good for him, Simon,' John said simply. 'I made him realise who he really was.'

'The police think I murdered him,' I said. 'But they're wrong. I just need to prove that. I know Frank meant a lot to you. You can help me find out who killed him.'

John looked at me doubtfully.

'At least answer my questions. It can't do any harm, and it may help.'

'OK,' John agreed reluctantly.

'Was there anything Frank was worried about before he died?'

'Yes, a whole bunch of stuff. He was under a lot of pressure. He wasn't taking it very well.'

'What sort of pressure?'

'He was convinced you were having an affair with Diane. He asked me about it. I said I didn't know, but it was clear you two got on awfully well, and you were working a lot together.'

'He gave me a hard time over that,' I said. 'He seemed to be going a bit over the top.'

'I thought so, too. But you know how much he doted on Lisa. And then of course he and I had that big fight. I never saw him again after that.' John flinched, struggling to maintain control. 'He called me the next day, but we didn't resolve anything. Then when I called him back, there was no reply.'

'I'm sorry,' I said. 'What about Revere?'

John took in a deep breath. 'There was something there that was bugging him, too. I don't know what it was. We tried not to talk about Revere and the people there too much.'

'I'm amazed the police didn't find out about you and Frank.'

'They did. They found my fingerprints at Marsh House. I said I'd been there working on deals with Frank. But when the cops interviewed my neighbours, they soon realised we had been together here. Plus they checked Frank's computer and found emails that made the situation pretty clear.'

'So didn't that make you a suspect?'

John nodded. 'For a day or so. But a neighbour had seen me here the afternoon Frank was killed, and I went out with some friends in the evening. So, after a while they gave up on me, and started asking about you. I did say that there had been some tension between you and Frank in recent months. They asked if you had ever threatened him, and I said absolutely not.'

'I suppose I should thank you.'

John shrugged. 'I was only telling the truth.'

'But now they know he was gay, can't they investigate that angle? Another gay lover, or something.'

'I was the only man Frank was with,' John snapped. 'I told the police I was sure of that.'

I sighed. Far from my discovery pointing suspicion away from me, somehow it only seemed to reinforce what Mahoney already believed.

'John, if you think of anything that might help me discover who killed Frank, can you let me know?'

'All right. I will.'

THE NEXT DAY at work Mahoney came in, set up camp in Frank's office for the morning, and seemed to be interviewing everyone but me. John and Daniel each took their turn. I walked past a couple of times and saw two of Mahoney's assistants going through piles of Frank's files. I wondered what else he had discovered that I didn't know about. Mahoney was doing better than me. I was stuck.

Daniel came back into the office. He had been with Mahoney for about half an hour.

'What did he say?' I asked.

He smiled at me. 'He told me not to tell you.'

'Come on, Daniel.'

'OK. He asked lots of questions about you. And Frank. Nothing specific. He was just fishing. He went through deals you had done together. Net Cop, that kind of thing.'

Interesting. If he was checking out Net Cop, I wondered how long it would take him to link Nancy Bowman's description to Craig.

I couldn't stand working at my desk, knowing that down the corridor Mahoney was asking everyone questions about me, so I decided to get the train to Wellesley and visit Net Cop.

The place was buzzing. After so much uncertainty, the engineers now felt confident their designs would actually take shape. In fact, we needed to hire more engineers to oversee the assembly and testing. Craig already had people in mind, but they had to be persuaded to jump from their existing lucrative posts. I joined Craig in the sales job. It was fun. I really did feel part of Net Cop.

We were in Craig's office late in the afternoon, when Gina popped her head in. 'There's a Sergeant Mahoney here to see you.'

'I'll be with him in a minute,' Craig said. Then he turned to me and raised his eyebrows. 'What shall I tell him?'

'He knows about Frank and John Chalfont. John told me.'

'Shit. Oh, I forgot to tell you. Mahoney was an active contributor to NORAID. Still is, for all my dad knows.'

I frowned, but I wasn't surprised. NORAID had been raising funds for the IRA for years. A supporter was unlikely to have warm feelings towards a British soldier who had served in Northern Ireland. 'Good luck,' I said.

'Thanks. You'd better go get yourself a cup of coffee.'

I left Craig's office and stalked off to find someone to play table tennis with. The Net Cop company facilities included a bare room which housed a table-tennis table. I lost three straight games. These coders were bloody good. And my concentration was poor. I wondered what Craig and Mahoney were talking about. Had Mahoney and his men found anything else that would incriminate me? It wouldn't take much more to get me arrested.

Eventually I heard the sounds of Mahoney leaving. Craig came looking for me, and led me back to his office.

'Well, he did ask if I was the person with the camera seen down by the marsh. I told him I was. I said I was following Frank because he'd turned down Net Cop and I hoped I might find something to use as leverage. He made me go through my story backwards and forwards. I told him the same thing every time.'

'Did you say you saw me?'

'Yes. He liked that bit.'

I smiled grimly. 'Did he ask for the photos?'

'Yep. I gave him the negatives.'

'Was there one of me?'

'Of course. I got a picture of you arriving.'

'But not leaving?'

'As I said, I left right after you arrived.'

'Great.'

I WAITED for Diane at Sonsie's bar with trepidation. I had considered cancelling, but there was no point. Diane had to be faced some time.

'Hi,' she said, kissing me on the cheek. Her scent reminded me of her apartment, the music, the whisky, her.

'Hi.' My throat was tight.

I ordered her a beer to go with mine. She seemed relaxed and confident in a bright blue suit with a tight short skirt. I didn't feel relaxed and confident at all.

'How have you been?' she asked.

'Busy. Running around trying to find out who killed Frank. The more I find out, the more questions there are unanswered.'

Diane touched my hand. It sent a shock through my whole body. 'You've had a tough time. Has Lisa come back?'

'No,' I said, pulling my hand away. 'But I really wish she would. I miss her.' I took a deep breath. 'I want Lisa back very badly. I'm sorry about the other night. I almost did something I didn't want to do. No, no, that's not right, I wanted to do it at the time. I mean, something I shouldn't have even started. And I'm not going to make the same mistake again.'

For a long moment Diane remained still. Then she spoke in a low, reasonable voice. 'I guess that says it. But if Lisa's stupid enough to let you go, she has only herself to blame. I like you, Simon. I think we could be good together. Just remember that.'

I didn't know whether Diane was putting a brave face on her rejection, or whether she didn't care one way or the other. That was the trouble with Diane. You never really knew.

'So, what are we going to do about Revere?' she asked. 'Lynette Mauer has told me she'll continue to invest in Revere, as long as I'm in charge.'

'Well done,' I said. 'Gil took me for a drink at his club last night. He wanted me to promise I would back whoever took over, whether it's you or someone else. He seemed to have discounted Art.'

Diane's eyebrows shot up. 'Someone else?'

'Yes. He's talking about perhaps getting in an experienced venture capitalist from outside to take over the firm.'

Diane frowned. 'Hmm.'

We finished our beers in silence as Diane's brain whirred. I was thinking about how much I could trust her. I really didn't know.

We left the bar, and Diane set off on foot back to her apartment, while I grabbed a passing cab. When I arrived home the answering machine was winking.

One message. 'Hi, Simon, it's John. I think I've got something on BioOne you might find interesting. Can you come round to my place tomorrow evening, and we can talk about it? Say about eight?'

I ARRIVED at John's building in the South End a little early. I buzzed his apartment number at the entrance to the building, but there was no reply.

It was cold, and I tried to go in the gallery next door, but they were just locking up. Then the door to John's building swung open, and a man came out. He was thin with close-cropped dyed blond hair. A diamond stud gleamed in his ear. I walked past him, and climbed the stairs to John's apartment, to wait for him there.

John's door was ajar. Wondering why he hadn't answered the buzzer, I pushed the door open. 'John?'

I walked in.

'John!' He was lying face down on the floor in the middle of his living room, a blood-soaked hole high in his back.

I rushed over to him. His face was pressed against the floor, a pool of blood near his mouth. His eyes were staring dully at nothing. Stupidly, I felt his neck for a pulse, desperately asking myself whether I should try mouth-to-mouth or CPR. There was no point. His neck was still warm, but he was very dead. I dropped to my knees next to him, closed my eyes, and put my face in my hands.

I heard a noise behind me, and spun round. A black woman in a tight dress stood in the doorway. She saw me, and screamed.

'He's dead,' I said. 'Call the police.'

She nodded and rushed from the apartment.

Within the next half-hour, a stream of other people arrived. One of them, a detective named Sergeant Cole, asked me questions about how I'd found the body, and then asked me to wait in the tiny hallway downstairs. A uniformed policeman stood next to me. After a while, Cole came down the stairs again. He was small, with a young face, but greying hair. He asked me to come to the station with him so he could take a full statement, and we drove off together in an unmarked car.

Within a couple of minutes we reached the police station, and I was led to an interview room. Cole joined me with another detective. They were both businesslike but friendly.

'Mr Ayot, do you mind answering a few questions?'

'Not at all,' I said.

Cole reached for a card from his wallet and began to read from it. 'You have the absolute right to remain silent. Anything you say can and will be used against you in a court of law.'

This took me aback. 'Hey, you don't suspect me, do you? I can explain what happened,' I protested.

Cole raised his hand in a placating gesture. 'That's great. But before you do, I need you to tell me you understand your rights. Now are you willing to talk to me?'

I knew Gardner Phillips would advise me to say nothing. But I was sick of being the cops' favourite suspect. It seemed to me best to tell them what had really happened so they could leave me alone.

'OK,' I said. 'Go ahead.'

Cole asked me to go through how I knew John, how I had entered the building, whether I had noticed anything. He took down details of my description of the man who had let me into the building. With a shiver, I realised this could have been John's murderer.

'And you were going to meet Mr Chalfont for what? Dinner?'

'No. He said he wanted to talk to me about something to do with work. He asked me to come round at eight.'

Cole had caught something in what I had said. A slight hesitation, perhaps. 'Something to do with work? What exactly?'

I took a deep breath. They would find out sooner or later, so I explained to Cole about Frank's murder. Cole's interest was quickened. His colleague was scribbling furiously.

When I'd finished, Cole smiled. 'Thank you very much, Mr Ayot. We'll just type this up, and then you can sign it.'

They left me in the interview room: badly lit, bare walls, bare table, uncomfortable chair, and a smell of urine and disinfectant.

I waited. An hour went by. I began to get impatient. The guy must type at five words a minute! I asked a cop in the corridor outside what was happening, and he promised to get back to me.

Finally, the door opened. Cole came in clutching some neatly typed sheets of paper. Following him was a shambling form I recognised instantly.

'Great to see you again, Mr Ayot,' Mahoney said, his eyes twinkling. He sat down opposite me. 'We'd like to ask you some more about your relationship with John Chalfont.'

I was tired, and I wanted to get out of there. 'OK,' I said.

'Did you know that Frank Cook and John Chalfont had a homosexual relationship?'

'Yes.'

'How long have you known that?'

'Three days.'

'Did you discuss this knowledge with John Chalfont?'

'Yes. On Thursday evening. At his apartment.'

'What did you talk about?'

'I asked him whether he had killed Frank. He said he hadn't. He talked about what he felt for Frank and I asked him whether he had any clue as to who might have murdered him.'

'And did he have any ideas?'

'Not then. But he did leave a message on my answering machine yesterday night that he had found out something interesting about BioOne. That's why I went to see him.'

'I see. Can you let us have the tape from the machine?'

I shrugged. 'OK.'

'Thank you. Have you any idea what he might have found out?'

'No.'

'There was no sign that anyone broke into the apartment. We think it's likely the murderer was someone he knew. Like it was with Frank Cook.' Mahoney paused. 'Mr Ayot, did you shoot John Chalfont?'

I looked Mahoney straight in the eye. 'No, I didn't.' I thought for a moment. 'What about the man I saw leave the building?'

'He lives there. He was just going out for the evening. Mr Ayot, did John Chalfont suggest that he had found something that could implicate you in the murder of Frank Cook?'

'No!' I replied. I turned to Cole. 'I want to speak to my lawyer.'

A spark of irritation flared in Mahoney's eyes. 'We'll talk later,' he said, and left the room.

It took a while to track down Gardner Phillips. He was at his weekend house somewhere or other. I finally got through to him. As expected, he told me to keep quiet until he got there. Which took two hours, spent alone in the poxy interview room.

As I waited for Phillips, I began to panic that I would never see freedom again. If they didn't get me for one murder, now it looked like they'd get me for the other.

Phillips arrived at last. I was hugely relieved to see him.

I quickly explained what had happened. 'Are they going to let me out?' I asked when I had finished.

'You bet they are.' He looked angry. 'They haven't arrested you because they don't have any evidence. And it just makes no sense that you would have shot John Chalfont and then waited there for the cops. There's nothing to stop you from leaving right away. I'll go and talk to them.'

He was back twenty minutes later. 'OK, let's go.'

I smiled. 'Thanks.'

Phillips's voice became stern. 'You know you shouldn't have spoken to them at all.'

I sighed. 'I suppose not. Sorry.'

He drove me back to my apartment, dropped me off, and took the tape from my answering machine away with him to give to the police.

I went straight for the shower, trying to wash off the evening in the police station. It was only then that the full significance of John's murder really sank in. It seemed so unfair. He was the archetypal nice guy, friendly to everyone. I would miss him. I saw again those dull blue eyes, the pale face, the trickle of blood. A cold feeling of revulsion and fear crept over me. Like Mahoney, I was sure that the two murders were connected. And, like Mahoney, I suspected I might be close to the connection. But I didn't know how. For the first time I sensed that my own life was in danger.

Monday morning was horrible. The meeting was short. Gil, looking exhausted, said a few words about John's death. Everyone was stunned. I left the office as soon as I could, I had work to do.

I took the 'T' to Central in Cambridge, and walked the few blocks to Boston Peptides.

I asked for Henry Chan and he was with me in a moment.

'Hello, Simon. How are you? What can I do for you?'

He had a huge moon face with very large square glasses, and eyes that always seemed surprised. He had been born in Korea and educated at the best universities the East Coast had to offer. He had tempted Lisa out of Stanford to join him at Boston Peptides, and since then had acted as a kindly, but quietly demanding, mentor. He was dressed in a white coat, and underneath it a shirt and tie.

'Can you spare me a few minutes, Henry?'

'It's about Lisa, I take it,' he said. 'Come through.'

He led me rapidly down the corridor towards his office, a small box filled with paper, computer equipment and a desk and two chairs. I sat in one and he sat in the other.

'I hear Lisa's left you. I'm sorry.'

'I also hear she's left you. Or rather you dumped her. Why did you do that? Didn't she do the important work on BP 56?'

Henry sighed. 'Your wife is a very intelligent woman. She made a tremendous contribution here.' He hesitated. 'BioOne is a very different company from Boston Peptides. She wasn't going to fit in. That became obvious. There was nothing I could do.'

'Henry! You were her boss. Why didn't you stand up for her? You could have gone too.'

Henry Chan took off his glasses and slowly rubbed his eyes. 'I did seriously consider resigning. But the thing is, Boston Peptides is everything to me. I've devoted my academic career to it. My house is mortgaged to the rafters for it. And with BioOne's support, I believe I can make something of it. When BioOne took us over we both had a choice: we could either fight them and lose, or stick with them and make something out of our technology. Lisa decided to fight. I decided to stick it out. Believe me, I don't like the way they do things any more than Lisa does.'

'What is it Lisa didn't like?' I asked.

'I'm sorry, Simon. Remember I work for BioOne now.'

'You've heard about Lisa's father's murder?'

Henry nodded, a slow downward movement of his huge head.

'I'm sure you also know that I'm the principal suspect?'

Another nod.

'I'm trying to prove my innocence, not just to the police, but also to Lisa. I need to get her back. Well, now someone else at Revere has been killed. And I think the connection between the two murders might have something to do with BioOne.'

Henry looked at me thoughtfully. 'OK. But what I tell you doesn't go any further than this room, and you mustn't name me as your source, whoever you talk to.'

'All right. Tell me a bit about what's wrong with BioOne.'

Henry paused. 'I think what Lisa and I both find most difficult is the secrecy. You see, in an ideal world scientists would share their discoveries with their peers as and when they make them. That way the scientific world as a whole can progress much faster than any one scientist working in isolation. But people are constantly afraid that someone else will steal their ideas. Once you start talking about companies with stock prices, then openness of information becomes even more difficult to achieve.'

'But all biotech companies must be secretive,' I said.

'That's true to some extent. Although at Boston Peptides we don't make a big issue of it. We're all here to find a treatment for Parkinson's disease, and if we can help other scientists without harming the prospects for our own projects, we will. BioOne is different. Their whole culture is permeated with secrecy. It's extraordinary. There are dozens of scientists working in different groups who are allowed no contact with one another. All their research results are passed to the centre, and they are only made available to others in the company on a need-to-know basis. It creates an atmosphere of competition and insecurity that produces results. But most of all, it concentrates all the power in the centre, with Thomas Enever.'

'What about Jerry Peterson, the chairman?'

'He has no idea what's really going on. Neither does your man, Art Altschule.'

'But surely some things must be made public? The company is quoted after all. And doesn't the Food and Drug Administration need data from the clinical trials?'

'Oh yes. The FDA needs truckloads of information. But most of that comes from the Clinical Trials Unit. They report directly to Enever and no one else.'

'What's this Enever like? I've only met him briefly. Lisa said he got caught fiddling some experiment results a few years ago.'

'That was never proved,' Henry replied. 'He published some research showing that neuroxil-3, an early form of neuroxil-5, might reduce the production of free radicals in the brains of patients with Alzheimer's. Other scientists couldn't reproduce the results, and a year later Enever was forced to publish a retraction. But Enever was never shown to have actually manipulated the data. I think he succumbed to the oldest temptation for any scientist: wanting a certain result so badly that he fails to notice contradictory data.'

'How did Lisa get herself fired?'

'She badgered Enever into letting her look at some of the research data for neuroxil-5, to see whether it could be used to treat Parkinson's. Then she had some questions about the data. You know what Lisa's like; she doesn't stop until she has the answers she wants. I tried to tell her to give up on it, but she wouldn't listen.'

'And what specifically was she worried about?'

'Look, Simon,' said Henry, looking at me carefully. 'You know I can't tell you anything that isn't publicly available. Especially if it is only unsubstantiated guesses.'

'So you think Lisa's concerns were nothing more than that?'

'Lisa had tremendous intuition. But sometimes she forgot she was a scientist. If you test the hypothesis, and find the scientific data doesn't substantiate it, then it's nothing more than speculation.'

'And the data didn't support her hypothesis?' I asked.

'Not in my opinion, no,' said Henry. 'Simon, I don't think Lisa would ever have got used to things here. She's gone to an excellent post. I'm convinced she'll be much happier there.'

Henry's eyes blinked behind his large glasses as I said goodbye and stood up to go. I wasn't a scientist but I trusted Lisa's intuition. As I walked back past her old lab, I pushed open the door and looked in. Half a dozen scientists were working in there. One of them was Kelly. She rushed up to me.

'Simon, will you get out of here! If someone recognises you we'll be in big trouble.'

'OK, OK,' I said as she propelled me down the corridor. 'Kelly, do you know where Lisa's staying?'

'Yes. But I'm not telling you where. Now get out!'

'Kelly, I've got to talk to you.'

'No you don't,' she said. 'Now please go.'

I WAITED FOR HER on the corner of Massachusetts Avenue and Boston Peptides' street, near the deli where I knew Lisa usually bought her lunch. It was a bit of a long shot. I had no idea whether Kelly frequented the same place. I stood there and read the *Globe*. Then I read the *Wall Street Journal*. Then a three-day-old *Daily Mirror*. I was just debating whether to buy *Business Week* when I saw her.

'Kelly!'

'Simon! I thought I told you to beat it.'

'You did. But I want to talk to you.'

'Simon, you are very bad news. Someone might see us.'

'OK,' I said, and grabbed hold of her arm. I steered her down a narrow alley and away from the busy street. 'They won't see us now.'

Kelly leaned back against a brick wall. 'I can't talk to you.'

'At least tell me how Lisa is,' I said. 'I'm worried.'

'You should be.' Kelly's eyes were hard. 'The poor woman's a mess. And from what I hear, you made her that way.'

Anger and frustration flooded through me. 'Kelly, I didn't kill her father. I didn't get her fired.' I tried to regain my composure. 'Kelly, she's got it all wrong. And I have to show her that.'

Kelly was listening, watching me suspiciously.

'I think her father's death had something to do with BioOne,' I continued. 'Something to do with whatever Lisa was asking questions about. You have to help me find out what that something was.'

'No way,' said Kelly. She turned and walked out of the alleyway. 'You're not getting me into trouble too.'

'Kelly. At least tell me where Lisa is staying.'

'If she wants you to know where she's living, she'll tell you. Now beat it or I'll scream. And I can scream.'

Kelly was serious. I gave up.

I RETURNED to the office.

John's desk looked strangely tidy. Empty.

Daniel followed my glance. 'The cops have been all over it. They took a ton of documents away. There's been pandemonium here. Gil is furious. I think he's just as angry about John and Frank having an affair as about John getting killed. Art went off for lunch and hasn't been seen since, and Ravi looks like a scared rabbit. Only Diane is keeping cool. And me of course.'

'Of course.'

'I mean, people are frightened. First Frank, then John. It could be any one of us next. Actually, it will probably be you.'

'Thanks a lot, Daniel. That possibility hadn't escaped me.'

'Be careful, Simon.' Daniel's tone was serious, for once.

'There's not a lot I can do,' I said. 'But can you do me a favour? Can you find out some stuff about BioOne for me?'

'BioOne? What's that got to do with anything?'

'I'm not sure. You know Lisa was fired from Boston Peptides?'

'Yeah. Art told me. Tell her I'm sorry when you see her.'

'That's unlikely,' I said. 'She's gone back to California.'

'Oh,' said Daniel. 'Not good.'

'Not good at all,' I agreed. 'Anyway, she was fired for asking awkward questions about BioOne's wonder drug.' I leaned forward. 'John phoned me before he died. He left a message. Said he had found out something about BioOne that might interest me. But I never got a chance to talk to him. Is there anything funny going on there? Something wrong with neuroxil-5, perhaps?'

'I don't think so,' answered Daniel. 'Everyone I come across seems to think the drug is working very well in the clinical trials. But I'm no biotech expert. I just do the number-crunching, remember.' Daniel paused. 'I can poke around discreetly if you like.'

I smiled thankfully. 'That would be great, Daniel.'

ART'S DOOR WAS OPEN. I knocked. He was back from lunch. A faint smell of alcohol hung in the room.

'What can I do for you, Simon?' He looked at his watch. 'I've got a few calls to make.'

'It won't take long. I just wanted to ask you about BioOne. I wondered if you could tell me what's wrong with neuroxil-5?'

Art frowned. 'Nothing. All the trial results so far have been excellent, and we are expecting great things when the Phase Three trial results are published. I checked with Dr Enever last month, when Frank talked to me. There is nothing wrong with neuroxil-5.'

'Frank asked you about neuroxil-5? What did he ask?'

Art looked as though he regretted mentioning it. 'Same as you. Was there anything wrong with the drug.'

'Have you told the police this?'

'No. Why?'

'Didn't you think it was suspicious?' I asked. 'Frank asked you a question casting doubt on Revere's most important investment, and shortly afterwards he was murdered.'

Art shook his head. 'No, Simon, I saw no reason to be suspicious. Frank was playing political games. Revere is what it is today because of BioOne. My investment. Frank wanted to discredit me, and so he went for my investment. Trouble was, he had no evidence. And let me tell you something. BioOne is at a very delicate stage right now. The last thing it needs is someone like you going around asking difficult questions.' He jabbed a finger at me angrily. 'If you go suggesting to anyone that there is something wrong with neuroxil-5, by the time I'm done with you, you'll wish you were still prancing around on ponies at the Queen's tea parties.'

'No, Art. If there is something wrong with neuroxil-5, I'll find it. And you won't be able to stop me.'

I left him standing at his desk red-faced and shaking and made my way back to my office deep in thought.

Gil passed me in the corridor. He nodded to me curtly.

On impulse, I stopped him. 'Gil? Do you have a moment?'

'Hm.' His eyes focused on me. 'What is it?'

'Are you confident about BioOne?'

Gil looked surprised. 'Why do you ask?'

'It was just something John was worried about before he died. Are you sure everything really is as solid as it seems?'

'Yes, I guess I am. That's not to say there won't be hitches, there always are. But BioOne is a big winner.'

'The company has never made a profit. It's only real asset is neuroxil-5. What if there were something wrong with the drug. BioOne would be worth nothing, wouldn't it?'

Gil smiled tiredly. 'You're right to be cautious, especially with biotech. There are dozens of biotech companies whose drugs have been shown to be no better than a pill made of sugar. But I have a good feeling about BioOne.'

He headed off back to his office and his problems, and I to mine. But I wasn't convinced. If only I knew what Lisa had discovered. How could I uncover the problem with neuroxil-5 myself?

An answer came to me.

I TOOK THE TRAIN out to Brookline, found Aunt Zoë's house and rang the bell. She answered in a moment with a warm smile.

'How nice to see you. Come in, come in.' She called into the recesses of the house. 'Carl! We have a visitor!'

Carl bustled into the hallway. 'Simon!' he said. 'How's Lisa?'

'Fine,' I lied.

The last time I had seen the living room, it had been crowded with Frank's mourners. Looking at Zoë now, I could see a resemblance to her brother: she was tall, long-limbed, with the same kindly hazel eyes. There was something warm and approachable about her. I saw why she was Lisa's favourite aunt.

Zoë made us all coffee, and I indulged in small talk with the two of them. I said Lisa was in California doing some research work, and left it at that. Zoë seemed to have no problems following the conversation. Apart from her initial well-disguised confusion over who I was, there was no sign that her brain was steadily decaying.

After a few minutes I steered the conversation round to the purpose of my visit. 'You remember my firm backed BioOne, the company that makes neuroxil-5?' I began. 'I wondered if Zoë has noticed any problems since she started taking it?'

'I don't think so, do you, dear?' said Carl, turning to Zoë.

'No,' she said. 'The hospital haven't come across anything out of the ordinary. Ever since Lisa called, I've been keeping a good look out for any problems, but I feel fine. And the good news is that I don't seem to be getting any worse up here.' She tapped her temple.

'That is good news,' I said. 'You said Lisa called you?'

'Yes,' said Carl. 'She said she wasn't sure, but she was worried that neuroxil-5 could have some dangerous side effect. She said she couldn't be specific. Zoë and I talked it over with our doctor, and we decided that we'd carry on with the drug. The doctor assured us that the FDA monitors these trials very thoroughly.'

'Do you know what this side effect might be, Simon?' Zoë asked, a brief look of worry crossing her face.

I paused, pondering how to answer. 'No. Sorry. It's just a suspicion from things I've seen at work.'

Zoë turned to Carl. 'Maybe I should stop taking the stuff?'

Carl took his wife's hands. 'When Frank introduced you to this drug, it gave us some hope. I don't want to give up on that hope. Sure, it might be dangerous. But it's the best shot we've got.'

Zoë looked at her husband and turned to me. 'Carl's right. But you will let us know if you discover anything more, won't you?'

I promised I would, and left.

DEEP IN THOUGHT as I walked home that evening, I turned off Charles Street into the warren of little tree-lined roads that make up the 'flat' of Beacon Hill. I turned the corner onto my short street and slowed to reach for my keys in my trouser pocket. I fumbled and dropped them. I bent down to pick them up.

At that moment, I heard a crack, crack, crack to my right, and the thud of brickwork shattering above my head. The fragments of brick spattered my face. I threw myself to the ground behind a parked four-wheel drive. More cracks of an automatic rifle, and the sound of bullets smashing into the metal of the car and shattering the glass. I crawled under it, my body pressed down hard against the cold tarmac, my heart thumping. Silence. Then I heard the sound of rapid footsteps on the other side of the road. I pulled myself to my feet and, crouching, dashed up the street behind the parked cars and stopped behind a parked motorcycle. An engine roared into life a few yards up the road. A burst of gunfire shattered windows above me. Close. Very close.

The car accelerated down the road. I heard car doors slamming, people running, and within a minute the road was a mess of flashing lights. A young man in jeans and a casual black jacket ran up to me.

'Are you OK?'

I recognised him as the Hispanic I had seen following me through the Common weeks ago.

I stood up. 'Yes,' I said. 'I think so.' I touched my face with my fingertips. Blood. 'Thank you.' I managed a smile.

'Looks like the guy got away. He was a pro; you were lucky.'

I stood up and took a few deep breaths to slow my racing heart. I let myself into my apartment and poured myself a stiff whisky.

A parade of people came and went, Cole, Mahoney's Boston partner, the Hispanic, who said his name was Martinez, and a paramedic who cleared up my scratched face. Eventually Mahoney himself arrived. 'So, you were shot at?' he began brightly.

'I believe that's what happened,' I replied.

'Lucky we had some people watching you.'

'I didn't know I had my own personal bodyguard. How long has this been going on for?'

'Oh, three weeks or so. On and off. More off than on, really. It's expensive tailing people.'

'Well, I'm glad you had the spare cash this evening.'

Mahoney sat down. 'Any idea who it was?'

'Your friend here said it was a professional. I don't know any professional killers. For that matter I don't know anyone who owns an automatic rifle.' Except for Art Altschule, I thought suddenly.

Mahoney noticed my hesitation. 'What is it?'

I told him about Art's interest in guns.

'We'll check that out,' he said. 'Is there anything else we should know about Mr Altschule?'

'No, not really. He doesn't like me.'

Mahoney raised his eyebrows. 'Why not?'

'I've been asking awkward questions about BioOne.'

'BioOne, eh?' Mahoney looked at me closely. 'What's the problem with BioOne?'

'I don't know. That's why I was asking Art.'

'Assuming we're talking about a contract killer here,' he went on, 'who else do you think might have hired him?'

'I don't know. The person who killed Frank and John, maybe?'

'But that was someone who knew them. They were both shot in the back with handguns. This is a totally different MO.'

'You're the detective. I'm just the poor bugger getting shot at.'

'We'll no doubt be talking again,' he said as he stood up to leave.

I WAS IN THE OFFICE early, by seven o'clock. Usually no one showed up before about a quarter to eight, so I went straight to Art's office.

A wooden filing cabinet had five drawers marked 'BioOne'. It was locked. Damn!

I searched around for a key. Couldn't find one. I tried his desk. The drawers were locked too. I had an idea. I quickly strode back to my own desk. In one corner of the drawer, next to a spare set of house keys, were my own desk keys, which I never used. I hurried back to Art's office and tried them on his drawers.

None of them worked. I checked my watch. A quarter to eight. I should be at my own desk by now. I checked that the office was exactly as I found it, and slipped out.

Just in time. I passed Art in the corridor.

I sat at my desk, trying to work out what to do. The only person with a key to Art's files was Art. And there was no reason for him to give it to me. Unless . . .

I made my way back to his office and knocked.

'Yes?' He was drinking a cup of coffee and scanning the *Wall Street Journal*.

'Can I borrow your key to the supplies closet?' The supplies closet was a large cupboard where some of the more valuable office supplies were kept: computer equipment and so on.

'Can't you get a key from Connie?'

'Not in yet.'

Art grunted, and pulled out his keys. He fiddled with one of them, trying to detach it. Damn. I needed the lot.

'I'll bring them right back,' I said.

'All right.' Art threw me the whole bunch.

I caught them and nipped out. Then I took the elevator down to the street, and hurried round the corner to a small hardware store. There were three keys on Art's ring that looked like they might open filing cabinets or desk drawers. I had all three copied.

It seemed to take the man for ever, but eventually I was back up in Revere's offices. I knocked on Art's door, and handed him his keys back. He was on the phone.

At about a quarter to ten I saw Art enter the elevator, jacket on. I slipped into his office, closing the door behind me.

The first thing I did was check his diary. He had an appointment at eleven at Revere's offices. That meant he would be back within an hour. I would have to be quick.

I tried the keys on the BioOne filing cabinet. The second one fitted. There were five large drawers. I started looking through them. There was so much information: the early papers on Revere's initial investment, a whole drawer full of documents related to the Initial Public

Offering, Annual Reports, monthly management accounts, forecasts.

It was taking too long, and I wasn't getting anywhere. If BioOne had secret misgivings about neuroxil-5, it wouldn't appear in these publicly available documents. Where would it be? Either in a copy of clinical trial results or in recent correspondence.

I searched, but I couldn't find any clinical trial data. It wasn't surprising really, from what I knew of Enever. But in the bottom drawer was the BioOne correspondence file. This was more interesting. Most of the correspondence was between Art and his old friend Jerry Peterson, and it was mostly about the stock price. Art had become quite upset about the downward lurch and had persuaded Jerry to give the analysts nods and winks that BioOne was optimistic about the Phase Three trials.

I put the file back and locked the cabinet. Nothing there to suggest that there were any concerns about neuroxil-5. Ten o'clock. I should really leave now. But it wouldn't take a moment to check Art's desk.

I tried the remaining two keys. One of them worked. I slid open the bottom drawer. Three bottles of Jack Daniel's: one empty, one half empty, and one full. I slammed that drawer shut and then froze. I could hear footsteps in the corridor outside. Oh, shit.

Art swung open the door to his office, and stopped dead when he saw me. My mind darted through a thousand excuses, and instantly rejected them all. This wasn't the time to lie.

Eventually he spoke. 'What the hell are you doing?'

'Looking for information on BioOne,' I replied. 'I asked you about it. You wouldn't tell me.'

His heavy face reddened in front of me. 'So you thought you'd poke around among my personal belongings to see what you could find? How did you get into my desk?' His eyes were on the bottom drawer. At least part of his anger came from the fear and now the knowledge that I would stumble on his whisky collection.

I looked down at the copied key still in the lock.

He felt for his keys in his pocket. 'You son of a bitch.'

He lunged towards me and pulled me to the floor. I hit my head on the side of the desk on the way down and was dazed for long enough for him to pin me to the ground. I just had time to move my face as he brought his fist crashing down on the side of my head.

Art was strong. I bucked and wriggled, but I couldn't throw him off. He hit me again, this time on the mouth. As he moved his hand to pin down my shoulder, I lunged and bit it hard.

He screamed, and pulled his hand away. I bucked, he lost his balance, and I pushed myself out from under him. He climbed to his feet, and reached for the top drawer of his desk, the only one I hadn't checked. He pulled out a small pistol, and pointed it at me.

Jesus! 'Art . . . It's not worth it. If you shoot me—'

'Shut up!'

'OK,' I said, holding my hands in front of me in a calming gesture.

'What the hell is going on here?' It was Gil. He stood in the doorway taking in the scene before him. 'Art, put that gun down!'

Art looked at Gil, and slowly put the gun down on the desk. 'This son of a bitch broke into my desk. He was trying to steal confidential information. I caught him at it.'

'Is this true, Simon?'

I took a deep breath. 'Yes.'

'Go back to your office and wait. Art, come with me to my office.' I left the room.

Twenty minutes later, I was in Gil's office. 'I'm very disappointed in you, Simon,' he said. 'We should be able to come to work at Revere without worrying about one of our colleagues going through our belongings. What were you doing?'

'I'm still trying to find out who killed Frank and John,' I replied.

'That's the police's job. I told you the other evening how important you are to this firm, how much we need you more than ever now, and what do you do? Snoop around, antagonise one of my partners.' Gil was red now. I had never seen him so angry.

'Someone tried to kill me last night,' I said flatly. 'They shot at me outside my apartment.'

Gil paused, at a loss for what to say. Then he spoke in a low, determined voice. 'You have your problems, Simon, and I have mine. You do what you have to do, and I'll do the best I can to ensure this firm survives. But as of this moment, you are suspended from this firm until further notice. Please leave the building. Now.'

THE FUTURE didn't look good. No wife, no job, and, unless I was very careful, a bullet in the head. I had to get whoever had killed Frank and John before they got me. Only then could I hope to get my life back into some kind of order.

When I arrived home the light on my answering machine was flashing. For a foolish second I thought it might be Lisa. It wasn't.

'Hi, Simon, it's Kelly.' Her voice, usually strong and confident, was subdued. 'I'd like to talk to you. Give me a call.'

I dialled Boston Peptides' number straight away, and we agreed to meet for lunch at a café near Harvard Square.

It was a vegetarian establishment, infested by students. Although I was early, Kelly was already waiting outside. We muttered greetings and then joined the end of the queue at the food counter in silence. I chose a salad, and Kelly some kind of quiche, and we sat down at the only free table.

'I shouldn't have come,' she said.

'I'm glad you did. You must have a good reason.'

'I think I have.' Kelly picked at her quiche. 'Lisa's in a bad way and she holds you responsible. I've been thinking a lot about it, and I'm not sure she's right. I kind of trust you. And I think you should know what Lisa was worried about. What got her fired. You never heard any of this from me, OK?'

'OK,' I nodded.

'As soon as BioOne took over Boston Peptides, Lisa wanted to get hold of some of the data on neuroxil-5. She wanted to see if she could use it in her work on Parkinson's. At first Enema said no way. No one is allowed to know anything unless they absolutely have to. But Lisa can be pretty persuasive.'

I smiled.

'He was very careful what data he would let her see. It was mostly from some of the early animal experiments, on aged rats. But as Lisa studied the information, she noticed something than Enema seemed to have missed. Several months after taking the neuroxil-5, quite a few of the rats died. Most of them died of natural causes. But a higher number than usual died of strokes.'

I raised my eyebrows.

'At first Lisa spoke to Henry about it. He told her to talk to Enema. Which she did.'

I could see where this was going. 'And Enema said there was nothing wrong.'

'That's right. He said that Lisa's observations weren't statistically significant. When she asked for more data he said that it had been thoroughly analysed and there was nothing to be worried about.'

'But that didn't satisfy Lisa?'

Kelly smiled. 'You know her. She wouldn't be satisfied until she had seen the data itself. When Enema refused to show it to her, she accused him of not checking the numbers carefully enough.'

'So he fired her?'

'Not surprisingly,' said Kelly.

It didn't surprise me at all. I knew that she had given Henry Chan a similarly difficult time over the years, but he had much more patience than Enever. I now understood why he felt Lisa wouldn't fit into the BioOne culture.

'Do you think Lisa was right to be concerned?' I asked Kelly.

'I didn't see the data myself, but I've worked with Lisa for two years. I trust her hunches. There may be something there.'

'Can you help me find out?' I asked.

Kelly looked down at her plate. 'Unlike Lisa, I don't have another job to go to if I get fired.'

'Hmm. Have the clinical trials shown the same problem to be present in humans?'

'I don't know. The Phase One and Two clinical trials probably involved only about a hundred people, total. It is possible that something that affected a small minority of patients might slip through unnoticed. That's why they have these massive Phase Three trials going on now, with a thousand patients or more. Only Enever will know the results of them.'

I was disappointed. It was hard to see how I, single-handedly, could break through BioOne's wall of secrecy.

'There is one thing you could do,' Kelly said. 'I'm pretty sure that the Phase Two trial was written up in the *New England Journal of Medicine*. There will probably be a list of the clinicians involved. Many will be signed up for the new trial. You could go and talk to some of them.'

'Thanks,' I said. 'I'll try it.'

We ate our food.

'How's Boston Peptides getting on without Lisa?' I asked.

'We miss her. BP 56 is going well. We're getting the first responses from human volunteers. It looks like the drug is safe, although it seems to cause depression in some people.'

'Depression?'

'Yes. It can reduce the levels of serotonin in the brain.'

Depression. Lisa had been taking BP 56. I remembered her fragility after Frank's death, the way she had lost her temper with me, her uncharacteristic irrationality, her black moods. A chemically induced depression, combined with all those other pressures, must have been very hard to cope with. No wonder she had cracked and run away. 'It's not serious enough to fail the drug, is it?'

'Oh, no,' said Kelly. 'There are ways around it. It may be as simple as prescribing Prozac in combination with BP 56.' She looked at her watch. 'I've got to go. Do you mind if you wait here for a couple of minutes before you leave? I don't want anyone to see us together.'

'OK,' I said. 'You go. And thank you.'

She left. I waited a few moments, and thought through what Kelly had told me. In some ways, this news that Lisa had been suffering from biochemically induced depression made me feel better. When she came off the drug, I should have a much better chance of persuading her to come back to me. But I still needed to prove that I hadn't killed Frank. And I still needed to find out if Lisa's hunch was right, if neuroxil-5 was killing some of the people it was supposed to be curing. That would be a disaster. For the Alzheimer's patients taking it, for BioOne, and for Revere.

THE *New England Journal of Medicine* was on the Internet. I found the article Kelly had mentioned. The title was 'A Controlled Trial of Neuroxil-5 as a Treatment for Alzheimer's Disease'. It described the Phase Two clinical trial on eighty-four patients and suggested that the results were encouraging. At the end there was a list of the six medical centres participating, together with the clinicians responsible.

It took an hour of fiddling about on the Internet before I had the names and addresses of these six centres. Four of them were in New England, one was in Illinois, and one in Florida. It was five o'clock. I resolved to see the four New England centres the next morning.

I made myself a cup of tea and picked up the mail that had arrived that morning. There was one letter with an address in handwriting that I knew very well.

Lisa's.

I opened it carefully, hardly daring to read it.

Dear Simon,

I have some news for you. I went to my family doctor today, and there is no doubt about it. I'm pregnant.

I felt you had a right to know as soon as I did. But you should also know that it doesn't change my decision to stay away from you. I hope that here in California I can start a new life for myself and for the baby. I have felt so horrible recently, but at least now I have something to live for.

Please don't try to contact me. I need to be away from you right now. I hope that I will get to the stage where I can see you again and talk to you again, but I'm not there yet. Lisa.

I read the letter over again, to make sure I had got it right. A turmoil of emotions bubbled inside me, including joy that I was going to be a father. I knew I would be a good father, and Lisa would be a good mother. I could imagine the three of us laughing together.

If Lisa ever gave us the chance.

Through the long night, it was difficult to fight the fear that whoever had tried to kill me would try again. I felt small and alone in my bed, our bed. I so desperately wanted Lisa's warm body next to me, her embrace to give me comfort and courage.

So I was going to be a father. Who was I kidding? I wouldn't last a week, let alone nine months.

Very early the next morning, I packed a bag and called a cab to take me to Logan airport.

At the Hertz office there I rented a bland white Ford and I drove round Route 128 until I came to a rest stop, and pulled up in the parking lot. I pulled out my cellphone and managed to make appointments to see three of the four Alzheimer's centres on my list.

First was Dr Herman A. Netherbrook of one of the smaller universities that littered Boston. His small office was in a medical research unit on the campus and he was about sixty, with the weary cynicism that afflicts stale schoolteachers and, presumably, academics. He welcomed me politely and I gave him one of my cards.

'Revere Partners is one of the investors in BioOne, who are conducting the Phase Three trial of their neuroxil-5 drug for Alzheimer's disease. A trial in which you are participating, I believe?'

'Indeed we are. We monitor the patients very carefully.'

'Of course. And have you encountered any adverse events?' I knew that adverse events had to be reported as soon as they occurred.

Netherbrook walked over to a filing cabinet, and pulled out a folder. 'Let me see. We have thirteen patients enrolled in the study. We have had two adverse events. One patient had a heart attack and another is showing signs of developing diabetes. But in a sample of elderly patients, that is only to be expected.'

'Any strokes?'

'Strokes?' He glanced at his file. 'No, none.'

'Thank you, Dr Netherbrook.'

I left, feeling slightly foolish, and drove off to a specialist Alzheimer's Research Clinic in Springfield, in central Massachusetts.

Dr Fuller turned out to be about thirty-two, blonde, with long legs and a soft southern accent. She seemed wasted on geriatrics.

She said that one of her ten patients enrolled in the trial had suffered a mild stroke after nine months. One stroke out of a total of twenty-three patients. That didn't prove anything.

On to Hartford and a Dr Pete Korninck. He was a genial man with a beard and iron-grey hair that curled over his ears. One of his sixteen patients had developed a liver complaint, and another had died of a heart attack.

'How about strokes?' I asked.

'None. At least not among the Alzheimer's patients.'

'What do you mean?'

'Well, we have some patients who suffer from multi-infarct dementia, also known as "mini-strokes". Over the years these can cause damage to the brain, which has similar effects to Alzheimer's. The two are often confused. These patients have "mini-strokes" all the time. And sometimes they get big strokes.'

'Presumably you exclude these patients from your study?'

'Where we can, yes. But there's no doubt some of them creep in. You can only really identify Alzheimer's for sure after an autopsy.'

'Have you had to reclassify any of your Alzheimer's patients in this way?'

'Yes, three.'

'And you told BioOne this?'

'Of course.'

I left Hartford, and drove east, stopping briefly for a cup of coffee. It had been a long day, but I thought I might still have time to see the fourth clinic on the list, in Providence, Rhode Island.

Dr Catarro wasn't available, but his assistant Dr Palmer was. He agreed to meet me at his office.

He was a dark thin man who could have been anything from twenty-five to forty.

'Thank you for waiting for me, Dr Palmer.'

'Not at all,' he said. He looked tired.

'Hard day?'

'Since Dr Catarro died in a car accident last month, every day has been a hard day. We haven't found a replacement yet.'

'I'm sorry,' I said. 'What happened?'

'He was driving home late one night, and he hit a tree on a road near Dighton. He was only a mile away from home. They think he must have fallen asleep at the wheel. He left his wife and two girls.'

'How awful,' I said, lamely.

Palmer's eyes dropped downwards. Then he looked up. 'Now, how can I help you?'

'Oh, yes. I believe Dr Catarro was taking part in a clinical trial conducted by BioOne. I wonder if I could ask you about it?'

'I won't be able to help. We discontinued the trial after Tony died. I had too much other stuff to do. I sent the records back to BioOne.'

I was disappointed. 'Do you happen to know if there were any adverse events?'

'Yes, there were,' said Palmer. 'Tony was involved in a disagreement with BioOne over the reporting of strokes.'

'Strokes?'

'Yes. A number of our patients had them. A couple were fatal. BioOne suggested that the patients concerned had been misdiagnosed as Alzheimer's patients, and were really suffering all along from mini-strokes. But the autopsy showed the two who died definitely did have Alzheimer's. They had the neurofibrillary tangles that you only get with Alzheimer's disease.'

'Do you know how this disagreement was resolved?' I asked.

'It wasn't,' said Palmer. 'It was one of the reasons I decided to drop the trial.'

'Thank you, Dr Palmer, that was very interesting,' I said, and left.

I WAS VERY CURIOUS. It was too much of a coincidence that Dr Catarro had died in the middle of asking questions about BioOne. Car accidents could be faked.

I dialled Information and got the number and address of a Dr Catarro in Dighton. I drove straight there. I didn't feel good about barging in on a widow, but I had no choice.

I found the white-painted clapboard house and rang the bell.

Mrs Catarro came to the door. She was small and blonde. Her face was carefully made-up, but looked fragile.

'Yes?' she asked.

'Mrs Catarro, my name is Simon Ayot. I'd like to ask you a couple of questions about your husband.'

She looked at me doubtfully, but the smart suit, friendly smile and English accent seemed to do the trick. 'Very well, come in.'

She led me into a living room and I sat down.

'Were you a friend of Tony's?' she asked.

'No, I wasn't. But I'm interested in a project he was working on before he died. Do you know if your husband was worried about the neuroxil-5 trial he was working on?'

She thought for a moment. 'Yes, he was, as a matter of fact,' she said. 'He used to talk about that a lot. It made him quite upset.'

'Did he say what the problem was?'

'As I recall, four of his patients had suffered strokes after taking the drug, then two had subsequently died, and the company that made it, what was it . . . BioOne, was doing all it could to hide the results. He was going to go to the Federal Authorities.'

'But it never came to that?'

'No,' she said.

'Thanks very much. If you do think of anything more to do with the trial, do give me a ring.'

I pulled out a card, scribbled in my cellphone number, and handed it to her.

'Oh, Revere Partners. You'll have known poor Frank Cook, then?'

'Yes.' I paused. 'Yes, I did. Did *you* know him?'

'Yes. Well, Tony knew him better. He'd known him for years. We saw him at a friend's house just before Tony's accident. Come to think of it, just before Frank was murdered.'

I froze. 'Did your husband talk to Frank about the clinical trial?'

She thought a bit. 'I think they had a long conversation about it. Frank was involved in it in some way. Like you, I assume.'

I nodded. 'That's right, Mrs Catarro.'

She looked at me suspiciously. 'You don't think . . .'

I sighed. 'I don't know. That's what I'm trying to find out. If I discover anything, I'll let you know.'

I left her on her doorstep, her fragile face looking as though it was on the verge of shattering.

I CHECKED into a motel on the outskirts of Providence, had an anonymous supper in a cheap anonymous restaurant, and felt safe.

I was now pretty certain that I knew why Frank had been killed. Dr Catarro had told him of his concerns about BioOne. Frank had asked questions and someone had killed him. And then Dr Catarro. I had asked questions, and they had tried to kill me.

Who was responsible? The list of possibilities was headed by two people: Art Altschule and Thomas Enever. But I still had no proof.

Even though it was late, I dialled Aunt Zoë's number. Carl answered, sounding tense.

'Carl? It's Simon Ayot.'

'Oh, Simon, how are you?'

'I'm sorry I'm calling so late . . .'

'That's OK. I've just come back from the hospital.'

'The hospital?' I knew what was coming next. 'Is it Aunt Zoë?'

'Yes,' said Carl, his voice strained. 'She had a stroke last night. The damage was massive. She's in a coma, and they don't think she'll come out of it.'

Despair overwhelmed me. 'I'm so sorry, Carl,' I said quietly.

There was silence on the other end of the line for a moment. 'That wasn't the side effect you were thinking about, was it, Simon?'

I couldn't lie to him. He'd find out soon enough. 'Yes,' I said.

'Damn!' Carl exclaimed. Then he gave a sigh. 'I guess I shouldn't have told Zoë to go on with the treatment, huh?'

'You didn't know, Carl. Neither did I.'

I BOUGHT the *Wall Street Journal* the next morning and read it over one of those great American breakfasts that you can get in cheap diners. Out of habit I scanned the NASDAQ quotes. BioOne's stock was up nineteen dollars to sixty-three!

I searched the paper for the story. BioOne had announced a marketing agreement with Werner Wilson, a huge pharmaceutical company with one of the largest sales forces of its kind in the country. Contingent on a successful outcome of the Phase Three trial of neuroxil-5, Werner Wilson was going to sell neuroxil-5 in the United States, as well as 'a promising new treatment for Parkinson's disease', which would be Lisa's BP 56. The deal gave extremely favourable terms to BioOne. The Wall Street analysts loved it, and so did the stock market. If they only knew.

I finished my breakfast, and went out to the little white Ford, which was doubling as an office. I called Daniel at Revere.

'What's up, Simon? Where are you?'

'On the road,' I replied. 'Listen, Daniel. I've been to some of the clinics that are participating in the Phase Three trial. And I think Lisa was right. There is a problem. Some people taking the drug have suffered strokes.'

'Ooh, that's bad. Did you see the BioOne stock price this morning?' he asked.

'Yes, sixty-three.'

'It's not going to be up there very long if this gets out.'

'No, it isn't. But keep it quiet for now, Daniel. I don't have hard evidence. I need the clinical trial data on the Phase Two trial, and the adverse events on Phase Three. Can you get that from BioOne?'

'I don't know, Simon. You know what Thomas Enever is like.'

'It's important, Daniel. Steal it if you have to.'

There was silence at the other end of the phone.

'Daniel?'

'This is heavy. You getting fired. People getting killed. It wouldn't be smart to steal BioOne documents. Sorry, Simon. Got to run.'

The bastard hung up. As usual, he was thinking of himself first. We hadn't discussed his personal holdings of BioOne stock, but at sixty-three dollars he was finally in profit. I was sure he would now sell, and

I was furious that I had given him the information to dig himself out of that hole when he had been unwilling to lift a finger to help me.

The trials data I needed was in the BioOne building in Cambridge. How could I get at it? I had seen the security. There was no way past that. I had an idea. I called Craig.

I DROVE OUT to Woodbridge, bought some groceries at the Star Market, and drove on to Marsh House, which seemed a good place to lie low. It would be foolish to go back to my apartment in Boston if I wanted to stay alive.

It was a crisp, clear day. The autumnal light reflected off the yellows and oranges of the marsh grass, so that it seemed to shimmer. The creek twinkled at the end of the jetty. No one was about.

I used Lisa's key to unlock the door. The house was cold. I found some wood, fed the stove, and lit it. I made myself a sandwich for lunch, and waited for Craig.

He came armed with a powerful laptop computer. He set it up on the kitchen table, and in no time it was up and running.

I watched him as he nosed around the BioOne web site, taking note of email addresses, and so on.

'Can I help?' I asked him.

'Yeah. Pizza. Extra anchovies. And good coffee.'

So I drove into Woodbridge and got a pizza. There was a kind of deli which ground exotic coffees, so I bought a quarter-pound of arabica and returned to the house with it.

'I think I can see a possible way in,' he said. 'There's a new link between BioOne's network and Boston Peptides', isn't there?'

'Yes. BioOne took them over very recently.'

'Excellent. That means they probably haven't got a cast-iron connection. It would really help if I had the password of someone in the Boston Peptides network,' Craig said.

'Hold on.'

I called Kelly.

'You shouldn't call me at work,' she whispered urgently.

'Kelly, I need your password for the computer system. I'm pretty sure now that Lisa was right about neuroxil-5. To be certain, I need to get into BioOne's computer.'

'Simon. I'll get fired.'

'Kelly. Patients will die.'

There was silence. 'OK. But it's kind of embarrassing.'

'Tell me.'

'Leonardodicaprio. One word.'

'I see what you mean.' Craig passed a note to me. 'Oh, and try to use the system as little as possible over the next twenty-four hours.'

She sighed. 'OK.'

'All right!' said Craig when I told him. 'Now what I'm going to do is try to log on to BioOne's connection, pretending to be a Boston Peptides' machine. Watch.'

He typed furiously and then, with a flourish, pressed enter. Numbers were dialled, modems screeched, lines of meaningless letters scrolled down the screen. After about a minute, it all stopped.

'We're in!' exclaimed Craig.

'I'm impressed.'

'Let's start with this guy Enever's email.'

It took a while, but eventually the screen was filled with Enever's emails. There were hundreds of them.

'OK, which ones do you want?'

'I can't tell without reading each one,' I said, shaking my head.

'OK. We'll download the lot, then.'

Craig downloaded the emails onto the Net Cop machine in Wellesley. When he'd finished, he rubbed his hands. 'Now for the Clinical Trials Unit.'

I'd asked him to look for data on the Phase Two clinical trial for neuroxil-5, and any early results for the Phase Three trial. It proved difficult. After a couple of hours, he took a break. 'This is going to be much harder,' he said, pouring himself a cup of coffee. 'It's much better protected than Enever's email, but I'll get it.'

Four hours later, he still hadn't. It was nearly midnight. I was exhausted, but I felt morally bound to stay awake and be supportive.

'Shit!' shouted Craig. 'These bastards know what they're doing.'

I yawned. 'Look, Craig. You've tried hard, I really appreciate it. But let's just give up.'

'No way. I'm not quitting till I get you that data.'

'But you'll be up all night!'

'Probably,' said Craig. 'I've done it before. But you get some sleep. Yawning your head off a couple of feet from my ear does not constitute help. Trust me. Go to bed.'

He was right. At least if I got some sleep I might not be quite so useless in the morning. 'Thanks, Craig. Wake me if you get anywhere.'

But it was the alarm clock that jolted me out of my sleep at six thirty. I pulled on some clothes, and went downstairs to the clatter of Craig's fingers on the keyboard. 'No luck?'

Craig turned to me. 'No,' he snapped. He didn't look tired, but he looked angry.

'Have you been at it all night?'

'I went for a walk about three. Didn't help.'

'Let me make you some coffee,' I said. 'Thanks for trying.'

Craig sipped noisily, his eyes glazed, his mind still on the problem. I felt refreshed by my sleep.

'Don't worry about it, Craig,' I said. 'You never know, there might be some stuff in Enever's emails. Someone might have sent him some of the clinical trial.'

Craig stopped in mid slurp. 'That's it!' he exclaimed. He leapt back to his keyboard.

'What are you doing?'

'Composing a message from Enever, asking the Clinical Trials Unit for the data. They send it. We read it.'

It was still early. We had to wait for the people in the Clinical Trials Unit to get into work, read their mail, and do something about it. At last, at 8.33am, a response came.

Dr Enever: Here is the data you requested. Can I give you the rest in hard copy, or do you need it in spreadsheet form? Jed

A large spreadsheet of figures was attached.

'Well, I think we need the rest in spreadsheet form, don't you?' said Craig with a smile as he composed a response. We sent it and watched for a response from the Clinical Trials Unit.

It didn't come. Instead, MESSAGE SENT flashed on the screen. 'What message?' I looked at Craig.

He checked the 'Sent Messages' file. It was from Enever, the real Enever this time, to Jed.

Jed: I didn't ask for all this data. Who told you to send it? Enever

'Uh-oh,' said Craig. 'Time to go.'

He quickly downloaded Jed's first email and its spreadsheet attachment, and left BioOne's system.

'Will they know we were there?' I asked.

'I hope not,' Craig said. 'But I don't want to risk going back in.'

'That's OK. I'm sure we've got a lot of good stuff already.'

Craig began packing up his computer.

'Are you going home now for a rest?' I asked.

'Oh, no. If I can't pull an all-night hacking run any more, I'm not fit to run the company.'

'Thanks for all your help.'

'No problem.' He paused at the door. 'Stay alive,' he said, and then he was gone.

I STARTED on the BioOne files right away, using my own laptop. Craig had given me a password so that I could access them on the Net Cop system any time I wanted.

There was a mass of information: columns of dense figures and statistics. It was good stuff, but I couldn't understand most of it. Someone else would have to look through it, someone who would be able to sort the interesting from the irrelevant, and who could analyse what they found.

The time had come to see Lisa. I had held off physically tracking her down until I had evidence to give her that I was still the man she had married, that I hadn't killed her father. I was now pretty close to having that evidence. But I needed her help if I was to make sure that more Alzheimer's sufferers like Aunt Zoë didn't die.

Perhaps she'd be amenable to reason. I could only hope.

I wrote a one-page note and stuck it in an envelope, packed my bags and left. I drove to the airport and two hours later I was on a flight to San Francisco.

12

Lisa's mother lived in a small wooden town house on Russian Hill, which, technically, had a view of the Bay and Alcatraz. It was true that from one of the upstairs windows you could just see some water and one corner of the fortress-island.

I rang the bell. There was no answer at first, and I wondered if she would be in. I knew she worked a couple of days a week.

Finally she answered, patting her hair in place and smoothing down her dress. The automatic smile disappeared when she saw me. 'Simon! What are you doing here?'

'I'm looking for Lisa.'

'Oh, Simon! You shouldn't have come all this way! You know I can't tell you where she is.'

'Well, I have. Can I come in?'

'Oh, yes, of course.' She led me into the kitchen. 'Do you want some coffee? I was just making some.'

'Yes, please.'

She busied herself with percolators and filters.

'How is Lisa?' I asked.

'Not good.'

'I'd like to help.'

She turned to me. 'I don't think you can. Her life has been turned upside-down, Simon. Frank's death, losing her job, Frank's . . .' she paused, 'sexuality. Rightly or wrongly she holds you responsible.'

'So she knows about Frank and John?'

'Yes. A detective flew out here to interview her.'

'That must have been so hard.' I looked closely at her mother. 'But you knew all the time, didn't you?'

She nodded. 'It took a while to dawn on me. Mind you, I think it took a while to dawn on him. It was almost a relief. Frank was adamant we shouldn't tell the kids. But now, since his death, it's just so difficult for her. And for Eddie, of course.'

'She can't really think I killed him, can she?'

'I don't know whether she thinks it through that rationally. She's afraid you might have. She just wants to leave it all behind.'

'What about you?' I asked. 'You don't think I killed him do you?'

Ann slowly shook her head.

'Then, just let me tell you why I want to see her. The reason Lisa was fired from BioOne was that she suspected a drug they are developing is dangerous. I've been investigating, and I think she might be right. I've collected a mass of information that I don't understand. I'd like her to look at it. It could prove her right. And more importantly, we could save lives. Did you hear about Aunt Zoë?'

'No,' said Ann. 'What happened?'

'She had a stroke. Carl thinks she won't make it.'

'Oh, no!'

'She was taking neuroxil-5. She suffered from the side effects. You know Lisa. You know how important this would be to her.'

Ann poured the coffee and sat down in silence. Then she seemed to make up her mind. 'She's living with her brother.'

EDDIE'S APARTMENT was in Haight-Ashbury. I wanted to give Lisa time to return from her lab in Stanford, so I spent several hours wandering around the area, drinking coffee, browsing in shops. The Haight had been the centre of the 1967 Summer of Love, and nostalgia for that time was everywhere, from Grateful Dead memorabilia shops to places to buy quaint drug accessories.

I was not looking forward to meeting Eddie. It was clear that the guilt and anger that he had felt at his father's death had been channelled into hatred of me. Lisa's staying with him could hardly have warmed her feelings towards me.

I pressed the buzzer at the entrance to his building, a pink

Victorian terraced house. There was a camera. He could see me.

'What do you want?' His voice was harsh.

'To see you,' I said.

There was a pause. 'Come on up,' the buzzer said.

His apartment was on the second floor. He opened the door and flashed a broad ironic smile. 'Come in, come in, old chap.'

I followed him into the living area. It was a mess of magazines, mugs, glasses and low furniture. I recognised Lisa's bag in a corner, and some of her clothes next to it.

'Let me get you a beer.' He headed towards the kitchen area and the refrigerator. I followed a couple of steps behind.

'I take it Lisa isn't back from Stanford yet?'

'No. And she won't want to see you.' He took one bottle of beer out of the refrigerator, opened it, and drank.

'I'd like to wait for her.'

Suddenly he spun round and landed a blow on the side of my head. It knocked me to one side. My first impulse was to fly back at him, but I resisted and stood up straight.

'Eddie! Simon! Stop it!'

I turned round. Lisa stood in the doorway. Her eyes were tired, her shoulders weary. I wanted to pull her to me and hold her tight.

'Simon, get out,' she said, matter-of-factly.

'That's what I was just telling him to do,' said Eddie.

I knew there was no chance of talking her round now. I handed her an envelope with the note I had written that morning. 'Read this.'

She stared at it, ripped it once, and threw it into the bin.

I kept my cool. 'You were right, Lisa, there is something wrong with neuroxil-5. Aunt Zoë had a stroke a couple of days ago as a result of taking it. That letter contains instructions for how to get access to BioOne's files on the trials. I can't analyse the information. You can.'

Her eyes widened. 'Aunt Zoë? No! Is she going to be all right?'

'Carl doesn't think so.'

'Oh, no!' She glanced down at the bin, and then, with an effort, composed herself. 'I won't listen to what you have to say, Simon. I want you out of my life. Now go back to Boston.'

It was painful to hear these words from someone I loved so much. But I had expected them.

'All right, I'm leaving now. But read the letter. And meet me in the coffee shop round the corner at ten o'clock tomorrow morning.'

'I won't be there, Simon.'

'Bye,' I said, and I left the apartment.

I ARRIVED at the coffee shop half an hour early, after an appalling night's sleep in a cheap hotel worrying whether Lisa would come. The café walls were orange, adorned with posters of dolphins and whales gliding through shimmering seas. The food was organic, and the coffee came in the standard forty different combinations.

I asked for a simple cup of black coffee and opened the *Wall Street Journal*. BioOne stock was down four to fifty-nine.

I finished the coffee and ordered another. Ten o'clock came and went, then ten thirty, then eleven. I nervously read and reread the same pages of the *Journal*. She obviously wasn't coming. But I couldn't leave. Everything I had done over the last month, the risks I had taken, the trouble I had caused, had all been with the intention of winning Lisa back. What if I couldn't convince her? I stayed put, as though remaining in that café was the only thing left for me to do.

Another coffee, decaf this time. And an organic Danish. My stomach needed something for the coffee to bite into.

It started to rain. Big San Franciscan drops of water that swiftly turned the street into a landscape of streams and lakes.

The café was beginning to fill with the lunch crowd. The waiters looked as if they were about to throw me out, so I ordered a grilled vegetable sandwich.

At two o'clock, I gave up. I barged out into the waterlogged street, raindrops splattering my hair. I didn't know where I was walking.

'Simon!' I almost didn't hear it, didn't believe it. 'Simon!'

I turned. It was Lisa running towards me, her bag swinging in the rain. She stopped in front of me, panting. I tried a smile. She returned it quickly, nervously. Water dripped off her nose and chin.

'Thank God you waited. I thought you'd go back to Boston.'

I shrugged. I allowed myself to smile again.

Lisa glanced up at the rain. 'Let's go inside.' She looked towards the café.

'I can't go back in there,' I said. I noticed a scruffy diner further down the street. 'How about that?'

She grimaced. 'OK. Actually, I'm starving.'

She ordered a hamburger; we sat in silence as we waited for the food. There was so much to say.

'I read those files,' she said at last. 'I didn't have time to go through the data thoroughly, but my gut feeling is that when the analysis is done it'll show the drug is dangerous. I'm almost certain that neuroxil-5 causes strokes in some patients if used over a six-month period or longer.'

'Aunt Zoë had been taking it for seven months.'

Lisa nodded. 'Poor Aunt Zoë. I'll really miss her.'

We were both quiet for a few moments.

'Didn't Enever pick any of this up?' I said.

'Nowhere does he mention the problem directly. But from his actions, I'd say he began to notice that the adverse events were getting out of line. He persuaded some clinicians to reclassify their patients as suffering from mini-strokes rather than Alzheimer's, then removed the strokes from the statistics.'

'So he knowingly fiddled the figures?'

'I wouldn't say that, exactly. He may have genuinely believed that the patients were misdiagnosed, or he may have convinced himself.'

'Hm. Anything from Catarro?'

'Some emails about the two stroke deaths. Enever suggested the patients might have suffered from mini-strokes. There's nothing from Catarro about the autopsies.'

'But the autopsy records should be easy to get.'

Lisa's hamburger arrived, and she munched on it nervously.

'You were right,' I said.

'Yes,' she replied. She gave me a smile. 'Thank you for proving it.'

'You read in my note how Dr Catarro spoke to your father just before he died,' I said quietly.

Lisa nodded and bit her lip.

'I didn't kill him,' I said.

She looked down. 'Simon. You were right. This neuroxil-5 stuff is important. But I don't want to talk about us, OK?'

I sighed. 'How have you been feeling since you came out here?'

'Better. I mean, I still feel awful about Dad. And I'm angry about Boston Peptides . . .' She paused. 'But the world doesn't seem quite as black as it did.'

'Has Kelly spoken to you about the BP 56 trials?'

Lisa shook her head, but I had caught her interest.

'They're going well apart from one thing. Apparently, the drug causes depression in some of the volunteers who are taking it. It can reduce the levels of serotonin in the brain.' Now I had all her attention. 'When did you start taking it?'

'You remember. About a week after Dad died.'

'And did you stop when you came out here?'

'Yes. When I was fired from Boston Peptides there didn't seem much point any more.' She put her head in her hands. 'No wonder I felt so bad. Why didn't I realise what was happening?'

'There was a lot else going on,' I said. 'You weren't exactly in a position to think clearly.'

'I guess I wasn't.' She looked up thoughtfully.

'Now can I tell you why I didn't kill your father?' I said quietly.

'Simon, I said—'

'I have a right to tell you. Just once. All you need to do is listen.'

She took a deep breath. 'OK.'

'Three people have been murdered in the last couple of months: your father, John Chalfont and Dr Catarro. The one thing that links all three is BioOne. Dr Catarro discovered that too many of his patients were dying after taking neuroxil-5. He mentioned this to your father. Your father made his own enquiries. He asked Art among others about the drug. So someone killed both of them.'

Lisa was listening quietly now.

'Then John discovered something suspicious about BioOne, which he wanted to tell me about. So he was murdered. And when I was getting closer to what has happened, they tried to shoot me.'

'Shoot you?' Lisa exclaimed. 'Oh, my God!' She put her hand over her mouth. 'Why would anyone do that?'

'If neuroxil-5 fails to get FDA approval, BioOne will be worthless. That will be very bad for a lot of people.'

'But what about the gun I found in our closet, Simon?'

'I don't know about that,' I said. 'Someone must have put it there.'

'But who? How?'

I shook my head. 'I don't know.'

Lisa was silent for a moment. 'Eddie's sure you did it.'

'I know. But what about John? And Dr Catarro? Why would I kill them? And why would I try to get myself shot?'

'I don't know.'

We were coming to the moment when I would know whether everything I had been doing had been worth while.

I took a deep breath. 'Now, do you think I murdered your father?'

Lisa looked down and fidgeted with a paper napkin.

'Lisa? Look at me. Answer me.'

She looked up. A small nervous smile touched her lips. She shook her head. 'No. I don't think you killed him.'

I couldn't believe it! I wanted to leap into the air and shout. But I controlled myself. I knew I still had a long way to go.

I looked at her empty plate. 'A hamburger?' I asked. 'I thought you never ate that kind of stuff.'

'It's my craving,' Lisa said. 'Burgers and fries.'

'How are you?' I asked. 'How's the baby?'

Her hand fell to her stomach. 'I'm lousy. I've been throwing up almost every morning.' Then she looked up and her eyes gleamed. 'I saw the baby, Simon. I had an ultrasound on Friday. It's real. It has a head and it moves and everything!'

I wished I'd been there, but I couldn't say it. It had stopped raining outside. 'Come on, let's get out of here.'

We left the diner and walked. I didn't care where we went.

'I wasn't going to come,' Lisa said. 'I took your letter out of the trash can, like you knew I would. I was up all night working through those files. I realised there was definitely something wrong with neuroxil-5. But I still couldn't face seeing you. And then ten o'clock passed, and I felt worse and worse. In the end, after what had happened to Aunt Zoë and everything you'd done to get the information, I knew I had to see you,' she said. 'And you were still there!'

I reached for her hand and squeezed it. 'Only just.'

We walked through puddles, weaving our way past other pedestrians. Above us, blue sky was ripping through the black clouds. Isolated streams of sunshine illuminated the newly watered Victorian buildings of the Haight, giving the faded hippiedom a new glister.

'What have you been doing?' she asked. I told her. I talked long and hard. All the thoughts that had been rushing round my head over the previous week burst out in a torrent. Lisa was the only person in the world I had ever been able to tell everything to: it felt so good to talk to her again.

We entered Golden Gate Park. We walked across to the Japanese Tea Garden and sat on a bench next to a miniature bridge over a tiny stream. The sun had emerged now. I put my arm round her and pulled her close.

'I'm sorry, Simon,' she said. 'Can I come back?'

My heart leapt. I kissed her.

WE TOOK A TAXI back to my hotel. We fell on each other, expressing with our bodies what we couldn't say in words. Afterwards, as she lay softly in my arms, I didn't want to move, never wanted to leave this drab hotel room, this nondescript queen-size bed, and Lisa, the woman I loved.

'It was horrible without you, Simon.'

'It was awful for me too.'

'I thought you'd changed. Or, even worse, that you never were the man I thought you were. You haven't changed, have you?'

'No,' I said, stroking her hair.

'I'd lost Dad like that too. He turned out to be a different man than I thought he was.'

'No, Lisa, that's not true. Your father always loved you. He had one secret he kept from you, but he kept it from himself also. And it had nothing to do with you. Don't think of him as someone different. He would have hated it.'

She kissed me on the cheek and nestled into my chest.

They were all there in the large conference room: Gil, Art, Diane, Ravi and Daniel from Revere, and Enever and Jerry Peterson from BioOne. Gardner Phillips had called everyone to his offices first thing on Monday morning at my request.

He stood up, shook my hand, and indicated that we should take our seats at the head of the long table. He sat on my right.

'Thank you for coming, ladies and gentlemen. I think you all know my clients Simon Ayot and his wife, Lisa Cook. They have some information about BioOne to share with you. Simon.'

I smiled at the assembled group. Diane returned my smile, Ravi looked vague, Daniel fascinated, and the others all glowered. Gil stared at me through his thick lenses, his forehead pulled down in deep furrows over his eyebrows. Enever looked furious. Not exactly an eager audience.

'I have bad news,' I began. 'Lisa and I have uncovered evidence that BioOne's drug neuroxil-5 is dangerous to human life.'

There was a stir around the room. 'Prove it,' demanded Enever.

'We will,' I said. Then I told them about my own investigations and explained that Lisa had been able to get hold of data that had confirmed her initial suspicions.

Enever was quick with the counterattack. 'What data?'

'I can't be specific,' Lisa replied. Gardner Phillips had warned us to stay well clear of how we had got hold of the information. 'But I can assure you there can be no question as to the conclusions.'

Enever snorted. 'That's absurd. Your "conclusions" are all unsubstantiated. They have no validity at all.'

'Don't you have any concerns about the incidence of strokes in patients taking neuroxil-5 for more than six months?' Lisa asked.

'No, of course not,' Enever replied. 'It's easy to misdiagnose ministrokes as Alzheimer's.'

'What about Dr Catarro's two stroke patients who were shown to have Alzheimer's at their autopsies?'

'Two elderly people dying of a stroke is no more than a statistical blip. He was just being difficult.'

'It was convenient he had his accident, then, wasn't it?'

'Too right,' muttered Enever. Then, as eyebrows were raised round the table, 'Look, I'm sorry the guy died. But he was a fool, all right?'

Enever's insensitivity was playing into our hands, but he hadn't admitted anything yet.

Gil spoke for the first time. 'You realise how serious these allegations are? If they are true, then BioOne's stock price would collapse immediately. The results would be catastrophic for all of us.'

'I know,' I said. 'I wish BioOne was a success. But it isn't. And the sooner we face up to that fact, the better. Every day this trial continues there's a chance that another patient will have a stroke.'

'You son of a bitch, Ayot.' It was Art. He looked edgy. Sober, but edgy. 'You've always had it in for BioOne. You're jealous, that's all. A damn stupid reason for destroying this firm's best investment.'

'Hold on, Art.' It was Gil. 'We can't gamble with other people's lives. Right now, we don't know. So what I suggest is that Dr Enever gives all the information he has to Ravi to look at. If Simon and Lisa's conclusions are found to be accurate, we will stop the trial.'

There was silence round the table.

'Ravi?' Gil looked at him for his reaction.

'Safety is the most important issue in developing any new drug,' he said. 'From what Simon and Lisa say, there must be real doubts. We have to address those right away.'

'Diane? Do you agree?'

She nodded.

Gil took a deep breath. 'Art?'

'No way!' Art almost shouted. 'This will destroy the stock price. It will destroy BioOne. Hell, it will destroy Revere. You can't do it, Gil.'

Some of the weariness left Gil's face. He sat up straighter, more determined. 'Jerry?'

Jerry Peterson looked at Enever, who was scowling deeply. Then he shrugged. 'I want you to give all the information we have on neuroxil-5 to Ravi by tomorrow, Thomas,' he said.

'Thank you,' said Gil, and the meeting broke up.

Everyone let the consequences of the decision that had just been taken sink in. Small groups formed and began earnest discussions.

Diane walked up to Lisa and me. I could feel Lisa stiffen.

'It's a bad day for Revere,' she said. 'But if there is a problem with the drug, we can't pretend it will go away. Gil was right.'

I nodded. 'Revere will lose millions. Hundreds of millions.'

We stood together in silence for a moment, contemplating the gloomy future of the firm. Then she glanced at Lisa. 'Good luck,' she said with a quick smile, and turned to find Gil and Ravi.

'Bitch,' muttered Lisa.

I didn't contradict her.

IT WAS WONDERFUL to wake up the next morning in our own bed, together. It took us a while to get up, but eventually I stumbled into the shower and Lisa went hunting for breakfast. Twenty minutes later, I heard the door slam. I stepped out of the shower, and grabbed a towel. 'What did you get, Lisa?'

Lisa always got whatever was freshest from the bagel bakery, which made breakfasts a bit of a lottery. But as long as it wasn't rye with caraway seeds I was happy.

No answer.

'Lisa?'

I walked through to the kitchen. Lisa had put the bag of bagels on the table and was staring at the newspaper. Wordlessly, she handed it to me.

BIOTECH BOSS FOUND DEAD, shouted the headline. Underneath was a picture of a grimacing Enever. I scanned the article. Dr Thomas Enever had been found hanged in his apartment. The police were tightlipped, but it was clear what had happened.

'Suicide,' I said.

Lisa nodded.

'Is there anything linking him to your father?'

'Nothing there,' she said. 'But I'm sure there will be.'

GIL CALLED ME later that day, and asked me to come in to Revere the next morning. All was forgiven, and there was work to be done.

Ravi's analysis confirmed Lisa's opinion. There were signs that as the length of time a patient took neuroxil-5 increased, so did the chances that he or she would suffer a stroke. Jerry Peterson was left with no choice. The trials were stopped immediately, the Phase Three data was called in for further analysis, and the FDA was informed. All this was outlined in a press announcement.

The stock dived from fifty-nine dollars to one and three-eighths, slashing the value of the company from nearly two billion dollars to around fifty million. The value of Revere's stake was reduced from $340 million to eight and a half. Nobody had escaped unscathed, except possibly for Daniel. I was sure the bastard had sold at the top.

There was plenty in the story of Thomas Enever's death to scare investors. The press had dug deep and quickly found buried secrets. The faked neuroxil-3 experiment. The hijacking of the Australian research institute's ideas. And the murders of Frank Cook and John Chalfont. The police did their best to sound vague, but the press had found their murderer. Thomas Enever had killed to defend the drug he had stolen.

I called Helen and told her we would be able to fund her appeal. She was overjoyed.

But all this was too late for Aunt Zoë. She died on Tuesday, a week after her stroke.

IT WAS THURSDAY evening. I saved my file, and turned off my machine. I'd done enough work for one day. I was just putting on my coat, when I realised I didn't have my house keys with me. Henry Chan had offered Lisa her old job back, and it was her first day. I knew there was little chance that she would be home when I got back. I was supposed to be meeting Kieran and the boys at the Red Hat later on that evening, and I wanted to go home to get changed. I was considering my options, the best of which seemed to be to go to the Red Hat early, when I remembered the spare set of keys in my desk drawer. As I dropped them in my trouser pocket, it dawned on me. That was how the gun had been planted! Someone had borrowed my house keys from my desk.

Not Thomas Enever. Someone at Revere.

IT WAS A BIG night at the Red Hat. Kieran was there, of course, and half a dozen others, all ex-business school.

I was asked lots of questions and, aided by plenty of beer, talked freely. Frank and John's murders, Enever's suicide and BioOne's collapse made for a better story than job offers and stock options.

I remained the centre of attention for an hour or so, and then Greg Vilgren spoke up. He was an American who had been posted to London with a big investment bank, and was on a brief visit back to Boston.

'Hey. Did you guys hear about Sergei Delesov?' Blank looks round the table. 'It was in the papers in London. He was murdered about a month ago.'

'Wow!' said Kieran. 'I always thought he was a bit of a shady character. What happened?'

'It was a contract killing,' Greg said. 'I didn't realise it, but apparently he was the youngest CEO of any bank in Russia.'

Notes were compared on Sergei. Nobody knew him much. Then

Kim spoke. She was a management consultant. 'Daniel Hall knew him, I think. He used to talk about his stock picks with him.'

'Really?' I said, leaning forward.

'Yeah. In fact, I think Daniel borrowed some money from Sergei, or from some people Sergei had introduced him to. To play the market.'

'Much money?'

'You know Daniel. More likely to be a hundred grand than ten.'

'Has he made his million yet?' Greg asked me.

'He gets close, then he blows it all,' I said. 'But he's a bright guy.'

'Hey, did he ever hit on you, Kimmy?' someone demanded.

'Daniel! No way,' said Kim, and the conversation deteriorated to its usual late-evening level.

NEXT DAY I watched Daniel in action. He was on the phone trying to say no to a hopeful entrepreneur.

The entrepreneur was persistent, and Daniel's patience wore out as it always did. 'I said no. No means no! N-O. No!' He slammed down the phone. 'What do these guys think we are, a charity?'

'I can't think where they'd get that idea from,' I said. 'Daniel, did you hear about Sergei Delesov? He was murdered. In Russia. Greg Vilgren told me last night.'

'Jesus! Not another one. It's a dangerous world out there. They're dropping like flies.' He didn't seem especially upset, but then you wouldn't expect that from Daniel.

'You knew him quite well, didn't you?'

'Nah. Crazy Rooskie. Do you remember he wore those Gucci loafers all the time?'

'Didn't he lend you some money?'

Daniel looked up sharply. 'Who told you that?'

'Kim Smith.'

Daniel grunted. 'I was down a few grand. He knew some people who could tide me over.'

'Some people?'

'Yeah. A loan company.'

'Why didn't you just go to a bank?'

'Jeez, Simon. What is this? An IRS investigation?'

'It just seems strange to borrow a few thousand dollars from some friends of a Russian, rather than top up your loan from the bank.'

'I was up to my limit with the bank. And my parents decided I was a lousy credit risk long ago. It was no big deal. I paid them back.'

Daniel made a show of looking over the papers on his desk, and I left him to them.

'What are you up to this weekend, Simon?' he asked after a couple of minutes.

'Oh, Lisa and I are going to Marsh House to sort out Frank's stuff. There's quite a lot to do. What about you?'

'Don't know yet.' Just then his phone rang, and he snatched it up.

WE DROVE up to Woodbridge first thing the next morning. The thin November sun burned through the last remnants of the morning fog to illuminate the watery landscape. The silence of the marsh lay like a heavy cloak all around us. The only movement was the occasional flapping of an egret hauling itself into the air. There weren't many left now; most of them had gone south for the winter.

It was cold inside. I wound the grandfather clock and lit the stove, and a steady warmth soon pushed its way through the building. The house wasn't really built for winter habitation, but the beginning of November was unseasonably warm, and the place was quiet, cosy and peaceful.

I had tried to call Jeff Lieberman the previous day without success. I had the number of his Riverside Drive apartment, so I tried him again. This time I got through.

'Hi, Simon.' He sounded tired.

'I didn't wake you, did I?'

'Yeah, but don't worry, you just beat the alarm by a couple of minutes. I didn't get home from the office until four last night. And they want me in again at eleven.'

'Jeff. Do you remember when Daniel came to New York in October?'

'Yes.'

'You definitely saw him, did you?'

'What do you mean? Yes, I did.'

'And that was the 10th of October, right?' The day Frank was killed.

'I can check with my diary. Yes. Here it is. October 10. Brunch. We were supposed to have dinner together, but he changed it.'

'He changed it?'

'Yeah. He called a day or so before, and said he'd met some "babe" who lived in New York, who he wanted to see that night.'

'Daniel? A babe?'

'I did try to pry, but he wasn't saying much. But, hey, everyone gets lucky sometime.'

'Did you see him that afternoon?'

'No. After brunch he headed off. I don't know where. Why all these questions?'

'Oh, nothing. I'll see you at the Net Cop board meeting next week.'

'Well?' asked Lisa as I put down the phone. She was perched on Frank's desk beside me trying to follow the conversation.

'Daniel switched dinner to brunch.'

We looked at each other. Lisa exhaled. 'So, what do we do now?'

'Well, the cops can check him out.'

'Do we call Mahoney?'

'I'd rather not. I think we should talk to Gardner Phillips first.'

I dialled the lawyer's home. His wife answered and said he was out on the golf course. I tried his cellphone. It was switched off. I called Mrs Phillips back, and asked her to make sure her husband called me as soon as he got in. It was urgent. She expected him back by eleven fifteen. I looked at the grandfather clock. A quarter to ten. An hour and a half. The waiting was difficult.

'I'm not hanging around here,' said Lisa. 'I'll go crazy. I'm going for a walk. Coming?'

'No, I'll stay here, just in case he comes back early.'

Lisa grabbed her coat and walked out of the door. I went upstairs to make sure the storm windows were securely fastened.

I heard the front door bang.

'Lisa! Did you forget something?' I ran down the stairs.

I stopped short. There, standing in the middle of the living room, his hands thrust deep into his city raincoat, was Daniel.

'Hello, Simon,' he said casually.

I fought to compose myself. 'Hello, Daniel,' I said in feigned welcome, as coolly as I could manage. 'What brings you here?'

He wasn't obviously carrying a gun. But he wasn't taking his hands out of his pockets either.

'Oh, I'm meeting some people for lunch at Woodman's in Essex, and I thought I'd drop by on the way,' he answered. An extremely unlikely story, I thought. 'Where's Lisa?'

'She had to go into the lab,' I replied. 'She'll be there all day.' If the worst came to the worst, I didn't want Daniel hanging around waiting for her to come back from her walk. 'Coffee?'

'Sure.'

I moved past him to get to the kitchen. As I fiddled about with coffee and filters, I thought it over. Another murder now would blow the case wide open again, something Daniel would want to avoid. He was here to check up on how much I knew. If I played it right, he might leave again.

We moved back into the living room, Daniel still keeping his hands in his pockets, and sat in chairs opposite each other.

'So this is where Frank was killed, huh?' Daniel looked around.

'Yes. Just there.' I pointed to the section of scrubbed floorboard in the dining area.

'And they still don't know for sure who did it, huh?'

'Not publicly. But I'm pretty certain they think it was Enever.'

'And you? What do you think?'

'I think it was Enever too. He had everything to lose from news about the side effects getting out. I'm sure it was him.'

Daniel watched me closely. Then, seeming to come to a decision, he pulled a stubby revolver out of his pocket.

'I don't believe you,' he said.

I stared at the gun. This was not looking good at all. If I had jumped him when we were both standing up only a few feet away from each other, he with his gun hidden in the folds of his coat, I might have stood a chance. But now we were sitting ten feet apart and he was pointing the weapon at my chest.

I swallowed. 'Why don't you believe me?'

'Because you are too smart for that. After the questions you were asking me yesterday, I'd have been happier with a story about how you knew Enever wasn't responsible but you'd stopped worrying about it once you'd cleared yourself.'

'I know you killed him, Daniel,' I said.

'Have you talked to the police?'

I shrugged.

'I need to know who you've spoken to.'

'I won't tell you.'

He jerked the gun at me. 'I'll pull the trigger.'

I glared at him. I wasn't going to let him get the better of me. 'I know you will. I still won't tell you.'

Daniel looked confused. He was thinking. 'You said Lisa is at the lab?'

'She's coming this evening.'

'I heard you call out to her when I came in.'

'I thought you must be her. I assumed she'd left the lab early.'

Daniel scanned the room. 'Is that your bag, then?' He nodded towards Lisa's black bag, lying on the floor.

'No,' I said simply.

'You're not being very truthful, are you, Simon? We'll wait here for her. She'll tell me who you've told.' He glanced at the old grandfather clock. It was five past ten. 'We'll wait till eleven. Then we'll see. This should be a good spot to watch out for her.'

And it was. From the living room there was a perfect view of the marsh. She would be bound to come into view on her way back.

We waited.

I knew why Daniel wanted to know who we had spoken to. If we hadn't told anyone, once he had got us out of the way he would stand a reasonable chance of continuing to lead a normal life. If anyone else did know, his best bet was to kill us and take the first plane to South America. Either way we ended up dead.

I had pieced together most of what Daniel had done, but I wanted to fill in the gaps.

'Why did you have to kill Frank? Was it because you'd borrowed money from the loan sharks Sergei Delesov introduced you to?'

'It was worse than that. I'd told them BioOne was a sure thing. The day afterwards, huge volume went through in the stock. Millions of dollars. If the bad news had broken about neuroxil-5 when they were still invested, I'd have been dead meat.'

'But they got out?'

'Yep. Thanks to your warning, I got them out in time, as well as myself. I don't think we'll be doing business together again, shall we say, but I'm still alive.'

'Yes.' I looked at him. 'But quite a few other people aren't.'

He just grunted. I thought through what must have happened. 'You changed dinner to brunch with Jeff in New York, and came back to Boston that afternoon to murder Frank? And some time afterwards you used my spare apartment keys to let yourself in to plant the gun in my closet?'

Daniel smiled thinly. 'Seemed like a good idea. It nearly worked.'

'Who killed Dr Catarro?'

'The Russians. And they were supposed to deal with you.'

'What about John? Why did you kill him?'

'I had to. He'd remembered something Frank told him about neuroxil-5. He called me to ask about it. He said he'd called you. I did what I had to do to survive.'

Thin, pale, nerdish, Daniel looked more at home with a keyboard than a gun. But I knew he was greedy, and had a self-centred morality. If the alternative was some Russian killing him, I could imagine him resorting to murder.

We sat in silence, waiting for Lisa. Daniel was trying to stay cool, but he was finding it difficult. He was fidgeting, and a film of sweat was building up on his upper lip.

Half past ten. The phone rang. A loud, pre-digital, old-fashioned clanging sound. Gardner Phillips. I moved towards it.

'Stay where you are!' Daniel snapped. 'Leave it!'

So I left it. Both of us stared at the telephone as it cried shrilly for attention. Thirty rings. Finally it went quiet. Daniel relaxed.

My mind raced. I hadn't told Phillips where I was, but he should be able to figure out the address from the phone number. He could have the cops here in twenty minutes. But why should he? I had said it was urgent, not a matter of life or death. He'd wait half an hour and call again. In half an hour I'd be dead.

A quarter to eleven. As the time when Daniel would shoot me drew nearer, so also did the chance that Lisa might not return until after his deadline. She might survive. Oh God, please let her survive.

Then I saw her. She was approaching the house from the side, the side I was facing, but in a few seconds she would pass right in front of the big living-room window, and Daniel couldn't fail to see her. Unless I distracted him. I kept my eyes on Daniel, but through my peripheral vision I could see her getting closer and closer.

When she was a couple of yards from the window, I made my move. 'I need coffee.' I stood up, and moved towards the kitchen.

'I said stay where you are!'

I walked on, slowly, my hands up in a calming gesture. 'OK. You can keep me covered. But I need that coffee.'

'Stay there, or I'll shoot!'

I could feel sweat breaking out all over me. He meant it. The bastard meant it.

Through the window, which Daniel was now turned away from, I could sense as much as see Lisa.

I sensed she stopped. She saw Daniel, then ducked out of sight.

'OK, OK,' I said, and slowly moved back towards the chair.

I sat in the chair again to wait. I wondered what Lisa would do. Get the hell out and call the cops, I hoped. I glanced at the old grandfather clock. Only two minutes to go. Too late for her to save me. But time for her to save herself and our child. Somehow, that knowledge gave me strength.

Daniel, realising that his self-imposed deadline was fast approaching, seemed to be steeling himself. He was tense, sweating.

The clock struck eleven.

Daniel stood up, the gun held out in front of him, shaking. 'Stand up!'

I stood up calmly.

Just then a car engine burst into life. I recognised the low growl of the Morgan's V8 engine. Lisa was going to get away!

'What's that? Lisa?'

I nodded and smiled.

'Did she see me?' His voice rose in something close to panic. Outside, the car was put into gear.

'You bastard!' he said. Outside the car engine revved. Then through the wooden walls of the house we could hear it explode, rushing towards us.

'What the—!'

There was an almighty crash. The wall of the living room erupted, and the dark green nose of the Morgan burst into the room. Wood flew everywhere, a chunk dealing Daniel a glancing blow.

He fired. I felt a sharp burn on my stomach, but I leapt and was on him. He was thin and wiry; I was strong, and bigger than him. I grabbed the hand holding the revolver and beat it against the floor until he let go of the gun. I grabbed it, and belted him over the head with the butt. He slumped onto the floor.

I rushed over to the Morgan, which was half in and half out of the house. The whole front of the car was concertinaed upwards. Behind the wheel was Lisa, motionless, her eyes shut, a cut on her head bleeding heavily.

I was seized with panic. 'Lisa! Are you all right?' Nothing. I touched her gently on the shoulder. 'Lisa! Lisa! Speak to me!'

She moved slightly and groaned. Her eyelids flickered. Relief flooded through me.

'Oh, Lisa, are you hurt? Please tell me you're not hurt!'

She shook her head. 'I don't think so,' she whispered.

I helped her out of the car and pulled her close to me.

'Thank you,' I said, holding her tight. She had risked her life and our child's life for mine. I couldn't ask more than that.

Epilogue

I was ten minutes late for the Monday morning meeting. I had had very little sleep over the weekend, and I was exhausted. Everyone was there: Diane, Ravi, Jim the new partner, and two new associates Kathleen and Bruce. No Gil. No Art. And no Daniel, who was into the second month of his life sentence.

Ravi was talking about Boston Peptides. Henry Chan and the rest of the management team, including Lisa, had bought the company out from the debris of BioOne, with Revere's backing. 'The prospects for BP 56 look excellent. It causes mild depression in some patients, but that's no problem if it's taken in conjunction with an antidepressant. We start Phase Two trials in September.'

'Simon?' Diane said from her position in Gil's old chair at the middle of the table, turning to me. 'How's Net Cop doing?'

'Craig has customers slavering over his prototype. Now all he needs to do is gear up for production. And the finance for that will come entirely from the Initial Public Offering.'

'Any price talk yet?'

'Forty-five dollars.'

Diane did some quick mental calculations. 'That puts a value on the company of two hundred and forty million, doesn't it? We'll have ten per cent of that. Not bad, Simon.'

And it wasn't bad. We would turn an initial $2 million investment into $24 million.

'Lynette Mauer will be pleased,' Diane said. 'I think she might bite at a new fund next year. With Net Cop, Boston Peptides and Tetracom, we're beginning to convince them that we know what we're doing without Gil.'

Gil was sailing five days a week, and had yet to go anywhere near a dialysis machine. But we were all determined that the firm he had started would thrive without him.

IT WAS EIGHT O'CLOCK and still light as I made my way back home. I was exhausted but I walked fast, eager to see Lisa and the baby.

I opened the door and called out. There was no reply. I dumped my briefcase and went through to the bedroom. Lisa was lying asleep, a breast exposed, the baby breathing gently next to her. I took off my clothes and crawled in beside them.

I kissed Lisa on the forehead. She didn't stir. Then I kissed the baby.

'Good night, Frank,' I said, and fell instantly asleep.

MICHAEL RIDPATH

Final Venture, a story about a young Englishman living and working in America, draws on Michael Ridpath's own experiences. Like Simon Ayot, his protagonist, he is married to an American and, although he lives in London, he has spent a lot of time in his wife's native country. He is fascinated, he says, by the way English people behave when they're in the United States. 'I think it changes their personalities. What's great about America is that you can reinvent yourself and shake off your background, whatever section of society you come from. I think it liberates people, allows them to be more themselves.'

Before becoming a full-time writer in 1994, Michael Ridpath worked in the City, for the most part as a bond trader, but also, again like Simon Ayot, as a venture capitalist. 'I'd been wanting to write about the world of venture capital for some time,' he says. 'It has always seemed amazing to me that many of the companies that are deemed to be successful can have market valuations of billions without actually earning any money. The most obvious examples today are the Internet companies, but it can be just as true for biotechnology firms.'

Ridpath says he found researching the biotech side of this, his fourth novel, fascinating. 'I spent weeks and weeks on it. Far too long. For the plot to work I needed to come up with an imaginary but plausible treatment for Alzheimer's disease. In the end, by reading a lot on the subject and trying out my ideas on people I knew in the field, I managed to do so. It was very gratifying!'

As a father of three young children, Ridpath says he enjoys the flexibility that comes with being a successful writer. What do his children think of the fact that their dad is a novelist? 'Well, all I can say is, when my daughter was asked at school what her favourite sound was, she said it was hearing her father tapping away on the keyboard!'

THE OTHER SIDE OF THE DALE

including Over Hill and Dale

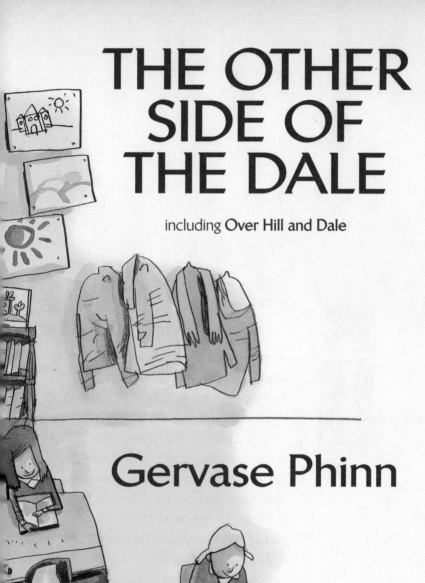

Gervase Phinn

In this fictionalised account of his early years as a school inspector, Gervase Phinn vividly describes the classrooms of the Yorkshire Dales, where children are often wiser than their teachers, and where many a lesson provokes laughter as well as learning. And back in the office, his colleagues are an unforgettable bunch: the irrepressible Sidney Clamp; Julie, the office chatterbox; and Connie, the caretaker from hell. Not to mention, the formidable Mrs Savage, scourge of the inspectors' office...

Prologue

At long last, after a two-hour search up and down the Dale, along muddy twisting roads, across narrow stone bridges, past swirling rivers and dribbling streams, and through countless villages, I had arrived at my destination. At the sight of the highly polished brass plate on the door bearing the words BACKWATERSTHWAITE SCHOOL, I heaved a sigh of relief and felt the sort of pioneering triumph that Christopher Columbus must have felt.

The austere building looked like any other large, sturdy Yorkshire country house. Beneath the grey slate roof, edged with purple lichen, tall windows faced the ever-watchful fields. From the grey and white limestone walls gillyflowers and tiny ferns creviced. A little beck trickled alongside as I made my way to the heavy oak door.

I lifted the great grey iron knocker in the shape of a ram's head and let it fall with a heavy echoing thud. A few seconds later the door was opened by a lean, stooping man with grey frizzy hair like a mass of wire wool. He looked as if he had survived the electric chair.

'Yes?'

'Mr Lapping?'

'Yes.'

'I think you were expecting me.'

'Are you the man who does the guttering repairs?'

'No, I am not! I am the man who does the school inspections. My name is Phinn, and I'm the newly appointed county inspector of schools for this area.'

'Are you indeed?'

'And I am making a number of initial visits to the schools in this part of the county. Yours is the first school I have on my list.'

'Is it indeed? I am most flattered.'

'Do you not remember, Mr Lapping? I wrote earlier last week saying I would be calling today?'

The tall figure scratched his frizzy hair. 'I do remember receiving a letter, now I come to think of it,' he said. 'Official looking, in a brown envelope. Yes, I believe I did.' He glanced at his watch. 'But you are a little late for visiting, Mr Flynn. The children go home at three thirty and it's getting on for half past four.'

'Yes, I'm sorry about the delay. I had difficulty finding the school.'

'Most people do,' replied the headteacher, nodding sagely.

'Never mind,' I shrugged. 'It was you I wished to speak to, Mr Lapping. Perhaps now that I know how to get here, I could arrange a further visit to see the children at work?'

'Yes, yes, of course,' he said with sudden eagerness. 'Do, do come in. We don't get many visitors up here once the summer holidays are over. I must admit I was quite surprised to see you at the door.'

I entered a large, bright classroom. Children's paintings, collages and beautifully written poems covered the walls. 'And as for coming to see the children at work,' he continued amiably, 'that would be very nice. We always enjoy visitors. Now I feel sure you would enjoy a cup of tea before you head off back down the Dale.'

'Yes, please,' I replied. 'But I don't intend to leave just yet. I would like to examine your School Development Plan before I go.'

'My *what*?' he asked.

'Your School Development Plan. The document which sets out your aims, objectives, targets and forward planning initiatives.'

'I haven't got one.' He gave a wan smile. 'I don't think I'd recognise one if it flew in the window, and that's the truth of it, Mr Flynn.'

'It's Phinn, actually,' I said.

'You'd better tell me about this School Development Plan of yours over this cup of tea I promised to make.'

So we sat in the small schoolroom by a window through which we looked upon great dark hills, and I outlined what the writing of a School Development Plan involved.

When I had finished the schoolmaster sighed. 'You know, Mr Phinn, I've been a teacher in this school for near on forty years. This school is a part of me. I live and breathe it. Look around. Outside is one of the most magnificent views in the world. Inside is a range and quality of work that speaks for itself. Every child in this school can read and write well, every child knows his or her tables, can paint and dance and sing, and they all get on, as you'll see on your next visit.' As I looked around me I knew these were no idle boasts. 'You town dwellers have a lot to learn about us country folk,' he continued. 'It's a different way of life. I'll do my best, Mr Phinn, but I reckon it'll be a while before you get your School Development Plan.'

I RETURNED a month later, skirting Brigg Rock and Hopton Crags, sheer and black and surrounded by tall ancient trees, to discover again the small school standing secure in its deep grey valley where the river, brown with recent rain, flowed unhurriedly beneath the arches of the slender bridge.

The morning I spent with the children was memorable. They sat open-mouthed as their teacher read a story in a soft and captivating voice, they answered questions with unusual perception, and they wrote the most moving poetry. Before I left, Daniel, a small nine-year-old with wide, unblinking eyes and hair as thick and bright as the bracken that covered the distant hills, approached me.

'Are thar t'scoil inspector?' he asked.

'Yes,' I replied, 'I am.'

'Well, can I tell thee summat?'

'Of course.'

'I just wanted to tell thee he's all right is Mester Lapping. He's a right good teacher, tha knaws.' I looked into the innocent eyes and smiled. 'Aren't tha goin' to write it down in tha big black book?' he continued. 'It's just that tha might forget.'

'No,' I replied, watching the tall, stooping figure who moved patiently and gently among his pupils. 'I won't forget.'

1

County Hall stood like many a Yorkshire town hall, sturdy and imposing, in the centre of the market town of Fettlesham. Surrounding it were formal gardens with well-tended lawns and neat footpaths. The interior was like a museum, hushed and cool, with long oak-panelled corridors and walls full of gilt-framed portraits of former councillors. It was really quite a daunting place.

'Just be yourself, answer the questions honestly—and remember to smile,' I thought to myself as I waited with the other candidates in the small anteroom to the Council Chamber. It was the good, sound, sensible advice I always gave to my students when, the term before they left school, I helped them to prepare for their job or college interviews. And if I'm not successful, I thought, well, it's not the end of the world, is it? I enjoy my present job and I've done pretty well to get a senior master's post in a flourishing comprehensive school before the age of thirty.

But I was not convincing myself. I really wanted this job as county inspector of schools (English and drama), and I'd been reasonably confident that I was well qualified and therefore in with a chance until I met the other applicants. They seemed infinitely more self-assured and better qualified than I. They sat in the anteroom, calm and composed, chatting amiably—mostly about themselves.

'I completed my PhD in early literacy problems,' a tall young woman was telling a distinguished-looking man. 'I feel certain I have read one of your books about qualitative and quantitative methods in the teaching of aphasic pupils.'

'Quite possibly,' he replied, stretching casually in his chair. 'I've written extensively and lectured widely on the topic of aphasia. My doctorate was in dyslexia.'

'Yes,' added another candidate, who sported a carefully trimmed beard. 'I remember you gave the keynote address on that very topic at the university where I lecture. It went down very well, I recall.'

'At which university do you lecture?' asked the self-assured young woman, suddenly looking in my direction.

'I don't lecture,' I replied. 'I'm a schoolteacher.'

'Really?' Three sets of eyes stared at me curiously. 'Have you published?'

'Nothing of any importance,' I replied. 'Just a few poems and stories for children, and an occasional article for an academic journal.'

'No, I didn't recognise the name,' remarked the expert in dyslexia, staring at his watch. 'I do wish they would get a move on. I really cannot abide waiting about.'

That was the end of any further dialogue, for the door opened and a tall, quietly spoken man entered and introduced himself. 'I am the Chief Education Officer of the county, Dr Brian Gore,' he said. 'I am so pleased you have all been able to attend for interview today.' He shook our hands warmly and chatted for a while, asking us if we had had a good journey. He then glanced at his watch. 'We will see candidates in alphabetical order, if you have no objections. The interview panel hopes to arrive at a decision today, so you may wish to wait for the outcome. Alternatively, you may wish to leave after your interviews and I will contact you at home this evening.'

I was the last candidate for interview so had a two-hour wait before I was called. Feeling a tight knot of fear growing in the pit of my stomach, I made for the gardens where I could get a breath of fresh air. An old man pushing a barrow-load of hedge clippings smiled as I approached.

'Champion day,' he said.

'Yes, indeed,' I replied. 'Lovely. The gardens look magnificent.'

'Well, I do try my best and you can't do more than that, can you?' he said, resting his barrow for a moment. 'Are you one of the new councillors then?'

'No, no! I'm here for an interview. School inspector's post.'

'School inspector, eh? I shall have to watch my p's and q's.' He laughed. 'Have you come far?'

'Just from Doncaster.'

'Not a town I know, Doncaster, but my father used to go to the races there. Do they still run the St Leger?'

'Yes, indeed, every year.'

For a while we chatted about the weather and the countryside and other commonplace topics, which thankfully took my mind off the fast-approaching interview.

'Well, I shall have to get on,' announced the gardener. 'I wish you well, young man. It's a lovely part of the country to work in and I hope you come in first in your own St Leger this morning.'

'That's kind of you,' I replied, 'but having seen the other runners I have a feeling I'm the rank outsider in this particular race.'

'The favourite doesn't always win, just remember that.'

'Well, I shall certainly try my best,' I said, smiling. 'And you can't do more than that, can you?'

'You can't, young man, you can't.'

For the next half-hour I walked around Fettlesham. It was a prosperous market town with a long main street full of smart dress shops and expensive jewellers. The estate agent's window displayed a selection of large farmhouses and detached 'executive' residences, which were way above the price range I could afford.

As I arrived back at the small anteroom, I paused outside the heavy mahogany door for a moment and listened to animated voices inside: the young woman and the expert on dyslexia were comparing details of their interviews.

'Quite tough questions, I thought,' the man was saying. 'The vicar's very astute and the old councillor at the end knew his stuff. That Dr Gore's sharp, isn't he? I think I did myself justice, though.'

'Did they ask you about dyspraxia?' asked the woman. 'I thought it was going to come up but they never asked anything about—' She stopped as I entered, and changed the subject to her recent research into learning difficulties.

Just then the bearded candidate came back from his interview. He was somewhat red-faced and breathless.

'Phew, what a grilling.' He sighed heavily and then, turning to me, said, 'Last man in!'

The council chamber was a magnificent circular room with a high domed roof. Ranks of highly polished wooden desks flanked a large central mahogany table at which Dr Gore and other members of the interview panel sat.

'Do take a seat, Mr Phinn,' said a solid, ruddy-faced individual in a thick tweed suit, 'and we will begin.'

The questions were wide-ranging but straightforward enough— about my qualifications, experience and expertise, my views on changes in the education system and recently published reports. Dr Gore sat gazing fixedly at me, with his long fingers steepled before him. When it came to his turn, the questions became more probing: What are the characteristics of a good school? How can you tell whether a teacher is effective or not? How should a teacher stretch and challenge a gifted pupil? How do you help the dyslexic child? What do you think is the role of a school inspector?

It was this last question that got me into a tangle.

'I think a school inspector is rather like Janus,' I replied.

'Like who?' asked an affable-looking cleric. 'Jesus?'

'No, Janus the Roman god. He is depicted with two heads looking in different directions.'

'I don't follow this line of thought. Are you saying a school inspector needs eyes in the back of his head?'

'Well, I suppose sometimes he does,' I replied giving the cleric a weak smile, 'but what I really mean is, he should look in one direction, to the schools and the teachers, to help, support and advise them, and at the same time he should look to the Education Committee to act as its monitor of standards. In a sense, he is both advisor and inspector rolled into one.'

'Sounds as if he needs to have a split personality,' commented a generously shaped councillor, chuckling.

As I returned to the room where the other candidates were waiting, I felt pretty certain that it had been a dire performance. I had tried to be clever and had come a cropper. I had been myself, I had attempted to answer the questions honestly, and I had smiled a great deal. But I should not have tried to be clever.

We did not have to wait long for the panel to reach its decision. Barely twenty minutes had elapsed when the door opened and Dr Gore entered.

'Mr Phinn,' he said quietly, 'could you return to the Council Chamber, please?'

I was walking on clouds as I followed Dr Gore back to the interview room.

'We would like to offer you the position of county inspector of schools,' said the solid, ruddy-faced individual in the thick tweed suit. I was speechless. 'We think you'll get on with the children and the teachers and be a real asset to the county. No disrespect to some of the other candidates, but we can't be doing with folk who think they are God's own gift to education.' I was still unable to say a word. 'Well, young man, has the cat got your tongue? Have you got an answer for us?'

'Y . . . yes,' I stuttered, 'I mean, yes, I would very much like to accept the position,' and I shook the large hand that was extended in my direction.

When I returned to the anteroom after a brief conversation with Dr Gore, all the others candidates had departed. But a few minutes later, as I made my way down the neat gravel path to the car park with a jaunty spring in my step, I met the gardener again.

'How did you get on?' he asked.

'I got the job,' I replied laughing. 'I actually got the job.'

'I thought you would,' he said. 'I'm a pretty good judge of character. I had my money on you from the start.'

'HELLO!' I CALLED hesitantly through an open door on the landing.

The school inspectors' office occupied the top floor of an Edwardian villa some distance from the main County Hall.

'Hello!' I called again, a little louder. There was still no reply. 'Hello! Is there anyone there?' There was still no answer so I popped my head round the door and peered into a small, cluttered office.

There were four heavy oak desks, four ancient wooden swivel chairs, four tall grey metal filing cabinets and a wall of dark, heavy bookcases crammed with journals and files. In the corner a computer hummed away on a small table. There was a half-drunk mug of tea on one desk, a shopping basket, handbag, a woman's scarf and a set of keys. I had written to the Office saying I would be calling in that

morning and, since I had received no reply, assumed it was convenient. However, it was clear no one was expecting me. I was just about
to do a little exploration when the shrill ringing of the telephone
made me jump. I waited a few moments before lifting the receiver.

'Hello?' I asked charily.

'Is that free school meals?' The voice was angry and strident.

'Pardon?'

'Free school meals. I want free school meals!'

'You have the wrong department,' I replied.

'Well, who am I through to then?'

'The inspectors' division.'

'I don't want the police! Why did they put me through to the
police? I asked for the Education.'

'This *is* the Education.' I attempted another explanation. 'It's the
education inspectorate.'

'And you don't deal with free school meals?'

'No, I don't deal with free school meals,' I sighed. 'I deal with
school inspections!'

'Well, who does deal with free school meals then?'

'I don't know. I'm new. But if you would like to leave your name
and number—'

'I'm in a telephone box!'

'Well if you could just hold the line for one moment—'

'Huh! Hang about in a draughty telephone booth that smells like a
public lavatory while you traipse off to find someone who'll be about
as much help as you? My brains aren't made of porridge, you know!'

The telephone went dead. Oh dear, I thought. I hope this is not a
flavour of things to come.'

'Mr Phinn?' I turned to find a young woman with blonde hair,
long metal earrings and a bright open smile, framed in the doorway.
'Is it Mr Phinn?'

'That's right,' I replied.

'I'm Julie,' she said. 'The inspectors' clerk. I've been looking all
over the office for you. You must have come up the back stairs.'

I shook her hand. 'I'm very pleased to meet you, Julie,' I said. 'I'm
sorry, I assumed the entrance was round the side.'

'That's all right. It's a bit of a maze in this building. Anyway, the
important thing is that you've found us. Here, let me move my things
out of the way.' She collected the shopping basket, handbag, scarf
and keys and dumped them on a chair, continuing her chatter as she
did so. 'I've been working in this office this week. It's got more space
than my room down the corridor. It's still the school holidays, so you

won't see the other inspectors until next week, I'm afraid.'

'I see. I just thought I'd spend a few days up here before the school term starts, find some digs, settle in and see if there is anything urgent I need to do.'

'Oh, there is,' replied Julie, laughing, and she pointed to the desk in the corner, which was piled high with papers. 'That's your place over there. The mountain started to grow as soon as everyone heard you'd been appointed. Mrs Young, the last English inspector, used to sit there. She's sunning herself in Spain at this moment, happily retired. Now, let me show you where everyone sits. Mr Clamp, the creative and visual arts inspector, is by the window next to Mr Pritchard, who covers mathematics, PE and games. Dr Yeats, he's the senior inspector, looks after history, geography and modern foreign languages, and that's his large desk in the middle.'

'I see,' I replied, not sure I'd remember any of this.

'Now, if you want to make a start on the paper mountain, I'll make us a cup of tea. I've prepared you a folder with some information about this and that, which you'll find in the top drawer. Dr Yeats has organised a programme for the second week. He'll take you round some schools with him to introduce you to various people. He also wants you to join him at some meetings to see how things work. He's really nice, is Dr Yeats. In fact, they all are in this office. Now, is that everything? Oh, yes, there's also a message for you from Mrs Savage.' Julie's voice took on a harder edge. 'She's Dr Gore's personal assistant. Not a person I warm to.'

Before I could ask what Mrs Savage might want, Julie headed for the door. 'Well, I'll let you get on. Give me a shout if you need anything. I'll be through with the tea in a minute.' Then she was gone.

I looked around the office in something of a daze, wondering where to start. A moment later Julie popped her head back round the door. 'I forgot to say—it's nice having you with us.'

I spent the entire day wading through letters, reports, questionnaires, publishers' catalogues, requests for references, minutes of meetings, agendas and details of teachers' courses.

'And it gets worse,' said Julie bringing me my fourth mug of tea.

'I've never seen so much paper in one place in all my life,' I groaned, stretching my arms in the air.

She smiled. 'Don't worry, it's not that bad. It's just that a lot of things have piled up over the weeks. It's always like this after the summer holidays. You'll soon have it cleared.'

'Do you think I should give Mrs Savage a ring?' I asked. 'It might be important.'

'If it was that important she'd have been over in person. No, it'll just be to fix a time to see Dr Gore.' Julie paused and stared at me for a moment. 'I didn't imagine that you'd look as you do. Your name conjures up a very different picture. I thought you'd be sort of French looking—dark and swarthy with an accent.'

'I'm sorry to disappoint you,' I laughed.

'Mr Clamp thought you would be a huge, red-headed Irishman and Mr Pritchard, a little, shy, bearded person. They had a bet on what you would look like. Dr Yeats has won. He said you would be just an ordinary, pleasant, agreeable chap.'

'Damned with faint praise, eh?'

'Actually, I reckon he had some sort of inside information. Anyway I'm sure you will settle in here. It's a very happy office. If there is anything else, Mr Phinn, anything at all, just ask.'

'You've been really helpful, Julie,' I replied. 'Thank you. I think you must have covered just about everything.'

'Did you find some digs, by the way?'

'Yes, on Richmond Road. I'll stay there until I find a flat to rent.'

'And is there a Mrs Phinn and lots of little Phinns?' she asked.

'No, there's no Mrs Phinn and no little Phinns,' I replied.

'Footloose and fancy free, eh? The world's your lobster, as my mother would say. Well, I'll let you get on.' And with that, Julie disappeared.

Thirty seconds later the telephone rang and I snatched up the receiver. This would be the call I was expecting from Mrs Savage.

'Hello?' I said cheerily.

'Is that free school meals?' The voice was angry and strident.

I cupped my hand over the receiver. 'Julie!' I yelled. 'Julie!'

2

Dr Harold Yeats, senior county inspector, stood six foot three inches in height. With his great broad shoulders, arched chest, heavy jaw and hands the size of spades, he looked more like an all-in wrestler than a school inspector. I found him waiting for me in the office the following Monday morning.

'Welcome, welcome!' he cried, shaking my hand vigorously. 'I must say when I saw the name Gervase Phinn on your application form, I imagined a rather lean, Oscar Wilde-like figure.'

'Julie told me you thought I would be just an ordinary-looking sort of chap,' I replied.

He roared with laughter. 'Ah, but that was after you were pointed out to me by the Chief Education Officer just after the interview. I observed you from his room, talking to the gardener. I had to admit to Dr Gore that it was something of a relief to find that you were just an ordinary, pleasant-looking chap. We could do with an injection of common sense and sanity in the office.'

Harold spent the morning with me going through my duties. I had joined a small team of inspectors responsible for different subjects in the curriculum. The main part of the job was to visit schools to check on the quality of the education and to give advice on how things might be improved. In addition to reporting to the Education Committee, inspectors had an advisory role which involved running courses, speaking at conferences, supervising young teachers and disseminating information from the Ministry of Education.

'My job this week,' explained Harold cheerfully as we headed for lunch in the County Hall canteen, 'is to help you settle in and get to know the ropes. Next week I'll take you with me to some meetings and we'll visit a few schools. Then, dear boy, you are on your own. But if there is anything you need to know, do please ask. And, of course, there's Julie,' he added. 'That young woman should not be underestimated. There is nothing Julie does not know about the workings of the school inspectorate. She's an absolute treasure.'

I must have looked very serious for Harold continued, 'You look rather pensive, Gervase. There's nothing wrong is there?'

'It's just the enormity of the job, Harold,' I said. 'There seems so much to do. I just hope I'm up to it.'

'Of course you're up to it, dear boy, you will fit in wonderfully well and be a great success. I have no doubts, no doubts at all about that.'

I just hope I prove him right, I thought to myself.

THE FIRST SCHOOL we visited the following Tuesday morning was a small, grey-stone primary school, set high on the moors above a vast panorama dotted with isolated farms and hillside barns.

'And we get paid for this, Gervase,' sighed Harold. 'It's like being on top of the world up here, isn't it? Beautiful, beautiful.'

When we arrived, we were greeted by a beaming caretaker.

'You're from the Education Office, are you?' he asked.

'Yes, yes,' replied Harold. 'I think the headteacher is expecting us.'

'Oh, oh, come this way, come this way,' said the overalled figure, dwarfed by Harold's great frame. 'We've *all* been expecting you. It's so good to see you.' The caretaker, poking his head round the school office door, announced with great enthusiasm to the school secretary, 'They're here, Mrs Higginbottom! The men from the Education. They're here! They've arrived!'

The secretary jumped up. 'Oh, good morning,' she said, beaming. 'It's so good to see you. The headteacher will be over the moon.'

We were overwhelmed by such a warm welcome.

'It's a recently appointed headteacher here,' Harold whispered confidentially. 'The new ones always tend to be very keen for inspectors to visit early on, to offer them advice.'

The headteacher, a tall, horsy-faced woman, strode into the room a moment later and greeted Harold with a vigorous handshake.

'At last!' she cried. 'I cannot tell you how pleased we are to see you here! You will have a cup of tea and a biscuit before you start, won't you—that's if you have the time.'

'Yes, yes,' replied Harold, 'that would be very acceptable.'

The headteacher nodded to the secretary, who departed to get the tea. 'It's just that I appreciate that your time is very precious.'

'Well, we're here for the remainder of the afternoon,' replied Harold. 'May I introduce my colleague, Mr Phinn.'

The headteacher shook my hand. 'I'm very pleased to meet you, Mr Phinn,' she said quickly, before returning her attention to Harold. 'Well, I think you'll find quite a lot needs doing,' she said. 'They are just not working and try as we might we can't get them to work. We've had such a lot of trouble this week.'

'That does sound serious,' said Harold.

'I've tried my best to get them to work but it's no good,' added the caretaker shaking his head. 'The weather might have had something to do with it, of course. They were frozen solid last winter.'

'Frozen solid?' Harold repeated.

'We thawed them out but they just froze again,' replied the head-teacher. 'Anyway, that's what you are here for, Mr Davies: to tell us why they won't work.'

'Yeats,' said Harold.

'I beg your pardon?'

'It's Yeats, Harold Yeats.'

'Aren't you Mr Davies from the Education Office—Premises and Maintenance—to see to the problem of the boys' lavatories?'

'No, no,' replied Harold. 'I'm Dr Harold Yeats, senior county inspector, to see about the curriculum. I wrote saying I would be calling with a colleague.' The headteacher's face took on the gloomy expression of a saint approaching certain martyrdom.

She cheered up a little, however, when Harold delivered a glowing report at the end of the afternoon, and she became positively jaunty when he promised to take up the cause of the boys' lavatories back at County Hall, as a matter of urgency.

'You will find in Education, Gervase,' he observed as we headed for the car, 'that sometimes lavatories take precedence over learning.'

OUR FINAL VISIT that day was to Hawksrill School, a tiny primary school deep in the heart of the Yorkshire Dales. We drove there along twisting, narrow roads, and through the open car window I could feel the warmth of the September sun and could catch the tang of leaf and loam and wood smoke. Now, after countless visits to hundreds of schools just like Hawksrill, I still feel the magic and wonder of the Dales that I felt that day.

We followed Mrs Beighton, the headteacher of the school, into a long room, bright and warm and full of colour, and were introduced to Mrs Brown, her assistant. Harold explained that we wished to listen to the children read, looking through their exercise books and asking them a few questions about their work.

'A pleasure,' replied the headteacher.

Harold and I went into the juniors' classroom, and soon the children came in chattering excitedly, their faces keen and happy. They hung up their coats, changed into their indoor shoes, exchanged reading books and sat talking to each other quietly until Mrs Brown called for their attention. She explained the task ahead.

I sat in the small reading corner and heard one child after another read to me, first from their own reading book and then from some I had brought. I was particularly impressed by John, a serious little boy of about seven or eight with a tangled mop of straw-coloured hair. During the break, Mrs Brown told me that he lived on a farm way out across the moors. It was a hard but happy life. He was expected, like most children from farming families, to help around the farm—feed the chickens, stack wood, muck out and undertake a host of other necessary jobs, and all that before he started his homework. When he was quite little, she told me, he had been woken by his father one night and taken into the byre to see for the first time the birth of a calf. The small, wet, furry bundle finally arrived and the vet held it up for the little boy to see.

'What do you think of that?' he had asked him. 'Isn't that a wonderful sight?'

John had thought for a moment before replying. 'How did it swallow the dog in the first place?'

ON THE FRIDAY, Harold and I compared notes. 'Do you think you will like this line of work, Gervase?' he asked.

'I'm sure I will,' I answered. 'I feel a lot more optimistic than I did last week. Thank you for looking after me. It's been so useful and quite fascinating.'

'It's been a pleasure. Well, it's getting late. We must be away. Next week you're on your own, and we'll meet again next Friday at about this time, to see how things are going. All right?' I nodded. 'And don't be afraid of asking for advice. Good night, Gervase. I think you'll fit in really well.'

'Good night, Harold, and thank you again.' I watched his great frame disappear through the door and heard his heavy footfalls descend the narrow stairs. I was tired but happy and knew in my heart that this was the job for me.

I was startled out of my reverie by the ringing of the telephone.

'Hello?' I said cheerily.

'Is that free school meals?'

'I do not believe it!' I said in a hushed voice. 'I just do not believe it!'

3

I first saw Sidney Clamp, the renowned inspector of creative and visual arts, that following week. He rushed into the office, puffing and panting, snatched his pile of letters, thrust some documents into Julie's hands for typing, hurriedly shook my hand and disappeared.

'Whoever was that?' I gasped.

'That,' Julie replied, sighing, 'is Mr Clamp. He often appears like the genie from the lamp and then disappears again.'

A week later, Sidney bolted past me on the long corridor at County Hall one lunch time, stopped suddenly, retraced his steps, stared at me for a moment and announced, 'Hello, Gervase, I thought it was you. Come along with me if you have a moment. I've something to show you.'

I was whisked along, with Sidney grasping my arm tightly and chattering excitedly. We arrived at a large room full of paintings, charcoal drawings, watercolours, sculptures and carvings.

'It's the art exhibition of children's and students' work,' he announced with obvious pleasure. 'At the end of each summer term, I collect a selection of artwork from the schools and colleges and then mount it and display it during the holidays to show the general public the high-quality work that well-taught young people achieve. Magnificent, isn't it?'

The exhibition did indeed look magnificent. It was a mass of brilliant colours and shapes, from the bold bright faces painted by the infants to the detailed oil paintings and twisted metal sculptures of the sixth-formers . When I turned to compliment Sidney on the display I found he had gone. I caught sight of him meandering between the exhibits, expounding, interpreting, explaining to visitors how the different effects had been created, his eyes bright with enthusiasm.

Later, Sidney and I walked to our cars together.

'I must admit,' he murmured, 'that when I heard the name Gervase Phinn, I had visions of a huge, red-headed, hot-tempered Irishman. Gervase Phinn,' he repeated. 'It has a sort of ring to it. *The Collected Poems of Gervase Phinn*. Mmmmm. Now take my name—Sidney Clamp. Not much of a ring to that, is there? It's not the sort of name to appear in the annals of Art History: Leonardo da Vinci, Pablo Picasso, Claude Monet, and—Sidney Clamp!'

'You could always change your name,' I suggested.

'Too late, too late,' he lamented, and gave me a mournful look. 'Too late for many things now.'

As we reached the car park he changed the subject.

'Harold tells me you've found a flat,' he remarked.

'Yes—it's above the Rumbling Tum café in the High Street. It's very noisy, but I've paid the rent for a couple of months. Eventually I hope to buy a place, but I don't want to rush into anything yet.'

'What sort of house have you in mind? Old? New? Large? Small? In the town? In the country?'

'I just don't know, to be frank. I've been so busy since I started that I haven't had time to think, never mind look for a house.'

'When you start looking seriously, I shall take it upon myself to give you my assistance. I am something of an expert on properties.'

'I shall know where to come,' I replied, smiling.

'And Julie tells me that you are unattached. No wife, fiancée, partner, girlfriend or children.'

'Yes, unattached at the moment. I've been so busy I haven't had time to think about that either.'

'Now that *is* serious. Never neglect your love life, Gervase. You cannot beat the love of a good woman. Wherever would I be without my Lila—my long-suffering wife of twenty-eight years. When you start looking seriously in the direction of the opposite sex, I shall take it upon myself to give you my undivided help and assistance. I am something of an expert on women. In fact, come to think of it, I am something of an expert in most things.' He eyed my battered Volvo. 'You aren't looking for a new car by any chance, are you?'

ONE BRIGHT Monday morning a few weeks later, the door of the office was flung open and there stood Sidney, beard bristling, eyes flashing. 'That Connie,' he boomed, 'has got to go!'

'Who?' I asked.

'Connie, the caretaker, site manager or whatever she calls herself. Have you not met her yet?'

'Ah, Connie!' I replied. 'Yes, I have met her.'

Connie was the caretaker of the Staff Development Centre, where all the courses and conferences for teachers were held. She was a woman of a certain reputation. In the fourth week of my new job, I had directed my first course at the Centre and she had watched my every move. I would look up from my lecture notes to see her face at the door; during the coffee break I found her hovering behind me. I almost expected to see her, arms folded, face scowling, duster in hand, waiting for me in the men's toilets. I had heard her talking on the telephone to a friend, explaining that she had a new inspector to break in and had to get him used to her systems. 'These clever artistic folk,' she said, 'are hopeless at clearing up after themselves.'

On hearing this I had scurried back to the room in which I had been working, made certain that the cups had been returned to the kitchen and the equipment had been safely put away.

Sidney, extrovert, unpredictable and creative, was the sort of man guaranteed to ruffle Connie's feathers, and he had experienced the sharp end of her tongue on many an occasion. On this particular Monday morning he was in a furious temper.

'Last Friday,' he snarled, throwing himself into his chair, 'I directed a highly successful course for infant teachers at the Staff Development Centre on the theme of "Creative Modelling in the Infant Classroom". I set the course members a practical task, to build a mythical creature, which I have to say they did with immense enthusiasm and inventiveness—and what do you think that dictator in the pink overall did?'

I turned in his direction and prepared myself for a long account of the disaster.

Sidney told me the infant teachers on the course had from kitchen rolls, plastic containers, tinfoil trays and bottle tops produced a huge dragon, which was proudly displayed near the entrance to the Centre. This very morning, armed with his camera, Sidney had returned to to take photographs of this stunning creation, only to find it had disappeared. He searched everywhere without success and finally ran Connie to earth to ask if she had seen the dragon.

'Dragon? No, I can't say that I have,' she had replied.

Sidney told Connie that she must have seen it. It was a four-foot-high, snakelike, fierce-faced creature constructed of waste material.

'Oh that!' Connie had replied casually. 'I put it in the bin.'

Sidney had exploded.

'Can you believe that, Gervase?' he demanded. 'She had consigned it to the rubbish tip! I said to her, "Connie," I said, "it was a work of art!" and do you know what she replied?'

'No, Sidney,' I said. 'But I feel certain you are going to tell me.'

'She looked at me, without a trace of remorse, regret or contrition, and she said, "Well, you should have written on it—*This is a work of art and not a load of old rubbish*—then I would have known not to throw it out."'

'I was lost for words. With hindsight, I should have replied, "Well, I should think you, of all people, would recognise a dragon!"'

IN THE PILE of mail one morning was a letter from a Miss Christine Bentley, headteacher of Winnery Nook Nursery and Infant School. She expressed the hope that I might call in and visit her soon, and included some delightful little poems written by the children. I looked at the map on the office wall and saw that my route to St Bartholomew's, an infant school I was to visit later that day, passed the village of Winnery Nook, so I decided to pop in during the morning and thank Miss Bentley for the poems.

Winnery Nook School was a modern, honey-coloured brick building with an orange pantile roof and large picture windows. The school was surrounded by fields and backed by a friendly belt of larch and spruce trees which climbed towards the high moors.

I arrived at morning playtime to hear the laughing of children in the small schoolyard, and I was just about to enter the main door when a very distressed-looking little girl of about five or six, her face wet with weeping, tugged at my jacket.

'They've all got big sticks!' she wailed piteously.

'Who's got big sticks?' I asked, surprised.

'All on 'em. They've all got big sticks!'

'Well, they shouldn't have big sticks,' I replied.

'I want a big stick!' she cried, sniffing and sobbing.

'No, you can't have a big stick. It's very dangerous.'

'I want a big stick!' she cried. 'They've all got 'em.'

At this point a very attractive young woman appeared from the direction of the playground.

'Whatever is it, Maxine?' she asked gently pulling the little child towards her. She then looked at me. 'It's Mr Phinn, isn't it?'

'Yes,' I replied. 'I'm looking for Miss Bentley, the headteacher.'

'That's me,' she replied, giving me such a smile that I was quite lost for words. She had the deepest of blue eyes and the fairest complexion I had ever seen, and a soft mass of golden hair.

'Mr Phinn?' she said. 'Mr Phinn?'

I returned from my reverie. 'Oh, yes, I'm sorry. I was distracted. I do hope you don't mind my taking you up on your invitation, Miss Bentley. I really did enjoy reading the children's poems and would love to er . . . look round the school if that's convenient.'

Before she could reply, the small child clutching her began to moan again. 'I want a big stick, Miss Bentley,' she pleaded.

'Of course you can have one,' the teacher replied, wiping away the little girl's tears. 'You weren't there when I gave everybody one. You don't think I'd leave you out, Maxine, do you? You come with me and I'll get you a nice big one. I won't be a moment, Mr Phinn.'

'A big stick?' I murmured. 'You're giving this little girl a big stick?'

The teacher gave a grin. 'She means a biscuit.'

The school was a delight: cheerful, optimistic and welcoming, and the creative writing was of very high quality. Maxine looked a very different little girl when I saw her again, smiling and contented and busily colouring with a large blue crayon.

'I've got a red crayon,' she said as I looked at her bright picture.

'It's a blue crayon. You've got a blue crayon,' I replied.

'It's red.'

'No, it's blue.' I took the crayon from her little fingers and held it against my suit. 'Like my suit, see—blue.'

'*That's* a blue crayon,' she said with great determination. 'I know that. I'm talking about my red one. It's at home. I've got a red crayon at home.'

I sighed, smiled and nodded. 'I see. What is your picture about?'

'A king and queen who live in a palace. Do you know how to write "queen"?'

'Yes,' I said and, borrowing her pencil again, carefully wrote the letters. 'Can you see it begins with a "q" and a "u" and when you put these two letters together they sound like "kwu".'

She nodded, copied down the word carefully and added, 'I know another word that starts with a "kwu".'

'Do you?'

'It's Kwistmas twee,' she replied, giggling.

This little girl, I thought to myself, really does take the biscuit.

At the end of the morning, I sat with the headteacher in her office, sipping tea and listening to her tell me about the school.

'I do hope you come to love this part of the world, Mr Phinn,' she said, 'and get to know the very special children who live here.'

'I'm sure I will,' I replied, and thought, I wouldn't mind getting to know you as well.

'Oh, how remiss of me,' said Miss Bentley, with a twinkle in those blue eyes as she passed me a plate of shortcake. 'Do have a big stick!'

IT WAS A CHILLY DAY as I drove along a twisting ribbon of road to a small school set deep in the Dales. Long belts of dark green firs glistened in an ocean of crimson heather and russet bracken, and grey wood smoke rose to the pale purple of the sky. It was a cold, bright, silent world.

Suddenly there was a loud crack and my windscreen shattered. I screeched to a halt. Climbing from the car I discovered a large pheasant lying on the bonnet, its claws sticking skywards. I was about to remove the bird when a red-cheeked character with a great walrus moustache appeared from behind a dry-stone wall, dressed in bright tweeds and with a shotgun under his arm.

'I say!' he boomed. 'Are you all right?'

I assured him that I was a bit shaken but no damage had been done apart from that to the windscreen.

'Good show!' he roared.

'It came from nowhere,' I said. 'I was—'

'Came from the sky, actually,' corrected my ruddy-cheeked companion. 'I bagged it. It's the October shoot. Lovely day for it. Plenty of game. Good sport. You're on my land, you see.'

'Oh, I'm sorry,' I apologised, 'I thought this was a public road.'

'It is, it is. It's just that it cuts through my land. Didn't you know it was the shoot? Out of county, are you?'

'Yes . . .'

'Anyway, not too much damage. Garage in the next village. Send the bill to me. No need to bother with insurance and that ballyhoo. Get in touch with the estate manager at Manston Hall. I'll tell him to expect your bill. I'm Lord Marrick, by the way. Take care.'

Before I could respond, he disappeared behind the dry-stone wall. I stared after him for a moment, then reached for the pheasant.

'I say!' The tweeded figure reappeared, snatched the pheasant from the bonnet of the car and made off with the aside: 'My bird, I think!'

I MET VALENTINE Courtnay-Cunninghame, the ninth Earl Marrick, properly some weeks later when I joined the interview panel for the appointment of a headteacher for High Ruston-cum-Riddleswade Endowed Church of England County Parochial Junior and Infant School. I arrived at the school at a time when a lively debate was taking place between the governors.

'Cost us a pretty packet just to place the advert in the paper!' boomed Lord Marrick as I entered. 'All those words in the name and every one to be paid for. Can't see why we can't just call it the village school or Ruston School, that sort of thing.'

'It's tradition, Lord Marrick,' responded the cleric to whom he was talking—a large, balding individual with a genial face and great bushy side whiskers. 'The school has always—'

'I'm all for tradition, vicar,' interrupted Lord Marrick, 'but I can't see the sense in this. I like things to be short and to the point.' Lord Marrick was still dressed in tweeds, but he now sported a large bow tie with pheasants, partridges and grouse flying on it.

'Shall we . . . er . . . make a start,' suggested the worried-looking woman at the head of the table. 'I don't think our school inspector has come all the way from Fettlesham to hear us squabble about the name of the school. Let me do a few introductions. I am Mrs Dingle-Smith, the Chairperson of the Governing Body.'

'Chairperson, I ask you!' grunted Lord Marrick. 'What's wrong with Madam Chairman?'

'Oh, please, Lord Marrick,' pleaded Mrs Dingle-Smith, 'we did discuss my title at the last governors' meeting.' Before the earl could reply, she hurried on, 'I believe you are acquainted with the rural dean, the Very Reverend Bernard Braybrook?'

'We met at my interview,' I said, praying that we would not get into the discussion about Janus again.

'And over here is another of our governors.' A diminutive, busy-looking woman in tweed suit and brogues shook my hand with amazing gusto.

'I'm Mrs Pole,' she said. 'Spelled P-o-w-e-l-l.'

'I'm Mr Phinn,' I replied. 'Spelled P-h-i-n-n.'

'And our other foundation governor,' continued Mrs Dingle-Smith, 'is the Earl of Marrick.'

'Met before!' roared the earl. 'Good to see you, Mr Phinn. Car all right, is it? Splendid, splendid. I move we get on with these interviews, Madam Chairman, otherwise we'll be here all night.'

Surprisingly, Lord Marrick said very little during the interviews. He simply stared rather menacingly at each of the candidates, grunting occasionally or nodding his head, and when it came to his turn to ask a question he snapped, 'Do you believe in standards?' All three candidates for the position of headteacher assured him that they did, at which point he nodded vigorously and growled, 'Glad to hear it!'

The last candidate was a rather intense, nervous young man in crisp white shirt, sober grey suit and dark blue tie. The stare on the earl's face became even more fixed. 'What's that on your tie?' he asked.

'I beg your pardon?' asked the startled candidate.

'The creatures! You have little animals all over your tie.'

'Oh, I see,' replied the candidate. 'They're natterjack toads.'

'Toads?' repeated Lord Marrick. 'Natterjack toads?'

'The natterjack toad is the emblem of CAPOW, the Countryside Association for the Protection of Wildlife. One of my hobbies is the preservation of endangered species.' Feeling a little more confident he chanced his arm. 'I see that you too like wildlife. I notice that your tie depicts a variety of birds indigenous to the area.'

'Oh, these?' replied the earl casually, lifting his tie to look at the pattern. 'I shoot 'em.'

'IT'S LADY MACBETH on the phone!' Julie called as she saw me appear in the office one morning at the beginning of November.

'Who?' I asked, puzzled.

'Mrs Savage and it's urgent—but everything's urgent to her.'

I snatched up the telephone. 'Hello, Gervase Phinn here.'

'Good morning, Mr Phinn,' said a calm, unhurried voice. 'Brenda Savage here, Dr Gore's personal assistant. The Chief Education Officer would like a word with you.'

The soft clear tones of the Chief Education Officer came down the line a few seconds later. 'I've been trying to have a word with you, Gervase, for the past few days but without success. There's something I need to discuss with you personally. I wonder if you could call over and see me tomorrow at about five o'clock?'

'Yes, of course, Dr Gore,' I replied.

The telephone clicked and he was gone.

'Dr Gore wants to see me,' I said to Julie.

'An audience with his eminence. It must be important.'

The following afternoon I anxiously entered the large, dark-panelled room of the Chief Education Officer. Glass-fronted bookcases lined one wall opposite a huge window that gave an uninterrupted view over Fettlesham. In the far distance were the moors.

'Sit down, will you, Gervase,' said Dr Gore. 'Thank you for coming to see me. Are you still enjoying the job?'

'Very much, thank you, Dr Gore.'

'You've been with us over half a term now, haven't you?'

'Yes, that's right,' I replied, wishing he would get to the point.

'Good, good. I've been receiving some admirable reports about you. Well now, Gervase, the principal reason for asking to see you was about this reading survey.'

'Reading survey?' I repeated.

'The County Education Committee members are deeply concerned at the recent Government White Paper on literacy and reading standards—that children cannot read as well as they could and that reading is not being taught effectively. Consequently I have agreed with them that we—and I am afraid that really means you—will present a short report to the Education Committee early in the spring. Now, I know that's a pretty short time scale but does it present a problem for you, would you say?'

'I shouldn't think so. It depends really on the number of schools in the sample, but—'

'The thing is, Gervase, you are the best person, as our inspector for English, to take responsibility for this report. You will need to devise a questionnaire for the selected schools about the methods used to teach reading, and you will need to hear a representative group. The Committee has decided to limit it to six- and seven-year-olds. The collation and analysis of the results can be done for you. Now, do you think you can manage it?'

'Yes,' I replied. 'I think so. I will start planning right away, Dr Gore.' I said.

'Well, that's settled then. We can make a start before Christmas. Mrs Savage will look after the admin so you will obviously need to liaise closely with her. Have you met Mrs Savage, by the way?'

'No, not yet,' I replied.

Dr Gore, steepled his fingers and nodded sagely. The room had become strangely quiet.

'Good, good,' he said suddenly. 'That's settled, then. Thank you for coming to see me, Gervase. I very much look forward to seeing your proposals and to reading your report.'

OVER THE NEXT few weeks, in between inspecting, advising, directing courses and joining interview panels, I set about planning the reading survey. With Harold's help, I selected a small random sample of schools in different parts of the county, chose a simple, easily administered test, and designed a questionnaire and a survey about reading interests and patterns. My suggestions were accepted by Dr Gore, who instructed me to go ahead. The next part of the process was potentially tricky. I needed to see Mrs Savage to get her to reproduce the material and send it out to the schools.

'Not something I would relish, liaising with Mrs Savage,' said Julie, screwing up her face as if waiting for an unpleasant smell to evaporate.

I approached the door on which were large black letters spelling out MRS B. F. SAVAGE, Personal Assistant to the Chief Education Officer. Fortunately, on the day I called Mrs Savage was at lunch. So I simply handed the draft copy of the questionnaire to her secretary.

The following day a memorandum arrived on my desk, stating that Mrs Savage had received the questionnaire, which she had reproduced, with 'various necessary amendments', and that she had arranged for a copy to be dispatched to each school, requesting that it be returned completed to her for analysis.

THE FIRST SCHOOL I visited as part of the survey was at Mertonbeck. It was a small village primary with high mullioned windows and a shiny grey slate roof. From the classroom window a great rolling expanse stretched to the faraway moors. The headteacher introduced me to the children, then set me up in a comfortable chair in the corner of the classroom.

'I'll send the children to you, Mr Phinn, one at a time,' she said. 'They really love to read.'

A little girl with long golden plaits and a face as speckled as a thrush's egg was the first to join me.

'Hello,' she said. 'I'm Amy. Miss said you wanted to see me.'

'Would you like to read to me, Amy?' I asked pleasantly.

'Why?' came the blunt reply. 'What for?'

'Well, that's why I'm here this morning—to hear the children read.'

'Is it your hobby?' I was asked.

'No,' I replied. 'It's my job.'

'It must be nice,' she mused, 'listening to people read all day.'

'It is,' I agreed.

I finally prevailed upon her to read and she did so in a clear and expressive manner. 'All right?' she asked.

'Splendid,' I replied. 'Thank you. You're a lovely reader, Amy.'

'I know,' she said. 'And I'm good at writing as well. Do you like writing, Mr Phinn?'

'Yes, Amy, I do like writing.'

'Do you write poems?'

'Yes.'

'Do you get the rhymes?'

'Sometimes.'

'And the rhythms?'

'Oh, I always get the rhythms.'

'Do you draw pictures around your poems?'

'No.'

'I do. I think it makes them look prettier on the page. Do you write poems about animals?'

'Amy,' I firmly said, chuckling. 'It's me who usually asks the questions, you know.'

She gave me the sweetest of smiles. 'I'm interested—that's all.'

The next child, a small boy with a crown of close-cropped black hair, was an excellent reader too. He read from his book with grim determination, in a loud and confident voice.

'You're a very good reader,' I commented, when he snapped the book shut. 'Do you like reading?'

'I do.'

'I see from your reading card you've read a lot of books this year.'

'I have.'

'Do you read at home?'

'Sometimes.'

It was like extracting blood from a stone. 'And what do you like reading about?' I asked cheerfully.

'Animals mostly.'

'Farm animals? Wild animals? What sort?'

'Cows. I live on a farm.' Then a slight smile came to his lips and his expression took on that of the expert in the presence of an ignoramus—a sort of patient, sympathetic, tolerant look. 'Do you know owt about cows then?' he asked.

'No,' I said feebly. I should have left it there but I persisted. 'Would you like to tell me about the cows on your farm?'

'There's not that much to tell really. Cows is cows.'

'You're not a very talkative little boy, are you?' I said.

'If I've got owt to say I says it, and if I've got owt to ask I asks it,' he replied.

THE FOLLOWING WEEK, on a sunny but cold morning, I visited St Helen's, a tiny Church of England primary school. I entered armed with my questionnaire, checklist, survey form and standardised reading test. In the small entrance area I pressed the buzzer at the reception desk, signed in and was soon in the headteacher's room looking at the serene countenance of Mrs Smith.

'You will find that we devote a great deal of time and effort to the teaching of reading, Mr Phinn,' she said. 'We pride ourselves on achieving good standards and I think you will find every child well on the road to reading.' I was not to be disappointed.

In the infants, I met Elizabeth. She was in that part of the classroom called the home corner, where children can dress up, get into role, practise talking, reading, writing and acting out parts. The home corner in this classroom was set out like an optician's shop. There were posters and signs, price lists and eye charts, a small desk with plastic till, appointment book and a large red telephone. Elizabeth was busy arranging some spectacles on a small stand.

'Hello,' I greeted her.

'Oh, hello,' she replied cheerily. 'Is it a pair of glasses you want?'

I hadn't the heart to say, 'No, I'm here to give you the Cathcart-Smitt Reading Test,' so I replied, 'Yes, that's right.'

'What sort have you in mind?'

'I think I'd like a pair that makes me look younger.'

'Well, we'll see what we can do.' Then she added, 'I shall have to test your eyes, you know.'

'I thought you might,' I replied.

'Can you read?'

Here was the school inspector come to test the child's reading and he was being tested himself. I nodded and was presented with a list of letters, which I read as she pointed to each in turn.

'You have very good eyes,' she said, as she rummaged in a box of frames. 'And you want some glasses to make you look young?' She finally decided on a pink pair, pointed at the ends, with diamanté studs. I tried them on and looked in the mirror. Elizabeth watched for a moment and then began giggling.

'Are you laughing at me?' I asked sadly, peering through the ridiculous pair of glasses. She nodded slowly and stopped giggling.

'I don't think it is very nice, you know, for you to laugh at your customers.' I pulled a strained face. 'I'm very upset.'

She stared for a moment before approaching me and then, patting me on the arm, whispered gently, 'It's only pretend, you know.'

Elizabeth then read to me in a clear, confident voice full of expression, and completed the reading test with flying colours.

THAT FRIDAY AFTERNOON, as I climbed the stairs to the inspectors' office, I felt weary after a week's work in schools. I had just about completed the last visit of the reading survey and had a weekend ahead of me to draft some early findings.

Julie saw me from her office and popped her head round the door. 'You've got a visitor.' She raised an eyebrow. 'Mrs "I could curdle milk with one of my stares" Savage. The Lucretia Borgia of the Education Department.'

I entered our office to find a tall, elegant, middle-aged woman, of strikingly good looks, casting a critical eye on the spider plant that sat on the windowsill. Mrs Savage was dressed in a stylish black suit, black stockings and shoes, and an assortment of expensive jewellery.

'Mr Phinn!' There was a clash of bracelets.

'Mrs Savage?' I replied.

'I thought that rather than communicate by memoranda we should meet face to face to discuss the collating of the results of the reading survey. I just cannot be doing with last-minute arrangements. I like things to be done efficiently and thoroughly.'

My mother had always advised that, when confronted by people bristling for an argument, the best plan of attack was to disarm them with graciousness and affability. It never failed to work. So I grinned toothily and replied in the softest of voices, 'I am sure that with your assistance, Mrs Savage, the collating will go exceptionally smoothly.' I motioned her to take a seat.

'It's just that I cannot impress on you too strongly how very important this report is, Mr Phinn.' Her voice was still strident. 'You are, of course, new to writing reports of this nature. Dr Gore has asked me to help you organise things.'

'Dr Gore, I know, regards your work very favourably.'

She allowed herself a slight smile. 'Well, I do endeavour to respond to requests promptly and efficiently. I may be a stickler but—'

'I think you are so right,' I cut in.

'You do?'

'But of course. And I know I will get the highest level of support from you.'

She was struck dumb with astonishment. I guessed she had been ready for a confrontation with this new, jumped-up inspector and the wind had been taken from her sails. On every occasion I readily accepted her suggestions and supported her ideas, all of which were, in fact, eminently sensible. After an hour, we had planned the report down to the finest detail and Mrs Savage was a different person.

'Your help has been invaluable, Mrs Savage,' I concluded, smiling.

'Well, it is nice to be appreciated, I'm sure,' she replied. Julie looked up from her desk as we passed. 'And should there be anything else, please do not hesitate to ask. You have my extension number.'

As Mrs Savage clattered down the stairs, jangling her bangles,

Julie shook her head. '"And if there is anything else,"' she minced in imitation, '"do not hesitate to ask." And as for you, Mr Phinn, you really did lay it on thick.'

'Well,' I replied, 'in my experience, people always appreciate recognition for what they do and respond much better to a kind word and a smile. I found Mrs Savage perfectly pleasant and more than helpful. I think her bark must be worse than her bite.'

'You think so, do you?' replied Julie. 'Well, in *my* experience, her bite is worse than her bark. My advice is to stay well clear of her. Beware of the woman in black.'

I should have heeded Julie's prophecy.

'BY THE WAY, Gervase,' said Sidney one Friday morning before the monthly inspectors' meeting, 'I saw the delectable Miss Bentley of Winnery Nook yesterday.'

'Oh, did you?' I replied, trying to sound casual.

'You didn't waste much time getting in there, did you? When I mentioned our new dynamic inspector, she said she had already met you. I believe hers was one of the first schools you visited.'

'Yes, that's right. If you must know, I received a welcoming letter from Miss Bentley and some poems from the children, and thought I'd call in to thank them.'

'And what did you think of the comely Miss Bentley?'

'She seems very nice.'

'Very nice? Very nice?' David Pritchard looked up from his papers. 'You are supposed to be our resident expert on the English language, one of the richest, most descriptive, most beautiful and powerful languages in the entire world, and all you can come up with is "very nice"?' David, county inspector for mathematics, PE and games, was a small, good-humoured Welshman with a head of silver hair, dark eyes and a big, splayed boxer's nose. At our first meeting he had taken me to lunch and during that one lunch-hour I had learned all I needed to know about our office and its workings. 'Don't you think, Gervase,' he now went on, 'that Miss Bentley of Winnery Nook is just exquisite—like some pale porcelain figurine?'

'I visited in my professional capacity. That sort of thing just never entered my head.'

'Good grief!' Sidney spluttered. 'You do sound an old stuffed shirt. I mean, how old are you, for goodness sake—ninety-five?'

'Thirty-one.'

'Thirty-one, attractive, educated, good-natured and, most important, single and unattached—you're love's young dream, dear boy!'

'Please don't go on, Sidney.'

'You want to get in there. Ask the divine Miss Bentley out.'

'It wouldn't be right. I mean, it could compromise a professional relationship. It's not ethical.'

'Thirty-one and acting as if he's in his dotage.'

Luckily, our discussion was curtailed when the giant frame of Harold Yeats appeared through the door.

'Colleagues,' he proclaimed, 'shall we begin the meeting?'

The conversation about Miss Bentley did start a train of thought, though. I mean, why shouldn't I ask her out? But then again, she might have a boyfriend or be engaged and I would make a fool of myself. I just did not know what to do.

The situation was resolved, or so I thought, the following Sunday, while I was at an auction at Roper's Saleroom in Collington, the nextdoor town, where there were some early editions of children's books for sale. I collected children's stories, picture books and poetry anthologies, and I thought I would see if there was anything of interest. At least it would get me out of the flat for a couple of hours.

The auction room was a long, elegant building set back from the road. As I headed for a table piled with books, I caught sight of Miss Bentley gently stroking the top of a highly polished mahogany table. She did indeed look exquisite. I watched her move around the room with a languid easy grace, and felt a stream of powerful emotions. She must have sensed that someone was watching for she looked up, saw me staring, waved and then came over.

'Hello,' she said, giving me a stunning smile. 'I thought it was you. So you're interested in antiques, are you?'

'Well, no, not really. I came to look at some children's books. I collect early editions.'

'And have you seen anything you fancy?' she asked.

'Well there's a first edition of *Un Drôle de Chien* but I guess it will be out of my price range.' My voice sounded wavery. Pure nerves.

She smiled and was just about to reply when a tall, fair, good-looking man approached. 'Not much here, I'm afraid. Did you see anything, Chris?' he asked, ignoring me.

'There's a nice Georgian table, not too big, which would probably fit into your study. Oh Miles, this is Gervase Phinn. He's a school inspector.'

'Really? You're that man that puts the fear of God into the poor teachers, are you?' commented Miles, brushing back his hair like a male model.

'Not really,' I replied.

'It must be dreadfully dull sitting at the back of classrooms ticking little checklists all day. And those beastly, noisy children everywhere. Still, each to his own. What are you interested in?' he added in a bored voice. 'Are you here for a particular piece of furniture?'

'No, no,' I replied. 'I'm looking at some old books.'

'Really? Old books?' I could see he wasn't the slightest bit interested. 'Well, we must make tracks.' He took Christine's arm and began to lead her away. 'There's nothing I like, Chris, so we might as well go and get something to eat. There wasn't anything you wanted, was there?'

'Yes, there was, as a matter of fact,' she said, releasing herself and flicking through the catalogue. 'There's a Copeland china plate.' She looked up and smiled in my direction. 'I collect plates. Miles says I have enough crockery to cover the fields of his farm.'

'Come on, Chris, it will take ages to reach that part of the sale. If you're really interested in even more plates and Mr Glynn here is staying on to bid for his old books, perhaps he could bid for you. We could reimburse him later.'

'I should be delighted,' I replied.

'Oh, could you?' cried Christine. 'That is kind. But don't go above thirty pounds, will you? It's lot 237, I think, but I'll just check.' She ran a long, delicate finger down a page in the catalogue. 'Yes, that's right. There's also "a blue plate of unknown provenance", lot 239. You could go to twenty pounds for that. And if you manage to buy the plates, you could pop round with them. There'll be coffee and a biscuit waiting.' Her eyes twinkled as she mentioned the biscuit.

'Oh, do come on, Chris,' urged Miles, tugging at her arm. With that, they left, chattering no doubt about the inspector who collected old books. I must have seemed deadly dull.

The book I was interested in fetched a price way above what I was prepared to pay. I could have left the auction room there and then—goodness knows I had enough to do—but I stayed to bid for the plates. I sat thinking about Christine and feeling a strange dull ache in the pit of my stomach. I had never felt like this about anybody before.

My thoughts were abruptly interrupted by the auctioneer's announcement: 'Lot 238: a Davenport toy tea set painted with Pratt coloured decoration, comprising four cups and saucers . . .'

Oh Lord, I had missed the first plate I had been asked to bid for. My mind had been on other things. Then I heard the auctioneer announce the next item: 'Lot 239, an attractive pale blue patterned plate of unknown provenance.'

Right, I thought, I'll not go away empty-handed. A big, purple-faced individual raised a finger as fat as a sausage when the auctioneer started the bidding at twenty pounds. I raised my hand.

'Twenty-five pounds!' shouted the auctioneer.

'Thirty!' barked the purple-faced individual.

'Thirty-five!' I called out.

'Forty!'

'Forty-five!' I was determined to buy the plate. Before I knew it, the bidding was up to fifty pounds.

'Sixty!' I shouted with a defiant ring to my voice.

At last, old purple face shook his head.

As I signed the cheque for the plate, the purple-faced individual sidled up. 'Nice plate,' he said. 'Very nice plate. Unusual figures. Nice bit of patterning as well.'

'Yes,' I replied, 'I'm sure my friend will like it.'

'Pity about the crack,' he grunted.

THAT EVENING I sat looking at the plate, wondering what to do. In my opinion, it was very ugly. The three stiff Chinese figures looked quite out of proportion, the perspective of the bridge was all wrong and the trees were crude to say the least. Worst of all, there was a long hairline crack right across the centre.

I telephoned Miss Bentley the following Monday.

'Hello, Winnery Nook Nursery and Infant School.'

'Miss Bentley?' There was that nervousness in my voice again. 'It's Gervase Phinn here. I'm afraid I missed the first plate you were interested in. But I did get the other. The one of unknown provenance.'

'Oh, excellent,' she said. 'How much did you pay for it?'

'As you said, twenty pounds.'

'I'm delighted. Thank you so much for taking the trouble.'

'No trouble,' I replied. 'It was a pleasure.'

'Well, there's no rush to get the plate to me but when you are passing, drop in. The coffee—and biscuit—are waiting.'

'I'll look forward to that,' I replied. 'I really will.'

4

It was the run up to Christmas, and I had volunteered to narrate the Christmas story to the infants at the small Roman Catholic primary school at Netherfoot. Thanks to Dominic, a massively freckled boy with ginger hair that stood up like a lavatory brush, I never reached the end. He positioned himself at my feet on the carpet in the reading corner, and his questions and comments came fast and furious.

I began: 'It was cold and dark that December night many years ago, on the hillside where the icy winds whistled through the trees—'

'I can whistle,' said Dominic puckering up his lips.

'And the grass was frosted and stiff with cold—'

'Do you want to hear me whistle?'

'Not now, I don't,' I said, 'perhaps later.' I continued with the story. 'Matthew, the little shepherd boy, huddled in a dry hollow with his sheep to keep warm. High above him the dark sky was studded with millions of tiny silver stars—'

'Miss Stirling gives you a star if you do good work,' said Dominic.

'These weren't that sort of star,' I said. 'These were like diamonds sparkling in the darkness. This was the night that Jesus was to be born.'

'I've heard this story!' exclaimed Dominic. 'I know what happens.'

'We all know what happens, Dominic,' I responded, 'and we are going to hear what happens again.'

'Why?'

'Because we are. Now, let's get on with the story.'

'Was baby Jesus induced?' asked Dominic.

'No, he wasn't induced.'

'I was induced.'

'Well, baby Jesus wasn't induced.'

'How do you know?'

'Because it was a long time ago and they didn't induce babies then.'

'Why?'

I sighed wearily. 'Just listen to the story, Dominic . . . And then amid the diamonds that sprinkled the dark sky there appeared a great shining star, a star that sparkled and gleamed—'

'How much did the baby Jesus weigh?' asked Dominic.

'I've not got to the baby Jesus yet.'

'I was an eight-pounder. My granny said I was like a—'

'Dominic!' I said very quietly and slowly. 'Now just listen to the story. You are spoiling it for all the other children.'

'I know how this story ends,' he replied, undaunted.

'Then why don't *you* come out here and tell us all, Dominic,' I said, throwing in the towel.

And so he did. Like a seasoned actor he came out to the front of the class and recounted the Christmas story in such a simple, animated and confident way that we all listened in rapt silence.

'Once upon a time there was a man called Joseph and a lady called

Mary and they were friends and they had fun. Then they had a wedding and after the wedding they went home and had some lunch and a drink and then they set off for Bethlem on their honeymoon and they went on a donkey. When they got to Bethlem there was no room at the inn so they had to stay in a barn round the back and then Mary had a little baby and she called it Jesus and she put him in a manger and all the animals were around him and the big star shone and then the shepherds all came and then the three kings came and they all gave him presents because it was his birthday and baby Jesus had plenty of milk because there were lots of cows about.'

There was silence at the end of Dominic's story, then he looked at me and said, 'OK?'

'OK,' I replied, 'very OK.'

On my way out a little girl with blonde plaits approached me shyly. 'I liked that story,' she said.

'Did you?' I replied. 'I'm glad.'

'But Dominic tells it better than you do. Happy Christmas.'

LATER THAT WEEK, I arrived at a primary school just outside Fettlesham to find an extremely distraught headteacher.

'Oh dear, Mr Phinn,' she gasped, 'oh dear me. It looks as if we will have to cancel the party. Father Christmas has appendicitis.'

It turned out that Father Christmas was Mr Beech, the school crossing-patrol assistant, who every year took on the role. This year he had been rushed to hospital and his daughter had telephoned to say that he would not be able to oblige. There were tears in the headteacher's eyes. 'The children will be so disappointed. They are all so excited about Father Christmas coming.'

What could I do? I was the only available man. Nervously I donned the costume and after a strong cup of coffee entered the hall. The children squealed in delight when they saw the familiar red coat and cotton-wool beard. Everything went well until a bright little spark announced loudly, 'You're not real, you know.'

'Oh yes, I am!' I replied in a deep, jolly Father Christmas voice.

'Oh no, you're not,' she persisted, 'your beard's held on by elastic. I can see it. And Father Christmas has big boots. You're wearing shoes.'

'Ah, well, I got stuck in a snowdrift on my way here and my boots were so filled up with snow that I borrowed these shoes from Mr Beech.' School inspectors have to think on their feet when it comes to bright little buttons like this one.

'You can't have because Mr Beech has gone to hospital,' continued the child. 'My mum told me because he lives next door. You're not the real Father Christmas!'

The headteacher intervened and bailed me out by starting the singing. After three verses of 'Rudolf the Red-nosed Reindeer', each child came forward to receive a small present.

'What are the names of your reindeers?' asked a little boy.

'Well, there's Rudolf,' I started, 'and Donner and Blitzen and er . . .'

The headteacher, seeing that I was struggling, helped me out again by explaining that Father Christmas was rather deaf.

'Some of the snow from the snowdrift is still in his ears,' she said.

One child asked me if I knew her name and, when I replied that I did not, looked crestfallen. 'But I thought Father Christmas knows all the boys' and girls' names?'

The headteacher explained that Father Christmas's eyes weren't too good either and he had such a lot of letters to read.

One rather grubby little scrap asked if she could sit on my knee.

'No, Chelsea,' said the headteacher firmly. 'I don't think—' She was too late—the child had clambered up like a little monkey.

'Come on down, Chelsea,' said the headteacher. 'I don't think Father Christmas wants children on his knee. He's got a poorly leg.' Any more ailments, I thought, and I would be joining Mr Beech in the Royal Infirmary.

'Now, you be a very good little girl and sit on the floor, Chelsea,' I said in my jolly voice, 'otherwise all the other children will want to climb up.' Chelsea stayed put, however, and I chuckled uneasily until the child's teacher managed to prise her off.

After the children had sung me out to 'Jingle Bells' I was invited into the staff room. It was extremely hot in the red suit.

'Father Christmas, you were a great hit,' said the headteacher. The staff looked on and nodded. 'And we'd like to give you a little Christmas gift.'

'Oh no,' I said, 'it really isn't necessary.'

'Oh, but it is,' insisted the headteacher and presented me with a small bottle wrapped in bright Christmas paper.

I shook my gift. 'Aftershave?' I enquired. 'Is it aftershave?'

'No, Father Christmas,' the staff replied.

I tore off the wrapping to reveal a small brown bottle of medication. The label read: 'For infestation of the head.'

'Chelsea's just got over head lice,' said the headteacher. 'It's not advisable to be too close to her for the time being.'

The rest of the staff then joined in with a hearty 'Ho! Ho! Ho!'

I was already beginning to itch.

'I HAVE A CRYPTIC message for you, Gervase,' announced David Pritchard, peering over his half-moon spectacles.

It was late Tuesday afternoon and three days before school finished for the Christmas holidays. I was endeavouring to catch up on a backlog of correspondence and seemed to be making little progress. Harold Yeats, oblivious to everything around him, was tapping away on the computer, trying to complete a school report. Sidney Clamp was scribbling at his desk, trying to plan his next art course for early in the new year.

'I was asked to ask you what has happened to the plate?' David said. 'Does that make any sense?'

'Yes,' I replied, 'it does. Thank you, David.' I returned to the letter I was writing.

'It sounds very mysterious to me. Like a coded message,' he observed. 'Like some secret phrase used by spies. You are not with MI5 are you, Gervase? FBI? CIA? An undercover agent investigating corruption in the county?'

'David, I'm attempting to write an important letter.'

'It's just that Miss Bentley came over to me at the Staff Development Centre last week, looked deep into my eyes with those limpid pools of hers and said, '"Ask Mr Phinn what has happened to the plate." It's a most unusual thing for someone to say.'

Sidney's ears pricked up at the mention of Christine Bentley's name. 'The ravishing Christine Bentley of Winnery Nook!' he cried. 'And what were you doing visiting Winnery Nook again, Gervase? What was your excuse this time for going to see the most desirable unmarried woman in the whole county?'

'I have been into the school once, Sidney, only once.'

'What's this about a plate, then?' he asked. 'Or was the word "date"? Did she say, "What has happened to our date?"?'

'No, it was definitely plate,' said David.

'Gentlemen,' said Harold turning away from the computer screen to face us, 'do you think we could return to the serious business of report writing? It is nearly the end of term, there is much to do, it looks like snow, the roads are busy and I intend getting home at a reasonable hour this evening, so I would really appreciate a little less badinage.'

'Of course, Harold, old boy,' replied Sidney. 'It is a dreadfully demanding time of year, I do agree. And we all have such a lot on our plates.' He glanced mischievously in my direction.

We had just settled down to work again when the telephone rang. Harold snatched up the receiver. 'Hello, Harold Yeats here. Yes, yes, he's sitting next to me. I'll pass you over.' He gave me the receiver. 'Gervase, it's for you. Miss Bentley of Winnery Nook.'

Sidney and David both turned to stare.

'Now,' exclaimed Sidney, 'all will be revealed!'

'Hello,' I answered. 'Yes, yes, he did mention it to me . . . No, no, that's quite all right . . . Yes, I have meant to call in with it but have been so very busy . . . Yes, yes, well, that would be very nice. I should enjoy that . . . Yes, of course. I will see you tomorrow then. Goodbye.' I put down the receiver carefully. I then returned to my letter.

'Well?' asked Sidney.

'Do tell, Gervase,' pleaded David. 'Put us out of our misery.'

'You don't need to look at me like that,' I said. 'I've only been invited to a nativity play, tomorrow evening.'

'Invited to the nativity play by Miss Bentley of Winnery Nook,' sighed David, 'and the only one in the office to receive a Christmas card from Mrs Savage. My goodness, Gervase, just what *is* your secret with the opposite sex?'

'Gentlemen,' growled Harold, 'please!'

WINNERY NOOK NURSERY and Infant School looked very different from when I had last visited it early in the autumn. The surrounding fields and rocky outcrops were now hidden under a smattering of snow, and the belt of pines had a fine dusting of white.

I entered the school hall clutching the blue cracked plate and looking for Christine. A member of staff informed me that she was backstage getting the little ones ready for the play, but that a seat had been reserved for me in the front row.

Mums and dads, grannies and grandpas, aunties and uncles, neighbours and friends filled the school hall for the nativity play. It would be the fifth I had seen this term, but for them it was the highlight of the school year.

I found my seat just as the lights dimmed and a spotlight lit up the small stage. The curtain opened to reveal various Eastern-looking houses painted on a backdrop and two rather forlorn palm trees made out of papier mâché and green crêpe paper. The little boy playing Joseph entered wearing a brightly coloured towel over his head, held in place by an elastic belt with metal snake fastener. He took centre stage without a trace of nerves, stared at the audience and then beckoned to a worried-looking Mary, who entered pulling a large cardboard and polystyrene donkey.

'Come on!' urged Joseph. 'Hurry up!' He banged on the door of one of the houses. 'Open up! Open up!' he shouted loudly.

The innkeeper threw open the door. 'What?' he barked.

'Have you any room?'

'No!'

'You have, I saw t'light on.'

'I haven't.'

'Look, we've travelled all night up and down those sand dunes, through towns, over hills, in and out of rivers. We're fit to drop.'

'Can't help that, there's no room.'

'And I've got t'wife out here on t'donkey.' Joseph gestured in the direction of Mary, who was now staring at the audience, her face completely expressionless. 'So give us a room.'

'There's no room. How many more times do I have to tell you?'

'She's having babby, tha knaws.'

'Well, I can't help that, it's nowt to do with me.'

'I know,' replied Joseph sighing as he turned to the audience, 'and it's nowt to do with me, neither.'

To the surprise of the children there were roars of laughter from the adults in the audience. And so the play progressed until angels in white with cardboard wings and tinsel halos, shepherds with towels over their heads and cotton-wool beards, and wise men in coloured robes and shiny paper crowns gathered around Mary and Joseph to sing 'Away in a Manger' and bring a tear to every eye.

Following the performance, I went in search of the elusive Miss Bentley.

'It went really well,' I said when I found her.

'Thanks,' she replied, shaking my cold hand. 'It's nice to see you again.' Then she caught sight of the plate.

'One cracked blue plate of doubtful provenance,' I announced, and presented it to her.

'Oh, it's lovely,' she replied. 'It's really unusual. Thank you so much for bidding for it. It was sweet of you. I think we got a real bargain here, don't you think?'

'Yes,' I replied, remembering the full price I had paid. All that money for a piece of ugly, cracked pottery.

'And you got my cheque?'

'Yes, yes, thank you, and the lovely card.' This was followed by a rather embarrassed silence. I changed the subject. 'And what are you doing over Christmas?' I said casually. 'Are you going away?'

'Yes,' she replied, 'we are off to Austria, skiing. Miles is a first-class skier. He was an army champion. What are you doing?'

'Nothing at all special,' I replied. 'I'm spending a quiet Christmas with my brother and his family.' I sounded deadly dull and dreary again. 'Well, I must make tracks. Thank you for asking me to the nativity, Christine. Good night and a Happy Christmas.'

I walked out into the cold night. Army champion! Well, of course, he would be, I thought. The white moon lit up the landscape, luminous and still. Lights twinkled in windows and there was the smell of pine trees in the air. It was the magic atmosphere of Christmas.

'And I hope he breaks his bloody leg!' I said aloud.

Julie bustled into the office balancing a potted spider plant in one hand and a wire tray full of letters in the other.

'So what sort of Christmas did you have?' she asked, placing the mail on my desk and the plant on the filing cabinet.

'I spent Christmas with my brother's family. I slept for most of the time in front of the log fire. What was your Christmas like?'

'About as quiet as the D-Day landings. Arguments about presents, screaming children, family feuds over Christmas dinner, quarrels about which television programmes to watch. Whoever said that Christmas was a time of peace and goodwill to all men should have spent it with us. I'm glad to be back. There's a message from Dr Gore somewhere in that pile of papers, by the way, asking you to call him urgently.' As she headed for the door Julie turned and smiled impishly. 'Probably heard about your secret liaisons.'

'I'VE A LITTLE JOB for you, Gervase,' Dr Gore said, smiling at me across the desk.

I glanced at him despairingly. Dr Gore's 'little jobs' were never little.

'Now don't look so worried,' he murmured. 'It's just that I've received a letter from the Department of Education and Science asking if it would be convenient for the Minister of State to visit the county. He's trying to get a feel for things before he puts together a White Paper. He wants to learn something about the education system at ground level up here in the north.'

I sighed. It was easy to predict what was coming next.

'He'll be with us in five weeks' time and I would like you to manage the visit and arrange an itinerary. Harold Yeats felt, and I must say I agreed immediately, that you would be able to cope admirably with the responsibility for making the visit run smoothly.'

'That's very gratifying,' I replied. 'Of course, I'll do my best.'

'Good, good,' said Dr Gore. 'Now the Minister will only be here for the morning and I want him to leave with a favourable impression. Your task will be to present him with a picture of the life and work in our schools. You know the sort of thing—Mrs Savage will help you. There will be one of the Minister's assistants, probably one of Her Majesty's Inspectors, contacting you shortly to discuss arrangements.' He beamed across his desk. 'Now do keep me fully informed, won't you, Gervase?'

'Of course.'

'See—quite painless. I think you will find this little job most enjoyable.'

THE TASK, I had to admit, promised to be interesting and challenging, and I set about it with gusto. First of all, I dropped a memo to Mrs Savage asking for her help in producing a programme of events. Then I booked the Staff Development Centre, asked colleagues to call in the best displays of work they had seen recently during inspections, and arranged for a representative group of people to meet the Minister.

'There's been another woman wanting to speak to you!' shouted Julie from the outer office two days later. 'With a funny name. Sounded like Miss Deadly Stare. I got the number.'

I rang the number, which was a London one, and asked for a Miss D. L. Stare. I thought it was a reasonable guess.

'De la Mare,' corrected the receptionist in high-pitched, artificial tones. 'Miss de la Mare, Her Majesty's Principal Divisional Inspector of Schools. I'll put you through.'

'De la Mare,' came a strident voice down the line. I explained who I was. 'Right, now I am arranging things this end for the visit of the Minister of State and, of course, we all want things to go as smooth as clockwork, don't we?' Miss de la Mare then barked various requirements down the telephone. The Minister, Sir Bryan Holyoake, I was told, was a perfectionist. He did not like a deal of fuss, drank only mineral water, and was punctilious about keeping to schedule. The information filled me with dread.

I spent a full day at the Staff Development Centre the week before the visit, making certain everything was ready for the Minister's visit. There were colourful exhibitions in every room.

Connie pursued me like some manic guard dog. 'I can't see what all this fuss is about anyway,' she remarked. 'And I hope you're going to take all those staples out when you've finished.'

'Of course, Connie,' I replied.

'It's just that I like things to be left as people find them.'

'Of course, Connie,' I repeated.

'I've seen how you inspectors leave this place after your courses. That Mr Clamp, with the fancy ties, left a trail of destruction and debris behind him last week.'

'There will be no destruction and debris, Connie,' I replied. 'You can be certain of that.'

I had completed the last of the displays and was admiring the final effect when Mrs Savage arrived, dressed this time in cardinal red with matching accessories. Over the weeks we had got to know each other so well that we were now on first-name terms.

'This looks very impressive, Gervase,' she said scanning the walls. 'I have a feeling that this visit is going to be a great success. Here are the programmes and the itinerary for you to look over.'

'That's very kind, Brenda. It's saved me a trip into the office. Thank you very much. I think everything's in order and—'

'Is that your car?' Connie appeared from nowhere. 'That blue car—is it yours?'

'Yes, it is,' replied Mrs Savage brusquely. 'Why?'

'You're blocking the main entrance. You'll have to move it. It's a health and safety hazard.'

'I hardly imagine,' replied Mrs Savage in a patronising voice, 'that one small car, parked against the wall, could constitute a health and safety hazard.'

'Yes it would!' snapped Connie. 'If there was a fire it would prevent people from getting out.'

'Perhaps you could then explain,' responded Mrs Savage, 'how a small car, parked well away from the door, could possibly—'

'Rules are rules! So would you move it—please?'

'I have only popped in to deliver some papers,' Mrs Savage insisted. 'I shall be going in one moment. Now if you wouldn't mind—'

The formidable Brenda Savage, however, had met her match in Connie, who clearly did mind. 'There's a sign that says: "Do not block this entrance." It is there so people do not park their cars in front of the main door and cause a health and safety hazard.'

'Oh, for goodness sake!' cried Mrs Savage, scrabbling for the car keys in her handbag. 'I shall move the wretched car.' She gave Connie a look of undiluted venom.

'Well, just so long as you do,' replied Connie, quite undaunted, strutting off down the corridor, holding her feather duster like a field-marshal's baton.

ON THE MONDAY MORNING I waited nervously at the entrance of the Centre, and several large black cars pulled up in front of the main entrance at exactly 9.00am. Out of the first climbed the Chief Education Officer accompanied by the Right Honourable Sir Bryan Holyoake, MP. The Minister of State was quickly surrounded by a knot of dark-suited, serious-looking men who intermittently whispered things in his ear, in response to which he gave slight nods. He was barely through the door when Connie sidled into sight. A dreadful thought crossed my mind. Connie was going to tackle him about blocking the entrance and causing a health and safety hazard.

'Don't mention the car, Connie, for goodness sake,' I hissed. 'I will tell the driver myself to park away from the door. Please do not mention the car!'

She nodded, and the party moved slowly down the main corridor of the Centre, which was resplendent with displays of children's writing and painting.

In the main hall, where an extensive exhibition of models and constructions was arranged, the Minister wandered around, pursued by his blue-suited minions, occasionally glancing at the distant hills framed by the window. His companions continued to whisper in his ear and he continued to nod in response.

Connie appeared again, the twitching of her lips and her fidgeting fingers betraying her agitation.

'I do hope that old gentleman doesn't trip on the step,' she said. 'He doesn't look all that good on his feet. In fact, he didn't look too well at all, if you ask me. I bet he could murder a cup of tea. I think I'll just pop down and—'

'He doesn't drink tea, Connie, really.' I guided her away, back to the entrance.

'Is he *the* important visitor then?'

'His name is Sir Bryan Holyoake, Connie,' I replied, 'and he's the Minister of State for Education and Science.'

'He won't be any relation to Ivy Holyoake who owns the tripe shop down Fitzwilliam Road, I don't suppose?'

'I shouldn't imagine so,' I said.

I WAS ONCE TOLD by a grizzled old farmer that the county of Yorkshire is bigger than Israel and covers more acres than words in the Bible. It may be something of an exaggeration, but the county is certainly large, and in winter, when the strings of caravans have disappeared, you can travel mile after mile without seeing a soul.

It was on one such cold, raw February day, when the sky was steely grey and the air so icy it almost burnt your cheeks, that I visited Bartondale. The drive from the nearby market town was uphill all the way along a narrow, twisting, slippery road. Barton Moor Parochial School, an austere building of dark grey stone, was set high up among dark green hills flecked with snow. Nearby there was the hamlet of Barton Moor, a little cluster of houses and an ancient squat church, all surrounded by a fleecy mist.

The inside of the school was as warm and welcoming as the head-teacher, a large woman with the wonderfully Dickensian name of Miss Sally Precious.

'It's so good to meet you, Mr Phinn,' she said, shaking my hand vigorously. 'I'm so pleased to see that you have arrived safely. The roads are quite treacherous at this time of year.'

'Well, I'm delighted to be here, Miss Precious,' I replied. 'I thought I would arrive a little early before the children, to have a look around the school and discuss a few things with you.'

She nodded enthusiastically.

I was taken on a tour of the small school, which took less than fifteen minutes. Miss Precious chatted amiably, describing how she organised the curriculum, the methods she used to teach reading, how she developed handwriting skills and the strategies she employed to help the gifted children.

There were only two classrooms: one for the infants and one for the juniors. Both were long rooms with high beamed ceilings, both showed clear evidence of high-quality work. In the infant classroom I met a small, nervous-looking woman who was busy arranging a spray of flowers and ferns. She introduced herself as Mrs Durdon, 'the teacher of the little ones'.

In the junior classroom the small, high-set windows had been removed and replaced by a large picture window, which gave a magnificent view across the desolate moor and down into the valley. It was an awesome view.

'It's very beautiful in its own way, isn't it?' commented the head-teacher.

'It is,' I agreed. 'It must be fascinating to see how the seasons change from this classroom window.'

The noise of excited chatter outside interrupted our reverie. 'If you'll excuse me for a moment, Mr Phinn,' said Miss Precious, 'I can hear the first children arriving. Mrs Durdon and I like to welcome them each morning and say a few words to the parents.'

I was left alone and was still staring through the window when a small, serious-faced boy with thick-lensed glasses entered.

'Good morning,' he said. 'You must be the school inspector. Miss Precious said you would be coming today. I'm Joseph Richard Barclay.' He held out a small hand, which I shook.

'And I'm Mr Phinn.'

'I'm pleased to meet you, Mr Phinn,' he said. 'Were you looking at the moor?'

'Yes. It really is a desolate scene.'

'There was a famous battle there, you know, over four hundred years ago, between the Roundheads and the Cavaliers. A lot of men perished on that moor. They say the ground was red with blood.'

'Really?'

'It was called the Battle of Barton Moor but it was really only a skirmish. It wasn't your proper full-scale battle like Marston Moor or Naseby. The Cavaliers were pursued by the Roundheads up the valley but made a stand at Barton Moor.'

'You're quite the expert, aren't you, Joseph?'

The boy nodded seriously. 'I do like history. If you walk across the moor in the late afternoon, it's full of shadows and shapes, and some say the ghosts of dead soldiers wander about.'

I stared at my companion. He was a strangely old-fashioned looking boy of about eleven, with a strangely old-fashioned way of speaking. Eleven-year-olds generally do not use words like 'perished' and 'skirmish' and 'pursued'.

'Well,' he said suddenly, 'I must get on. I have to collect the register. If you'll excuse me.'

Through the classroom door I heard a hubbub of excited children as they hung up their coats and changed into their indoor shoes.

'Miss, t'watter in t'hen coops froz up last night. It were as 'ard as Brimham Rocks.'

'T'calf were born last night, miss—it's a really big 'un. Like a babby helephant, it were. I was up 'til ten with t'vet!'

'Miss, my mum says it's cold enough to freeze t'flippers off a penguin this mornin'.'

When the children caught sight of me, I was surrounded by the same lively chatter, full of the richness of a Dales' dialect.

'Come on, come on, chatterboxes!' said Miss Precious. 'You'll have plenty of time to talk to Mr Phinn later this morning.'

She turned to me. 'Could you start in Mrs Durdon's class with the infants, please, Mr Phinn, and join us after morning break?'

Mrs Durdon, despite her nervousness, proved to be a very good teacher. The classroom was neat and tidy and the standard of reading was high, as was the quality of the written work.

At playtime Mrs Durdon donned a thick black coat, heavy scarf, woolly hat and boots and, explaining that she was on yard duty that morning, hurried off in the direction of the small playground.

A cup of coffee in a fine china cup was awaiting me in the head-teacher's room.

'Now,' she said, taking two heavy, black leather-bound volumes from the shelf, 'I want you to have a look at the school log books. They are really fascinating and go back well over a century.'

She opened one of the books and passed it across her desk. The first page had the following entry:

September 5th, 1898
Took up my position as Headmaster of Barton Moor Parochial School in the County of York. 24 children on role, all from farming familys. Most of them iliterate.

'Isn't it just priceless.' Miss Precious smiled. 'See how he's spelt "illiterate" and "families" and "roll". It gets better.'

The next entry read:

September 6th, 1898
Morning spent on arithmetic, handwriting and scripture. Afternoon spent on rhetoric. I learned them a poem.

'This is really interesting,' I said. 'Have you thought of writing a short history of the school? It would make an excellent piece of research for the children.'

'We've done it,' she replied proudly. 'The children collected photographs and old maps, made copies of parish records and interviewed parents and grandparents. We discovered a host of fascinating characters from the past: eccentric parsons, colourful landlords of the local inn, a footpad who was hanged at York and the Lord of the Manor who ran off with a serving maid. We amassed a great deal of information and Joseph put it all together. I think you met Joseph Barclay earlier this morning. He's produced a very readable account of the school's history.' She reached up and plucked a booklet from the shelf. The chronicle was word-processed in bold clear lettering and written in a style unusually mature for an eleven-year-old. It was illustrated by small line drawings, carefully executed maps and photographs.

'It's good, isn't it?' Miss Precious said. 'You'll see Joseph's other work next lesson. I would be very interested to know what you think of it and I would really welcome some advice on his education. He's a very unusual little boy is Joseph Barclay.'

THE VERY PERSON we were talking about was busily tidying the books in the classroom when I arrived at the end of morning break.

'Hello, Mr Phinn,' he said.

'Haven't you been out to play, Joseph?' I asked.

'No, sir. I had a few jobs to do in the classroom.'

'It's good to blow a few cobwebs away, you know, get a breath of fresh air, have a run around in the morning.'

'Oh, I get enough fresh air. I walk a mile to school each morning and a mile home in the afternoon. That keeps me hale and hearty.' I smiled at the old-fashioned turn of phrase.

When the children had settled at their desks after the morning break, Miss Precious began her lesson.

'Now, children,' she said, 'Emily's mother has been gardening again, and she's found something.' Miss Precious turned to me. 'I should explain, Mr Phinn, that Emily, like most of the children in the class, lives close to Barton Moor and her garden goes right up to the site of the battlefield. Emily's mother has found some really interesting things. Tell us what your mother found yesterday, Emily.'

'Well,' began Emily, 'it's a sort of buckle. It's maybe from a belt or a bag. It's all rusted up but there is a little silver rose in the middle.'

'We'll add that to our collection, shall we, Emily, and when someone comes up from the university we can find out what it is.'

'So other things have been found, have they?' I asked.

'Yes, sir,' announced a boy, waving his hand as if hailing a taxi. 'My granddad found some lead musket balls and three brass buttons when he was mending a gate.'

'My dad found a sort of spear thing,' chimed in another. 'It was under the foundations when we built the extension. It's at the museum now. What was it called?' he said, turning to Joseph.

'It was a halberd,' replied Joseph. 'A sort of hatchet with a spike on the top, which would have been mounted on a long wooden pole.'

'That's it!' shouted the boy. 'A halberd.'

'Has anyone else found anything in their gardens?' I asked.

'I found a dead cat, sir!' announced a large boy with a placid face. This was received with some kindly laughter, but I noticed that it failed to bring a smile to Joseph's lips.

'I don't think somehow that a dead cat, Ben,' chuckled the teacher, 'dates back to the Battle of Barton Moor. Soldiers were not in the habit of taking their pets into battle with them.'

'Excuse me, miss,' interrupted Joseph, 'some of the commanders did take their pets into battle with them. Prince Rupert had a dog—it was a toy poodle—called Boy, which he sat on his saddle and he took everywhere with him, even into the thick of the fighting.'

'Do you know, Mr Phinn,' said Miss Precious amiably, 'Joseph has more history in his little finger than I've got in my entire head.'

I spent the remainder of the morning listening to the children read confidently and clearly, and examining their written work.

When it came to Joseph's turn, his record of the books he had read over the year was wide and challenging, mostly historical in theme. His reading was slow but without any hesitations at the difficult words. His writing was beautifully presented, accurate but entirely serious in theme.

'SO WHAT DID you make of our Joseph?' asked Miss Precious at lunch time. 'He's a most remarkable boy, isn't he?'

'He's one of the brightest children I have ever met,' I replied. 'Articulate and, for his age, immensely knowledgeable, very polite but . . .' I paused for a moment to try to think of the most appropriate word, 'I find him melancholy. A disconcerting child.'

'You are very perceptive, Mr Phinn. He's a pleasant boy, always helpful and courteous, but he has such a mournful, pessimistic nature. I just wish sometimes he'd run in panting and laughing like the others—but he never does.'

'Is he bullied?' I asked.

'Oh good gracious, no. The other children tolerate him remarkably well. They accept him for what he is. The boys tried at first to involve him in their games but he prefers to be alone. In summer he sits quietly reading on the bench in the playground, like an old man enjoying his retirement. In winter he potters about the classroom, cleaning the blackboard, sharpening the pencils.'

'What do his mother and father say?' I asked.

'Well, that's part of the problem, I feel,' sighed the headteacher. 'He lives with his grandparents. They're well meaning and caring and they try their best with him, but they're like many older people—they've slowed down and want a quiet life.'

'Well, I have to say, Miss Precious, that I don't think he could be in a better school than this. There is a spirit of happiness and endeavour here. The work Joseph undertakes is certainly challenging enough and he seems, in his own way, a contented child. He's a very unusual young man and I guess we'll all be hearing a great deal about him in the future.'

Before I set off for my appointment at the next school, I said goodbye to the teachers and children.

'Thank you so much for coming, Mr Phinn,' smiled Miss Precious.

'Do have a safe journey.' Then she added: 'Joseph, perhaps you would show Mr Phinn out and put the catch on the door after him.'

As we walked towards the entrance, Joseph asked, 'Are you writing a report on this school?'

'Yes, I am,' I replied.

'Well, if you want my opinion, I think this is a very good school with many positive features. Miss Precious really tries her best and works very hard.' It sounded like the comments from one of my own reports. 'I hope you'll put that in to your account of the school.'

'I shall certainly consider doing so, Joseph,' I said. At the door he held out a small hand.

'Well, I must get back to my work,' he said as I shook his hand. '"Time waits for no man", as my grandfather says.'

I arrived home late that evening when all was still and the air misty and cold. The lights of the shops and houses lit up the high street, casting bright bars of yellow across the road. My flat above the Rumbling Tum café was in darkness. I let myself in, but paused for a moment before I turned on the light. I could not stop thinking of a lonely little boy with thick-lensed glasses walking home along the narrow path that bordered Barton Moor.

'HELLO, WINNERY NOOK Nursery and Infant School.'

'Miss Bentley . . . er . . . Christine?'

'Speaking.'

'It's Gervase Phinn here. You left a message for me to ring you.'

'Oh yes, thanks. I must see you. I can't really explain over the telephone. There's a personal matter I need to discuss with you. Can you call in some time?'

My heart began to beat nineteen to the dozen. 'I can call in today after school, if that's convenient. It would be about six o'clock.'

'That will be fine. I usually stay late on a Monday. I look forward to seeing you then.'

Whatever could she want? I thought. What was the personal matter? What was there to discuss? I racked my brains to think of what it could be about.

Just before six I arrived at Winnery Nook. The school was deserted and silent. I sat in the car daydreaming, wondering what could be so urgent and personal. Over the last few months I had seen Christine very briefly at a couple of courses, and of course I had received the card and cheque for the plate, but I had had no chance to see her for any length of time since Christmas. She had certainly been in my thoughts, though.

A sudden tap on the car window made me jump. 'Are you going to sit out here all evening?' It was Christine. Flustered and embarrassed, I clambered from the vehicle. 'I've been watching you from my room,' she said. 'You can come inside, you know. I don't bite.'

I followed her into the school and down the corridor to her room. She motioned for me to take a seat.

'I've had a tiring day,' I said, in a feeble attempt to explain the odd behaviour. 'I was just sort of unwinding.'

'Are you still enjoying the job?' she asked.

'Oh yes, very much,' I replied, but I could not cope with pleasantries. I just had to know why she wanted to see me. 'What is it . . . er . . . you wanted to speak to me about?'

'It's that plate!' she exclaimed. 'The one you bought for me.'

'This is all about the plate?'

'The plate, yes. Look, let me explain. We had a school fundraising event a week ago, along the lines of that television programme where people bring paintings, glass and china and other family heirlooms to be talked about and then valued by experts. We arranged for a valuer from Burton's Fine Arts in Fettlesham to come, and I brought the blue patterned plate. Well, when Mr Burton saw it he went really quiet, and asked how much I had it insured for. He said later that when he first saw it, he nearly fainted. That plate, Gervase, is a Delft blue patterned plate, probably made at the end of the seventeenth century, and it would fetch over six hundred pounds at auction.'

'That old plate? But it had a crack right the way down it!'

'That's a kiln crack according to Mr Burton and will not affect the value all that much.'

'Well, that's incredible.'

'So you see my dilemma,' sighed Christine. 'I feel I ought to give you some money. After all, you bought it. Without you I wouldn't have it at all.'

'Well, I only bid for it—you wanted it. I wouldn't have looked twice at it had I been on my own.'

'Yes, but—'

'There are no "buts". The plate is yours. I merely bought it on your behalf and you've paid me for it.'

'You really are kind, Gervase,' she said. 'I must do something to thank you.'

'You can treat me to a meal some time,' I answered.

She gave a disarming smile, 'Yes, I'll do that. I'd like that very much. Would you like to come round for supper? I haven't asked you before because, well, I wondered if it was the right sort of thing to do—inviting round a school inspector . . . What about this Sunday? Have you anything on in the evening?'

'N-no,' I stammered, 'I don't have anything on.'

'Right then, Sunday it is. Come about seven. I'll send you a map showing directions. I live with my parents in Collington.'

I gulped. 'Are you sure Miles won't mind?' I asked gingerly. 'You inviting me round for supper. I mean, won't he mind?'

'I couldn't care less whether Miles minds or not,' she replied. 'After our dreadful holiday in Austria, where all I heard was how expensive everything was and how good he was at skiing, I became heartily sick of him. We don't see each other any more.'

It was fortunate that no one else was outside the school or they would have jumped out of their skins at hearing the whoop of joy that I emitted when I got back to my car.

6

Early in March I was asked by Harold Yeats to give the opening talk on the Newly Qualified Teachers course, all about some of the qualities I considered the good teacher should possess.

I spent the preceding weekend planning the lecture carefully. Good teachers, I thought, should be committed, hardworking, enthusiastic, dedicated and well organised. They should have good discipline, be able to command respect and, of course, relate well to children. And they should encourage their pupils to chance their arm, to experiment, to try out ideas without fear of being criticised. My lecture finished, therefore, with a heartfelt plea for young, keen teachers to take a few measured risks.

One young teacher who heard me speak that Monday morning certainly took the advice to heart. I was visiting St Anthony's Boys' Secondary Modern School to observe the morning lessons of a newly qualified young teacher called Miss Isleworth.

'I heard you speak on the course last week, Mr Phinn,' she said when I arrived, 'and I did so enjoy your talk.'

'Thank you very much,' I replied.

'You know you mentioned about good teachers taking risks?'

'Yes.'

'Did you really mean it?'

'Most certainly. I don't think we move forward unless we do.'

'Well,' said Miss Isleworth with a great drawing-in of breath, 'I'm certainly going to take risks this morning.'

'Really?'

'I have quite an adventurous drama lesson planned with thirty-five thirteen-year-old-boys. I just hope it will be all right.'

I reassured her as we walked across the playground in the rain to the drama studio—a grandiose name for a temporary classroom, perched on four large concrete blocks and sited on a muddy patch of ground. The glass in the windows was painted black.

'What is the theme of the drama lesson?' I enquired as we went in out of the rain.

'We're re-enacting the sinking of the *Titanic*,' she replied.

It was my turn for a great drawing-in of breath. 'Good heavens!' I said. 'That *is* a pretty adventurous undertaking.' The sinking of the *Titanic* in a wooden hut with thirty-five teenage boys. She really *is* taking risks, I thought with some concern.

It was pitch-black inside the hut. The drumming of the rain on the wooden roof was all that could be heard.

'Oh dear,' sighed Miss Isleworth, as she searched for the light switch, 'I don't think they've turned up.'

'I can hear breathing,' I whispered. The teacher clicked on the lights to reveal all the pupils frozen in a tableau. They were arranged on five large, grey staging blocks, which presumably represented the *Titanic*. In a corner three boys stood behind drums and assorted percussion instruments. Another boy controlled a large spotlight on a stand.

'Just relax for a moment will you, boys,' said Miss Isleworth. 'I am really really pleased to see the way you have prepared for the play.' She turned in my direction. 'This is Mr Phinn, who will be joining us this morning. There's a chair in the corner, Mr Phinn.'

'Miss, can we start?' asked an excited little figure on the highest block. He wore a battered bus conductor's cap.

'In a moment, Dean. First, let me recap what we are doing this morning. This is the climax of the drama where the great ship hits the iceberg. The night is still, the sea is calm. It is dark and most of the passengers are in bed. On the bridge Captain Smith and his first officer peer into the night. Are you ready on the lights?'

'Yes, miss!'

'Right then, action!'

First, darkness. Then a spotlight picked out two small figures— Dean and another boy on the highest staging block.

'It's a cold night, Captain Smith, and no mistake,' said the boy.

'It is indeed, especially for the time of year,' replied Dean.

'In the Atlantic.'

'On our maiden voyage.'

'To America.'

'In 1912.'

'On the unsinkable *Titanic*.'

Lights illuminated the other pupils on the different blocks. Some mimed sleeping, others were walking the deck.

Dean peered into the darkness. 'What's that then?' he asked.

'What?'

'That in the water in front of us.'

'It's . . . it's an iceberg!'

'Stop engines!' they both shrieked. This was followed by booming drums, clashing cymbals, screams and shouts. All the pupils in the various staging blocks lurched forward, struggling as they sank beneath the icy waters. All was still. Then the spotlight picked out a lad with his hands in his pockets, standing in the water ahead of the *Titanic* and looking around self-consciously.

'Robert,' called Miss Isleworth, 'what are you doing?'

'I was away last week, miss,' came the reply. This was followed by good-humoured groans and laughs.

'Right, everybody!' shouted the teacher. 'We'll run through this again. Robert, you get on the *Titanic*.' Robert joined the captain and the first officer on the highest block.

'You're not here!' Dean snapped. 'This is the bridge. There's only us two up here.'

Robert descended a block. 'And you're not here either!' said another boy. 'This is first class and we're full up.'

Down another block went Robert. 'This is the engine room and there's no room for you down here either.'

Robert appealed to Miss Isleworth. 'Miss, there's *nowhere* for me to go!'

'He can be a seal in the water, miss,' suggested a helpful individual in first class.

'I'm not being a seal. I want to be on the *Titanic*,' moaned Robert.

Miss Isleworth, thinking on her feet, called Robert over. 'You can go in the galley, Robert,' she said. 'You can be cooking when the *Titanic* hits the iceberg.'

So Robert assumed the lowest position, looking distinctly unhappy with his assigned role.

'Right, let's go through it again,' said Miss Isleworth. Again, darkness, and the spotlight picked up the two figures on the bridge.

'It's a cold night, Captain Smith, and no mistake.'

'It is indeed, especially for the time of year.'

As they continued, lights illuminated the other pupils on the different blocks. Robert was moving his hands as if poking an imaginary fire.

Dean peered into the darkness. 'What's that then?'

'What?'

'That big thing in the water in front of us.'

'Blinking heck! It's a great mountain of ice coming our way. It's an iceberg. It's . . . it's an iceberg!'

'Stop engines!' they both shrieked. Booming drums, clashing cymbals, screams and shouts. All the pupils lurched forward, struggling as they sank beneath the icy waters. All except Robert, who was still cooking in the galley.

'Robert!' shouted Miss Isleworth. 'What *are* you doing?'

'I'm cooking the chips on the *Titanic*, miss.'

There was a groan from the captain, officers, passengers and crew.

'Robert,' said the teacher, 'the *Titanic* has hit the iceberg. The front of the ship has been ripped open, the watertight compartments are flooding, the icy waters are rushing in, people are panicking to get to the lifeboats—and you are cooking chips in the galley.'

'Yes, miss.'

'Well, just think what you *would* be doing. Imagine what it would be like in the galley when the disaster happens.'

'Yes, miss.'

'Right, let's go through it one more time,' said Miss Isleworth.

'Again, miss? We're going through it again?' asked an angry Captain Smith, pulling his bus conductor's hat off his head.

'Last time,' the teacher assured him.

First, darkness. Then the spotlight picked up two small figures on the highest staging block.

'It's a cold night, Captain Smith,' said the first officer in a very matter-of-fact voice.

'It is indeed,' sighed the other.

Light illuminated the other pupils, miming but with little enthusiasm—except for Robert who was busy cooking chips in the galley.

Dean peered into the darkness. 'What's that then?'

'What?'

'That big thing in the water in front of us.'

'Could be an iceberg, I suppose.'

'Shall we stop engines?'

His companion sighed again. 'Might as well.'

There followed a few lukewarm drum beats, the odd scream and a shout. All the pupils leaned forward half-heartedly before slowly disappearing beneath the icy waters. All was still. The spotlight picked out a lone figure gradually sinking with one arm held aloft. It was Robert. Then 'glug, glug, glug' and he was gone.

'Robert,' asked Miss Isleworth, 'what was the arm all about?'

'I was holding the chip pan up, miss,' he explained. 'Didn't your mum tell you that if hot fat hits water, it can be very dangerous?'

I ARRIVED at Mrs Savage's palatial office in the County Hall Annexe late one March afternoon. The first draft of the guideline booklet on 'The Teaching of Spelling' was ready and I had been asked to call to collect it for its final check before printing. Her desk was a vast affair in rich mahogany. There were filing cupboards and cabinets, an expensive-looking bookcase, an occasional table and two easy chairs. Long pale curtains hung at the window.

Mrs Savage's secretary was just getting ready to go home. She told me to make myself comfortable: Mrs Savage would be along at any moment.

It had been a tiring day. I had driven up and down the Dales, missed lunch and was ready for a hot bath and something to eat. The clock on the County Hall bell tower struck six and I had just about decided to give up and go home when the door opened and she breezed in. She was in a scarlet suit with enormous shoulder pads and great silver buttons. This was 'power dressing' taken to extremes.

'Sorry to have kept you waiting. But my little den is quite comfortable, isn't it?' she said, closing the door behind her. 'I cannot work in an environment that isn't homely. I just don't know how you survive in that cramped little office with those noisy, difficult individuals around you. Dr Yeats is pleasant enough—but the other two! I really don't know how you can stand it.'

Before I could reply she moved to her desk. 'But we don't want to talk about your colleagues, do we?' She smiled like a shark. 'Now, let's get a cup of coffee organised. Then we can make ourselves comfortable. I'll ring down and see if someone can arrange it.'

'No, I won't have anything. Actually, I'm in rather a hurry. I have a lot of work to do this evening and I haven't eaten today.'

'It's not good to miss a meal. And you know what they say about all work and no play.' The tone of voice changed to a softer lilt. 'You know, Gervase, I really feel you and I liaise rather well.'

'Pardon?'

'I was only saying to dear Dr Gore this morning that there are some people with whom one can work, and others one cannot. I feel you are one of the former. We do work well together, don't we?' She skirted the desk and moved in my direction. 'We have a certain rapport. Do you feel the same about me?' She fluttered her eyelashes.

Good gracious, I thought, this cannot be happening. 'Well . . . er . . . I do think we managed to work well together on the Minister's visit, but on a strictly professional and—'

'Exactly! Exactly!' She moved closer. 'That's just what I mean. We sort of clicked, didn't we?'

'Clicked?' I moved back a step. 'Er . . . now about the guidelines . . .'

'You know, Gervase, we relate. We talk the same language. We dance to the same music.' I moved back another step. 'Do you like dancing, Gervase?' she asked.

I was lost for words. 'Well, I . . . I . . .'

'You certainly look like a good mover to me.'

'Well, I . . . I . . .'

'There's the County Ball at the end of the month.'

'Really, the County Ball?'

'I've been asked, in my capacity as the PA to the CEO to distribute the tickets, and I was wondering—'

I predicted how this sentence was going to end so made a pre-emptive strike. 'You know, I have always wanted to be able to dance but this leg of mine gives me so much trouble. An old rugby accident, a nasty break, never been quite right, you know. I have to have an operation when they can fit me in.'

'My mother always told me to beware of people with operations,' she replied, moving even closer. 'They always want to show you their scars.'

One more step, and my back would be against the door.

'In any case, the County Ball is not an occasion for wild jigs and rowdy reels. The dancing is very often slow and stately.'

'About the guidelines, Mrs Savage . . .'

'It's a quite wonderful occasion. The highlight of the year. Exquisite food, beautiful music. Everybody who is anybody will be there.'

Well, I certainly won't, I said to myself.

'I used to go to it every year when Conrad was alive.'

'Conrad?'

'My dear departed. You knew I was a widow, didn't you, Gervase? That I live all on my own. You live alone, don't you?'

'I do, yes, but I like living alone. I really like living alone. I enjoy the peace and quiet after a hard day's work.'

'We had such a short time together, Conrad and I—before his untimely death.'

'I'm very sorry,' I said. 'But about the guidelines—'

'Gervase, I was wondering if you might like—'

I made a second pre-emptive strike. 'My goodness!' I exclaimed, pulling at the door, 'I quite forgot. I'm supposed to be meeting Sidney Clamp at six and just look at the time. I must make tracks.' Before she could answer I gabbled on. 'I'll collect the guidelines another time. Must rush. Bye!' and made as fast an exit as I could.

'COULD YOU ASK Mrs Savage to send over the draft copy of the spelling guidelines?' I asked Julie the next morning.

'She left a note asking you to call for them.'

'Yes, I saw it, but I haven't the time today, I'm afraid.'

'Well, you could pop over now. The Annexe is on your way.'

'Julie, I have not the time to go over now. Please give Mrs Savage a ring and ask her to send them over.' I paused. 'And should Mrs Savage call, I am *not* in.'

Over the next few weeks I avoided Mrs Savage sedulously. If I saw a glimpse of a red dress in the main corridor of County Hall I scurried into the gents'. If I heard a sharp voice emanating from a room I was passing, I hurried on like an Olympic walker. Still, it was inevitable that we should meet again—and it was at Castlesnelling High School that our paths crossed.

I had been asked to write a report on the state of the library and on my first visit had been shown into a bare, cold, featureless room with a few ancient tomes and dogeared textbooks scattered along the high wooden bookcases. There was a pervasive smell of dust, and the books on the shelf, with titles like *Wireless Studies for Beginners*, *Life in the Belgian Congo*, and *Harmless Scientific Experiments for Girls*, bore witness to the fact that there had not been a clear-out of old and inappropriate material for some time. The newly appointed Head of Library and Resources, Mr Townson, gestured with upturned hands as we surveyed the room.

'Well,' he said, 'you can see what needs doing.' He was a young, dapper man who was obviously keen to change things. 'The Head has persuaded the Governors to release some capital to improve things and I would be so grateful for any advice you could give.'

I wrote a full report with recommendations and, a few weeks later, returned to the school to deliver the good news that the county would refurbish the room, help stock it with a good balance of appropriate texts and install some computers.

I entered the library to find Mrs Savage in a powder-blue suit with shoulder pads that would not have disgraced an American footballer. She was ensconced in the one easy chair, basking in a pale ray of sunlight that made her earrings sparkle. My heart sank.

'Do you know Mrs Savage?' Mr Townson asked innocently.

'Yes, yes, indeed,' I replied. 'Good morning.'

She gave me a cold look. 'Good morning, Mr Phinn,' she replied, making it clear that we were no longer on first-name terms.

'Brenda has been so very helpful,' Mr Townson explained enthusiastically. 'We've been revamping the school library prospectus and various other documents. She's been a real gem.' He turned and smiled warmly at the seated figure.

'It's nice to be appreciated,' she commented caustically. 'Quite often people take one for granted.'

'Mrs Savage is helping me to sort out the library,' continued Mr Townson.

Mrs Savage made a sort of humming noise before looking at her watch as if entirely bored.

'If it's not convenient,' I began, 'I can call—'

'No, no!' Mrs Savage rose to her feet. 'I was about to go.' She swept towards the door but turned on her high heels. 'I will be in touch, Simon,' she said sweetly. She nodded in my direction, 'Goodbye, Mr Phinn.' Then she was gone.

'An absolutely delightful woman,' enthused the young Mr Townson rubbing his hands. 'She's been so supportive and sympathetic. Cannot do enough for me.'

I ran my finger along a shelf on which were a number of books on the art of ballroom dancing.

'Do you dance by any chance, Mr Townson?' I asked casually, plucking a tome from the shelf.

'Yes, I do, as a matter of fact. Why?'

'Oh, nothing,' I replied. 'Nothing at all.'

7

'Oh no!' cried Harold, looking up from the memorandum he was reading. 'It's the Fettlesham Show in a month. That is something I could well do without.'

'Why?' I asked innocently. 'It sounds really interesting. I've seen it advertised in every shop and post office in the county so it must be a pretty big affair. I thought I might spend a Saturday—'

'Dear, oh dear,' sighed Harold, clearly not listening to a word I was saying. 'It completely slipped my mind. The Fettlesham Show!'

'Harold!' I said in a loud voice. 'What is so upsetting about the Fettlesham Show?'

'What is so upsetting about the Fettlesham Show is that I have to spend all day Saturday manning the County Education Tent, answering questions, giving advice about little Johnny who can't read very well and little Janet who has difficulties with her number work. It's an exhausting and thoroughly tiresome business.'

'From the posters,' I said, 'I thought it was an agricultural show— horses, hounds, dog competitions—that sort of thing.'

'It *is* an agricultural show, but there are all sorts of other displays and exhibitions.'

'It sounds really interesting. I might just go.'

Harold looked up. 'The word "might" does not come into it, Gervase. You *will* be going.'

'I will?'

'You'll be attending the Fettlesham Show, along with the other inspectors. You have been assigned your own little job.'

'I have?'

'Yes, indeed. Sidney will be adjudicating the art competition, David's organising the children's sports and you have been dragooned into judging the poetry competition. Hard luck. For the last few years they have had some local poet, Priscilla Pollard or somebody or other, very popular by all accounts. She's into trees and daffodils and frisking lambs. Anyway, this year she says she can't do it, for some reason.'

'I'm surely not expected to read hundreds of children's poems, am I?' I exclaimed. 'I just haven't the time. Not in the next few weeks.'

'Don't worry, Gervase,' Harold reassured me. 'You judge the final short list of poems. The organisers do all the preliminary reading and come up with the best ten. You just turn up at the show, judge the poems, say a few words, smile pleasantly and present book tokens and rosettes to the five prize-winners. It's a very pleasant day out, I should imagine.'

THE SATURDAY of the show was sunny and windless. Beneath the cloudless summer sky, marquees and tents were scattered across a wide open field. People were grooming horses, brushing sheep and washing cattle. Others were arranging cakes on long trestle tables, or putting the final touches to amazing floral creations. In one corner of the field, a large notice announced: POETRY COMPETITION THIS WAY.

Inside, the tent was crowded, stuffy and noisy. I peered in every direction until I spotted a vigorous, red-faced woman with a bay window of a bust and a large badge with STEWARD written on it.

'I'm Gervase Phinn,' I said, 'the judge of the poetry competition.'

'Oh, the adjudicator,' she exclaimed. ''Bout time too. I'm Joan Pickersgill. The final ten poems have been selected. We've got some really lovely efforts this year so your task won't be easy. You need to pick five out of the ten and then place them in reverse order.'

'Is this him?' barked a lean, middle-aged woman with narrow eyes, as she pushed her way through the crowd. She was dressed in a green waxed jacket and carried a vicious-looking shooting stick. 'Are you Mr Chinn?' she yapped.

'Phinn,' I corrected. 'My name is Gervase Phinn. I'm the county school inspector for English and drama.'

'School inspector, are you? Well, we're looking for the best poem not the best handwriting or spellings, you know.'

'Yes, I appreciate that,' I replied.

'We usually have Philomena Phillpots, the Dales poetess,' said Mrs Pickersgill. 'Wonderful writer. Have you come across her?'

'No, I can't say that I have.'

'Well, she's very popular, very popular indeed, and has published proper poems. She does the insides of birthday cards as well.'

'Does she really?' I replied, wishing I was in the Education Tent with Harold. Anything was better than this.

'Now, this is the way we do it, Mr Phinn,' said Mrs Pickersgill, referring to her clipboard. 'It goes like clockwork if we stick to the proper agreed routine. The children assemble at ten thirty—and you move from one to another, read his or her poem and have a little chat with the young poet—not too long or it will take all day. Then you say a few words to the children and parents about the high standard of the entry. Finally you announce the winners in reverse order and present the rosettes and the book tokens. Is that clear?'

'Crystal,' I replied.

'Jolly good. You tootle off and browse the poems.'

The ten poems ranged from the exceptional to the very ordinary, so I satisfied myself that it would be an easy task after all. If these poems had been short-listed, what on earth were the others like, I thought. I quickly selected the five I considered to be the best, and when the time came for me to do my circuit of the tent, Mrs Pickersgill's voice came through the loudspeakers. 'Attention!

Attention everybody! The poetry judging is about to commence!'

The noise subsided, there was a hushed silence and I could feel all eyes upon me. The first poem was rhyming doggerel and extended over three pages. It started:

> All over the land it began to snow,
> Up on the hills and way down below,
> Away from the town where the lights did glow,
> Away from the wood where there lived a crow.
> I did not like the crow, oh no,
> But I liked playing in the snow.

'You have obviously put a great deal of time and effort into this poem,' I told the tall, serious-looking author.

'She made up all the rhymes herself,' said the woman standing next to her, presumably her mother. 'Every one.' I smiled and moved on.

The next poem was clearly lifted from 'The Lake Isle of Innisfree'. It began:

> I will arise and go now,
> And go to Fettlesham,
> And a small house I'll build there . . .

'Did you write this poem yourself?' I asked a cheerful-looking youngster with a tangle of ginger curls and a freckled face.

'Oh yes, mester,' he replied firmly. 'Definitely wrote it myself.'

'It's just that it reminds me of a poem I have read before—a poem by W. B. Yeats. Do you know it?'

'This Yeats must have got the idea from our Sam,' interposed his father, an angry-looking man with a face the colour and texture of a walnut. I moved on.

The third trite little verse was surrounded by drawings of little cartoon lambs and fluffy white sheep:

> On their fresh, green grassy banks
> The little lambs are at their pranks,
> Hear the little lambkins bleat,
> See them jump on woolly feet.
> Oh what joy those lambkins bring
> To the world when it is Spring.

Next to the poem's author stood a tall woman wearing a long, floral-print dress. She stared fixedly at me as if waiting for some kind of recognition. Next to her was a girl of about eleven, also attired in a long, floral-print dress.

'Do you live on a farm?' I asked the little poet.

'No,' she replied sullenly.

'What made you write a poem about lambs?'

'Don't know,' she answered in the same tone of voice.

I was getting nowhere so, having smiled weakly at mother and daughter, I moved on. Finally I came to the last of the ten. It was quite clearly the best—the most truthful and the most arresting:

> I love my grannie.
> She has hair like silver,
> And skin like gold,
> Eyes like emeralds,
> And teeth like pearls.
> She is a very precious person.
> My grannie calls me
> Her little treasure,
> But she is mine.
> And I love her very much.

'What did your grannie say when you showed her your poem?' I asked its small author.

'She said I wouldn't get much for her if I tried to sell her.'

I chuckled and asked the little girl some questions about her poem. She answered easily and I had no misgivings that this was her own, unaided work.

I had now completed the circuit and had the five winners fixed in my mind. I stepped up confidently onto the small dais, referred to my notes and took a deep breath to announce the results.

'Ladies and gentlemen, boys and girls,' I began, 'it gives me great pleasure to announce the winners of the poetry competition. All the children have tried extremely hard and produced some very high-quality verse. I know you will want to join me in giving them a hearty round of applause.' There was a ripple of lukewarm hand-clapping.

'And so, without further ado, these are the winning poems.' To light hand-clappings I announced the four runners-up. Then: 'And the first prize, for a gentle, carefully written piece of verse, goes to Amy Tunnicliffe for her delightful poem about her grannie.'

The announcement was greeted with one or two slow claps and an assortment of whispers and tut-tutting. By the time I had presented the rosettes, the book tokens and shaken the prize-winners' hands, the crowd had dispersed. A few people, mainly parents of the competitors, remained behind mumbling and shaking their heads.

'Not a popular choice,' announced Mrs Pickersgill.

'It may not be the most popular choice, Mrs Pickersgill,' I retorted, 'but in my opinion the poem is far and away the best.'

'It doesn't rhyme though, and is on the short side,' she growled.

'The quality of a poem doesn't depend on its length any more than on its rhymes.'

'Philomena Phillpots, the Dales poetess, felt that a piece of writing wasn't a poem unless it rhymed.'

'Well, I beg to differ with Philomena Phillpots, the Dales poetess.'

'But she has had her poems published,' persisted Mrs Pickersgill. 'It's just that she couldn't judge the poems today because her daughter Pollyanna submitted an entry. She had to declare an interest. Pollyanna's was the poem about the lovely little lambkins.' She gestured with a sweep of her hand to two figures both wearing long floral-print dresses. They glared across the tent at me.

For the remainder of the afternoon I tried to enjoy myself, but as I moved from stall to stall I kept hearing mention of the result of the poetry competition wherever I went.

'You tell me what a policeman knows about poetry. They had an inspector judging this year! They should be out catching criminals, not judging poetry!'

'He must know the mother, that's all I can think. I mean, it didn't even rhyme.'

'That poem about the crow brought tears to my eyes. That should have won.'

As I headed for the Education Tent to seek out Harold, I caught sight of Lord Marrick, striding towards me.

'Now then, Gervase!' he boomed. 'Come and let me buy you a drink. My prize Belgian blue has just won the cup for best bull. I'm as pleased as Punch.' Before I could argue, his arm was through mine and we were heading for the beer tent. When I emerged a good hour later, feeling much more at peace with the world, I bumped into Harold, looking extremely hot and flustered.

'Ah, Gervase!' he gasped, taking my arm. 'I'm panting for a stiff drink. You will not believe the time I've had.'

It was nearly three when I finally extracted myself from the beer tent and as I left, somewhat unsteady on my feet, who should I walk slap into but Mrs Pickersgill and her lean companion. I smiled warmly as I passed them, and caught a snippet of their conversation.

'I just knew he'd been drinking,' snorted Mrs Pickersgill.

'I thought he smelt like a brewery when he came into the tent,' replied her companion. 'Probably had difficulty reading the poems through that cloud of alcohol, never mind judging them.'

 **8**

'How are you, Gervase?' Dr Gore asked softly. 'How have you found your first year with us?'

'Oh . . . er . . . very well, thank you, Dr Gore,' I replied, shifting nervously in my chair. He continued to smile and in the silence that followed I heard the slow ticking of the clock on the wall, and the slight buzzing of a faulty fluorescent light in the outer office. 'I think, well, quite good actually, quite successful . . .' My voice trailed off. 'Not too bad,' I said finally.

'Good, good,' the CEO said. 'I expect you are wondering why I sent for you so early in the new academic year?' he continued.

'Yes, I *was* wondering,' I replied nervously.

THE MORNING had started off so well. I had arrived bright and early at the Education Office in Fettlesham that first day of the new term, keen to be back at work. A warm September sun shone in a cloudless sky, the air was fresh and still, the birds were singing and everything seemed right with the world. Over the summer break, I had managed to clear my desk of the mountain of paperwork. Reports had been completed, guidelines written, courses planned, documents filed away. I surveyed my empty desk with a real sense of achievement.

Then, as I sat down, thinking about the quiet, uneventful, stress-free day ahead of me, I heard a clattering on the stairs, and a moment later Julie tottered in on absurdly high-heeled shoes.

'I don't know about you,' she said, 'but I could murder a strong cup of coffee.' Without waiting for an answer she disappeared out of the room.

A few minutes later, when I was sorting through my morning's mail, she returned with two steaming mugs. I watched as she set one mug down on my desk and cupped her hands round the other.

'How was your holiday?' I said.

'Don't ask!'

'Not too good then?' I hazarded, reaching for the coffee.

'Awful! I went to Majorca with my boyfriend. The hotel was only half built and the pool was full of screaming children. We had a karaoke every night until two in the morning with a tone-deaf Dutchman singing "I Did It My Way" and a woman from Dudley who sounded like a sheep about to give birth. And if you got down after eight o'clock in the morning you could say goodbye to the sun loungers. We'll go to Skegness next year in his auntie's caravan. Anyway, what was your holiday like?'

'Oh, I managed to get away for a few days,' I told her.

Before I could elaborate, Julie dived in with her characteristic bluntness. 'And did you see much of that sexy teacher you were taking out?'

'Unfortunately, not a great deal,' I replied, smiling.

Over the summer holidays Christine had spent three weeks in Chicago staying with a cousin and a further week writing up a dissertation for a masters degree. We had enjoyed a day walking on the North York Moors and been to the theatre and out to dinner a couple of times. This term I was determined to see a whole lot more of her.

'So what's happening with you two, then?' asked Julie. She was not one to beat about the bush. 'Are you getting it together? Is it serious?'

'I'm not sure . . .' I started.

Julie folded her arms and pulled a face. 'Typical of men that—it's always the woman who has to make the decisions.'

I decided to change the subject. 'Am I the only one in the office this morning?'

'Just you. Mr Clamp's planning his art course, Mr Pritchard's meeting with the newly qualified teachers and Dr Yeats is at a conference. There's not much mail either, by the look of it.'

'So,' I said happily, 'it looks like a quiet start to the term.'

'Not necessarily,' said Julie. 'Mrs Savage phoned last Friday.' Her voice became hard-edged. 'She wondered where you were. I said, "People do take holidays, you know." If she'd bothered to look at those wretched inspectors' engagement sheets I have to send over to Admin every week, she'd have seen that you were on leave. She just likes the sound of her own voice. It gets under my skin. And speaking of skin, I reckon she's had her face done.'

'*Mrs Savage?*'

'Mrs Savage. When I saw her last week in the staff canteen I didn't recognise her. Her skin's been stretched right back off her face. She looks as if she's walking through a wind tunnel. All those wrinkles have disappeared. And I think she's had that rhinosuction because she looks a lot thinner as well.'

'Liposuction,' I corrected.

'She's that thick-skinned, I think I was right first time.'

'Julie!' I snapped. 'Did she say that Dr Gore wanted to see me?'

'At nine o'clock prompt. That's what Lady High and Mighty said.'

'Did she say what he wanted?'

'I never gave her the chance. I keep all conversations with that woman as short as possible. It's probably one of his little jobs.'

I was well acquainted with Dr Gore's little jobs—and they were never 'little'. I prayed that this was not one of them.

TEN MINUTES after my meeting with Dr Gore, Julie was waiting for me at the top of the stairs. 'Well?'

'One guess.'

'A little job?'

'Right first time.'

'I'll put the coffee on.'

I followed her into the office. 'Actually, it's not too bad,' I said cheerfully. 'Dr Gore has asked me to organise the visit of one of Her Majesty's Inspectors for later this term. He wants to look at some schools as part of a national information-gathering exercise on literacy standards. I just have to nominate a number of schools and arrange things, nothing massively demanding in that. I can ring round the schools this morning and get a letter off to the Ministry. The only fly in the ointment is having to liaise with Mrs Savage.'

Julie pulled a face and clattered out of the office. 'Forget the coffee,' she said. 'I'll get the brandy.'

ONE BRIGHT MORNING a week later I was looking through my post when I came upon a frighteningly official-looking envelope. The letter inside had a black embossed heading—The Ministry of Education—and ended with a large flourish of a signature. I recognised the name, Miss W. de la Mare, from the previous year.

In the letter, Miss de la Mare requested that I arrange a series of visits to schools 'which demonstrate good practice in the teaching of reading and writing' and which 'show good breadth and balance in the curriculum'. She was particularly interested in poetry.

I knew just the school for her to visit: Backwatersthwaite Primary, one of the first schools I had called at last year. I had visited the school again a couple of times during the year and had been immensely impressed by the quality of the education. The children answered questions with enthusiasm and perception, read with expression and wrote the most vivid poetry.

I replied promptly, suggesting five schools to visit and offering to accompany Miss de la Mare on the Backwatersthwaite visit. I certainly did not want her to spend half the day driving backwards and forwards in search of the elusive school.

A couple of days later a second letter arrived, informing me that Miss de la Mare was grateful for the list of suitable schools and for my offer to accompany her on one of the visits, but she would prefer to go alone. I immediately telephoned the headteachers at the chosen schools forewarning them of the HMI's visitation.

'Well, thank you very much,' sighed George Lapping down the line. 'Thank you very much indeed. I know now who my friends really are.' I could guess from his tone that he was secretly pleased, despite his pretence of displeasure.

'You should be very flattered that I recommended your school, George,' I replied. 'It's a mark of the excellent work that your pupils achieve. As Shakespeare would have it, "Some are born great, some achieve greatness and some have greatness thrust upon them."'

'But I am having an *HMI* thrust upon me. Gervase, I can't be doing with visitors. They interrupt my teaching routine. Anyway, I have to go now. There are children to teach. I'll let you know how I get on.' With that the line went dead.

'MISS, WHO'S THAT funny man at the back of the classroom?' The speaker was a small, stocky boy of about nine or ten with a shock of thick, red hair.

'That's not a funny man, Oliver,' replied Mrs Peterson, colouring a little; 'that's Mr Phinn.'

'Well, who is he, miss?' asked the child.

'He's a visitor, come to see how well we are getting on.'

'But what does he do, miss?' persisted the little boy, staring intently at me. 'He's just sitting there not doing anything.'

'That's because he's a school inspector and—'

'And he just sits and watches people then, does he, miss?'

'Well, yes, he does, but he has lots of other things to do. Mr Phinn listens to children read, for example.'

'Listens to children read?' Oliver repeated. 'And does he get paid for it, miss?'

'Yes,' replied the teacher wearily, 'he does get paid for it, Oliver, but come along now, settle down, there's a good boy.'

Oliver shook his head like an old man despairing at the excesses of youth, before commenting, 'Nice little number that.'

I was sitting in the junior classroom of Highcopse County Primary School, the second week into the new school term, watching the children settle at their tables.

It was a gloriously sunny September morning, and through the open classroom window I could see a great rolling sweep of green, dotted with lazy sheep, rise to the austere, grey-purple fells beyond. An old stone farmhouse crouched against the lower slopes, and a kestrel hovered in the warm air. It was idyllic. The boy was right—it was a 'nice little number'.

I was brought back from my reverie by the teacher's voice. 'Now, is everyone ready?' she asked. 'Will you all face the front and pay attention? Do stop shuffling your feet, Penny, and Oliver, don't do that with your pencil, please. You know what happened last time . . . Thank you. It will not have escaped your notice, children, that we have a very special visitor in school today.' The children looked warily in my direction. My smile was greeted by a sea of solemn faces. 'Our special visitor is called Mr Phinn, and he will be hearing some of you read, looking at your writing and having a little chat about the work you have been doing. That's right, Mr Phinn, isn't it?'

'It is indeed,' I replied.

'Oliver!' snapped Mrs Peterson, 'will you stop doing that with your pencil? I have told you once and I don't want to have to tell you again. We do not want a repetition of last term's incident, do we?'

'No, miss,' answered the child brightly.

'Oliver managed to get a piece of wax crayon lodged in his ear, Mr Phinn, and we had the devil's own job to get it out, didn't we, Oliver?'

'Yes, miss.' There was no trace of contrition in the cheerful voice.

'Peter, turn round please, dear, and pay attention. And do you know, Mr Phinn, when I asked Oliver what he was doing pushing a wax crayon in his ear, he replied, "To see if it fitted."' The teacher pursed her lips. 'Now then, Oliver, you can perhaps remember what I said Mr Phinn does for a living?'

'Not a lot, by the sound of it, miss,' replied the child seriously.

The teacher sighed. 'Can you remember what I said his job was called?' she asked sharply.

'Yes, miss. He's a suspecter.'

AFTER MORNING PLAYTIME I joined the infant class in a spacious room with colourful displays depicting fairy-story characters covering the walls. There were low tables with small, orange melamine chairs at each, a selection of bright picture books on a trolley, a big plastic tray for sand and another for water, and at the front a square, old-fashioned teacher's desk.

The five- and six-year-olds were in the charge of a serious-looking teacher in a grey jumper and dark brown skirt, called appropriately Mrs Dunn. She had iron-grey hair pulled back severely and wore a pained expression. The children read competently and their writing, though slightly below the standard I would have expected, was sound enough. There was a great deal of copied writing, a few simple stories, but no poetry.

At the end of the morning I returned to Mrs Peterson's class to make my farewells. The teacher beamed as I entered her room.

'Now, children, look who's back—it's Mr Phinn.'

'I've just popped in to say goodbye, Mrs Peterson.'

'It's been a pleasure, Mr Phinn. We do like to have special visitors, don't we, children?' One or two children nodded unenthusiastically. 'It's been a real treat for us and I hope it is not too long before you come back and see us again. That would be nice, children, wouldn't it? My goodness, Mr Phinn, we do have such a lot of fun in this classroom, don't we, children?' The class stared impassively. 'We really do have so much fun, don't we?' There were a few nods. 'Yes, we do, children! We're always having fun.'

As I passed Oliver on my way out, I heard him mutter, 'I must have been away that day.'

 9

'You've had a telephone call,' announced David, when I arrived at the office one damp, depressing, October afternoon. 'You have been summoned to an audience with the Bride of Frankenstein.'

'Oh, no,' I moaned. 'Whatever does Mrs Savage want now?'

'You are to go over and see her at six o'clock. She was insistent.'

'I can't seem to escape from the woman,' I said, banging down my briefcase. 'I get messages and memos every other day.'

'She's perhaps taken a shine to you,' said David, finding the whole situation highly amusing. 'You want to watch out.'

'Huh!' I grunted.

'Or a certain young, attractive headteacher might start getting a trifle jealous.'

'David, I've already had the third degree from Julie about my love life. Could we leave Christine out of it, do you think?'

'My goodness,' said David, taking off his reading glasses and folding them on the desk in front of him, 'someone is in a rather fraught condition this afternoon.'

I had never divulged to my colleagues the dreadfully embarrassing confrontation that had taken place in Mrs Savage's office a few months ago. Since then I had kept my distance and, on the few occasions our paths had crossed, Mrs Savage had remained coldly formal. I had sensed, however, that beneath the icy exterior there was something still simmering.

It was with some trepidation, therefore, that I headed for the dreaded meeting. The trip from our office to County Hall was a pleasant stroll on a bright summer's day, and a bracing walk on a fresh winter's morning, but today was dark and the wind drove the rain at a slant, thoroughly soaking me.

I found Mrs Savage sitting stiffly at her desk, a computer humming away on a console beside her.

'Do come in, Mr Phinn, and take a seat,' she said. 'I won't be a moment.' There was a note of sharp command in her voice. I sat in one of the easy chairs, while she scratched away with a sharp pencil, glancing up occasionally as if to make sure I was still there. I had not seen her since the previous term and, as Julie had remarked recently, she seemed to have lost weight and a number of wrinkles and creases into the bargain. Dressed in a pale green silk suit splashed with great crimson poppies, she certainly was a striking-looking woman.

'Now then, Mr Phinn,' she said suddenly, looking up from her papers, 'thank you for coming up to see me.'

'That's all right, Mrs Savage,' I replied, attempting to sound relaxed. 'I believe you mentioned that it was urgent?'

'It is,' she said sharply. 'It's about the Feoffees.'

'I beg your pardon?'

'The Feoffees,' she repeated. It was clear that she had no intention of enlightening me as to what a Feoffee actually was. Well, two can play at that game, I thought.

'What have the Feoffees got to do with me, Mrs Savage?' I asked.

'As you may be aware, Mr Phinn, Lord Marrick, the Vice-Chairman of the Education Committee, is to take up the office of Chief Lord of the Feoffees in the New Year.' She paused for effect.

'Really?'

'Next year is the five hundredth anniversary of the foundation of the Feoffees, and Lord Marrick is keen to mark this very significant juncture in the Feoffees' history by hosting an open day at Manston Hall at the end of May. He wants various events, involving a wide range of local institutions and organisations, to celebrate such an auspicious occasion.'

'I see,' I said, nodding. 'And how do I come in?'

'Dr Gore wishes you to attend a planning meeting at Manston Hall in November. Of course, Dr Gore would have represented the

Education Department himself but it is impossible for him to attend. He has been asked by the Minister of Education to sit on a government committee and will be exceptionally busy for the foreseeable future. Dr Gore would not normally have delegated such an important task, but he understands that you had a number of dealings with Lord Marrick last year so his lordship is not unfamiliar to you.'

'I see,' I said again.

'Dr Gore would like this matter expedited immediately.' She leaned over her desk and clasped her hands before her. 'He has also, Mr Phinn, asked me to liaise with you over this.' Her voice took on a sharper edge. 'I sincerely hope that we will, in fact, liaise and that you will not take it upon yourself, as you did with the HMI visits, to do everything on your own.'

I had guessed that she would raise that little matter. 'Yes, of course, Mrs Savage,' I said pleasantly.

There was a portentous pursing of the lips. Mrs Savage eyed me for a brief moment before continuing. 'Dr Gore has asked me to deal with all the administration. I have already informed Lord Marrick that you will be representing the Education Department and I shall send you the agenda and the papers for the meeting just as soon as I receive them.' She gave me a frosty look. 'I would be very appreciative, Mr Phinn, if you would see to it that I am kept fully informed. It makes my life so much easier if I know what is happening, when it is happening and how it is happening. I hope I make myself clear.'

'Perfectly clear, Mrs Savage.'

'Good,' she said.

I stood up to go.

'One moment, Mr Phinn, I haven't finished with you yet.' She gave a small, quick smile before rising from her chair. I felt a tingle of apprehension. Was she going to leap across the desk, launch herself on top of me in wild abandon, drag me onto the thick shagpile carpet, throw me over the occasional table? I stepped back as she moved stealthily around the desk like a predatory cat. I could smell her heavy perfume. My apprehension turned to cold fear.

'What about a date?' she asked.

'Date?' I whispered. 'What date?'

'You need a date for the meeting at Manston Hall.'

'Ah,' I sighed, 'that date.'

'The 25th of November at ten o'clock.'

I was rooted to the spot.

'Is there something else, Mr Phinn?' asked Mrs Savage.

'No, nothing,' I replied, and headed at a brisk pace for the door.

SIDNEY AND DAVID were putting on their coats when I arrived back at the office.

'You managed to escape unscathed then,' David commented. 'What did Mrs Savage want?'

'Have you heard of the Feoffees?'

'Are they a pop group?' asked David.

'I once went out with an amazing American girl at Oxford called Fifi,' sighed Sidney. 'Had wonderful muscles and flaming red hair.'

'Will you two be serious for a moment,' I said. 'I have to attend a meeting at Manston Hall. Evidently Lord Marrick is becoming the top Feoffee, whatever that involves, and wants to arrange some events to celebrate it. Could it be some sort of Masonic order?'

'Probably a Yorkshire version of the druids,' Sidney suggested. 'Old men in white sheets dancing around the monoliths at Brimham Rocks. Like the daft sort of thing the Welsh go in for. Dressing up in those funny costumes and waiting for the eclipse.'

'Daft!' exclaimed David. 'I'll have you know that the druids are part of a cultural tradition that stretches back centuries. The Celts—'

'Oh, please spare us the Celts,' begged Sidney, 'or we'll be here all night.' He turned towards me. 'Oh, by the way, I met Mrs Peterson on my art course yesterday. She was not best pleased with your report on her school.'

'What did she say?' I asked.

'That your report was full of criticisms,' Sidney told me.

'It wasn't that bad,' I said glumly. 'My report judged the school to be sound enough but there needed to be more variety in the work. In particular, the teachers didn't bother at all with any poetry.'

'She also said you were not very impressed with Mrs Dunn.'

'Not very impressed with Mrs Dunn! She never smiled the whole lesson!' I exclaimed. 'But all I wrote was that the teacher of the infants could be a little livelier.'

'An unusual woman, Mrs Dunn,' said David. 'I remember meeting her on one of my mathematics courses, and I recall saying to Mrs Peterson what a good teacher she was but that she was such a serious person and didn't sparkle. "I don't employ Christmas tree fairies, Mr Pritchard," she replied tartly. "I employ teachers."'

'And Mrs Peterson said that you said the children were unusually quiet,' continued Sidney.

'Well, they were. There was only one child who got a word in.'

'Mrs Peterson said that was because you frightened them.'

'What?'

'She said you sat at the back with your big black clipboard like someone about to take the measurements for a coffin.'

'You seem to have taken an unusual interest in my visit to Highcopse School, Sidney. It appears you have gone through the report with Mrs Peterson in some detail.'

'Just forewarning you, old boy, that's all.'

'Oh heck, I'll give her a ring later and sort it out.'

'Might be a wise move,' added David, nodding sagely, 'bearing in mind that her husband is County Councillor George Peterson. He's on the Education Committee. One of the most tiresome members.'

At this point a heavy laboured tread could be heard on the stairs leading up to the office, and a moment later Harold breezed in, wet and windblown, but smiling a great toothy smile. The senior county inspector was a walking encyclopaedia and turned out to know everything there was to know about the Feoffees. He became quite animated when asked to explain what they were.

'A very interesting group of men, the Feoffees,' he enthused. 'It was originally a body of prominent landowners and gentry, founded in the reign of Henry VII to keep law and order. All justice in a town was administered by the Feoffees and they ensured that the sick and needy were cared for. They were responsible for no end of things— repair of bridges and roads, keeping the water supply fresh, isolating plague victims, making sure the pillories and ducking stools were kept in good working order—'

'That's fine,' I interrupted, 'but what is their function today?'

'Well, it is largely a charitable institution. Why are you so interested in the Feoffees anyway, Gervase?'

I explained about the meeting with Mrs Savage, and my involvement in the forthcoming celebrations.

'I see,' said Harold. 'It sounds a very interesting undertaking. I would have very much liked to have attended that meeting myself.'

'Well, I'm glad she didn't approach me!' said Sidney. 'It sounds a complete and utter waste of time! What has all this got to do with education? I thought our job was to inspect schools not join a group of anachronistic, undoubtedly well-heeled geriatrics who—'

'Sidney,' snapped Harold, 'it has everything to do with education! First, the Feoffees are part of our rich cultural heritage. Furthermore, they still help the poor, particularly orphans and deprived children. They also give scholarships and bursaries to deserving causes.' The clock on the County Hall tower began to strike seven but Harold, who had now got the bit firmly between his teeth, continued undeterred. 'The Feoffees number amongst their ranks of anachronistic, well-heeled geriatrics our own Dr Gore, so when you ask—'

'For whom the bell tolls,' interrupted Sidney, 'it tolls for me to get on home. Seven o'clock and I might, with any luck, have missed the traffic. Oh, and Harold, I do hope the Feoffees have ensured that Hawksrill Bridge is still standing and that there aren't too many crowding around the pillories. I need to get back in time for the football.'

'What an end to the week,' I sighed.

'I have had a most enjoyable week, actually,' said Sidney. 'The art course was a great success, all schools visited, reports completed, letters written, documents filed.'

'And pigs fed and ready to fly,' added David.

THE FOLLOWING MONDAY I telephoned Mrs Peterson's school.

'Hello, Mrs Peterson, it's Gervase Phinn here.'

'Oh, hello, Mr Phinn. How are you?'

'I'm very well, thank you. Now, er, Mrs Peterson, my colleague Sidney Clamp has had a word with me. He tells me that you are rather upset about the report I wrote after my visit.'

'I wasn't upset,' she said sweetly, 'just a little disappointed.'

'Would you like me to call in and discuss it with you?' I asked.

'Oh no, there's no need for that. I know how busy you are. I do appreciate your comments about poetry, but you see it's not one of Mrs Dunn's strong points. Not mine either, if I'm truthful. So what would be really useful, rather than suggesting what we should be doing, would be for you to come and show us just what you mean.'

'In what way?'

'Well, could you take the children for a poetry lesson? Do a demonstration?'

I walked straight into that little trap, I thought. 'Well, yes, I suppose I could,' I replied.

'Next week?'

I flicked through my diary. 'Thursday morning?'

'Splendid. I look forward to seeing you then. Mrs Dunn will be so excited.' The headteacher rang off. I could imagine Mrs Dunn's reaction at the thought of my taking her class for poetry and the word 'excitement' did not spring readily to mind.

IT WAS A BRIGHT, clear morning when I arrived at Highcopse School the following week, and a fat pheasant strutted along the craggy limestone wall bordering the school. A squirrel ran up the trunk of an ancient tree by the road, and high above, in a vast and dove-grey sky, the rooks screeched and circled. Here was poetry indeed.

The junior class was ready and waiting, paper in front of them, pencils poised. I spent the first part of the morning encouraging the children to write poetry based on several large prints of paintings by famous artists which depicted figures and faces. I asked them to concentrate on the distinctive features, dress, facial expressions and surroundings, prompting them through questions like, 'Who is this person? Where does she live? Is she feeling happy or sad? How would you describe the expression?' In a relatively short time ideas covered the blackboard and helped the children compose some impressive pieces of writing. Mrs Peterson was taken aback when she read one little girl's poem which was based on the large colour print of Mary Cassatt's 'Child with a Red Hat'.

> It looks as if her head's on fire.
> Great flaming hat as red as a furnace.
> Tongues of yellow in the golden hair,
> Like burning corn.

Another child's poem was based on 'The Ironers' by Degas.

> She yawns with a mouth like a gaping cave,
> In a face as fat as a football.
> She has the fists of a boxer
> And arms as thick as tree trunks.
> It must be all that ironing.

Mrs Peterson took me aside. 'I must say Mr Phinn, the children have written lovely poems. You have brought out their creativity.'

I was feeling pleased with myself when I appeared after morning playtime in the classroom of Mrs Dunn. I gathered the small children around me in the reading corner and we talked about several large photographs of animals that I had brought with me. We were going to look at each picture in turn, talk about the colours and shapes and then write poems. I did not, however, get very far. When I held up a photograph of a mole, a large round child called Thomas remarked casually that his granddad killed moles.

'Does he really?' I replied equally casually and attempted to move on. 'Now look at his little fat black body. He's an unusual little creature, the mole. Can you see his big flat paws like pink spades and—'

'They dig and dig wi' them claws,' explained Thomas. 'Do a lot o' damage to a field, do moles. Some farmers put down poison but me granddad traps 'em and hangs up their bodies on t'fence.'

I decided to look at another picture. 'Here we have a grey squirrel. I saw a squirrel this morning peeping from between the branches of the tree outside. Look at his large black eyes and long bushy—'

'Tree vermin,' commented the same boy. 'My granddad shoots them an' all. They eat all t'corn put out for t'hens. Rats wi' bushy tails, that's what squirrels are. My granddad goes out in t'morning with his shotgun, shoots 'em and hangs up their bodies on t'fence.'

'Just listen a moment, will you, Thomas,' I said, catching sight of Mrs Dunn sitting at the back of the room with a self-satisfied smile on her face, enjoying my discomfiture. 'We can perhaps talk about that later on, but for the moment let's look at the picture and think of the shapes and colours in it.' I selected a large photograph of a dormouse and decided on a pre-emptive strike. 'And what about dormice, Thomas? Does your granddad kill those as well?'

'No, he quite likes dormice. They don't really do any harm.'

Thank goodness for that, I thought. 'Right then,' I said cheerfully, 'let's all look at this shy little dormouse, clinging to a stalk of wheat. Look carefully at the colour of his fur and—'

'Sheba kills dormice, though,' said Thomas. 'Our farm cat. She plays with 'em. We try to get 'em off of 'er but she runs away.'

'I see,' I said wearily. 'Is there anyone else who would like to say anything about animals?'

A small, pixie-faced little boy sitting right under my nose raised his hand eagerly.

'Yes?' I said, looking into the keen little face. 'What have you to tell me?'

'I've got frogs on my underpants,' he announced proudly.

By the end of the morning the children had produced some short, interesting poems about the animals. Most were not about little, soft-furred moles, adorable little dormice, gambolling rabbits or playful squirrels, but were blunt, realistic descriptions of the animals that they knew so much about—far more than I ever would. They clearly did not need a set of photographs to prompt them.

'Thomas lives on the farm at the top of the dale,' explained Mrs Dunn as we headed in the direction of the school hall for lunch. She was quite animated. 'Like most farming children, he's been brought up to be unsentimental about animals.' She paused for a moment before adding, 'He has a great deal to say for himself, hasn't he? You might have guessed, Mr Phinn, he's Oliver's younger brother.'

At lunch I sat between Thomas and an angelic-looking little girl. The boy surveyed me for a moment. 'Meat and tatey pie for lunch,' he said rubbing his hands. 'I reckon you won't be 'aving any.'

'Why is that?' I asked, intrigued.

'You're probably one of those vegetarians. Me granddad doesn't like vegetarians. He says they take the meat out of his mouth.

"There's nothing better than a good bit o' beef on your plate or a nice bit o' pork on your fork." That's what my granddad says. He doesn't like vegetarians, my granddad.'

Woe betide any vegetarian foolish enough to cross his granddad's land, I thought to myself. They'd end up, along with the moles and the squirrels, hanging up on t'fence.

Before I could inform Thomas that I was not, in fact, a vegetarian, the little angel sitting next to me whispered shyly, 'I like rabbits.' She took a mouthful of meat and potato pie before adding quietly, 'They taste really good with onions.'

I am certain that I learned more from the children that morning at Highcopse Primary School than they did from me.

LATER THAT AFTERNOON, while collecting some documents from County Hall, I bumped into George Lapping.

'What are you doing here, George?' I asked. 'I thought you rarely ventured out of Backwatersthwaite.'

'I've been selected to sit on one of these advisory committees. It's on "Key Skills". Now what do I know about key skills? You're responsible, putting me in the spotlight and encouraging that HMI to visit me. I knew it would happen.'

'I meant to give you a ring. She's been, then, has she?'

'Oh, she's been all right,' he replied with a wry chuckle.

'Have you got a minute, George?' I asked him. 'Just let's pop into one of the empty committee rooms and you can fill me in.'

A moment later George was giving me a blow-by-blow account of the visitation of Miss Winifred de la Mare, HMI.

'For a start,' he began, 'I didn't remember receiving the letter she said she sent, saying when she would be coming, so it was a real shock when this large woman arrived on my doorstep, wearing thick brown tweeds, heavy brogues and a hat in the shape of a flowerpot.

'"You were expecting me!" she snaps.

'"Was I?" I replied.

'"Yes!" says she.

'"Oh!" says I.

'"I wrote you a letter," says she.

'"Did you?" says I.

'"Did you not get it?" she asks.

'"I might have," I replied.

'"It was very important," says she.

'"Was it?" says I.

'"Official!" says she. "In a large brown envelope."

'"Really?" says I.

'"The name is de la Mare," says she. "Do you not remember?"'

'"Can't say as I do," says I.'

'So what happened?' I asked.

'She followed me into the school, peering around her as if it were a museum, declined a cup of tea, plonked herself down on my chair, took her flowerpot off her head and got out this thick wedge of paper from her big black bag.

'"I'm ready to commence," says she.

'"Are you?" says I.

'"I am," says she.

'I pointed out to her that the children had not yet arrived so there was not much point in "commencing" anything, but at nine o'clock after the register she could get started. I asked her if she wanted to begin with the infants and work up, or the juniors and work down.

'"I wish to start with you, Mr Lapping," she says, fixing me with those gimlet eyes of hers. "I want to discuss the teaching of spelling, grammar and punctuation, approaches to poetry, drama and story writing, standards of literacy, and the level of comprehension."

'"Hang on, Miss Mare," I says.

'"De la," says she, "it's de la Mare."'

I shut my eyes and groaned inwardly—I could guess what was coming.

'"OK, Della," I says, "I don't have all that information at my fingertips you know."

'"Well, don't you think you ought to, Mr Lapping?" says she. "After all you are the headteacher!"

'"Well, it's a new one to me," says I. "It's the first time in nearly forty years of teaching that the nit nurse has wanted that sort of information from me."'

I winced. 'You thought she was the school nurse?'

'Well, of course I did. How was I to know she was one of these HMIs?'

'How did she react?' I hardly dared ask.

'She stared at me for a moment with a sort of glazed expression and then she smiled. '"Let's start again, Mr Lapping," she said. "My name is Winifred de la Mare, HMI."'

'We got on like a house on fire after that, particularly when she had met the children and read their poetry and stories. She liked what she saw so much she's coming back in the spring.'

'I am delighted,' I said. 'Maybe I could come out to meet her when she returns?'

'Oh, you'll be meeting her all right, Gervase,' George Lapping replied. 'She was very interested in the creative writing we were doing, said it was very innovative, so I told her I got the ideas from one of your literacy courses and I suggested that she might care to join the next one you direct. She said it was an excellent suggestion and that she will, no doubt, be getting in touch with you.'

'Well, thank you very much,' I replied.

'You should be very flattered,' he told me, with a mischievous ring in his voice. 'It's a mark of the excellent service you provide that I have recommended you.' With that, he made for the door, waving his hand dramatically. '"Some are born great, some achieve greatness and some have greatness thrust upon them."'

 **10**

There was a witch waiting for me outside Winnery Nook school. The hideous creature had long, knotted black hair cascading from beneath a pointed hat, a pale green face and a flowing black cape. As I approached, the ghastly crone smiled widely to reveal a mouthful of blackened teeth. 'Hello, Gervase, how nice to see you.'

Before me stood the woman I was pretty sure I loved. Beneath the green make-up, the tangle of hair and the cloak was Miss Christine Bentley, and even dressed as a witch she looked wonderful. That particular morning I had agreed to visit her school as part of the Children's Reading Day celebrations to take the school assembly, talk to the children about stories and reading, and judge a fancy-dress competition the theme of which was fictional characters.

'I thought you were going to dress up for Children's Reading Day,' I teased, returning her smile.

'Cheeky thing!' she exclaimed. 'You had better come in. But any more clever comments of that kind and I'll put a spell on you.'

Christine had already put a spell on me, if only she knew it. I walked with her down the school corridor past excited, chattering children in all sorts of costumes.

'How was Chicago?'

'Marvellous,' Christine replied.

'And the dissertation?'

'All finished and sent off.'

We arrived at the main hall and were surrounded by colourful little characters all excited to show themselves off to the headteacher.

'Look,' Christine whispered, 'things are a bit frenetic at the moment, but I'm free this weekend. Let's go out and I can tell you all about it and you can tell me what sort of summer you've had.'

'That would be great,' I said. 'I'll give you a ring.'

'I must welcome the parents and children now, Gervase, so if you would like to wait in the staff room, I'll see you in a moment. Make yourself a cup of coffee.'

When I found Christine later, she was sitting with a child who was dressed in twisted yellow tights over which he wore a pair of close-fitting, electric-blue underpants. He had on a baggy white T-shirt with SUPAMAN written across the front in large, shaky letters.

'Well, *I* don't think you look a prat, Gavin,' said Christine.

'I do, miss,' whimpered Superman. 'Everyone says I look a prat.'

Christine caught sight of me. 'Well, look who is here!' she cried, beckoning me over. 'It's Mr Phinn.' Superman looked up, stifled his sobbing, and stared sorrowfully in my direction. 'Now, Mr Phinn is a very important visitor, Gavin, and knows everything because he's a school inspector and something of an expert on costumes. So shall we ask Mr Phinn what he thinks about your outfit?'

The child sniffed and nodded. 'Well, Mr Phinn,' said Christine, 'do you think Gavin looks a prat?'

'I certainly do not think he looks a prat!' I exclaimed.

The boy started to weep again. 'I do! Everybody says I do!'

'And I have in my pocket a special piece of paper which says you do not look a prat.' I reached in my jacket, produced a visiting card and wrote on it: '*Superman does not look a prat.*'

The little boy took it from me, scrutinised it for a moment and asked, 'Is that what it says?'

'It does,' I replied.

He tucked the card down the back of his electric-blue underpants, sniffed, smiled and scurried off.

Christine put her hand on my arm. 'That was sweet,' she said. 'Now, let's see how you fare taking the school assembly.'

The infants by this time had gathered in the hall and were sitting crosslegged in their resplendent costumes, facing the front.

'Good morning, children,' said Christine brightly.

'Good morning, Miss Bentley,' they chanted.

'Don't you all look wonderful this morning,' she said, scanning the rows of expectant, happy faces. 'Everyone looks really, really super. My goodness, what a lot of different characters we have in the hall today. It's going to be really hard to judge which of you is the best, so I have asked two of my friends to help me. I think you all know Mrs

Wainwright'—she indicated the Chairman of Governors sitting at the side—'and some of you may remember Mr Phinn who visited our school last year.'

Before us paraded a whole host of characters, from Long John Silver and Peter Rabbit to Toad of Toad Hall and Little Red Riding Hood. Last of all came the little boy in wrinkled yellow tights, electric-blue underpants and a T-shirt with SUPAMAN written across the front. I heard a few suppressed giggles and whispers from the other children and saw their smirks and smiles.

Mrs Wainwright and I awarded the first prize to the Little Mermaid, the second prize to Aladdin and the third prize to a very pleased little boy in yellow tights, electric-blue underpants and a T-shirt with SUPAMAN written across the front. As he scampered away he wore a great beaming smile.

I said my farewells to the children and Mrs Wainwright and headed for the door. Christine followed me out. She slipped her hand through my arm. 'Gavin won't stop talking about that for weeks. You're an old softie really, aren't you?' She gave me a quick peck on the cheek. 'I've got to go. Don't forget to ring me.'

A large, round-faced boy appeared from the hall. He wore a bright red blouse, baggy blue pants, large red floppy hat with a small silver bell on the end, and huge black shoes. A scarlet circle adorned each cheek. It was Noddy.

'Mr Phinn!' he gasped. 'Mr Phinn! I need one of those pieces of paper which you gave to Gavin which says I don't look a prat.'

MY NEXT APPOINTMENT was at Hawksrill Primary, deep in the heart of the Dales, and then I had to call in at the Staff Development Centre to plan a course for secondary school librarians with Mike Spiller, Principal Librarian for the county, and the children's writer, Irene Madley, who lived locally. I arrived at the unattractive red-brick building with only a few minutes to spare. As usual, the car park was littered with Connie's red and yellow cones and resembled the test course for advanced motorists.

Connie herself was awaiting my arrival, standing in the entrance hall, arms folded tightly over her chest, dressed in her usual brilliant pink nylon overall.

'Good afternoon, Connie,' I said in the most agreeable of voices. 'What a lovely day it is.'

'I wouldn't know, I've been inside cleaning,' she answered glumly.

'The weather has been perfect today,' I continued cheerfully. 'Beautifully mild and sunny.'

'Aye, that's as may be but I reckon we'll be paying for it next week.' Before I could respond, she launched into the attack. 'You came into the car park like a squirrel with its tail on fire. You want to slow down. It's a good job it isn't icy, or you'd have been into the wall and then the sparks would have really hit the fan.'

'I thought I was running a bit late for the meeting,' I explained.

'Well, there's only you here.' Connie set off up the corridor in the direction of the kitchen. 'You nearly had my bollards over. I put them bollards there for a reason, you know. They're to stop people from driving recklessly and from blocking my entrance.'

'I've parked well away from the entrance, Connie,' I assured her, 'and your bollards are all in place.'

'Just as well,' she snorted, flicking at windowsills as she walked ahead of me. 'I've put you in Room 9. And I suppose you'll be wanting a cup of tea.'

'That would be most welcome.'

'Well, you're out of luck with the biscuits. Mr Clamp polished off the last custard creams on Tuesday and I'm all out of garibaldis.'

Connie disappeared into the small kitchen and I heard her rattling and clattering as she made the tea.

'And did you and your husband have a nice holiday in Ireland this summer?' I shouted after her.

'No,' came the quick reply.

'You didn't enjoy it?'

'No, I didn't!' She emerged with a mug of tea which she thrust into my hand. 'Be careful, it's hot.'

'Well, I once had an absolutely marvellous holiday in Ireland,' I told her. 'What was your problem?'

'The crossing. I thought I was going to die, I really did. As soon as I set foot on that ferry I just knew I was going to be sick. We'd barely got out of the harbour when it started to move and it got worse and worse. I was up and down those steps like a shuttlecock. If I vomited once, I vomited ten times.' I took a sip of tea and attempted to look concerned. 'Up and down, up and down went that boat. I'll tell you, I've never been so glad to get my feet on terra cotta.' I spluttered, nearly choking on my tea. 'I told you that tea was hot,' she said.

'No, it's fine,' I replied, wiping my tie with a handkerchief, 'It's about time I checked that my colleagues have arrived.'

'And leave the room tidy,' Connie told me, disappearing into the kitchen where she resumed the clattering. I was halfway down the corridor when I heard her add, 'And I hope they've parked away from the entrance.'

FOLLOWING the planning meeting, I headed for home, Connie watching eagle-eyed from the window as I crawled out of the car park, negotiating the lines of strategically placed cones.

I was tired, but happy with the way Children's Reading Day had turned out, and as I pulled up outside my flat just as the clock at County Hall chimed nine, I thought that it would seem very lonely after such an eventful day. I parked behind a little green Morris Minor which I recognised immediately, and as I jumped out of my car the side window of the Morris slid down.

'Hello,' said Christine. 'I've just put the cauldron on. I wondered if you would like to join the Wicked Witch of the West for supper?'

11

The evening before my appointment with Lord Marrick and the Feoffees, the snow fell unexpectedly and in bitter earnest. Peering from the window of my flat, I watched the great flakes begin to form a thick carpet along the pavements.

I thought of the farmers. I had seen a Dales winter the previous Christmas. The icy wind had raged, the snow had piled into great mounds and drifts that froze, transforming the landscape into a vast ocean of crusted billows. I recalled seeing a farmer, his collie dog leaping at his heels, tramping through thick snow in a field behind a school, in search of his foundered sheep.

The next morning, 25 November, I was up bright and early. I pulled back the curtains to find the snow had stopped but had settled. The main road out of Fettlesham, however, looked to have been cleared and the weather forecast said there would be no more snow. I called to check if the meeting was still on and the telephone was answered by Lord Marrick's secretary, who confirmed that it was going ahead. She reassured me that the weather further up the dale was not too bad and that all the roads were passable. I decided to chance it and drive out to Manston Hall.

After I left the main Fettlesham–West Challerton road, the car skidded a few times, but thankfully there were no sharp inclines and I was soon crawling towards the tall ornate gates that marked the entrance to Manston Hall. Built in warm red brick, the house stood out square and bright in its vast white parkland, a beautifully proportioned building of extraordinary charm and beauty.

There were several large saloon cars, a Range Rover and a Rolls-Royce parked in front of the hall. My old Volvo estate looked out of place in such expensive company. I checked my hair in the rear-view mirror, straightened my tie, collected my notepad and climbed out.

The great black door to Manston Hall, flanked by elegant pillars, was opened by an ancient retainer, who gestured for me to enter.

While he pushed shut the heavy door and rearranged the draught-excluder in front of it, I gazed round the spacious entrance hall in wonder. The ceiling was a jungle of decorative plasterwork, and the floor of white inlaid marble matched the huge and magnificently carved chimneypiece, above which a full-length portrait in dark oils depicted a severe-looking man in military uniform.

'May I have your name, sir?' asked the retainer.

'Gervase Phinn,' I replied.

'If you would come this way, Mr Phinn.'

I followed his slow, measured steps down a long corridor. He opened a door and I was ushered through it into Lord Marrick's library, a panelled room with floor-to-ceiling shelving crammed with leather-bound books. A huge Persian carpet covered the dark, polished wooden floor. Before a roaring open fire stood a group of men in animated conversation.

Lord Marrick strode across to meet me.

'Mr Phinn. Gervase. Good of you to come. Dreadful weather, isn't it? Come along in and meet everyone.'

Taking my arm he led me towards the fireplace and began introducing me, as the education representative, to the frighteningly august group. There was Brigadier Lumsden, Archdeacon Richards, the High Sheriff, and finally Judge Plunkett, a painfully thin man with a face full of tragic potential. I shook hands, smiled at each one and wondered why I was there. What could an insignificant school inspector contribute to this gathering of the great and the good?

'Gentlemen!' boomed Lord Marrick. 'We appear to be all present and correct, so shall we make a start? If you would follow me, I'll lead the way.' We followed him into another equally magnificent room, in the centre of which was a long, highly polished table with balloon-backed rosewood chairs arranged round it.

'Now, gentlemen,' he began, when we were all seated. 'I appreciate your giving up valuable time to join me here this morning, particularly in this bloody awful weather, and I want to assure you that this meeting will be short and to the point. I want to mark the five hundred years of the Feoffees by a major event at Manston Hall on the last Saturday in May. I want the general public to know about those traditions that are so much a part of our cultural heritage. So could we throw a few ideas around regarding how the area for which each of you has responsibility can play its part in the celebration?'

During the next half-hour the ideas came fast and furious. The brigadier suggested a parade of army vehicles, and a display by the army motorcycle team; the high sheriff said he could arrange a march past by the police band, and a demonstration by dog-handlers and mounted police; the archdeacon offered a recital by the abbey choir; other suggestions came forth for exhibitions of local history, craft stalls and information stands of all kinds. Then there was a sudden silence and all eyes seemed to be on me.

'Mr Phinn,' Lord Marrick said suddenly. 'You have been very quiet. What can the Education Department offer?' I began by mumbling something about having to consult Dr Gore and my colleagues, but ended up agreeing to mount a display of children's stories based on famous characters from history, approach a couple of schools to ask them to perform some short plays on a historical theme, and enlist the help of my colleagues to arrange an exhibition on education down the ages, a gymnastics display and a performance by the County Youth Orchestra. That little lot would keep Mrs Savage busy, I thought to myself.

DURING THE PREVIOUS summer, we inspectors had the onerous task of analysing all the school reports from the preceding academic year in order to get a clear picture of how well, or otherwise, schools in the country were doing and whether standards were rising or falling. It was a great relief to me that the verdict on the state of English teaching in the county turned out to be positive. There was, however, just one area of the English curriculum that seemed to be neglected. Mrs Peterson and Mrs Dunn at Highcopse Primary School were not alone in spending little time on poetry. I decided, therefore, to mount a series of weekend courses to help teachers in this important area.

The first course was planned to take place in early December, and when the deadline came for final applications my in-tray was piled high with over fifty requests.

The Staff Development Centre had been booked well in advance, but I rang Connie to let her know how many teachers were antici-pated. Then I steamed ahead, ordered the materials, arranged for the course programme to be printed, and dispatched letters of accep-tance to the applicants.

Everything was going like clockwork—and then I received a letter from the formidable Miss de la Mare, Her Majesty's Principal

Divisional Inspector of Schools. She said she had been impressed with some of the creative writing she had observed in the few schools she had recently visited and mentioned her visit to Backwatersthwaite and the poetry lessons of the 'inspirational Mr Lapping'. She said she was compiling a national report on the teaching of the arts in primary schools and, as she had noticed that I was running a series of weekend poetry courses, she thought how useful it would be if she attended one. She concluded her letter: 'I have followed the normal protocol and contacted Dr Gore and he is happy for me to join you. I trust there will be no objection on your part?'

'No objection!' exclaimed Sidney with a hollow laugh, when I read him the letter. 'As if you are in any position to object.'

'And everything was going so smoothly,' I sighed. 'I could have well done without this.'

'Oh, that's always the way,' said David in his Prophet of Doom voice. 'There's always something or somebody who has to spoil things. I don't think I've ever run a course without a mishap. I remember the occasion when thirty teachers and I turned up all bright-eyed and bushy-tailed to find the Staff Development Centre all locked up and Connie away in Mablethorpe in her caravan for the weekend.'

'Ah, now that's one thing that won't happen,' I told him, 'I've checked the date with Connie.'

'I've had my share of disastrous courses,' said David morosely, 'Mind you, I've never been scrutinised by an HMI. Now that is deeply worrying. At least my disasters went unobserved.'

'I am sure that Gervase is greatly encouraged by all this,' remarked Sidney. 'I would just like to say that I will be directing my art course at the very same time as our young colleague is running his, and will be there at the Staff Development Centre to give him the benefit of my advice and support.'

'Huh!' snapped David. 'You'll not have time to be giving him any support. You'll be too busy arguing with Connie.'

Before Sidney could respond, I put my hand on his shoulder and said, 'That is really very kind of you, Sidney. I might just ask Miss de la Mare to pop into a few of your sessions. After all, she is interested in the arts as well.'

ON THE MORNING of the course I arrived at the Centre bright and early, checked the equipment, arranged the tables and chairs, and waited nervously for the first teachers to arrive. Even though I had run courses before, I could not help being rather on edge. Would my speakers turn up? If they did, would they be well received? Suppose the heating went off? I was deep into the things that might go wrong when the door opened and Connie made an entrance.

'There's a woman in reception wanting to see you. Sounded like "Fella Beware".'

'Miss de la Mare,' I whispered to myself. 'She's the HMI I told you about, Connie,' I said, jumping to my feet and hurrying to the door.

'Well, I hope her car hasn't blocked my entrance,' grumbled Connie, following me down the corridor.

Miss de la Mare was not as I had imagined. I expected her to be dressed, as George Lapping had described her, in thick brown tweeds, heavy brogues and a hat in the shape of a flowerpot. The woman waiting for me in the entrance was very different. She was plump and cheerful-looking, with a freckled face, and neatly bobbed silver hair. She was dressed in a coat as red as a letter box and wore a long multicoloured scarf round her neck.

She shook my hand vigorously. 'Winifred de la Mare. Good of you to let me come, Mr Phinn. Really looking forward to joining you. Oh, by the way, I noticed in the course booklet that there's an art course going on at the same time. Do you think your colleague would mind if I looked in this afternoon?'

'He would be delighted,' I replied gleefully.

She peered around her, 'I don't suppose there's a chance of a cup of tea? I've travelled a fair distance this morning.'

'Of course.' I turned to Connie, who was loitering in the background. 'I wonder if Miss de la Mare could—'

Before I could complete my request, Connie had set off in the direction of the kitchen, saying that if my visitor would care to follow her, she would put the kettle on. As they steamed off, I caught a snatch of their conversation.

'You keep this Centre very neat and tidy.'

'I try my best and you can't do any more than that.'

I knew from that moment that the course would be a success.

And indeed, my opening lecture and the morning workshops were well received. Miss de la Mare, despite her frequent interruptions, proved to be most amicable and involved herself fully in all the activities, joining the discussions and even tackling the writing tasks.

At lunch time I introduced her to Sidney. He was holding forth to several young women teachers who had gathered around him in the dining area. They were staring up at him, wide-eyed.

'Miss de la Mare,' I said, giving Sidney a surreptitious wink, 'may I introduce my colleague, who is the creative and visual arts inspector?'

Sidney's smile could have been seen a hundred yards away. 'I am delighted to meet you, Miss de la Mare,' he said. 'I hope you are enjoying the poetry course.'

'Very much,' she said briskly.

'Miss de la Mare is wondering if she might join you for the remainder of the day,' I said.

The smile waned a little. 'Join me?' he said.

'If you have no objection,' said Miss de la Mare.

I recalled my earlier conversation with Sidney. He really had no choice in the matter.

'I should be delighted,' he said.

BY THE TIME Sunday afternoon had arrived, I had seen relatively little of Miss de la Mare. She seemed to have been so captivated with Sidney's work that she had remained with him for all of Saturday afternoon and Sunday morning. For the last session of the poetry course, however, she reappeared, and later, in the staff room after all the teachers had made their farewells, she said, 'He's quite a character, Mr Clamp. An immensely creative man and very innovative. I did so enjoy my time with him. I have a mind to ask him to contribute to a national course on "The Arts in School" that I am directing next summer in Oxford. Do you think he would be interested?'

'I'm sure he would,' I replied. Sidney had made another conquest.

'You may care to come along too,' continued Miss de la Mare. 'I found those parts of the poetry course I attended most interesting. You certainly got them to think and to argue. So many people imagine that a poem *must* have something profound to say. Personally, though, I have always been of the opinion that a poem can be about anything and that anything can be a poem. You see, the reader brings so much to the verse, very often seeing things in it that the poet never intended.'

'Yes, I suppose so,' I said.

'I once visited a large primary school in the middle of a dreadfully depressing inner-city area.' Miss de la Mare continued, smiling at the memory. 'The work of the children consisted largely of arid exercises. There was the occasional story, the odd comprehension, but not a sign of a poem. And then I found this nervous little boy in the corner of the classroom. When I asked if I could examine his book he looked at me with large sad eyes and said very quietly, "No." I tried to coax him but he was adamant, saying he couldn't spell, his writing was untidy and he never got good marks. I eventually persuaded him to let me see his writing. The book was indeed very poor.

But then, at the very back I came upon a piece of writing that was a small masterpiece. I asked him if he had received any help with it, and he shook his head. I remember the words so well:

Yesterday yesterday yesterday
Sorrow sorrow sorrow
Today today today
Hope hope hope
Tomorrow tomorrow tomorrow
Love love love

'"What a wonderful little poem," I told him.

'He thought for a while, then stared up at me sadly and said: "They're my spelling corrections, miss."'

12

'I'm really going to make an effort with Christmas this year,' announced Julie, a week before the schools closed for the holidays.

'And why is that?' asked David, looking up from his papers.

'Because last year was so awful. I spent ages and ages looking for presents that in the end didn't suit and I wrote hundreds of cards to people I hadn't seen for ages and wasn't likely to ever see again. Well, this year I'm not sending any cards and I'm giving all my nephews and nieces money.' She looked up. 'You know the present I got from Paul last year?'

'I don't,' I said, 'but I guess you are about to tell us.'

'Red underwear! That's what I got. Skimpy red silk underwear. Now who in their right minds—apart from Mrs Savage and a French prostitute—would be seen dead in red underwear?'

'So what about Christmas Day itself?' I asked. 'Have you cancelled it?'

'We're going out to dinner. I want peace and quiet, no hassle, no noise, no stress.'

'And speaking of hassle, noise and stress,' said David, cupping a hand round his ear, 'I think I can hear our Sidney's dainty tread on the stairs.'

'And that's another thing,' said Julie, 'I've got a mountain of work to finish for Mr Clamp and I was hoping to get off a bit earlier tonight to finish my Christmas shopping.'

A moment later Sidney burst into the office. 'Happy Christmas!' he roared, throwing his briefcase on Harold's chair. 'I just love this time of year. The smell of pine trees in the air, carols and cribs, fairy lights, holly and mistletoe, and Santa's grotto, ho! ho! ho!' He pulled off his coat and flopped at his desk. 'Christmas makes you feel so well disposed to others. Why, at this time of year I could kiss Connie and hug Mrs Savage.' Sidney suddenly stopped. The three of us were staring at him silently. 'Is it something I've said?'

Julie placed a pile of papers on his desk. 'Dr Yeats wants the report on Loxley Chase School before the end of the afternoon. You have six letters to sign, the questionnaire on "Painters in Schools" to complete, your January course applications to check over and you still haven't finished the Arts Council response that Dr Gore asked you to do. Happy Christmas!'

'I've somehow gone back in time,' said Sidney dramatically, 'and found my way into the office of Ebeneezer Scrooge.'

Thereafter, the first part of the day was unusually quiet. Sidney settled down to his reports and letters and all that could be heard was the scratching of pens, the occasional sigh, and the scraping of a chair on the hard wooden floor. When the clock on the County Hall tower struck eleven o'clock, however, Sidney's pen bounced off the page in a flourish as he stabbed the final full stop to the Loxley Chase Report. He leaned back in his chair, placed his hands behind his head and began one of his all too familiar interrogations.

'I assume, Gervase, that over Christmas you are taking the Venus of Fettlesham, the Aphrodite of the education world, to some far-away, exotic location?'

'No,' I replied curtly.

'No?' he retorted. 'Is it a wet weekend in Whitby, then?'

'Actually, we are not spending Christmas together. I'm going to my brother's in Retford again. I'm hoping we can have a few days together in the New Year.'

'Barbados, Nice, St Tropez, Paris?'

'Settle.'

'Settle?' he cried. 'You're taking her to Settle? It's the potholing capital of the Dales. What are you intending doing? Creeping about on all fours underground with lamps on your heads?'

'Actually, Settle is spectacular in winter,' David told him. 'As a matter of fact, it was I who recommended it to Gervase. There's a very pleasant little hostelry there. The food is outstanding, the views magnificent and the owners friendly. Also, it's very romantic.'

'But it is still Settle,' groaned Sidney. 'Has she agreed to go?'

'I haven't asked her yet,' I said. 'I want it to be a surprise.'

'It'll be a surprise all right!' He changed the subject. 'And what have you got your inamorata for Christmas?'

'A locket,' I replied.

'Oh dear, oh dear. A locket! A locket is something you give your maiden aunt or a little girl for her first Communion. What you need for a beauty like Christine is something that expresses your simmering passion. An obscenely large bottle of French perfume, a huge box of Belgian chocolates, a—'

'Or something tasteful like red silk underwear?' suggested David.

'That's exactly the sort of thing,' enthused Sidney. 'Red silk underwear is an inspired suggestion.'

'There is no way I am giving Christine red underwear!' I said.

'But she will adore it!' cried Sidney, just as Julie appeared with his letters for signing. 'What woman could resist red silk underwear? Wouldn't you agree, Julie?'

Julie gave him a long, blistering look, then slowly left the office.

'You know, I think Christmas brings out the worst in some people,' sighed Sidney, shaking his head.

I DECIDED TO BROACH the subject of Settle with Christine that very evening. I had agreed to go with her to the Christmas production at Winnery Nook Junior School and was due to pick her up from her parents' house at seven o'clock.

I arrived a little before half past six. Rain began to fall as I drove up the curved gravel drive. Christine's mother opened the door to me with a warm smile and I was ushered down the long hallway and into the sitting room.

'What an evening,' she said. 'Come along in, Gervase. Christine won't be long. She arrived back late from school as usual, so she's still getting ready.'

It was a charming, elegant room and about as different as it possibly could be from my dark little flat. A large Christmas tree in the corner sparkled with silver tinsel and tiny lights, the mantelpiece was lined with cards, red and gold decorations hung from the walls. I sat in front of a welcoming log fire which crackled brightly in the grate.

'This room looks splendid,' I said.

'Oh, I just love Christmas,' Christine's mother replied, echoing Sidney. 'It really brings out the best in people, don't you think?'

'So you're all prepared for Christmas?' I asked.

'Just about. I told Christine you would be welcome to join us for the day, but she said you had already agreed to go to your brother's.'

'That's right,' I replied. 'I'm collecting my parents and my sister is coming down and we'll have a family Christmas in Retford. But thank you very much for inviting me.'

'Well, perhaps next year,' she said, smiling.

Let's hope I will still be on the scene next year, I thought.

'Ours will be a quiet affair,' Mrs Bentley continued. 'We never see a great deal of Christine at Christmas, to be truthful. She goes off on Boxing Day and—'

'Goes off?' I interrupted.

'Skiing, you know. She's gone skiing every Christmas since she left college. Didn't she tell you?'

'No,' I replied, crestfallen, 'she never mentioned it.'

'Oh dear,' said Mrs Bentley. 'I hope I haven't put my foot in it.'

'YOU NEVER TOLD ME you were going skiing after Christmas,' I remarked as I drove towards Winnery Nook Junior School a short while later.

'Oh, didn't I?' she replied innocently. 'Well, I knew that you were off to your family get-together in Retford. You didn't want to come, did you?'

'I might have done. Who are you going with?'

'Oh, just a friend,' she replied.

'What friend?' I could feel my heart thumping in my chest.

'Are you jealous?'

'No,' I said peevishly. 'Well, yes, I am as a matter of fact.'

'Alex. I'm going with Alex, an old college friend. So there. Now you know.'

'And what's this Alex like?'

'Tall, slim, attractive.' She paused. 'She's very nice.'

'Oh, it's a she, then?' I cried, vastly relieved.

'Of course it's a she, silly. I'm not likely to be going off skiing with another man, am I?' She moved closer. 'I'm not that sort of woman.'

'Oh well, that's different,' I said. 'I just thought that we might spend the last weekend together before schools start again. There's a really nice hotel that David recommended and—'

'I'm only going for a week, and will be back on the second.'

'So you'll come?'

'I'd love to. And where is this hotel?'

'Well, it's not Barbados, I'm afraid. It's near Settle.'

'I love Settle,' Christine said. 'I'll really look forward to it.'

'Good, that's settled, then,' I said.

We both laughed out loud.

'EXCELLENT NEWS, gentlemen!' Harold Yeats crashed through the door the next morning, making the three of us shoot up from our chairs.

'For goodness sake, Harold!' cried Sidney, retrieving the bundle of papers that he had scattered across the office floor in his alarm. 'I wish you wouldn't do that.'

'It's just that I have some really wonderful news!' exclaimed Harold, vigorously rubbing his large hands.

'Is it a pay rise?' asked David lugubriously.

'No, not a pay rise, David, but it is something that will, I have no doubt, bring a smile to that austere Welsh countenance of yours.'

'Mrs Savage has been given the sack.' announced David gleefully. 'Now that *would* bring a smile to my face.'

'No, no.' Harold rumpled his hair. 'Dr Gore has agreed, with the Education Committee's approval, for us to appoint another inspector, one to cover science and technology.'

'Oh, be still my dancing feet!' exclaimed David. 'You mean I will no longer be responsible for science and technology?'

'I thought that would please you,' said Harold.

'It is absolutely superb news, Harold. When will he start?'

'It will be after Easter. The advertisement goes into the *Education Supplement* after Christmas to allow time for the successful candidate to give a couple of months' notice to his employer.'

'He! His!' exclaimed Sidney. 'Don't you two think, in this age of equal opportunities, that it may very well be a woman who is appointed?'

Harold took a deep, steadying breath. 'It would, of course, be splendid if we were able to appoint a woman. Actually, when we were short-listing for the English post we all thought Gervase was—'

'A woman?' exclaimed Sidney.

'Well, er, yes,' Harold stuttered. 'I'm sure Gervase will be the first to admit he has a most unusual name and—'

'It's all right, Harold,' I laughed. 'I'm used to it. I often get letters addressed to Ms Phinn.'

'But of course, Harold,' persisted Sidney, 'it would be an extremely sensible move to have a woman on the team. After all, an attractive, intelligent young woman would add verve and colour to this drab cubicle we call an office.'

'Now who's being sexist?' spluttered David. 'Why has she got to be attractive, intelligent, young? It's not a beauty contest.'

'Look!' said Harold. 'I do wish you would stop nit-picking. Now, if you could all bear with me for one moment, without interrupting,

I shall explain the new procedures. Dr Gore feels we need to refine the selection process and he's going to try out some modern techniques. For the first part of the day, the short-listed candidates will sit a brief sociometric test before meeting a selection of primary school headteachers in an informal setting. Then, after morning coffee, each candidate will make a fifteen-minute presentation to the interview panel. Following this, lunch will be with three secondary headteachers and the candidates will again be assessed in an informal setting. In the afternoon they will sit a written paper. It should all be over by about five thirty.'

'Is that *all* they have to do?' asked Sidney. 'What about hang-gliding from the clock tower at County Hall or making a model of Buckingham Palace out of used matchsticks?'

'I have to admit that it does sound like the Spanish Inquisition!' exclaimed David. 'I'm certainly glad I didn't have all that carry-on to go through when I was appointed. If you were warm and breathing, then they gave you the job.'

'We have to move with the times,' said Harold. 'Now, I would like you all to be at the Staff Development Centre at about five thirty on the day of the interviews on March 1st.'

'St David's Day!' David murmured. 'Well, I hope we are not going to be long. We're having a Welsh evening at the Golf Club.'

'Why do you want us there, Harold?' I asked.

'It's for you three to meet the successful candidate,' Harold told us. 'Gervase, you mentioned that it would have been nice if you had been given the opportunity of meeting your future colleagues, so I intend to put that suggestion into practice.'

Julie, who had been standing by the door listening, raised her hand. 'Could I ask something, Dr Yeats?'

'Of course, Julie, what is it?'

'Where is he, she or it going to sit? On top of the bookcase? In a filing cabinet? On the windowsill? This office is already overcrowded. You'll never get another desk and cupboard in here.'

'Perhaps you could discriminate in favour of the smallest candidate, Harold,' suggested Sidney. 'Someone four foot tall and as thin as a rake.'

'And what about all the added typing and filing,' continued Julie, 'and all the extra running about I'll have to do?'

'Julie, Julie,' Harold reassured her, 'let's try to be positive. We are in desperate need of someone to take on the extra work. I am certain that all these little internal difficulties can be overcome. I shall have a word with Mrs Savage.'

'Oh, well, if you have a word with Mrs Savage,' said David sarcastically, 'she'll just wave her witch's broomstick, and everything will be fine. One could not hope for a kinder, more easy-going person than the ever-helpful Mrs Savage.'

Harold gave a great sigh. 'I just hope our new colleague has a sense of humour, thick skin and the patience of a saint.'

'So what was Settle like?' asked Sidney, the first week back after the Christmas break.

I was certainly not going to elaborate. 'Excellent,' I replied. 'We didn't go out much.'

'*Really?* Sounds like you had a very intimate time. And the locket?'

'She loved it.'

'Mmmm, and there was I thinking Miss Bentley was a woman of taste. Did she help you choose that horrendous suit you're wearing?'

'No, I bought it yesterday, as a matter of fact.'

'And you are intending going into schools in it, are you?'

'Of course, I am. Why shouldn't I?'

'Because you'll frighten the teachers and terrify the children.'

'I take it you don't like it, then?'

'Wherever did you get it?'

'It was in the January sales.'

'I assumed *that* much,' said Sidney. 'I should imagine that it has been in the January sales since Queen Victoria's time. I asked from where did you purchase the monstrosity?'

'From Fritters of Fettlesham.'

'Fritters of Fettlesham!' exclaimed my colleague. 'Fritters of Fettlesham! Are you aware that the only customers who frequent that antique emporium are decrepit old colonels, elderly clergymen and retired schoolmasters?'

I had to admit to myself that the suit was rather unusual. It was a sort of mustardy brown with a dark red, dog-tooth pattern.

'Are you wearing it for a bet?' persisted Sidney.

'Look, this suit may not be at the height of fashion, but it's incredibly warm and was remarkably cheap. What's more, the man in Fritters assured me it was the cosiest suit in the shop.'

'Cosiest!' exclaimed Sidney. 'You are not a teapot, Gervase.'

'Look, Sidney, I wanted something to insulate me against the cold this winter, and on mornings like today, this suit is ideal. It may not be particularly stylish, but I'll be as snug as a bug in a rug.'

'That's because it very probably was a rug before someone, with a bizarre sense of humour, turned it into a suit.'

At this point Julie bustled in with the morning mail. 'And what is *your* opinion of Gervase's attire, Julie, my dear?' Sidney asked.

'He looks like my Uncle Cyril,' she informed us casually, moving from one desk to the other filling the in-trays.

'Was he the doctor?' I asked.

'No,' she replied. 'He was the bigamist who ended up in prison.'

'I'm off,' I said, heading for the door, not wishing to prolong the conversation a moment longer.

'And don't go near the cliffs, will you, Gervase?' shouted Sidney after me. 'You'd be a hazard to shipping in that suit!'

THE WEEKS PASSED quickly and soon the day of the interviews for the new inspector arrived. Harold, smartly dressed and carrying a leather-backed clipboard, was in the office early, as were we all that morning, to find out who had been short-listed for the post.

'My goodness,' remarked Sidney. 'You look like a game-show host with that clipboard. So, who have you called for interview then?'

'Well, there are five up for the post, including, you will be pleased to hear, Sidney, some women. There's a Mr Carey Price-Williams—'

'Can't be doing with folk with double-barrelled names.'

'If I may continue?' Harold said. 'There's a Mr Thomas Wilson, a Ms Jennifer Black, a Dr Gerry Mullarkey—'

'I bet you any money we get the crusty old doctor,' sighed Sidney, leaning back in his chair. 'I can just picture the old buffer. He'll be a dusty physicist with glasses like the bottoms of milk bottles and grey hair sticking up like wire wool.'

'Actually, you couldn't be more mistaken,' Harold continued. 'Dr Mullarkey is extremely well qualified, with a wide range of experience and excellent references.'

'Wasn't Dr Mullarkey a villain in Sherlock Holmes, Gervase?' asked Sidney, going off on one of his tangents.

'No, that was Professor Moriaty,' I said.

'I wonder if he really exists. It's a very strange name, is Mullarkey. It sounds a tad suspicious to me. It could be a pseudonym.'

'Look,' interrupted Harold, 'I came in here for five minutes, not for a detailed analysis of each candidate. I must be off.'

'Hang on a minute, Harold!' cried Sidney. 'You have only mentioned four. Who's the fifth candidate?'

Harold consulted his clipboard. 'A Miss Gloria Goodwood.'

'Now *that's* more like it!' chortled Sidney. 'Gloria Goodwood. She sounds like the heroine in a romantic novel: young, alluring, with a mass of auburn hair over her alabaster shoulders.'

'If she is successful,' replied Harold, 'you will see Miss Goodwood at five thirty at the Staff Development Centre. I look forward to seeing you all later this afternoon to meet your new colleague.'

I SPENT THE DAY working on the plans for those events for which I was responsible at the Feoffees Pageant, which was to be held at Manston Hall at the end of May. Schools had provided me with a mountain of stories based on famous characters from history, and I sorted out a good selection. Pupils from three different schools were to perform plays on historical themes, Sidney had arranged for an exhibition of children's art, David a gymnastics display and the County Youth Orchestra would give a performance on the lawn at Manston Hall. The Education Department would be well represented.

All communication with Mrs Savage about the Feoffees Pageant had been undertaken by note and memorandum. I had been careful to record all the arrangements we had agreed upon, and had made certain Dr Gore had been sent a copy. My promise to liaise had been kept—even if I had ducked meeting with her in person.

AS INSTRUCTED, I arrived at the Centre at five thirty. Connie was standing in her familiar pose, with arms folded, in the centre of the entrance hall like some nightclub bouncer. She was facing up to Sidney and David, who had obviously arrived only seconds before.

'How are we on this beautiful, mild St David's Day?' Sidney was saying effusively. 'And here comes Mr Phinn, look you.'

'I'm very well, thank you. But if you're expecting something to drink, you're out of luck because there's no milk. All those councillors and candidates have gone through four pints of gold top and two boxes of garibaldis.'

'It's so good to find you in such a cheerful mood, Connie,' remarked Sidney. 'Now, what are the candidates like? Do tell.'

'Well, there's a big, hairy man who has a lot to say for himself. A bit like you, Mr Clamp, but he's Welsh.'

'Ever the flatterer, Connie,' Sidney murmured.

'There's a nicely spoken woman of about forty-five and a very sour-faced individual in a shiny suit.'

'Dr Mullarkey,' added Sidney knowingly.

'I don't know what he's called,' continued Connie, 'but he was very off-hand with me when I asked him to hextinguish his pipe. I can't see how he could make a very good inspector when he couldn't read any of the "No Smoking" signs I have around the Centre.'

'And the other candidates?' I enquired.

'There was a very friendly young woman. The only one to offer to help me dry the dishes. Very chatty and cheerful. I took to her.'

'That will be Glorious Goodbody,' purred Sidney.

'And what about the last one?' asked David.

'Look, Mr Pritchard!' snapped Connie. 'I don't spend all day standing about watching people, you know.'

'Of course, you don't, Connie. Perish the thought.'

'Anyway, I hope they're not going to be much longer. I've got to do the toilets before I finish. And would you three move into the staff room? I have the carpet out here to vacuum.'

As the hand on the Centre clock ticked towards six, Sidney, David and I huddled in the small staff room, getting increasingly impatient.

'You would think that after nine hours of interrogation they would have picked someone,' complained David.

'The appointment is a foregone conclusion anyway,' remarked Sidney. 'I could tell by the way Harold was so depressingly enthusiastic when a certain candidate was mentioned. I bet you a pound to a penny we get the dry old stick with the funny name.'

'I think you may very well be right,' agreed David. 'He said more about that Mullarkey fellow than all the others put together.'

'You don't think you two are prejudging this poor person a little?' I chimed in. 'He's probably a very decent sort. Just because he's got an unusual name doesn't mean—'

At that moment Harold Yeats burst into the room. 'I have some news!' he exclaimed. 'We have appointed Dr Gerry Mullarkey. So if you would care to make your way down to the lounge area, you can congratulate Dr Mullarkey and introduce yourselves.'

There was no sign of Dr Mullarkey in the lounge. Behind the kitchen hatch Connie could be heard banging pans about. The room was empty save for an extremely pretty, slender young woman with short, raven-black hair.

'Excuse me, we are looking for a Dr Mullarkey,' announced David.

'Have you seen him by any chance?' I asked.

'I wonder if he's already left,' suggested Sidney'

'I'm Dr Mullarkey,' said the young woman. 'Geraldine Mullarkey. Most people call me Gerry. I assume that you gentlemen are my new colleagues?'

Our mouths fell open.

'Oh, I say,' murmured Sidney, staring into the blue eyes. 'Oh, I say.'

David stepped forward. 'Good afternoon,' he said formally, offering his hand. 'I'm David Pritchard, inspector for mathematics, PE and games. The hairy one is Sidney Clamp, the inspector for visual and creative arts. The one who looks at this moment as if the hamster is dead but the wheel is still turning is Gervase Phinn, the inspector for English and drama. It is good to have you with us, Gerry. And if there is anything we can do for you, please ask.'

'There *is* something, actually. I have to catch a train from Fettlesham just after seven. I wonder if one of you could give me a lift to the station—that's if it's not too far out of your way.'

'No problem,' said David, 'I can easily drop you off.'

'Nonsense!' cried Sidney. 'You're going in the opposite direction. I can easily drop Geraldine off at the station.'

'It would be much easier for me to drop Gerry off,' I interrupted. 'I have a visit to make this evening at Brindcliffe Primary School, which is directly opposite the station.'

'Well, that's settled,' said Dr Mullarkey, collecting her briefcase. 'I'm sorry to have to rush. I'm really looking forward to working with you all.' She gave me a stunning smile. 'Shall we go, Gervase?'

Sister Brendan was headteacher of St Bartholomew's Roman Catholic Infant School in Crompton, a darkly depressing northern industrial town. She was a slight, fine-featured woman with small dark eyes and a sharp beak of a nose. Her school was surrounded by derelict building sites, dilapidated warehouses and row upon row of blackened red-brick terraced housing.

The school itself, adjacent to the little church, was a complete contrast. Like its headteacher, it was bright and welcoming, and on my first visit I had been immensely impressed by the high quality of the education. The walls were ablaze with children's paintings and poems.

When I was compiling my report, I had had difficulty in finding any issues for the headteacher and her staff to address. One area I did mention, however, was a greater encouragement of clear speaking. I suggested that the staff, while not denigrating the children's natural way of talking, might teach the pupils to speak with greater clarity. One means of doing this, I suggested, was through drama.

A couple of days after my meeting with Gerry Mullarky, I received a telephone call from Sister Brendan, who thanked me for 'a most useful report' and made a request.

'We would like some advice on drama, Mr Phinn. Could you come in for an afternoon, do you think?'

'Yes, of course, Sister,' I replied. 'I could drop off some helpful books with ideas for various drama activities and I'll happily talk things through with you and your staff.'

'I was thinking more of a practical demonstration,' she said.

'Perhaps you could take the children for a drama lesson.'

What could I say? 'Of course, Sister,' I replied, trying to sound enthusiastic, 'I'd be delighted.' It was like a rerun of Highcopse School when Mrs Peterson had inveigled me into teaching a poetry lesson. Well, that had gone well enough, I thought to myself.

I ARRIVED at St Bartholomew's on a cold but bright Friday morning. Sister Brendan was at the entrance to greet me.

'My goodness, Mr Phinn, you're the early bird,' she said, beaming widely. 'Come along in.' I followed her down the bright corridor and into the headteacher's room. 'Now, the plan this morning, Mr Phinn, if it is acceptable to you, is that we will have our assembly and then you can have the two top infant classes for drama.'

'Two whole classes!' I exclaimed.

'Well, I thought we ought to take full advantage of your kind offer to work with the children. Is there a problem with that?'

'No, no problem, Sister,' I replied, feeling slightly nervous at the thought of controlling sixty or so lively six- and seven-year-olds.

'Assembly this morning will be taken by Monsignor Leonard. He comes in every Friday to spend a little time with us. When I told him you were in school he wondered if he might stay to watch your drama session?'

'Yes, of course,' I replied.

'He'll be bringing with him Miss Fenoughty, who is his house-keeper, and the church organist. Of course, she just comes in with Monsignor Leonard for his weekly assembly and we make do with a tape the remaining days. I know it sounds a little uncharitable but I don't think I could cope with Miss Fenoughty every day of the week.'

'Oh dear. Why is that?'

Sister Brendan sighed. 'Well, she's rather deaf, you see, and she hammers on the keys as if there is no tomorrow. The piano fairly shudders. It's the same in church on Sunday. Last week the Ave Maria sounded like the "1812 Overture".' By now, I just could not stop myself from smiling.

'I can see you find it funny, Mr Phinn, but let me assure you Miss Fenoughty would try the patience of a saint.' Sister Brendan peered through the window. 'And speaking of saints, here comes Monsignor Leonard, who has to put up with Miss Fenoughty, morning, noon and night.'

Down the path to the school came the priest, a tall man in a shabby cassock, and a small woman of indeterminate age. I followed

Sister Brendan to the school entrance to meet them.

'Good morning, Sister. Good morning, Mr Phinn,' murmured the priest before stooping and shouting in his companion's ear: 'This is Mr Phinn, Miss Fenoughty. Do you remember, I mentioned him this morning at breakfast?'

'I knew a Bernadette Flynn who used to go to Notre Dame High School,' remarked the old lady, scrutinising me. 'Very talented girl.'

'It's Phinn, Miss Fenoughty, Mr Phinn,' corrected the priest.

'I also knew a Father Flynn. He was a lovely man.' She looked up at me. 'Are you any relation?'

Sister Brendan, like the statue of the Virgin Mary which dominated the entrance hall, raised her eyes saintlike to heaven.

SISTER BRENDAN had not exaggerated. Miss Fenoughty's rendition of 'All Things Bright and Beautiful' made the ground shake and the windows tremble. Quite a number of the children covered their ears. Monsignor Leonard gave a small homily about showing charity to those less fortunate, a prayer was said and the assembly was over. While Sister Brendan explained to the children what was to happen that morning and organised them for my drama session, I approached Miss Fenoughty and thought I'd show a little kindness to the less fortunate.

'You certainly play with gusto, Miss Fenoughty,' I said cheerfully.

'Who must go?' she snapped. 'I thought I was going to stay and watch the drama.'

'No, I meant your playing.' I raised my voice. 'It was very rousing.'

At this point Sister Brendan rescued me. 'Miss Fenoughty,' she said slowly and loudly, 'would you like to sit in the staff room while you wait for Monsignor Leonard? He's going to watch the drama.'

'I know he is, Sister Brendan,' she replied. 'Mr Flynn said it would be all right if I watched too.'

'Wouldn't you rather wait in the staff room?'

'No thank you, Sister,' she said firmly.

THE TWO TOP infant groups remained seated while the rest of the children returned to their classrooms. Monsignor Leonard joined Miss Fenoughty, who had ensconced herself at the rear of the hall on the only chair with arms.

'Now, children,' said Sister Brendan. 'We have with us this morning Mr Phinn. We are very fortunate, because Mr Phinn has taken time out of his very busy life as an inspector to teach a drama lesson.' She then joined the audience at the back of the hall.

'Good morning, children,' I said.

'Good morning, Mr Phinn,' they chorused.

'People who perform drama are actors and they take on acting parts,' I explained. 'They pretend to be other people and use their bodies, faces and voices to make up a story, just like in a theatre or in the cinema or on the television. Now, this morning *we* shall be acting out a story, but first we are going to do a few warm-up activities to get us in the right frame of mind.'

Until morning playtime I took the children through a series of different exercises. We visited dark dungeons and dusty attics, braved storms and swam rivers, climbed mountains and crawled through caves, dug gardens and threaded needles—a whole range of mimed performances which they clearly enjoyed. At break-time in the staff room, Sister Brendan seemed happy at the way things were going, and I was feeling a great deal more confident.

After playtime, the children gathered round me in a half-circle and I explained to them that we had been miming various actions, and now we were going to add words. As the focus of our drama I picked the poem by Robert Browning, 'The Pied Piper of Hamelin'. The poem has fifteen long verses and, as I was limited for time and the text is sometimes quite difficult, I read a little of the original to give the children a feel for the language and then retold the story myself to move things along: how the people of Hamelin, cursed with a plague of rats, crowded into the Council Chamber demanding action from the mayor and corporation, how a strange, tall figure with 'sharp blue eyes and light loose hair', draped in his coat of yellow and red, agreed to rid the town of the rats for the sum of a thousand guilders, and how he blew his pipe until the rats emerged.

I then told the children how the piper danced through the narrow streets, playing his shrill notes, followed by a sea of squeaking rats. I told them how he took the rats to the river's edge and how the creatures hurled themselves into the murky waters, how the Pied Piper came for his money and how the mayor laughed in his face.

The children listened with wide eyes and open mouths when I related how the Pied Piper's face darkened with anger, how he shook his fist at the city, how the skies clouded over and an icy wind began to blow.

And so we came to the dramatic conclusion to the tale: how the Pied Piper lifted his pipe to his lips and blew three long, clear notes. Then the children came out of the houses, skipping and running and dancing and clapping their hands, and followed the strange man in his coat of yellow and red up to the mountainside, where a great door opened and swallowed them all, all except for the little lame boy who was left behind.

> Alas, alas for Hamelin!
> There came into many a burgher's pate
> A text which says that heaven's gate
> Opes to the rich at as easy rate
> As the needle's eye takes a camel in!

'Now, there's a couple of difficult words in this verse,' I explained. '"Pate" is the old word for head and a "burgher" is—'

A boy with large round glasses waved his hand madly in the air. 'Mr Phinn! Mr Phinn!' he cried. 'I know that. It's something you eat with chips.'

Another child enquired loudly if they were having burgers for dinner.

'That's another kind of burger,' I told them. 'In "The Pied Piper", a burgher is a sort of council official. It was the burghers who refused to give the Pied Piper his thousand guilders.'

The children did not look as if they were any the wiser but I pressed on. I organised the children into various groups: the scurrying, squeaking rats, the mothers and children, cooks and councillors, the mayor and, of course, the Pied Piper. Everything seemed to be going smoothly, so then I asked several of the groups to perform their part of the poem for the others to watch.

The last group was to act out that part of the story when the mayor refuses to give the Pied Piper his thousand guilders. The little boy playing the Pied Piper was the child who had volunteered the answer about the burghers earlier. Now, with all eyes upon him, he looked extremely shy and nervous. If the boy playing the mayor was nervous he certainly did not show it. 'Well, Pied Piper, what do you want?' he called confidently from the centre of the hall.

'I have come for my money,' mumbled the Pied Piper as he sidled across the floor towards him.

'Well, you're not having it!' shouted the mayor.

'OK,' said the Pied Piper and walked quickly away.

'No! No! No!' shouted the other child. 'That's not what you do!' He appealed to me. 'Mr Phinn! Mr Phinn! That's not right, is it? He wouldn't just say "OK" and walk off, would he? He'd go barmy!'

I turned to the child with the large glasses. 'You would get quite angry, you know,' I said. 'You have got rid of all the rats and the mayor promised you the thousand guilders. Now he has refused to pay so you would not be very happy about that, would you?' The child shook his head. 'Let's try it again, and this time when you leave the Council Chamber, you must show how angry you are.'

All faces were turned to the Pied Piper as he stamped into the Council Chamber. His eyes were now slits behind the large glasses, his lips were pressed tightly together, his little body looked stiff and he held up a fist threateningly.

'Well, Pied Piper, what do you want?' demanded the mayor.

'I have come for my money,' shouted the Pied Piper.

'Well, you're not having it!' retorted the mayor.

'Go on, give me my money. You said you would.'

'Well, I've changed my mind. You're not having it!'

'I'll blow my pipe then.'

'You can blow your pipe until you burst, pal, you're not having any money and that's that!'

'Give me my money!'

'No! Clear off!'

'Well, you can stuff your thousand guilders!' roared the Pied Piper. 'You're a tight-fisted old bugger!'

All the adults in the hall fell into a stunned, frozen silence. Monsignor Leonard, Sister Brendan and Miss Fenoughty were like a tableau at the back. None of them moved a muscle.

Then, into the deathly silence, the small boy with the large glasses piped up. 'Is that better, Mr Phinn?' he asked.

Later, as I said my farewells in the school hall, I attempted to direct the conversation away from the morning's drama but without success. Miss Fenoughty was determined to discuss proceedings.

'I did enjoy this morning, Mr Flynn. I do so love that poem. I thought the little ones did very well, didn't you?'

'I did,' I replied, smiling weakly.

'And that little boy who played the part of the Pied Piper, he was a natural little actor. My goodness he really did sound the part, didn't you think?'

'I did,' I replied again.

'And fancy him remembering that word he'd asked you about.'

'Word?' I repeated.

'"Burgher". He remembered the word "burgher". Don't you recall at the end, didn't he shout at the mayor, "Give me my money, you mean old burgher"?'

I heard Monsignor Leonard splutter beside me, hastily burying his face in his handkerchief. Even Sister Brendan had to suppress a smile. Their enjoyment, however, was short-lived.

'You know, Sister,' exclaimed Miss Fenoughty, with a wild gleam in her eye, 'I've been thinking. I've got the score somewhere for the musical version of "The Pied Piper". Wouldn't it be a good idea to perform it for the parents? I would, of course, be pleased to act as musical director. What do you all think?'

We were as motionless as the statue of St Bartholomew of Whitby, who looked down upon us from his plinth at the front of the hall. It was the same St Bartholomew, the hermit, who took himself off to the Farne Islands in the twelfth century to escape the strident noises of the world and to spend his life in quiet meditation. I'm sure we all envied him at that moment.

DR MULLARKEY was due to take up her post as county inspector for science and technology in early June, a few days after the Feoffees' celebration, and Harold had organised some school visits before she started so she could get a feel for things and meet a few people.

This morning, a week before the end of the spring term, it was my turn to accompany Gerry, and I had arranged to take her into three primary schools to observe some design and technology work.

'I'm really looking forward to starting,' said Gerry, as we skirted the grey exterior of County Hall and walked towards the car park. 'Of course, I've got to find somewhere to live, so could do with a bit of advice about location and houses.'

'I'm the last one to ask. After eighteen months I'm still in my rented flat on the high street. I just don't seem to have found the time for house hunting.'

'I'll probably do that at the outset,' she said. 'Rent a flat or a little cottage, I mean.'

We walked in silence for a while. 'So, you've no family?' I asked.

'No, just me.'

The clock on the County Hall tower struck eight o'clock as I drove down Fettlesham High Street. I was soon onto a narrow twisting road, bordered by craggy grey limestone walls, beyond which the dark, undulating fields were covered in a light, fleecy mist, empty save for the occasional twisted hawthorn tree. The pale sun, shining through the clouds, made the whole landscape before us glisten.

'It's magnificent,' Gerry said quietly.

'It is, isn't it? I can never get used to it.'

The small stone primary school we were to visit first was in the very heart of the village of Tarncliffe, sandwiched between the post office-cum-general store and the squat, grey Primitive Methodist chapel. From the pavement the door opened directly into the one large classroom and passers-by could peer through the windows to see the pupils at work. We were given a warm welcome by the head-teacher and her assistant, who both shook our hands vigorously.

Gerry and I started with the junior-aged children, who were behind a large partition industriously constructing models. In the corner were two girls of about ten or eleven, who explained to us that they had been asked to design and produce a labour-saving device for use in the home. They had come up with the idea for a gadget that would tell the milkman the number of pints required each day. Their first, not very novel idea had been to design a clock-face with numbers round the rim and a hand that could be adjusted to point to the number of pints needed.

'But then,' explained one of the girls enthusiastically, 'what if you wanted some cream as well as milk?'

'Or orange juice?' added the other. 'Or eggs or yoghurt?'

'So the problem has become very complicated,' observed Gerry, looking at their plans. 'Have you managed to resolve it?'

'One solution would be to have different faces for a different things—but teacher said our design has to be cheap to produce.'

'This is a real problem,' said Gerry. 'Have you found an answer?'

'Oh, yes!' exclaimed one of the girls. 'Tessa had a brainwave.' She pushed a piece of paper in Gerry's direction. Gerry examined the sketch, nodded and observed, 'Ingenious' before passing it to me. The design was for a small square of plywood on which was written in bright capital letters: MILKMAN! SEE NOTE IN BOTTLE.'

In another corner of the room was the infant section.

'Would you like me to read to you?' asked a small girl, with wide, cornflower-blue eyes and a mass of blonde hair.

'Yes,' I replied, 'I would like that very much.'

'I'm a very good reader, you know,' she confided in me, while she searched in her bag for her book.

'Are you?'

'I read with expression.'

'Do you?'

'And I can do different voices.'

'Really? I expect you use dramatic pauses as well,' I said.

She looked up for a moment and then added seriously, 'I don't know what they are, but I probably can.'

She was indeed a very accomplished little reader and sailed through her book confidently and fluently. 'I *am* good, aren't I?' she announced when she had completed three pages.

'Very good,' I said.

'I'm good at talking as well.'

'I can tell that. I think your mummy's got a little chatterbox at home.'

'Oh, no!' exclaimed the child. 'My granny has asthma and I'm not allowed to keep pets.'

'I see,' I said chuckling and wondering what sort of animal she thought a 'chatterbox' was.

'My granny wobbles, you know,' the little chatterbox continued.

'Does she?'

'She has a special disease which makes her wobble and forget things. It's called "Old Timers' Disease".'

Gerry, who had joined me a few moments before, leaned closer and whispered in my ear. 'You know, Gervase, if I get Alzheimer's disease when I'm old I think I would like my grandchildren to say that I have got "Old Timers' disease". It sounds much friendlier, don't you think?'

'Excuse me,' said the little chatterbox, patting my arm, 'would your girlfriend like to hear me read?'

AT THE SECOND SCHOOL, Sheepcote Primary, Gerry looked through the children's work and discussed the science curriculum with the teacher while I moved around the classroom talking to the children about the tasks they were undertaking that morning. On the table, tucked in a corner, were two boys busy sewing. One looked as if he had been dragged through a hedge backwards. His shirt was hanging out, his socks were concertinaed around his ankles, his legs were covered in cuts and bruises, and his shoes were so scuffed I could not tell whether they were black or brown. His companion was a large, amiable-looking boy with a round moon of a face, dimpled elbows and knees, and fingers as fat as sausages. Both boys were surrounded by threads, cottons, fabrics, an assortment of needles, boxes of pins and scissors and both were sewing furiously.

'Hello,' I said brightly.

'Hello,' replied the larger boy. His companion continued to sew.

'And how are you?'

'Middlin' well.'

'And what are you two up to?' I asked.

'Samplers,' he answered. 'Victorian embroidery.'

'For Mother's Day on Sunday,' added the other.

'May I see?' I said, bending over to get a closer look.

'Can't be stopping,' said the untidy one, forcing the needle savagely through the canvas. 'Got to get it finished.' He turned to his friend. 'Pass us t'pink will tha, Dean?'

His companion searched through the coloured threads. 'All gone,' he replied. 'I needed it for mi roses.'

'And tha's used all t'purple, an all?'

'That were for mi lilac.'

'And tha's left me wi all t'blacks and t'browns and t'greys. Thanks very much!'

The boys, entirely oblivious of my presence, resumed pushing the large needles through the fabric as if their lives depended upon it.

'Just stop a moment, will you, please,' I told them.

The untidy one paused, looked up, and then returned to his sewing. 'I can't stop,' he told me. 'I've got to gerrit done.'

His companion, clearly pleased with his effort, held up a pale square of cream fabric. In large, uneven letters were the words: A MOTHER'S LOVE IS A BLESSING. The border was ablaze with a host of unrecognisable but extremely vivid flowers.

'I've just got mi name to put at t'bottom and I'm all done,' he announced proudly.

The other boy stopped sewing abruptly. 'Aye, well, I've been on this for four week and I'll be lucky to get it done for next year's Mother's Day, way things stand.'

'Why?' I asked.

'Because I've only just started mi border, and Dean's used all t'pinks and purples.'

'You could do animals instead of flowers,' suggested his companion. 'You don't need colours for sheep and cows and goats . . .'

'I'd need pink for t'pigs, though, wouldn't I?'

'I'm sure that, however it turns out, your mother will love your sampler,' I reassured him.

'If she gets it!'

'Well, I may see you boys later,' I said moving away. 'I thought I'd pop into the singing class during the lunch-hour.'

'Singing?' the untidy boy exclaimed. 'Singing! We don't go to no singing class! That's for t'cissies!' The other boy, putting the finishing touches to his large pink rose, nodded in agreement: 'Aye, choir's for t'cissies and t'lasses. You wunt catch us theer.'

CRAGSIDE PRIMARY, our final port of call, sat in the shadow of the massive sphinx-like Cawthorne Crag. There was a mouth-watering aroma of baking pastry permeating the building.

'The children learn to cook in this school, Mr Phinn,' explained the headteacher. 'I feel it is important that all children, and particularly boys, should know how to bake a loaf, make a pie, even cook a whole meal. They won't always have their mothers looking after them. Today, we are trying our hand at pastry.'

In the school kitchen, two boys in white aprons were helping a large woman with floury hands take their culinary efforts out of the oven.

'Do you like jam tarts?' one boy asked as I approached.

'Oh, I'm very partial to them.'

'Do you want one of mine?'

'You have to wait until they are cool, Richard,' said the woman with the floury hands, giving me a warning look.

'Tarts are better when they're hot, miss,' persisted the boy. He selected the biggest on the baking tray with a blob of dark red, which I supposed was jam, in the centre. It looked the most unappetising piece of pastry, but I could not go back now. The boy watched keenly as I took a bite. 'What do you think?' he asked.

It was difficult to speak as the dried-up confection coated my mouth. I coughed and sprayed the air with bits of pastry and dried jam. 'I have never tasted a tart like this in my life,' I assured him honestly, between splutters.

A great smile spread across his face. 'Would you like another?'

'No, thank you,' I replied quickly, 'one will be quite enough.'

At the end of the afternoon, as we were heading for the door, the little chef appeared with a brown paper bag in his hand. 'I've put one of my tarts in here for you, miss,' he said to Gerry, 'to have with your tea tonight.'

'That's very kind,' she said. 'Thank you very much.'

'And another one for you, sir,' he added.

'Thank you,' I replied.

'Funny thing is baking, isn't it?' the boy pondered, holding out his hands in front of him the better to examine them. 'You know, my hands were dead mucky before I started making my tarts and just look how clean they are now.'

13

Mrs Savage appeared very much at home in the entrance hall of Lord Marrick's stately home. She was dressed in an elegant cream coat over a flowing blue chiffon dress and a generous assortment of gold jewellery. Standing before the magnificently carved chimney-piece, she looked like the lady of the manor posing for a photograph.

'Ah, Mr Phinn,' she said, advancing. 'You are here at last.'

I glanced at my watch. 'It's only just gone eight,' I replied.

'As you know,' she answered haughtily, 'I like things to be done efficiently and thoroughly and not left to chance.'

It was the Saturday morning of the Feoffees Pageant at the end of May and the weather was perfect. Marquees and multicoloured tents were scattered on the green sward in front of Manston Hall. The event was to start at 11.00am, when the Feoffees would process in full regalia and Lord Marrick would officially open proceedings. Already the police bandsmen had arrived and stall-holders were busy arranging their wares on long trestle tables.

I followed Mrs Savage down the stone steps of the hall and towards a large marquee, outside which was a big sign announcing EDUCATION EXHIBITION. We were just about to enter the tent when a small man in a blue boiler suit addressed Mrs Savage. 'I've been looking for you.'

She gave him one of her condescending looks. 'Really?'

'Where do you want your tent, love?'

'I *beg* your pardon?'

'Your tent,' he repeated. 'Where do you want it putting?'

'What tent? I don't know anything about a tent.'

'Where you're doing your fortunetelling.'

'Do I look remotely like a fortuneteller?'

'I was told to look for a woman in blue and yella wi' lots o' bangles.'

'I suggest you look elsewhere. I am certainly not Gypsy Rose Lee.'

'Sorry, I'm sure,' said the man, disappearing hastily.

The art exhibition was magnificent. Sidney had produced a dazzling display of work, while, behind the Education marquee, teachers were preparing for the drama production, a troop of junior gymnasts was practising on large blue mats, and members of the Youth Orchestra were rehearsing for their performance.

'Well,' said Mrs Savage, smiling uncharacteristically, as we headed back towards the hall, 'I think everything is in order.'

I had to hand it to the woman. Things had been organised extremely well, and the Feoffees Pageant went like clockwork.

'Splendid! Splendid!' said Dr Gore later that morning as he entered the marquee where the children's work was displayed. 'It really does look impressive in here. Wonderful work. I just wanted to say how well everyone has done. I think we can say that the Education Department has held its own, eh?' He strode off, rubbing his hands enthusiastically. 'Splendid! Splendid!'

'I think the old man's pleased,' remarked Sidney phlegmatically.

I WAS IN LOVE. Since the first moment I had set eyes on Christine, I had been smitten. Over the twenty-one months I had known her, that love had become so powerful that in the middle of meetings at the Education Office my thoughts would drift to her. On a course, the words of the speaker would flow over me as my mind turned to Christine. And people were beginning to notice.

'Gervase!' cried Sidney, late one afternoon towards the end of the summer term. 'Are you with us? I've just asked you an important question and you continue to peer into the middle distance like Macbeth seeing the ghost of Banquo.'

'I'm sorry, Sidney, I was miles away.'

'You are unusually unforthcoming these days, Gervase,' remarked David. 'Is there something on your mind?'

'No, no, there's nothing on my mind.'

'Is it that dreadful headteacher from Henderson Road?' asked Sidney. 'She complains about all the inspectors, so I shouldn't worry.'

'No, nothing like that.'

'It'll be Mrs Savage, then,' said David. 'Has she been chasing you?'

'No, it's not Mrs Savage.'

'Well, what is it?' both my colleagues asked.

'I can't say. It's . . . it's . . . it's just that I'm in love!' I blurted out.

There was a stunned silence.

'In love?' repeated Sidney. 'Oh, that is serious. Is it a certain doctor of philosophy, with alluring Irish eyes and a smile like a rainbow?'

'No, it's not Gerry. I hardly know her.'

'Is it a certain well-preserved, power-dressed widow with a predatory look and a smile like a shark?'

'Mrs Savage? Do me a favour!'

'The *femme fatale* with the feather duster in the crackling nylon overall who inhabits the SDC?'

'Sidney, will you be serious!'

'Then it must be the delectable Miss Bentley of Winnery Nook.'

'You know very well it is.'

'Well, you want to look sharpish. She's an extremely attractive young woman. Very marriageable. If you don't pull your finger out, she'll go back to that dreadful soldier and give you the old heave-ho!'

'Now, does that make you feel a lot better, Gervase?' asked David sarcastically. 'You know, Sidney, with such sensitivity and understanding, you ought to work for the Samaritans.'

'I am only telling him to go for it. I mean, look at him. He's like a sick calf, mooning about the office.'

'Well, that's what love does for you,' said David. 'I recall someone

532

saying that love was like the measles—that it is something we all have to go through. I know I did.'

'More like the mumps with me!' exclaimed Sidney. 'Incredibly painful and all the more so when you're older. You see, Gervase, it's happening to you late in life so it's affecting you far worse.'

'Late in life!' I cried. 'I'm just over thirty, not in my dotage!'

'But as you get older, you get more picky. My advice, if you really love Christine, is to face up to things. Stop shilly-shallying, ask her straight out to marry you.'

'It's not as easy as that, Sidney,' I said, sighing. 'She might not be ready for . . . er . . . marriage. She's so involved with her work in school. She's a very independent woman. I know she likes my company and we enjoy the same things but—'

'Have you told her how lovely she is and that you can't stop thinking about her?' asked Sidney.

'No.'

'Have you told her that you can't live without her?'

'No.'

Sidney snorted. 'Then how, in heaven's name, is she to know how you feel? She might think that *you* are the one who isn't ready for marriage. She might think that *you* are too involved with your work.'

'Much as I am loath to admit it,' ventured David, 'Sidney, despite his bluntness, is perfectly right. I think you ought to take Christine out for a really romantic dinner in a remote country inn. Champagne, roses, soft music. That's the way it's done. I know the very place. A delightful French restaurant with superb food and magnificent views, not too far from here.'

'Is that the way you proposed?' I asked.

'Well, no, actually,' replied David. 'I asked Gwynneth in a bus shelter on a rainy Sunday afternoon in Pontypool.'

'Look, Gervase, do you really love her?' asked Sidney, suddenly turning very serious.

'Yes, I do,' I replied.

'Well, *why* don't you ask her to marry you?'

'I'm frightened she'll say no. I haven't got much money saved, I drive an old car and I live in a rented flat.'

Sidney got up from his desk and came and perched on the corner of my desk. 'That's not the real reason though, is it?'

'No,' I admitted. 'I'm just frightened that she doesn't love me.'

Sidney put his hand on my shoulder. 'Well, old boy, there's only one way to find out, isn't there?'

Sidney was right, of course. I could not delay any longer.

I BOOKED A TABLE at Le Bon Appetit restaurant in the picturesque village of Ribsdyke for the Saturday after next. Christine would be in a good mood because term would have ended and she would be looking forward to the long summer break. There would be soft music, subdued lights and, from our secluded table, we would watch the sun go down behind the noble fells. I would reach out and take Christine's hand in mine. Our eyes would lock. I would gaze into hers and whisper, 'Christine, darling, will you marry me?' Her eyes would fill with tears. 'Of course,' she would sigh.

It did not quite work out like that.

The taxi arrived late and it was without a doubt the oldest and smelliest in the fleet, reeking of diesel and stale cigarettes.

'I didn't know I were pickin' up t'Prince of Wales,' said the driver facetiously, when I complained about the state of the interior.

When we finally arrived at Christine's parents' house, I could see my future bride staring anxiously through the window.

'I thought you'd stood me up,' she said, as I hurried her down the path. Then she caught sight of the vehicle. 'And we're going by taxi. How nice.'

Le Bon Appetit was heaving. We squeezed through a crowd of loud young men in smart suits holding pints of lager, and were greeted by the head waiter. He was a small, dark-eyed, Gallic-looking individual, who eyed me superciliously as he ran a fat finger down his list of reservations.

'Ah, oui. Meester and Meesis Pinn.'

'Phinn!' I corrected.

'Meester Phinn. Eef you would like to come zees way, I will show you to your table.' We followed him through a noisy restaurant to a small table positioned between two larger tables full of laughing people and directly opposite the doors to the kitchens.

'Is there somewhere a little quieter?' I asked.

'Oh, no, no, no! I am afraid not. Le Bon Appetit ees always ver' busy at zer weekend.'

'It's fine,' said Christine squeezing into a chair.

After we had ordered them, the drinks took an age to arrive and, try as I might to have a conversation with Christine, my voice was drowned by the noise of the other diners, the banging of the swing doors to the kitchen, and the overloud background music. To make matters worse, the waiter, another small Gallic-looking individual, insisted on taking us through the menu in maximum, dreary detail.

When finally the loud drone came to a halt, he took my order and strode away with a flourish.

'Sounds delicious,' shouted Christine across the table.

'David recommended this place,' I shouted back. 'I didn't think it would be quite so crowded.' At this point there were shrieks of laughter from the office party at the next table.

'Would you care to see the wine list, sir?' The wine waiter was shouting also, as he offered an enormous leather-bound volume.

'Just a bottle of dry house white, please,' I replied. I could not contemplate listening to him working through the catalogue of wines.

The restaurant grew noisier and noisier and hotter and hotter, and when the food finally arrived, my mussels numbered five, Christine's soup looked as appetising as grey dishwater, the main courses were barely warm and the white wine was too sweet.

'I'm really sorry about this, Christine!' I shouted across the table. 'I wanted this evening to be so special.'

'To be what?' asked Christine.

'Sorry, what did you say?'

'You said something about wanting the evening to be. . .'

'Special! I wanted it to be special. And there was something very particular I wanted to ask you. Something I've been wanting to say for weeks now—'

'Would you care to 'ear what we 'ave for dessert?' It was the waiter again.

No, I felt like saying, let me guess. 'Would you like a pudding, Chris?' I asked.

'No, thanks, just coffee, please.'

'Could we just have coffee, please,' I said to the waiter. 'And is there anywhere less crowded and noisy for us to have it?'

'Oh, no, no, no! I am afraid not. Le Bon Appetit ees always ver' busy at zer weekend.'

This was just impossible. I could not possibly ask her here.

'Shall we skip the coffee?' suggested Christine helpfully. 'We could go back to my house. I make an excellent cup and I know Mum and Dad would love to see you again.'

'No coffee, then, thank you,' I told the waiter. 'Just the bill, please.'

Turning back to Christine, I said, 'Yes, let's go back to your house for coffee.' I had not planned for the evening to end like this. How could I propose with Christine's parents making polite conversation over coffee? 'I'll just go and rustle up the taxi. I ordered it for eleven, but we don't want to be hanging about here for the next hour.'

Having persuaded the head waiter to ring for the taxi, I headed for the only quiet place in the building: the gents. I had to get my thoughts straight. In the deserted cloakroom, I splashed cold water over my face and stared into the mirror. Perhaps Christine's parents would leave us to ourselves and then I could pop the question. I had rehearsed what I would say so many times I knew it backwards. I looked in the mirror, smiled and said out loud, 'I think you know how I feel about you. You're always in my thoughts, you're forever in my dreams. I love you. I've loved you since I first saw you.' I paused for effect. 'I just cannot live without you. Will you marry me?'

There was a loud flushing noise, a cubicle door opened and a man with a clarety complexion and heavy jowls emerged with a bemused expression and joined me at the washbasin.

'I'm afraid I can't,' he said, washing his hands vigorously. 'I'm married already. I've been married for forty-five years. But thank you for asking—I shall always treasure the memory.' Then, chuckling, he left me to my thoughts.

The evening had been a total disaster. What could possibly happen next? I had not long to wait. At the bar, having settled the bill, I became aware of a familiar voice.

'Could you order me a taxi, please, to collect us in about thirty minutes?' It was Dr Gore.

'Dr Gore!' I exclaimed.

The Chief Education Officer smiled and came down the bar to join me. 'Hello, Gervase, I didn't see you there. I take it you too have been celebrating the end of term? Are you here with your colleagues?'

'No, no, just with a friend,' I replied.

'Well, you must come and join us for a coffee.'

'That's very kind, but I'm expecting a taxi—'

'I'm sure that you have time for a cup of coffee. In any case, if your taxi does arrive it can wait for ten minutes or so. I won't take no for an answer. You run along and fetch your friend. We're through the archway, in a little alcove.'

'And where have you been?' Christine demanded in a mock angry voice when I arrived back at the table. 'I've been sitting here for ages.'

'I'm really sorry. I met Dr Gore and just couldn't get away. He's asked us to join him for coffee. Do you mind awfully?'

'Of course not.'

I led Christine through the crowd in the direction of the secluded alcove where Dr Gore had said he was sitting. This was where Christine and I should have been, I thought crossly.

'He's over there,' said Christine.

I stopped in my tracks when I saw who was with the CEO. At a pretty table, bathed in pink light from a nearby lamp, sat a stream-lined figure in acid-green silk. It was Mrs Savage.

Dr Gore stood as we reached the table. 'Ah, there you are,' he said. 'Good, good. Miss Bentley, how very nice to see you. Gervase never mentioned who his friend was. Come, come, do take a seat. I've ordered some more coffee.'

We sat down on chairs pulled up by Dr Gore. 'You know Brenda, of course, Gervase,' he continued jovially. He turned to Christine. 'This is my personal assistant, Brenda Savage.'

She gave a smirk before extending a hand like some member of royalty. 'Delighted to meet you,' she said.

'And this is Christine Bentley,' Dr Gore told her. 'One of our most distinguished and hard-working headteachers.'

'Hello,' said Christine warmly. 'I think I saw you with Dr Gore when he came to talk at the Headteachers' Conference.'

'That's right,' said Mrs Savage. 'I spend a lot of time with Dr Gore.' She gave me what could only be termed a challenging look.

Dr Gore and Mrs Savage, I thought to myself. Well, well. The evening was collapsing into a complete shambles—but what a story I would have to tell David and Sidney.

I could have cheered when I saw the little French waiter heading in our direction.

'Meester and Meesis Pinn, your taxi is 'ere.'

I thanked Dr Gore for the coffee, shook his hand, wished him a pleasant summer holiday, and smiled weakly at Mrs Savage.

Christine slid her hand into mine and we headed for the door. 'That was an unexpected meeting, wasn't it?' she said. 'Fancy coming across Dr Gore and Mrs Savage. Do you think there's something going on between them? He's a widower, isn't he?'

'Christine—'

'Of course, it might be just be a sort of thankyou meal—'

'Christine! I'm totally uninterested in Dr Gore and Mrs Savage at this moment. There really is something I have to ask you. Could we just sit down for a moment?' We found an empty table near the bar. I took a deep breath and tried to remember the words I had endlessly rehearsed. My mind went blank. 'I know this is not the best place to say this, but I really have to say it now. It's just that I think you are the most beautiful, wonderful, amazing person I've ever met and, well, I love you. I can't stop thinking about you. It's making me ill.'

'Oh?'

'Will you marry me, Christine? You may want to think about it—'

'No,' Christine replied immediately.

'No?' Her answer was like a bullet to the heart.

'No, I don't need to think about it. Of course I'll marry you.'

'*You will?*' I shouted, loud enough to turn the entire restaurant silent. 'You'll marry me?'

'Of course I will.'

Making his way to the bar was the claret-faced man who had heard the final rehearsal of my speech in the gents.

'Well done, lad,' he chuckled, thumping me on the back.

This was followed by a clatter of clinking glasses and applause from the rest of the diners. I caught sight of Dr Gore raising a brandy glass in our direction.

We let the taxi wait and stood with our arms around each other on the little humpbacked bridge in front of the restaurant. In the clear moonlight, the swirling waters beneath were speckled with leaves, while old dead oaks, garlanded in ivy, stood upright to the sky and willows shivered in the breeze. The smells of wet wood and honeysuckle mingled in the summer air.

Christine's blue eyes were bright with pleasure and her hair shone golden in the moonlight. I stooped to kiss her.

'I'd like six,' I said, wrapping my arms around her waist.

'Six what?' Christine asked.

'Children. I'd like six children.'

'Let's think about that later, shall we?' she replied.

'You *do* want children?' I asked.

'Of course, but not at this moment and I might want eight.'

'Ey up! Are tha ready or what?' said a loud voice from the road.

I turned to face the taxi driver. 'I've got a lot o' calls toneet,' he said. 'Can't be messin' abaat whilst tha looks at t'river. It'll still be theer in t' mornin'. So let's be 'avin' thee.'

Christine and I laughed so loudly that he jumped with surprise. 'Are you two all right?'

'We're champion, aren't we, Chris?' I exclaimed robustly, in true Yorkshire fashion. 'Just champion!'

GERVASE PHINN

The amusing anecdotes about school-teachers, schoolchildren and fellow school inspectors that fill the pages of Gervase Phinn's delightful fictionalised memoirs, give insight into his thirty years in education. For fourteen of those years he taught in secondary schools in Rotherham, before taking on an advisory role in language teaching. In 1988 he became North Yorkshire's senior general inspector for English and drama, and he currently works as a freelance educational consultant as well as being visiting professor in education at the University of Teesside.

Talk to Gervase Phinn about education and you quickly realise it is his passion—second only to his wife Christine (whom he met in just the way he describes in *The Other Side of the Dale*) and four children. He feels very strongly that today's teachers get a bad press: the vast majority are immensely hard-working and dedicated but don't make the headlines. He is also convinced that teaching is 'the most important role in society, because a teacher can transform a child for good or ill'. If he were Secretary of State for Education, he says the first thing he would do would be to raise teachers' morale by reassuring them that they are doing an excellent job.

'The best teachers are enthusiastic, caring, sensitive and supportive. And they have the interests of all children, however damaged or repellent, at heart. I'm encouraging my three youngest, two of whom are already at university, to go into the profession. It's the best job in the world. I know for me there could be no other.'

The success of his first two books has propelled Gervase Phinn into the public eye, and he now has a calendar filled, outside his working hours, with speaking engagements and campaigns for children's charities. He plans to write more books in the 'Dales' series very soon.

ACKNOWLEDGMENTS AND PICTURE CREDITS: *The Bombmaker:* pages 6–8: Science Photo Library/Shark Attack. *Relative Strangers:* pages 152 and 153: Background girl: Pat Horner/photonica; pictures, left to right: baby: Mel Yates/Telegraph Colour Library; woman; man with girl: The Photographers Library; man swinging child: Anthony Nagelmann/Telegraph Colour Library; page 279 (left: Joyce Hopkirk, right: Val Corbett) © Caroline Forbes. *Final Venture:* pages 280 and 281: male figures: The Photographers Library; skyscrapers: Julian Cotton Photo Library/A. Bouchet. *The Other Side of the Dale:* pages 422 and 423: Warwick Johnson-Cadwell/Eastwing; page 539 Derry Brabbs.

DUSTJACKET CREDITS: Spine from top: Science Photo Library/Shark Attack; Pat Horner/photonica; The Photographers Library; Warwick Johnson-Cadwell/Eastwing. Back cover: (Phinn): Derry Brabbs.

Printed by Maury Imprimeur SA, Malesherbes, France
Bound by Reliures Brun SA, Malesherbes, France

208AD